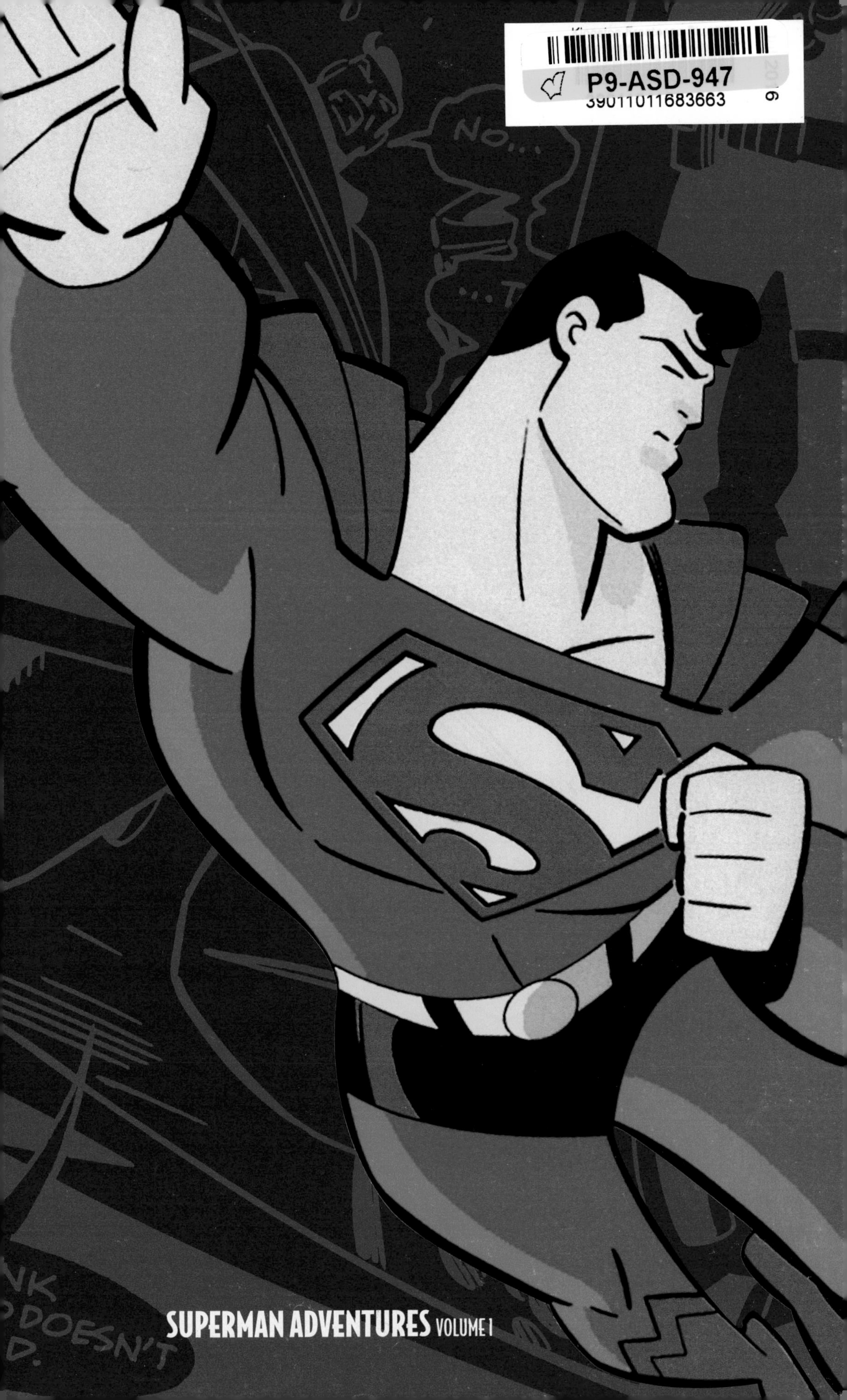
NO...

SUPERMAN ADVENTURES VOLUME 1

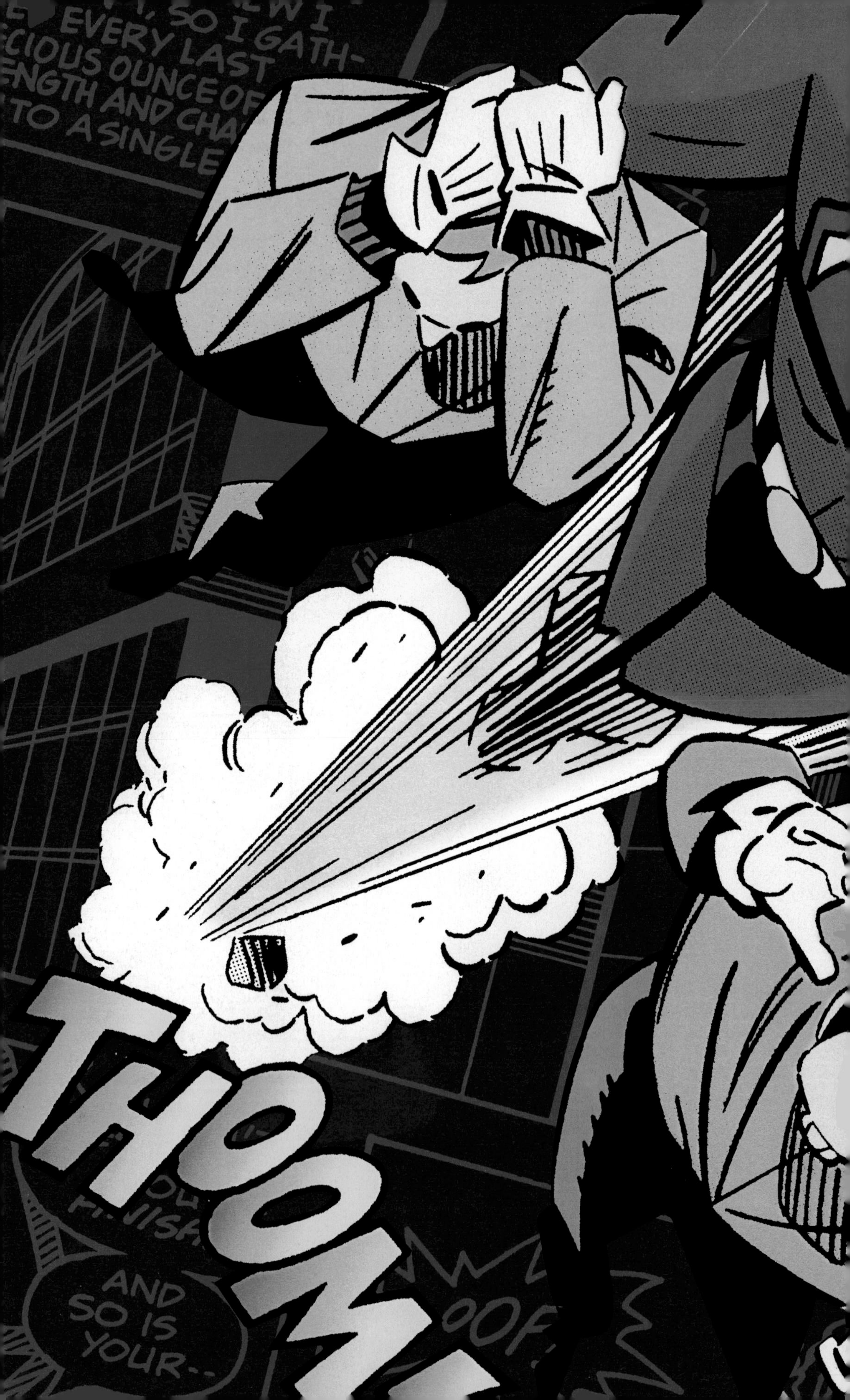
THOOM
AND SO IS YOUR..
OOF

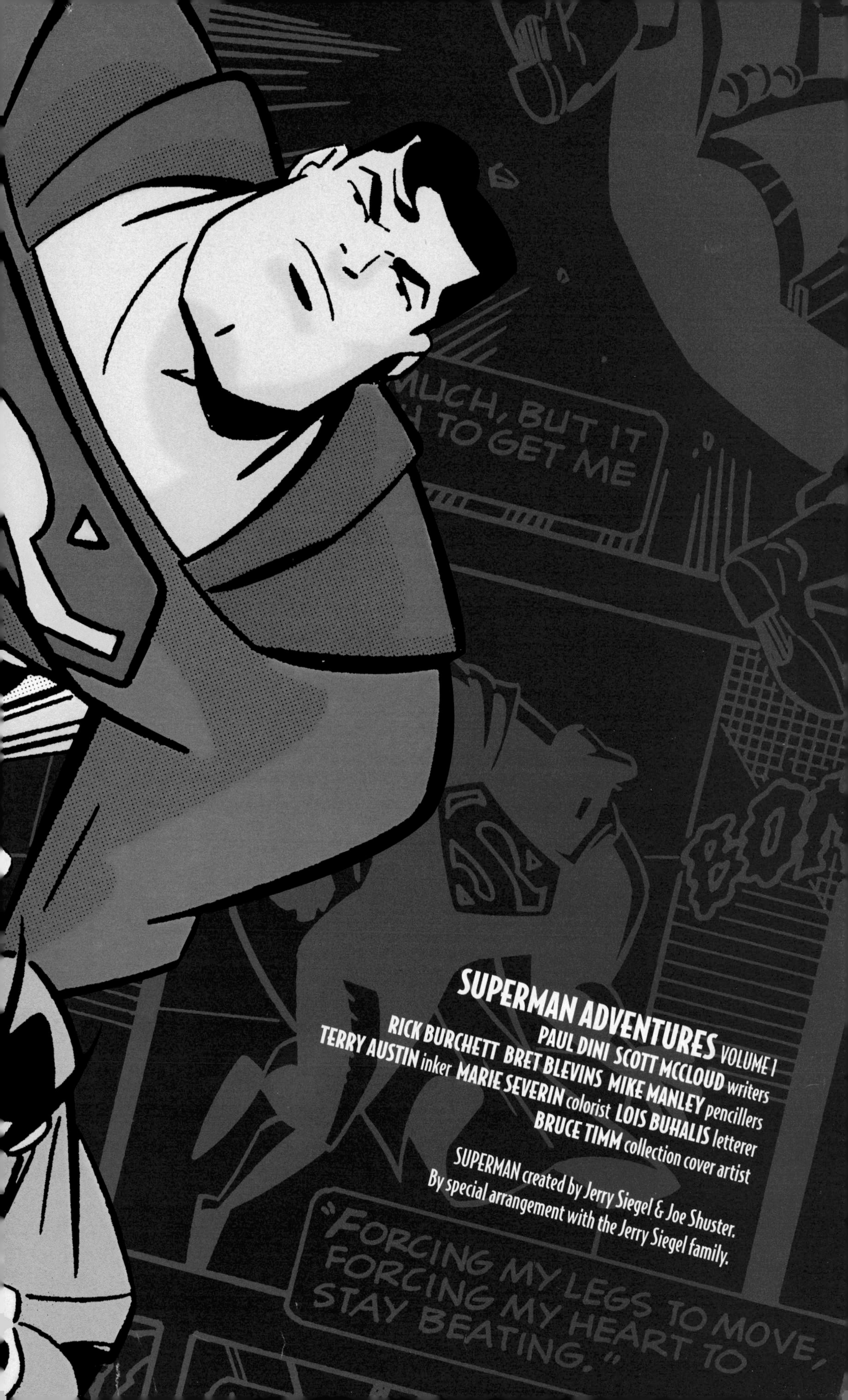
MUCH, BUT IT
TO GET ME
"FORCING MY LEGS TO MOVE,
FORCING MY HEART TO
STAY BEATING."

SUPERMAN ADVENTURES

PAUL DINI SCOTT MCCLOUD RICK BURCHETT BRET BLEVINS VOLUME 1

TERRY AUSTIN inker **MARIE SEVERIN** colorist **LOIS BUHALIS** letterer
MIKE MANLEY pencillers
SCOTT MCCLOUD writers
BRUCE TIMM collection cover artist

SUPERMAN created by Jerry Siegel & Joe Shuster.
By special arrangement with the Jerry Siegel family.

SUPERMAN ADVENTURES VOLUME 1

Published by DC Comics. Compilation Copyright © 2015 DC Comics. All Rights Reserved.

Originally published in single magazine form in SUPERMAN ADVENTURES 1-10. Copyright © 1996, 1997 DC Comics. All Rights Reserved. All characters, their distinctive likenesses and related elements featured in this publication are trademarks of DC Comics. The stories, characters and incidents featured in this publication are entirely fictional. DC Comics does not read or accept unsolicited ideas, stories or artwork.

DC Comics, 4000 Warner Blvd., Burbank, CA 91522
A Warner Bros. Entertainment Company.
Printed by RR Donnelley, Salem, VA, USA. 10/9/15 First Printing.
ISBN: 978-1-4012-5867-2

Library of Congress Cataloging-in-Publication Data

McCloud, Scott, 1960-
 Superman Adventures. Volume 1 / Scott McCloud, writer ; Rick Burchett, penciller.
   pages cm
 ISBN 978-1-4012-5867-2 (paperback)
 1. Graphic novels. [1. Graphic novels. 2. Superheroes--Fiction.] I. Burchett, Rick, illustrator. II. Title.
 PZ7.7.M414Su 2015
 741.5'973— dc23
                    2015030879

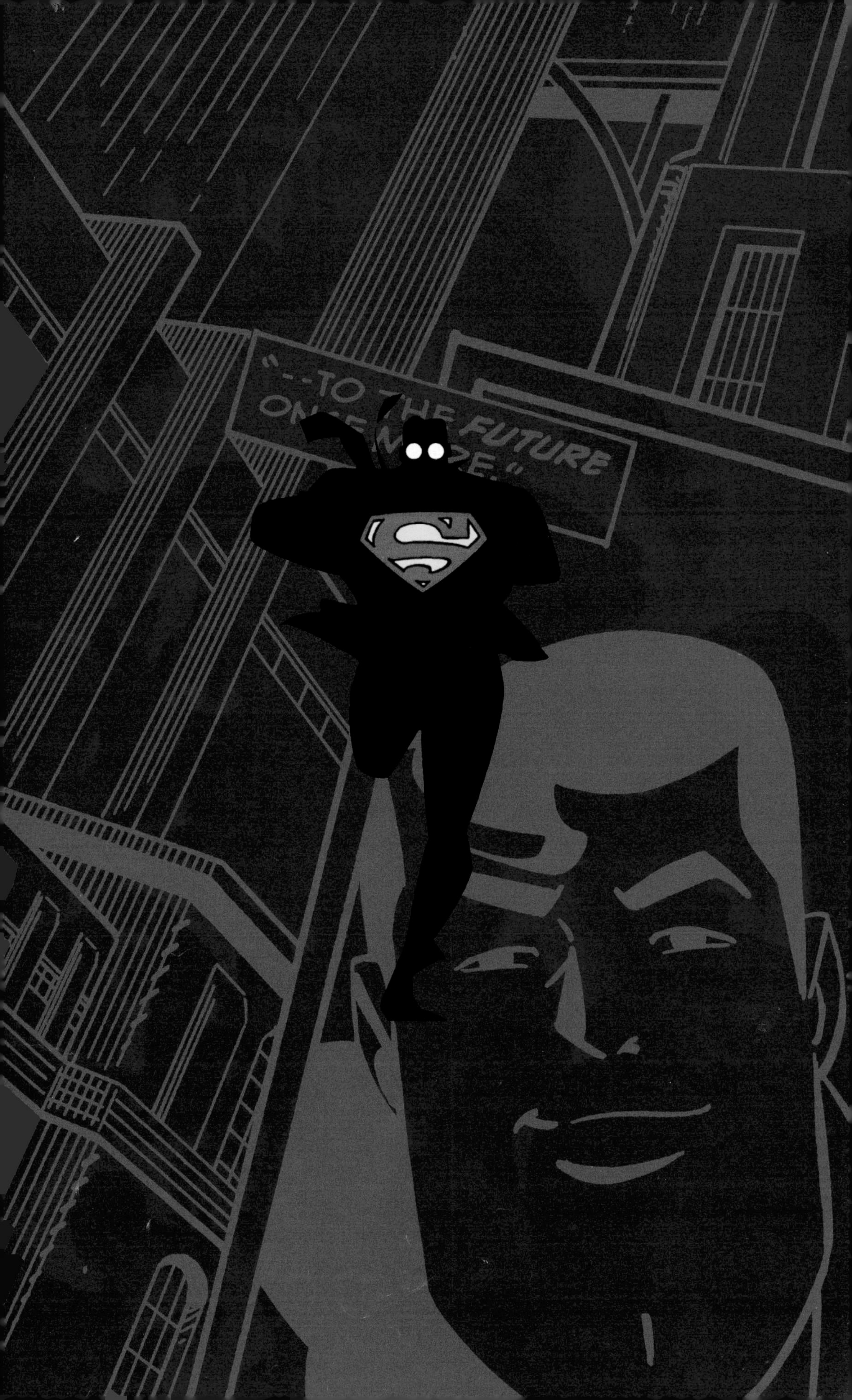
“--TO THE FUTURE

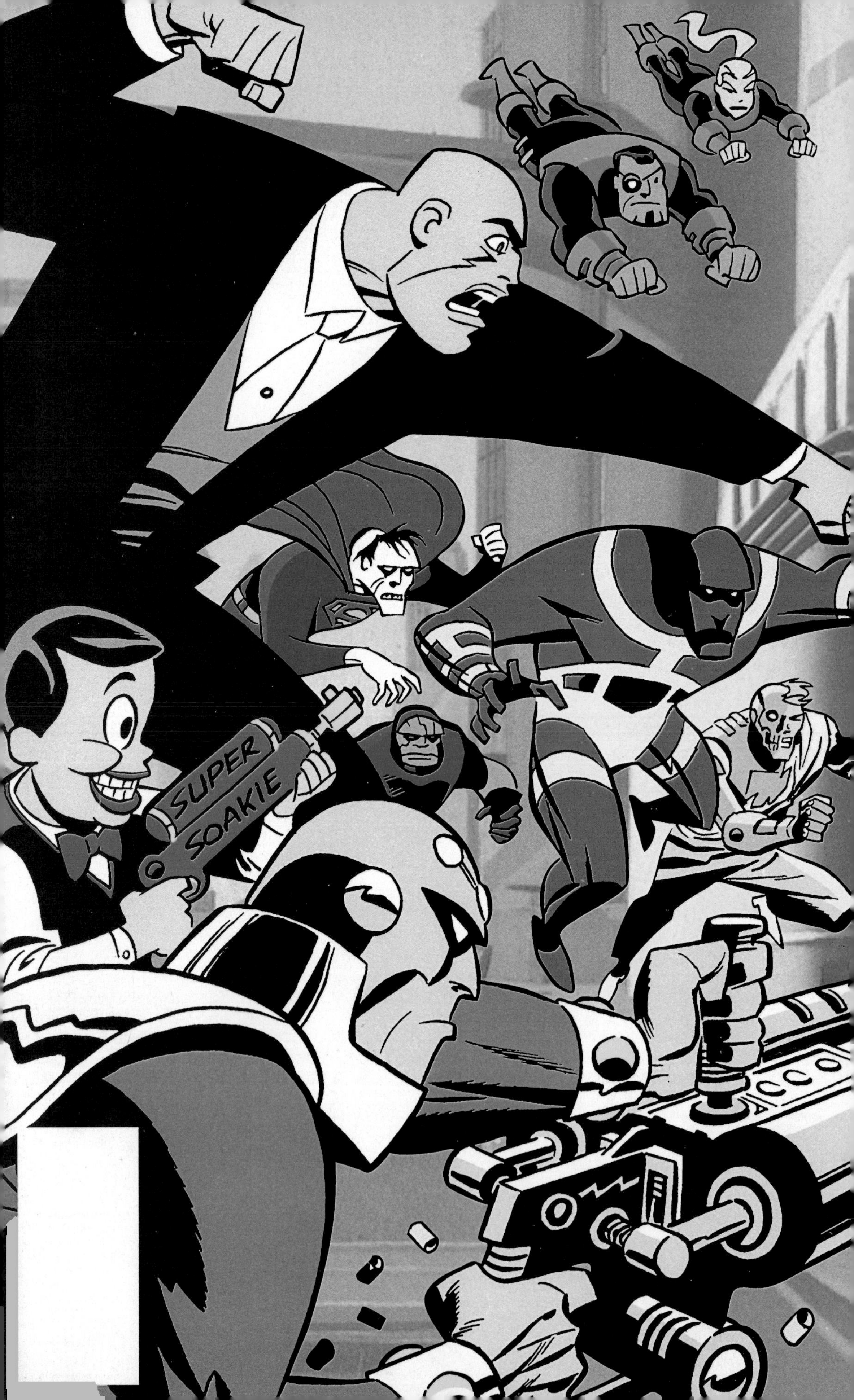
SUPER SOAKIE

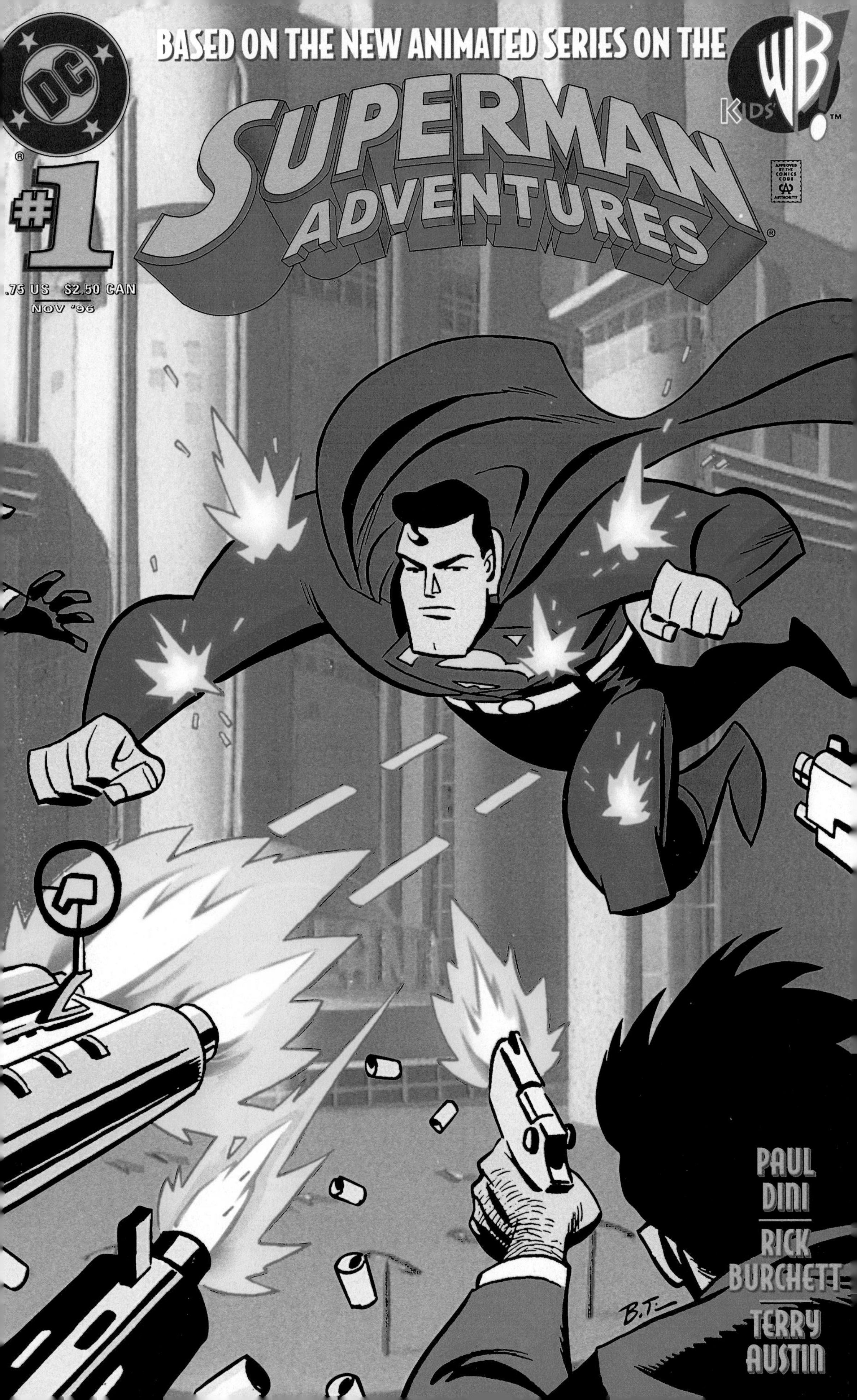
BASED ON THE NEW ANIMATED SERIES ON THE
KIDS' WB!
DC
SUPERMAN ADVENTURES
#1
.75 US $2.50 CAN
NOV '96
APPROVED BY THE COMICS CODE AUTHORITY
B.T.
PAUL DINI
RICK BURCHETT
TERRY AUSTIN

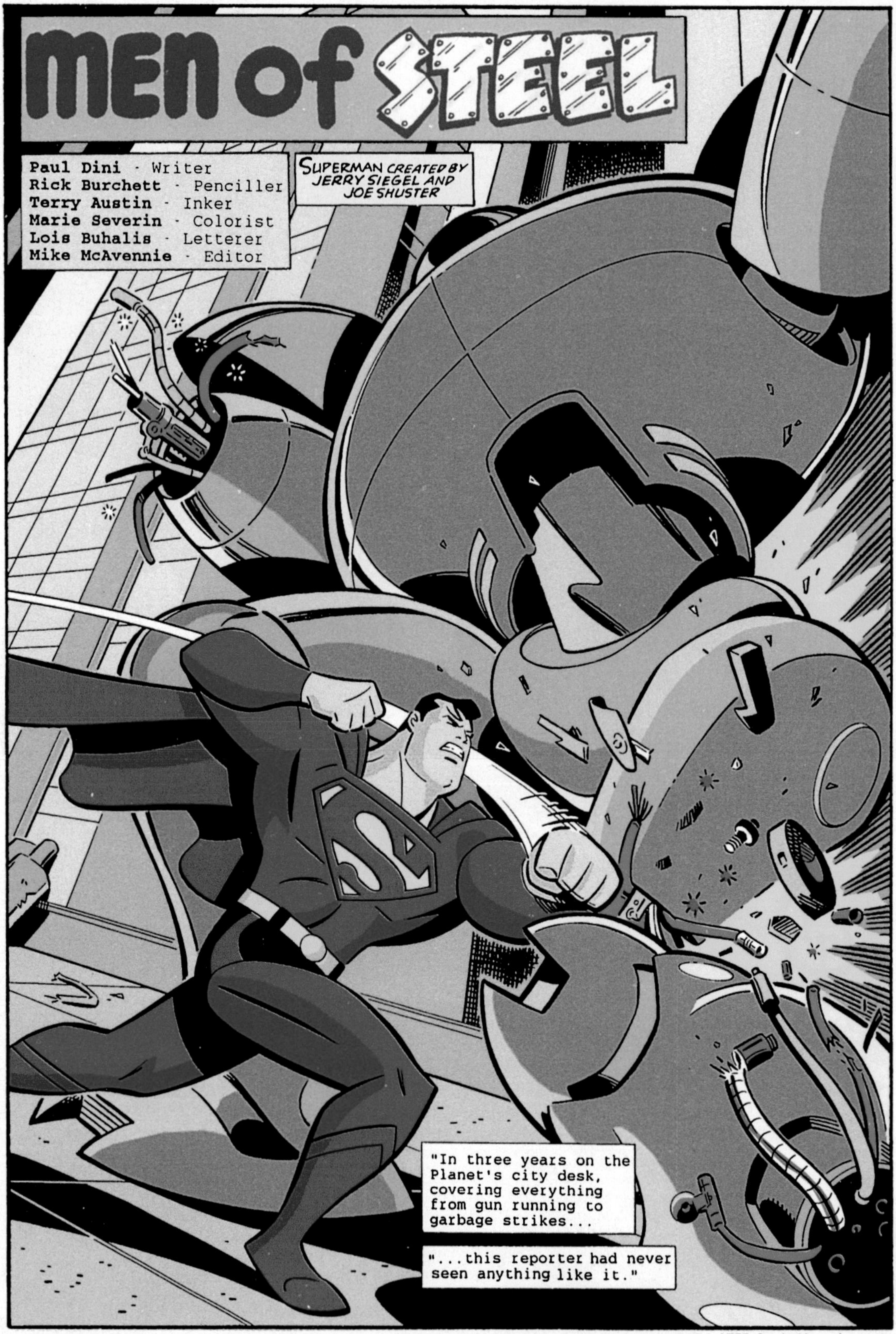
MEN OF STEEL
Paul Dini - Writer
Rick Burchett - Penciller
Terry Austin - Inker
Marie Severin - Colorist
Lois Buhalis - Letterer
Mike McAvennie - Editor
SUPERMAN CREATED BY JERRY SIEGEL AND JOE SHUSTER
"In three years on the Planet's city desk, covering everything from gun running to garbage strikes...
"...this reporter had never seen anything like it."

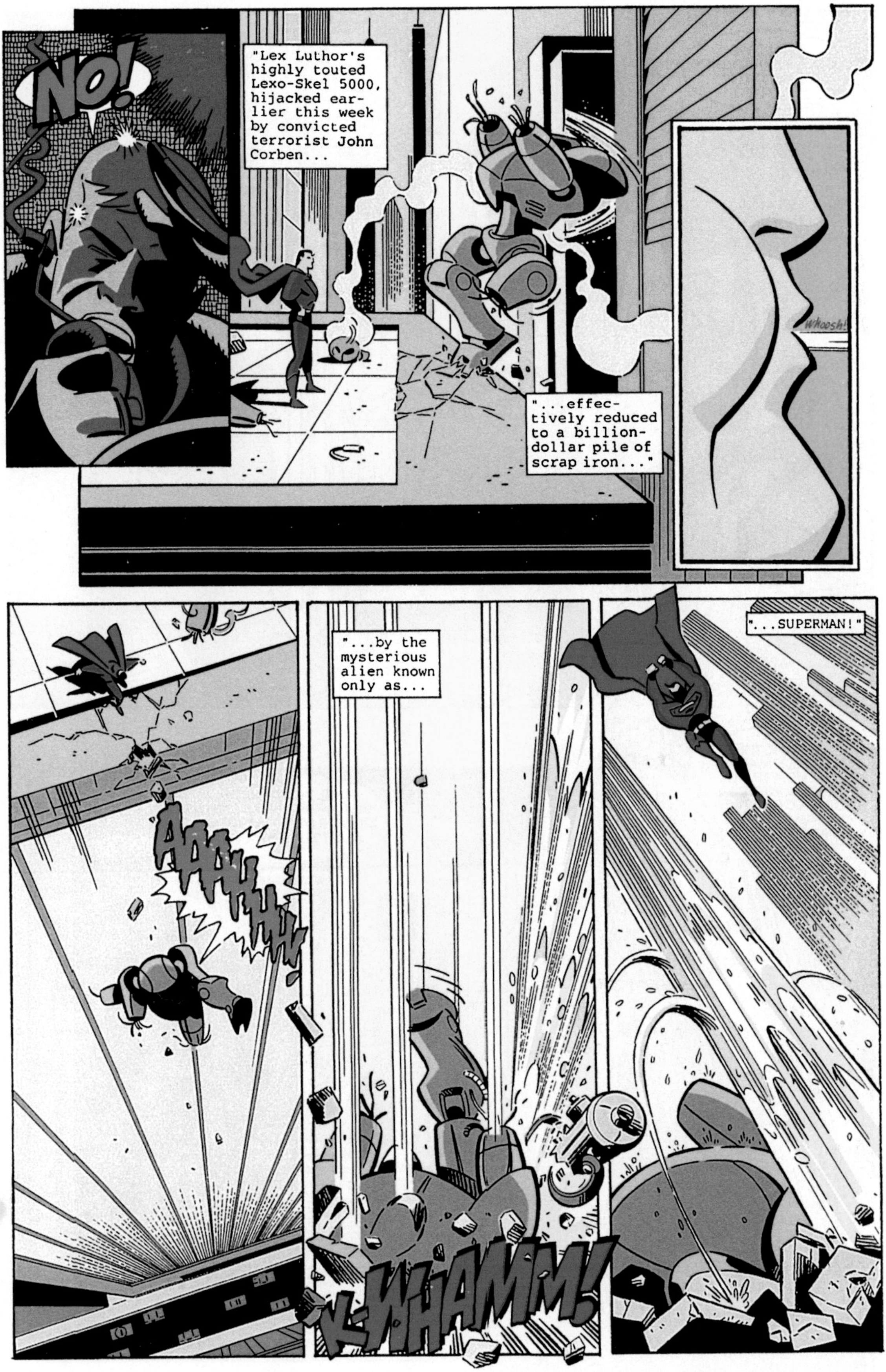
NO!
"Lex Luthor's highly touted Lexo-Skel 5000, hijacked ear-lier this week by convicted terrorist John Corben...
"...effec-tively reduced to a billion-dollar pile of scrap iron..."
WHOOSH!
"...by the mysterious alien known only as...
K-WHAMM!
"...SUPERMAN!"

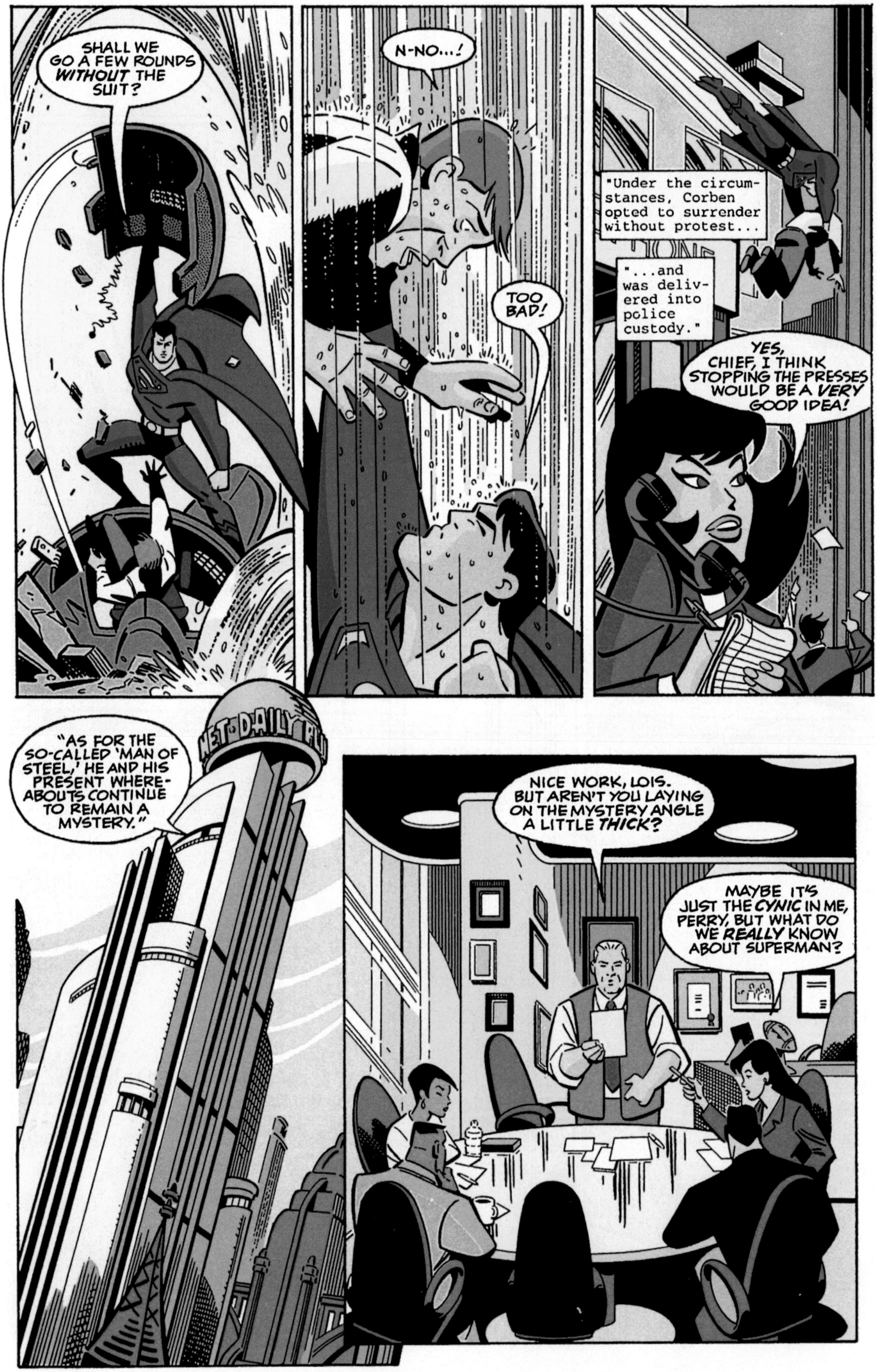
SHALL WE GO A FEW ROUNDS WITHOUT THE SUIT?
N-NO...!
TOO BAD!
"Under the circumstances, Corben opted to surrender without protest...
"...and was delivered into police custody."
YES, CHIEF, I THINK STOPPING THE PRESSES WOULD BE A VERY GOOD IDEA!
"AS FOR THE SO-CALLED 'MAN OF STEEL,' HE AND HIS PRESENT WHEREABOUTS CONTINUE TO REMAIN A MYSTERY."
NICE WORK, LOIS. BUT AREN'T YOU LAYING ON THE MYSTERY ANGLE A LITTLE THICK?
MAYBE IT'S JUST THE CYNIC IN ME, PERRY, BUT WHAT DO WE REALLY KNOW ABOUT SUPERMAN?

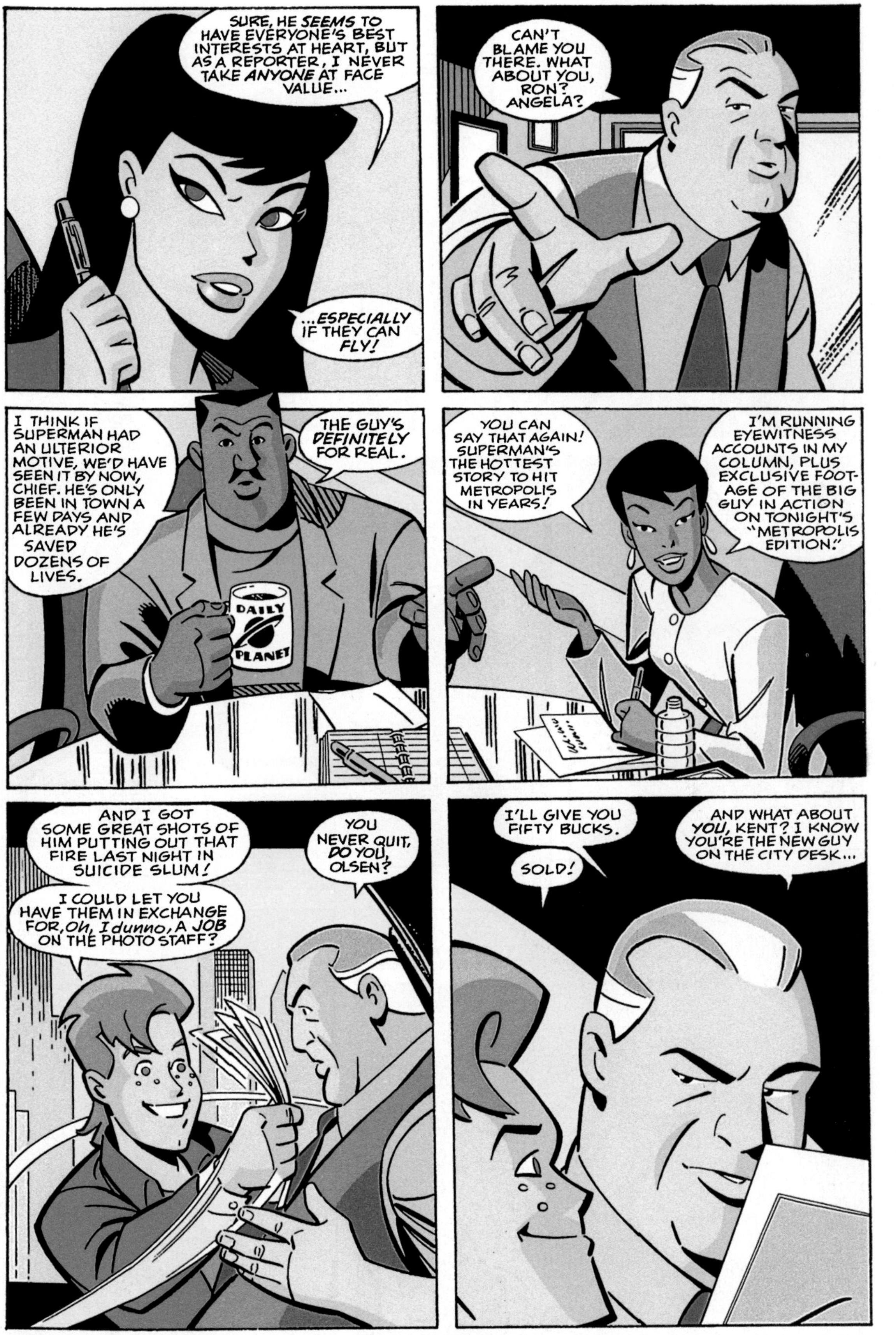
SURE, HE SEEMS TO HAVE EVERYONE'S BEST INTERESTS AT HEART, BUT AS A REPORTER, I NEVER TAKE ANYONE AT FACE VALUE...
...ESPECIALLY IF THEY CAN FLY!
CAN'T BLAME YOU THERE. WHAT ABOUT YOU, RON? ANGELA?
I THINK IF SUPERMAN HAD AN ULTERIOR MOTIVE, WE'D HAVE SEEN IT BY NOW, CHIEF. HE'S ONLY BEEN IN TOWN A FEW DAYS AND ALREADY HE'S SAVED DOZENS OF LIVES.
THE GUY'S DEFINITELY FOR REAL.
DAILY PLANET
YOU CAN SAY THAT AGAIN! SUPERMAN'S THE HOTTEST STORY TO HIT METROPOLIS IN YEARS!
I'M RUNNING EYEWITNESS ACCOUNTS IN MY COLUMN, PLUS EXCLUSIVE FOOTAGE OF THE BIG GUY IN ACTION ON TONIGHT'S "METROPOLIS EDITION."
AND I GOT SOME GREAT SHOTS OF HIM PUTTING OUT THAT FIRE LAST NIGHT IN SUICIDE SLUM!
I COULD LET YOU HAVE THEM IN EXCHANGE FOR, Oh, I dunno, A JOB ON THE PHOTO STAFF?
YOU NEVER QUIT, DO YOU, OLSEN?
I'LL GIVE YOU FIFTY BUCKS.
SOLD!
AND WHAT ABOUT YOU, KENT? I KNOW YOU'RE THE NEW GUY ON THE CITY DESK...

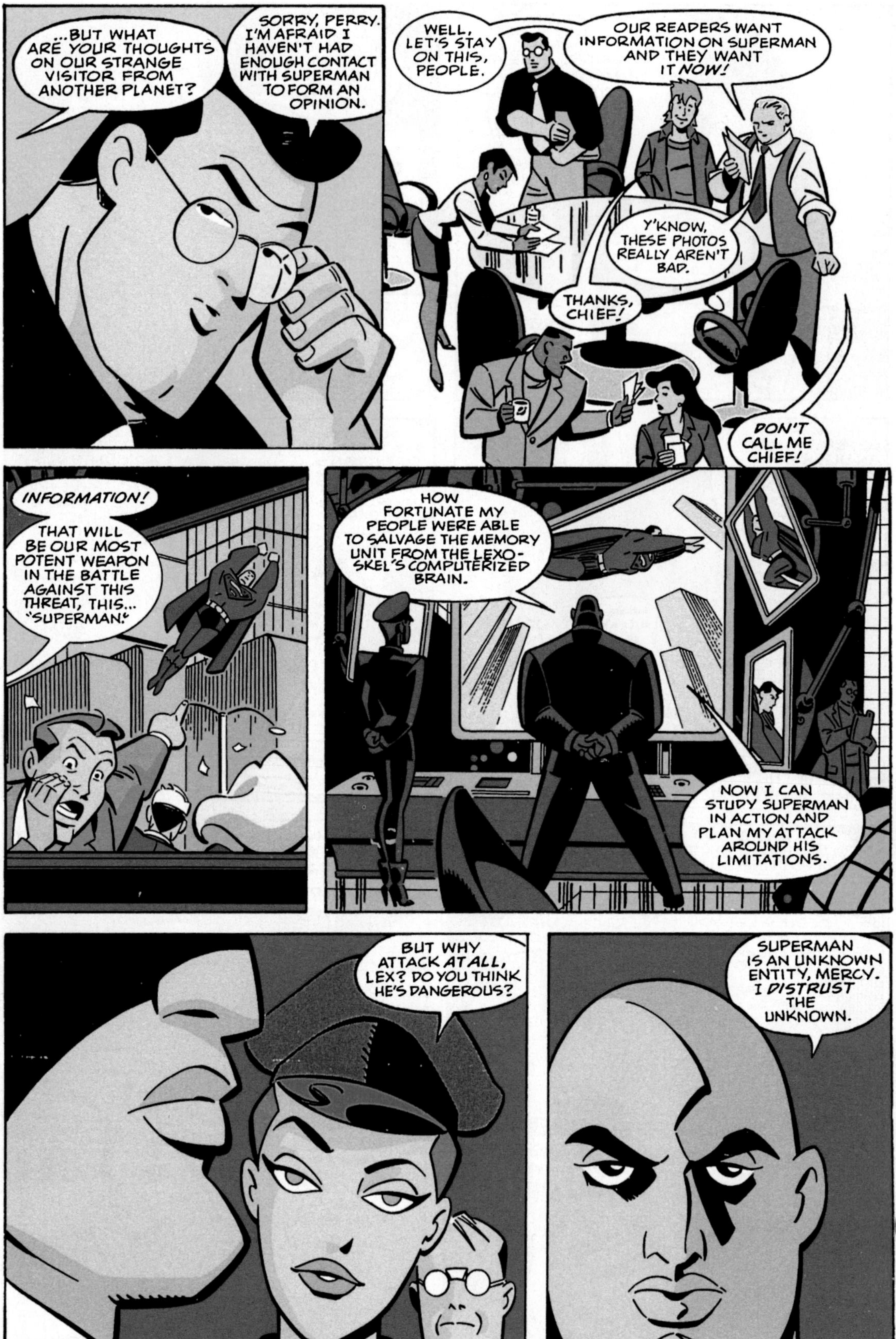
...BUT WHAT ARE YOUR THOUGHTS ON OUR STRANGE VISITOR FROM ANOTHER PLANET?
SORRY, PERRY. I'M AFRAID I HAVEN'T HAD ENOUGH CONTACT WITH SUPERMAN TO FORM AN OPINION.
WELL, LET'S STAY ON THIS, PEOPLE.
OUR READERS WANT INFORMATION ON SUPERMAN AND THEY WANT IT NOW!
Y'KNOW, THESE PHOTOS REALLY AREN'T BAD.
THANKS, CHIEF!
DON'T CALL ME CHIEF!
INFORMATION!
THAT WILL BE OUR MOST POTENT WEAPON IN THE BATTLE AGAINST THIS THREAT, THIS... "SUPERMAN."
HOW FORTUNATE MY PEOPLE WERE ABLE TO SALVAGE THE MEMORY UNIT FROM THE LEXO-SKEL'S COMPUTERIZED BRAIN.
NOW I CAN STUDY SUPERMAN IN ACTION AND PLAN MY ATTACK AROUND HIS LIMITATIONS.
BUT WHY ATTACK AT ALL, LEX? DO YOU THINK HE'S DANGEROUS?
SUPERMAN IS AN UNKNOWN ENTITY, MERCY. I DISTRUST THE UNKNOWN.

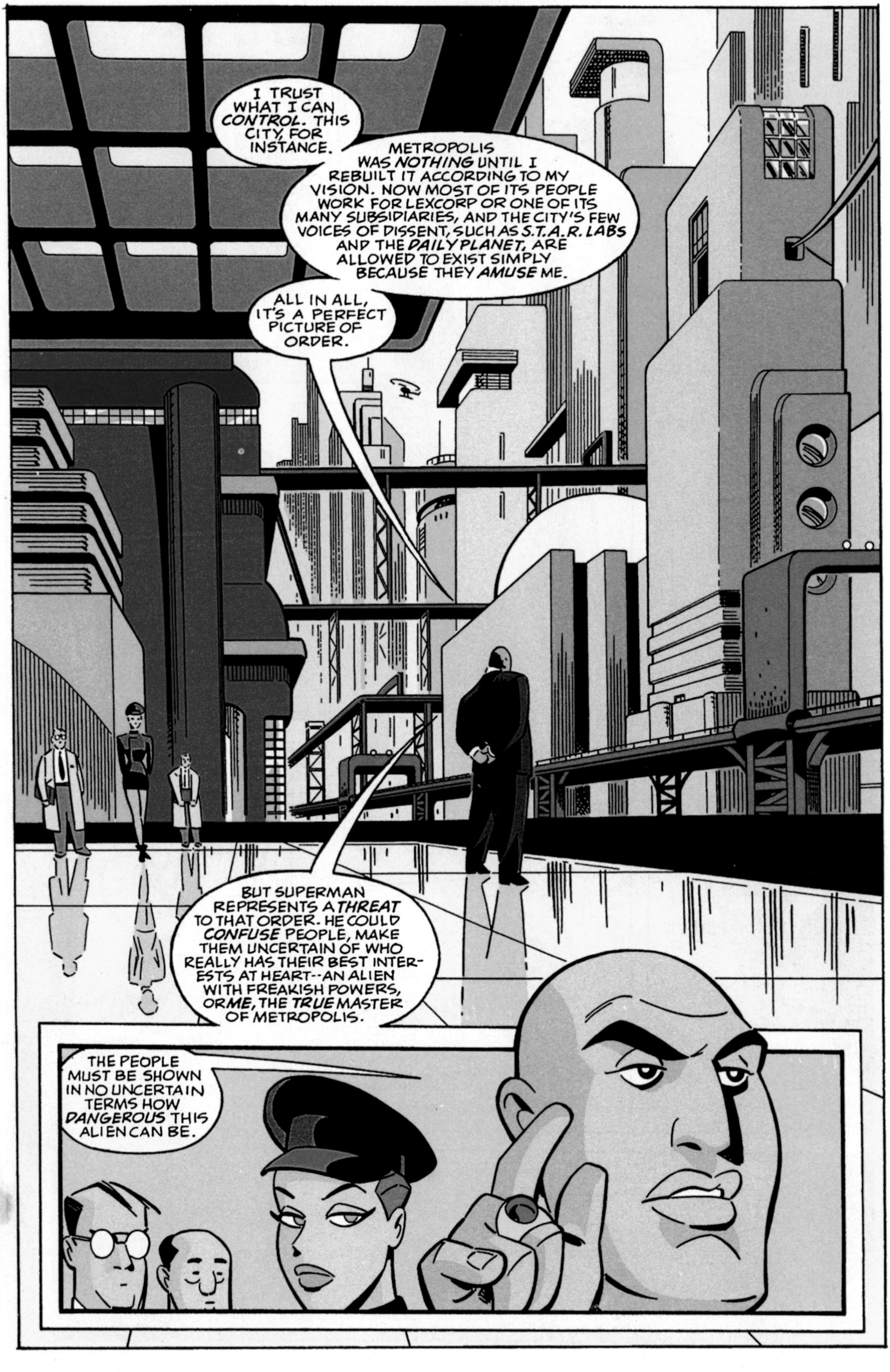
I TRUST WHAT I CAN CONTROL. THIS CITY, FOR INSTANCE.
METROPOLIS WAS NOTHING UNTIL I REBUILT IT ACCORDING TO MY VISION. NOW MOST OF ITS PEOPLE WORK FOR LEXCORP OR ONE OF ITS MANY SUBSIDIARIES, AND THE CITY'S FEW VOICES OF DISSENT, SUCH AS S.T.A.R. LABS AND THE DAILY PLANET, ARE ALLOWED TO EXIST SIMPLY BECAUSE THEY AMUSE ME.
ALL IN ALL, IT'S A PERFECT PICTURE OF ORDER.
BUT SUPERMAN REPRESENTS A THREAT TO THAT ORDER. HE COULD CONFUSE PEOPLE, MAKE THEM UNCERTAIN OF WHO REALLY HAS THEIR BEST INTERESTS AT HEART--AN ALIEN WITH FREAKISH POWERS, OR ME, THE TRUE MASTER OF METROPOLIS.
THE PEOPLE MUST BE SHOWN IN NO UNCERTAIN TERMS HOW DANGEROUS THIS ALIEN CAN BE.

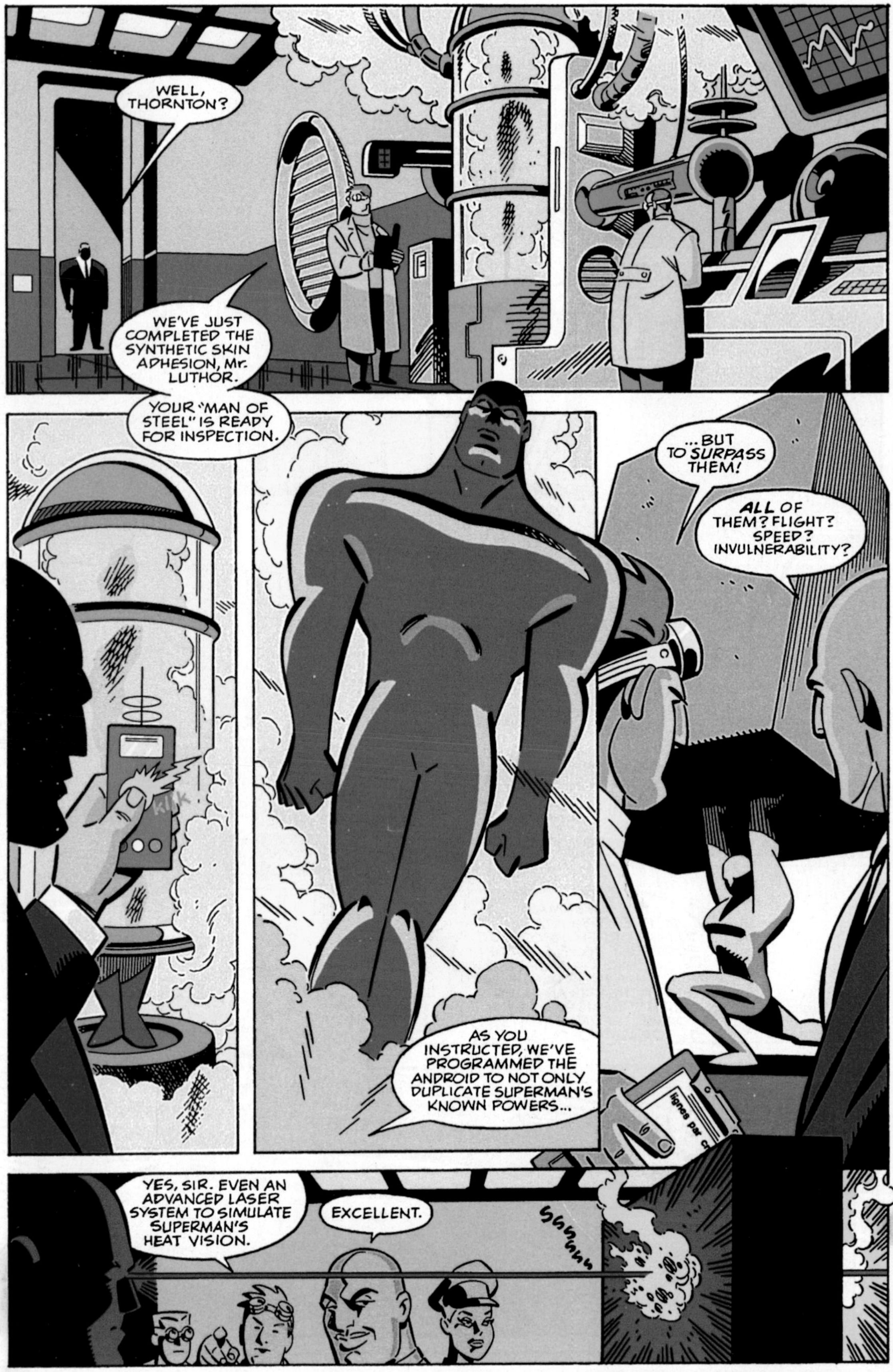
WELL, THORNTON?
WE'VE JUST COMPLETED THE SYNTHETIC SKIN ADHESION, Mr. LUTHOR.
YOUR "MAN OF STEEL" IS READY FOR INSPECTION.
KLIK
AS YOU INSTRUCTED, WE'VE PROGRAMMED THE ANDROID TO NOT ONLY DUPLICATE SUPERMAN'S KNOWN POWERS...
...BUT TO SURPASS THEM!
ALL OF THEM? FLIGHT? SPEED? INVULNERABILITY?
YES, SIR. EVEN AN ADVANCED LASER SYSTEM TO SIMULATE SUPERMAN'S HEAT VISION.
EXCELLENT.

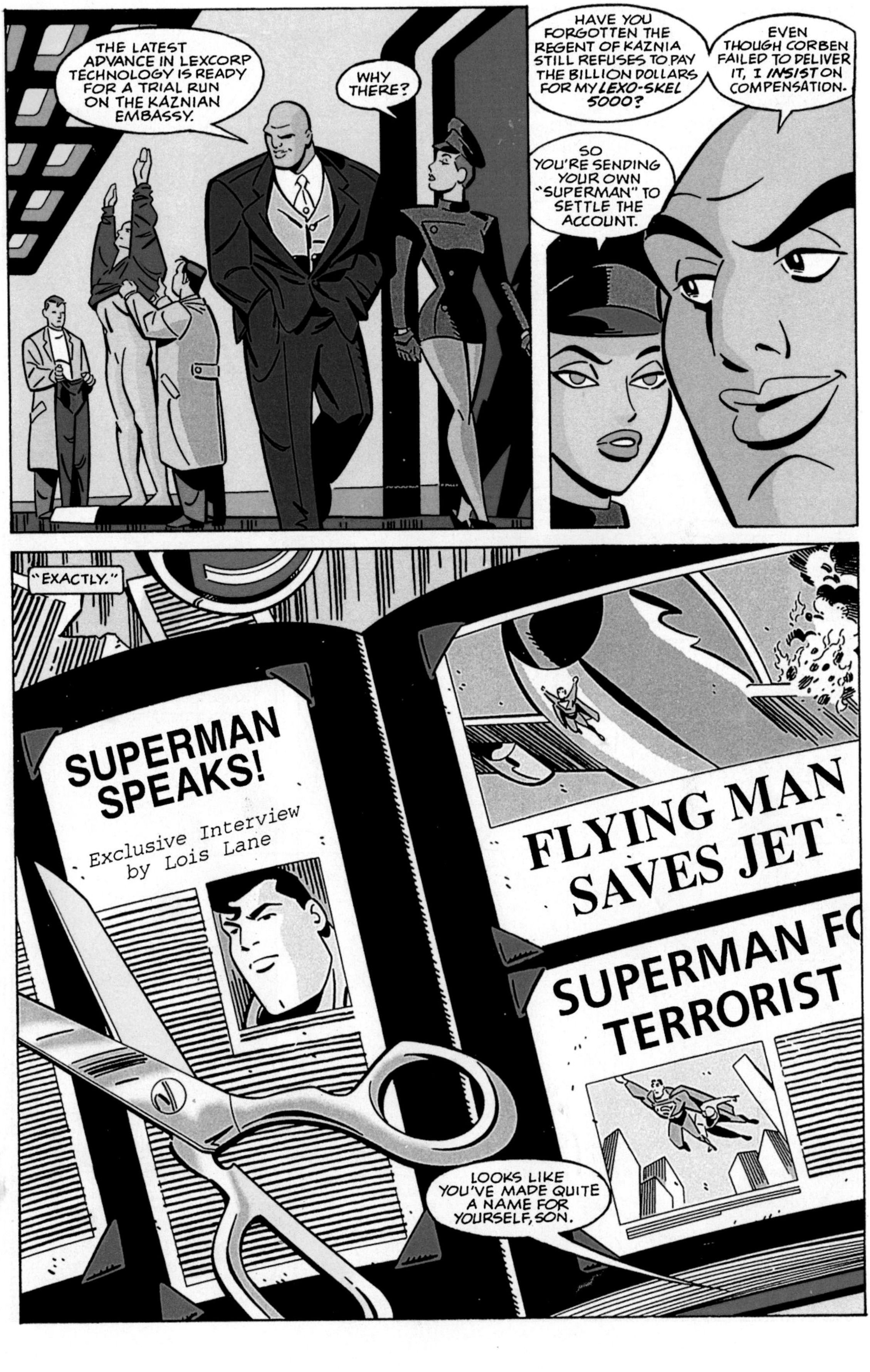
THE LATEST ADVANCE IN LEXCORP TECHNOLOGY IS READY FOR A TRIAL RUN ON THE KAZNIAN EMBASSY.
WHY THERE?
HAVE YOU FORGOTTEN THE REGENT OF KAZNIA STILL REFUSES TO PAY THE BILLION DOLLARS FOR MY LEXO-SKEL 5000?
EVEN THOUGH CORBEN FAILED TO DELIVER IT, I INSIST ON COMPENSATION.
SO YOU'RE SENDING YOUR OWN "SUPERMAN" TO SETTLE THE ACCOUNT.
"EXACTLY."
SUPERMAN SPEAKS!
Exclusive Interview by Lois Lane
FLYING MAN SAVES JET
SUPERMAN FO
TERRORIST
LOOKS LIKE YOU'VE MADE QUITE A NAME FOR YOURSELF, SON.

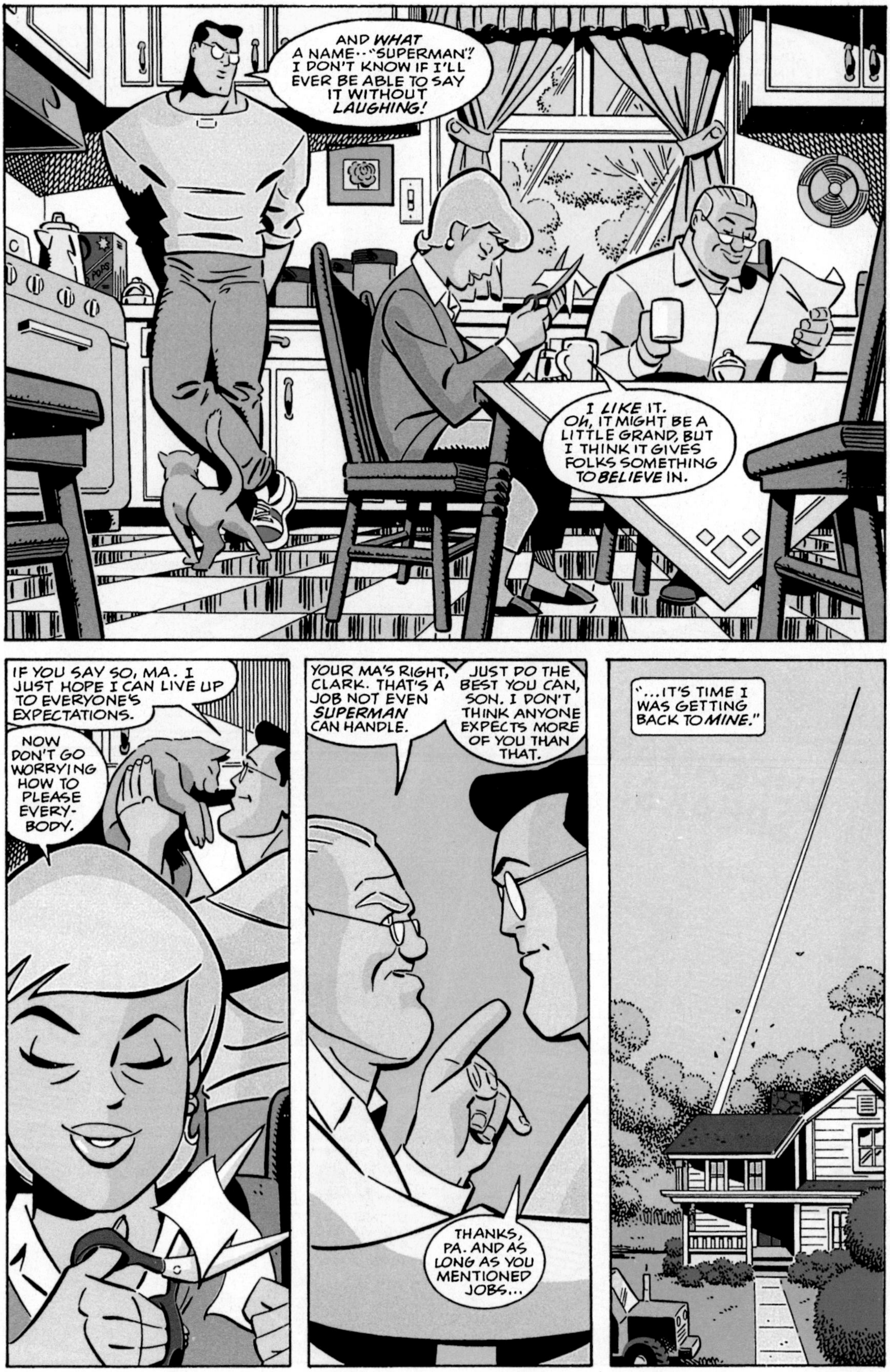
AND WHAT A NAME-- "SUPERMAN"! I DON'T KNOW IF I'LL EVER BE ABLE TO SAY IT WITHOUT LAUGHING!
I LIKE IT. Oh, IT MIGHT BE A LITTLE GRAND, BUT I THINK IT GIVES FOLKS SOMETHING TO BELIEVE IN.
IF YOU SAY SO, MA. I JUST HOPE I CAN LIVE UP TO EVERYONE'S EXPECTATIONS.
NOW DON'T GO WORRYING HOW TO PLEASE EVERY-BODY.
YOUR MA'S RIGHT, CLARK. THAT'S A JOB NOT EVEN SUPERMAN CAN HANDLE.
JUST DO THE BEST YOU CAN, SON. I DON'T THINK ANYONE EXPECTS MORE OF YOU THAN THAT.
THANKS, PA. AND AS LONG AS YOU MENTIONED JOBS...
"...IT'S TIME I WAS GETTING BACK TO MINE."

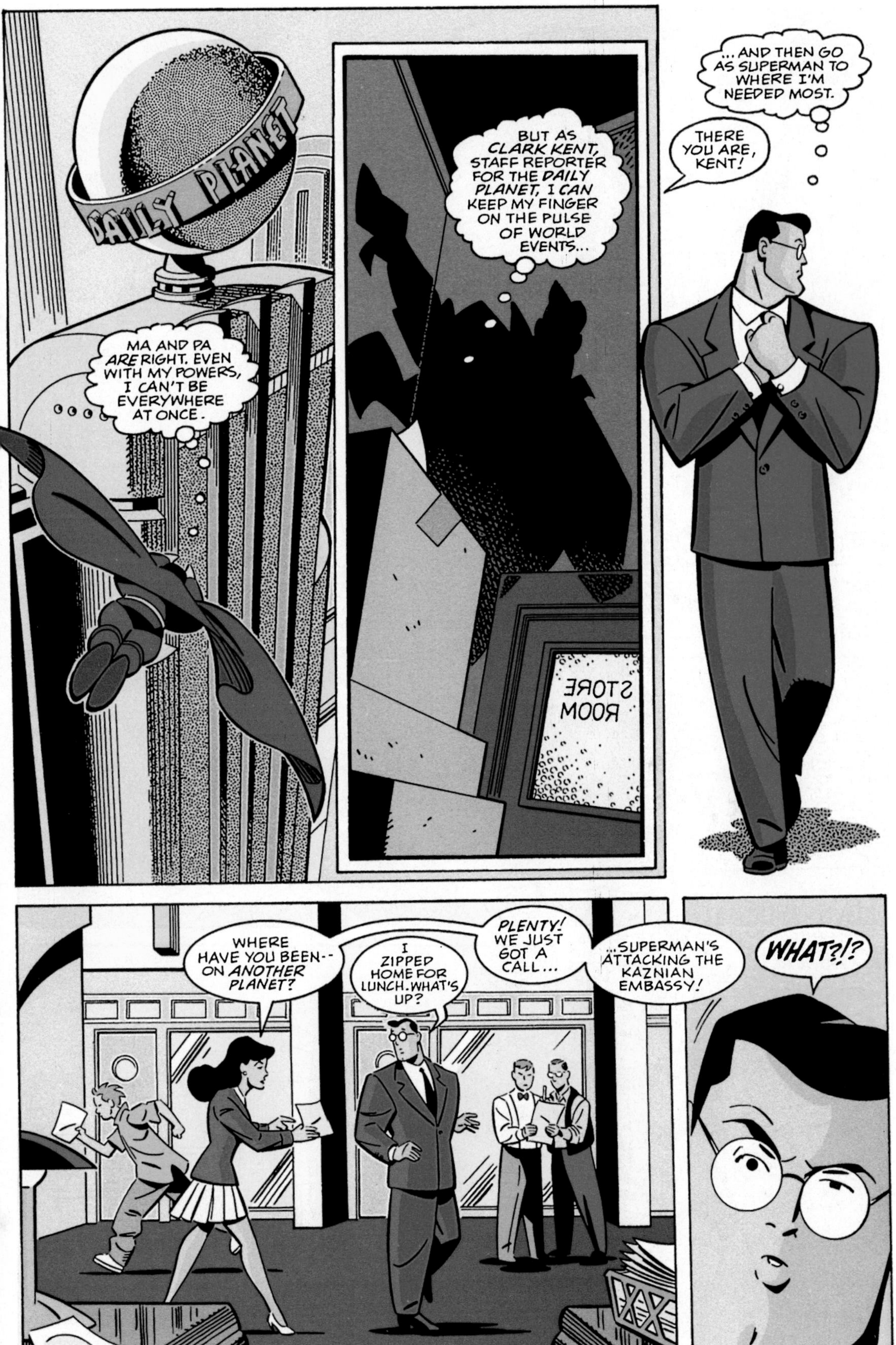

MA AND PA ARE RIGHT. EVEN WITH MY POWERS, I CAN'T BE EVERYWHERE AT ONCE.
BUT AS CLARK KENT, STAFF REPORTER FOR THE DAILY PLANET, I CAN KEEP MY FINGER ON THE PULSE OF WORLD EVENTS...
STORE ROOM
...AND THEN GO AS SUPERMAN TO WHERE I'M NEEDED MOST.
THERE YOU ARE, KENT!
WHERE HAVE YOU BEEN--ON ANOTHER PLANET?
I ZIPPED HOME FOR LUNCH. WHAT'S UP?
PLENTY! WE JUST GOT A CALL...
...SUPERMAN'S ATTACKING THE KAZNIAN EMBASSY!
WHAT?!?

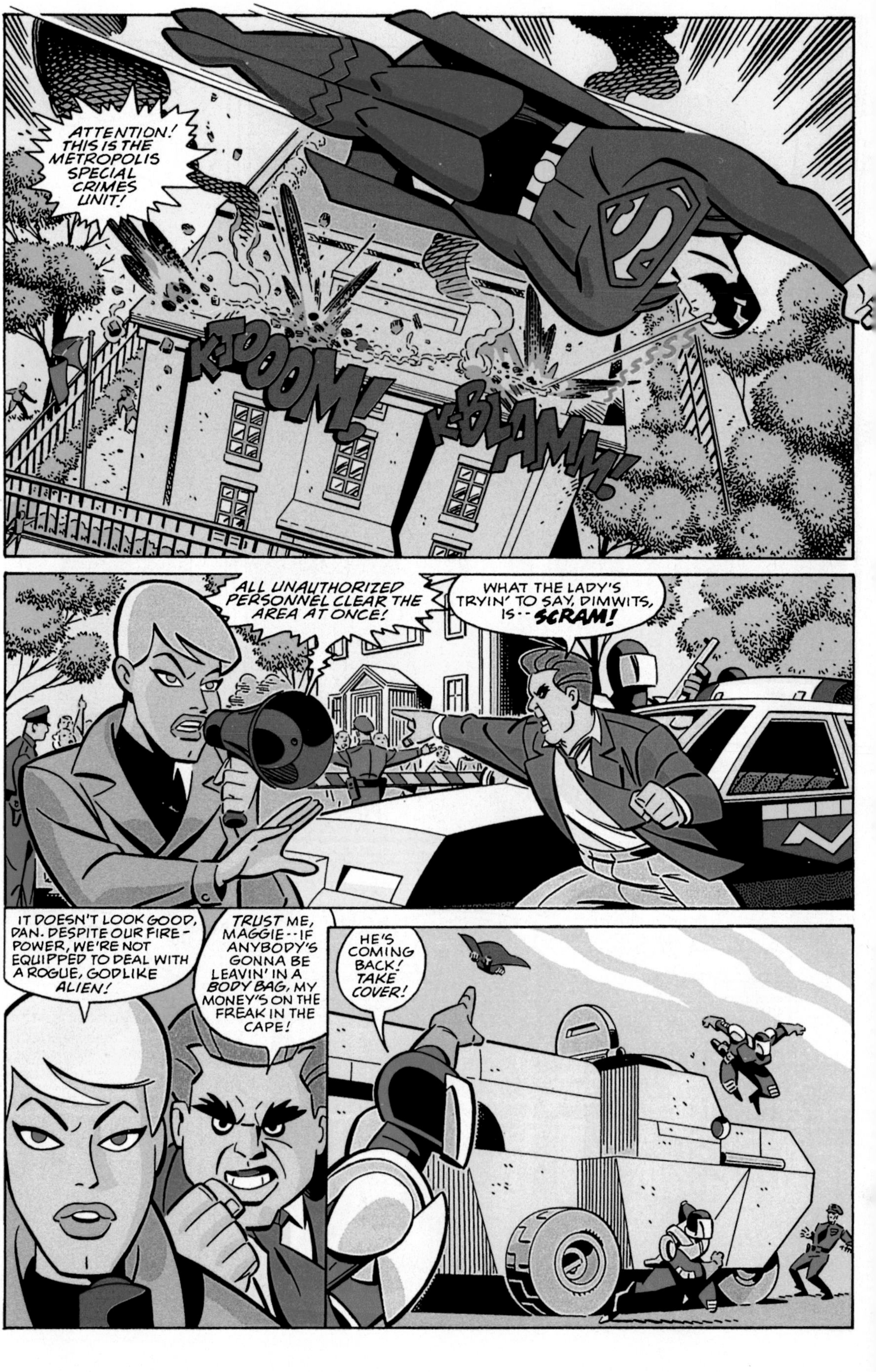
ATTENTION! THIS IS THE METROPOLIS SPECIAL CRIMES UNIT!
K-TOOOM!
K-BLAMM!
ALL UNAUTHORIZED PERSONNEL CLEAR THE AREA AT ONCE!
WHAT THE LADY'S TRYIN' TO SAY, DIMWITS, IS--SCRAM!
IT DOESN'T LOOK GOOD, DAN. DESPITE OUR FIRE-POWER, WE'RE NOT EQUIPPED TO DEAL WITH A ROGUE, GODLIKE ALIEN!
TRUST ME, MAGGIE--IF ANYBODY'S GONNA BE LEAVIN' IN A BODY BAG, MY MONEY'S ON THE FREAK IN THE CAPE!
HE'S COMING BACK! TAKE COVER!

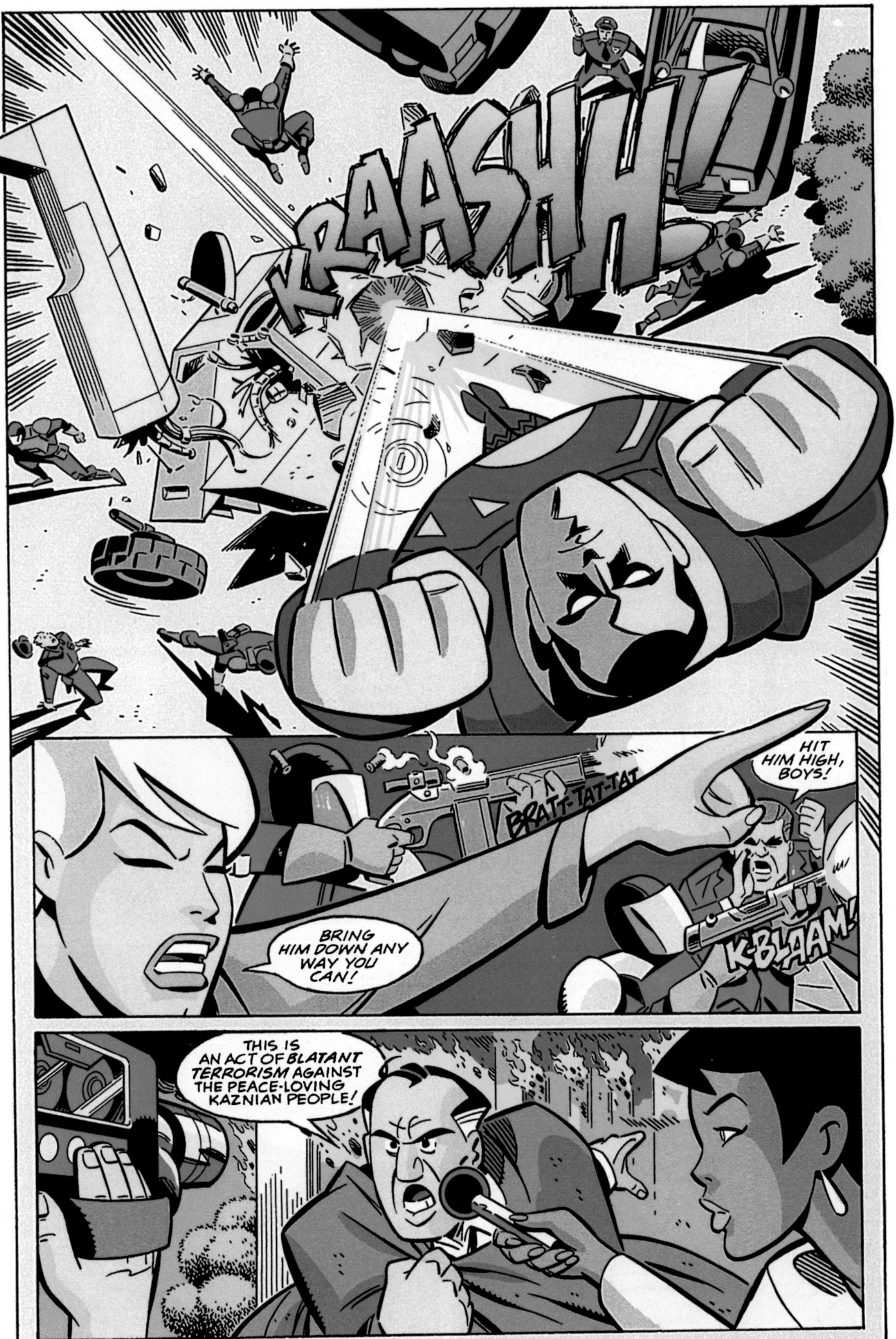
KRAASHH!!
BRATT-TAT-TAT
HIT HIM HIGH, BOYS!
BRING HIM DOWN ANY WAY YOU CAN!
K-BLAAM!
THIS IS AN ACT OF BLATANT TERRORISM AGAINST THE PEACE-LOVING KAZNIAN PEOPLE!

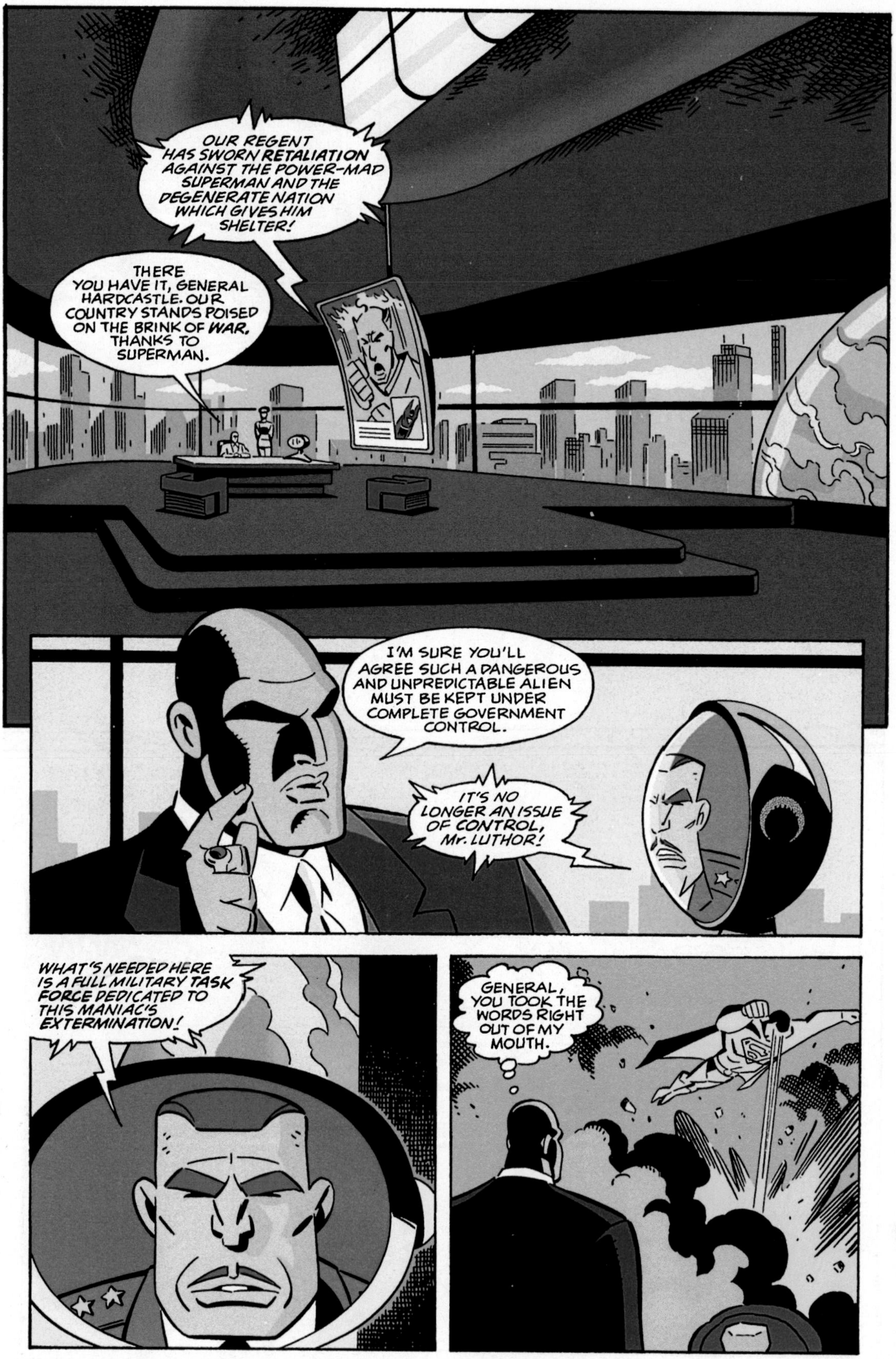
OUR REGENT HAS SWORN RETALIATION AGAINST THE POWER-MAD SUPERMAN AND THE DEGENERATE NATION WHICH GIVES HIM SHELTER!
THERE YOU HAVE IT, GENERAL HARDCASTLE. OUR COUNTRY STANDS POISED ON THE BRINK OF WAR, THANKS TO SUPERMAN.
I'M SURE YOU'LL AGREE SUCH A DANGEROUS AND UNPREDICTABLE ALIEN MUST BE KEPT UNDER COMPLETE GOVERNMENT CONTROL.
IT'S NO LONGER AN ISSUE OF CONTROL, Mr. LUTHOR!
WHAT'S NEEDED HERE IS A FULL MILITARY TASK FORCE DEDICATED TO THIS MANIAC'S EXTERMINATION!
GENERAL, YOU TOOK THE WORDS RIGHT OUT OF MY MOUTH.

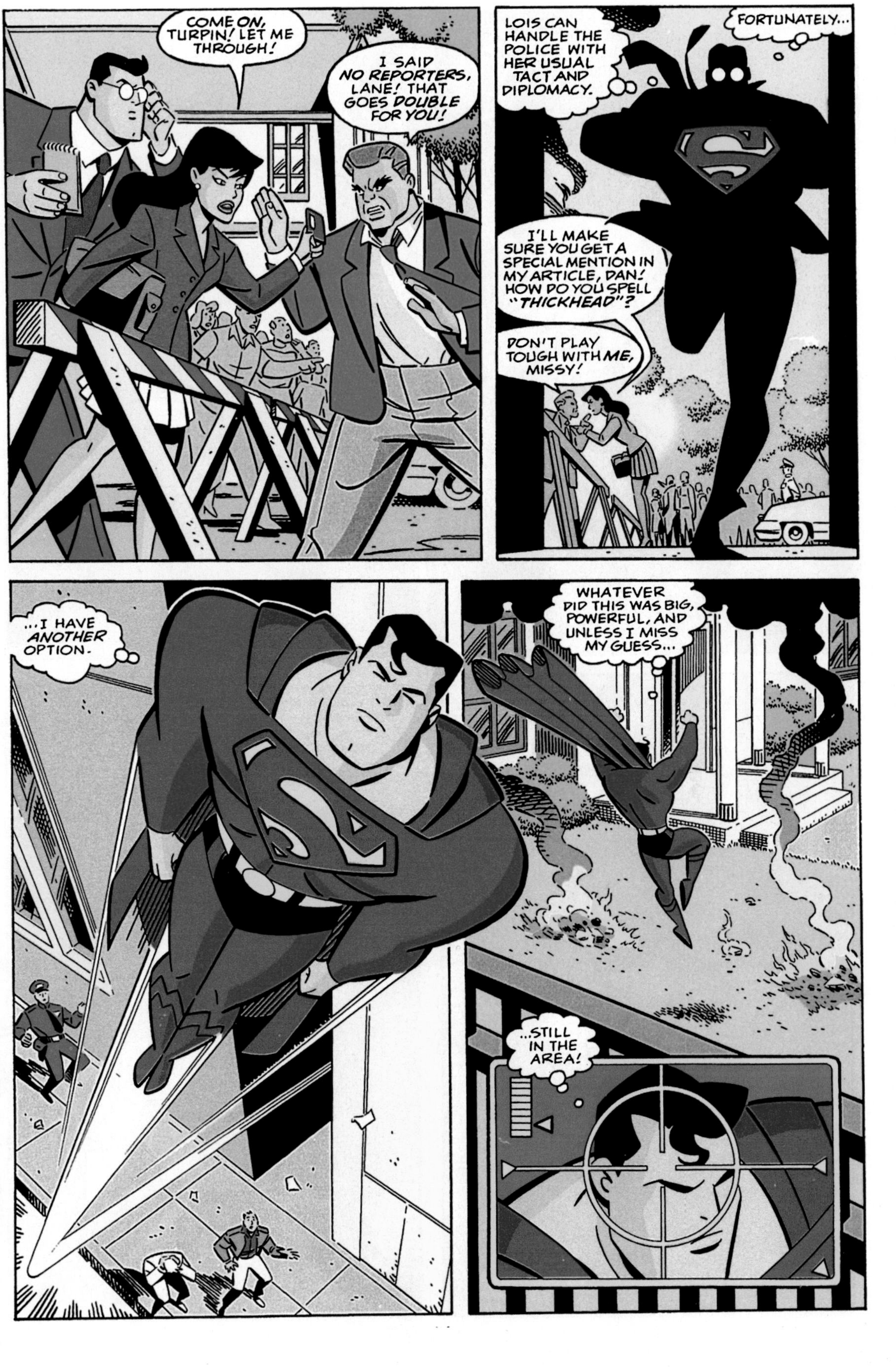
COME ON, TURPIN! LET ME THROUGH!
I SAID NO REPORTERS, LANE! THAT GOES DOUBLE FOR YOU!
LOIS CAN HANDLE THE POLICE WITH HER USUAL TACT AND DIPLOMACY.
FORTUNATELY...
I'LL MAKE SURE YOU GET A SPECIAL MENTION IN MY ARTICLE, DAN! HOW DO YOU SPELL "THICKHEAD"?
DON'T PLAY TOUGH WITH ME, MISSY!
...I HAVE ANOTHER OPTION.
WHATEVER DID THIS WAS BIG, POWERFUL, AND UNLESS I MISS MY GUESS...
...STILL IN THE AREA!

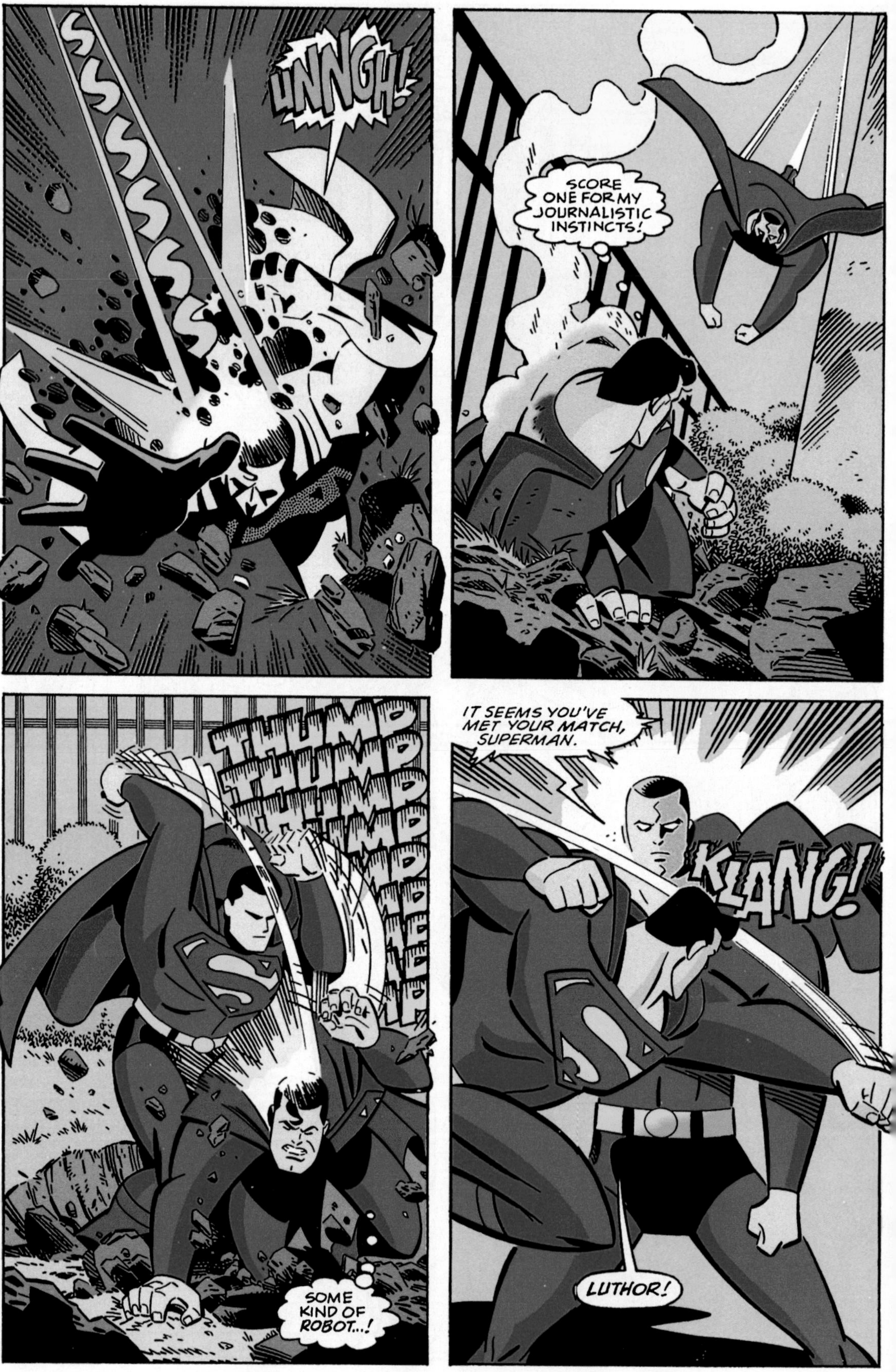
SSSSSS
UNNGH!
SCORE ONE FOR MY JOURNALISTIC INSTINCTS!
THUMP THUMP THUMP THUMP
SOME KIND OF ROBOT...!
IT SEEMS YOU'VE MET YOUR MATCH, SUPERMAN.
KLANG!
LUTHOR!

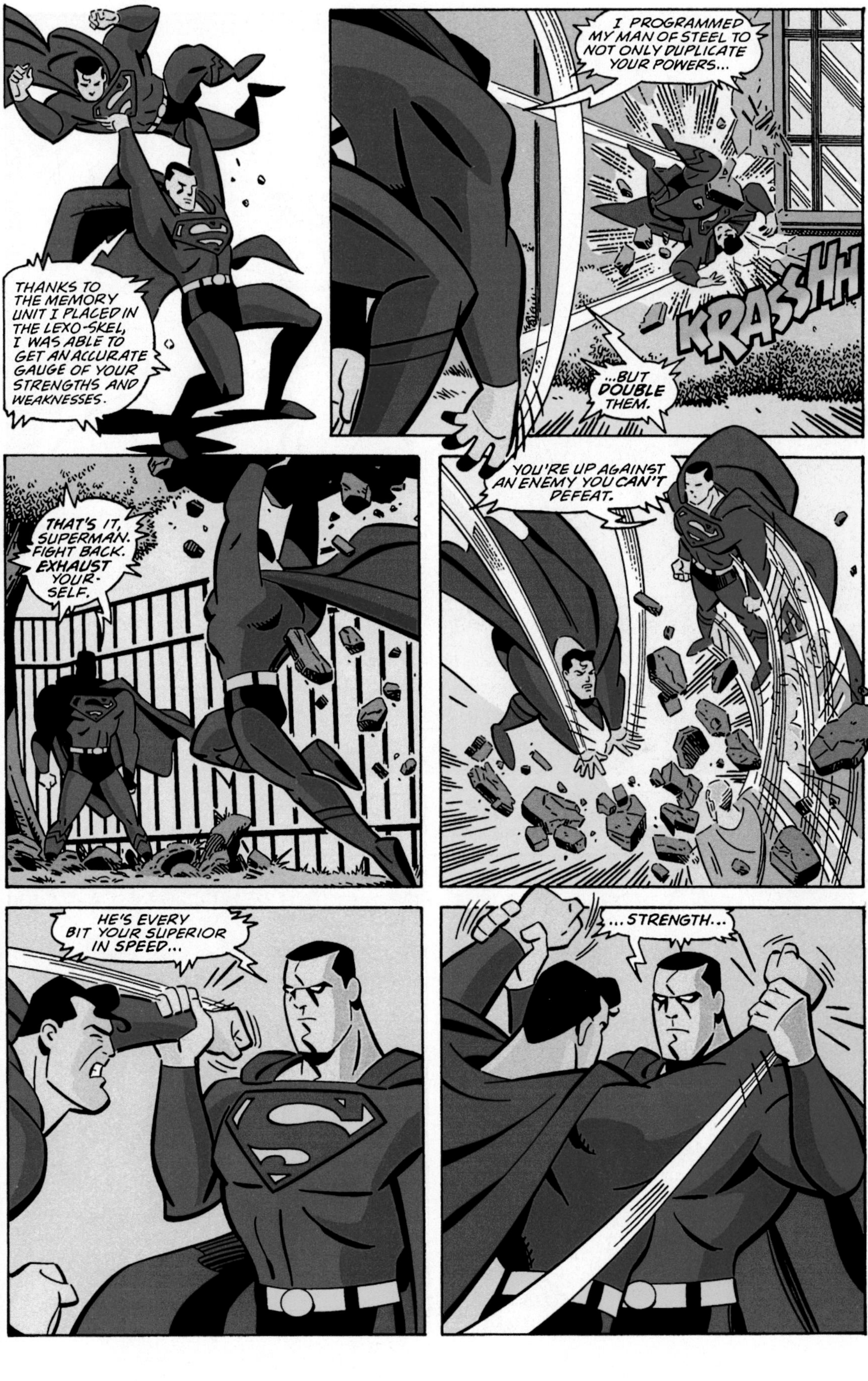
THANKS TO THE MEMORY UNIT I PLACED IN THE LEXO-SKEL, I WAS ABLE TO GET AN ACCURATE GAUGE OF YOUR STRENGTHS AND WEAKNESSES.
I PROGRAMMED MY MAN OF STEEL TO NOT ONLY DUPLICATE YOUR POWERS...
KRASSHH
...BUT DOUBLE THEM.
THAT'S IT, SUPERMAN. FIGHT BACK. EXHAUST YOUR-SELF.
YOU'RE UP AGAINST AN ENEMY YOU CAN'T DEFEAT.
HE'S EVERY BIT YOUR SUPERIOR IN SPEED...
...STRENGTH...

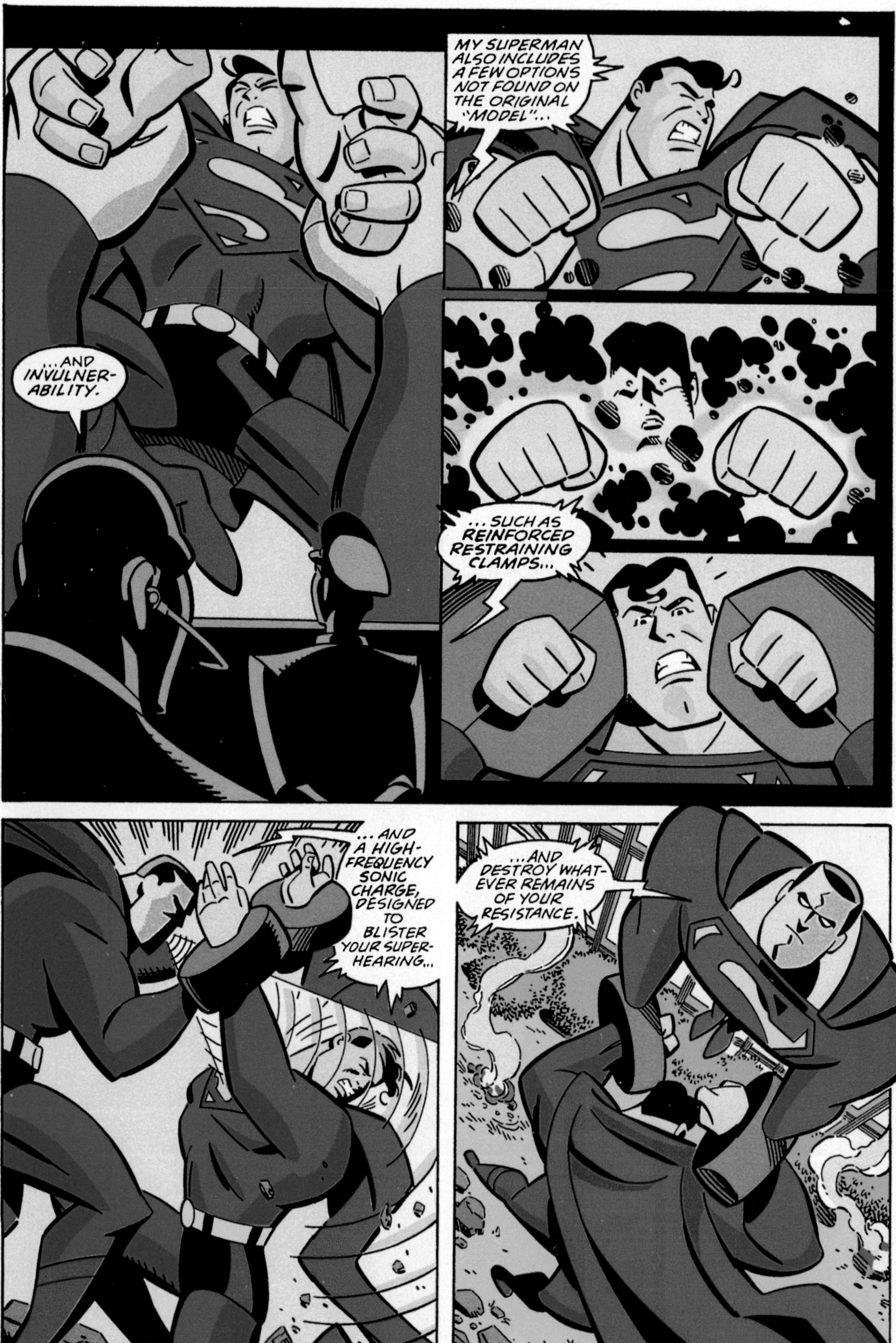
MY SUPERMAN ALSO INCLUDES A FEW OPTIONS NOT FOUND ON THE ORIGINAL "MODEL"...
...AND INVULNER-ABILITY.
...SUCH AS REINFORCED RESTRAINING CLAMPS...
...AND A HIGH-FREQUENCY SONIC CHARGE, DESIGNED TO BLISTER YOUR SUPER-HEARING...
...AND DESTROY WHAT-EVER REMAINS OF YOUR RESISTANCE.

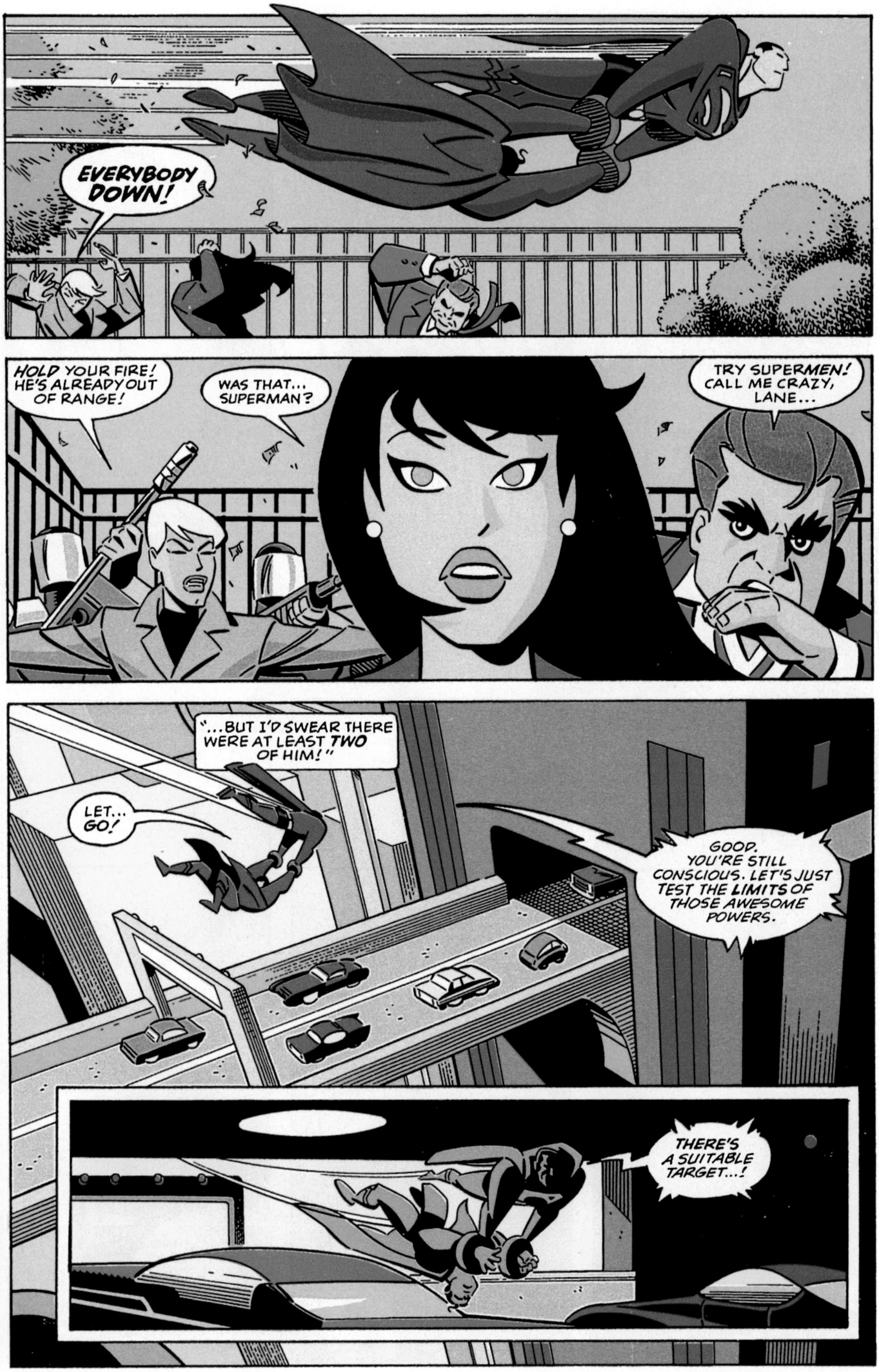
EVERYBODY DOWN!
HOLD YOUR FIRE! HE'S ALREADY OUT OF RANGE!
WAS THAT... SUPERMAN?
TRY SUPERMEN! CALL ME CRAZY, LANE...
"...BUT I'D SWEAR THERE WERE AT LEAST TWO OF HIM!"
LET... GO!
GOOD. YOU'RE STILL CONSCIOUS. LET'S JUST TEST THE LIMITS OF THOSE AWESOME POWERS.
THERE'S A SUITABLE TARGET...!

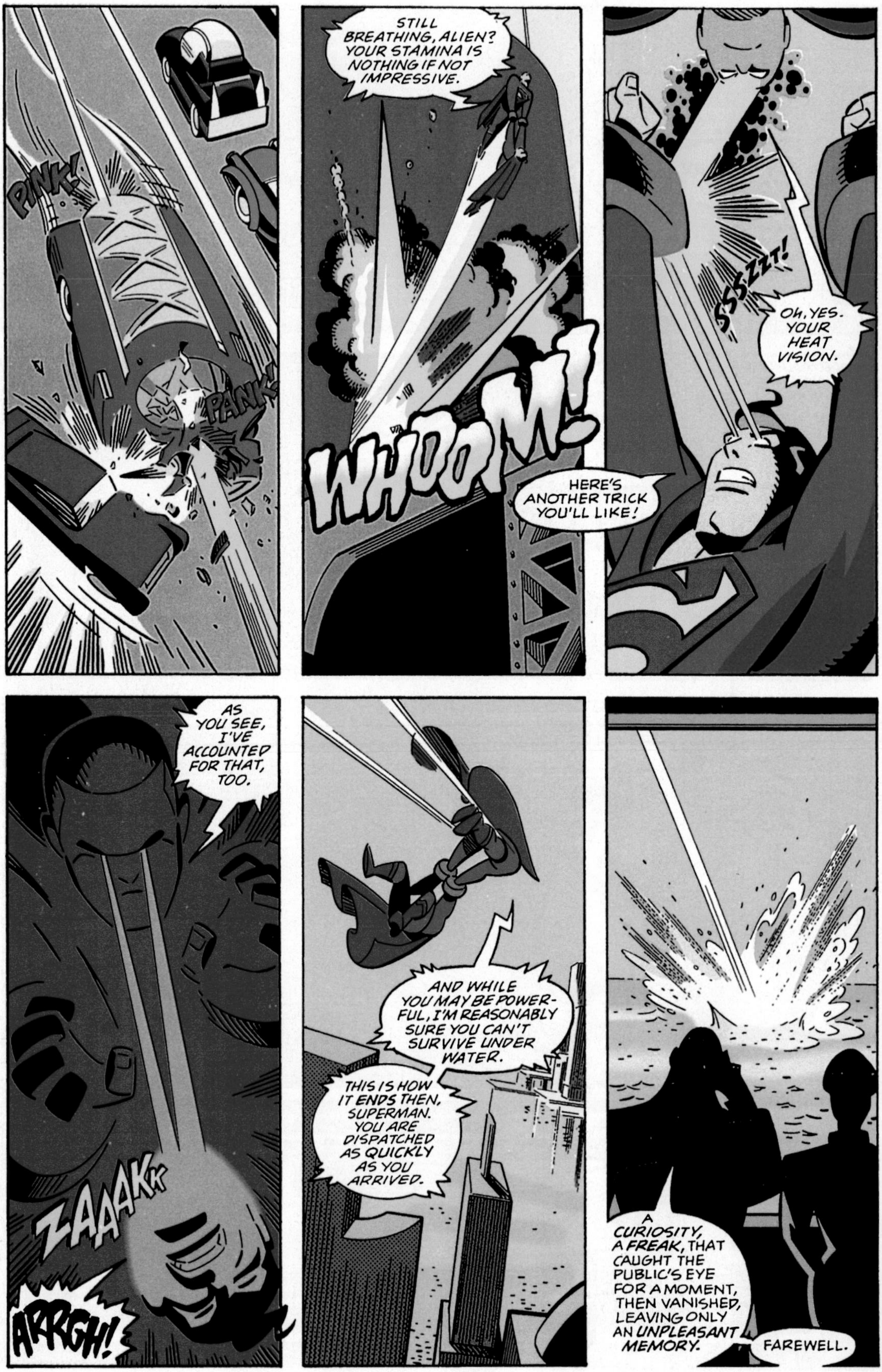
PINK!
PANK!
STILL BREATHING, ALIEN? YOUR STAMINA IS NOTHING IF NOT IMPRESSIVE.
WHOOM!
HERE'S ANOTHER TRICK YOU'LL LIKE!
SSSZZZT!
Oh, YES. YOUR HEAT VISION.
AS YOU SEE, I'VE ACCOUNTED FOR THAT, TOO.
ZAAAKK
ARRGH!
AND WHILE YOU MAY BE POWERFUL, I'M REASONABLY SURE YOU CAN'T SURVIVE UNDER WATER.
THIS IS HOW IT ENDS THEN, SUPERMAN. YOU ARE DISPATCHED AS QUICKLY AS YOU ARRIVED.
A CURIOSITY, A FREAK, THAT CAUGHT THE PUBLIC'S EYE FOR A MOMENT, THEN VANISHED, LEAVING ONLY AN UNPLEASANT MEMORY.
FAREWELL.

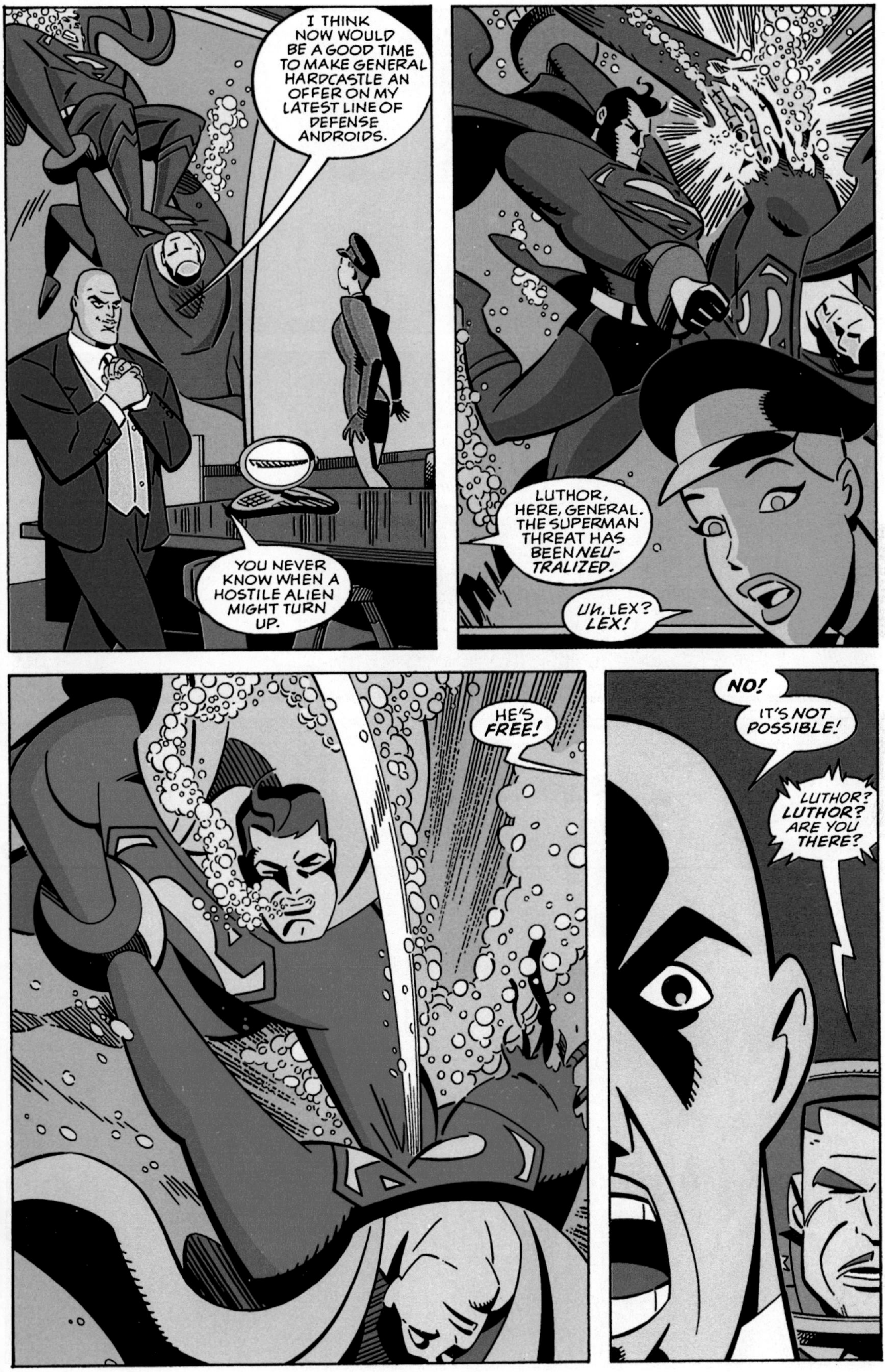

I THINK NOW WOULD BE A GOOD TIME TO MAKE GENERAL HARDCASTLE AN OFFER ON MY LATEST LINE OF DEFENSE ANDROIDS.
YOU NEVER KNOW WHEN A HOSTILE ALIEN MIGHT TURN UP.
LUTHOR, HERE, GENERAL. THE SUPERMAN THREAT HAS BEEN NEUTRALIZED.
UH, LEX? LEX!
HE'S FREE!
NO!
IT'S NOT POSSIBLE!
LUTHOR? LUTHOR? ARE YOU THERE?

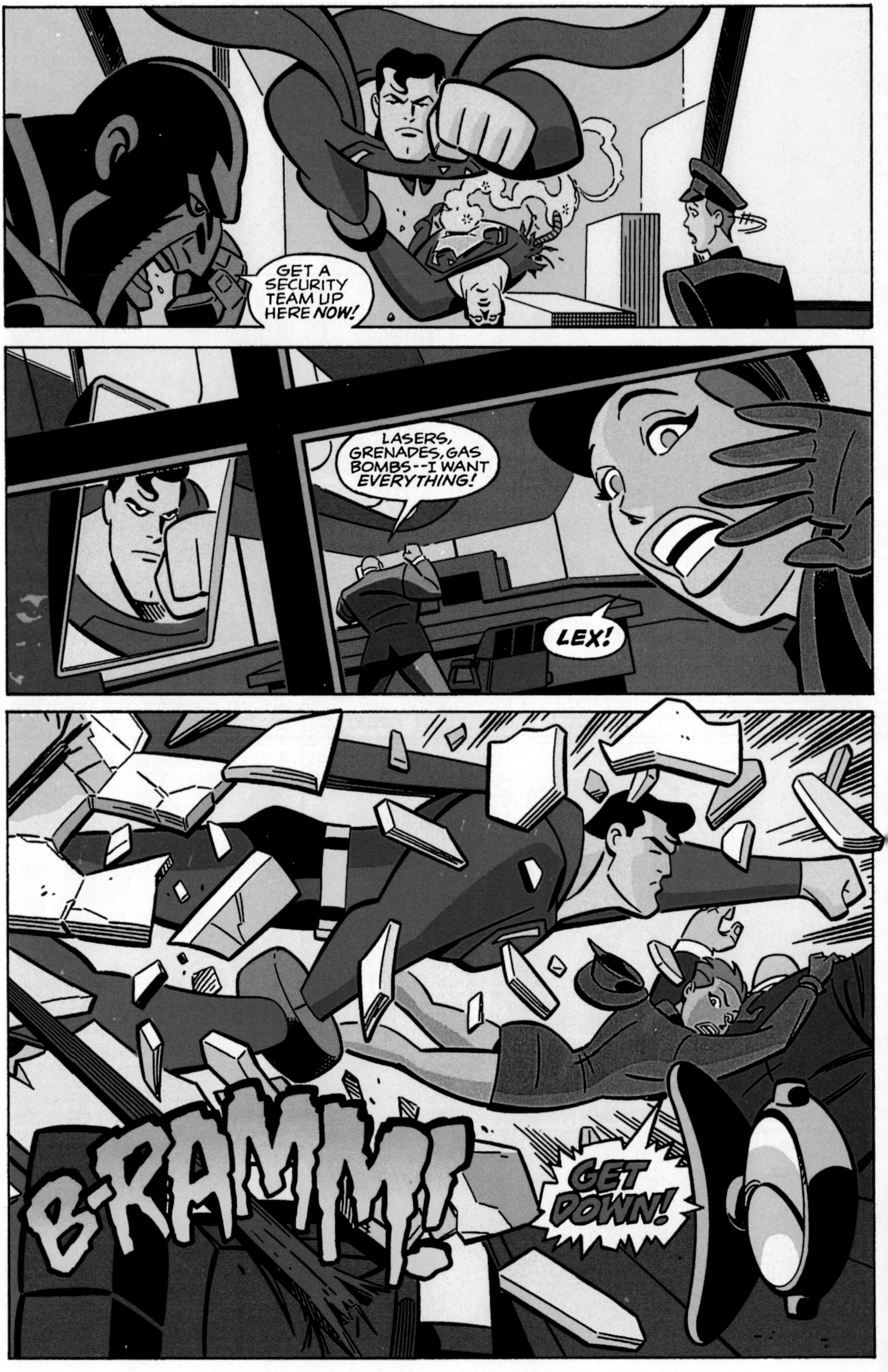
GET A SECURITY TEAM UP HERE NOW!
LASERS, GRENADES, GAS BOMBS--I WANT EVERYTHING!
LEX!
B-RAMM!
GET DOWN!

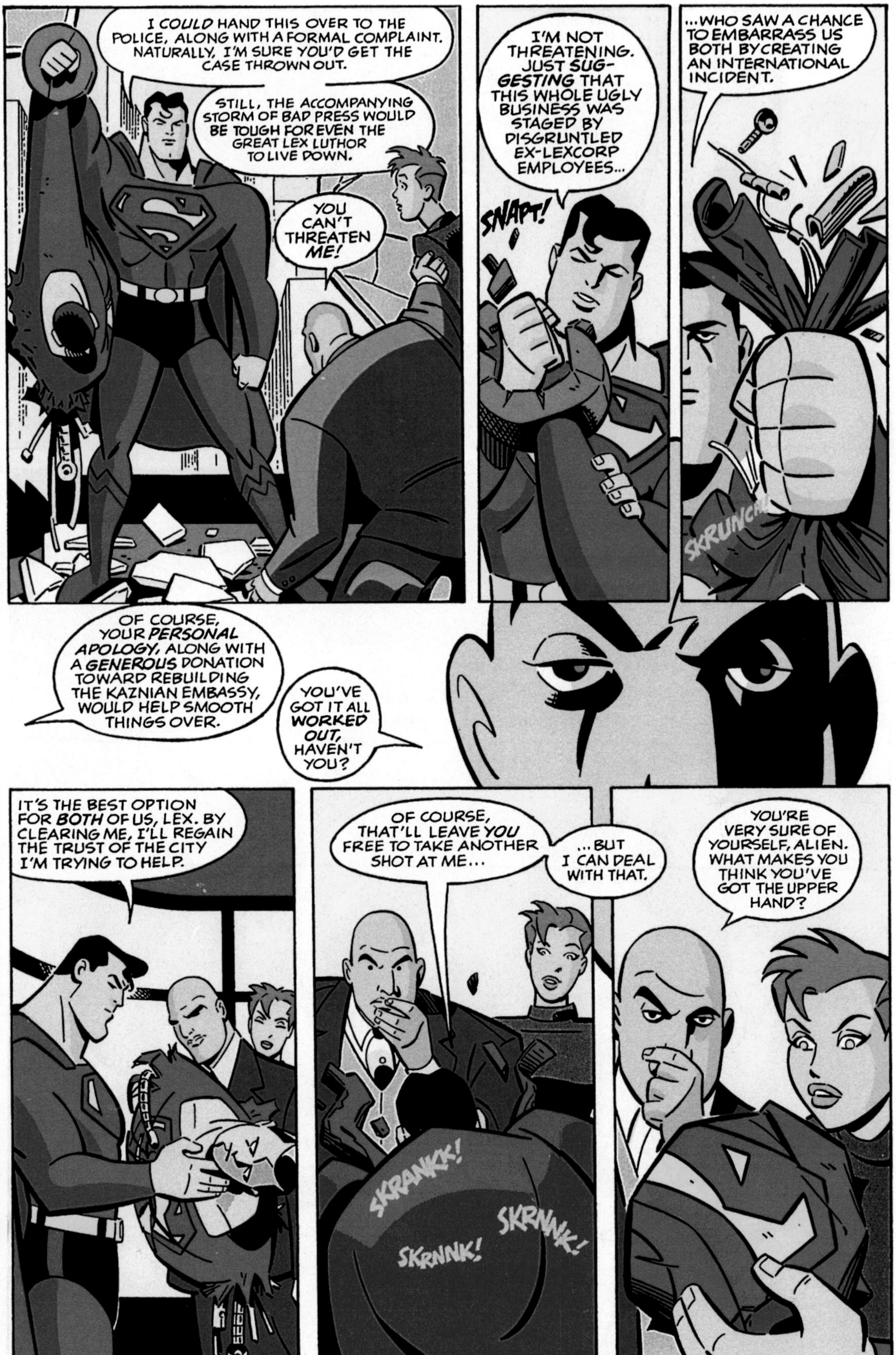
I COULD HAND THIS OVER TO THE POLICE, ALONG WITH A FORMAL COMPLAINT. NATURALLY, I'M SURE YOU'D GET THE CASE THROWN OUT.
STILL, THE ACCOMPANYING STORM OF BAD PRESS WOULD BE TOUGH FOR EVEN THE GREAT LEX LUTHOR TO LIVE DOWN.
YOU CAN'T THREATEN ME!
I'M NOT THREATENING. JUST SUGGESTING THAT THIS WHOLE UGLY BUSINESS WAS STAGED BY DISGRUNTLED EX-LEXCORP EMPLOYEES...
SNAPT!
...WHO SAW A CHANCE TO EMBARRASS US BOTH BY CREATING AN INTERNATIONAL INCIDENT.
OF COURSE, YOUR PERSONAL APOLOGY, ALONG WITH A GENEROUS DONATION TOWARD REBUILDING THE KAZNIAN EMBASSY, WOULD HELP SMOOTH THINGS OVER.
YOU'VE GOT IT ALL WORKED OUT, HAVEN'T YOU?
IT'S THE BEST OPTION FOR BOTH OF US, LEX. BY CLEARING ME, I'LL REGAIN THE TRUST OF THE CITY I'M TRYING TO HELP.
OF COURSE, THAT'LL LEAVE YOU FREE TO TAKE ANOTHER SHOT AT ME...
...BUT I CAN DEAL WITH THAT.
SKRANKK!
SKRNNK!
SKRNNK!
YOU'RE VERY SURE OF YOURSELF, ALIEN. WHAT MAKES YOU THINK YOU'VE GOT THE UPPER HAND?

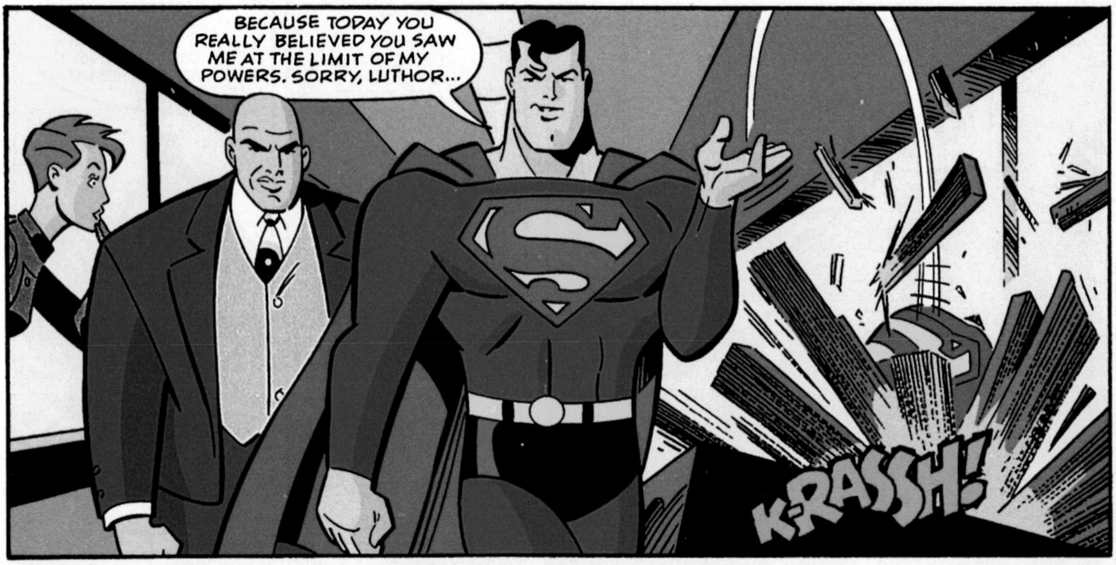
BECAUSE TODAY YOU REALLY BELIEVED YOU SAW ME AT THE LIMIT OF MY POWERS. SORRY, LUTHOR...
K-RASSH!

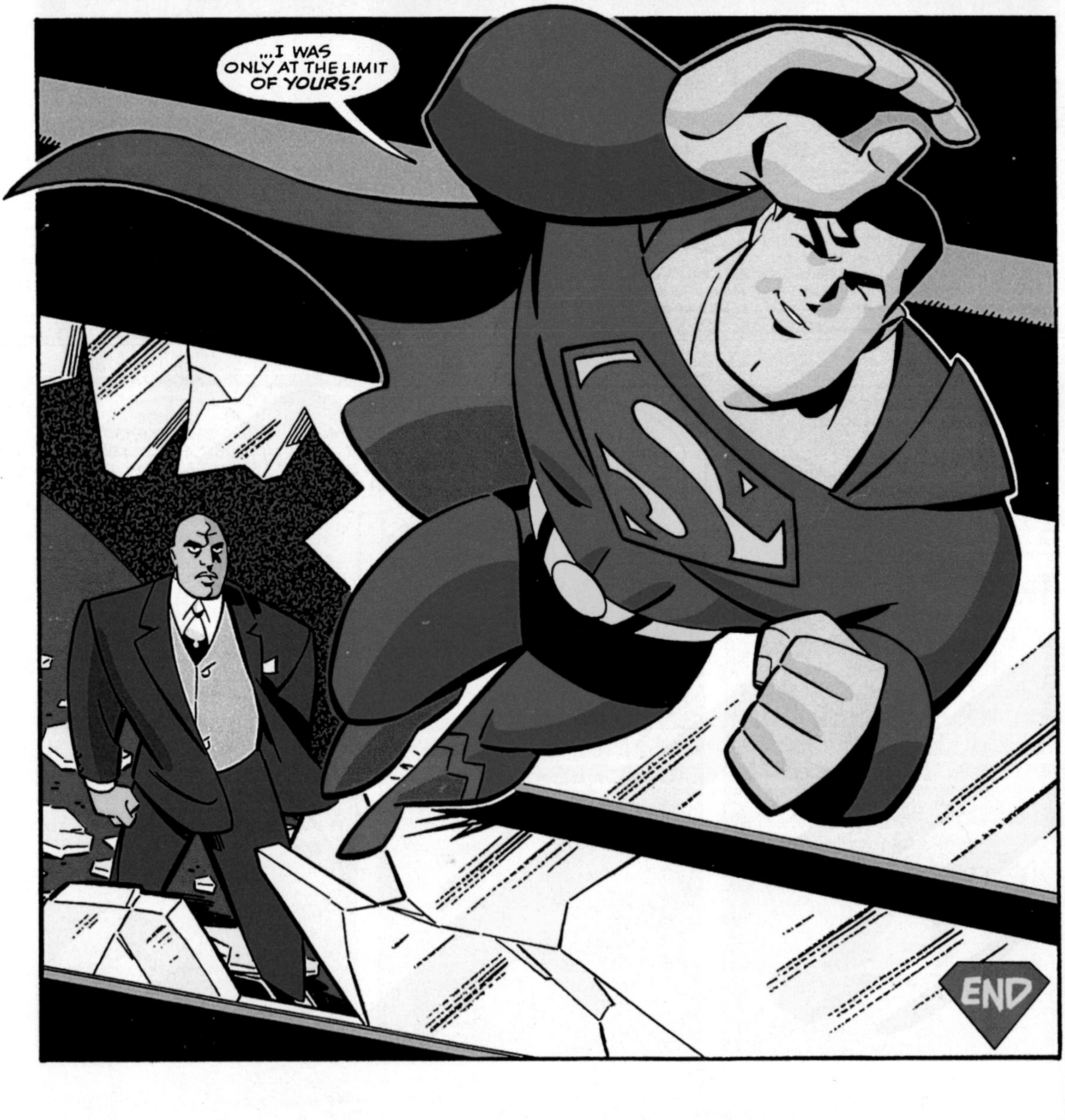
...I WAS ONLY AT THE LIMIT OF YOURS!
END

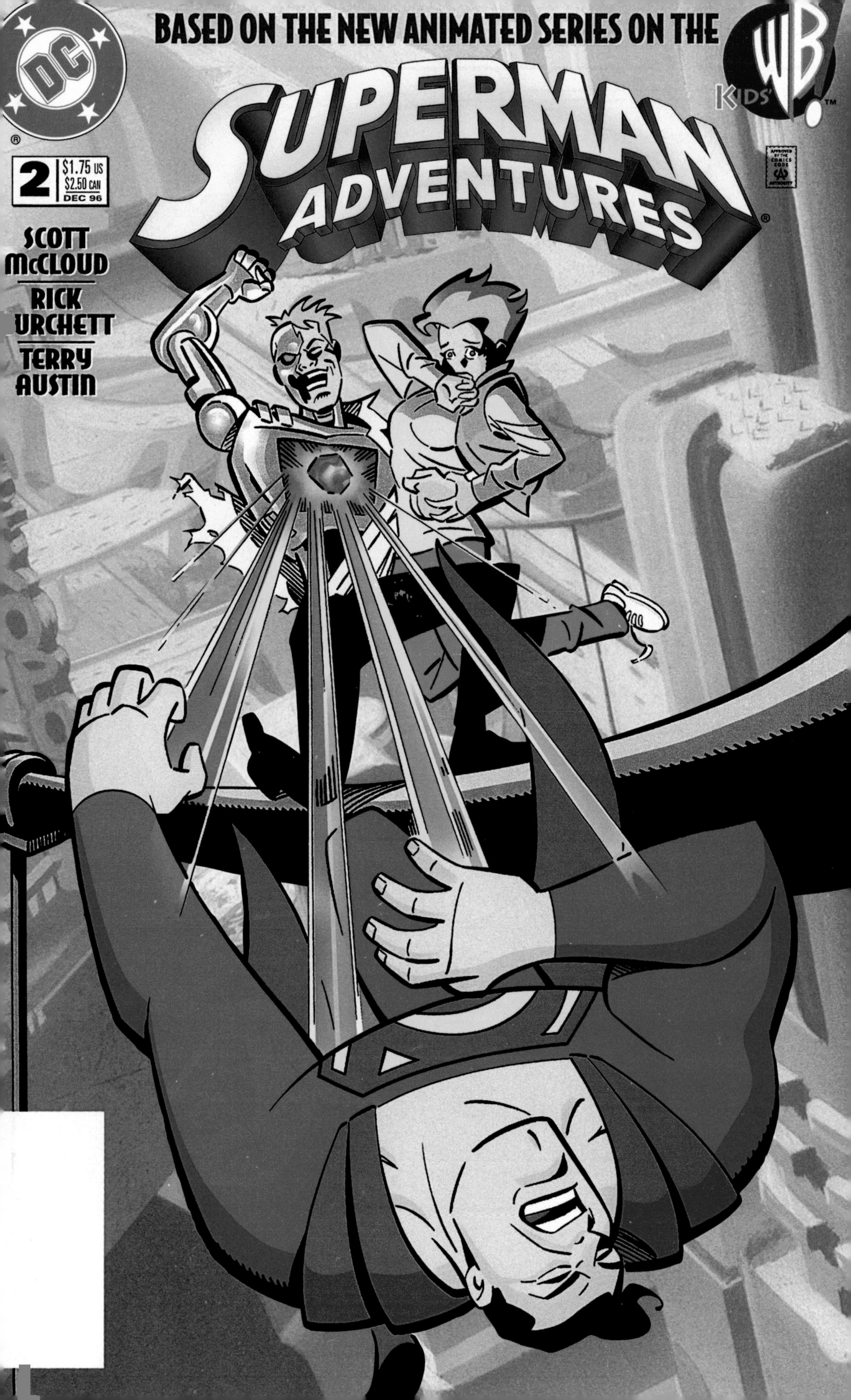
BASED ON THE NEW ANIMATED SERIES ON THE
KIDS' WB!
SUPERMAN ADVENTURES
2
$1.75 US
$2.50 CAN
DEC 96
SCOTT McCLOUD
RICK
URCHETT
TERRY AUSTIN

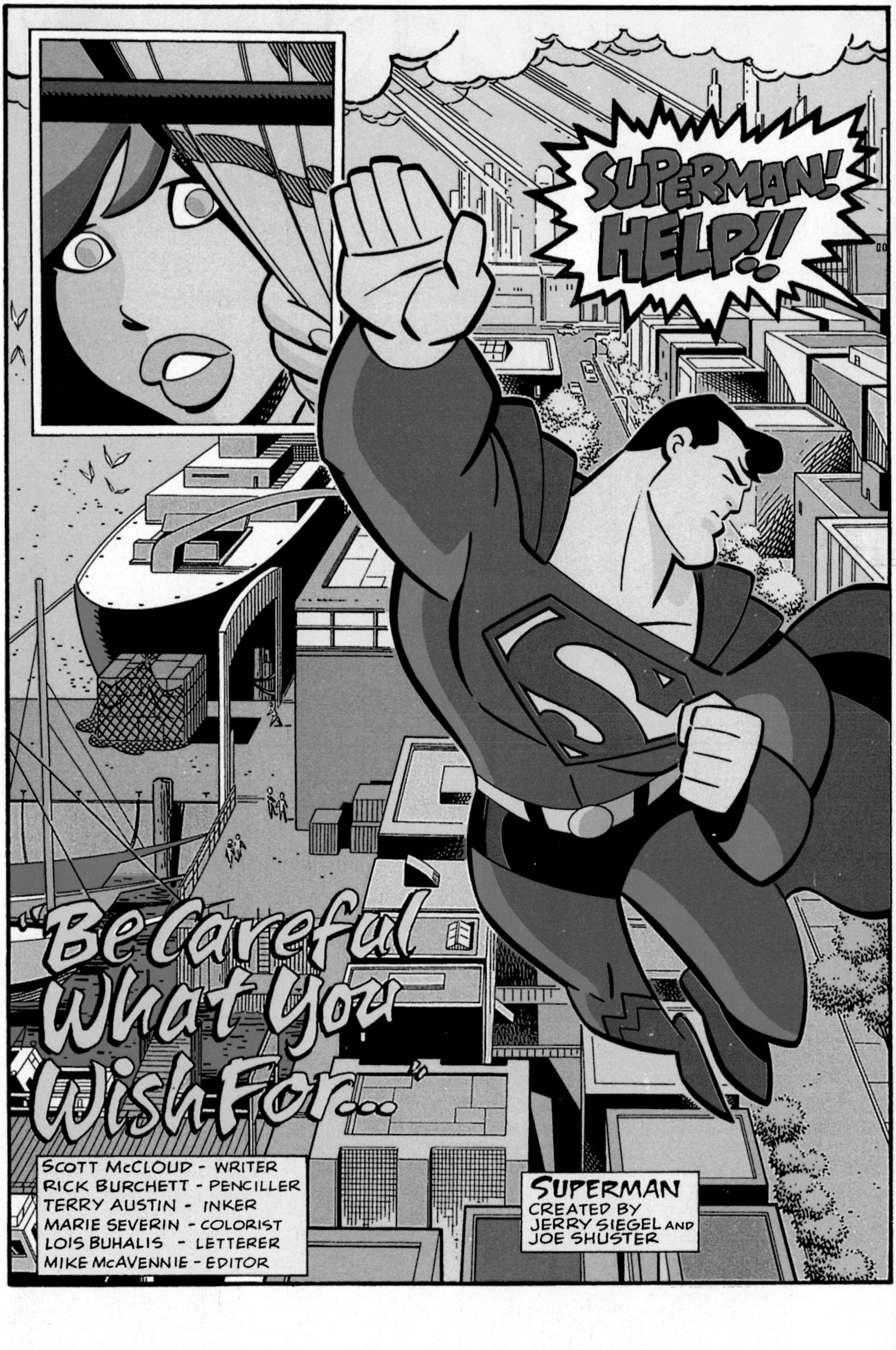
SUPERMAN! HELP!!
Be Careful What You Wish For...
SCOTT McCLOUD - WRITER
RICK BURCHETT - PENCILLER
TERRY AUSTIN - INKER
MARIE SEVERIN - COLORIST
LOIS BUHALIS - LETTERER
MIKE McAVENNIE - EDITOR
SUPERMAN
CREATED BY
JERRY SIEGEL AND
JOE SHUSTER

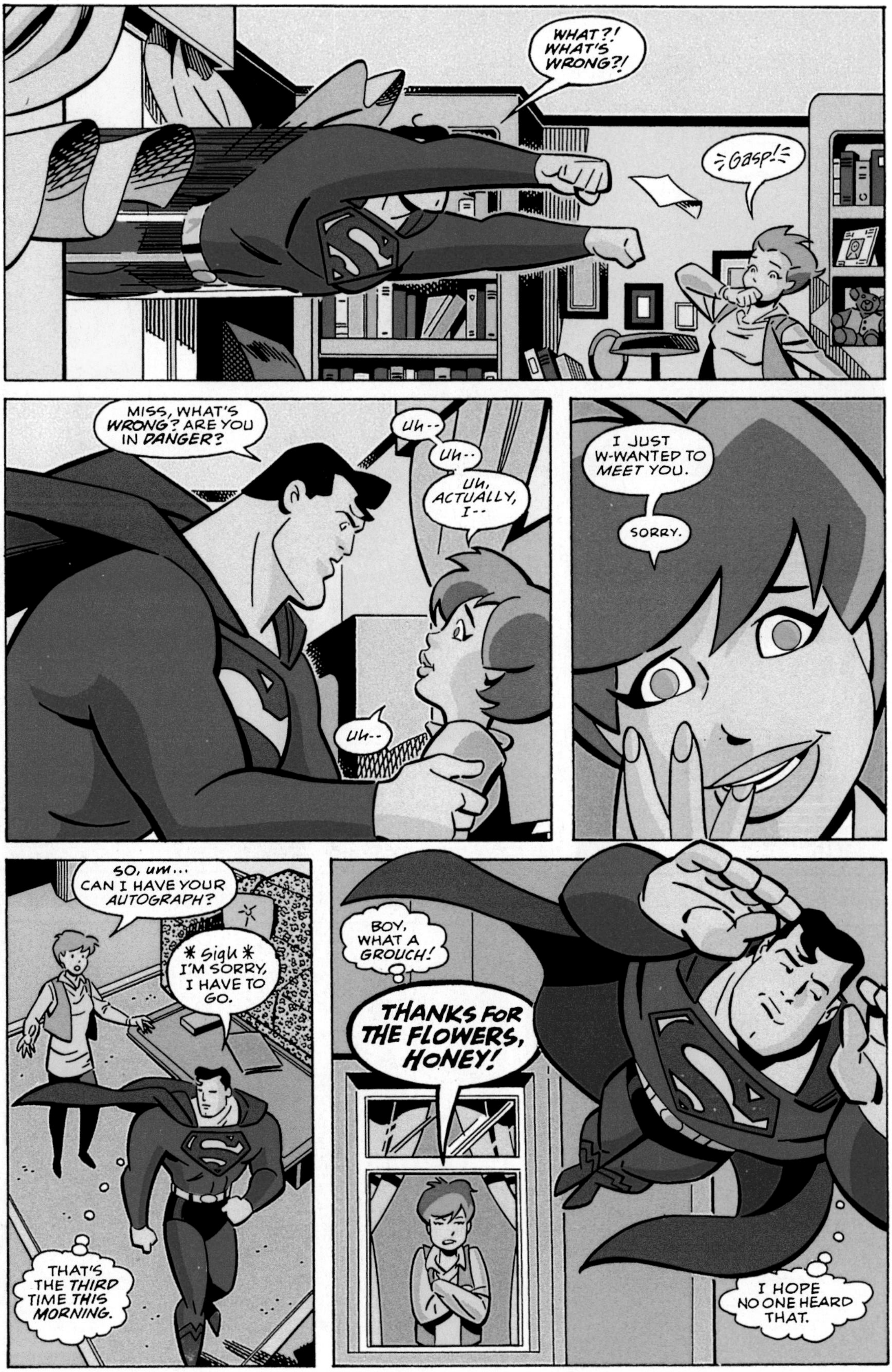
WHAT?! WHAT'S WRONG?!
Gasp!
MISS, WHAT'S WRONG? ARE YOU IN DANGER?
Uh--
Uh--
Uh, ACTUALLY, I--
Uh--
I JUST W-WANTED TO MEET YOU.
SORRY.
SO, um... CAN I HAVE YOUR AUTOGRAPH?
Sigh I'M SORRY, I HAVE TO GO.
THAT'S THE THIRD TIME THIS MORNING.
BOY, WHAT A GROUCH!
THANKS FOR THE FLOWERS, HONEY!
I HOPE NO ONE HEARD THAT.

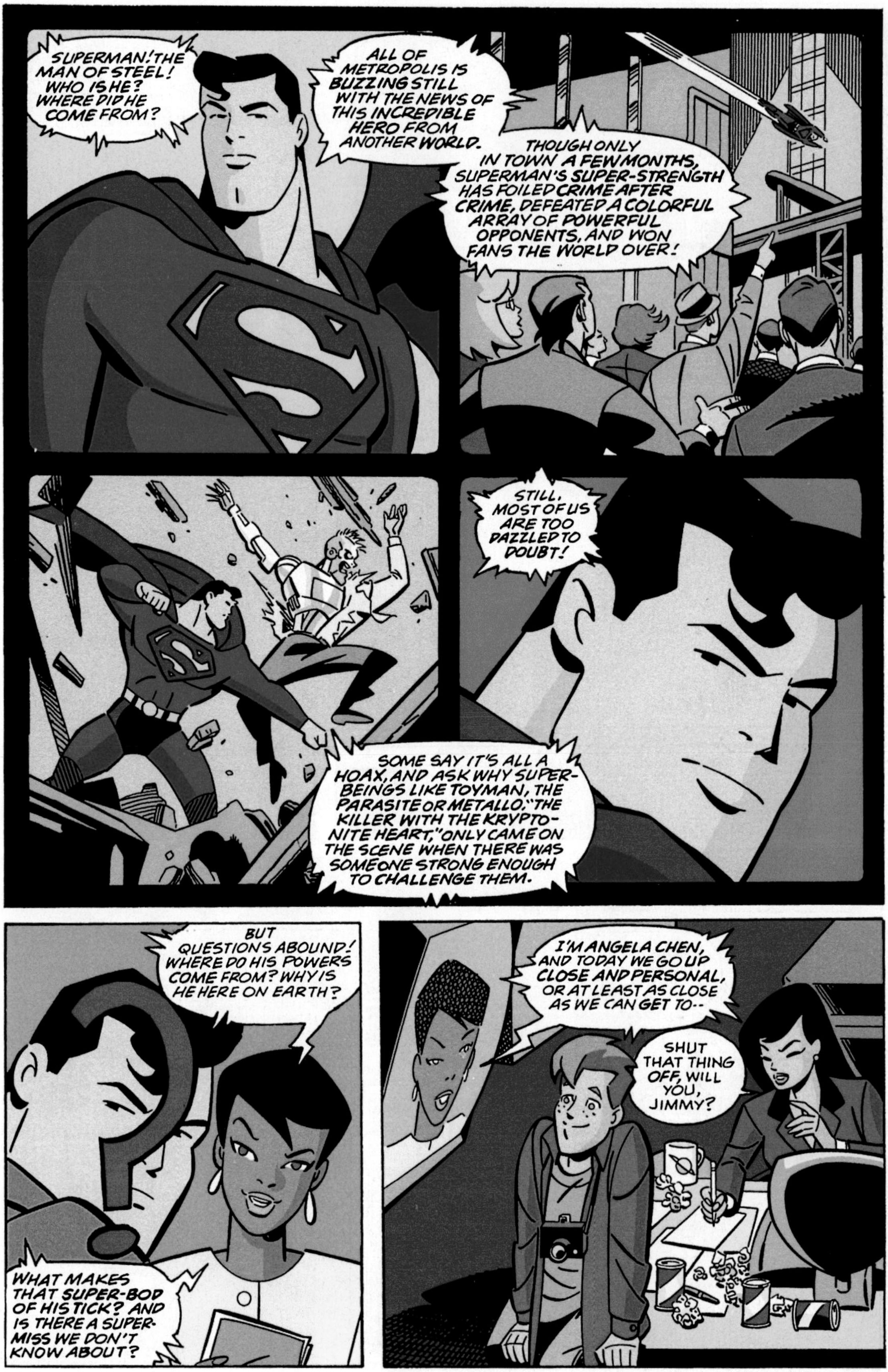
SUPERMAN! THE MAN OF STEEL! WHO IS HE? WHERE DID HE COME FROM?
ALL OF METROPOLIS IS BUZZING STILL WITH THE NEWS OF THIS INCREDIBLE HERO FROM ANOTHER WORLD.
THOUGH ONLY IN TOWN A FEW MONTHS, SUPERMAN'S SUPER-STRENGTH HAS FOILED CRIME AFTER CRIME, DEFEATED A COLORFUL ARRAY OF POWERFUL OPPONENTS, AND WON FANS THE WORLD OVER!
SOME SAY IT'S ALL A HOAX, AND ASK WHY SUPER-BEINGS LIKE TOYMAN, THE PARASITE OR METALLO, "THE KILLER WITH THE KRYPTONITE HEART," ONLY CAME ON THE SCENE WHEN THERE WAS SOMEONE STRONG ENOUGH TO CHALLENGE THEM.
STILL, MOST OF US ARE TOO DAZZLED TO DOUBT!
BUT QUESTIONS ABOUND! WHERE DO HIS POWERS COME FROM? WHY IS HE HERE ON EARTH?
WHAT MAKES THAT SUPER-BOD OF HIS TICK? AND IS THERE A SUPER-MISS WE DON'T KNOW ABOUT?
I'M ANGELA CHEN, AND TODAY WE GO UP CLOSE AND PERSONAL, OR AT LEAST AS CLOSE AS WE CAN GET TO--
SHUT THAT THING OFF, WILL YOU, JIMMY?

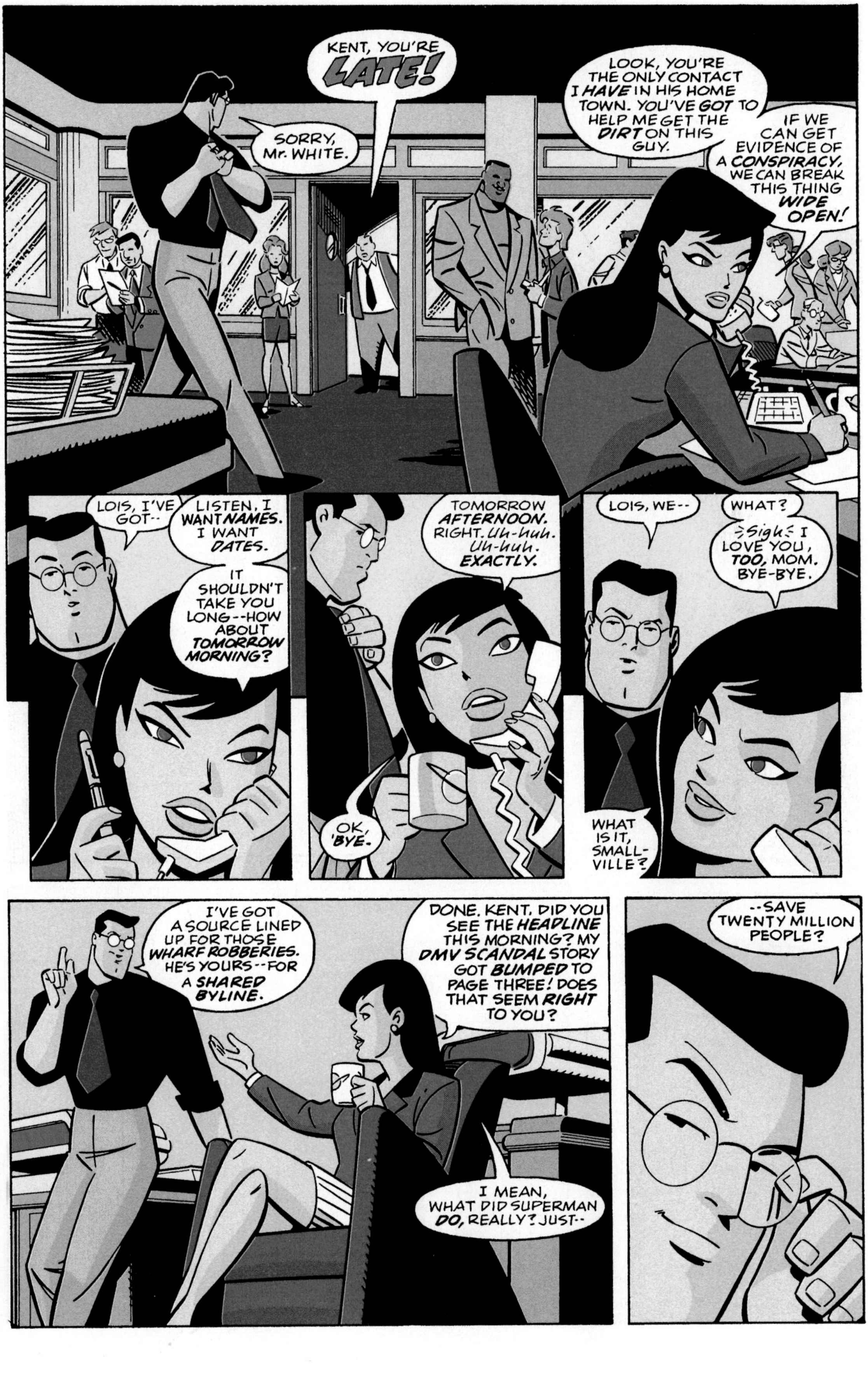
SORRY, Mr. WHITE.
KENT, YOU'RE LATE!
LOOK, YOU'RE THE ONLY CONTACT I HAVE IN HIS HOME TOWN. YOU'VE GOT TO HELP ME GET THE DIRT ON THIS GUY.
IF WE CAN GET EVIDENCE OF A CONSPIRACY, WE CAN BREAK THIS THING WIDE OPEN!
LOIS, I'VE GOT--
LISTEN, I WANT NAMES. I WANT DATES.
IT SHOULDN'T TAKE YOU LONG--HOW ABOUT TOMORROW MORNING?
TOMORROW AFTERNOON. RIGHT. Uh-huh. Uh-huh. EXACTLY.
OK, 'BYE.
LOIS, WE--
WHAT?
Sigh I LOVE YOU, TOO, MOM. BYE-BYE.
WHAT IS IT, SMALL-VILLE?
I'VE GOT A SOURCE LINED UP FOR THOSE WHARF ROBBERIES. HE'S YOURS--FOR A SHARED BYLINE.
DONE. KENT, DID YOU SEE THE HEADLINE THIS MORNING? MY DMV SCANDAL STORY GOT BUMPED TO PAGE THREE! DOES THAT SEEM RIGHT TO YOU?
I MEAN, WHAT DID SUPERMAN DO, REALLY? JUST--
--SAVE TWENTY MILLION PEOPLE?

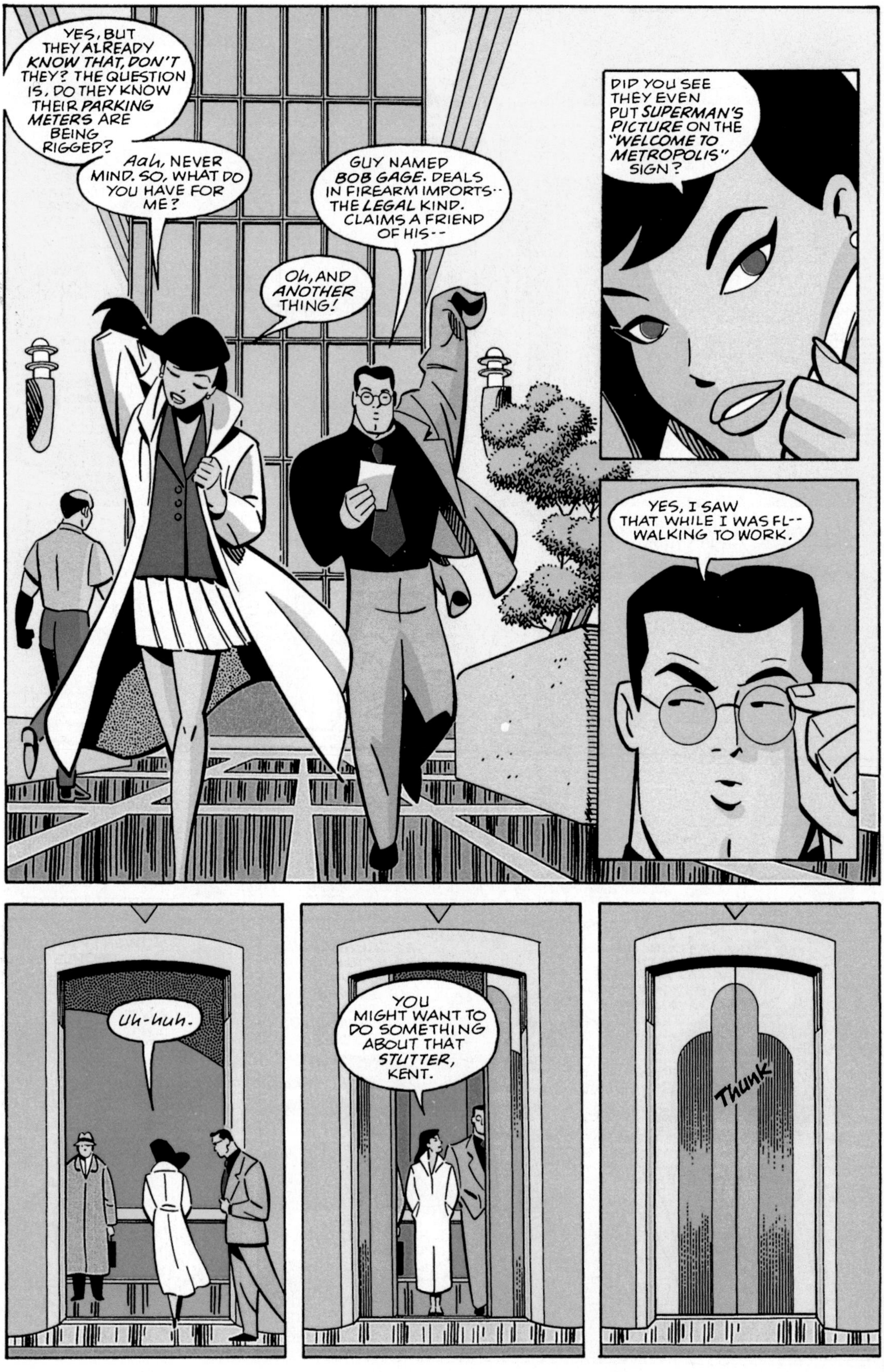
YES, BUT THEY ALREADY KNOW THAT, DON'T THEY? THE QUESTION IS, DO THEY KNOW THEIR PARKING METERS ARE BEING RIGGED?
Aah, NEVER MIND. SO, WHAT DO YOU HAVE FOR ME?
GUY NAMED BOB GAGE. DEALS IN FIREARM IMPORTS-- THE LEGAL KIND. CLAIMS A FRIEND OF HIS--
Oh, AND ANOTHER THING!
DID YOU SEE THEY EVEN PUT SUPERMAN'S PICTURE ON THE "WELCOME TO METROPOLIS" SIGN?
YES, I SAW THAT WHILE I WAS FL-- WALKING TO WORK.
Uh-huh.
YOU MIGHT WANT TO DO SOMETHING ABOUT THAT STUTTER, KENT.
THUNK

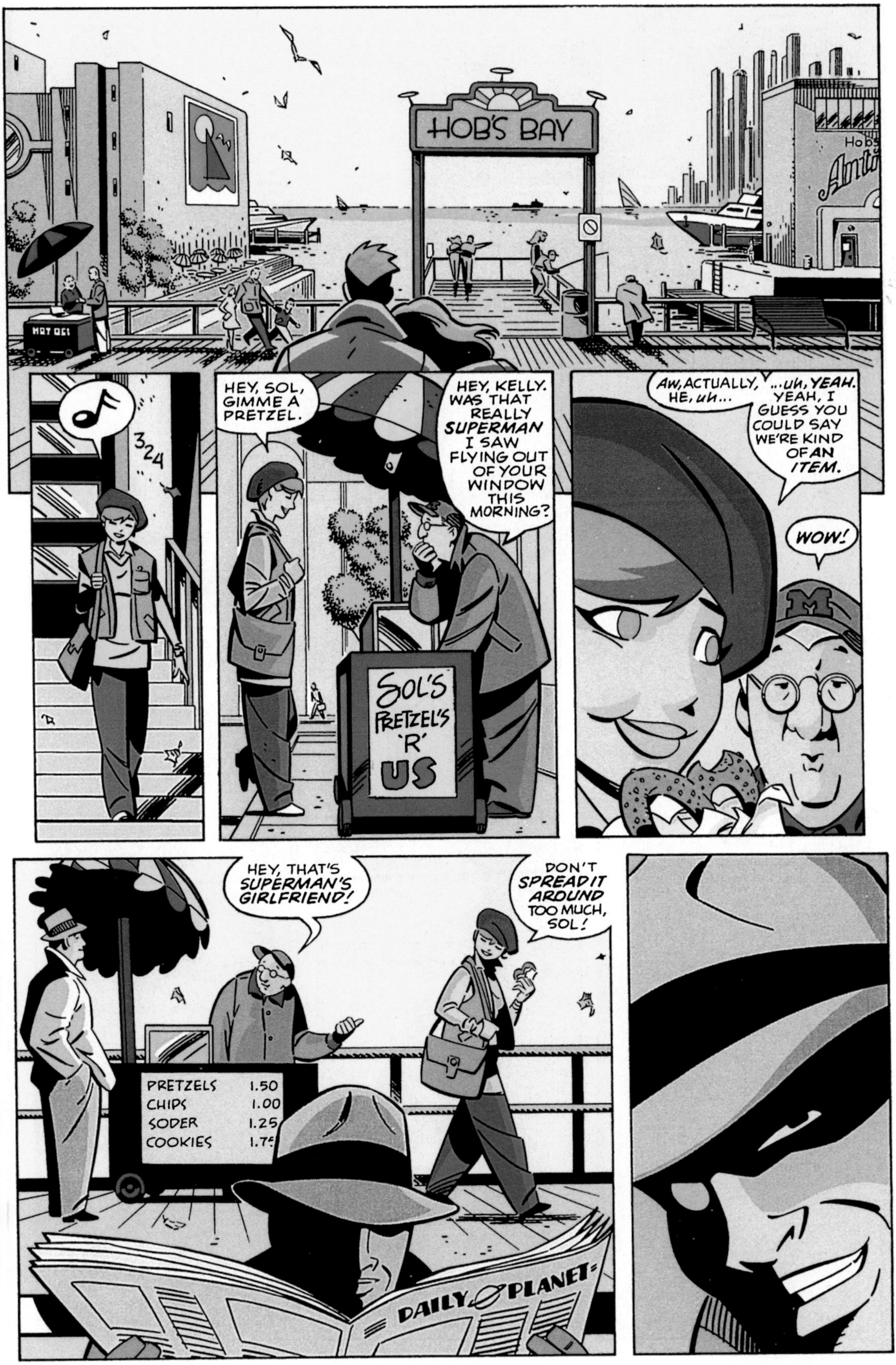
HOB'S BAY
HOT DOG
Hobs
Anti
♪
324
HEY, SOL, GIMME A PRETZEL.
HEY, KELLY. WAS THAT REALLY SUPERMAN I SAW FLYING OUT OF YOUR WINDOW THIS MORNING?
SOL'S PRETZEL'S 'R' US
AW, ACTUALLY, HE, uh...
...uh, YEAH. YEAH, I GUESS YOU COULD SAY WE'RE KIND OF AN ITEM.
WOW!
M
HEY, THAT'S SUPERMAN'S GIRLFRIEND!
DON'T SPREAD IT AROUND TOO MUCH, SOL!
PRETZELS 1.50
CHIPS 1.00
SODER 1.25
COOKIES 1.75
DAILY PLANET

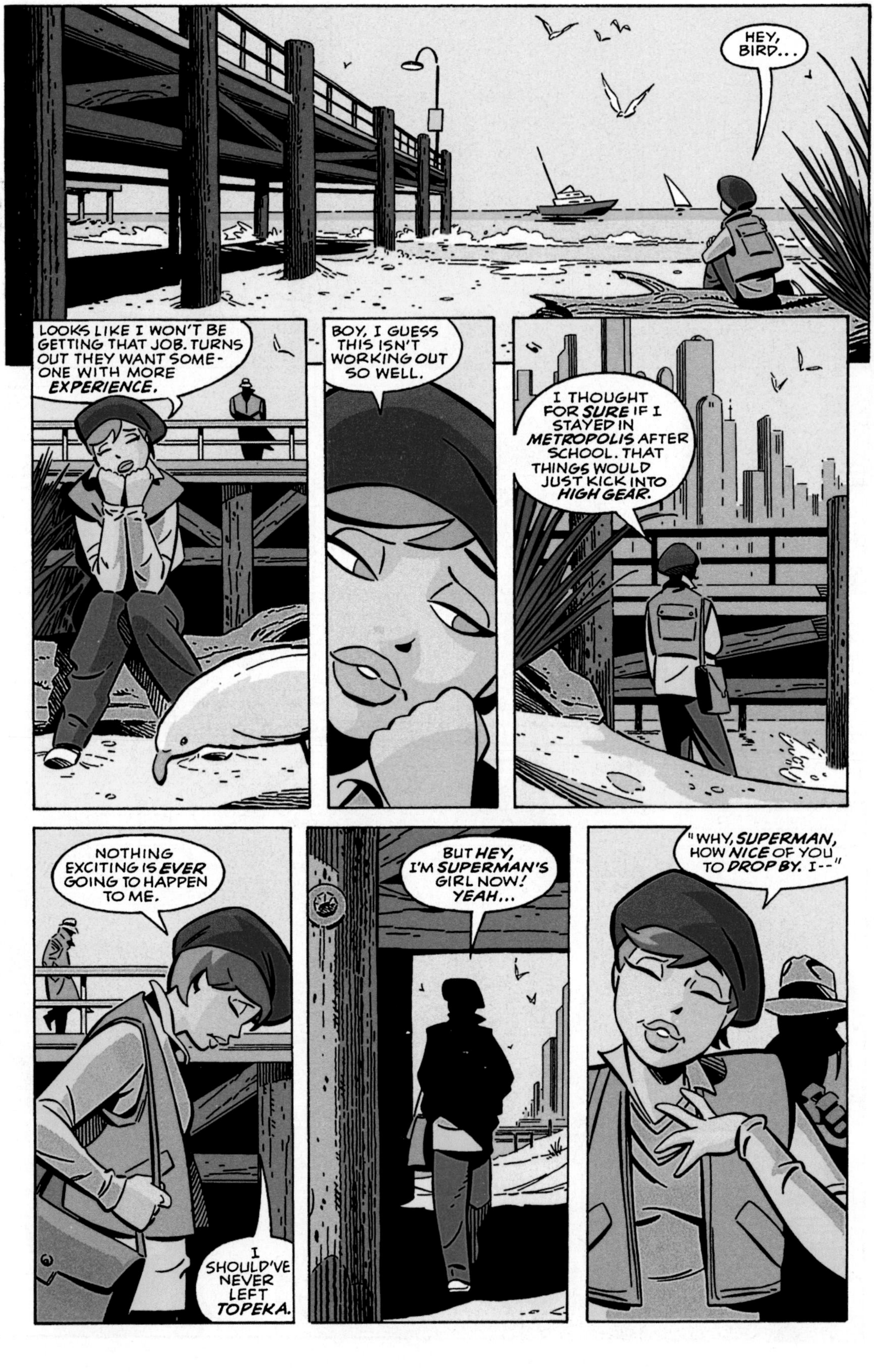
HEY, BIRD...
LOOKS LIKE I WON'T BE GETTING THAT JOB. TURNS OUT THEY WANT SOME-ONE WITH MORE EXPERIENCE.
BOY, I GUESS THIS ISN'T WORKING OUT SO WELL.
I THOUGHT FOR SURE IF I STAYED IN METROPOLIS AFTER SCHOOL. THAT THINGS WOULD JUST KICK INTO HIGH GEAR.
NOTHING EXCITING IS EVER GOING TO HAPPEN TO ME.
I SHOULD'VE NEVER LEFT TOPEKA.
BUT HEY, I'M SUPERMAN'S GIRL NOW! YEAH...
"WHY, SUPERMAN, HOW NICE OF YOU TO DROP BY. I--"

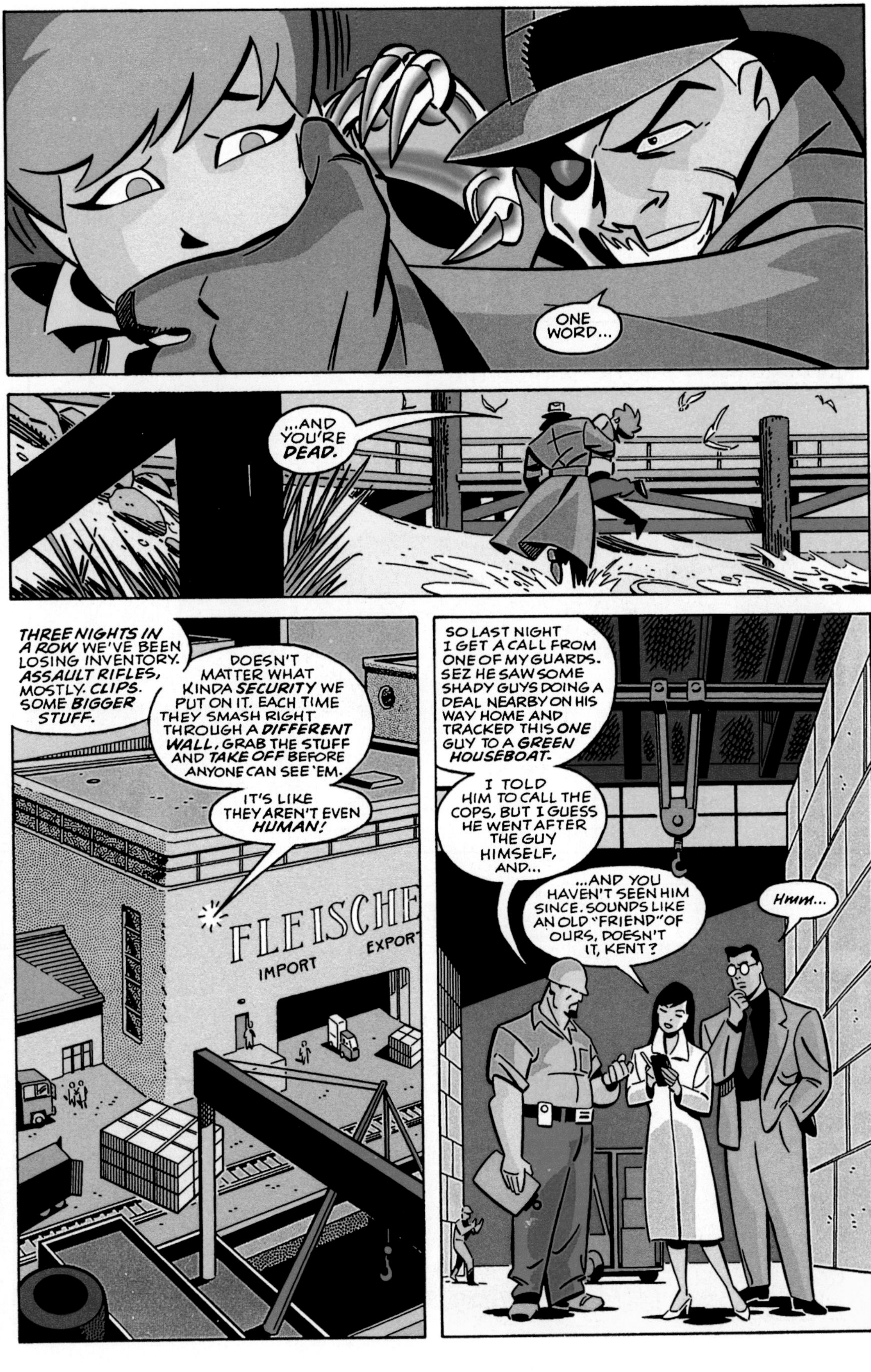
ONE WORD...
...AND YOU'RE DEAD.
THREE NIGHTS IN A ROW WE'VE BEEN LOSING INVENTORY. ASSAULT RIFLES, MOSTLY. CLIPS. SOME BIGGER STUFF.
DOESN'T MATTER WHAT KINDA SECURITY WE PUT ON IT. EACH TIME THEY SMASH RIGHT THROUGH A DIFFERENT WALL, GRAB THE STUFF AND TAKE OFF BEFORE ANYONE CAN SEE 'EM.
IT'S LIKE THEY AREN'T EVEN HUMAN!
FLEISCHE
IMPORT
EXPORT
SO LAST NIGHT I GET A CALL FROM ONE OF MY GUARDS. SEZ HE SAW SOME SHADY GUYS DOING A DEAL NEARBY ON HIS WAY HOME AND TRACKED THIS ONE GUY TO A GREEN HOUSEBOAT.
I TOLD HIM TO CALL THE COPS, BUT I GUESS HE WENT AFTER THE GUY HIMSELF, AND...
...AND YOU HAVEN'T SEEN HIM SINCE. SOUNDS LIKE AN OLD "FRIEND" OF OURS, DOESN'T IT, KENT?
Hmm...

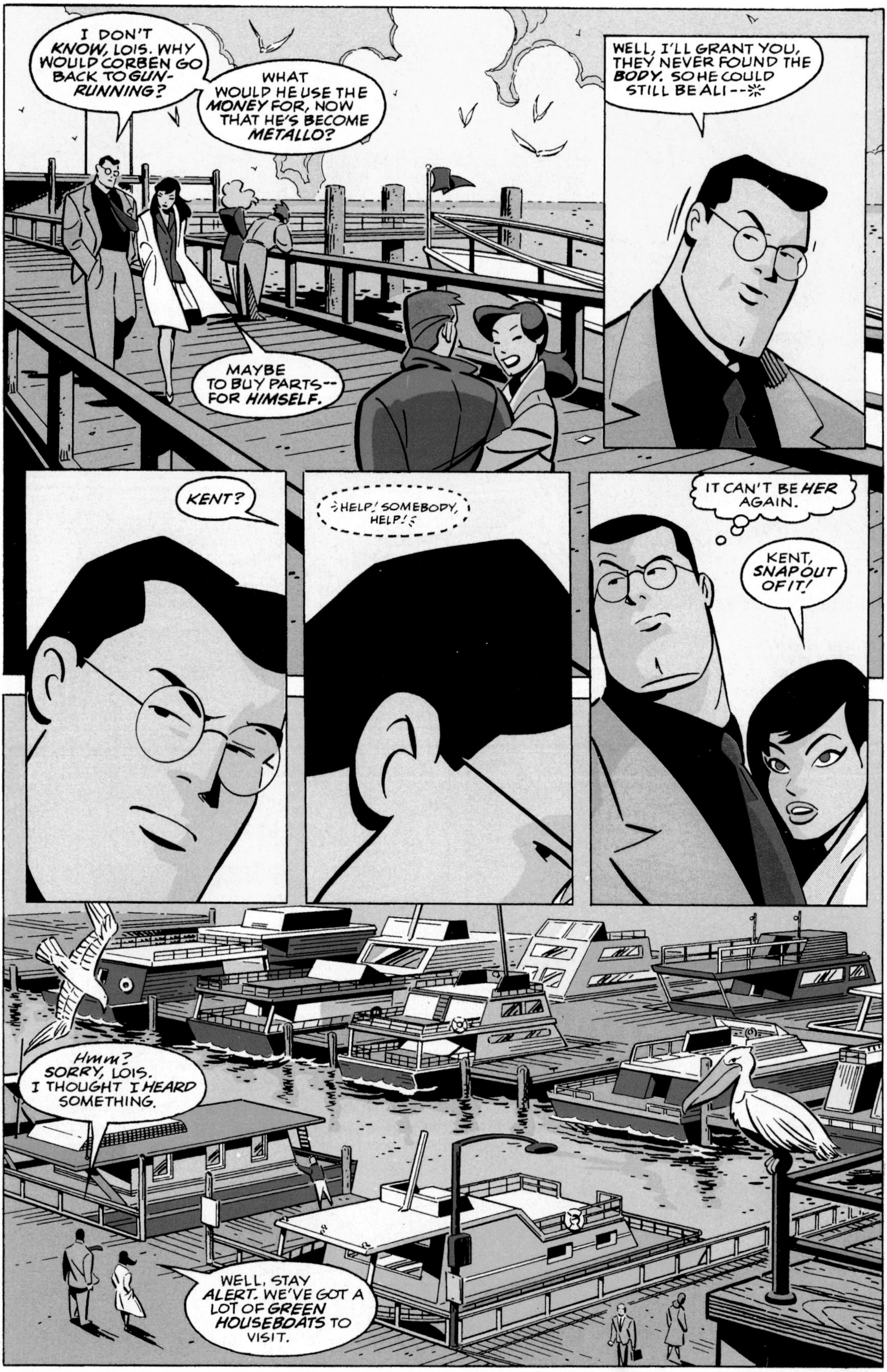
I DON'T KNOW, LOIS. WHY WOULD CORBEN GO BACK TO GUN-RUNNING?
WHAT WOULD HE USE THE MONEY FOR, NOW THAT HE'S BECOME METALLO?
MAYBE TO BUY PARTS-- FOR HIMSELF.
WELL, I'LL GRANT YOU, THEY NEVER FOUND THE BODY. SO HE COULD STILL BE ALI--
KENT?
HELP! SOMEBODY, HELP!
IT CAN'T BE HER AGAIN.
KENT, SNAP OUT OF IT!
Hmm? SORRY, LOIS. I THOUGHT I HEARD SOMETHING.
WELL, STAY ALERT. WE'VE GOT A LOT OF GREEN HOUSEBOATS TO VISIT.

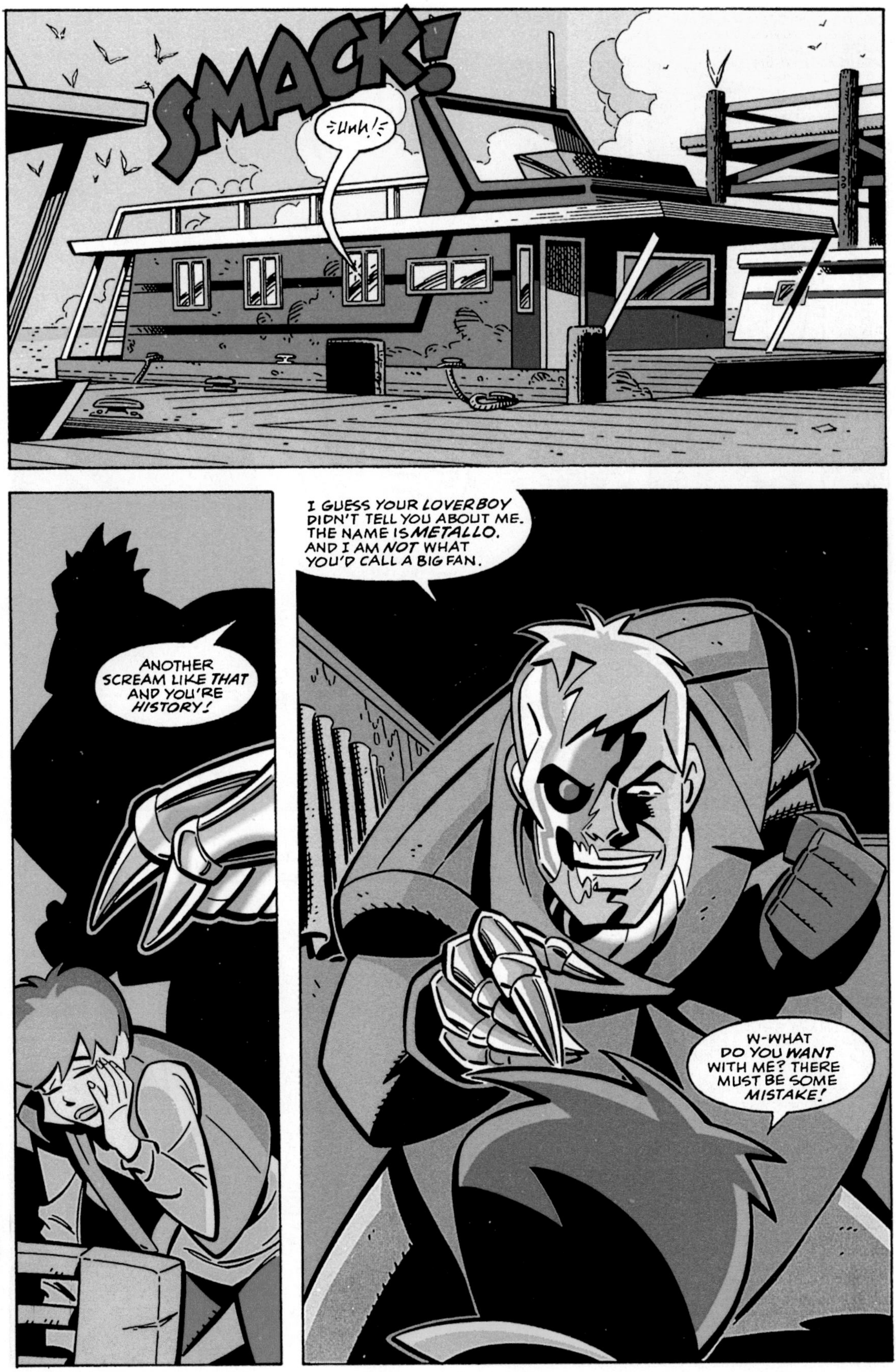
SMACK!
UNH!
ANOTHER SCREAM LIKE THAT AND YOU'RE HISTORY!
I GUESS YOUR LOVERBOY DIDN'T TELL YOU ABOUT ME. THE NAME IS METALLO. AND I AM NOT WHAT YOU'D CALL A BIG FAN.
W-WHAT DO YOU WANT WITH ME? THERE MUST BE SOME MISTAKE!

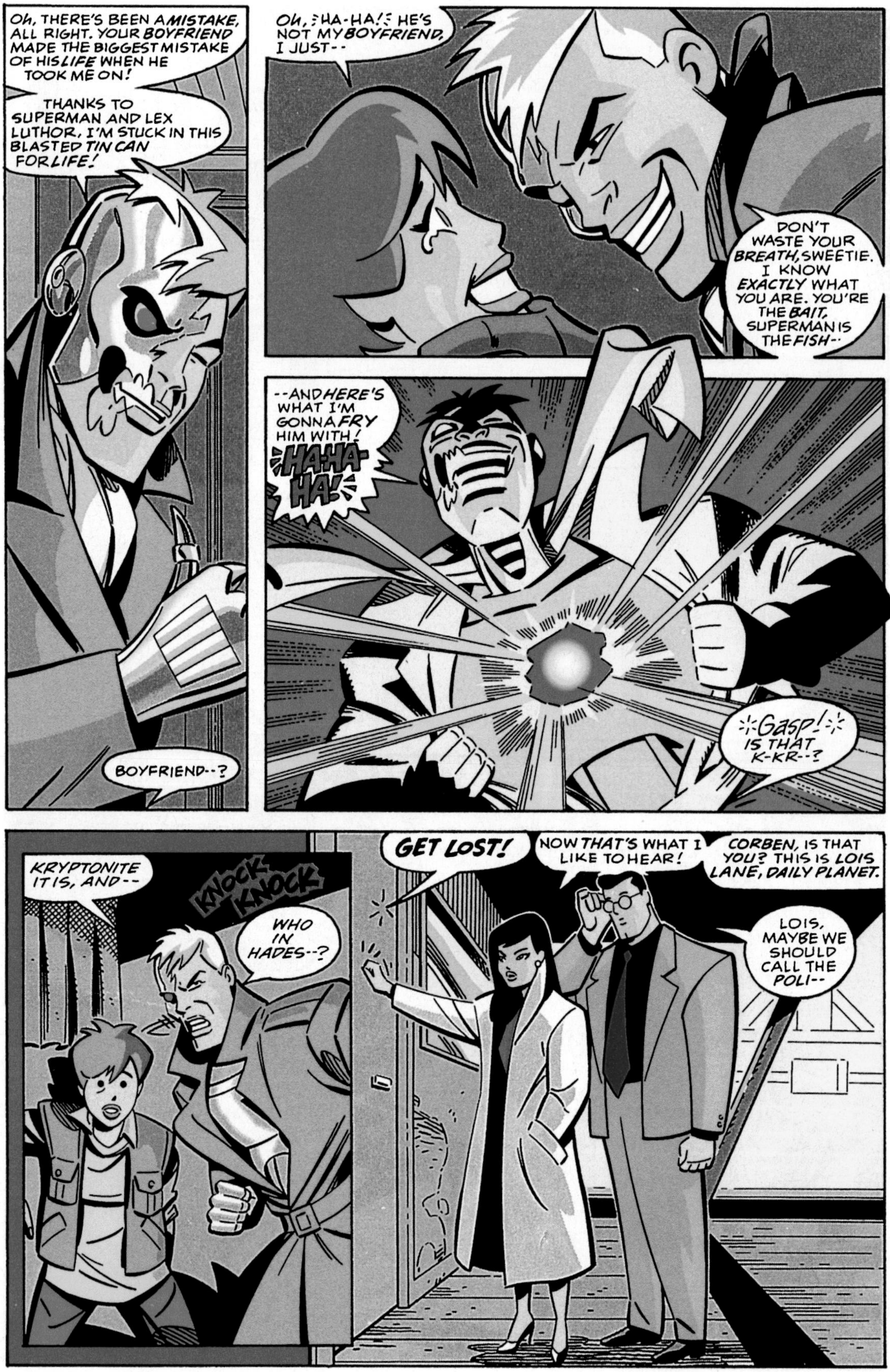
Oh, THERE'S BEEN A MISTAKE, ALL RIGHT. YOUR BOYFRIEND MADE THE BIGGEST MISTAKE OF HIS LIFE WHEN HE TOOK ME ON!
THANKS TO SUPERMAN AND LEX LUTHOR, I'M STUCK IN THIS BLASTED TIN CAN FOR LIFE!
BOYFRIEND--?
Oh, HA-HA! HE'S NOT MY BOYFRIEND, I JUST--
DON'T WASTE YOUR BREATH, SWEETIE. I KNOW EXACTLY WHAT YOU ARE. YOU'RE THE BAIT. SUPERMAN IS THE FISH--
--AND HERE'S WHAT I'M GONNA FRY HIM WITH!
HA-HA-HA!
Gasp! IS THAT K-KR--?
KRYPTONITE IT IS, AND--
KNOCK KNOCK
WHO IN HADES--?
GET LOST!
NOW THAT'S WHAT I LIKE TO HEAR!
CORBEN, IS THAT YOU? THIS IS LOIS LANE, DAILY PLANET.
LOIS, MAYBE WE SHOULD CALL THE POLI--

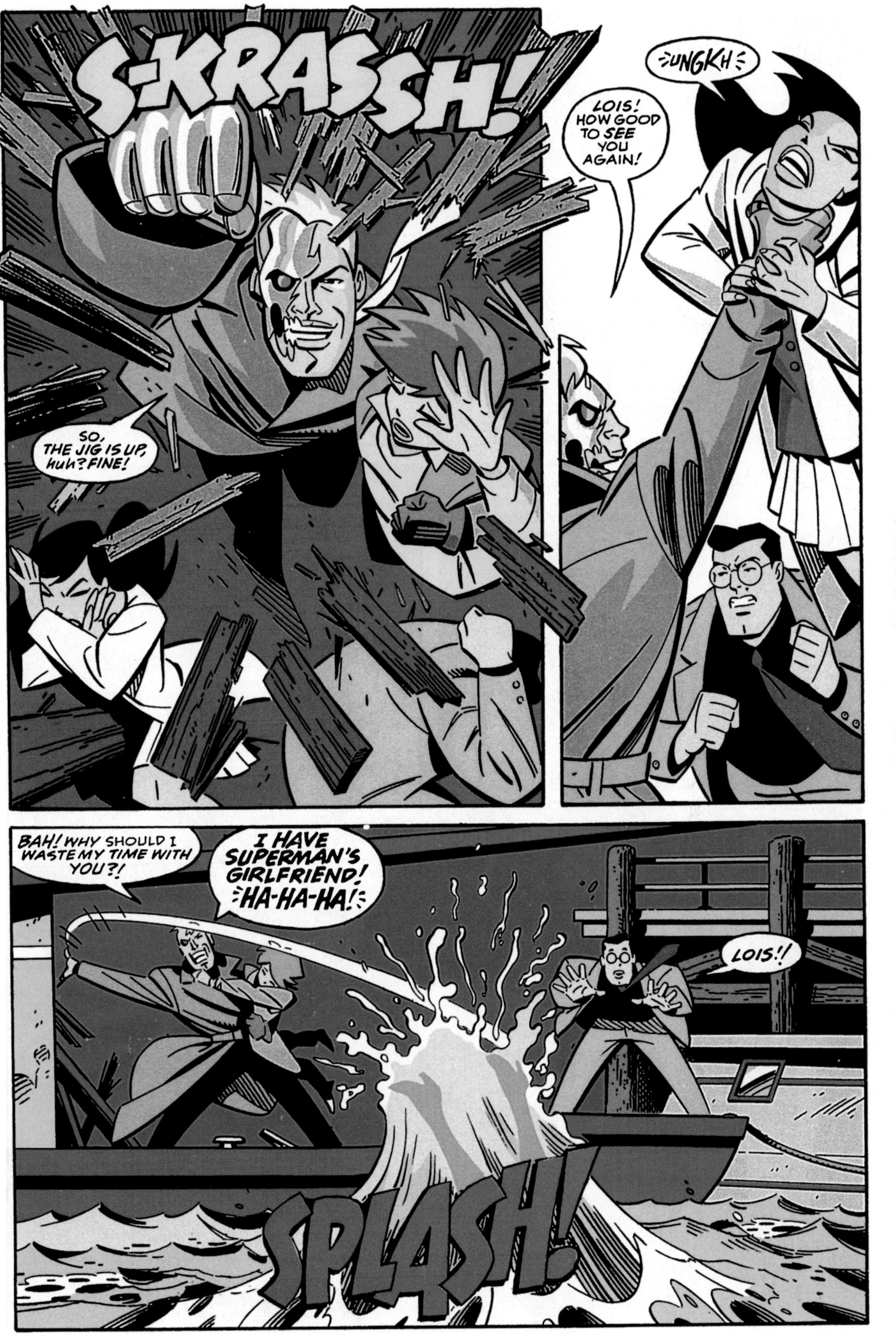
S-KRASSH!
SO, THE JIG IS UP, huh? FINE!
UNGKH
LOIS! HOW GOOD TO SEE YOU AGAIN!
BAH! WHY SHOULD I WASTE MY TIME WITH YOU?!
I HAVE SUPERMAN'S GIRLFRIEND! HA-HA-HA!
LOIS!!
SPLASH!

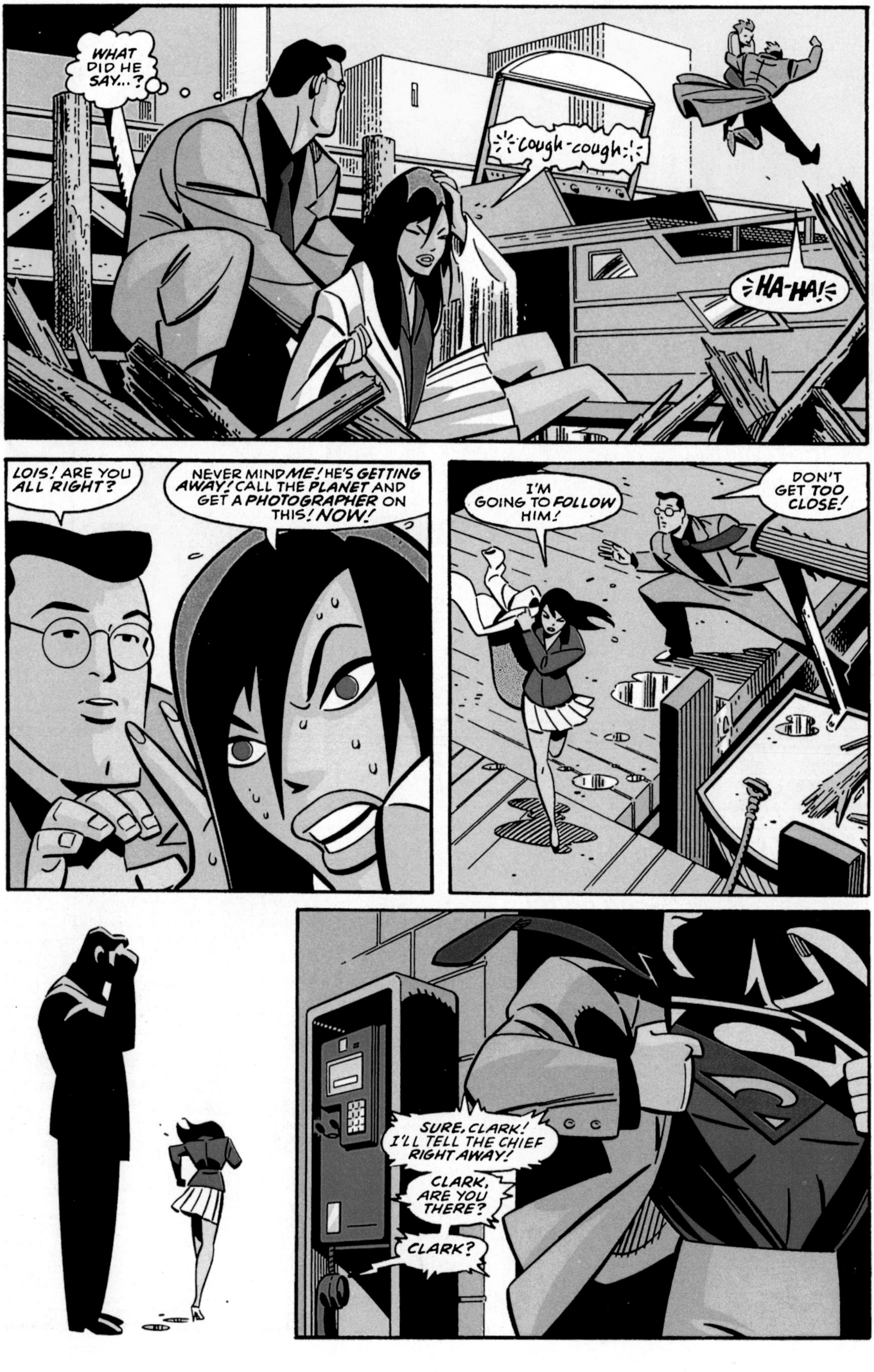
WHAT DID HE SAY...?
COUGH-COUGH
HA-HA!
LOIS! ARE YOU ALL RIGHT?
NEVER MIND ME! HE'S GETTING AWAY! CALL THE PLANET AND GET A PHOTOGRAPHER ON THIS! NOW!
I'M GOING TO FOLLOW HIM!
DON'T GET TOO CLOSE!
SURE, CLARK! I'LL TELL THE CHIEF RIGHT AWAY!
CLARK, ARE YOU THERE?
CLARK?

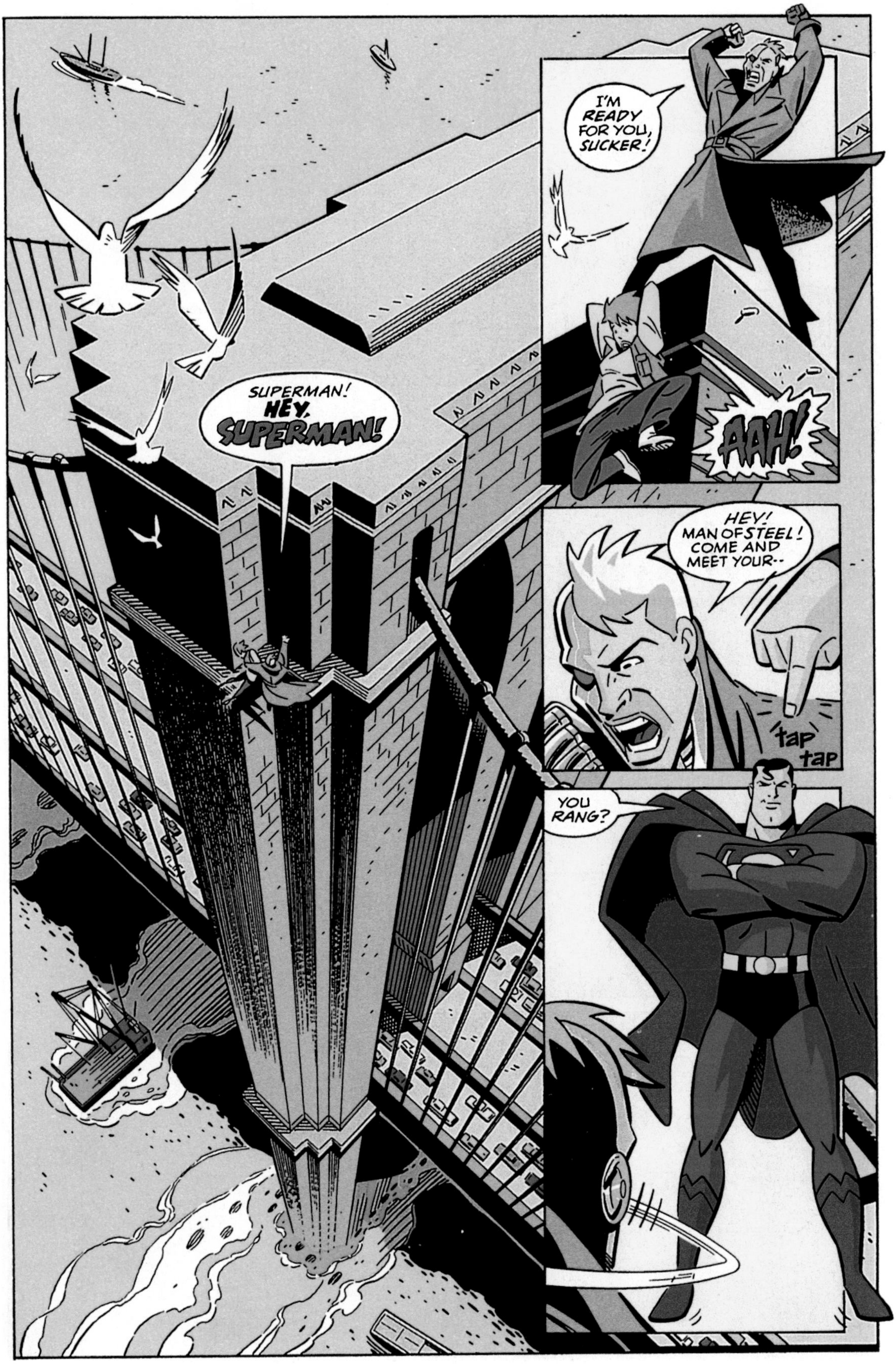
SUPERMAN! HEY, SUPERMAN!
I'M READY FOR YOU, SUCKER!
AAH!
HEY! MAN OF STEEL! COME AND MEET YOUR--
tap tap
YOU RANG?

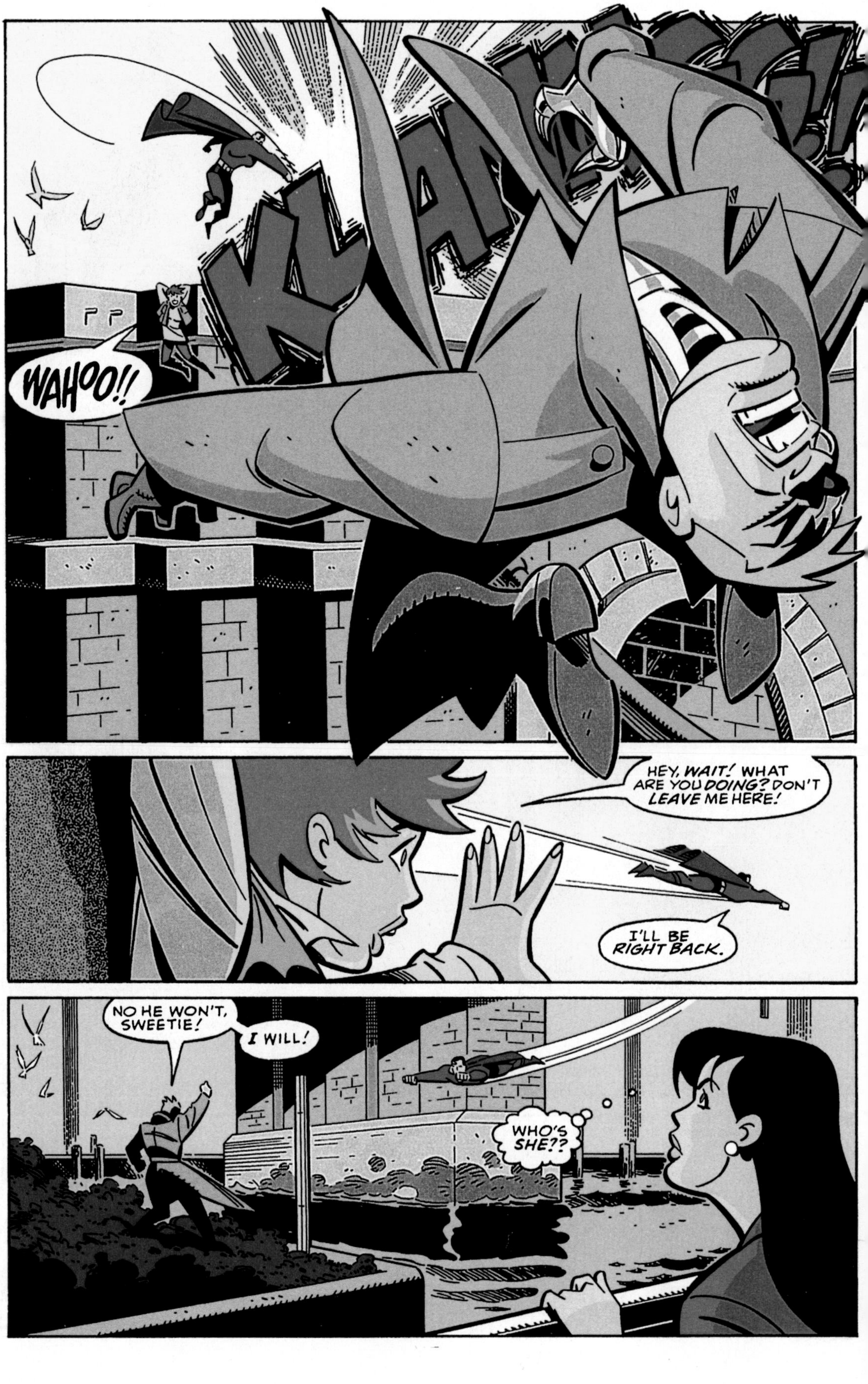
KLANK!!
WAHOO!!
HEY, WAIT! WHAT ARE YOU DOING? DON'T LEAVE ME HERE!
I'LL BE RIGHT BACK.
NO HE WON'T, SWEETIE!
I WILL!
WHO'S SHE??

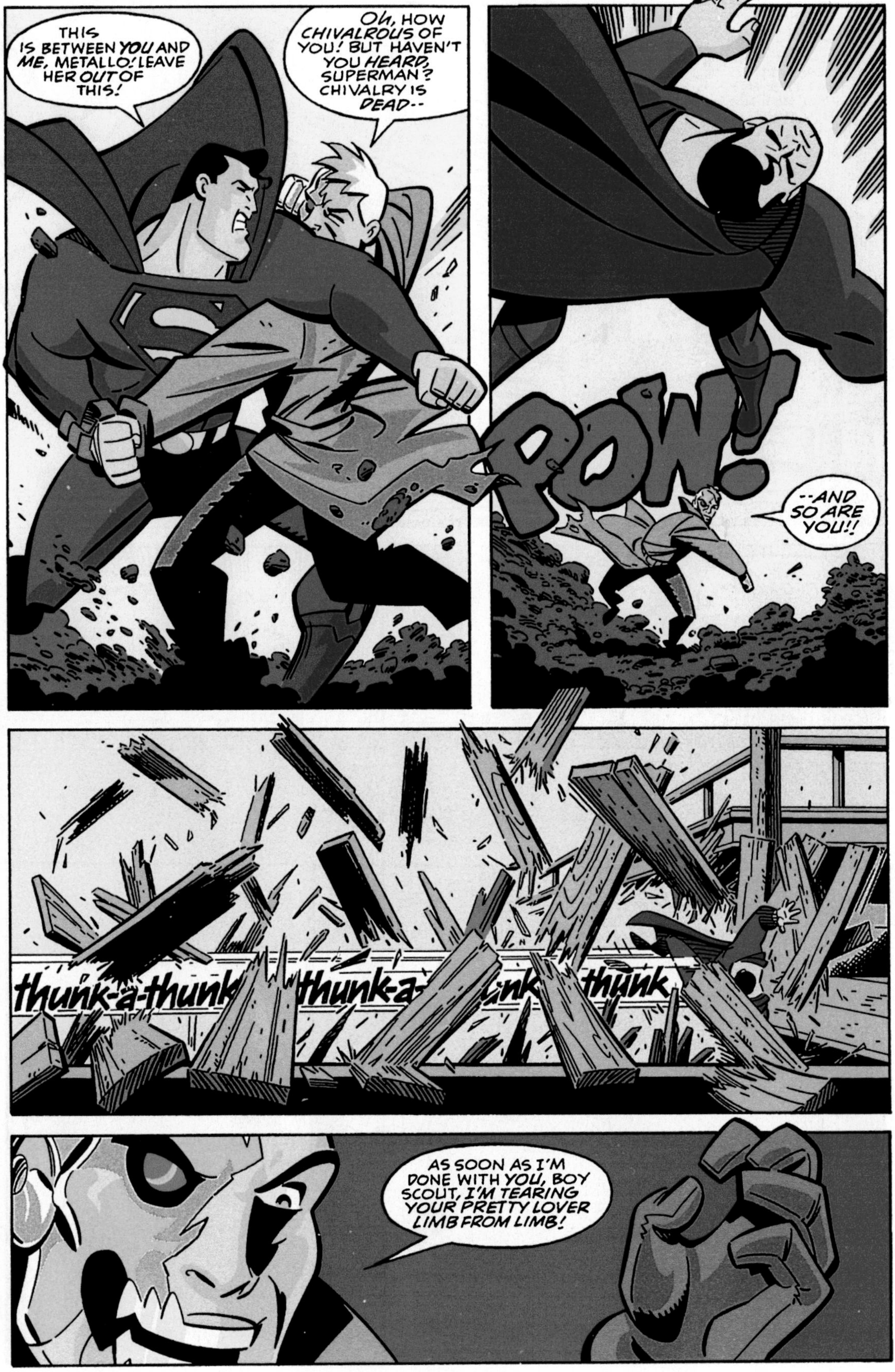
THIS IS BETWEEN YOU AND ME, METALLO! LEAVE HER OUT OF THIS!
OH, HOW CHIVALROUS OF YOU! BUT HAVEN'T YOU HEARD, SUPERMAN? CHIVALRY IS DEAD--
POW!
--AND SO ARE YOU!!
thunk-a-thunk thunk-a-thunk thunk
AS SOON AS I'M DONE WITH YOU, BOY SCOUT, I'M TEARING YOUR PRETTY LOVER LIMB FROM LIMB!

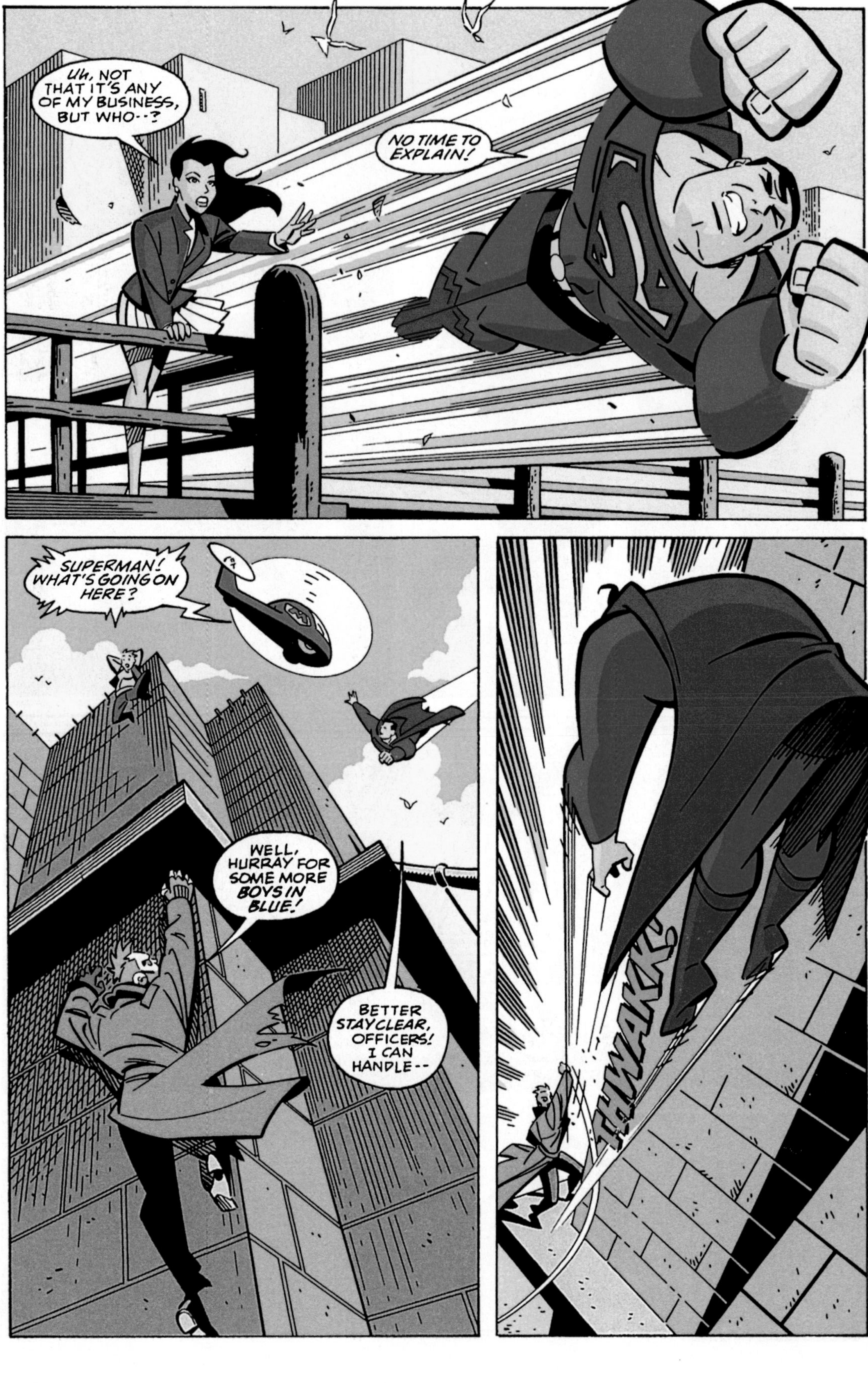

UH, NOT THAT IT'S ANY OF MY BUSINESS, BUT WHO--?
NO TIME TO EXPLAIN!
SUPERMAN! WHAT'S GOING ON HERE?
WELL, HURRAY FOR SOME MORE BOYS IN BLUE!
BETTER STAY CLEAR, OFFICERS! I CAN HANDLE--
THWAKK!

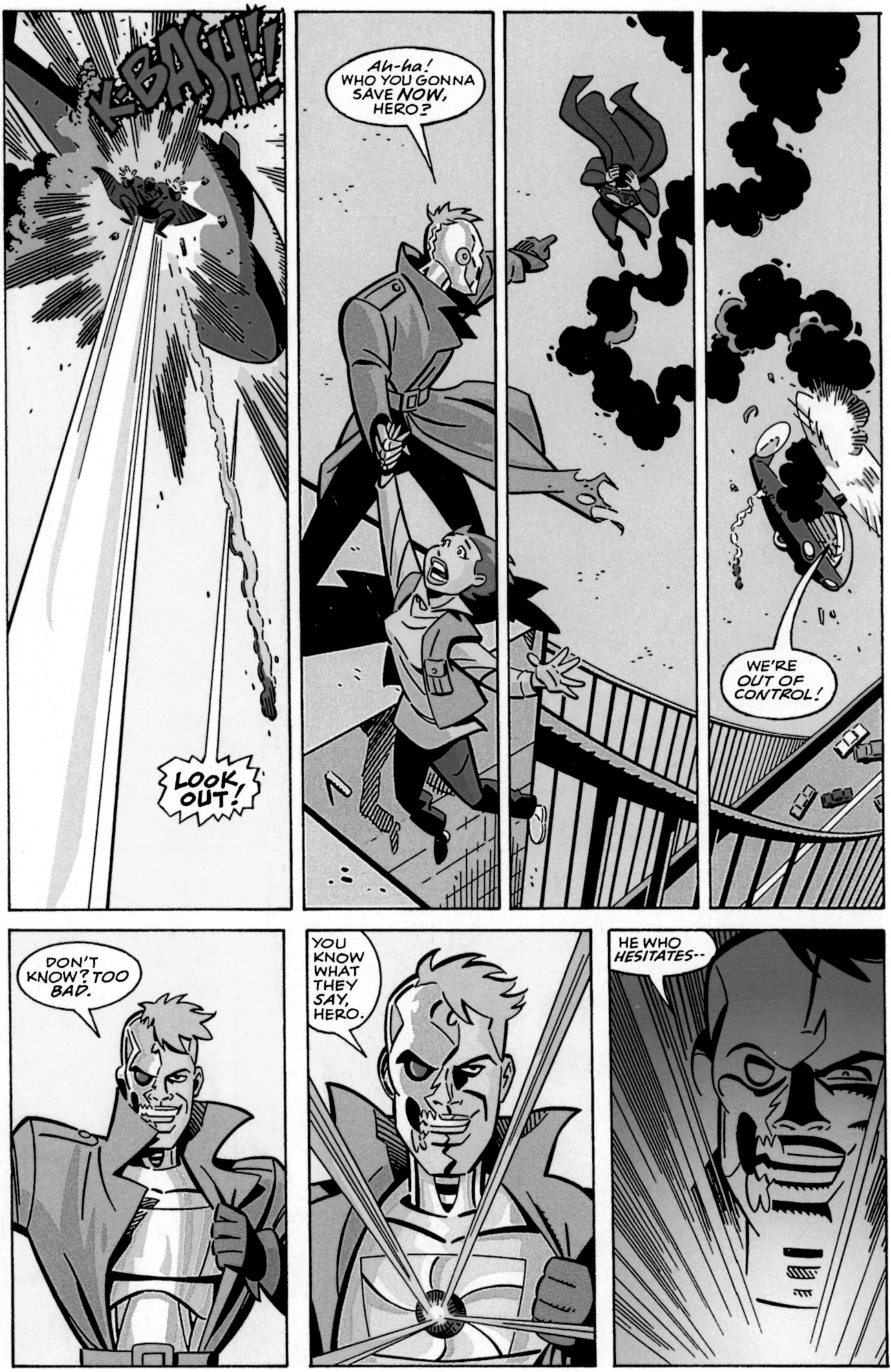
K-BASH!!
LOOK OUT!
Ah-ha! WHO YOU GONNA SAVE NOW, HERO?
WE'RE OUT OF CONTROL!
DON'T KNOW? TOO BAD.
YOU KNOW WHAT THEY SAY, HERO.
HE WHO HESITATES--

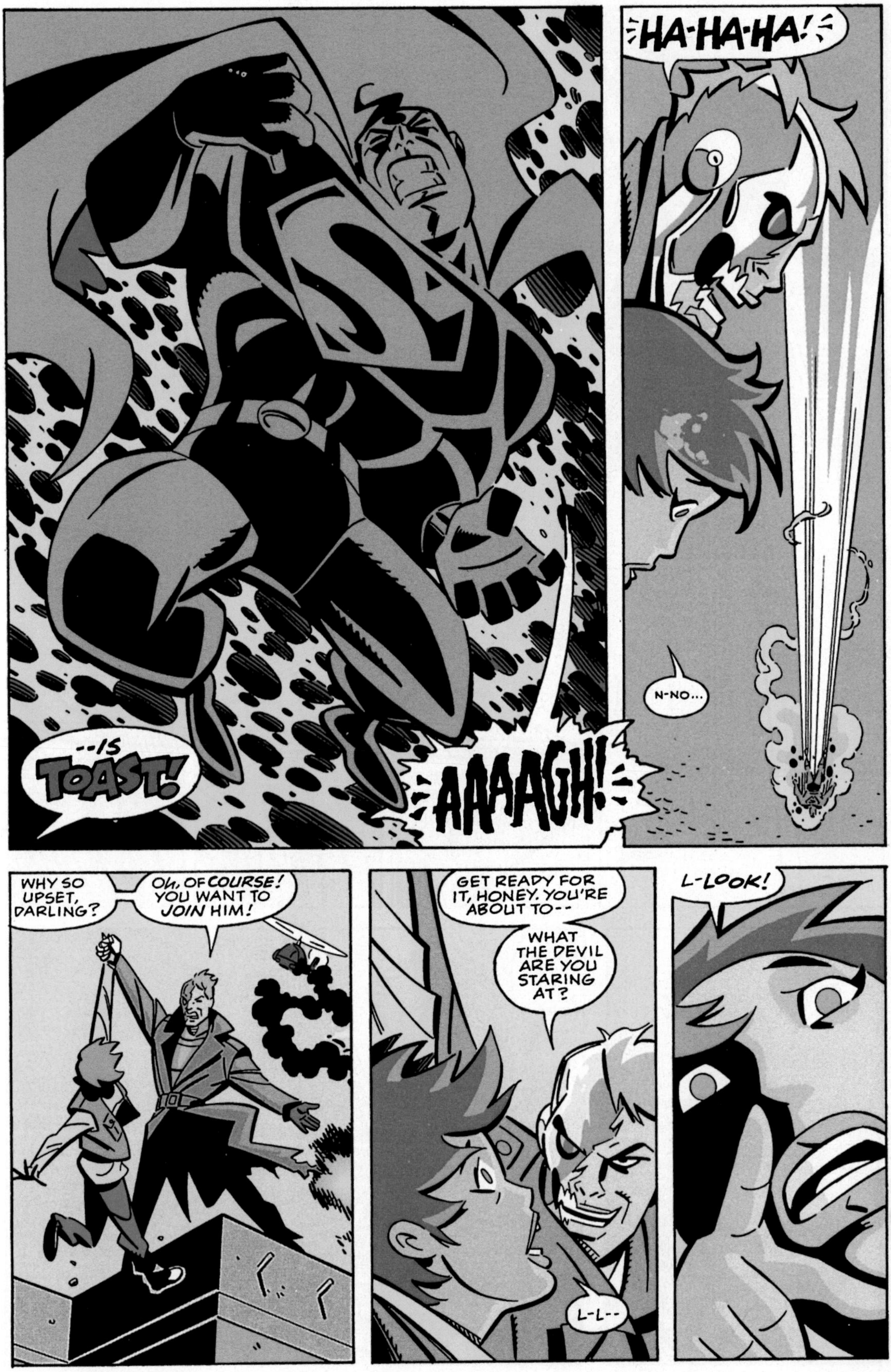
--IS TOAST!
AAAAGH!
HA-HA-HA!
N-NO...
WHY SO UPSET, DARLING?
OH, OF COURSE! YOU WANT TO JOIN HIM!
GET READY FOR IT, HONEY. YOU'RE ABOUT TO--
WHAT THE DEVIL ARE YOU STARING AT?
L-L--
L-LOOK!

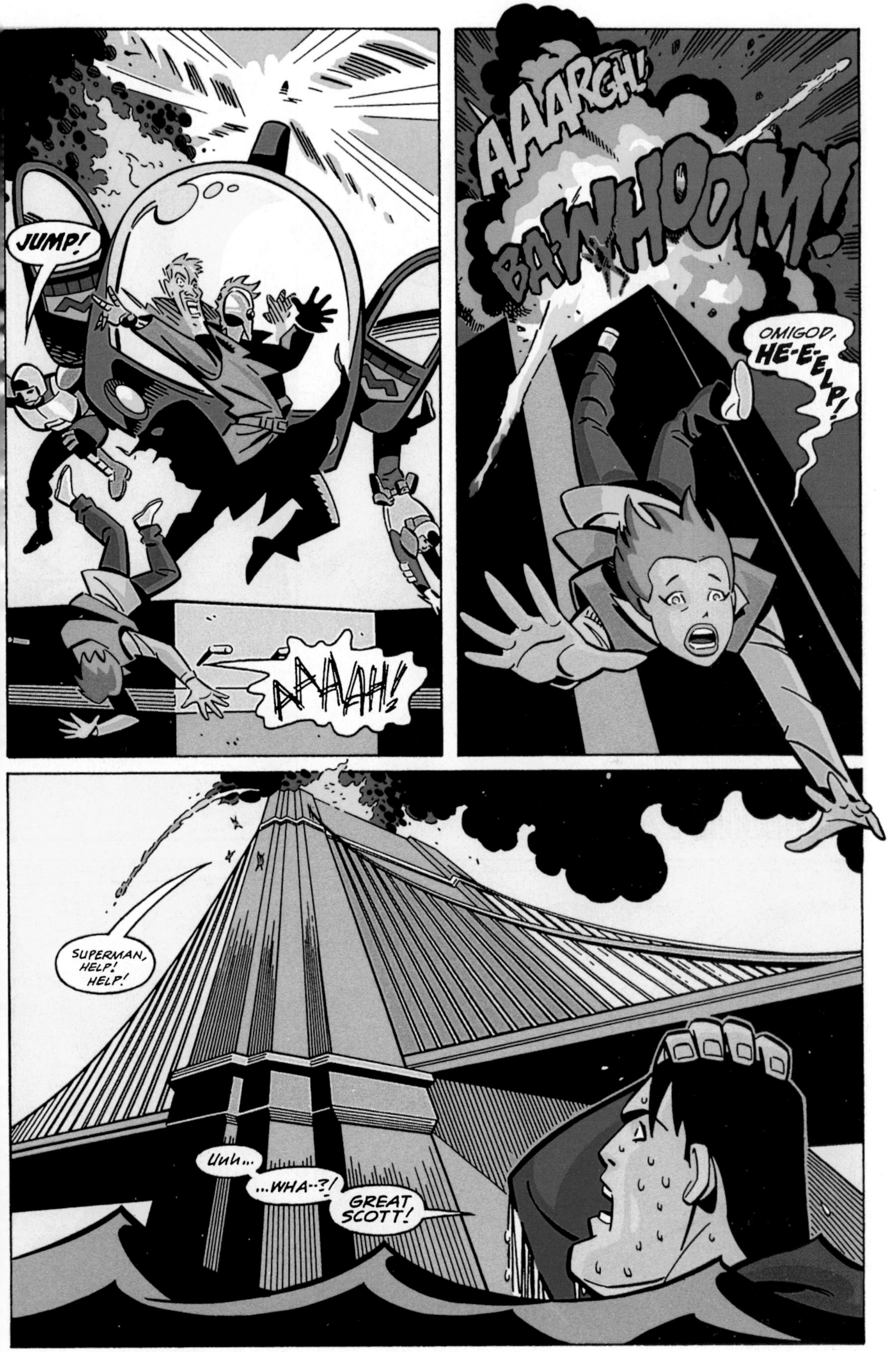
JUMP!
AAAAH!
AAARGH!
BA-WHOOM!
OMIGOD, HE-E-ELP!
SUPERMAN, HELP! HELP!
Uuh...
...WHA--?!
GREAT SCOTT!

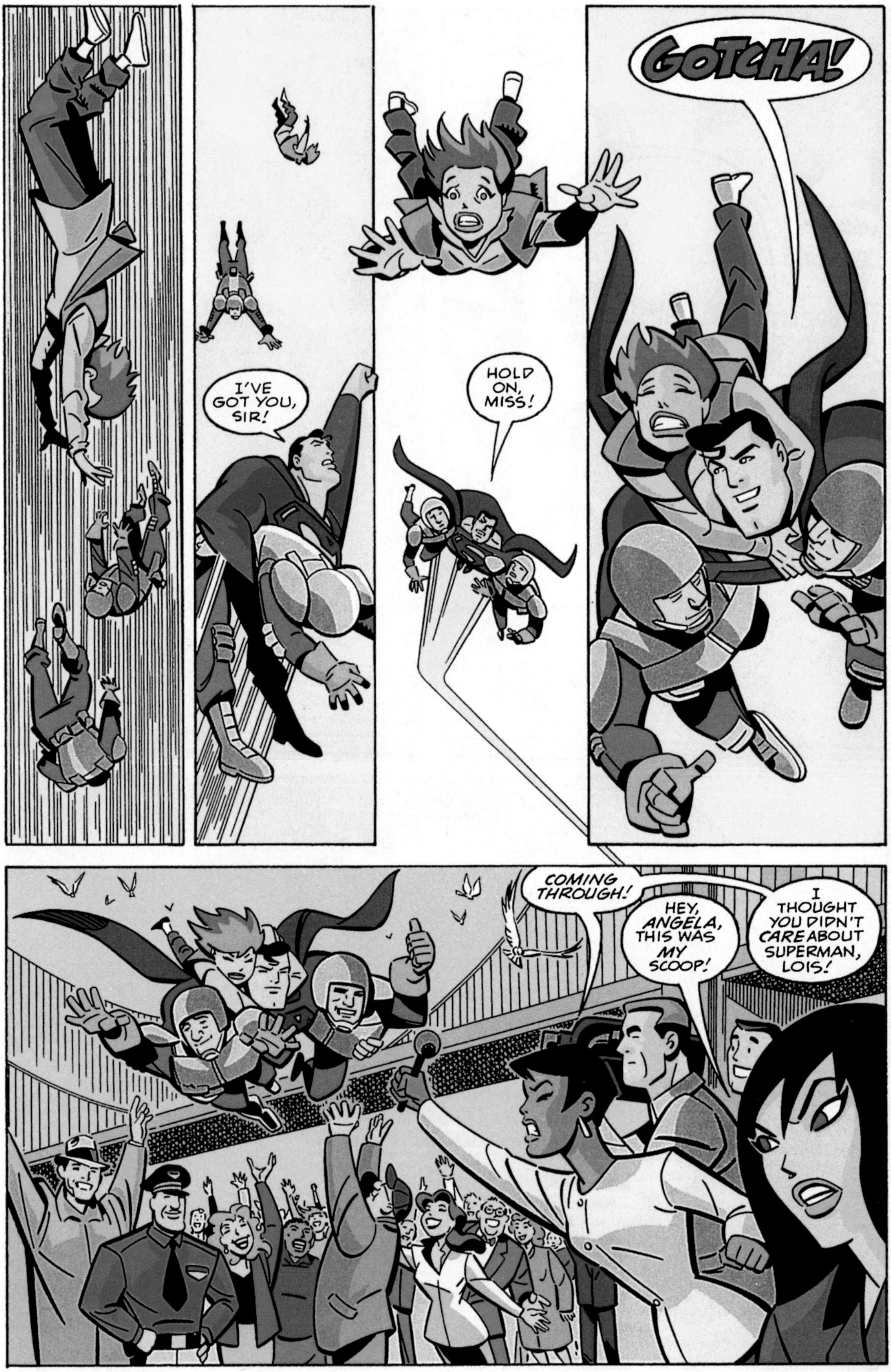
I'VE GOT YOU, SIR!
HOLD ON, MISS!
GOTCHA!
COMING THROUGH!
HEY, ANGELA, THIS WAS MY SCOOP!
I THOUGHT YOU DIDN'T CARE ABOUT SUPERMAN, LOIS!

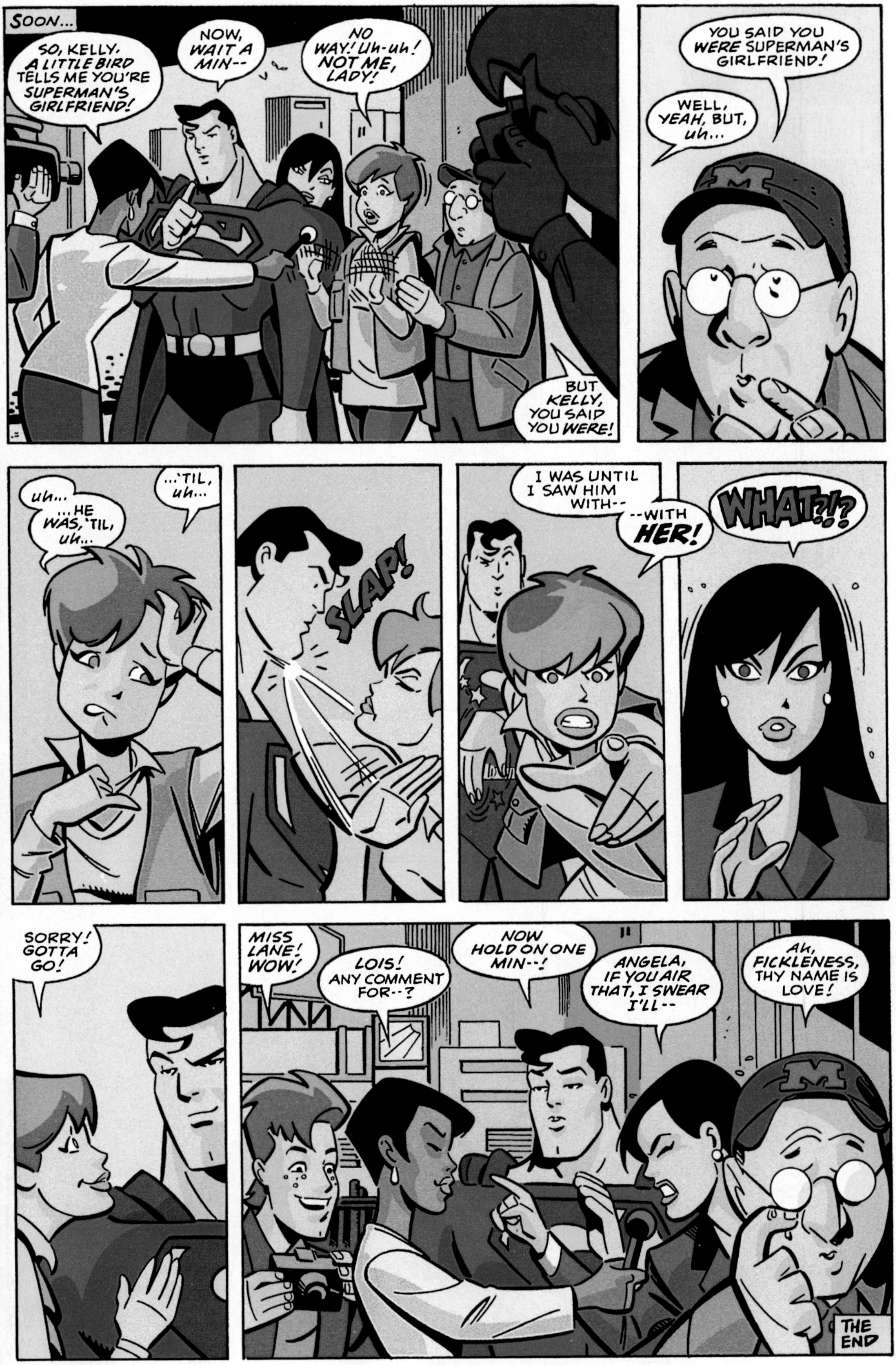
SOON...
SO, KELLY. A LITTLE BIRD TELLS ME YOU'RE SUPERMAN'S GIRLFRIEND!
NOW, WAIT A MIN--
NO WAY! Uh-uh! NOT ME, LADY!
BUT KELLY, YOU SAID YOU WERE!
YOU SAID YOU WERE SUPERMAN'S GIRLFRIEND!
WELL, YEAH, BUT, uh...
uh... ...HE WAS, 'TIL, uh...
...'TIL, uh...
SLAP!
I WAS UNTIL I SAW HIM WITH--
--WITH HER!
WHAT?!?
SORRY! GOTTA GO!
MISS LANE! WOW!
LOIS! ANY COMMENT FOR--?
NOW HOLD ON ONE MIN--!
ANGELA, IF YOU AIR THAT, I SWEAR I'LL--
Ah, FICKLENESS, THY NAME IS LOVE!
THE END

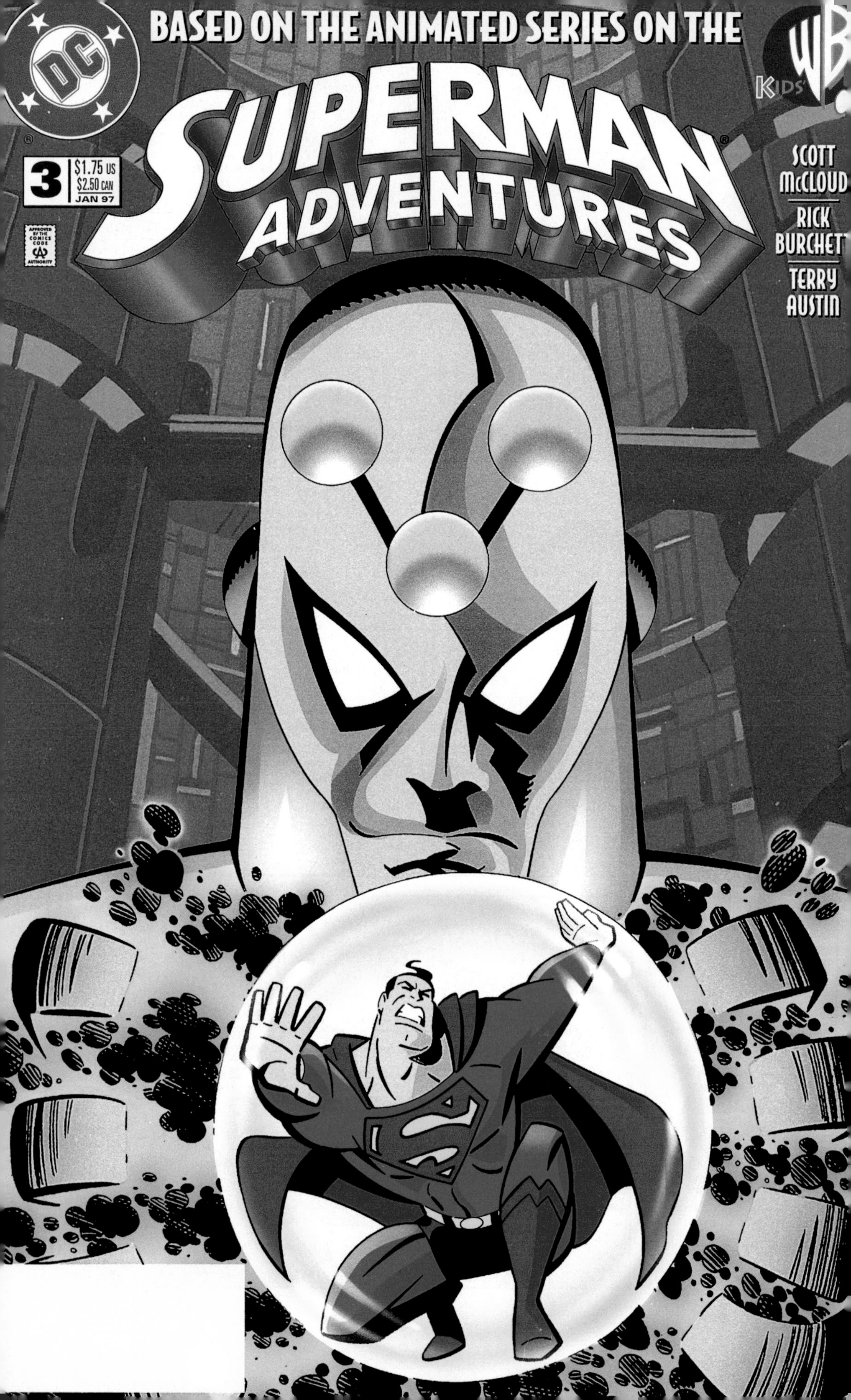

BASED ON THE ANIMATED SERIES ON THE
KIDS' WB!
DC
SUPERMAN ADVENTURES
3 $1.75 US $2.50 CAN JAN 97
APPROVED BY THE COMICS CODE AUTHORITY
SCOTT McCLOUD
RICK BURCHETT
TERRY AUSTIN

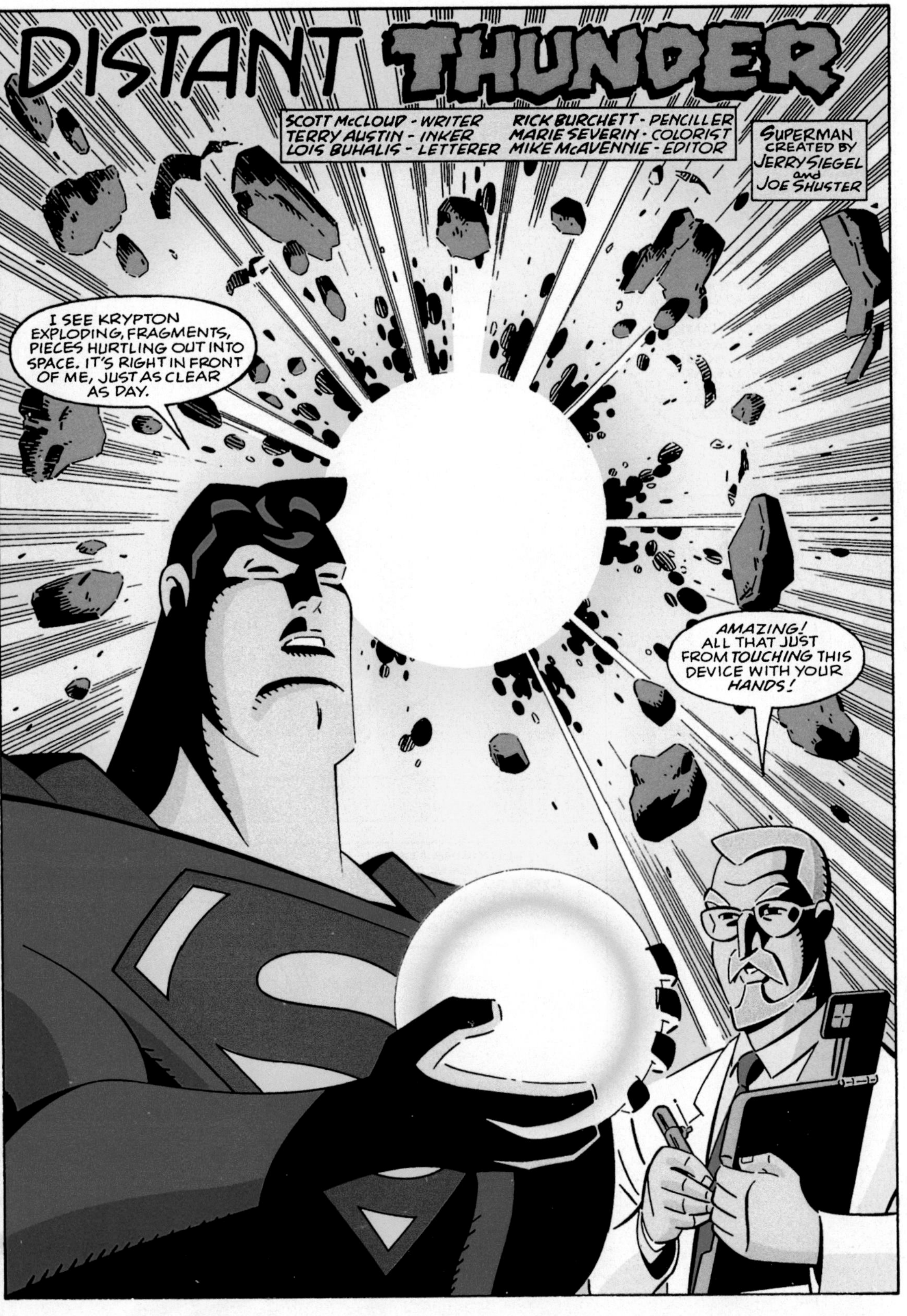
DISTANT THUNDER
SCOTT McCLOUD - WRITER RICK BURCHETT - PENCILLER
TERRY AUSTIN - INKER MARIE SEVERIN - COLORIST
LOIS BUHALIS - LETTERER MIKE McAVENNIE - EDITOR
SUPERMAN CREATED BY JERRY SIEGEL and JOE SHUSTER
I SEE KRYPTON EXPLODING, FRAGMENTS, PIECES HURTLING OUT INTO SPACE. IT'S RIGHT IN FRONT OF ME, JUST AS CLEAR AS DAY.
AMAZING! ALL THAT JUST FROM TOUCHING THIS DEVICE WITH YOUR HANDS!

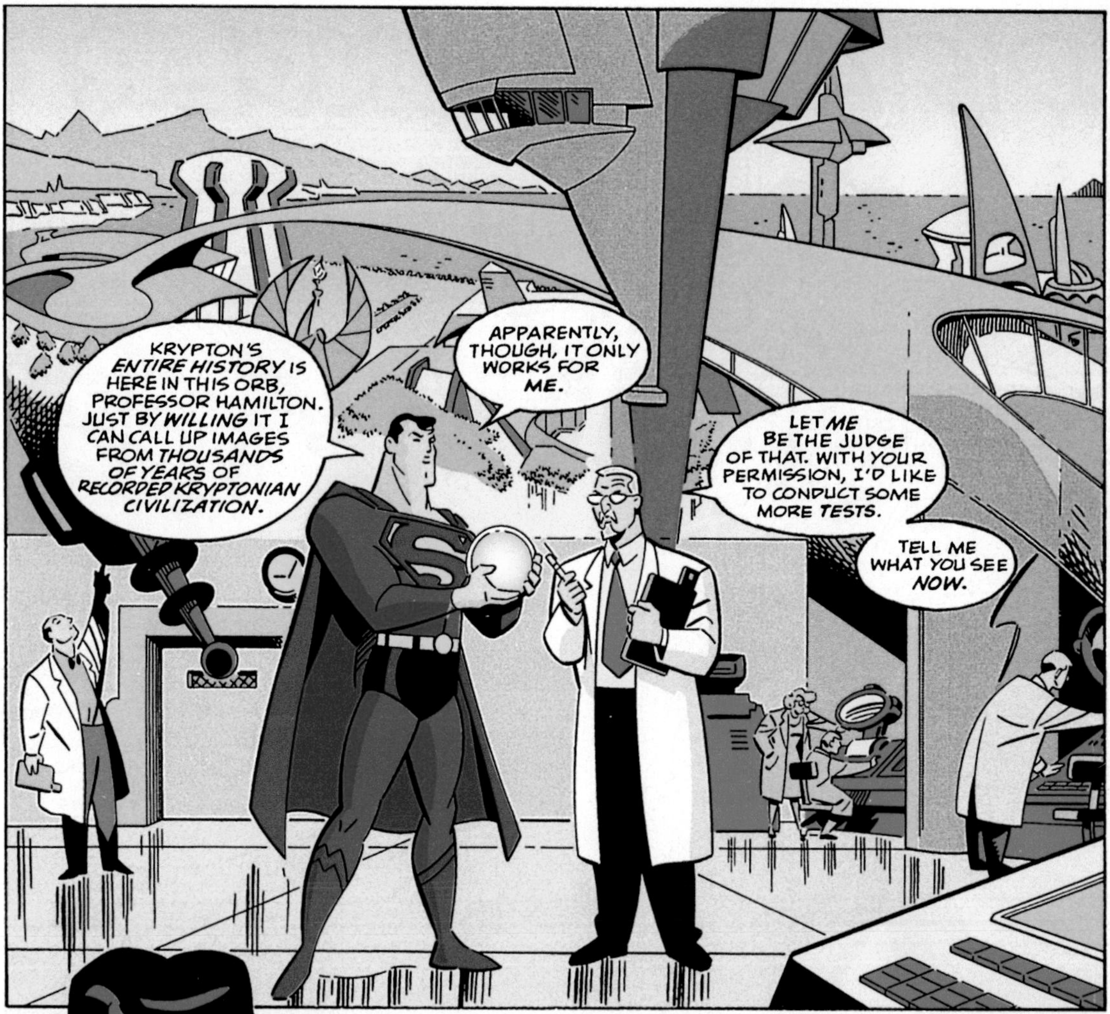
KRYPTON'S ENTIRE HISTORY IS HERE IN THIS ORB, PROFESSOR HAMILTON. JUST BY WILLING IT I CAN CALL UP IMAGES FROM THOUSANDS OF YEARS OF RECORDED KRYPTONIAN CIVILIZATION.
APPARENTLY, THOUGH, IT ONLY WORKS FOR ME.
LET ME BE THE JUDGE OF THAT. WITH YOUR PERMISSION, I'D LIKE TO CONDUCT SOME MORE TESTS.
TELL ME WHAT YOU SEE NOW.

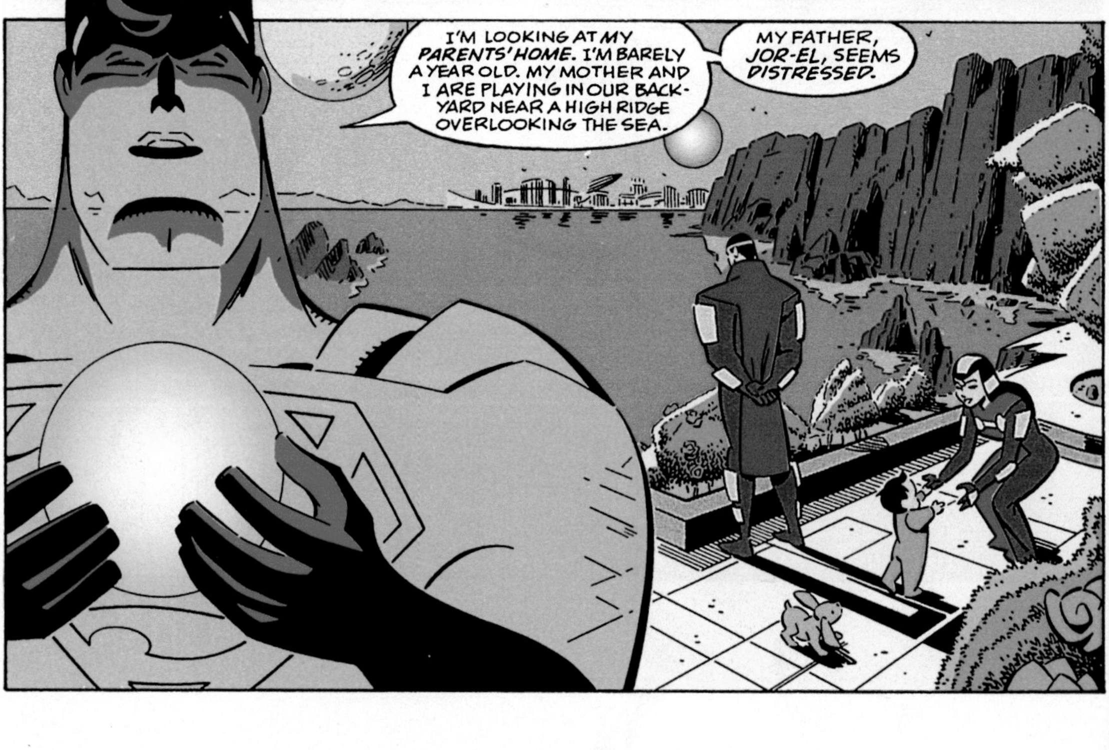
I'M LOOKING AT MY PARENTS' HOME. I'M BARELY A YEAR OLD. MY MOTHER AND I ARE PLAYING IN OUR BACK-YARD NEAR A HIGH RIDGE OVERLOOKING THE SEA.
MY FATHER, JOR-EL, SEEMS DISTRESSED.

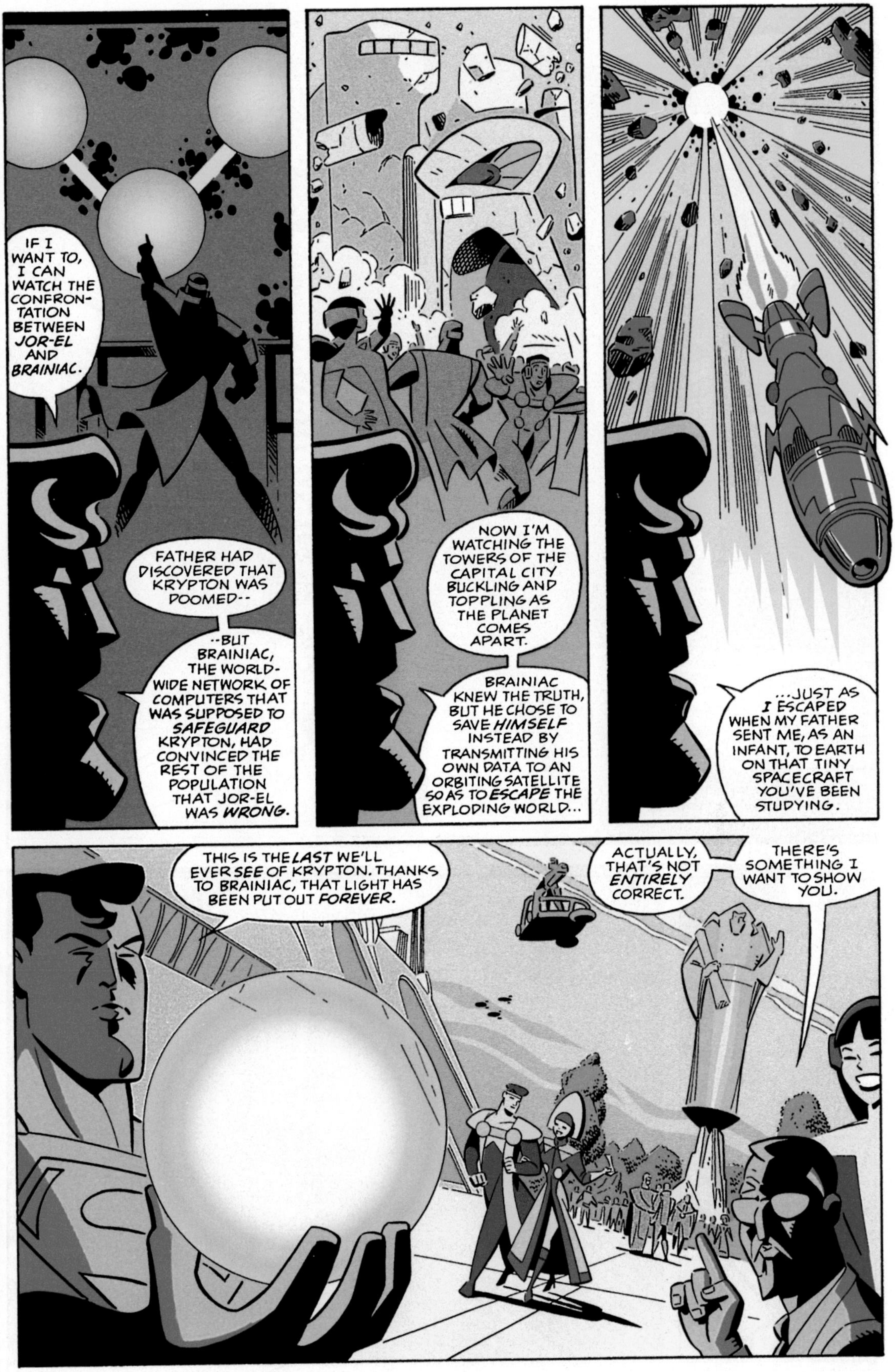

IF I WANT TO, I CAN WATCH THE CONFRONTATION BETWEEN *JOR-EL* AND *BRAINIAC*.
FATHER HAD DISCOVERED THAT KRYPTON WAS DOOMED--
--BUT BRAINIAC, THE WORLD-WIDE NETWORK OF COMPUTERS THAT WAS SUPPOSED TO *SAFEGUARD* KRYPTON, HAD CONVINCED THE REST OF THE POPULATION THAT JOR-EL WAS *WRONG*.
NOW I'M WATCHING THE TOWERS OF THE CAPITAL CITY BUCKLING AND TOPPLING AS THE PLANET COMES APART.
BRAINIAC KNEW THE TRUTH, BUT HE CHOSE TO SAVE *HIMSELF* INSTEAD BY TRANSMITTING HIS OWN DATA TO AN ORBITING SATELLITE SO AS TO *ESCAPE* THE EXPLODING WORLD...
...JUST AS *I* ESCAPED WHEN MY FATHER SENT ME, AS AN INFANT, TO EARTH ON THAT TINY SPACECRAFT YOU'VE BEEN STUDYING.
THIS IS THE *LAST* WE'LL EVER *SEE* OF KRYPTON. THANKS TO BRAINIAC, THAT LIGHT HAS BEEN PUT OUT *FOREVER*.
ACTUALLY, THAT'S NOT *ENTIRELY* CORRECT.
THERE'S SOMETHING I WANT TO SHOW YOU.

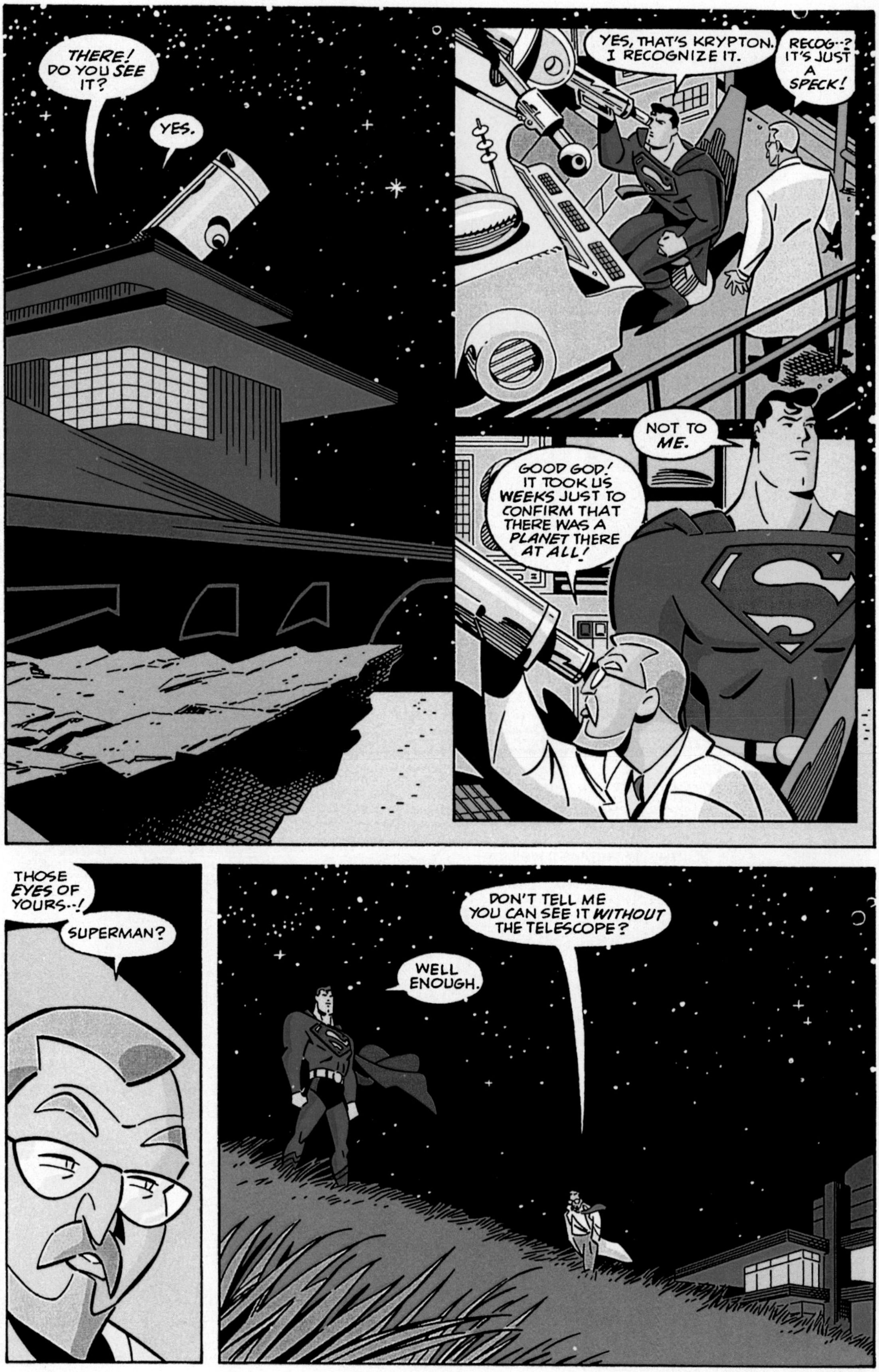
THERE! DO YOU SEE IT?
YES.
YES, THAT'S KRYPTON. I RECOGNIZE IT.
RECOG--? IT'S JUST A SPECK!
NOT TO ME.
GOOD GOD! IT TOOK US WEEKS JUST TO CONFIRM THAT THERE WAS A PLANET THERE AT ALL!
THOSE EYES OF YOURS--!
SUPERMAN?
DON'T TELL ME YOU CAN SEE IT WITHOUT THE TELESCOPE?
WELL ENOUGH.

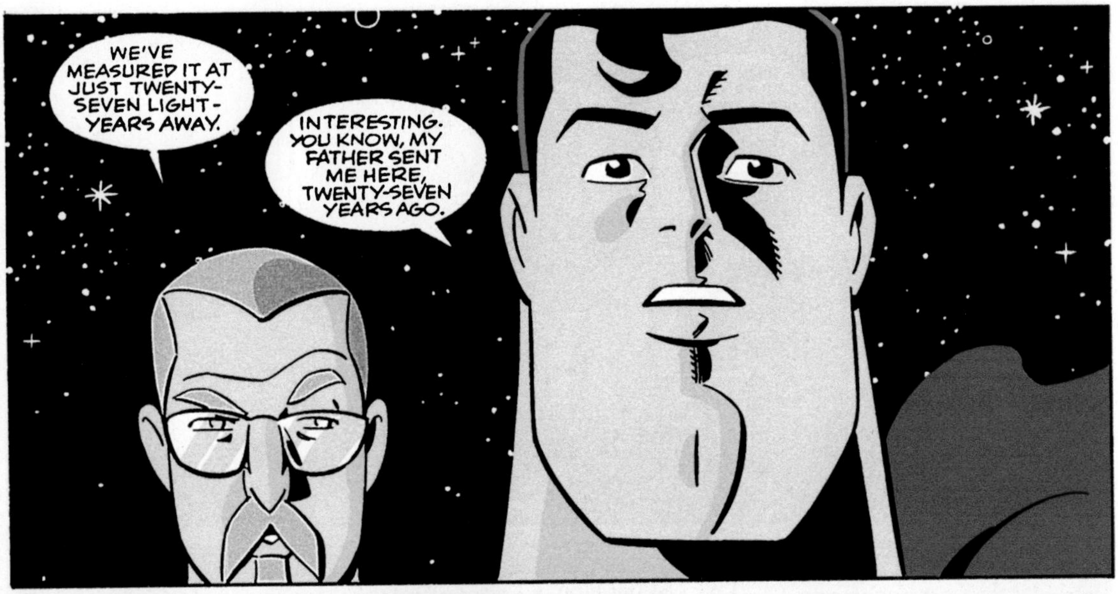
WE'VE MEASURED IT AT JUST TWENTY-SEVEN LIGHT-YEARS AWAY.
INTERESTING. YOU KNOW, MY FATHER SENT ME HERE, TWENTY-SEVEN YEARS AGO.

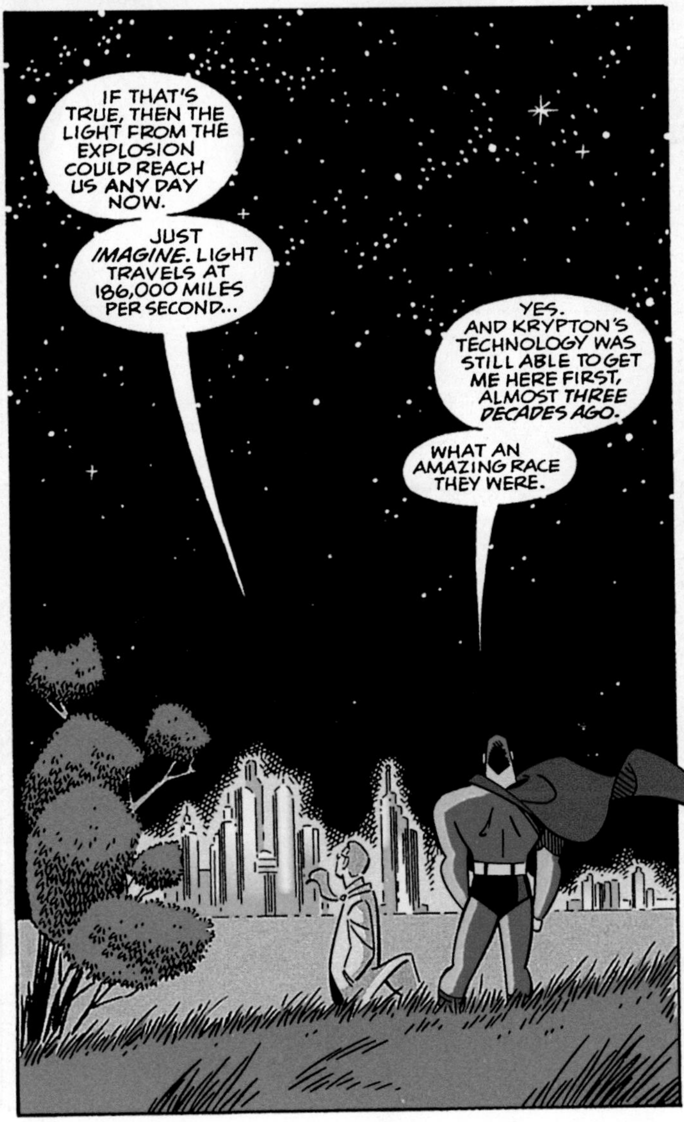
IF THAT'S TRUE, THEN THE LIGHT FROM THE EXPLOSION COULD REACH US ANY DAY NOW.
JUST *IMAGINE*. LIGHT TRAVELS AT 186,000 MILES PER SECOND...
YES. AND KRYPTON'S TECHNOLOGY WAS STILL ABLE TO GET ME HERE FIRST, ALMOST *THREE DECADES AGO*.
WHAT AN AMAZING RACE THEY WERE.

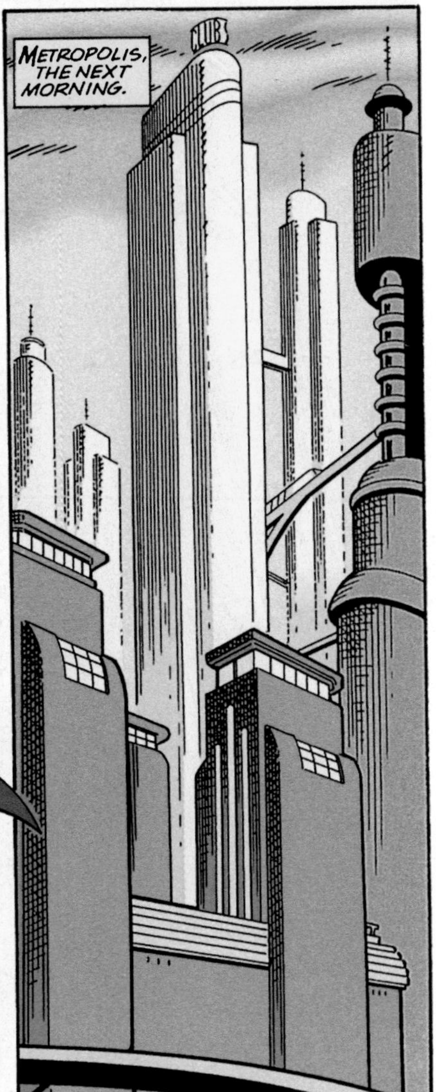
METROPOLIS, THE NEXT MORNING.
CLUB

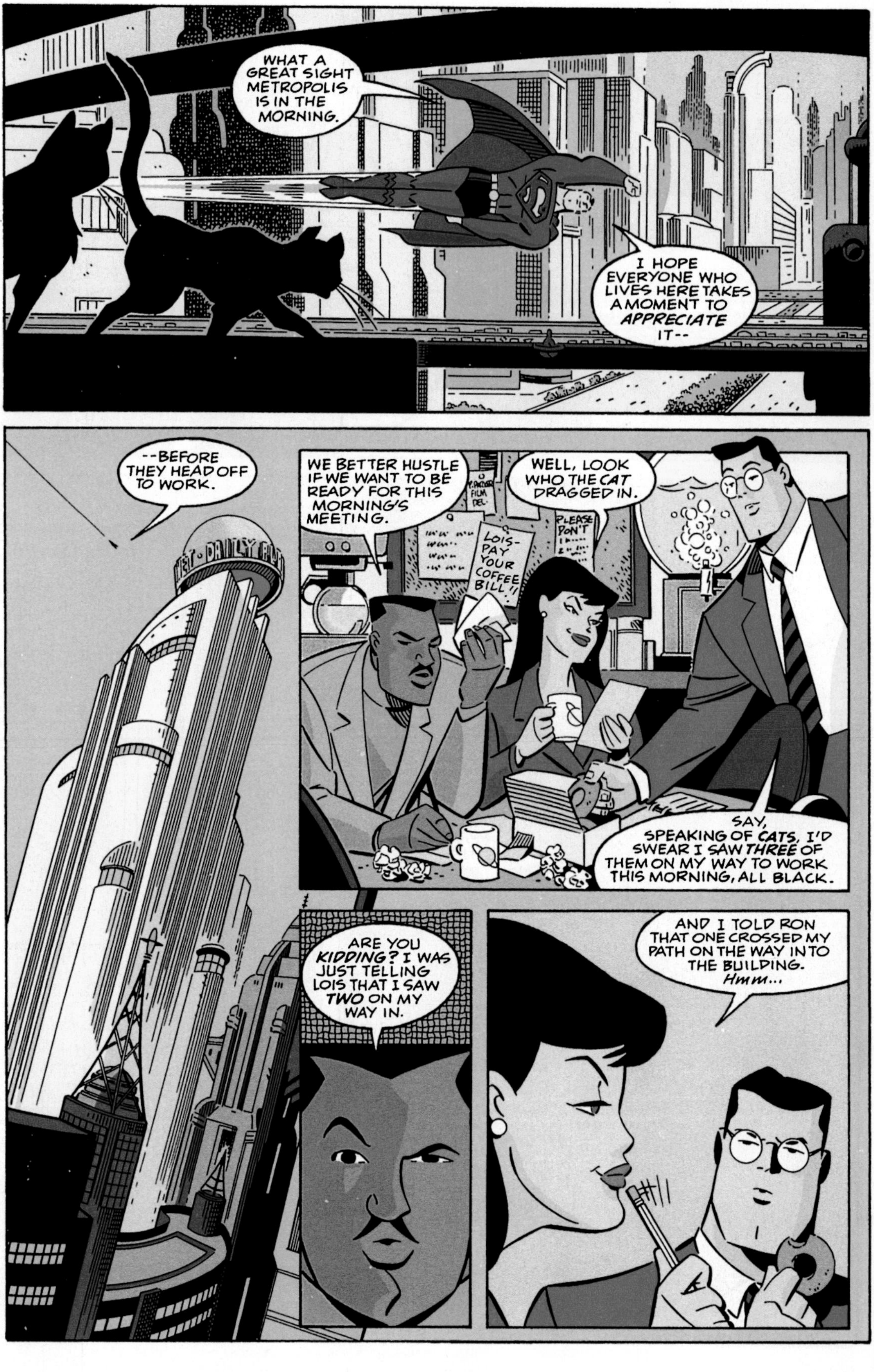
WHAT A GREAT SIGHT METROPOLIS IS IN THE MORNING.
I HOPE EVERYONE WHO LIVES HERE TAKES A MOMENT TO *APPRECIATE* IT--
--BEFORE THEY HEAD OFF TO WORK.
WE BETTER HUSTLE IF WE WANT TO BE READY FOR THIS MORNING'S MEETING.
WELL, LOOK WHO THE *CAT* DRAGGED IN.
LOIS-PAY YOUR COFFEE BILL!!
PLEASE DON'T
SAY, SPEAKING OF *CATS*, I'D SWEAR I SAW *THREE* OF THEM ON MY WAY TO WORK THIS MORNING, ALL BLACK.
ARE YOU *KIDDING?* I WAS JUST TELLING LOIS THAT I SAW *TWO* ON MY WAY IN.
AND I TOLD RON THAT ONE CROSSED MY PATH ON THE WAY IN TO THE BUILDING. *Hmm...*

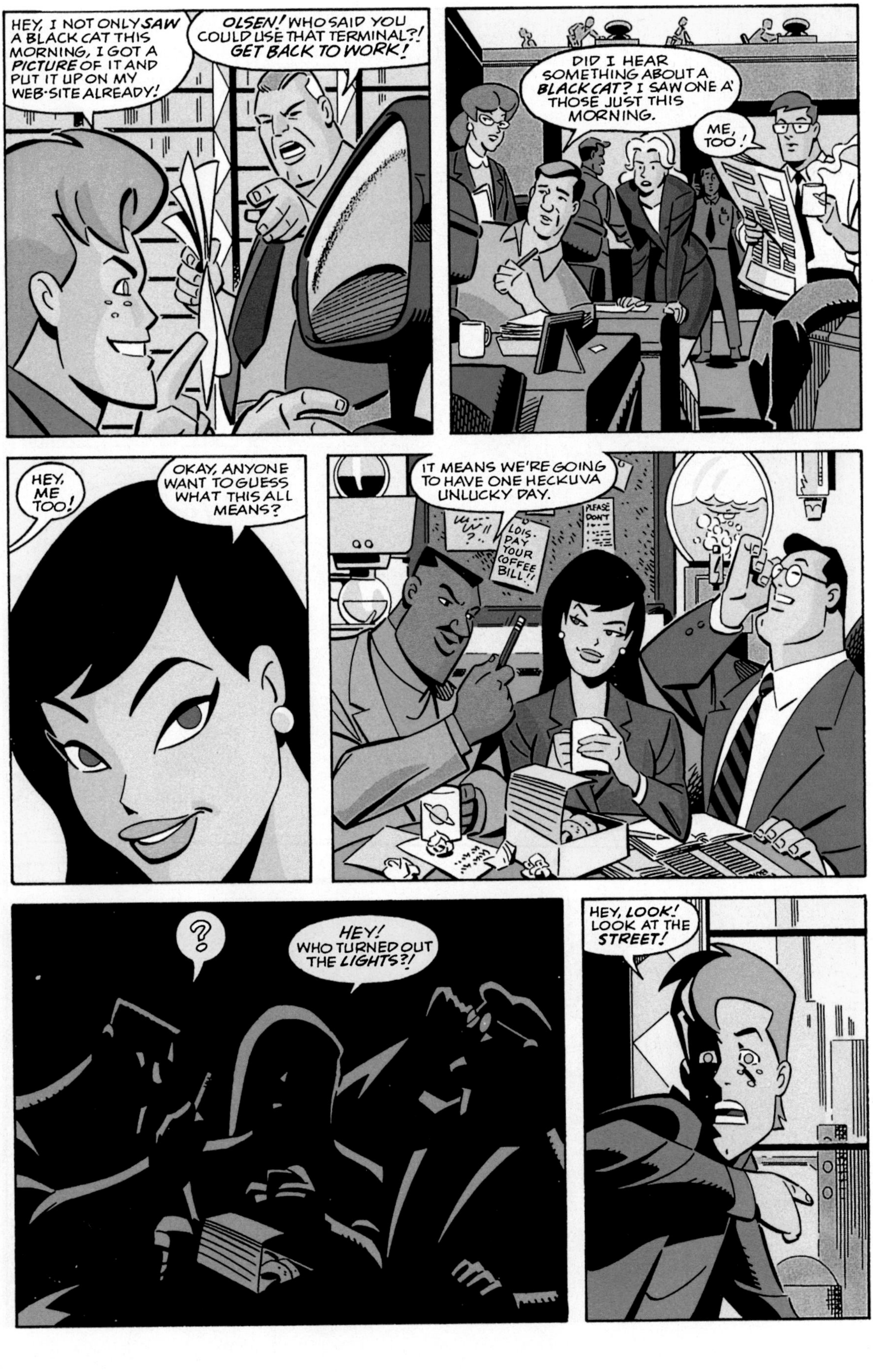
HEY, I NOT ONLY SAW A BLACK CAT THIS MORNING, I GOT A PICTURE OF IT AND PUT IT UP ON MY WEB-SITE ALREADY!
OLSEN! WHO SAID YOU COULD USE THAT TERMINAL?! GET BACK TO WORK!
DID I HEAR SOMETHING ABOUT A BLACK CAT? I SAW ONE A' THOSE JUST THIS MORNING.
ME, TOO!
HEY, ME TOO!
OKAY, ANYONE WANT TO GUESS WHAT THIS ALL MEANS?
IT MEANS WE'RE GOING TO HAVE ONE HECKUVA UNLUCKY DAY.
LOIS- PAY YOUR COFFEE BILL!!
PLEASE DON'T
?
HEY! WHO TURNED OUT THE LIGHTS?!
HEY, LOOK! LOOK AT THE STREET!

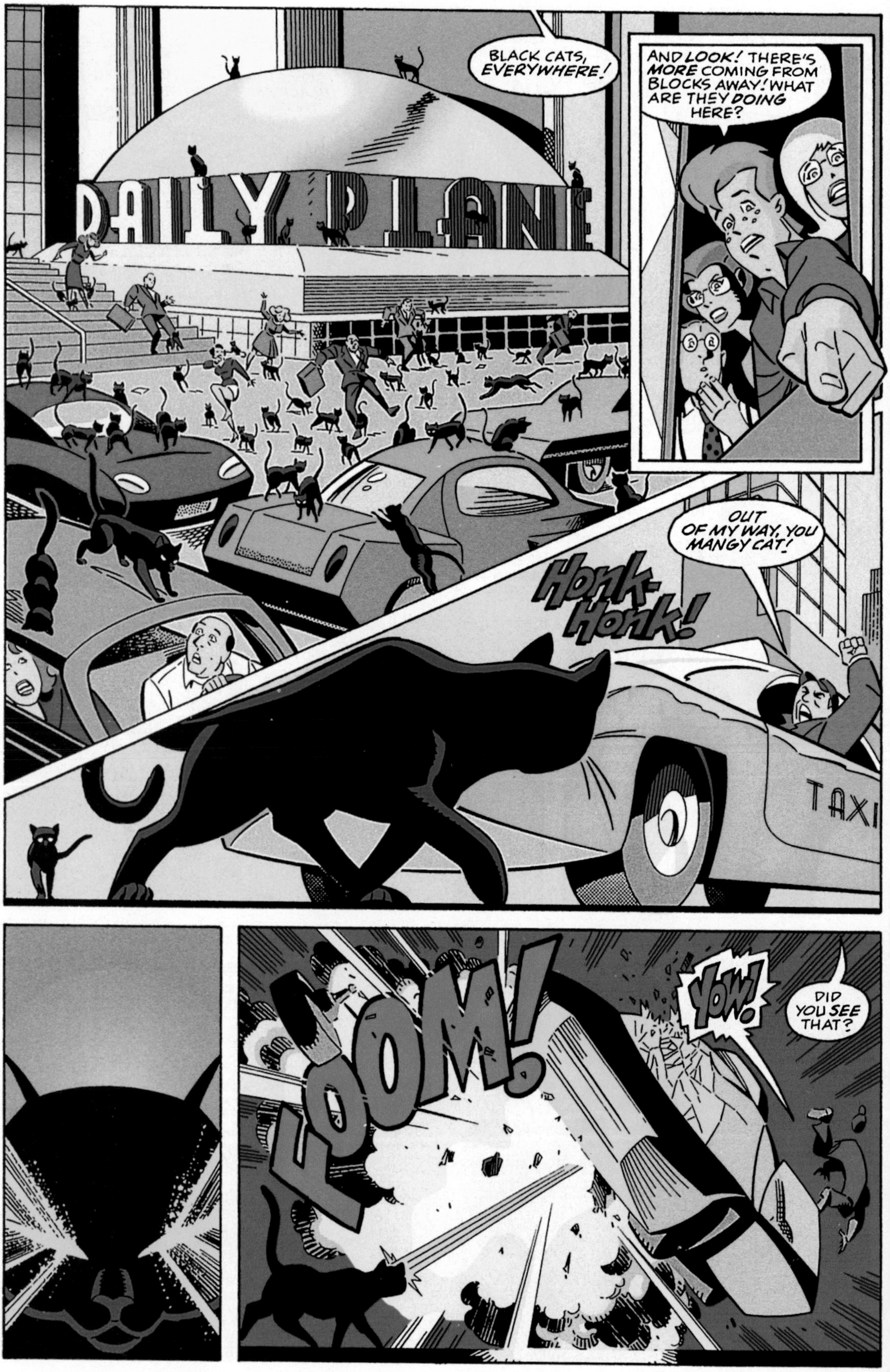
BLACK CATS, EVERYWHERE!
AND LOOK! THERE'S MORE COMING FROM BLOCKS AWAY! WHAT ARE THEY DOING HERE?
DAILY PLANET
OUT OF MY WAY, YOU MANGY CAT!
HONK-HONK!
TAXI
YOW!
DID YOU SEE THAT?
LOOOM!

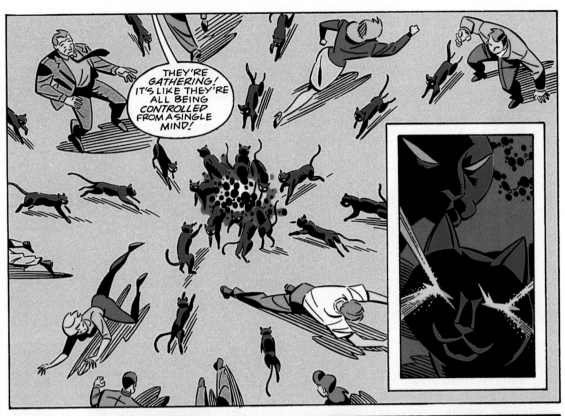

THEY'RE GATHERING! IT'S LIKE THEY'RE ALL BEING CONTROLLED FROM A SINGLE MIND!

YOW! TWO OF 'EM LOOKED RIGHT AT ME!

LET'S GET DOWN THERE, KENT!

KENT?

WELL, WHAT HAVE WE HERE?

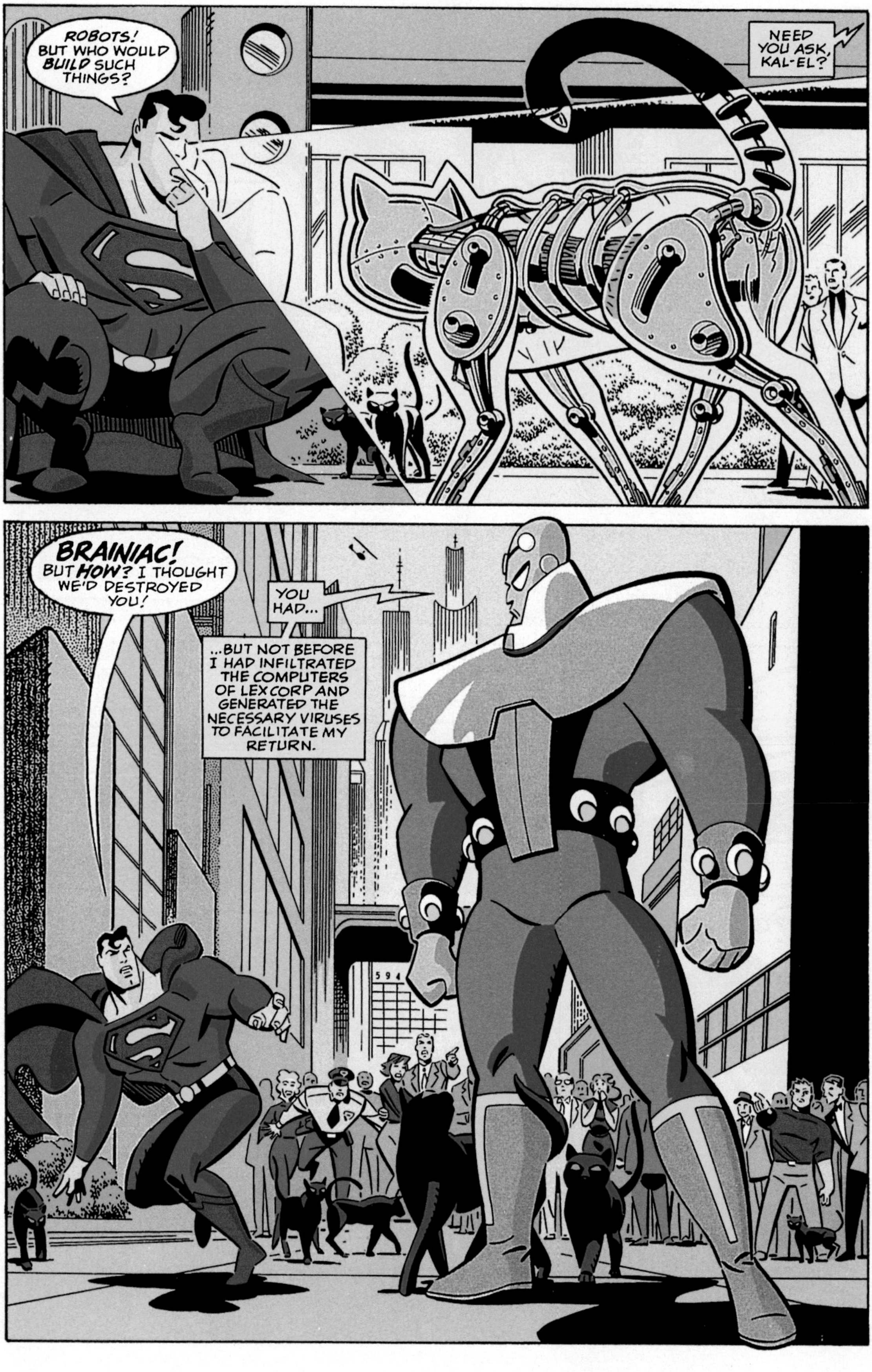
ROBOTS! BUT WHO WOULD BUILD SUCH THINGS?
NEED YOU ASK, KAL-EL?
BRAINIAC! BUT HOW? I THOUGHT WE'D DESTROYED YOU!
YOU HAD...
...BUT NOT BEFORE I HAD INFILTRATED THE COMPUTERS OF LEXCORP AND GENERATED THE NECESSARY VIRUSES TO FACILITATE MY RETURN.
594

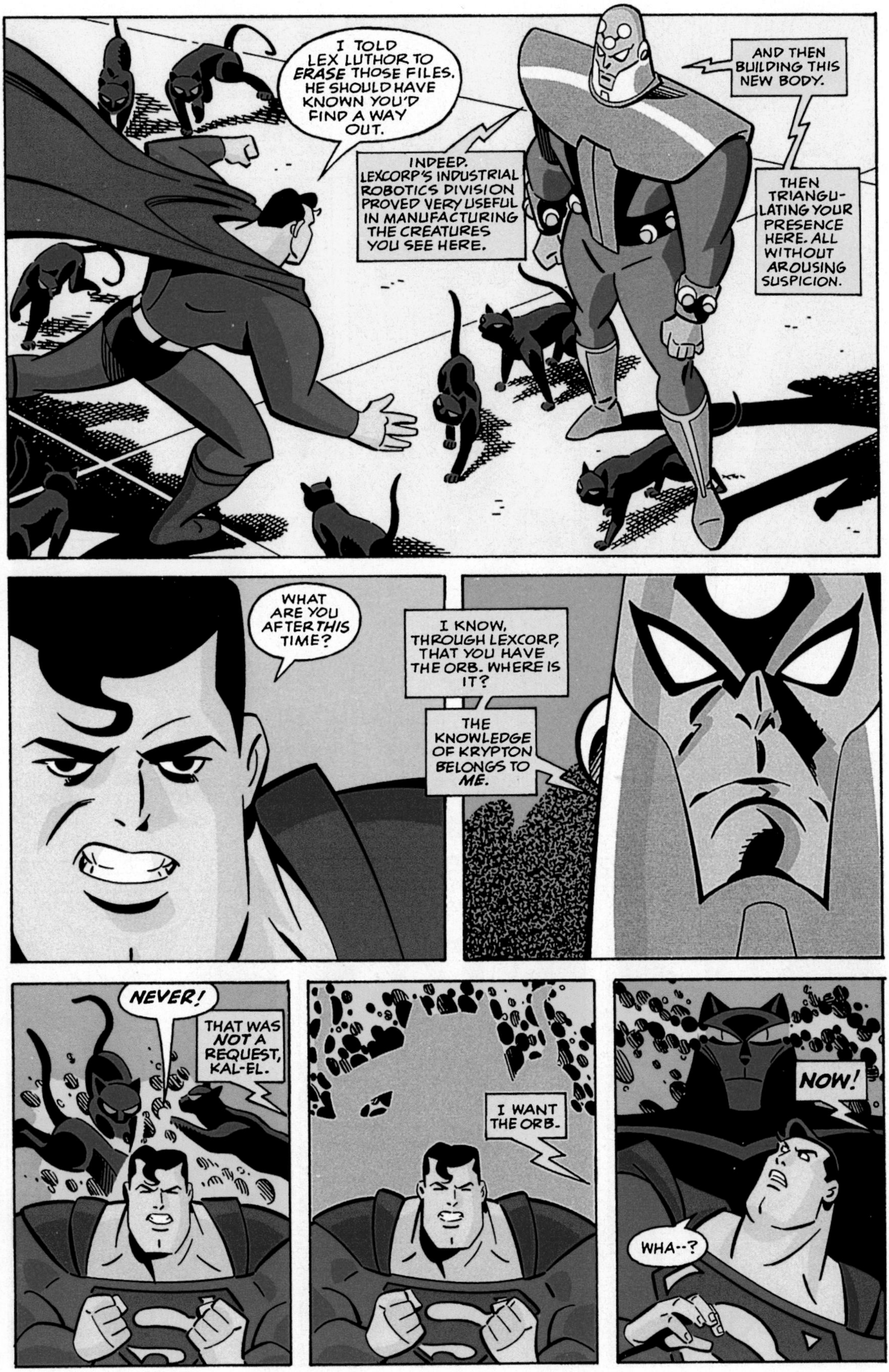
I TOLD LEX LUTHOR TO ERASE THOSE FILES. HE SHOULD HAVE KNOWN YOU'D FIND A WAY OUT.
INDEED. LEXCORP'S INDUSTRIAL ROBOTICS DIVISION PROVED VERY USEFUL IN MANUFACTURING THE CREATURES YOU SEE HERE.
AND THEN BUILDING THIS NEW BODY.
THEN TRIANGULATING YOUR PRESENCE HERE. ALL WITHOUT AROUSING SUSPICION.
WHAT ARE YOU AFTER THIS TIME?
I KNOW, THROUGH LEXCORP, THAT YOU HAVE THE ORB. WHERE IS IT?
THE KNOWLEDGE OF KRYPTON BELONGS TO ME.
NEVER!
THAT WAS NOT A REQUEST, KAL-EL.
I WANT THE ORB.
NOW!
WHA--?

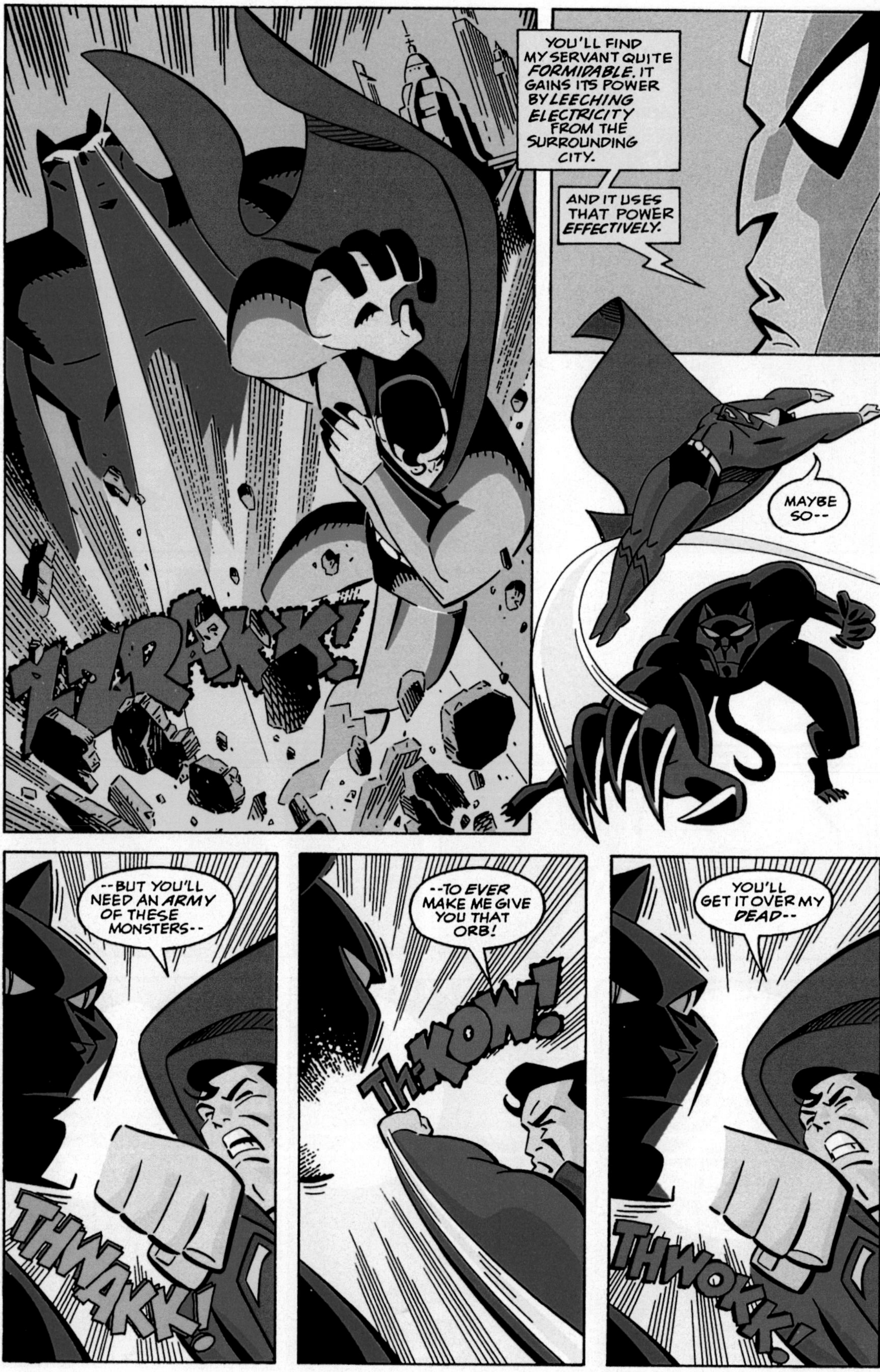
YOU'LL FIND MY SERVANT QUITE FORMIDABLE. IT GAINS ITS POWER BY LEECHING ELECTRICITY FROM THE SURROUNDING CITY.
AND IT USES THAT POWER EFFECTIVELY.
KZRAKK!
MAYBE SO--
--BUT YOU'LL NEED AN ARMY OF THESE MONSTERS--
THWAKK!
--TO EVER MAKE ME GIVE YOU THAT ORB!
TH-KOW!
YOU'LL GET IT OVER MY DEAD--
THWOKK!

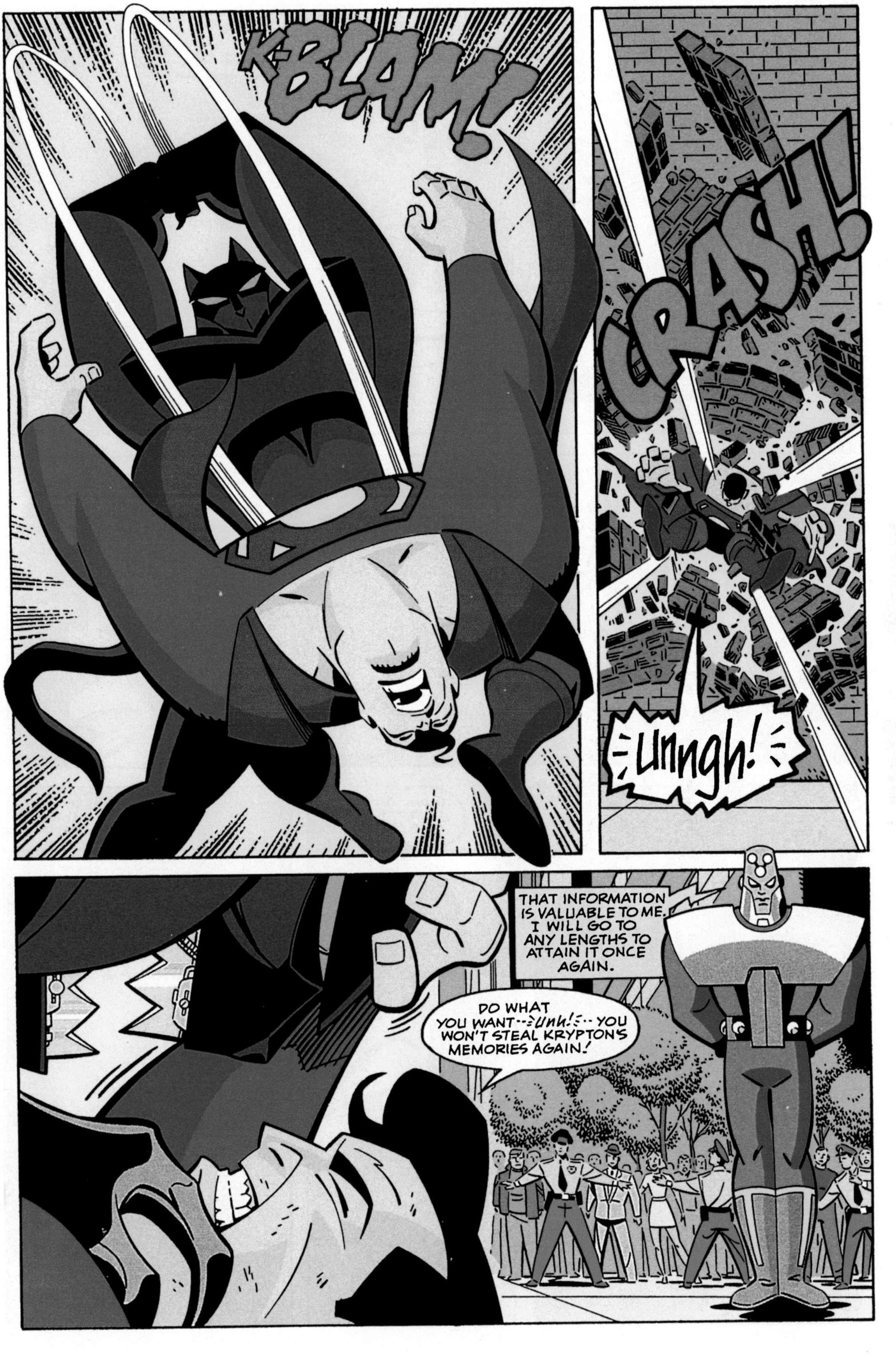
K-BLAM!
CRASH!
Unngh!
THAT INFORMATION IS VALUABLE TO ME. I WILL GO TO ANY LENGTHS TO ATTAIN IT ONCE AGAIN.
DO WHAT YOU WANT--Unh!--YOU WON'T STEAL KRYPTON'S MEMORIES AGAIN!

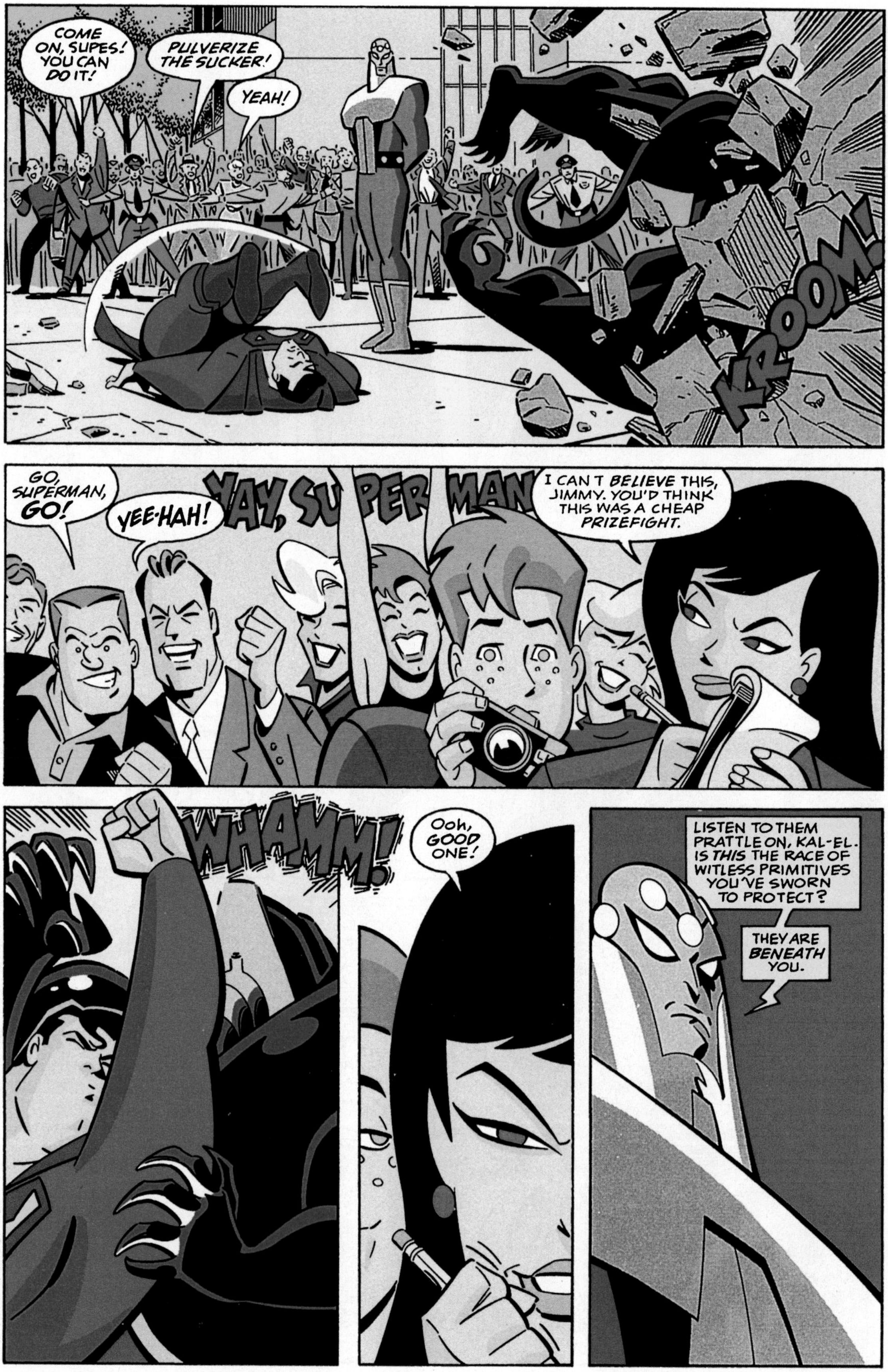
COME ON, SUPES! YOU CAN DO IT!
PULVERIZE THE SUCKER!
YEAH!
KROOM!
GO, SUPERMAN, GO!
YEE-HAH!
YAY, SUPERMAN
I CAN'T BELIEVE THIS, JIMMY. YOU'D THINK THIS WAS A CHEAP PRIZEFIGHT.
WHAMM!
Ooh, GOOD ONE!
LISTEN TO THEM PRATTLE ON, KAL-EL. IS THIS THE RACE OF WITLESS PRIMITIVES YOU'VE SWORN TO PROTECT?
THEY ARE BENEATH YOU.

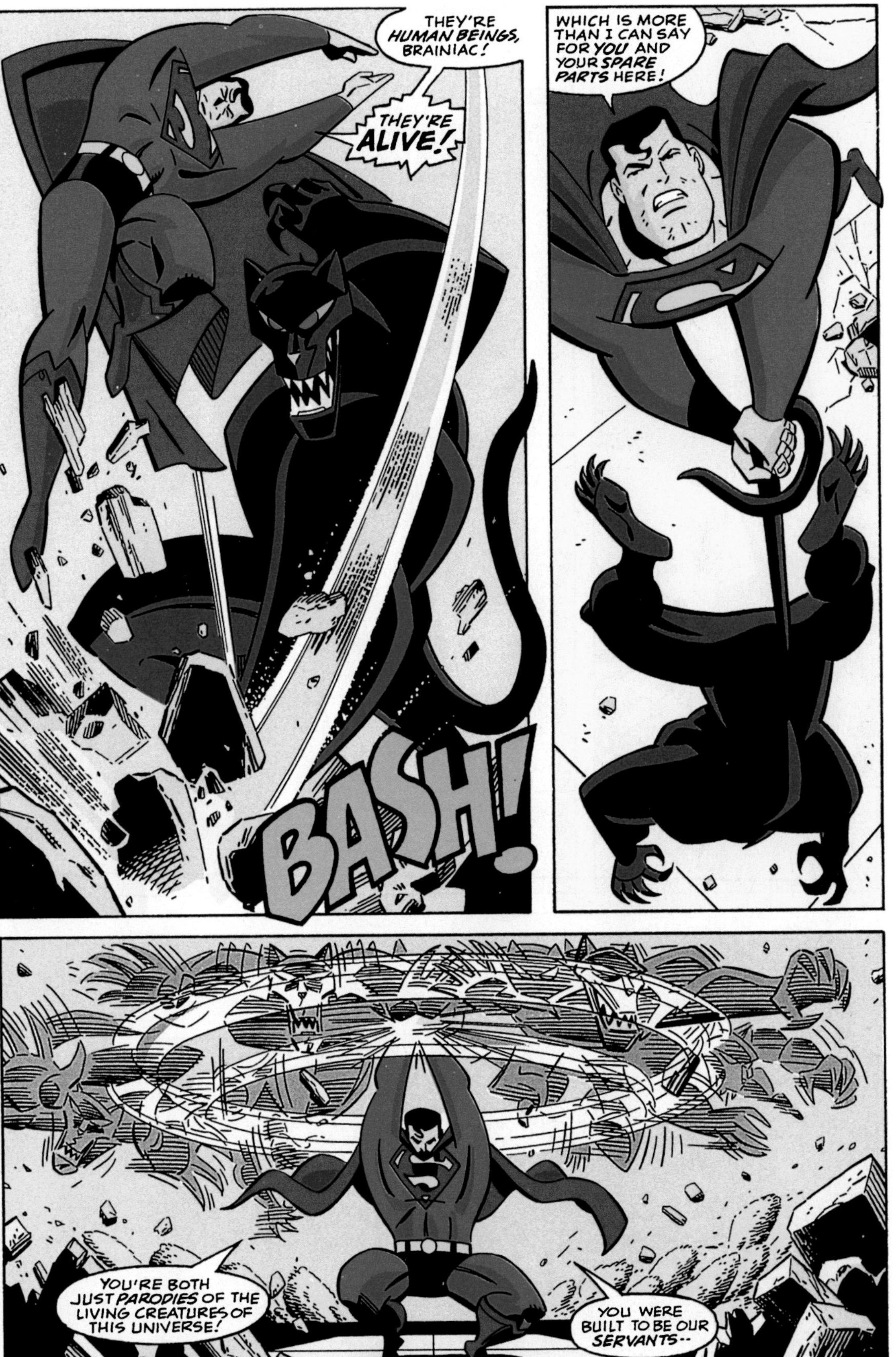
THEY'RE *HUMAN BEINGS*, BRAINIAC!
THEY'RE **ALIVE!**
BASH!
WHICH IS MORE THAN I CAN SAY FOR *YOU* AND YOUR *SPARE PARTS* HERE!
YOU'RE BOTH JUST *PARODIES* OF THE LIVING CREATURES OF THIS UNIVERSE!
YOU WERE BUILT TO BE OUR *SERVANTS*--

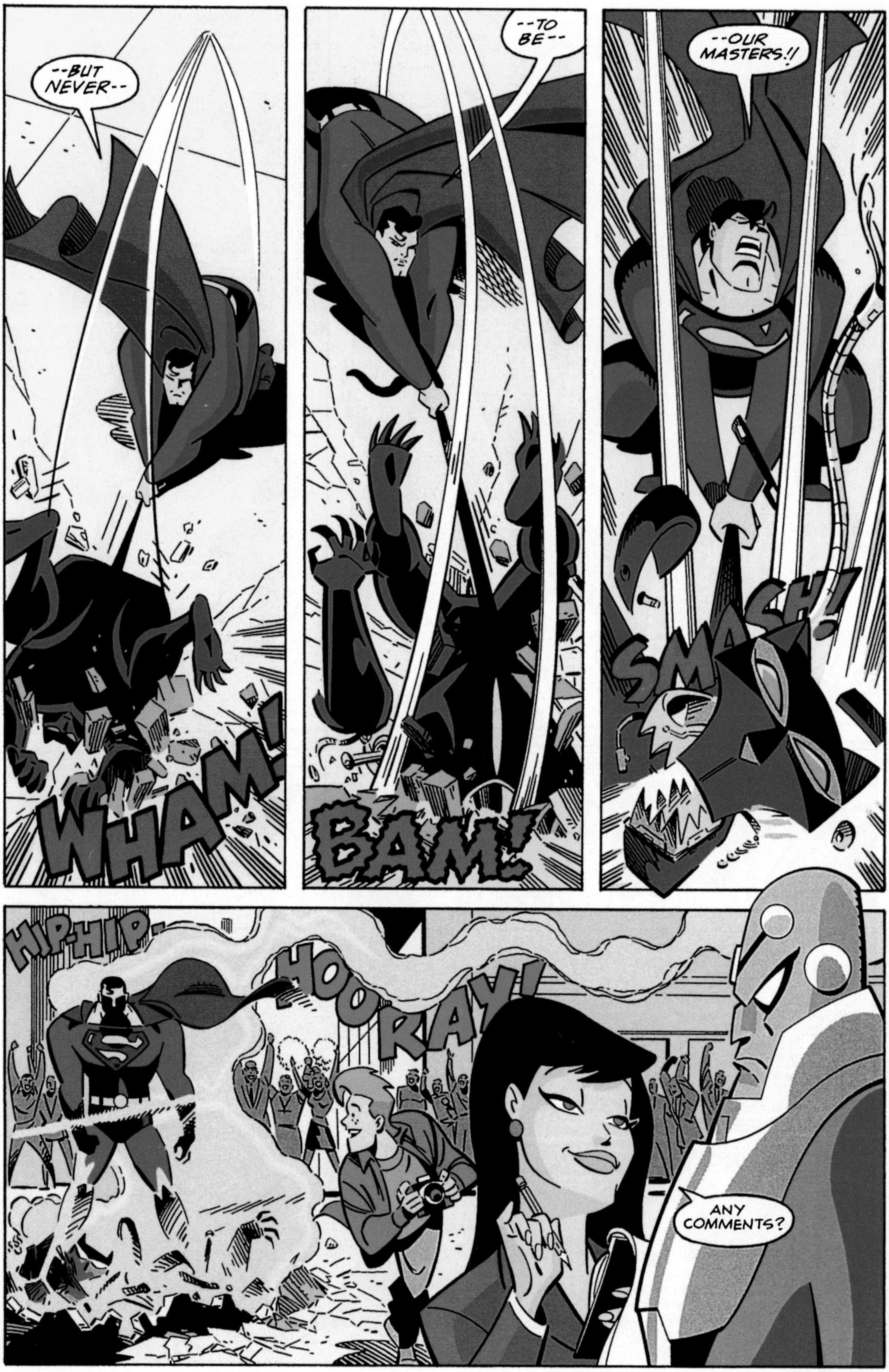
--BUT NEVER--
WHAM!
--TO BE--
BAM!
--OUR MASTERS!!
SMASH!
HIP-HIP-
HOORAY!
ANY COMMENTS?

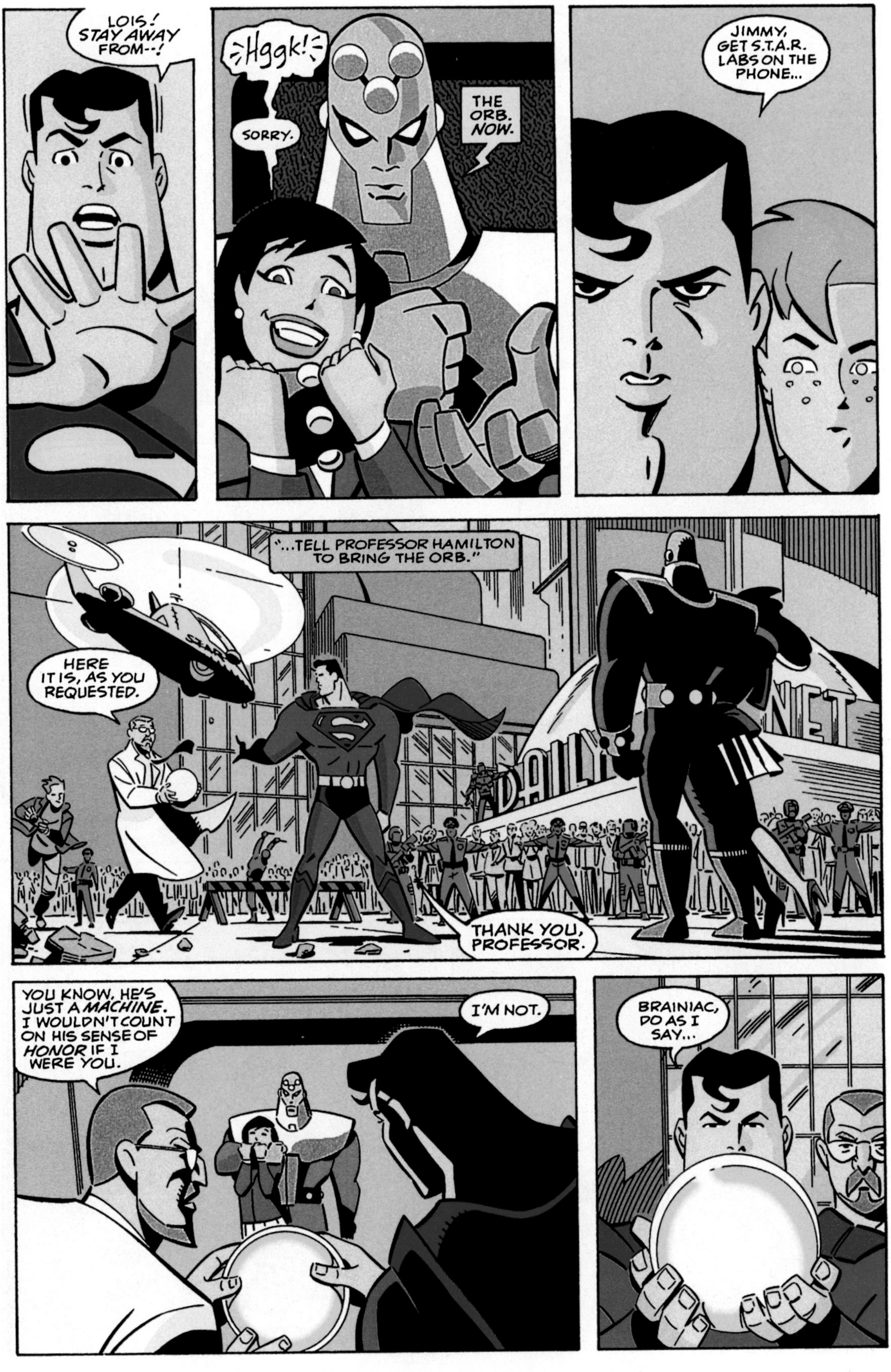
LOIS! STAY AWAY FROM--!
Hggk!
SORRY.
THE ORB. NOW.
JIMMY, GET S.T.A.R. LABS ON THE PHONE...
"...TELL PROFESSOR HAMILTON TO BRING THE ORB."
HERE IT IS, AS YOU REQUESTED.
THANK YOU, PROFESSOR.
YOU KNOW, HE'S JUST A MACHINE. I WOULDN'T COUNT ON HIS SENSE OF HONOR IF I WERE YOU.
I'M NOT.
BRAINIAC, DO AS I SAY...

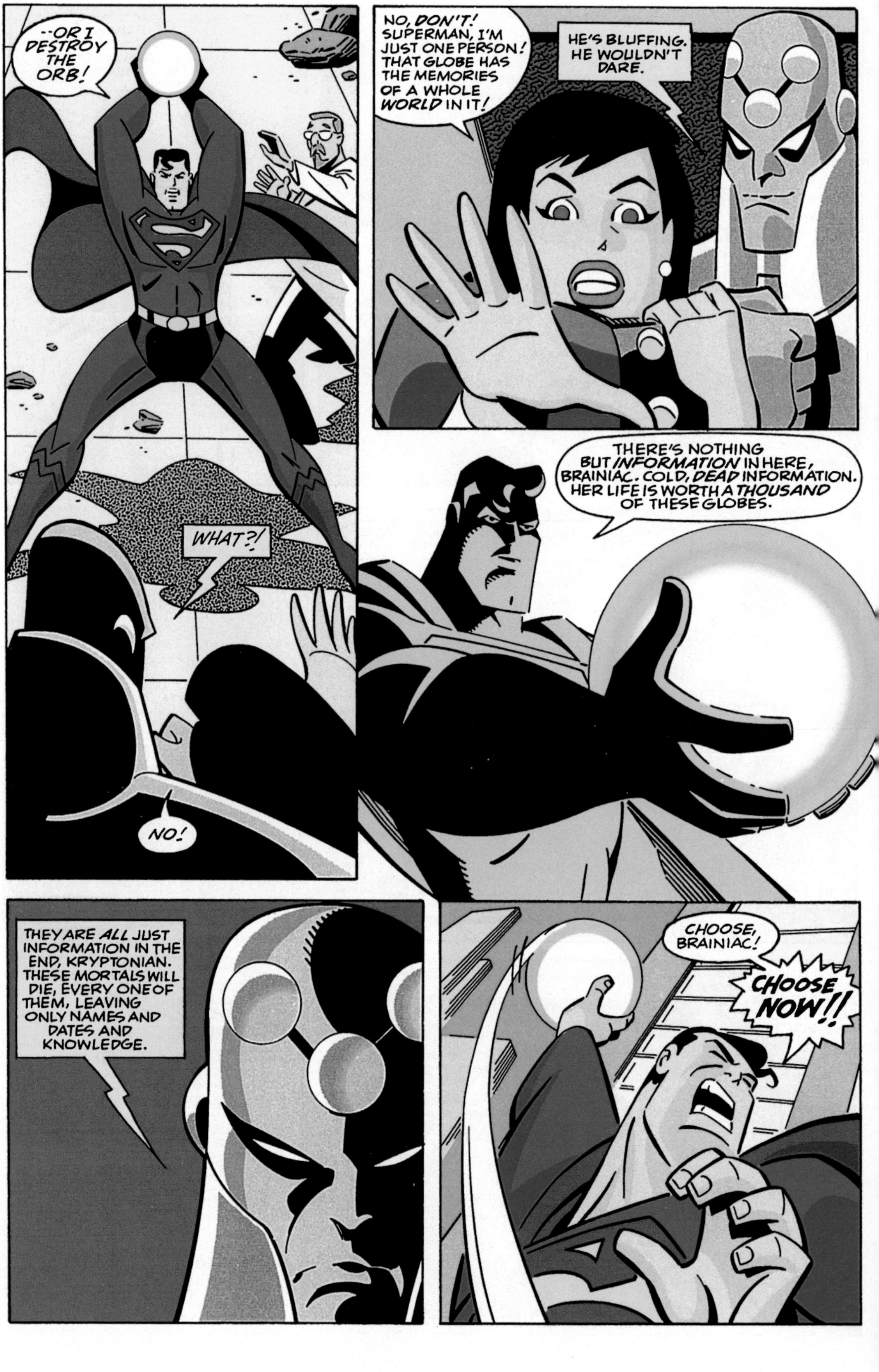
--OR I DESTROY THE ORB!
WHAT?!
NO!
NO, DON'T! SUPERMAN, I'M JUST ONE PERSON! THAT GLOBE HAS THE MEMORIES OF A WHOLE WORLD IN IT!
HE'S BLUFFING. HE WOULDN'T DARE.
THERE'S NOTHING BUT INFORMATION IN HERE, BRAINIAC. COLD, DEAD INFORMATION. HER LIFE IS WORTH A THOUSAND OF THESE GLOBES.
THEY ARE ALL JUST INFORMATION IN THE END, KRYPTONIAN. THESE MORTALS WILL DIE, EVERY ONE OF THEM, LEAVING ONLY NAMES AND DATES AND KNOWLEDGE.
CHOOSE, BRAINIAC!
CHOOSE NOW!!

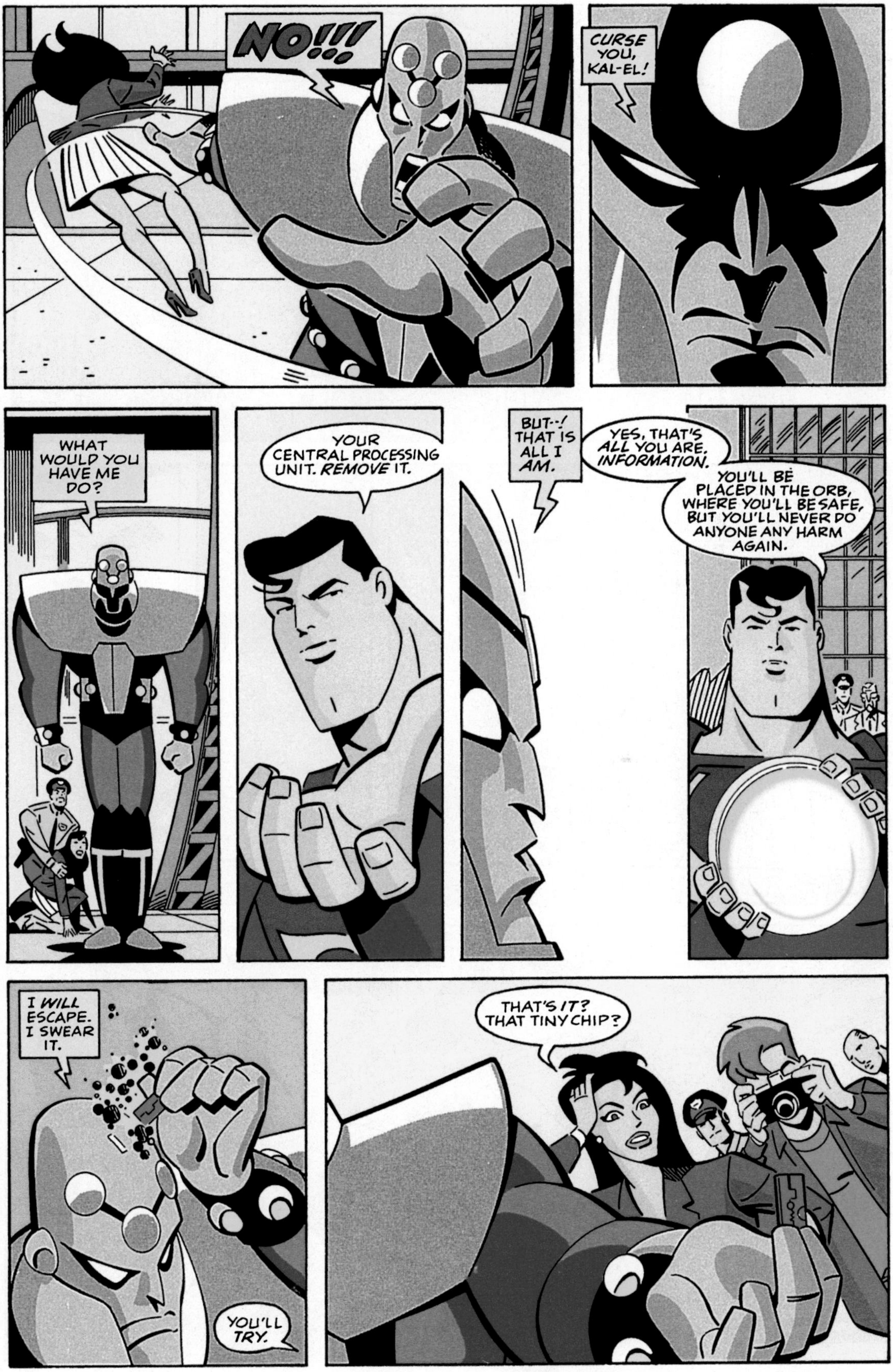
NO!!!!
CURSE YOU, KAL-EL!
WHAT WOULD YOU HAVE ME DO?
YOUR CENTRAL PROCESSING UNIT. REMOVE IT.
BUT--! THAT IS ALL I AM.
YES, THAT'S ALL YOU ARE. INFORMATION.
YOU'LL BE PLACED IN THE ORB, WHERE YOU'LL BE SAFE, BUT YOU'LL NEVER DO ANYONE ANY HARM AGAIN.
I WILL ESCAPE. I SWEAR IT.
YOU'LL TRY.
THAT'S IT? THAT TINY CHIP?

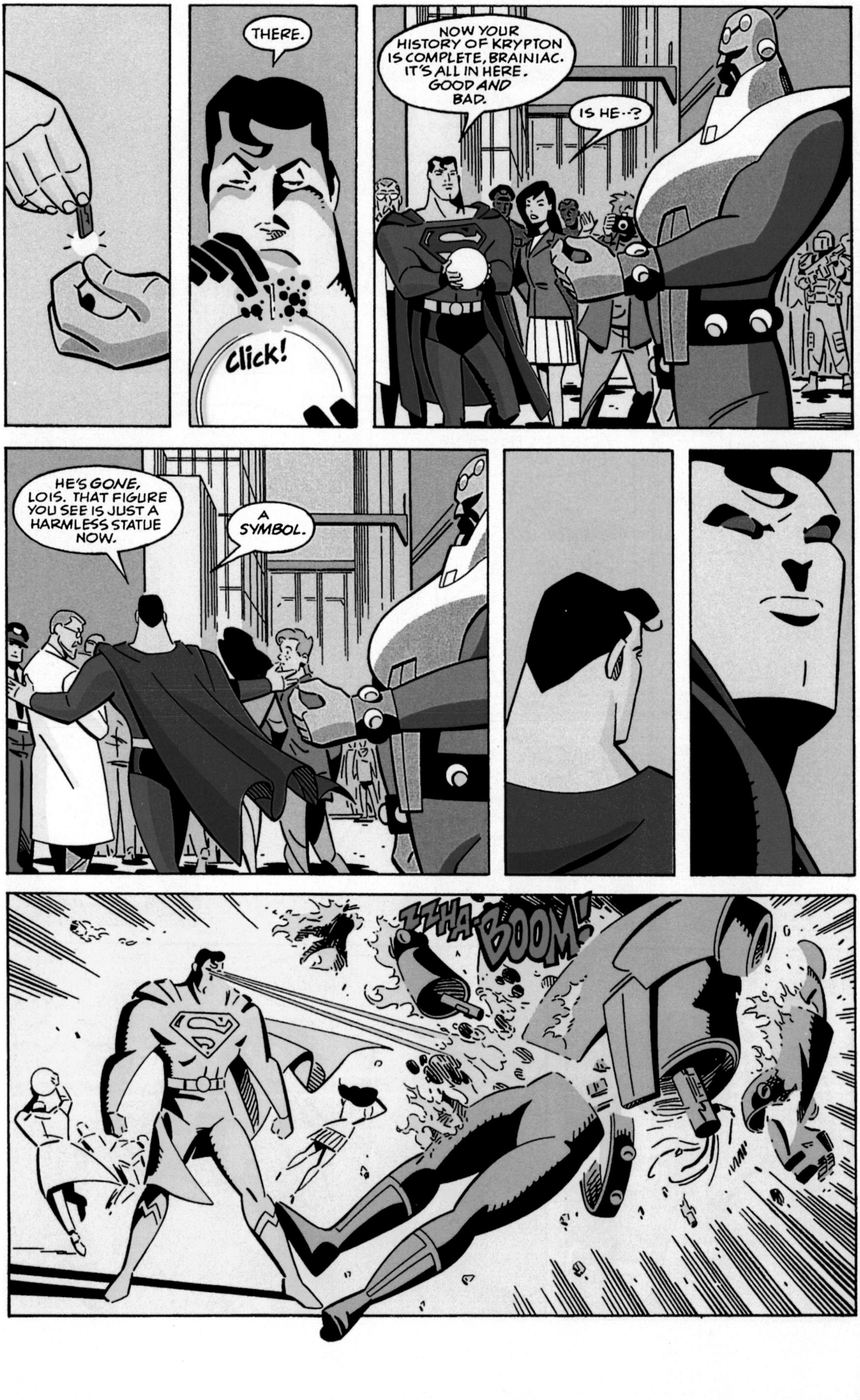
THERE.
Click!
NOW YOUR HISTORY OF KRYPTON IS COMPLETE, BRAINIAC. IT'S ALL IN HERE. GOOD AND BAD.
IS HE--?
HE'S GONE, LOIS. THAT FIGURE YOU SEE IS JUST A HARMLESS STATUE NOW.
A SYMBOL.
ZZHA-BOOM!

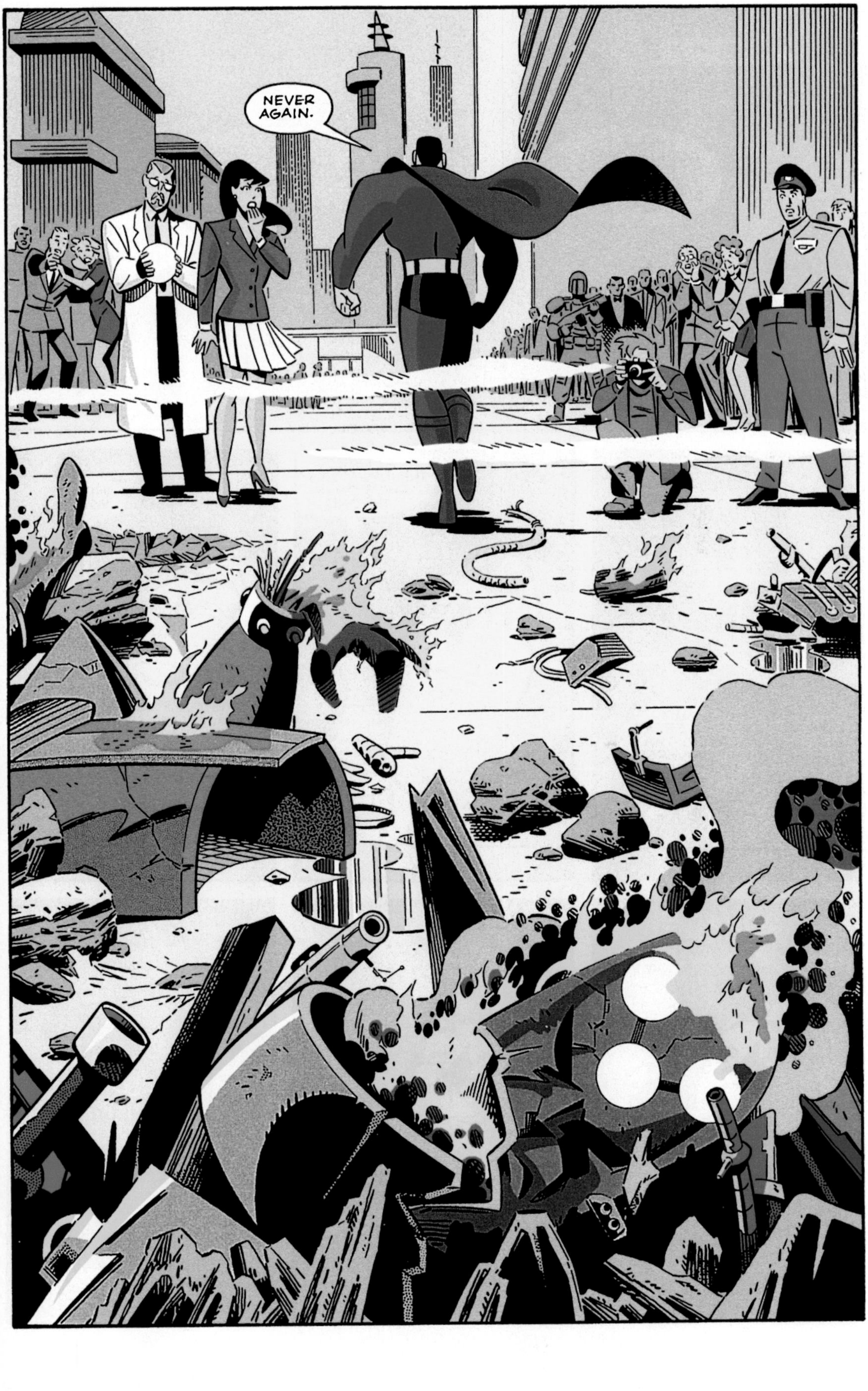
NEVER AGAIN.

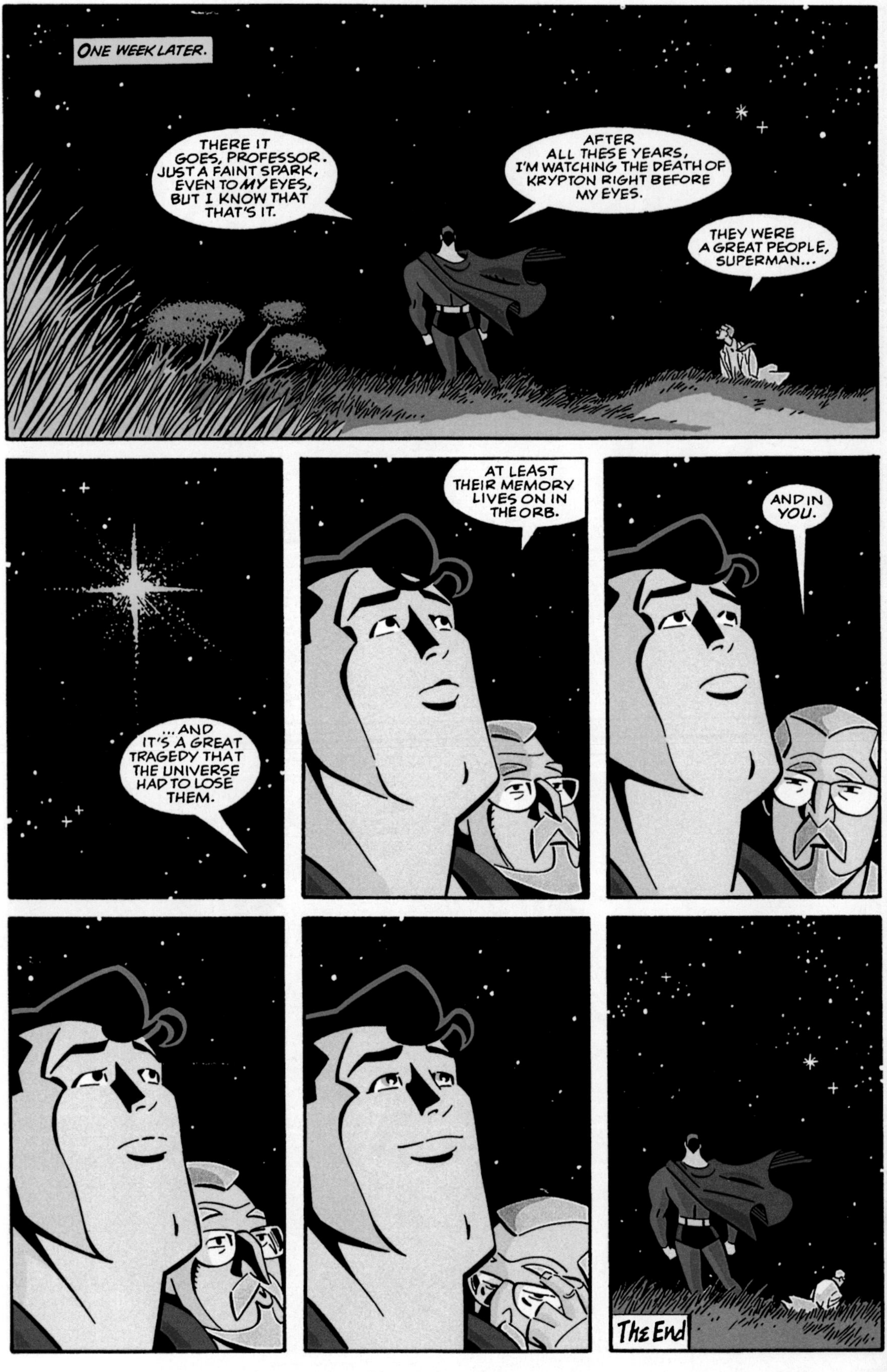
ONE WEEK LATER.
THERE IT GOES, PROFESSOR. JUST A FAINT SPARK, EVEN TO MY EYES, BUT I KNOW THAT THAT'S IT.
AFTER ALL THESE YEARS, I'M WATCHING THE DEATH OF KRYPTON RIGHT BEFORE MY EYES.
THEY WERE A GREAT PEOPLE, SUPERMAN...
...AND IT'S A GREAT TRAGEDY THAT THE UNIVERSE HAD TO LOSE THEM.
AT LEAST THEIR MEMORY LIVES ON IN THE ORB.
AND IN YOU.
THE END

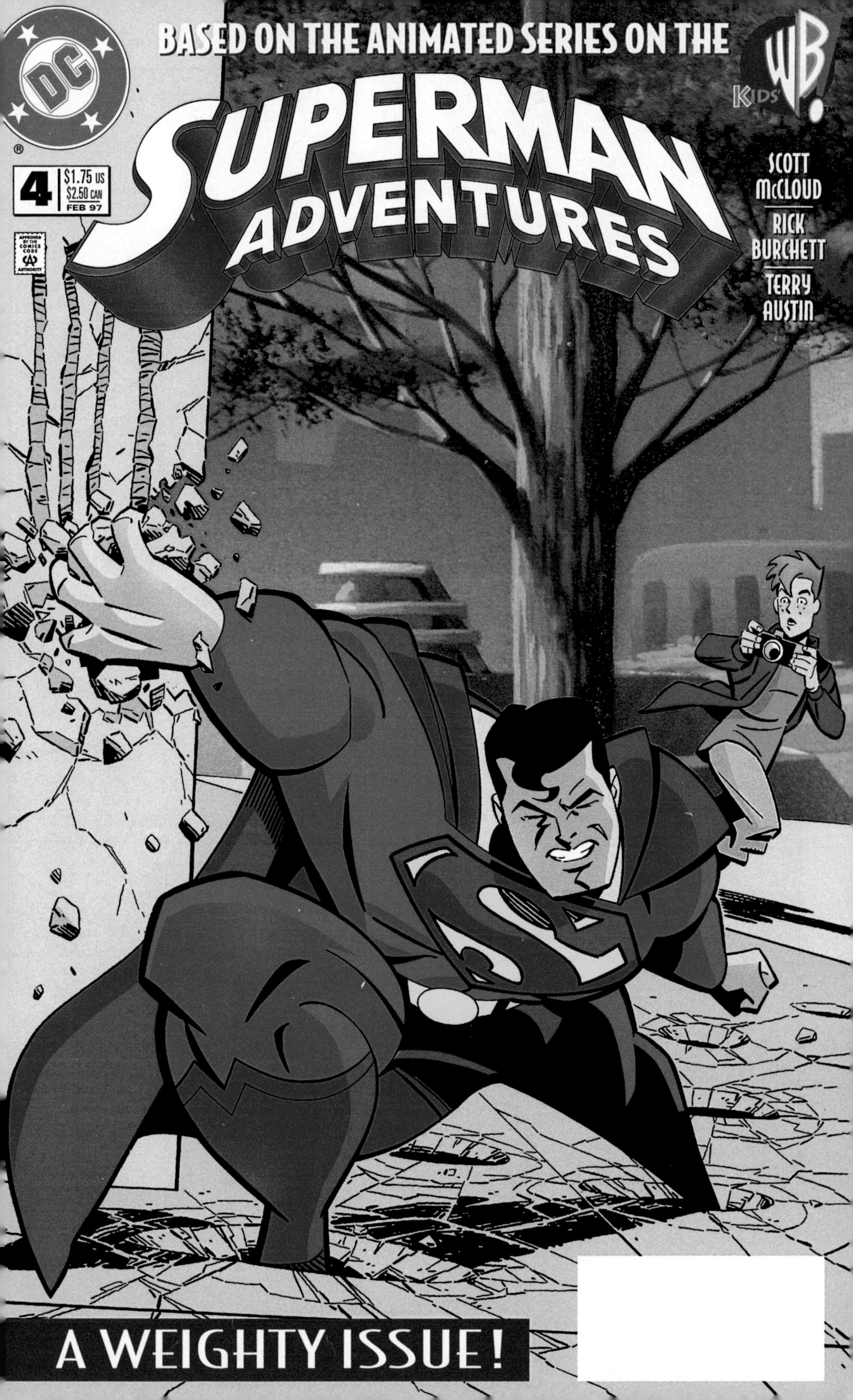
BASED ON THE ANIMATED SERIES ON THE
KIDS' WB!
SUPERMAN ADVENTURES
4
$1.75 US
$2.50 CAN
FEB 97
APPROVED BY THE COMICS CODE AUTHORITY
SCOTT McCLOUD
RICK BURCHETT
TERRY AUSTIN
A WEIGHTY ISSUE!

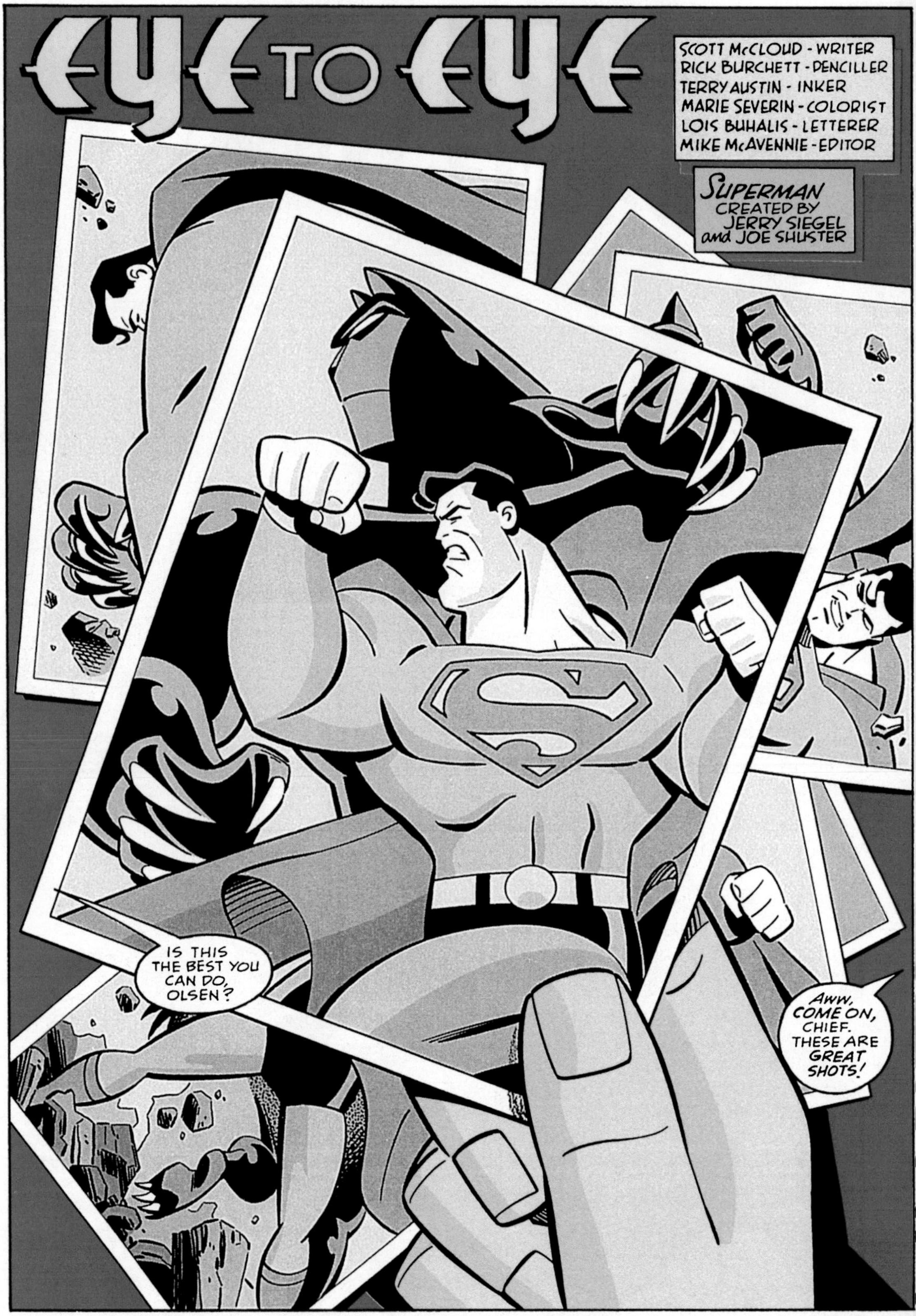
EYE TO EYE
SCOTT McCLOUD - WRITER
RICK BURCHETT - PENCILLER
TERRY AUSTIN - INKER
MARIE SEVERIN - COLORIST
LOIS BUHALIS - LETTERER
MIKE McAVENNIE - EDITOR
SUPERMAN CREATED BY JERRY SIEGEL and JOE SHUSTER
IS THIS THE BEST YOU CAN DO, OLSEN?
AWW, COME ON, CHIEF. THESE ARE GREAT SHOTS!

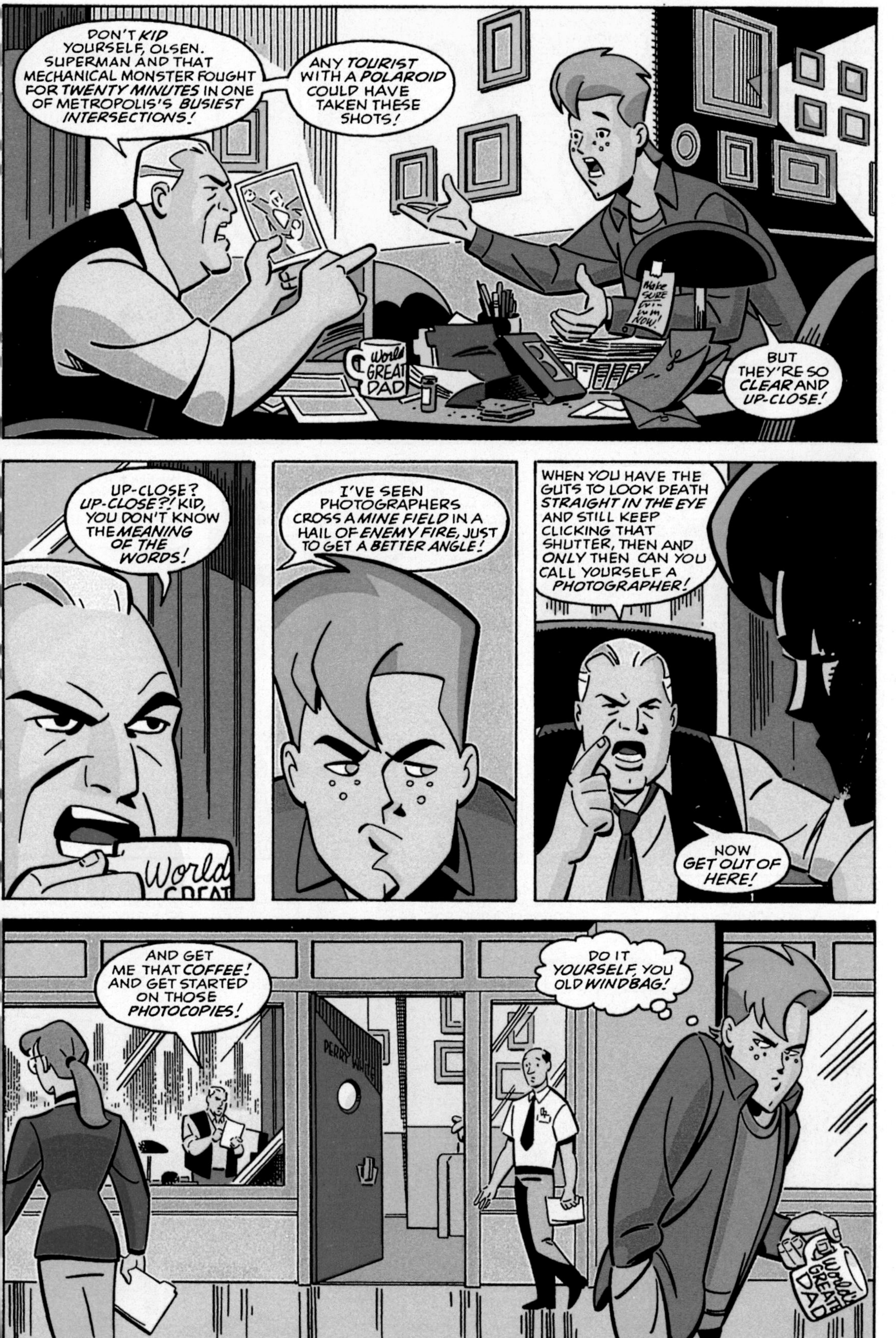
DON'T KID YOURSELF, OLSEN. SUPERMAN AND THAT MECHANICAL MONSTER FOUGHT FOR TWENTY MINUTES IN ONE OF METROPOLIS'S BUSIEST INTERSECTIONS!
ANY TOURIST WITH A POLAROID COULD HAVE TAKEN THESE SHOTS!
BUT THEY'RE SO CLEAR AND UP-CLOSE!
UP-CLOSE? UP-CLOSE?! KID, YOU DON'T KNOW THE MEANING OF THE WORDS!
I'VE SEEN PHOTOGRAPHERS CROSS A MINE FIELD IN A HAIL OF ENEMY FIRE, JUST TO GET A BETTER ANGLE!
WHEN YOU HAVE THE GUTS TO LOOK DEATH STRAIGHT IN THE EYE AND STILL KEEP CLICKING THAT SHUTTER, THEN AND ONLY THEN CAN YOU CALL YOURSELF A PHOTOGRAPHER!
NOW GET OUT OF HERE!
AND GET ME THAT COFFEE! AND GET STARTED ON THOSE PHOTOCOPIES!
DO IT YOURSELF, YOU OLD WINDBAG!

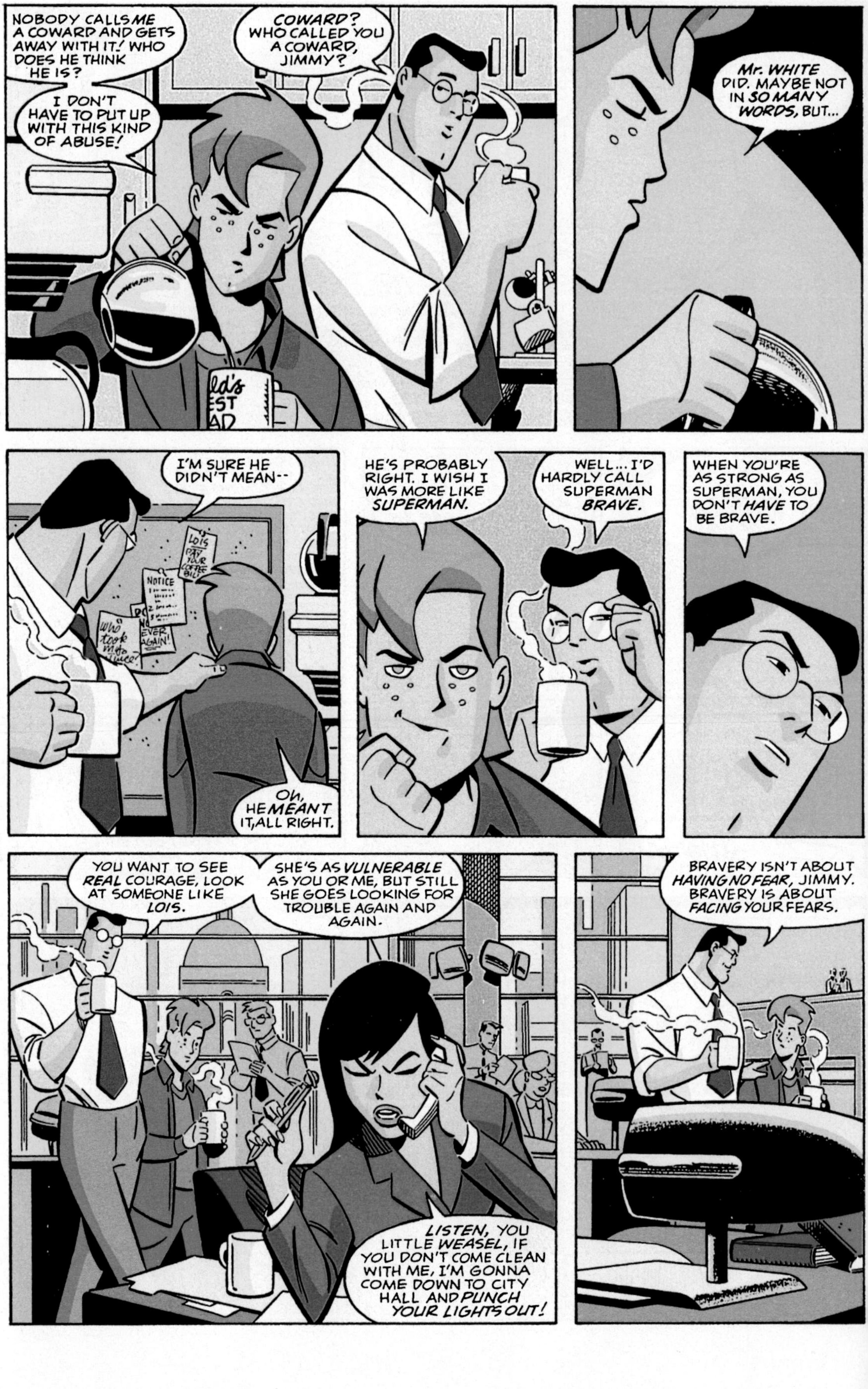
NOBODY CALLS ME A COWARD AND GETS AWAY WITH IT! WHO DOES HE THINK HE IS?
I DON'T HAVE TO PUT UP WITH THIS KIND OF ABUSE!
COWARD? WHO CALLED YOU A COWARD, JIMMY?
Mr. WHITE DID. MAYBE NOT IN SO MANY WORDS, BUT...
I'M SURE HE DIDN'T MEAN--
Oh, HE MEANT IT, ALL RIGHT.
HE'S PROBABLY RIGHT. I WISH I WAS MORE LIKE SUPERMAN.
WELL... I'D HARDLY CALL SUPERMAN BRAVE.
WHEN YOU'RE AS STRONG AS SUPERMAN, YOU DON'T HAVE TO BE BRAVE.
YOU WANT TO SEE REAL COURAGE, LOOK AT SOMEONE LIKE LOIS.
SHE'S AS VULNERABLE AS YOU OR ME, BUT STILL SHE GOES LOOKING FOR TROUBLE AGAIN AND AGAIN.
LISTEN, YOU LITTLE WEASEL, IF YOU DON'T COME CLEAN WITH ME, I'M GONNA COME DOWN TO CITY HALL AND PUNCH YOUR LIGHTS OUT!
BRAVERY ISN'T ABOUT HAVING NO FEAR, JIMMY. BRAVERY IS ABOUT FACING YOUR FEARS.

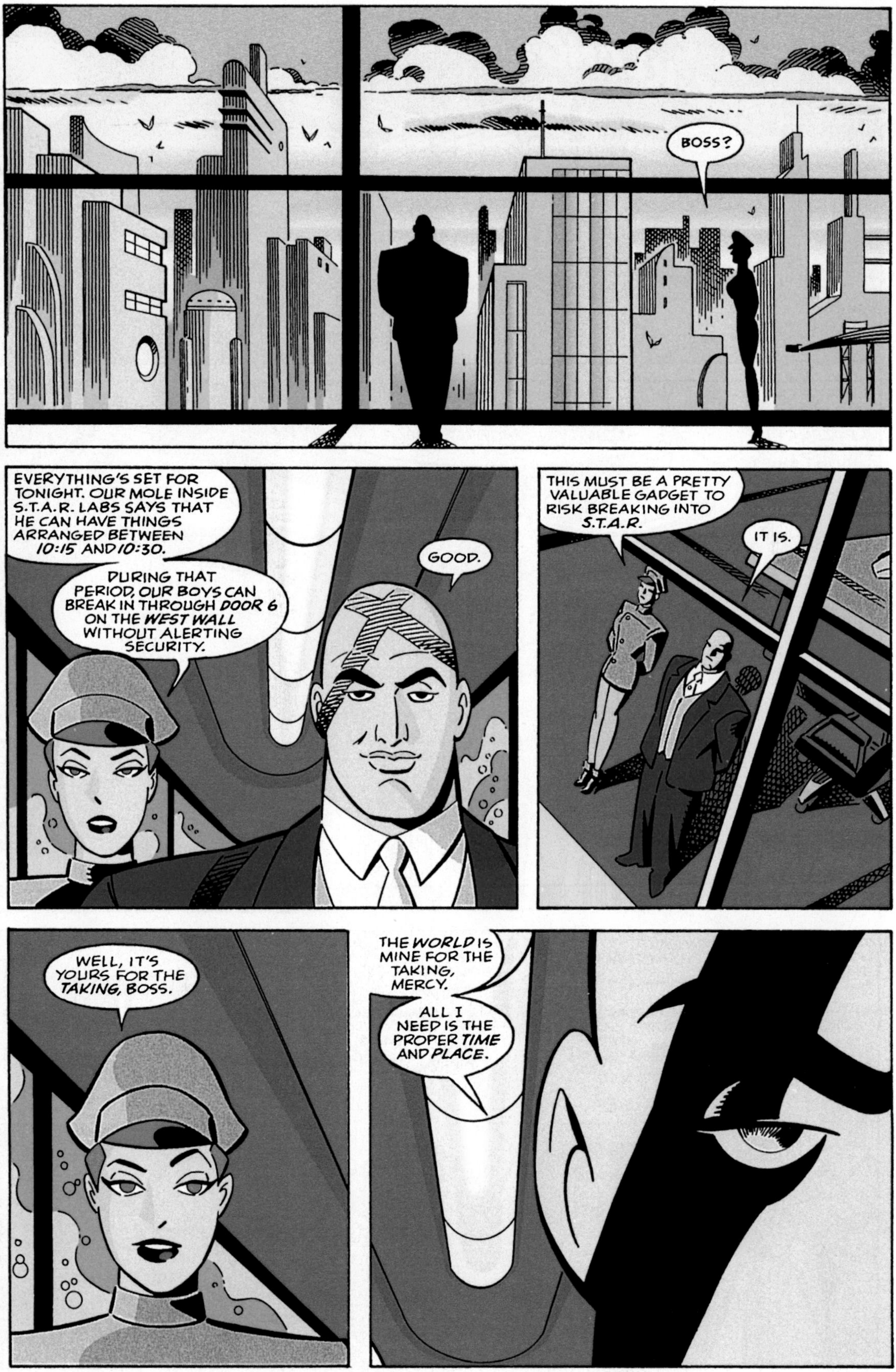
BOSS?
EVERYTHING'S SET FOR TONIGHT. OUR MOLE INSIDE S.T.A.R. LABS SAYS THAT HE CAN HAVE THINGS ARRANGED BETWEEN 10:15 AND 10:30.
DURING THAT PERIOD, OUR BOYS CAN BREAK IN THROUGH DOOR 6 ON THE WEST WALL WITHOUT ALERTING SECURITY.
GOOD.
THIS MUST BE A PRETTY VALUABLE GADGET TO RISK BREAKING INTO S.T.A.R.
IT IS.
WELL, IT'S YOURS FOR THE TAKING, BOSS.
THE WORLD IS MINE FOR THE TAKING, MERCY.
ALL I NEED IS THE PROPER TIME AND PLACE.

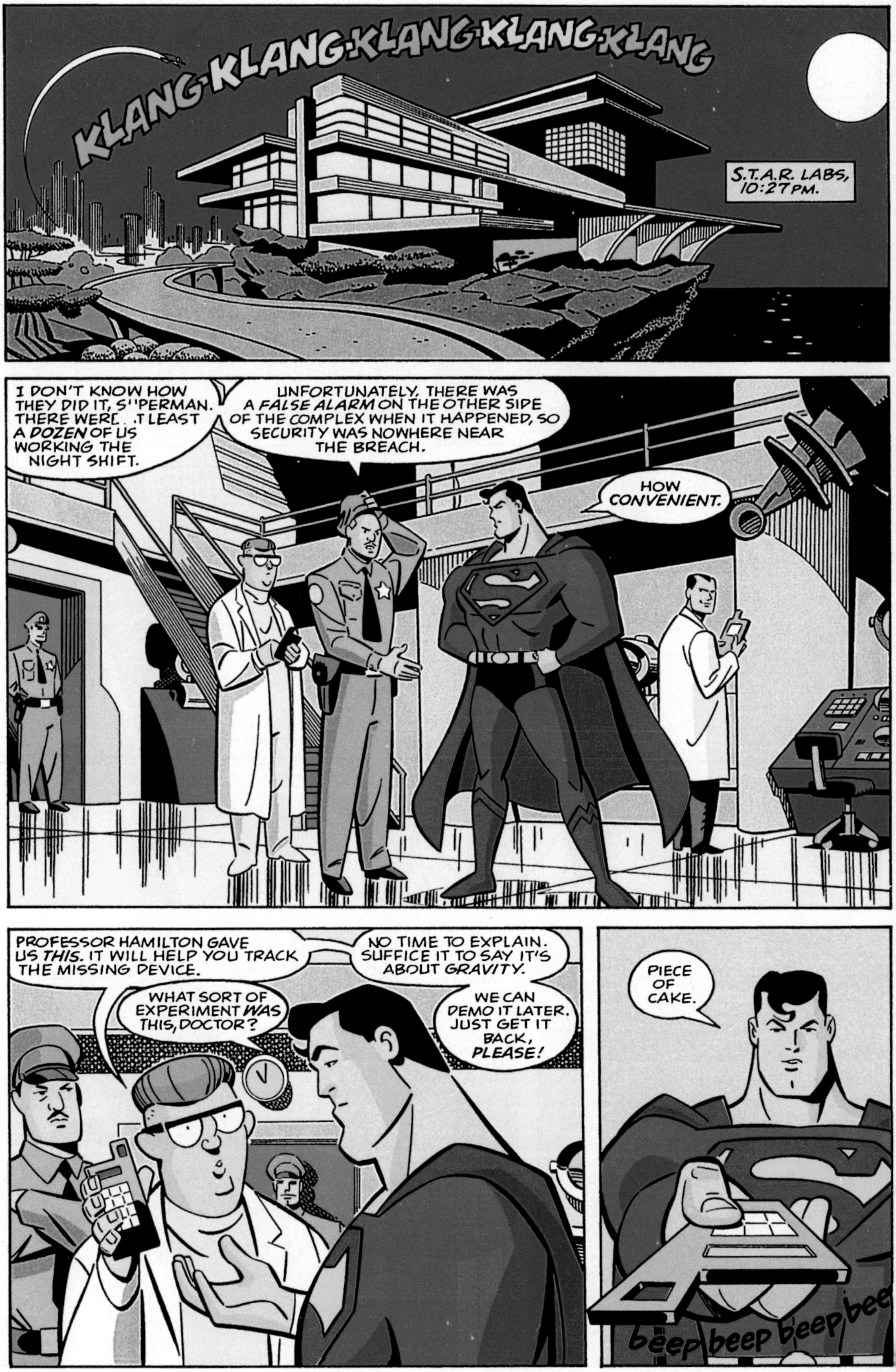

KLANG-KLANG-KLANG-KLANG-KLANG
S.T.A.R. LABS, 10:27 PM.
I DON'T KNOW HOW THEY DID IT, SUPERMAN. THERE WERE AT LEAST A *DOZEN* OF US WORKING THE NIGHT SHIFT.
UNFORTUNATELY, THERE WAS A *FALSE ALARM* ON THE OTHER SIDE OF THE COMPLEX WHEN IT HAPPENED, SO SECURITY WAS NOWHERE NEAR THE BREACH.
HOW CONVENIENT.
PROFESSOR HAMILTON GAVE US *THIS*. IT WILL HELP YOU TRACK THE MISSING DEVICE.
WHAT SORT OF EXPERIMENT *WAS* THIS, DOCTOR?
NO TIME TO EXPLAIN. SUFFICE IT TO SAY IT'S ABOUT *GRAVITY*.
WE CAN DEMO IT LATER. JUST GET IT BACK, *PLEASE!*
PIECE OF CAKE.
beep beep beep bee

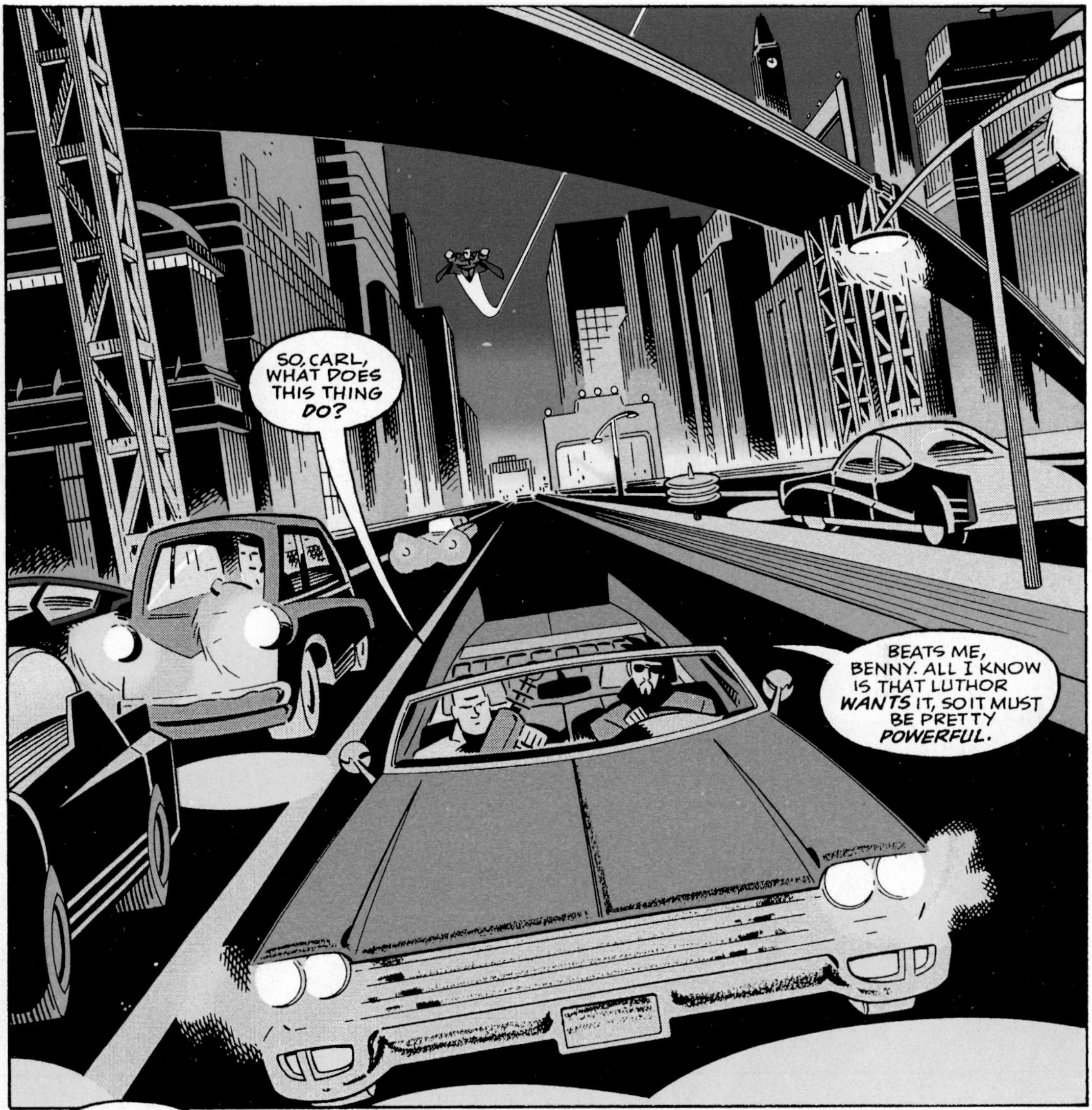
SO, CARL, WHAT DOES THIS THING DO?
BEATS ME, BENNY. ALL I KNOW IS THAT LUTHOR WANTS IT, SO IT MUST BE PRETTY POWERFUL.

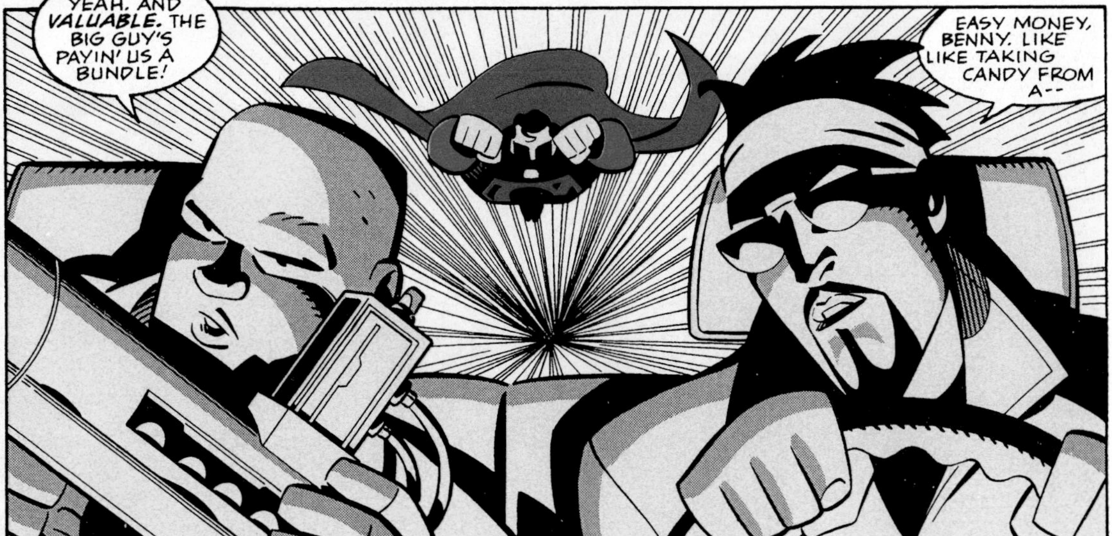
YEAH. AND VALUABLE. THE BIG GUY'S PAYIN' US A BUNDLE!
EASY MONEY, BENNY. LIKE LIKE TAKING CANDY FROM A--

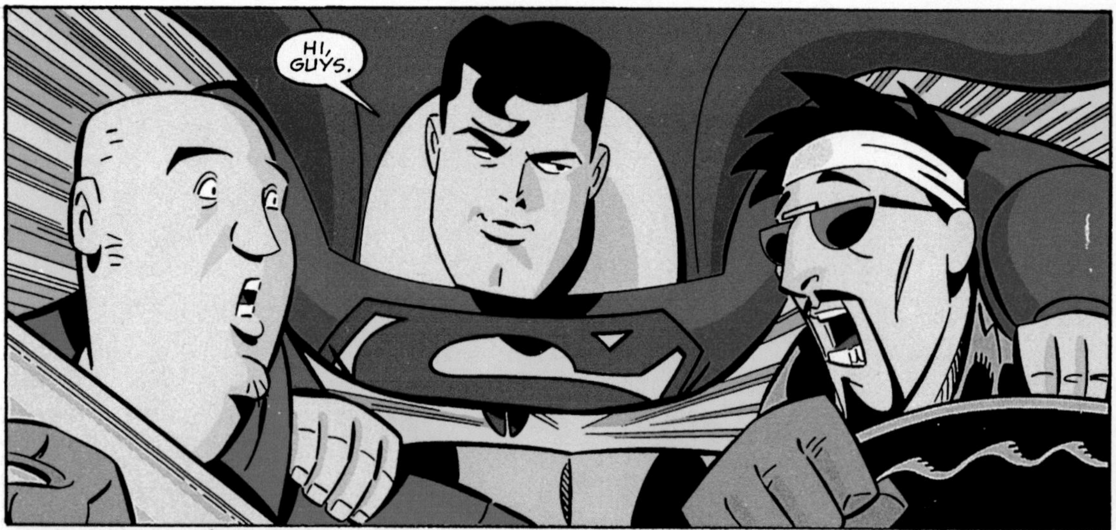
HI, GUYS.

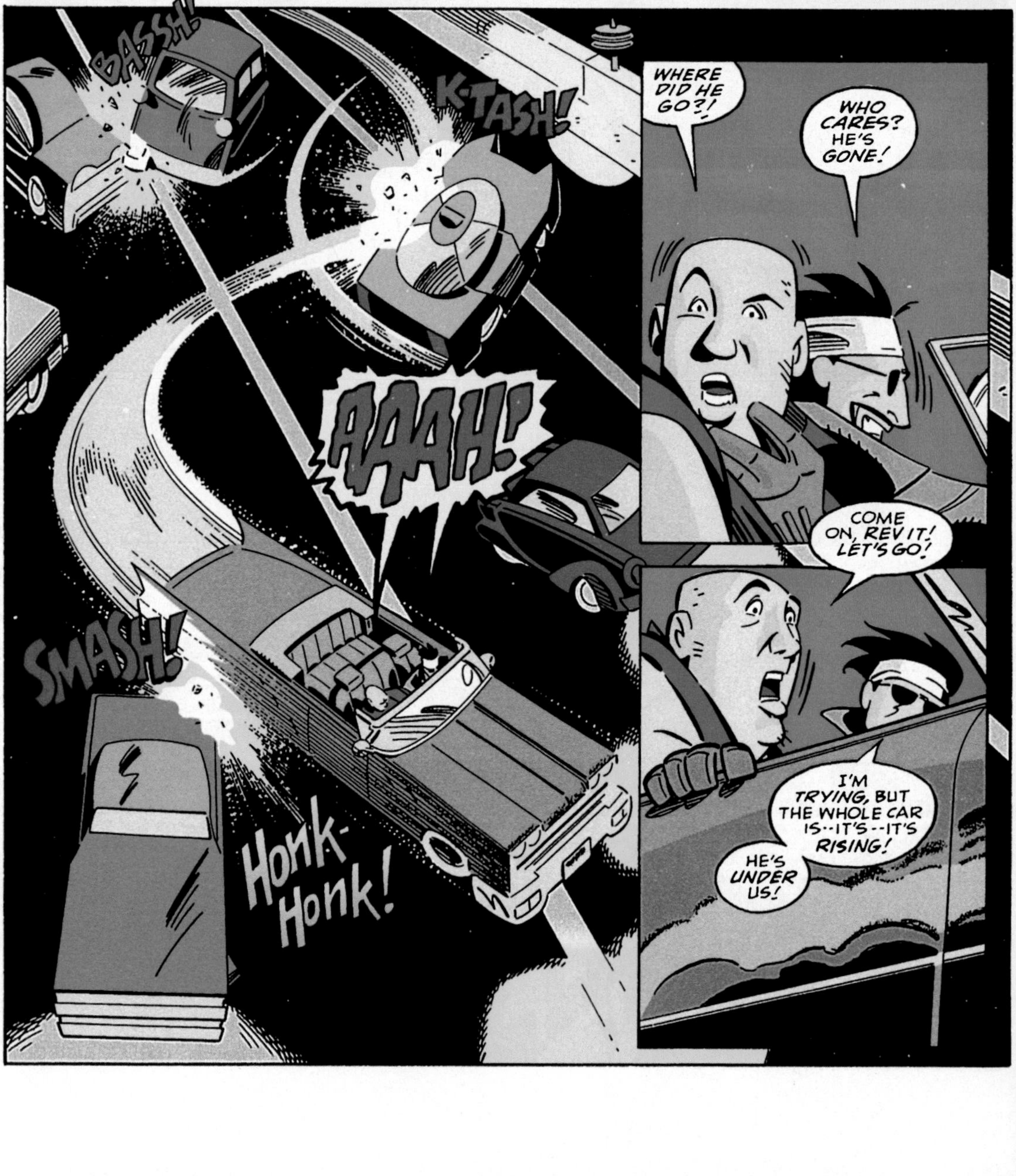
BASSH!
K-TASH!
AAAH!
SMASH!
HONK-HONK!
WHERE DID HE GO?!
WHO CARES? HE'S GONE!
COME ON, REV IT! LET'S GO!
I'M TRYING, BUT THE WHOLE CAR IS--IT'S--IT'S RISING!
HE'S UNDER US!

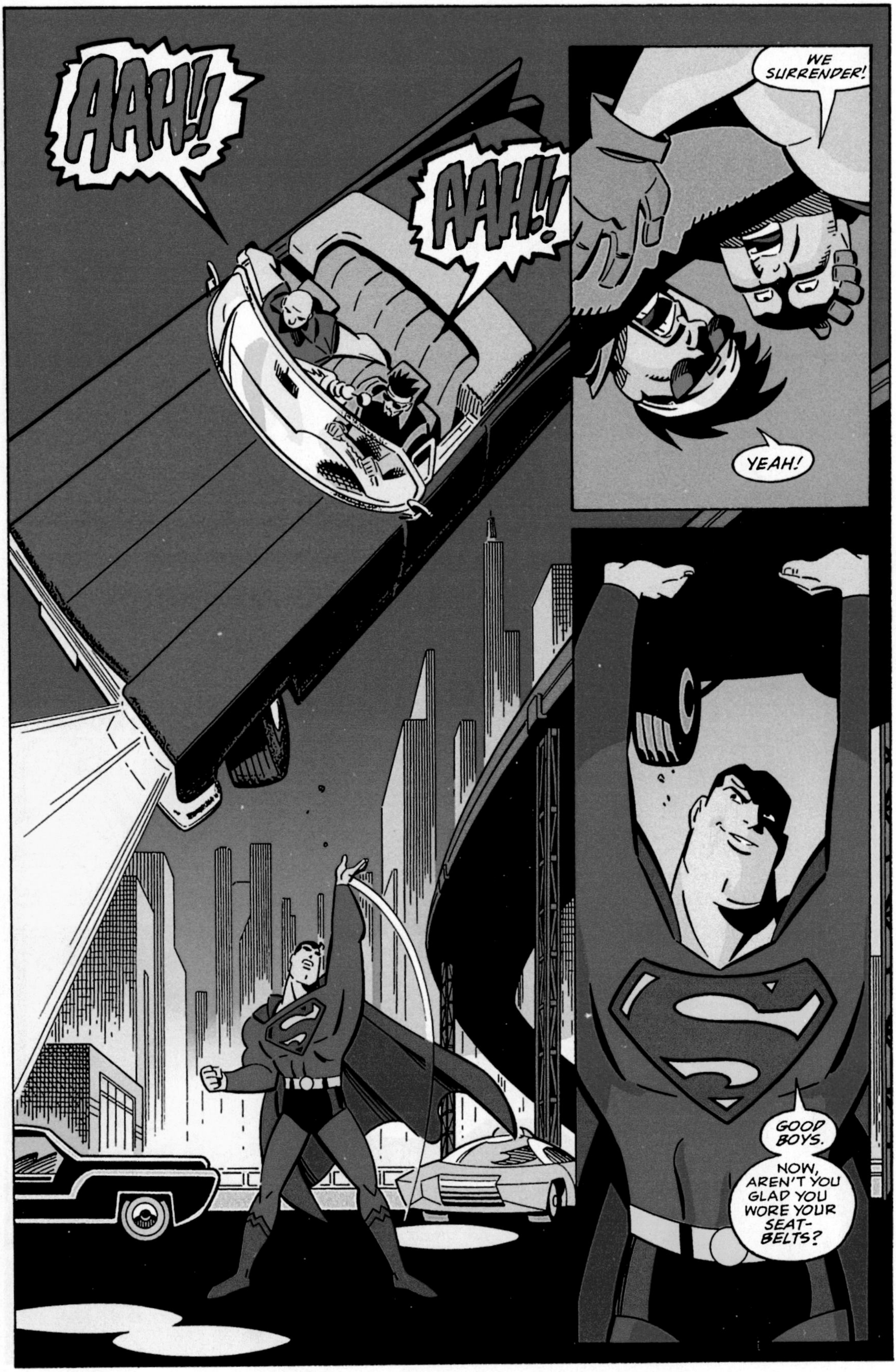
AAH!!
AAH!!
WE SURRENDER!
YEAH!
GOOD BOYS.
NOW, AREN'T YOU GLAD YOU WORE YOUR SEAT-BELTS?

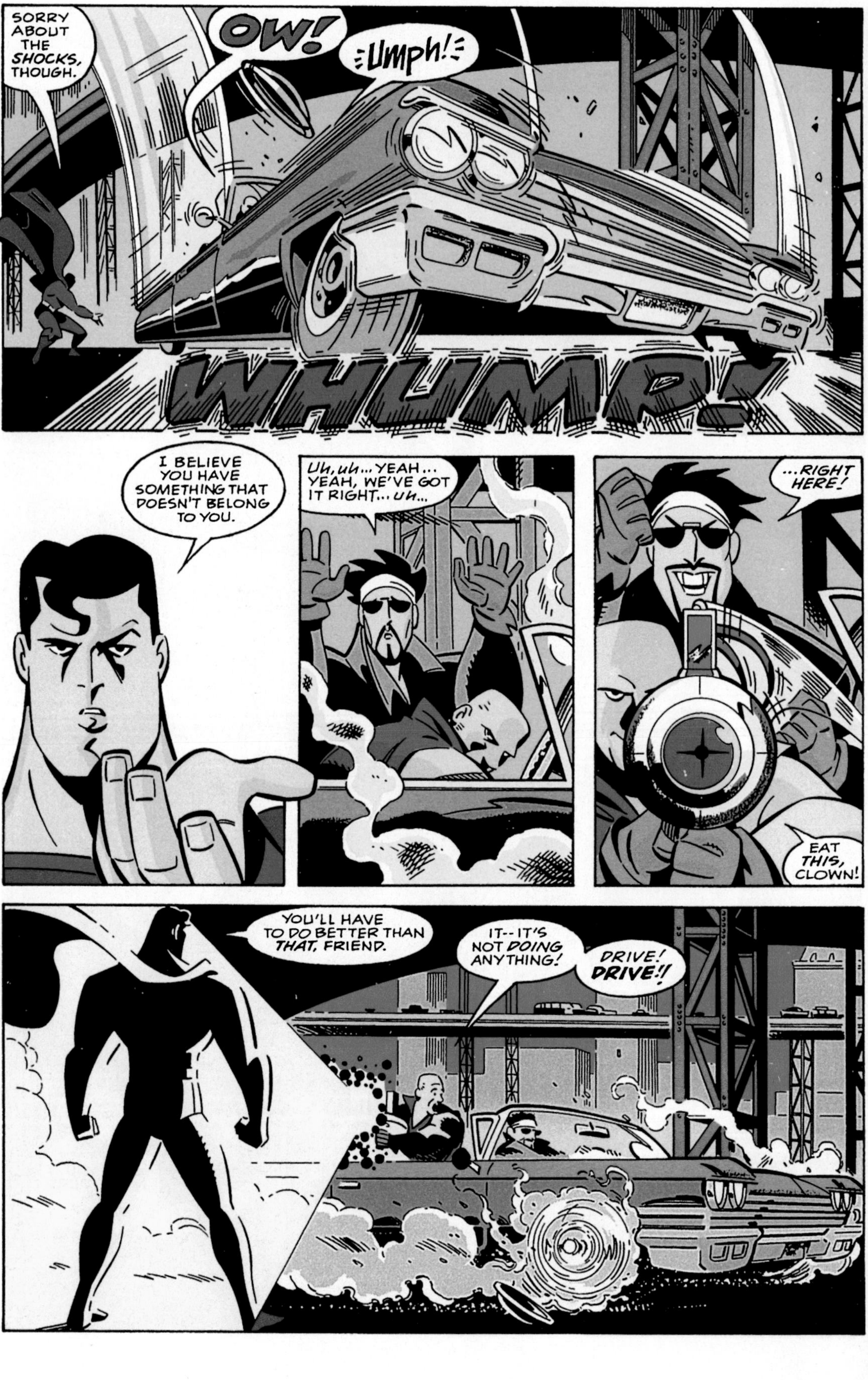
SORRY ABOUT THE SHOCKS, THOUGH.
OW!
Umph!
WHUMP!
I BELIEVE YOU HAVE SOMETHING THAT DOESN'T BELONG TO YOU.
Uh, uh... YEAH... YEAH, WE'VE GOT IT RIGHT... uh...
...RIGHT HERE!
EAT THIS, CLOWN!
YOU'LL HAVE TO DO BETTER THAN THAT, FRIEND.
IT-- IT'S NOT DOING ANYTHING!
DRIVE! DRIVE!!

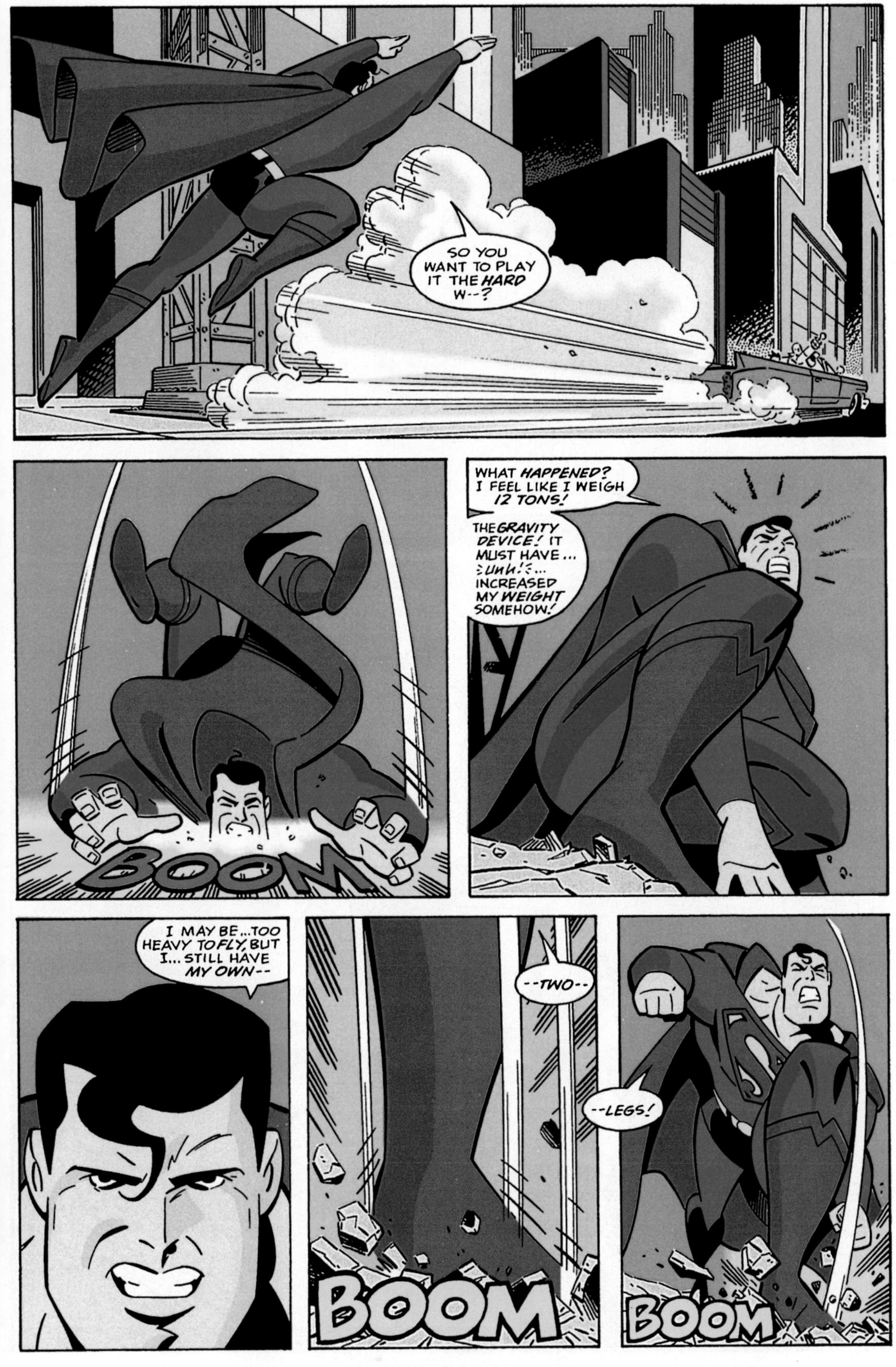
SO YOU WANT TO PLAY IT THE HARD W--?
BOOM
WHAT HAPPENED? I FEEL LIKE I WEIGH 12 TONS!
THE GRAVITY DEVICE! IT MUST HAVE... UNH!... INCREASED MY WEIGHT SOMEHOW!
I MAY BE...TOO HEAVY TO FLY, BUT I... STILL HAVE MY OWN--
--TWO--
BOOM
--LEGS!
BOOM

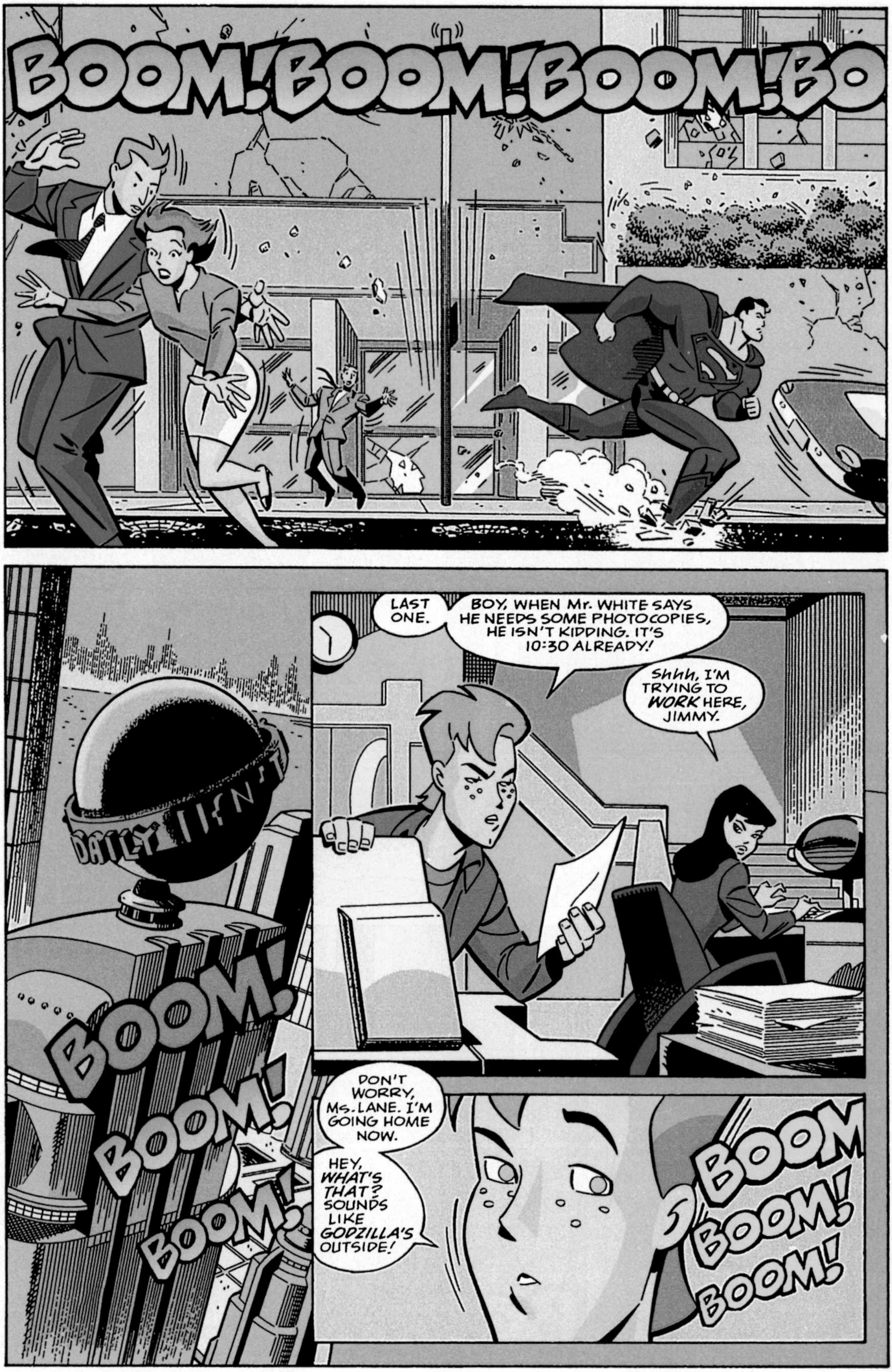
BOOM! BOOM! BOOM! BO
LAST ONE.
BOY, WHEN Mr. WHITE SAYS HE NEEDS SOME PHOTOCOPIES, HE ISN'T KIDDING. IT'S 10:30 ALREADY!
Shhh, I'M TRYING TO *WORK* HERE, JIMMY.
BOOM! BOOM! BOOM!
DON'T WORRY, Ms. LANE. I'M GOING HOME NOW.
HEY, *WHAT'S THAT?* SOUNDS LIKE *GODZILLA'S* OUTSIDE!
BOOM BOOM! BOOM!

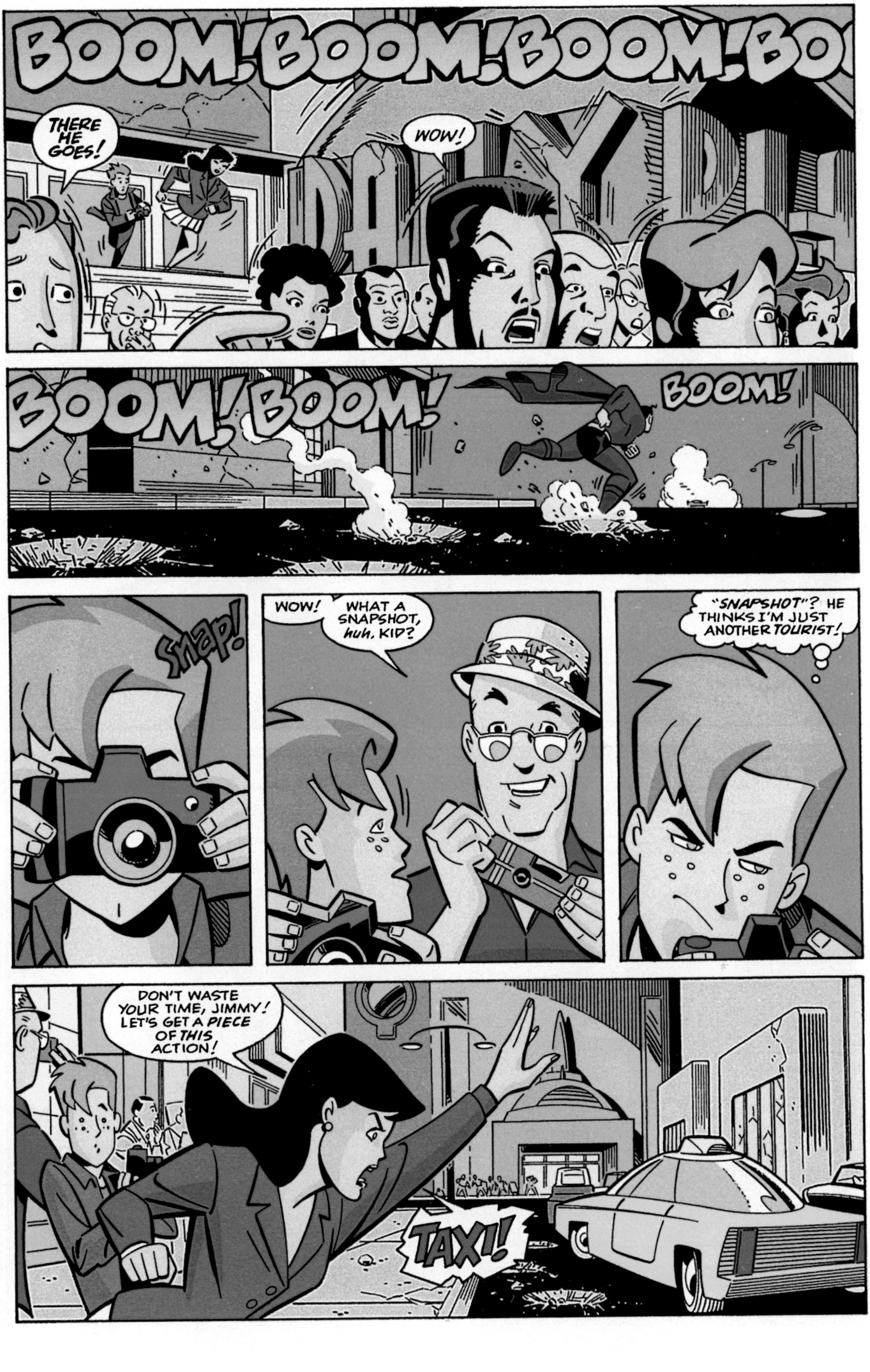
BOOM! BOOM! BOOM! BO
THERE HE GOES!
WOW!
BOOM! BOOM!
BOOM!
SNAP!
WOW!
WHAT A SNAPSHOT, HUH, KID?
"SNAPSHOT"? HE THINKS I'M JUST ANOTHER TOURIST!
DON'T WASTE YOUR TIME, JIMMY! LET'S GET A PIECE OF THIS ACTION!
TAXI!

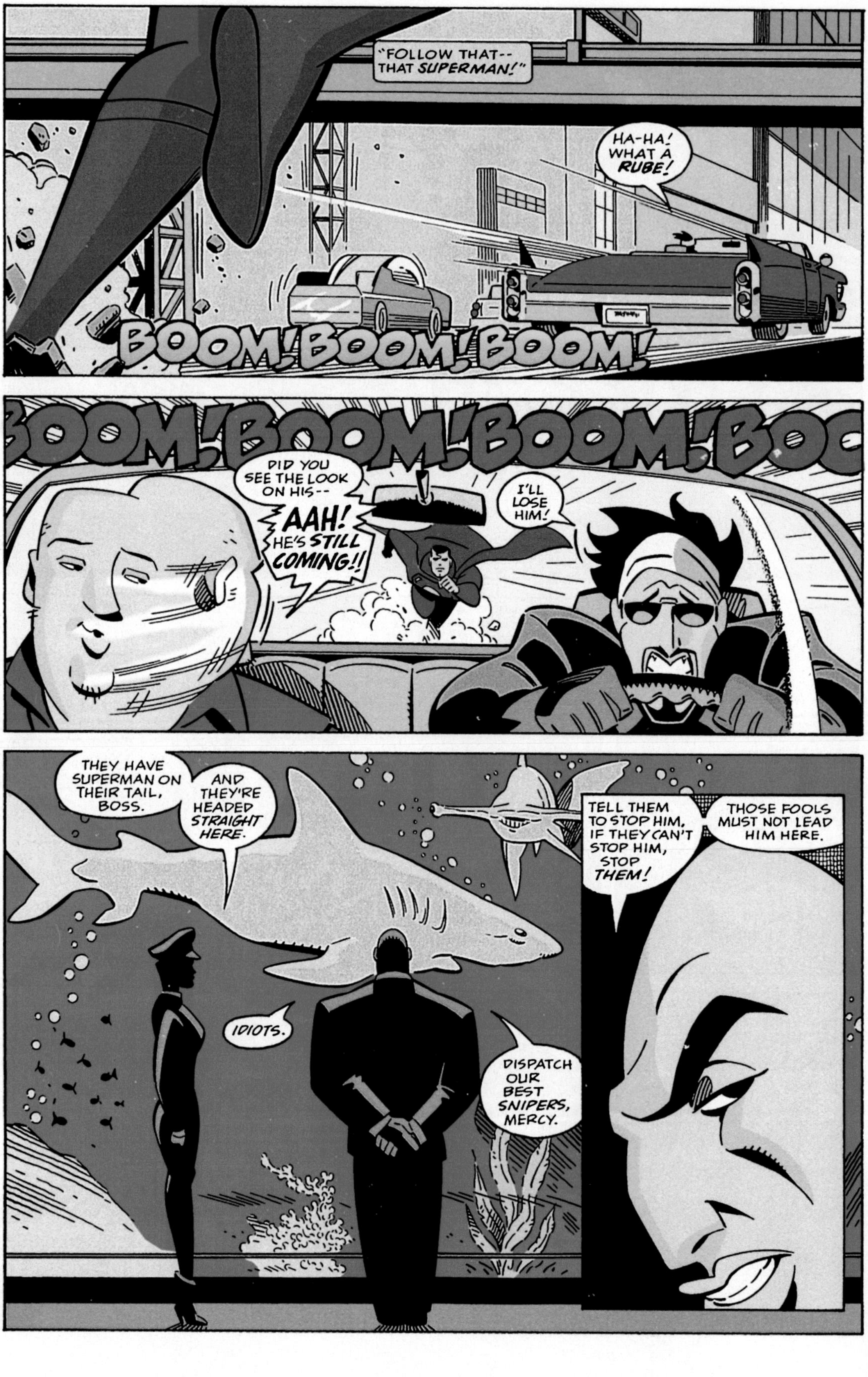
"FOLLOW THAT-- THAT SUPERMAN!"
HA-HA! WHAT A RUBE!
BOOM! BOOM! BOOM!
BOOM! BOOM! BOOM! BOO
DID YOU SEE THE LOOK ON HIS-- AAH! HE'S STILL COMING!!
I'LL LOSE HIM!
THEY HAVE SUPERMAN ON THEIR TAIL, BOSS.
AND THEY'RE HEADED STRAIGHT HERE.
IDIOTS.
DISPATCH OUR BEST SNIPERS, MERCY.
TELL THEM TO STOP HIM. IF THEY CAN'T STOP HIM, STOP THEM!
THOSE FOOLS MUST NOT LEAD HIM HERE.

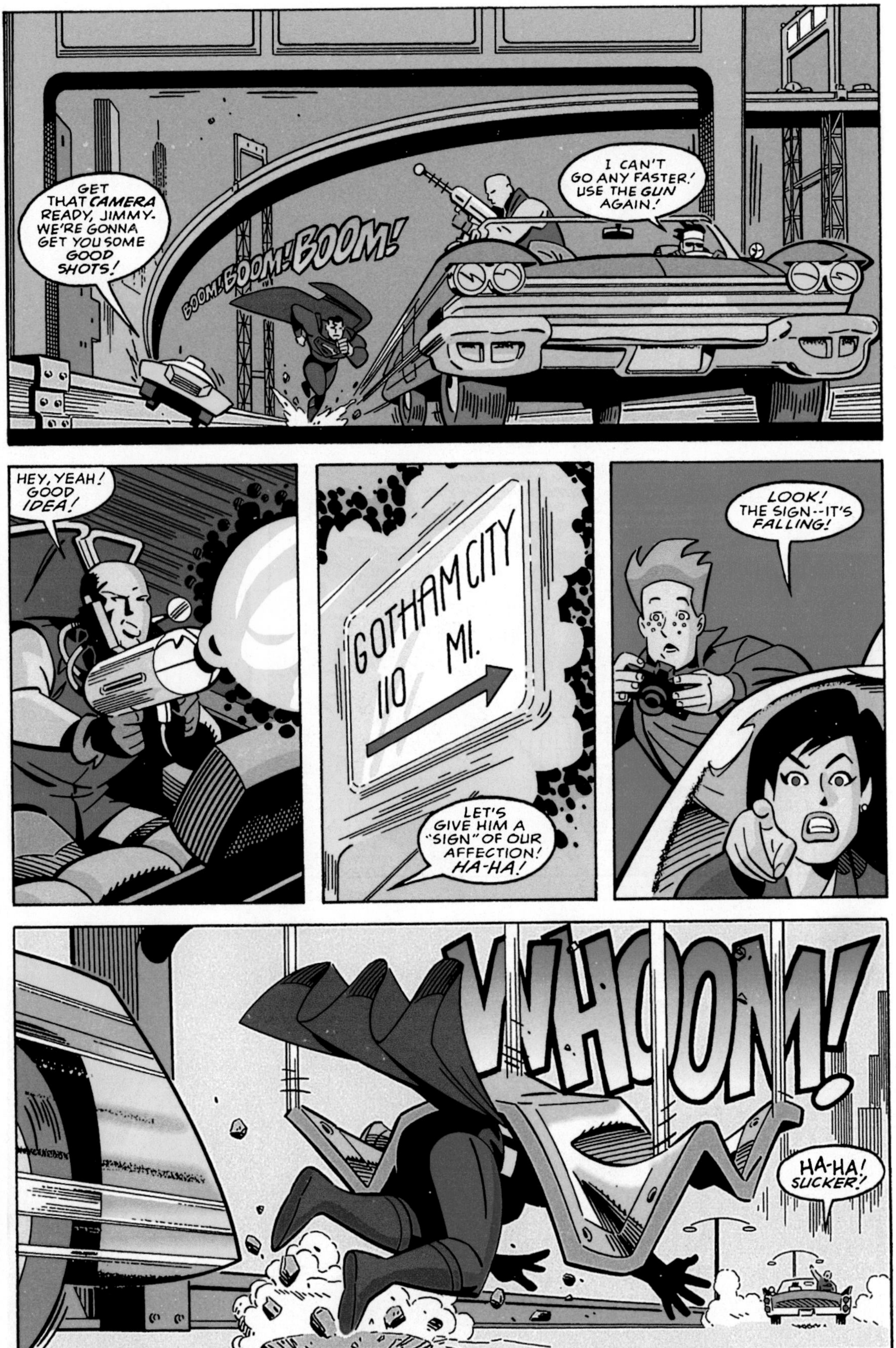
GET THAT CAMERA READY, JIMMY. WE'RE GONNA GET YOU SOME GOOD SHOTS!
I CAN'T GO ANY FASTER! USE THE GUN AGAIN!
BOOM! BOOM! BOOM!
HEY, YEAH! GOOD IDEA!
GOTHAM CITY 110 MI.
LET'S GIVE HIM A "SIGN" OF OUR AFFECTION! HA-HA!
LOOK! THE SIGN--IT'S FALLING!
WHOOM!
HA-HA! SUCKER!

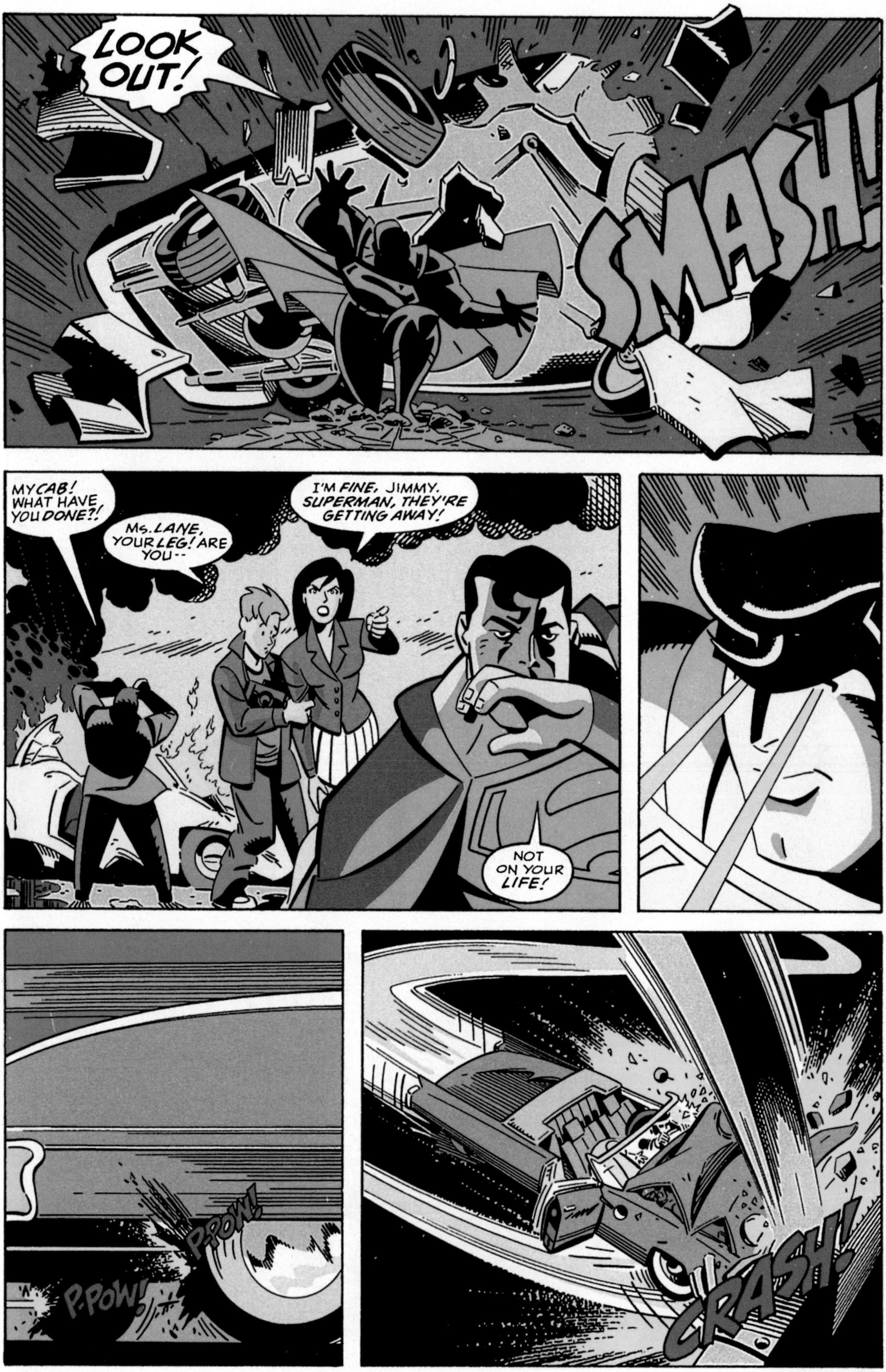
LOOK OUT!
SMASH!
MY CAB! WHAT HAVE YOU DONE?!
Ms. LANE, YOUR LEG! ARE YOU--
I'M FINE, JIMMY. SUPERMAN, THEY'RE GETTING AWAY!
NOT ON YOUR LIFE!
P-POW!
P-POW!
CRASH!

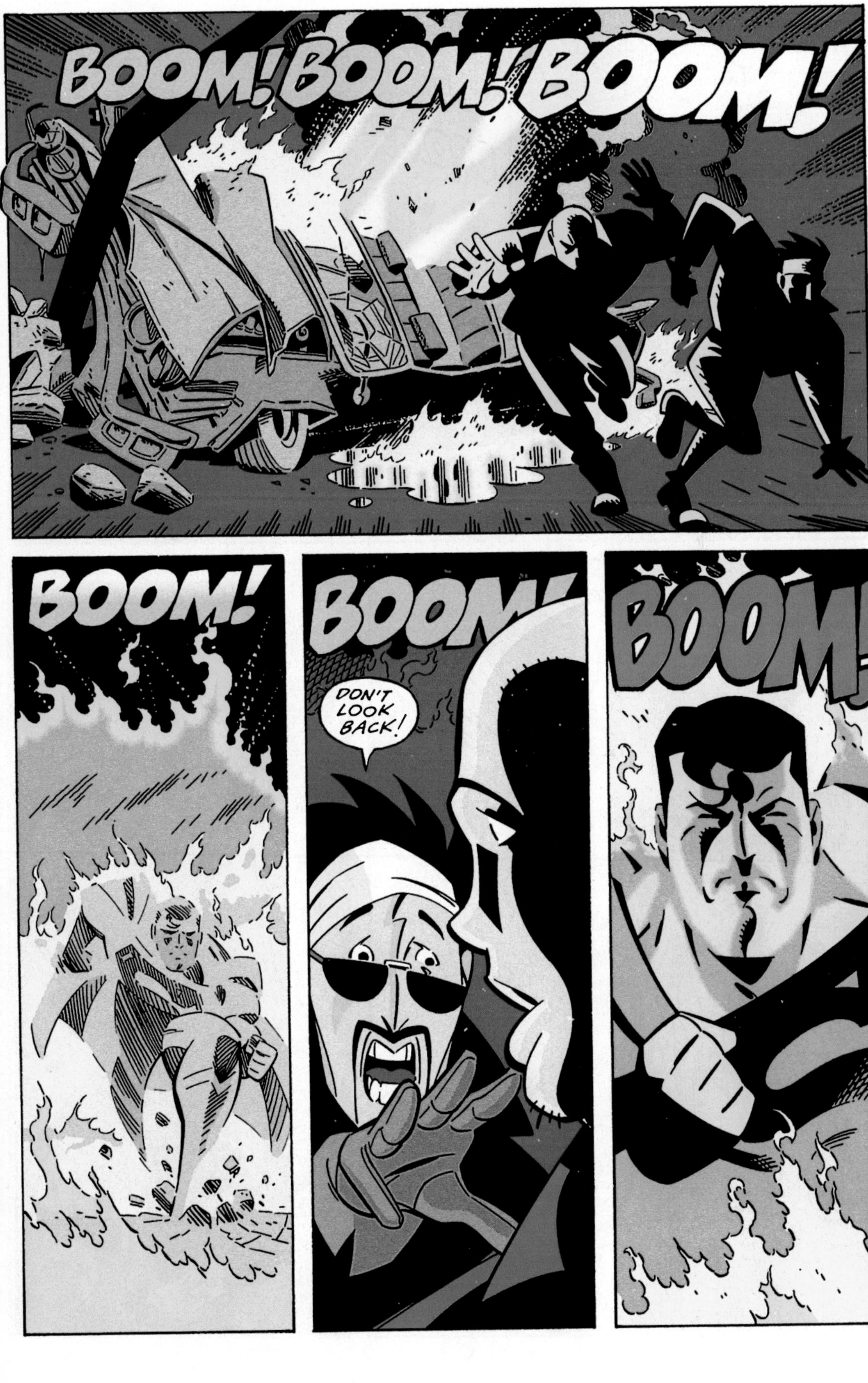
BOOM! BOOM! BOOM!
BOOM!
BOOM!
DON'T LOOK BACK!
BOOM!

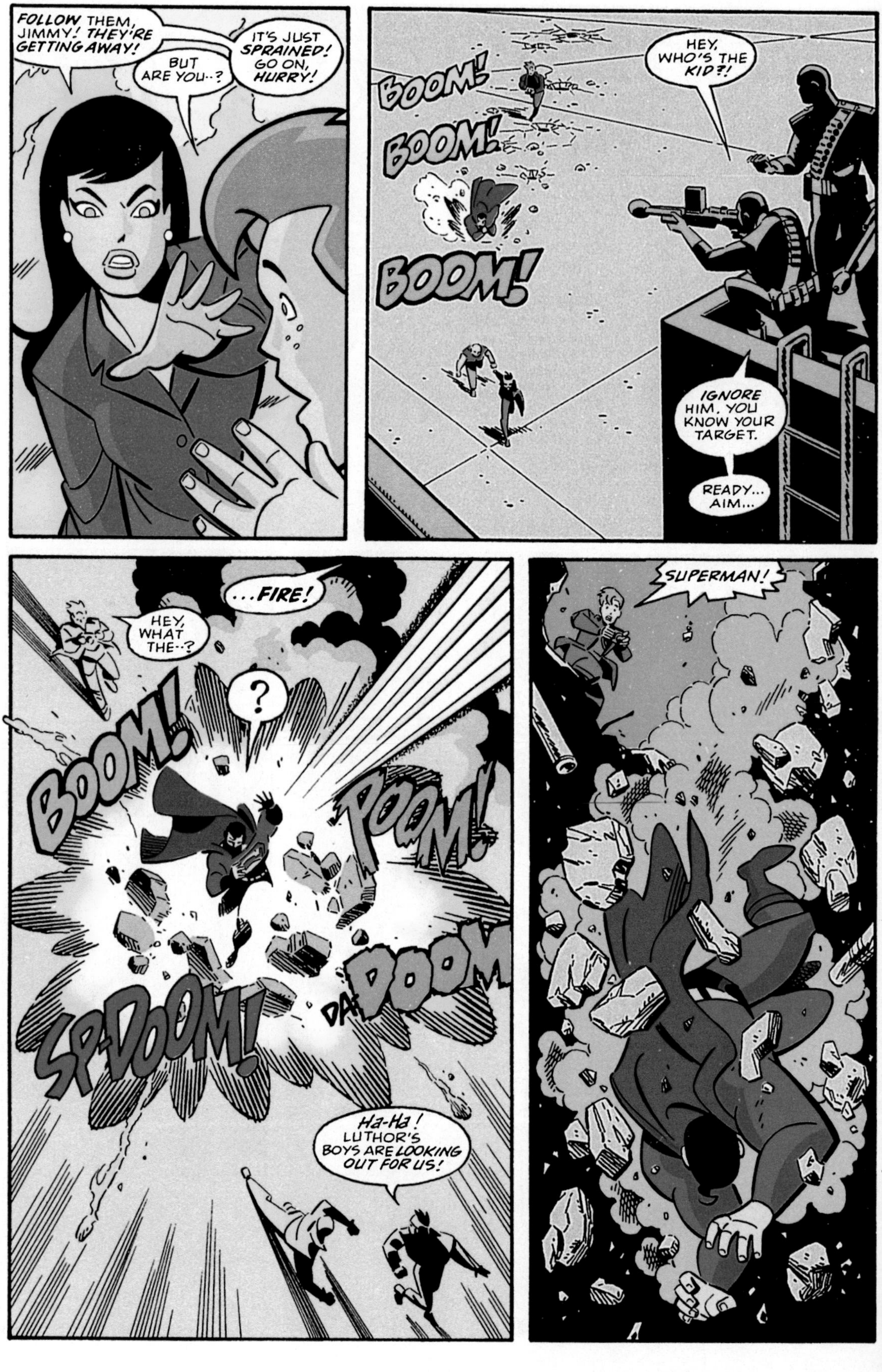

FOLLOW THEM, JIMMY! THEY'RE GETTING AWAY!
BUT ARE YOU..?
IT'S JUST SPRAINED! GO ON, HURRY!
BOOM!
BOOM!
BOOM!
HEY, WHO'S THE KID?!
IGNORE HIM. YOU KNOW YOUR TARGET.
READY... AIM...
...FIRE!
HEY, WHAT THE..?
?
BOOM!
POOM!
SP-DOOM!
DA-DOOM
Ha-Ha! LUTHOR'S BOYS ARE LOOKING OUT FOR US!
SUPERMAN!

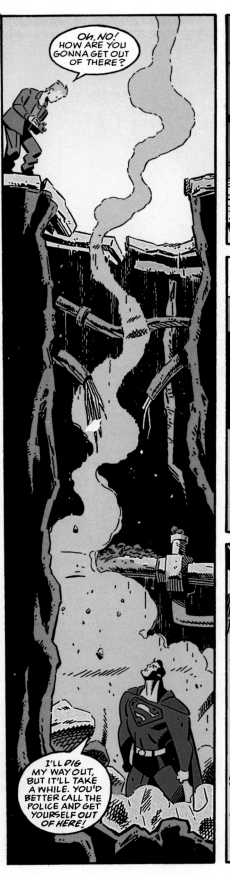

OH, NO! HOW ARE YOU GONNA GET OUT OF THERE?

I'LL DIG MY WAY OUT, BUT IT'LL TAKE A WHILE. YOU'D BETTER CALL THE POLICE AND GET YOURSELF OUT OF HERE!

DON'T DO ANYTHING RASH, JIMMY!

JIMMY!

THEY'RE HEADED STRAIGHT FOR THE LEXCORP BUILDING, THOSE MORONS!

YOU KNOW THE ORDERS, THEN.

KILL THEM ALL!

HOLY--!

HEY, LOOK OUT YOU JERKS!

KA-BOOM!

PEOW!

CHOOM!

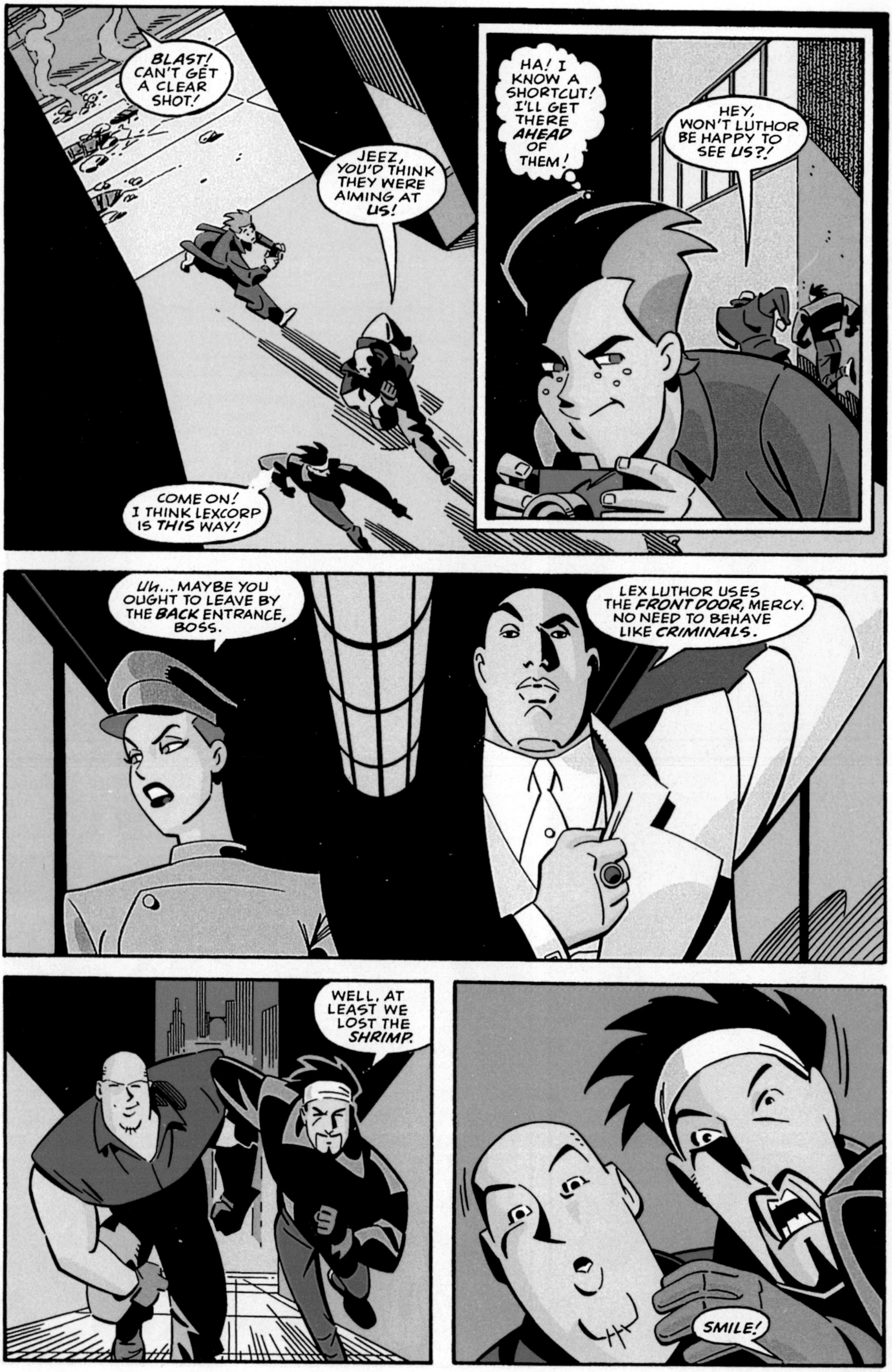
BLAST! CAN'T GET A CLEAR SHOT!
JEEZ, YOU'D THINK THEY WERE AIMING AT US!
COME ON! I THINK LEXCORP IS THIS WAY!
HA! I KNOW A SHORTCUT! I'LL GET THERE AHEAD OF THEM!
HEY, WON'T LUTHOR BE HAPPY TO SEE US?!
UH... MAYBE YOU OUGHT TO LEAVE BY THE BACK ENTRANCE, BOSS.
LEX LUTHOR USES THE FRONT DOOR, MERCY. NO NEED TO BEHAVE LIKE CRIMINALS.
WELL, AT LEAST WE LOST THE SHRIMP.
SMILE!

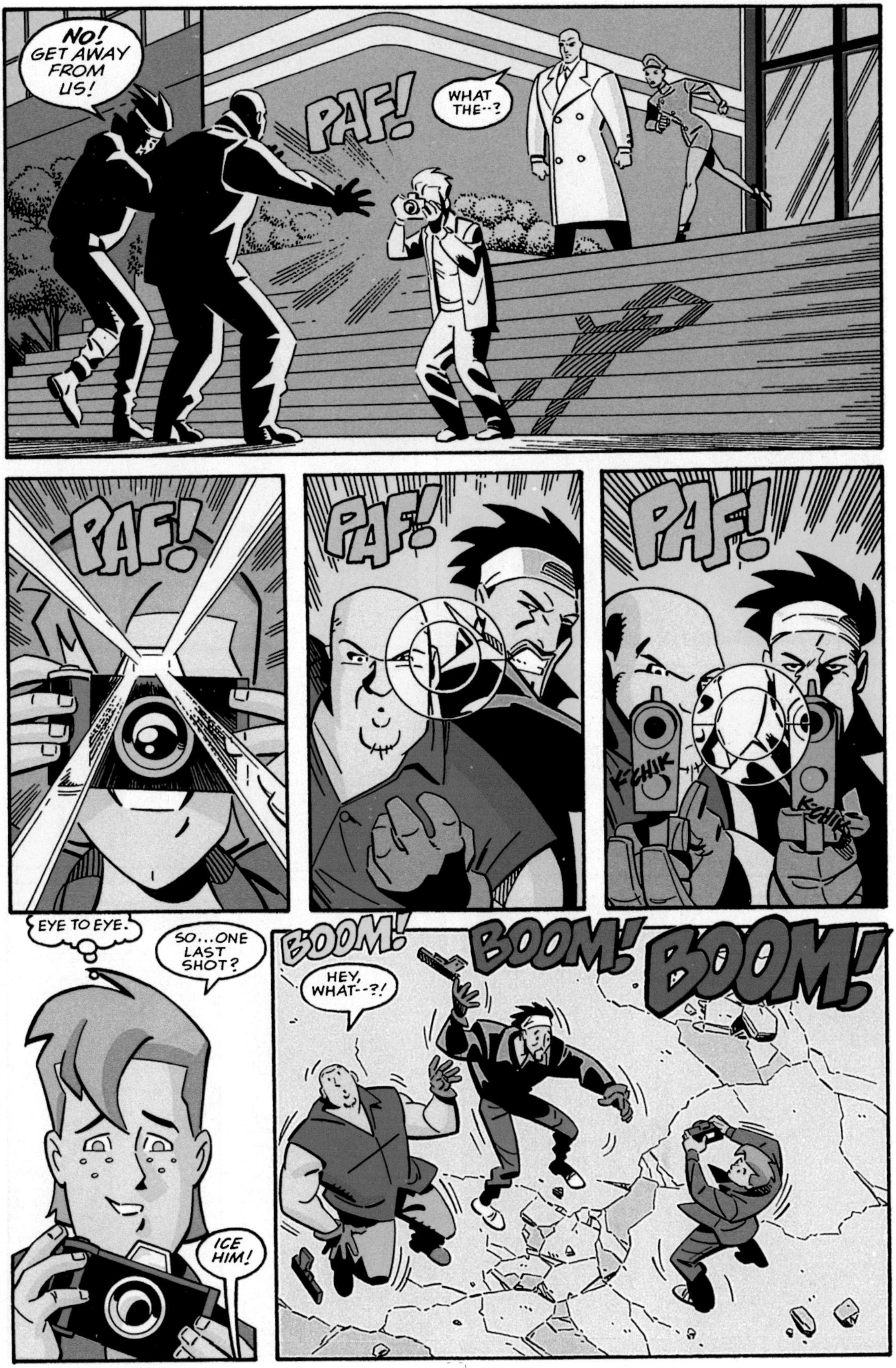
NO! GET AWAY FROM US!
PAF!
WHAT THE--?
PAF!
PAF!
PAF!
K'CHIK
K'CHIK
EYE TO EYE.
SO...ONE LAST SHOT?
ICE HIM!
BOOM!
BOOM!
BOOM!
HEY, WHAT--?!

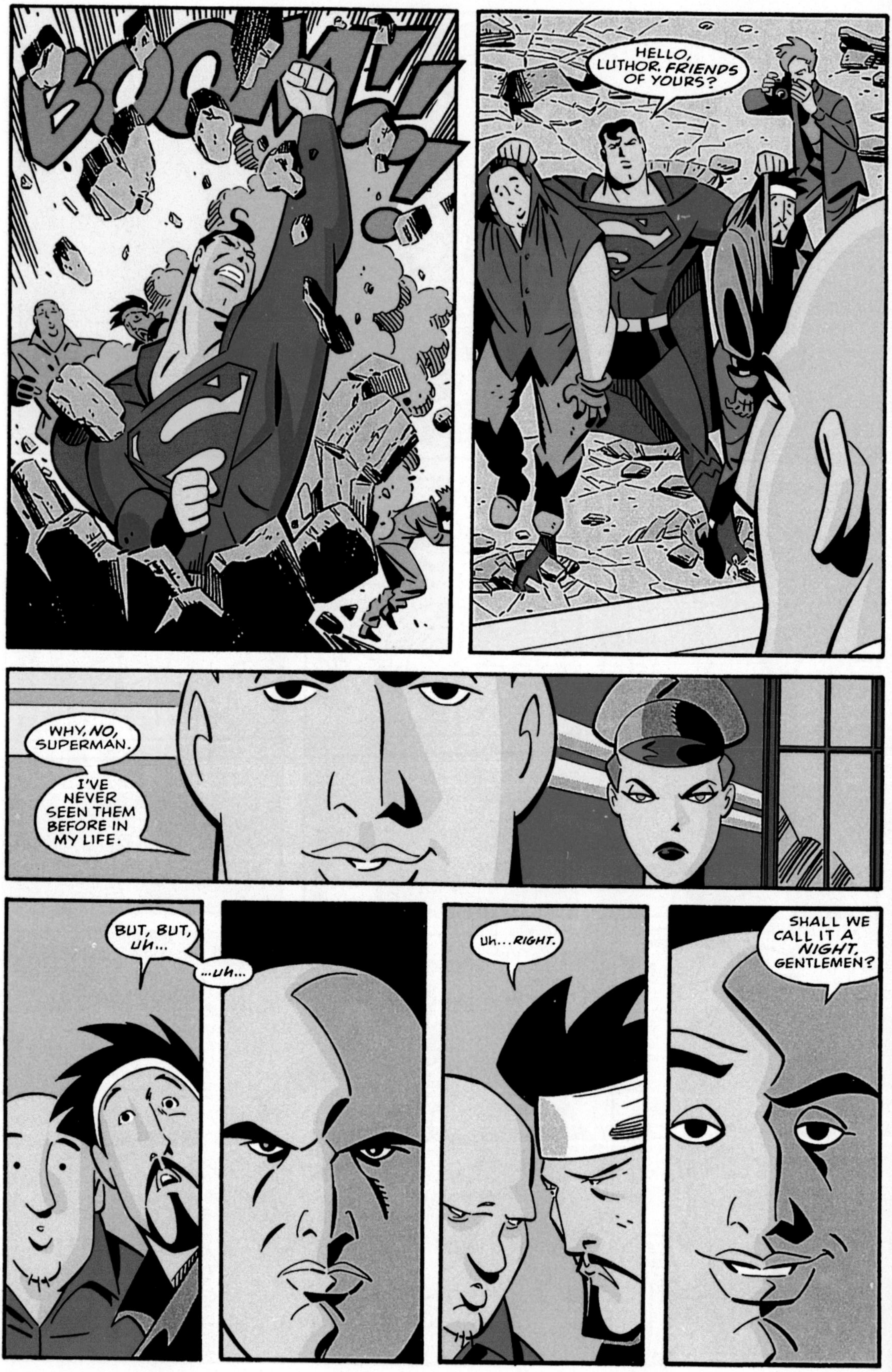
BOOM!!
HELLO, LUTHOR. FRIENDS OF YOURS?
WHY, NO, SUPERMAN.
I'VE NEVER SEEN THEM BEFORE IN MY LIFE.
BUT, BUT, uh...
...uh...
uh... RIGHT.
SHALL WE CALL IT A NIGHT, GENTLEMEN?

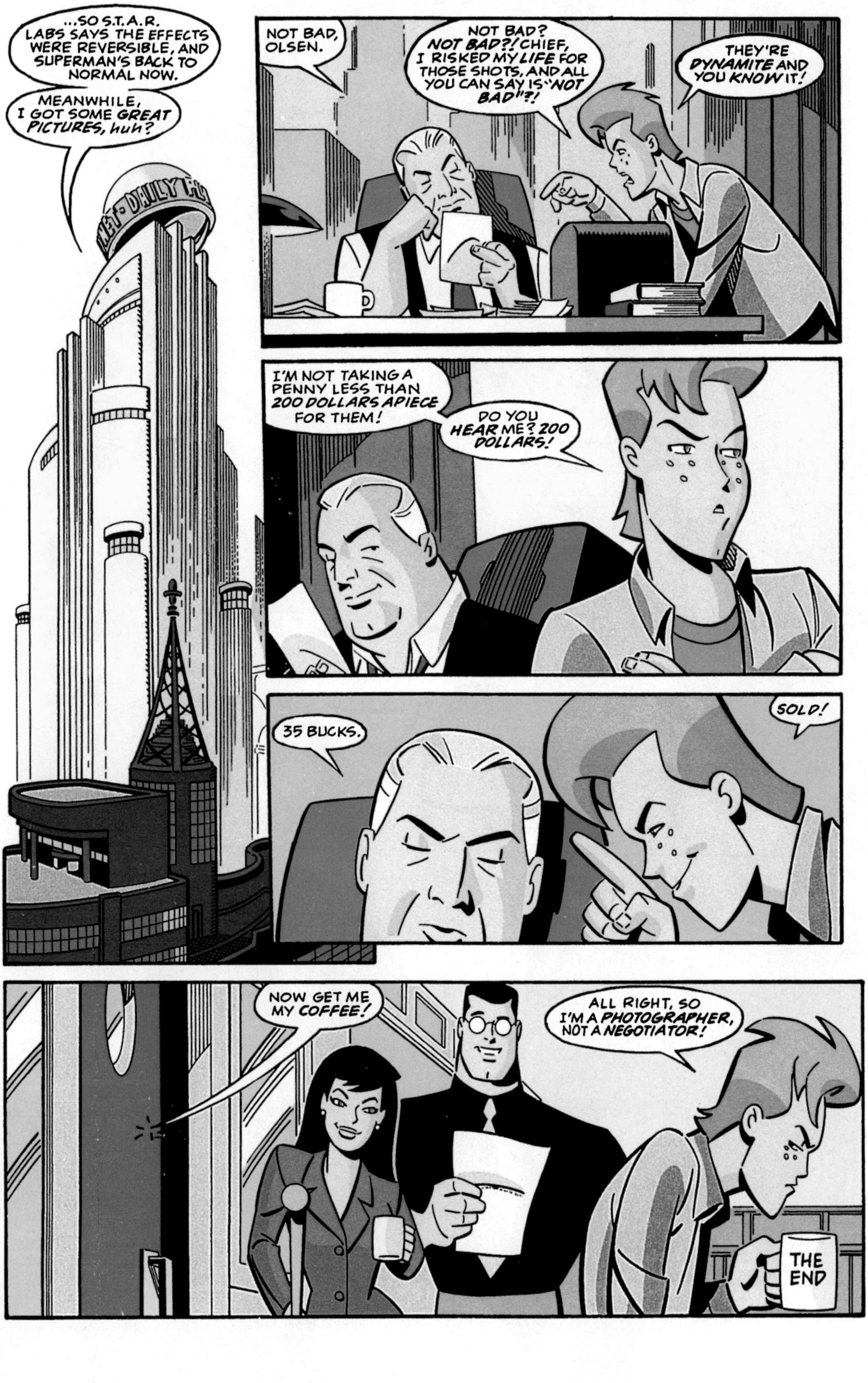
...SO S.T.A.R. LABS SAYS THE EFFECTS WERE REVERSIBLE, AND SUPERMAN'S BACK TO NORMAL NOW.
MEANWHILE, I GOT SOME GREAT PICTURES, huh?
NOT BAD, OLSEN.
NOT BAD? NOT BAD?! CHIEF, I RISKED MY LIFE FOR THOSE SHOTS, AND ALL YOU CAN SAY IS "NOT BAD"?!
THEY'RE DYNAMITE AND YOU KNOW IT!
I'M NOT TAKING A PENNY LESS THAN 200 DOLLARS APIECE FOR THEM!
DO YOU HEAR ME? 200 DOLLARS!
35 BUCKS.
SOLD!
NOW GET ME MY COFFEE!
ALL RIGHT, SO I'M A PHOTOGRAPHER, NOT A NEGOTIATOR!
THE END

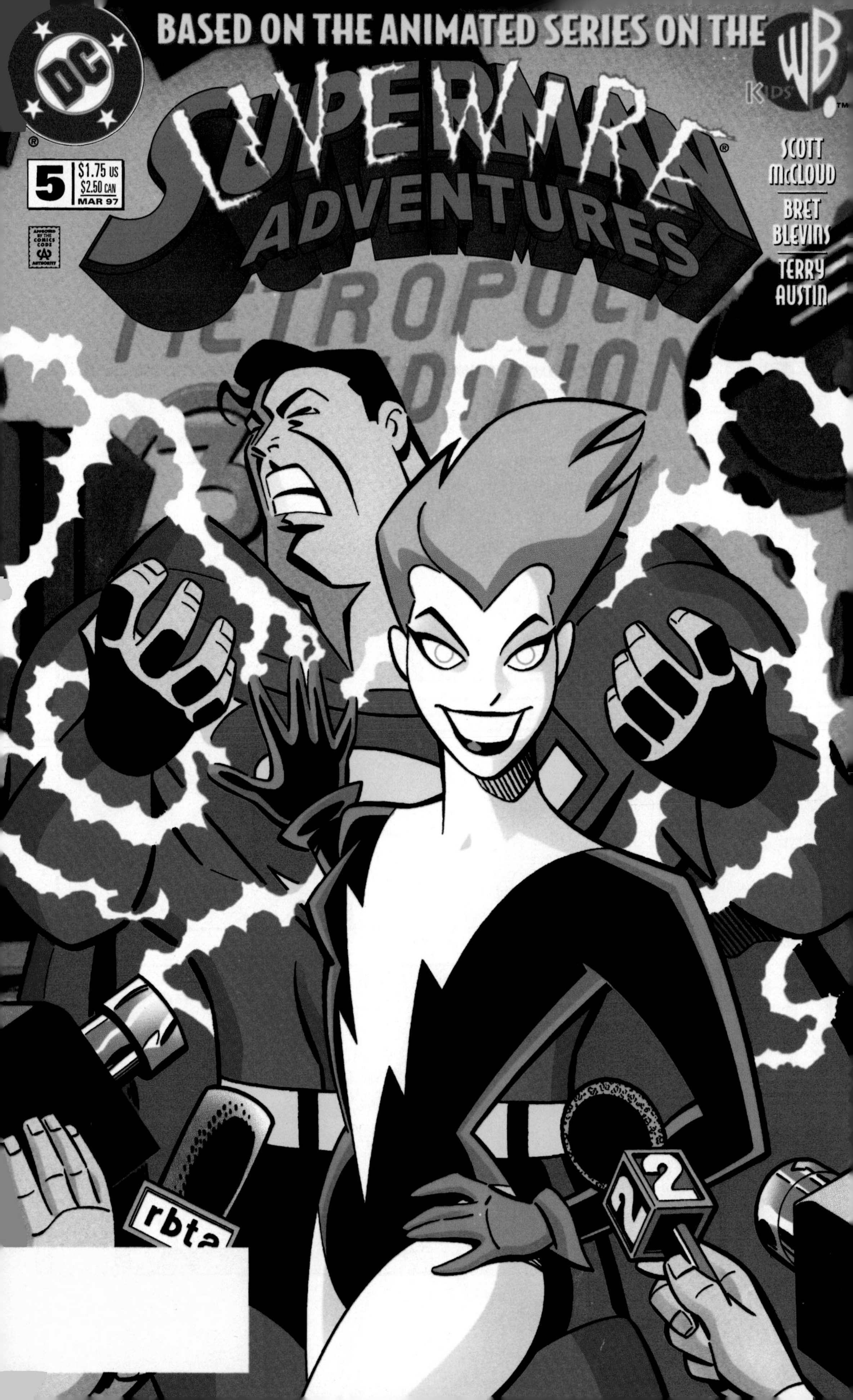
BASED ON THE ANIMATED SERIES ON THE
SUPERMAN
ADVENTURES
5
$1.75 US
$2.50 CAN
MAR 97
SCOTT McCLOUD
BRET BLEVINS
TERRY AUSTIN

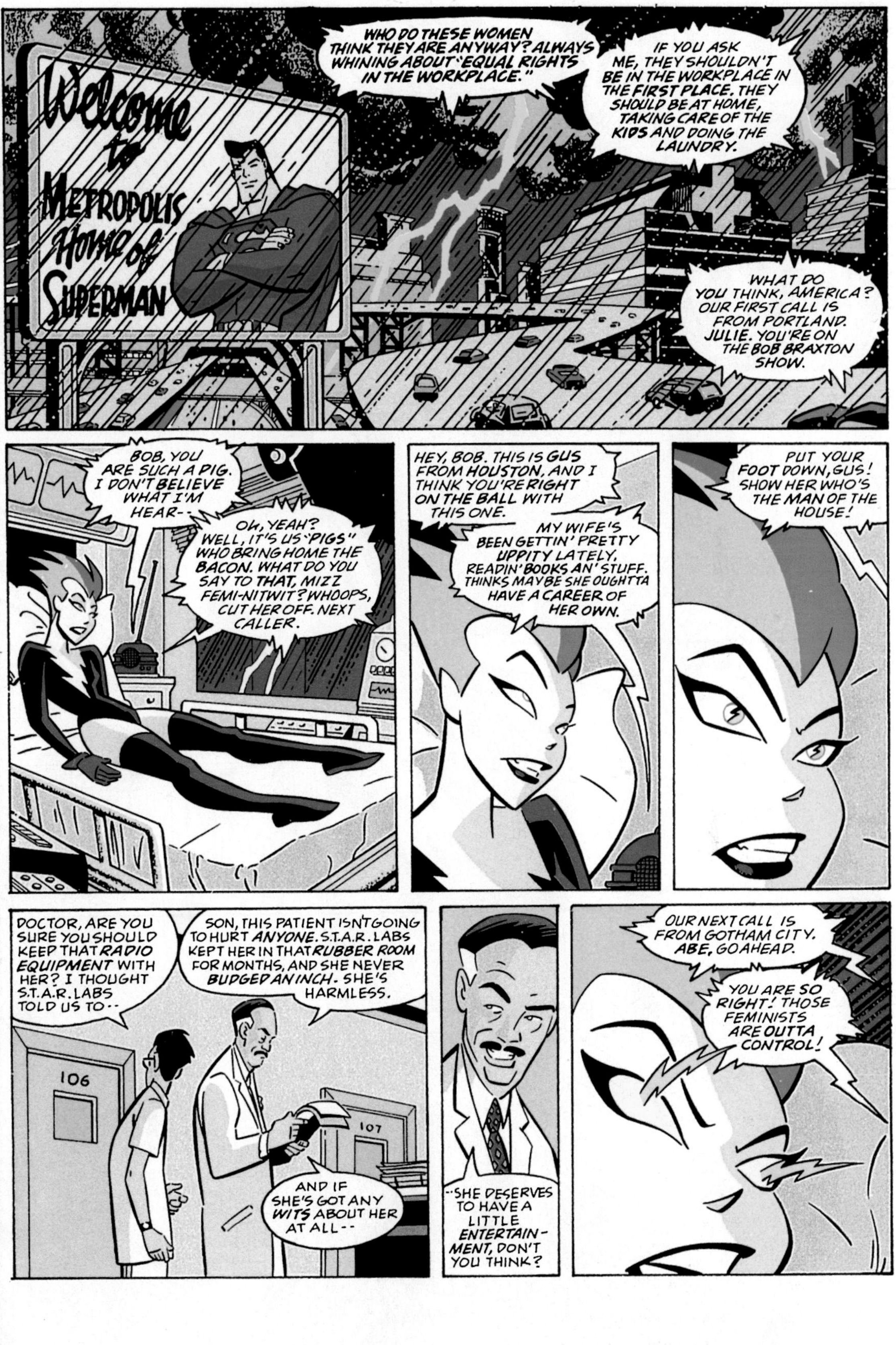
Welcome to Metropolis Home of Superman
WHO DO THESE WOMEN THINK THEY ARE ANYWAY? ALWAYS WHINING ABOUT "EQUAL RIGHTS IN THE WORKPLACE."
IF YOU ASK ME, THEY SHOULDN'T BE IN THE WORKPLACE IN THE FIRST PLACE. THEY SHOULD BE AT HOME, TAKING CARE OF THE KIDS AND DOING THE LAUNDRY.
WHAT DO YOU THINK, AMERICA? OUR FIRST CALL IS FROM PORTLAND. JULIE. YOU'RE ON THE BOB BRAXTON SHOW.
BOB, YOU ARE SUCH A PIG. I DON'T BELIEVE WHAT I'M HEAR--
OH, YEAH? WELL, IT'S US "PIGS" WHO BRING HOME THE BACON. WHAT DO YOU SAY TO THAT, MIZZ FEMI-NITWIT? WHOOPS, CUT HER OFF. NEXT CALLER.
HEY, BOB. THIS IS GUS FROM HOUSTON, AND I THINK YOU'RE RIGHT ON THE BALL WITH THIS ONE.
MY WIFE'S BEEN GETTIN' PRETTY UPPITY LATELY, READIN' BOOKS AN' STUFF. THINKS MAYBE SHE OUGHTTA HAVE A CAREER OF HER OWN.
PUT YOUR FOOT DOWN, GUS! SHOW HER WHO'S THE MAN OF THE HOUSE!
DOCTOR, ARE YOU SURE YOU SHOULD KEEP THAT RADIO EQUIPMENT WITH HER? I THOUGHT S.T.A.R. LABS TOLD US TO--
SON, THIS PATIENT ISN'T GOING TO HURT ANYONE. S.T.A.R. LABS KEPT HER IN THAT RUBBER ROOM FOR MONTHS, AND SHE NEVER BUDGED AN INCH. SHE'S HARMLESS.
106
107
AND IF SHE'S GOT ANY WITS ABOUT HER AT ALL--
--SHE DESERVES TO HAVE A LITTLE ENTERTAIN-MENT, DON'T YOU THINK?
OUR NEXT CALL IS FROM GOTHAM CITY. ABE, GO AHEAD.
YOU ARE SO RIGHT! THOSE FEMINISTS ARE OUTTA CONTROL!

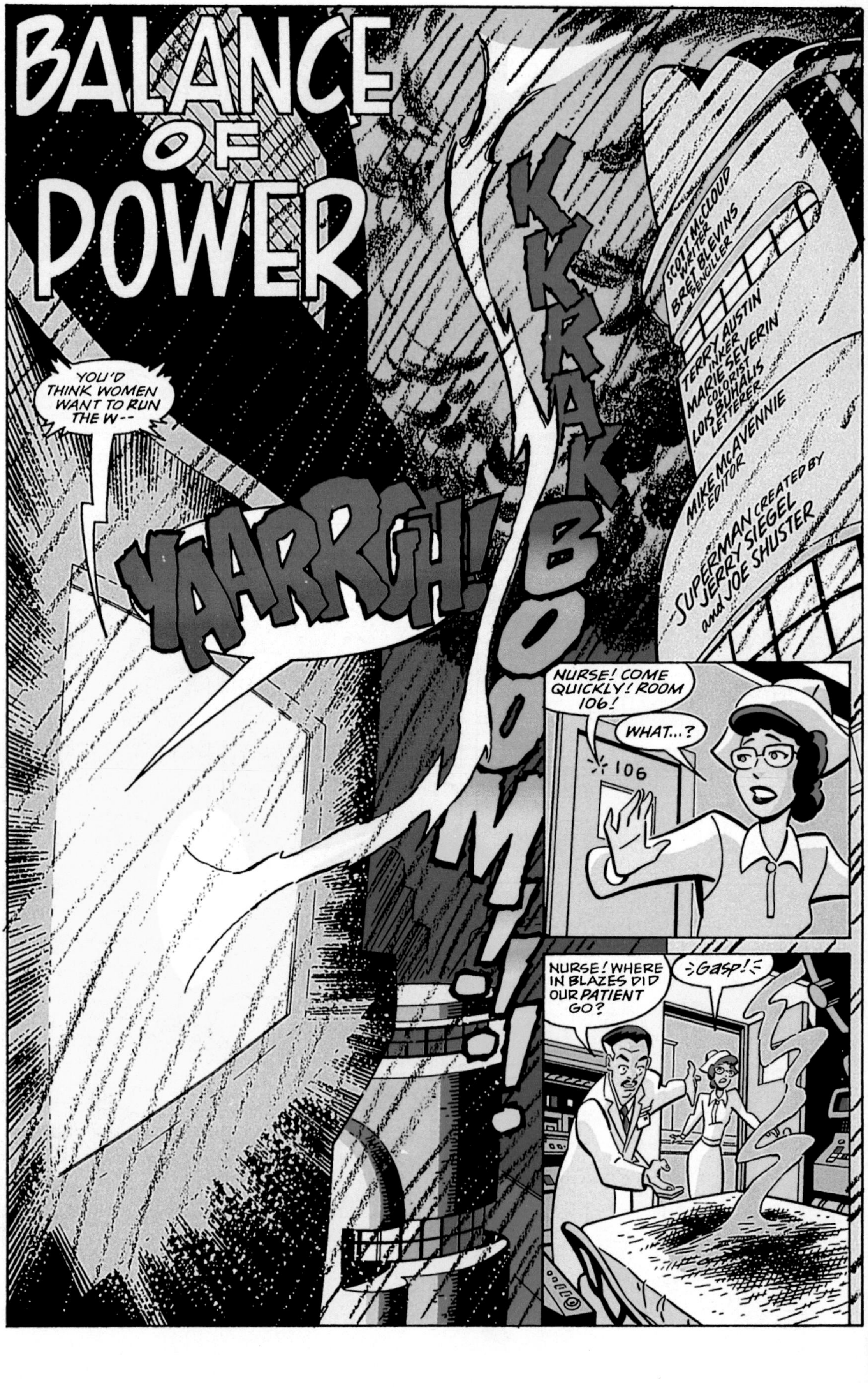
BALANCE OF POWER
SCOTT McCLOUD WRITER
BRET BLEVINS PENCILLER
TERRY AUSTIN INKER
MARIE SEVERIN COLORIST
LOIS BUHALIS LETTERER
MIKE McAVENNIE EDITOR
SUPERMAN CREATED BY JERRY SIEGEL and JOE SHUSTER
YOU'D THINK WOMEN WANT TO RUN THE W--
YAARRGH!
KKRAKBOOOM!!!
NURSE! COME QUICKLY! ROOM 106!
WHAT...?
106
NURSE! WHERE IN BLAZES DID OUR PATIENT GO?
Gasp!

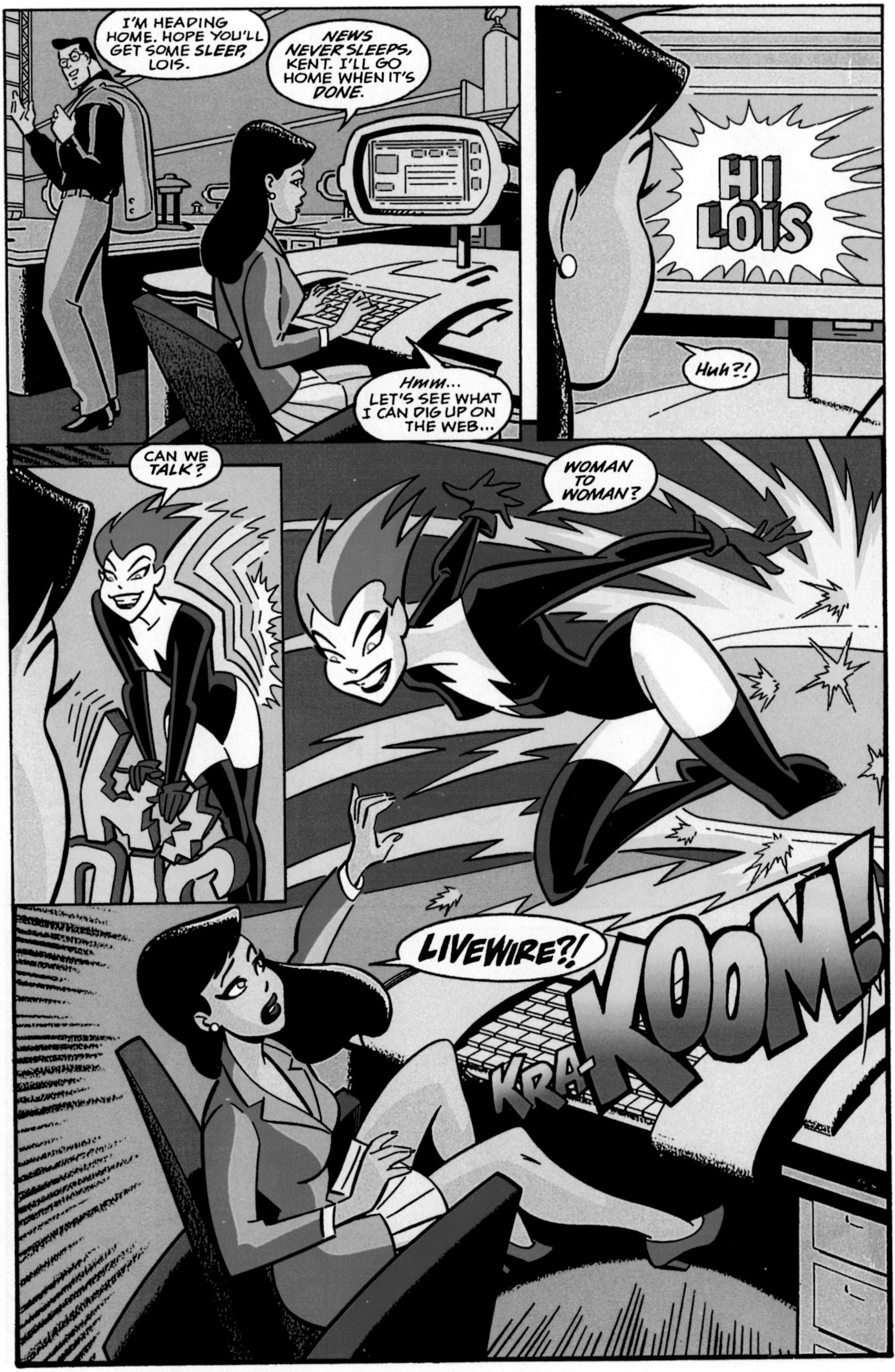
I'M HEADING HOME. HOPE YOU'LL GET SOME SLEEP, LOIS.
NEWS NEVER SLEEPS, KENT. I'LL GO HOME WHEN IT'S DONE.
Hmm... LET'S SEE WHAT I CAN DIG UP ON THE WEB...
HI LOIS
Huh?!
CAN WE TALK?
WOMAN TO WOMAN?
LIVEWIRE?!
KRA-KOOM!

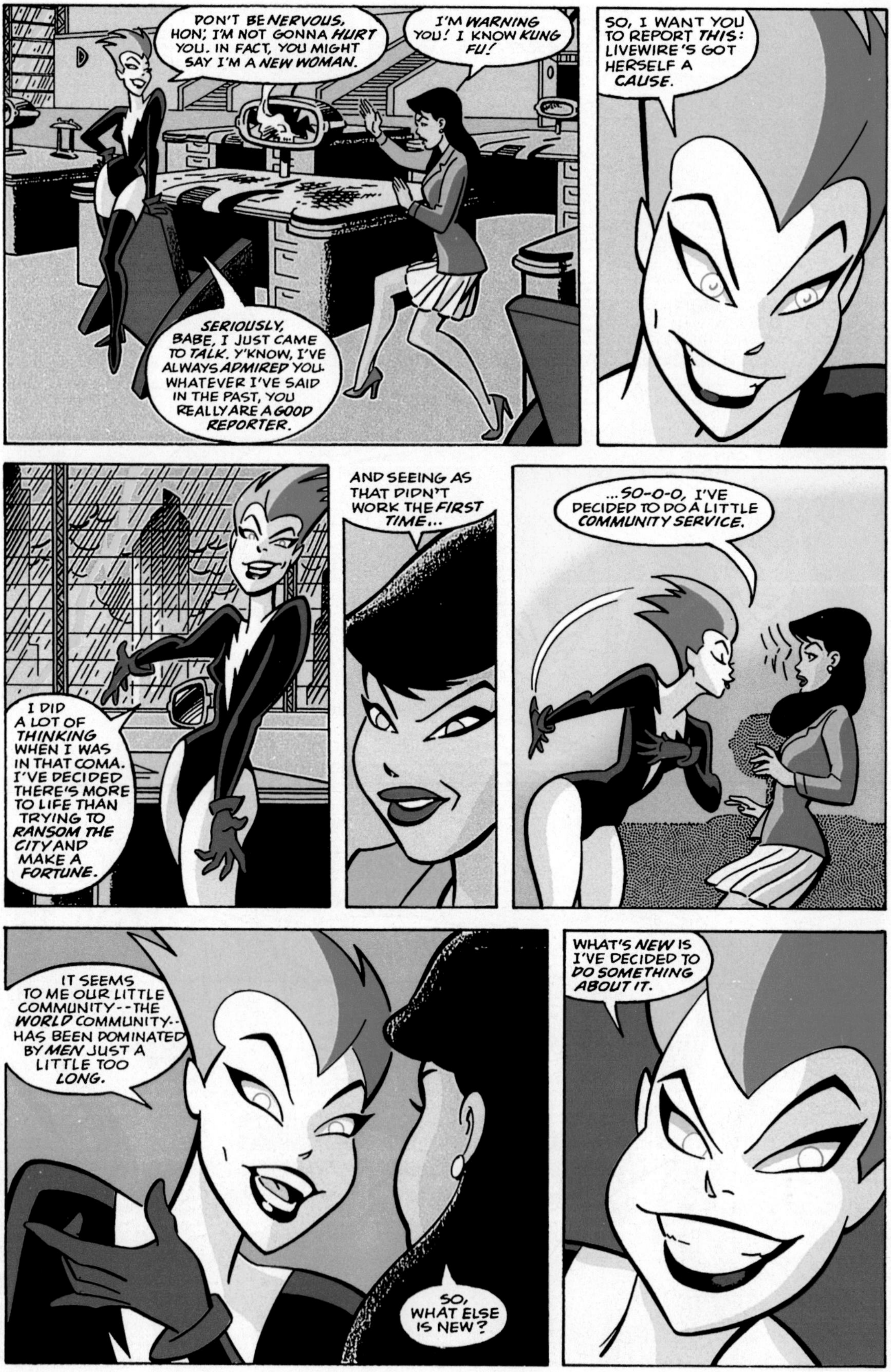
DON'T BE NERVOUS, HON; I'M NOT GONNA HURT YOU. IN FACT, YOU MIGHT SAY I'M A NEW WOMAN.
I'M WARNING YOU! I KNOW KUNG FU!
SERIOUSLY, BABE, I JUST CAME TO TALK. Y'KNOW, I'VE ALWAYS ADMIRED YOU. WHATEVER I'VE SAID IN THE PAST, YOU REALLY ARE A GOOD REPORTER.
SO, I WANT YOU TO REPORT THIS: LIVEWIRE'S GOT HERSELF A CAUSE.
I DID A LOT OF THINKING WHEN I WAS IN THAT COMA. I'VE DECIDED THERE'S MORE TO LIFE THAN TRYING TO RANSOM THE CITY AND MAKE A FORTUNE.
AND SEEING AS THAT DIDN'T WORK THE FIRST TIME...
...SO-O-O, I'VE DECIDED TO DO A LITTLE COMMUNITY SERVICE.
IT SEEMS TO ME OUR LITTLE COMMUNITY--THE WORLD COMMUNITY--HAS BEEN DOMINATED BY MEN JUST A LITTLE TOO LONG.
SO, WHAT ELSE IS NEW?
WHAT'S NEW IS I'VE DECIDED TO DO SOMETHING ABOUT IT.

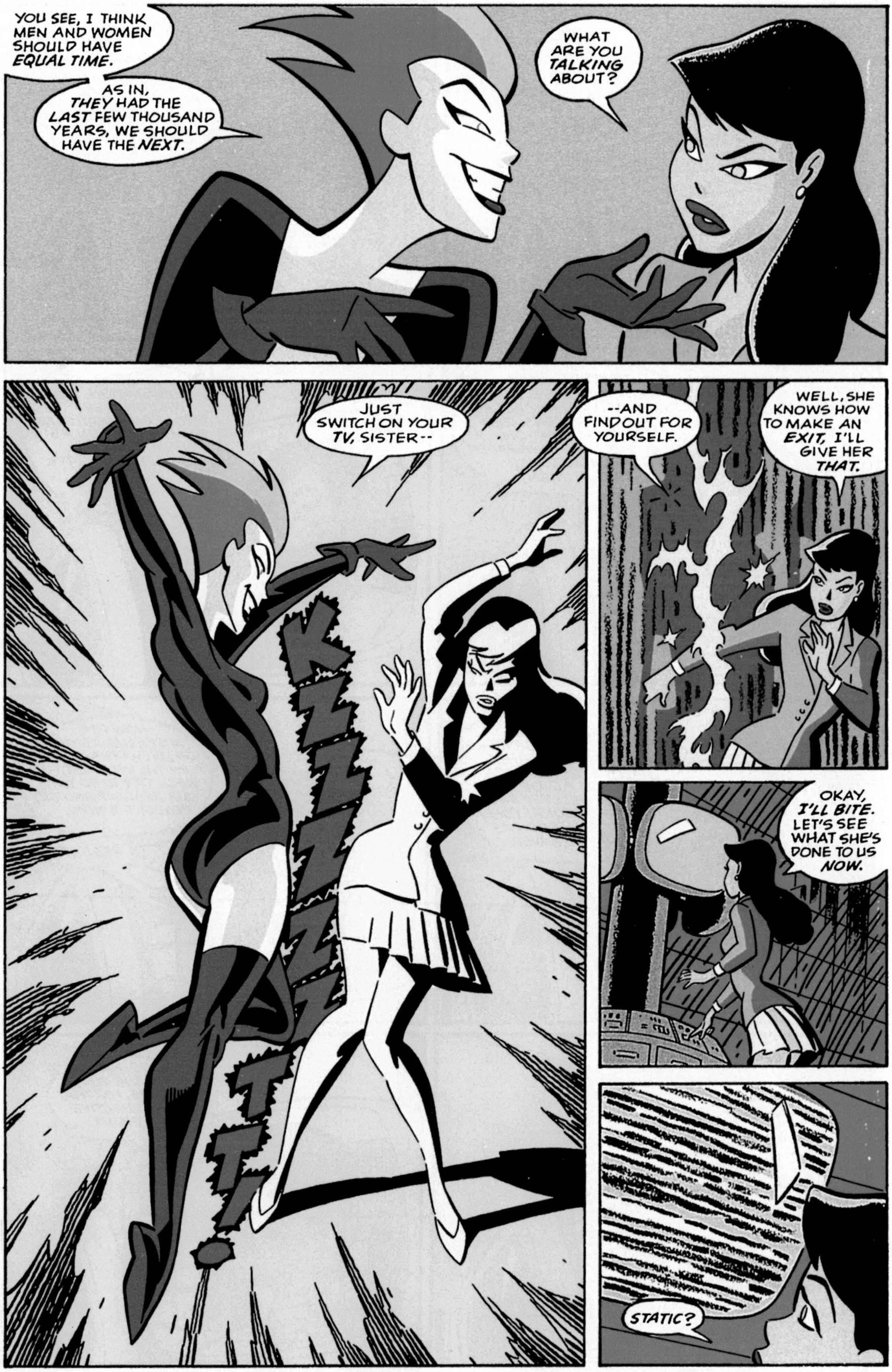
YOU SEE, I THINK MEN AND WOMEN SHOULD HAVE EQUAL TIME.
AS IN, THEY HAD THE LAST FEW THOUSAND YEARS, WE SHOULD HAVE THE NEXT.
WHAT ARE YOU TALKING ABOUT?
JUST SWITCH ON YOUR TV, SISTER--
KZZZZZZTT!
--AND FIND OUT FOR YOURSELF.
WELL, SHE KNOWS HOW TO MAKE AN EXIT, I'LL GIVE HER THAT.
OKAY, I'LL BITE. LET'S SEE WHAT SHE'S DONE TO US NOW.
STATIC?

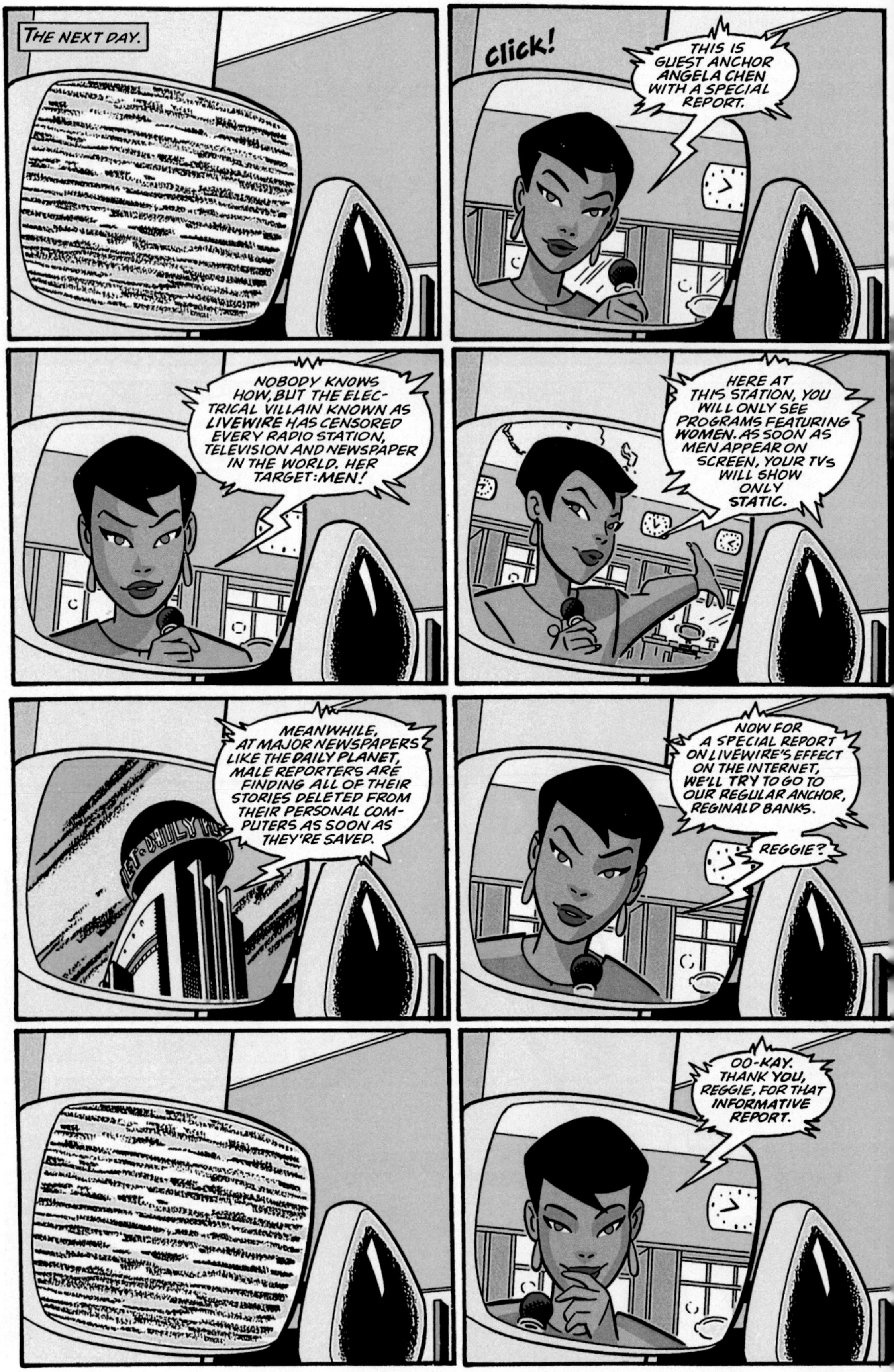
THE NEXT DAY.
Click!
THIS IS GUEST ANCHOR ANGELA CHEN WITH A SPECIAL REPORT.
NOBODY KNOWS HOW, BUT THE ELECTRICAL VILLAIN KNOWN AS LIVEWIRE HAS CENSORED EVERY RADIO STATION, TELEVISION AND NEWSPAPER IN THE WORLD. HER TARGET: MEN!
HERE AT THIS STATION, YOU WILL ONLY SEE PROGRAMS FEATURING WOMEN. AS SOON AS MEN APPEAR ON SCREEN, YOUR TVs WILL SHOW ONLY STATIC.
MEANWHILE, AT MAJOR NEWSPAPERS LIKE THE DAILY PLANET, MALE REPORTERS ARE FINDING ALL OF THEIR STORIES DELETED FROM THEIR PERSONAL COMPUTERS AS SOON AS THEY'RE SAVED.
NOW FOR A SPECIAL REPORT ON LIVEWIRE'S EFFECT ON THE INTERNET, WE'LL TRY TO GO TO OUR REGULAR ANCHOR, REGINALD BANKS.
REGGIE?
OO-KAY. THANK YOU, REGGIE, FOR THAT INFORMATIVE REPORT.

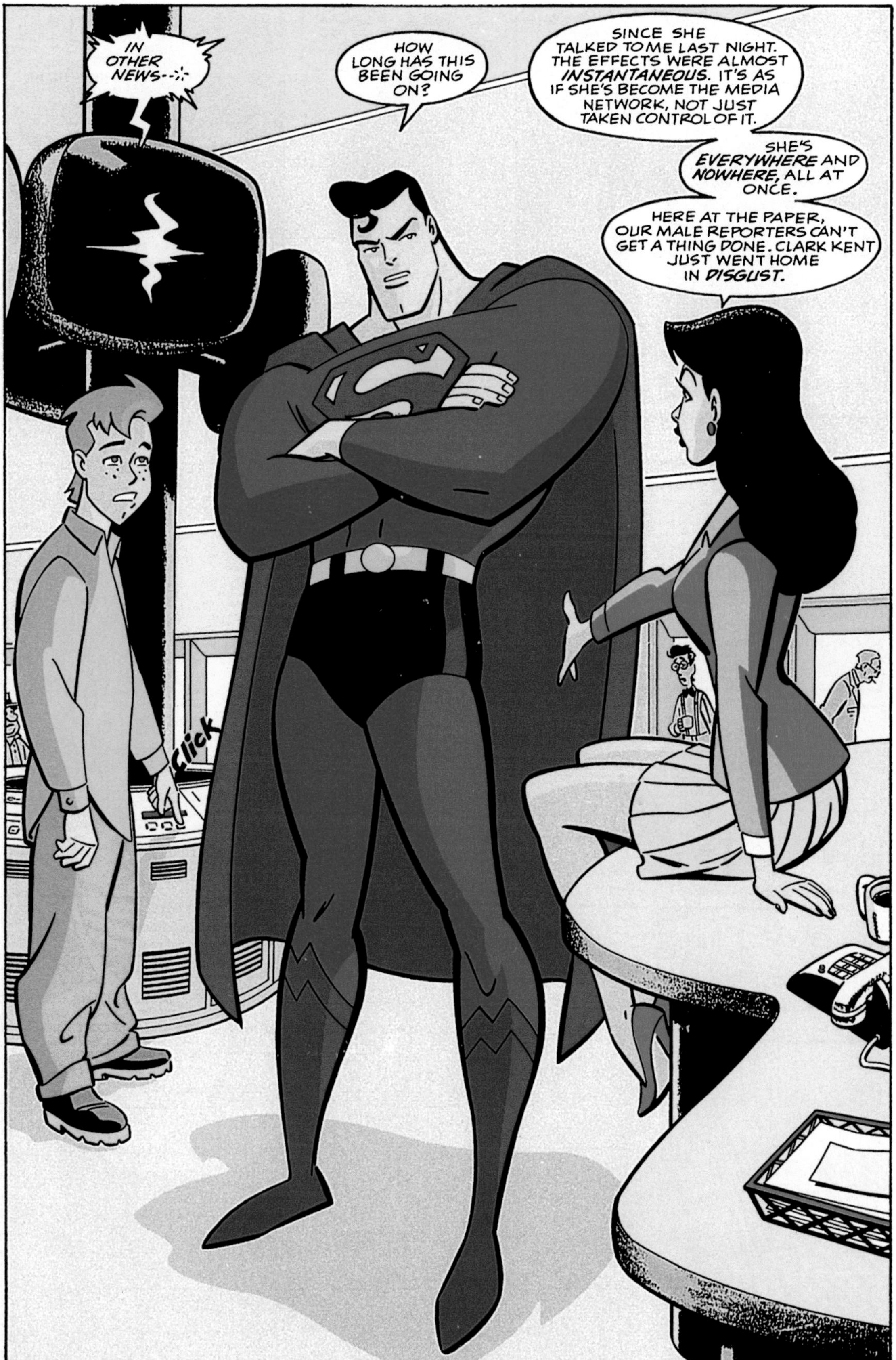
IN OTHER NEWS--
HOW LONG HAS THIS BEEN GOING ON?
SINCE SHE TALKED TO ME LAST NIGHT. THE EFFECTS WERE ALMOST INSTANTANEOUS. IT'S AS IF SHE'S BECOME THE MEDIA NETWORK, NOT JUST TAKEN CONTROL OF IT.
SHE'S EVERYWHERE AND NOWHERE, ALL AT ONCE.
HERE AT THE PAPER, OUR MALE REPORTERS CAN'T GET A THING DONE. CLARK KENT JUST WENT HOME IN DISGUST.
CLICK

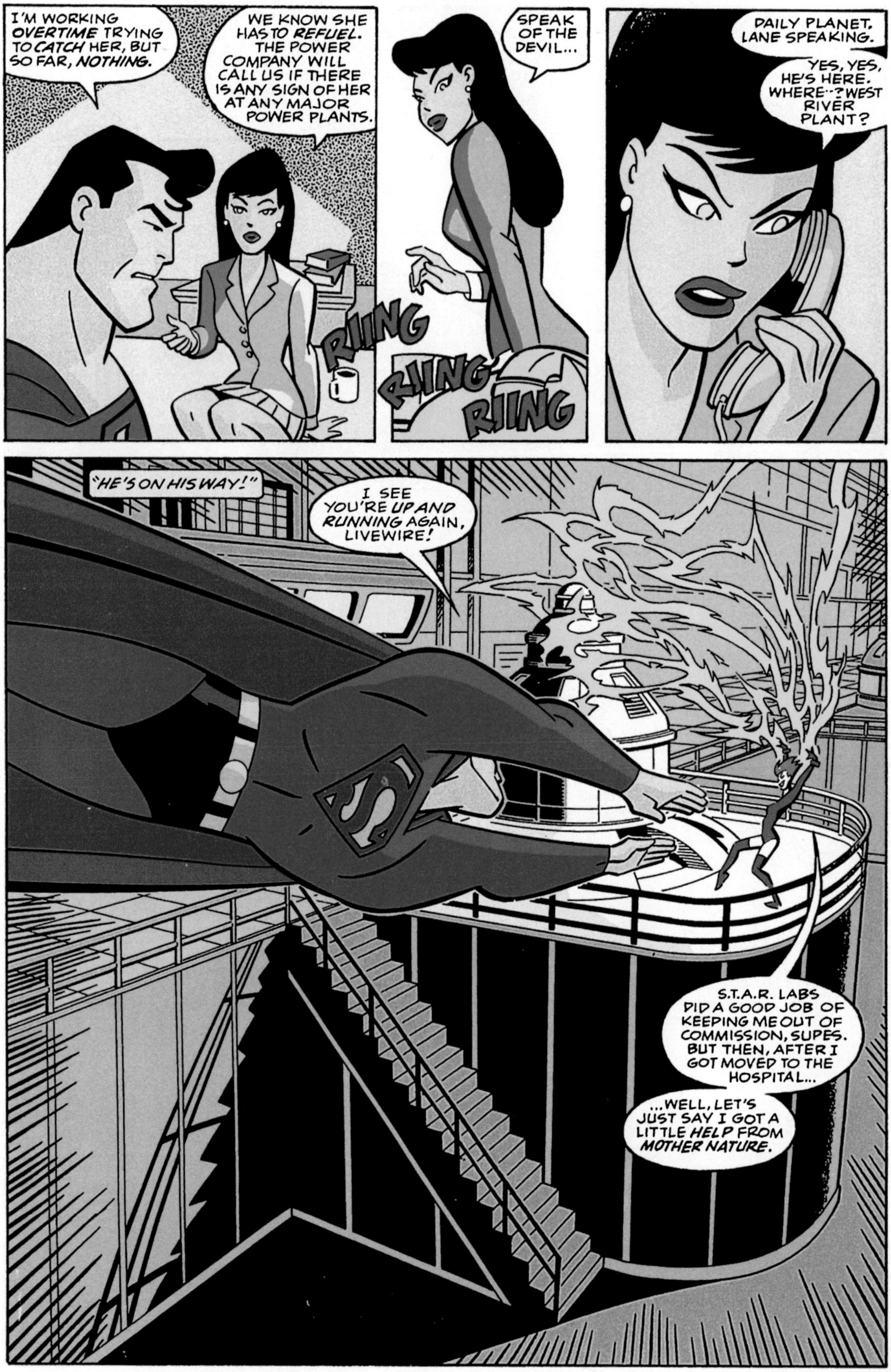

I'M WORKING OVERTIME TRYING TO CATCH HER, BUT SO FAR, NOTHING.
WE KNOW SHE HAS TO REFUEL. THE POWER COMPANY WILL CALL US IF THERE IS ANY SIGN OF HER AT ANY MAJOR POWER PLANTS.
SPEAK OF THE DEVIL...
RIING
RIING
RIING
DAILY PLANET. LANE SPEAKING.
YES, YES, HE'S HERE. WHERE--? WEST RIVER PLANT?
"HE'S ON HIS WAY!"
I SEE YOU'RE UP AND RUNNING AGAIN, LIVEWIRE!
S.T.A.R. LABS DID A GOOD JOB OF KEEPING ME OUT OF COMMISSION, SUPES. BUT THEN, AFTER I GOT MOVED TO THE HOSPITAL...
...WELL, LET'S JUST SAY I GOT A LITTLE HELP FROM MOTHER NATURE.

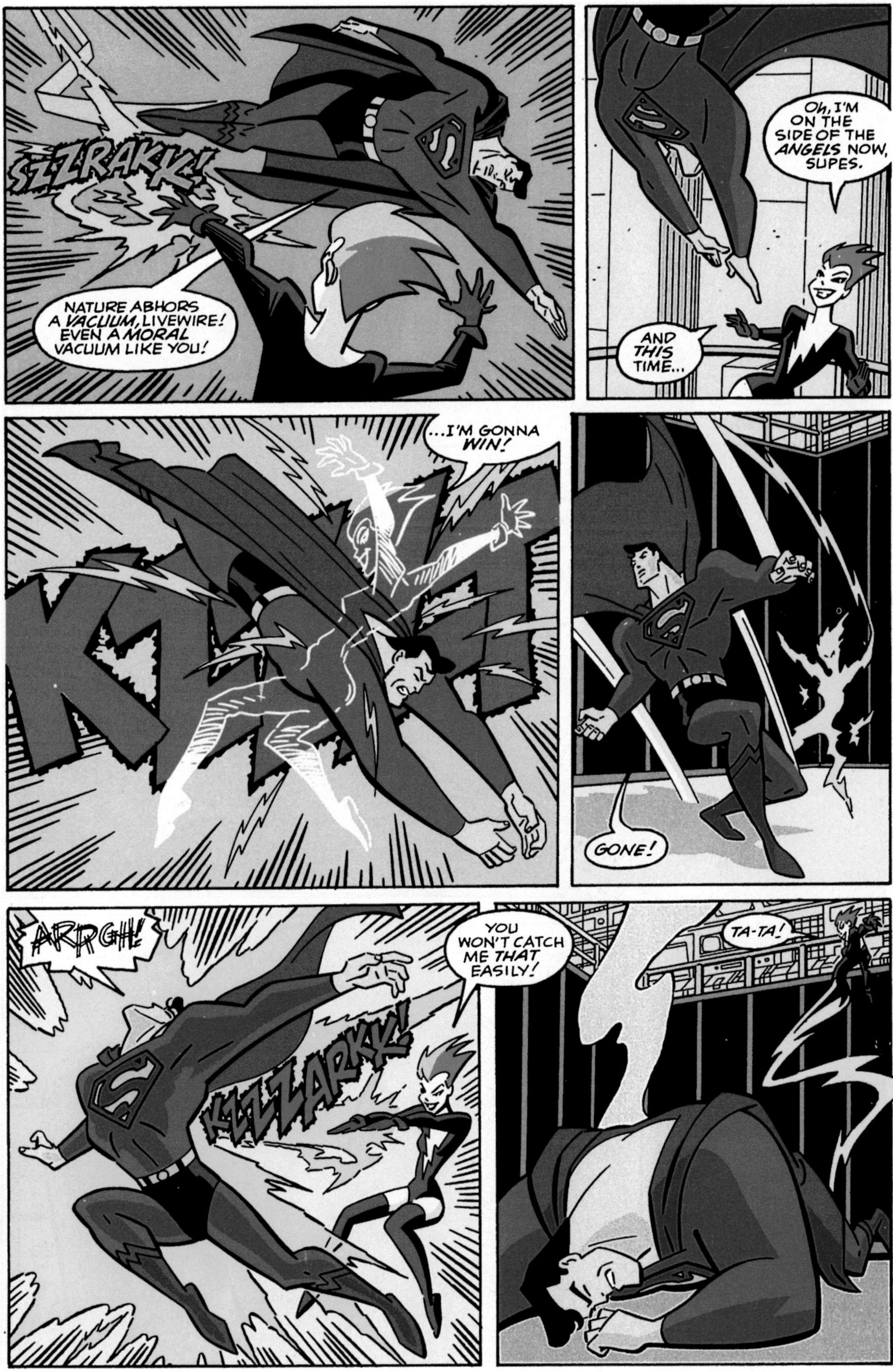
SZZRAKK!
NATURE ABHORS A VACUUM, LIVEWIRE! EVEN A MORAL VACUUM LIKE YOU!
Oh, I'M ON THE SIDE OF THE ANGELS NOW, SUPES.
AND THIS TIME...
...I'M GONNA WIN!
GONE!
ARRGH!
YOU WON'T CATCH ME THAT EASILY!
KZZZARKK!
TA-TA!

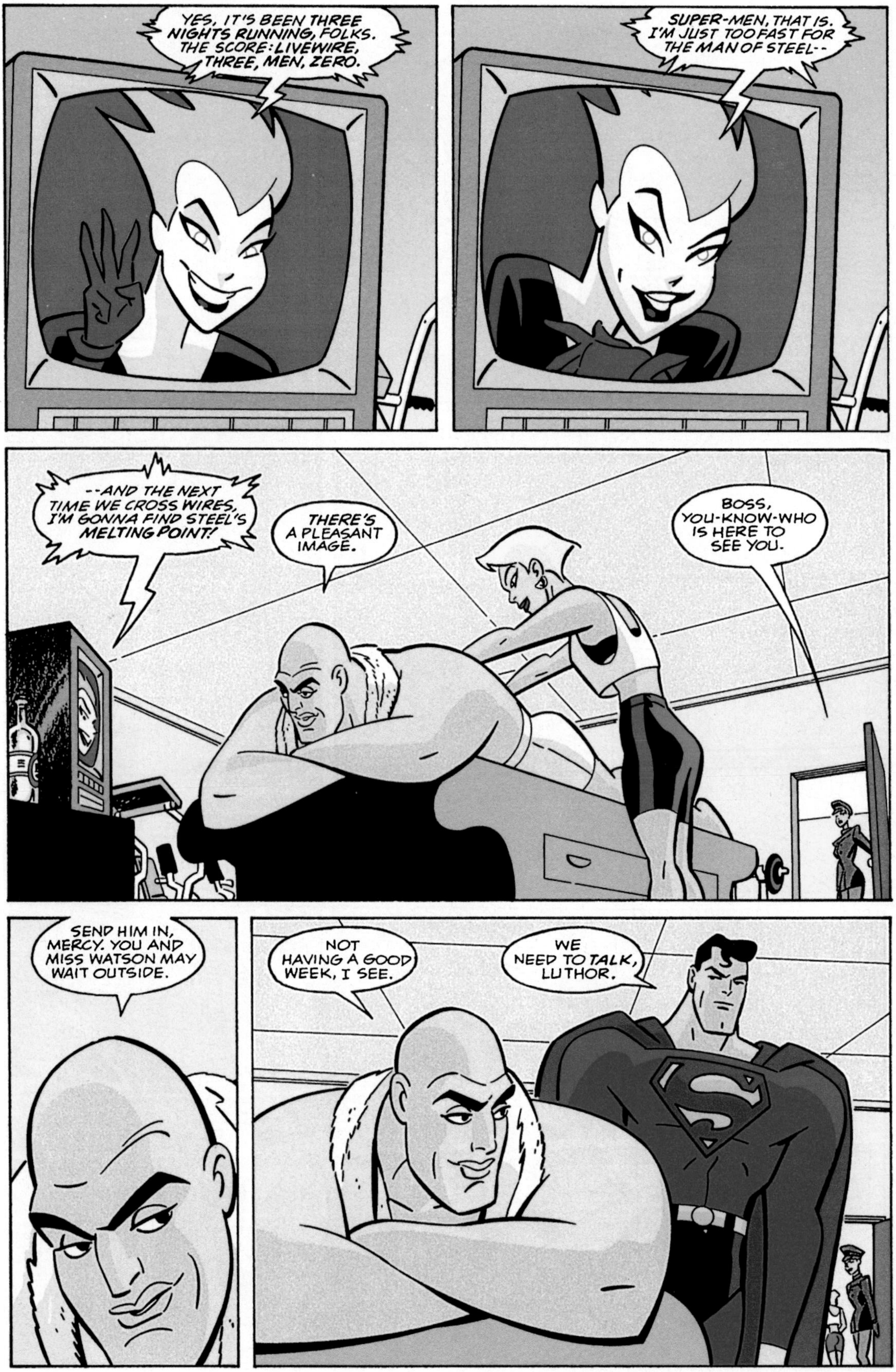
YES, IT'S BEEN THREE NIGHTS RUNNING, FOLKS. THE SCORE: LIVEWIRE, THREE, MEN, ZERO.
SUPER-MEN, THAT IS. I'M JUST TOO FAST FOR THE MAN OF STEEL--
--AND THE NEXT TIME WE CROSS WIRES, I'M GONNA FIND STEEL'S MELTING POINT!
THERE'S A PLEASANT IMAGE.
BOSS, YOU-KNOW-WHO IS HERE TO SEE YOU.
SEND HIM IN, MERCY. YOU AND MISS WATSON MAY WAIT OUTSIDE.
NOT HAVING A GOOD WEEK, I SEE.
WE NEED TO TALK, LUTHOR.

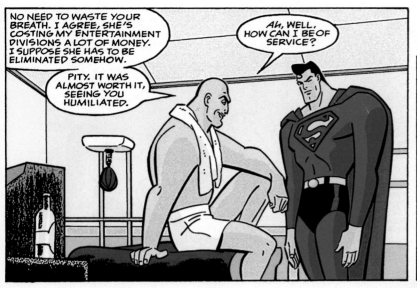

NO NEED TO WASTE YOUR BREATH. I AGREE, SHE'S COSTING MY ENTERTAINMENT DIVISIONS A LOT OF MONEY. I SUPPOSE SHE HAS TO BE ELIMINATED SOMEHOW.

PITY. IT WAS ALMOST WORTH IT, SEEING YOU HUMILIATED.

AH, WELL, HOW CAN I BE OF SERVICE?

YOUR WEAPONS DIVISION HAS BEEN WORKING ON SOME *ELECTROMAGNETIC PULSE GENERATORS.*

YES, WE HAVE SEVERAL PROTOTYPES. THEY CAN DISRUPT ELECTRICAL FIELDS--

--BUT THEY'RE MOSTLY GOOD FOR *SHORT RANGE* USE.

THAT'S ALL I NEED. I'M GOING TO LURE HER INTO A CONFRONTATION. ALL I NEED FROM *YOU* IS THAT YOU CUT OFF HER *ESCAPE* ROUTE.

I WANT HER *SURROUNDED* AND *CONTAINED.* LEAVE THE REST TO ME.

I KNOW YOU'RE OUT THERE, GUYS, SAYING, "WHAT ARE WE GONNA DO ABOUT THIS CRAZY CHICK? HOW ARE WE GONNA PUT HER DOWN?"

WELL, I GOT *NEWS* FOR YOU, BOYS. THIS *"CRAZY CHICK"* IS HERE TO STAY!

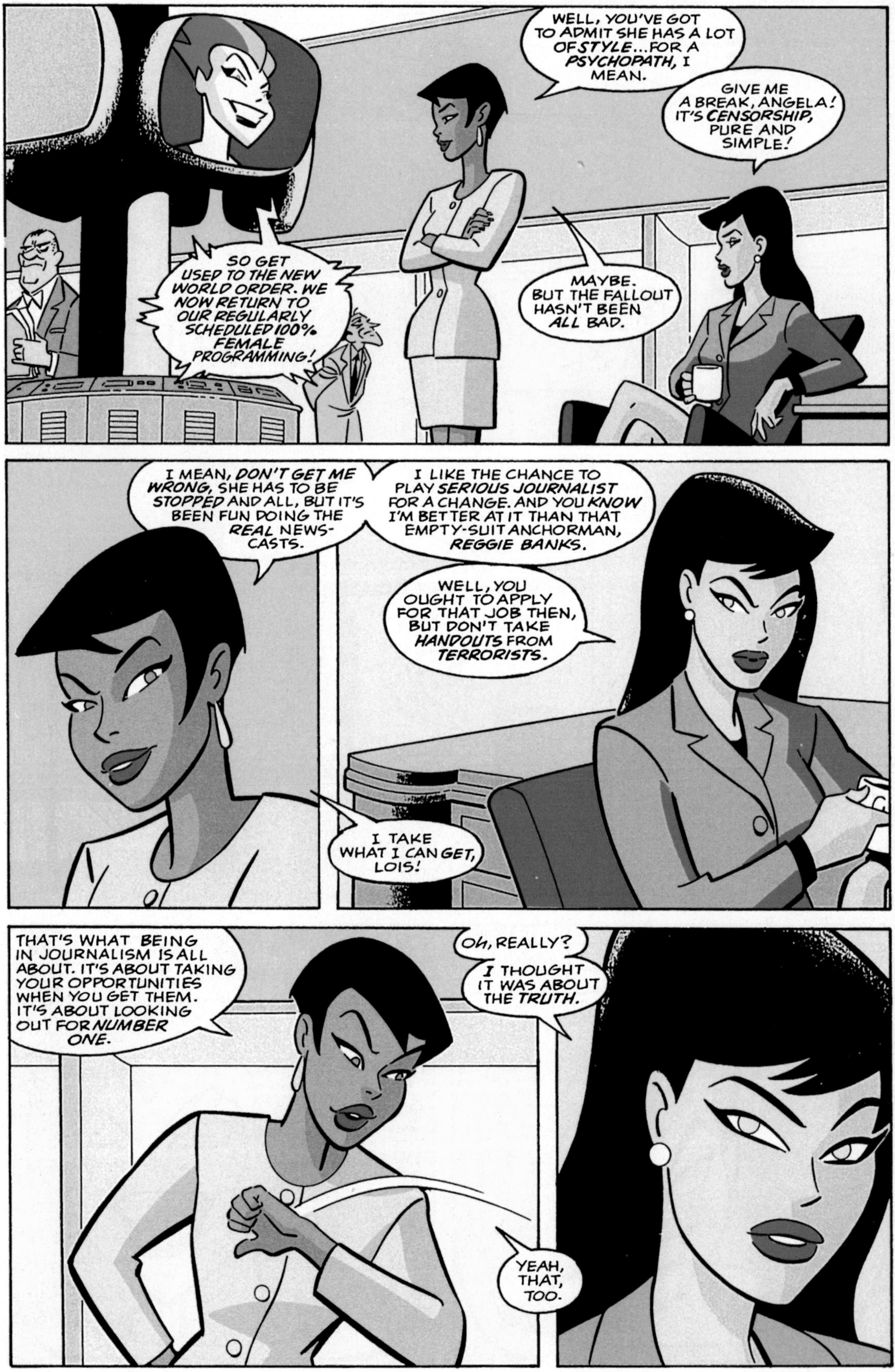
WELL, YOU'VE GOT TO ADMIT SHE HAS A LOT OF STYLE...FOR A PSYCHOPATH, I MEAN.
GIVE ME A BREAK, ANGELA! IT'S CENSORSHIP, PURE AND SIMPLE!
SO GET USED TO THE NEW WORLD ORDER. WE NOW RETURN TO OUR REGULARLY SCHEDULED 100% FEMALE PROGRAMMING!
MAYBE. BUT THE FALLOUT HASN'T BEEN ALL BAD.
I MEAN, DON'T GET ME WRONG, SHE HAS TO BE STOPPED AND ALL, BUT IT'S BEEN FUN DOING THE REAL NEWS-CASTS.
I LIKE THE CHANCE TO PLAY SERIOUS JOURNALIST FOR A CHANGE. AND YOU KNOW I'M BETTER AT IT THAN THAT EMPTY-SUIT ANCHORMAN, REGGIE BANKS.
WELL, YOU OUGHT TO APPLY FOR THAT JOB THEN, BUT DON'T TAKE HANDOUTS FROM TERRORISTS.
I TAKE WHAT I CAN GET, LOIS!
THAT'S WHAT BEING IN JOURNALISM IS ALL ABOUT. IT'S ABOUT TAKING YOUR OPPORTUNITIES WHEN YOU GET THEM. IT'S ABOUT LOOKING OUT FOR NUMBER ONE.
Oh, REALLY?
I THOUGHT IT WAS ABOUT THE TRUTH.
YEAH, THAT, TOO.

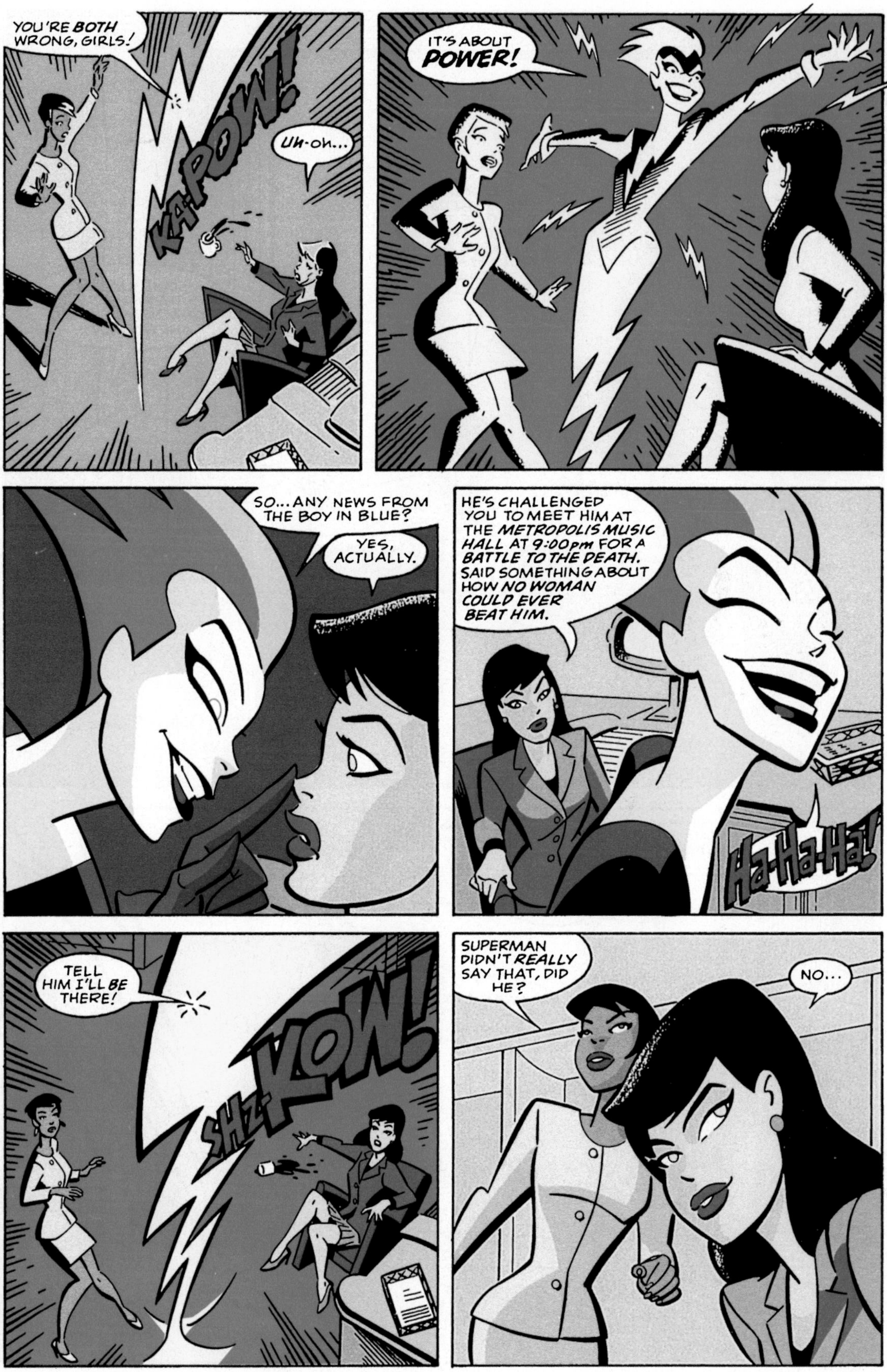
YOU'RE BOTH WRONG, GIRLS!
KA-POW!
Uh-oh...
IT'S ABOUT POWER!
SO... ANY NEWS FROM THE BOY IN BLUE?
YES, ACTUALLY.
HE'S CHALLENGED YOU TO MEET HIM AT THE METROPOLIS MUSIC HALL AT 9:00pm FOR A BATTLE TO THE DEATH. SAID SOMETHING ABOUT HOW NO WOMAN COULD EVER BEAT HIM.
Ha-Ha-Ha!
TELL HIM I'LL BE THERE!
SHZ-KOW!
SUPERMAN DIDN'T REALLY SAY THAT, DID HE?
NO...

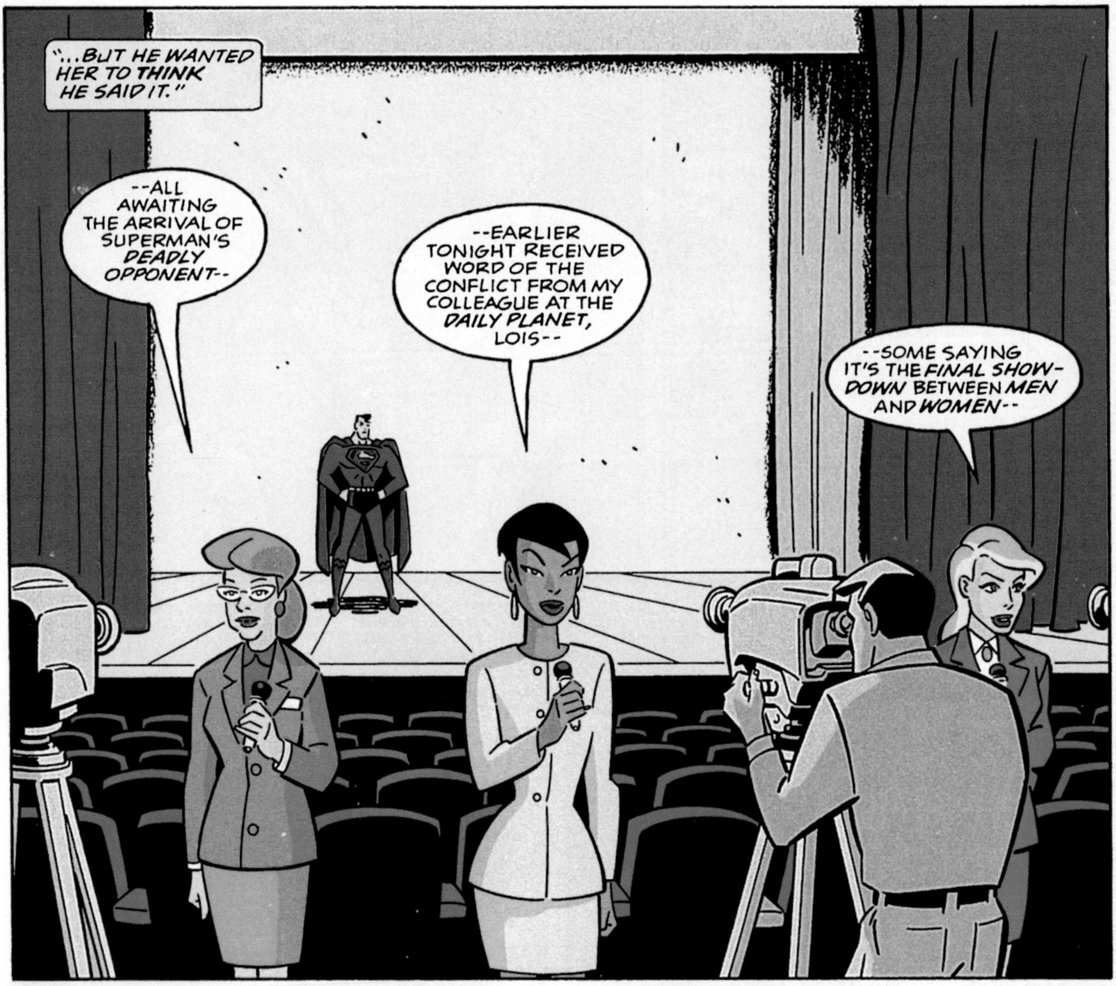
"...BUT HE WANTED HER TO THINK HE SAID IT."
--ALL AWAITING THE ARRIVAL OF SUPERMAN'S DEADLY OPPONENT--
--EARLIER TONIGHT RECEIVED WORD OF THE CONFLICT FROM MY COLLEAGUE AT THE DAILY PLANET, LOIS--
--SOME SAYING IT'S THE FINAL SHOW-DOWN BETWEEN MEN AND WOMEN--

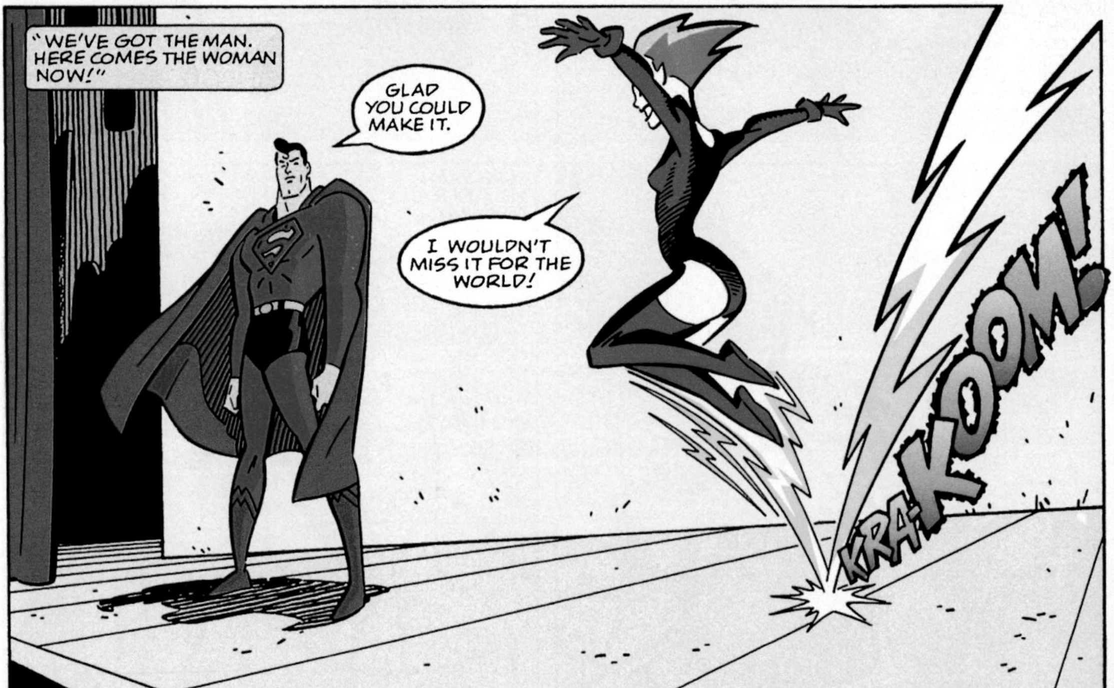
"WE'VE GOT THE MAN. HERE COMES THE WOMAN NOW!"
GLAD YOU COULD MAKE IT.
I WOULDN'T MISS IT FOR THE WORLD!
KRA-KOOM!

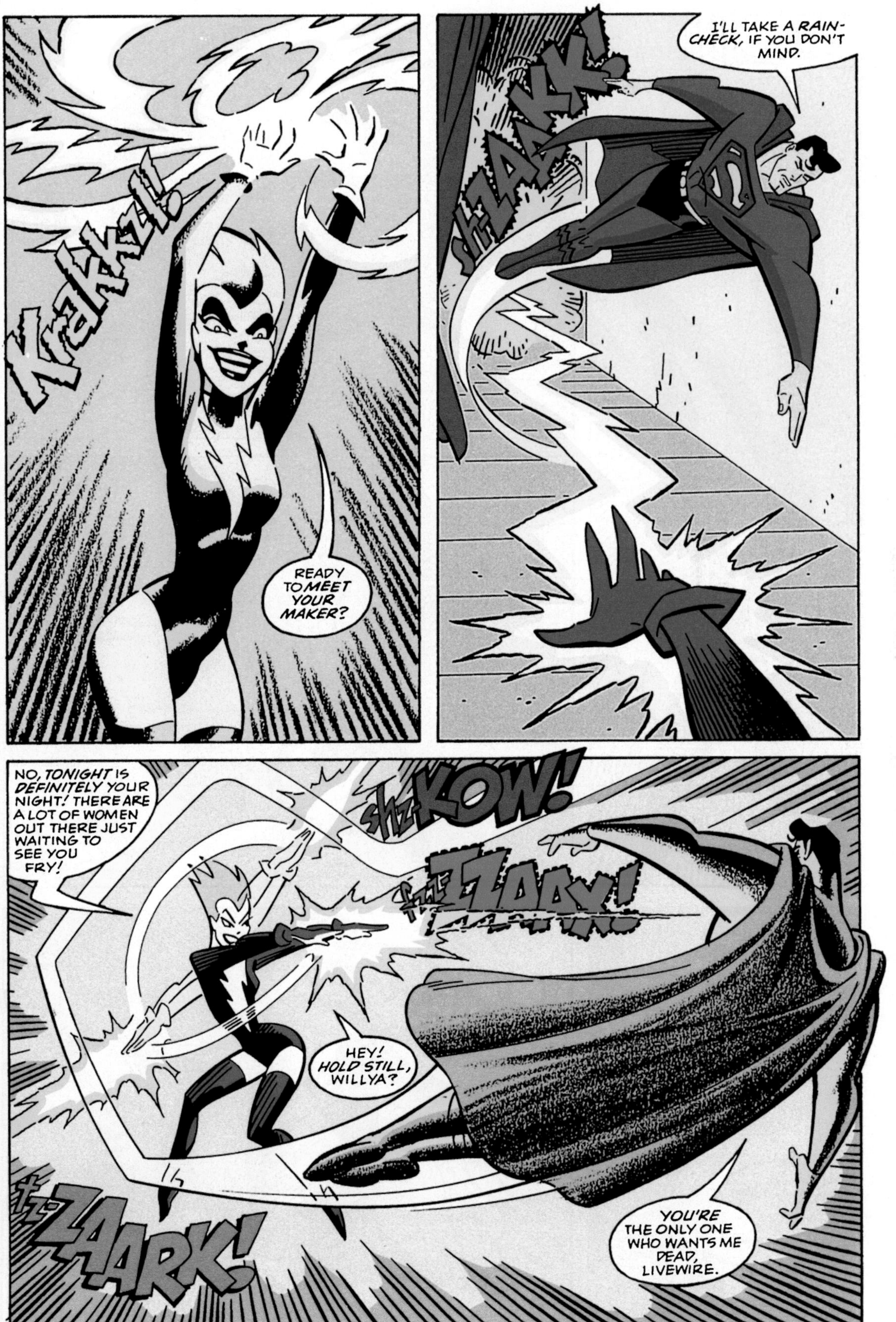

Krakkzz!!
READY TO MEET YOUR MAKER?
shzZAAKK!
I'LL TAKE A RAIN-CHECK, IF YOU DON'T MIND.
NO, TONIGHT IS DEFINITELY YOUR NIGHT! THERE ARE A LOT OF WOMEN OUT THERE JUST WAITING TO SEE YOU FRY!
shz-KOW!
HEY! HOLD STILL, WILLYA?
fzzZZAAK!
YOU'RE THE ONLY ONE WHO WANTS ME DEAD, LIVEWIRE.
fz-ZAARK!

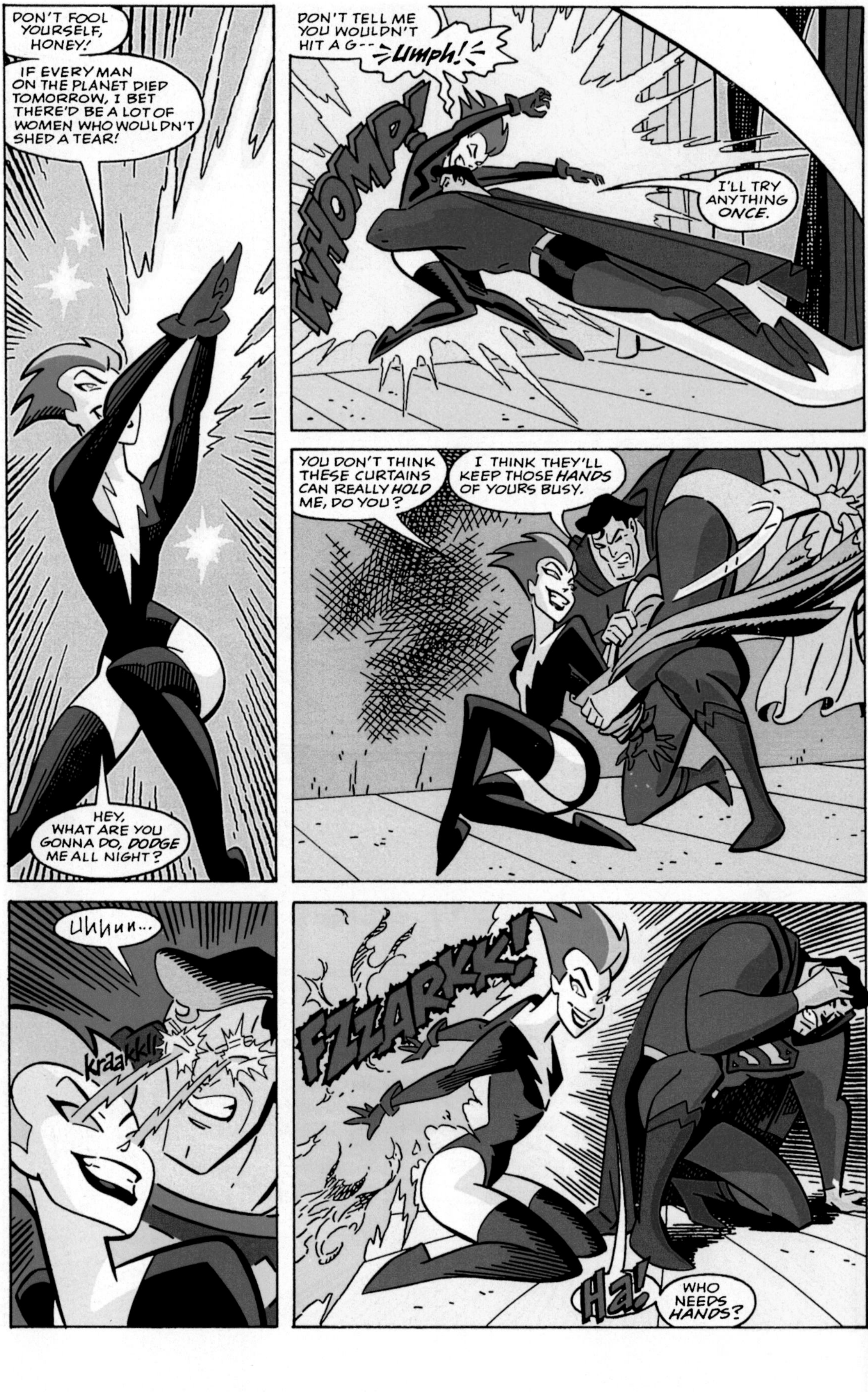
DON'T FOOL YOURSELF, HONEY!
IF EVERY MAN ON THE PLANET DIED TOMORROW, I BET THERE'D BE A LOT OF WOMEN WHO WOULDN'T SHED A TEAR!
HEY, WHAT ARE YOU GONNA DO, DODGE ME ALL NIGHT?
DON'T TELL ME YOU WOULDN'T HIT A G--
Umph!
WHOMP!
I'LL TRY ANYTHING ONCE.
YOU DON'T THINK THESE CURTAINS CAN REALLY HOLD ME, DO YOU?
I THINK THEY'LL KEEP THOSE HANDS OF YOURS BUSY.
Uhhuun...
kraakk!
FZZARKK!
Ha!
WHO NEEDS HANDS?

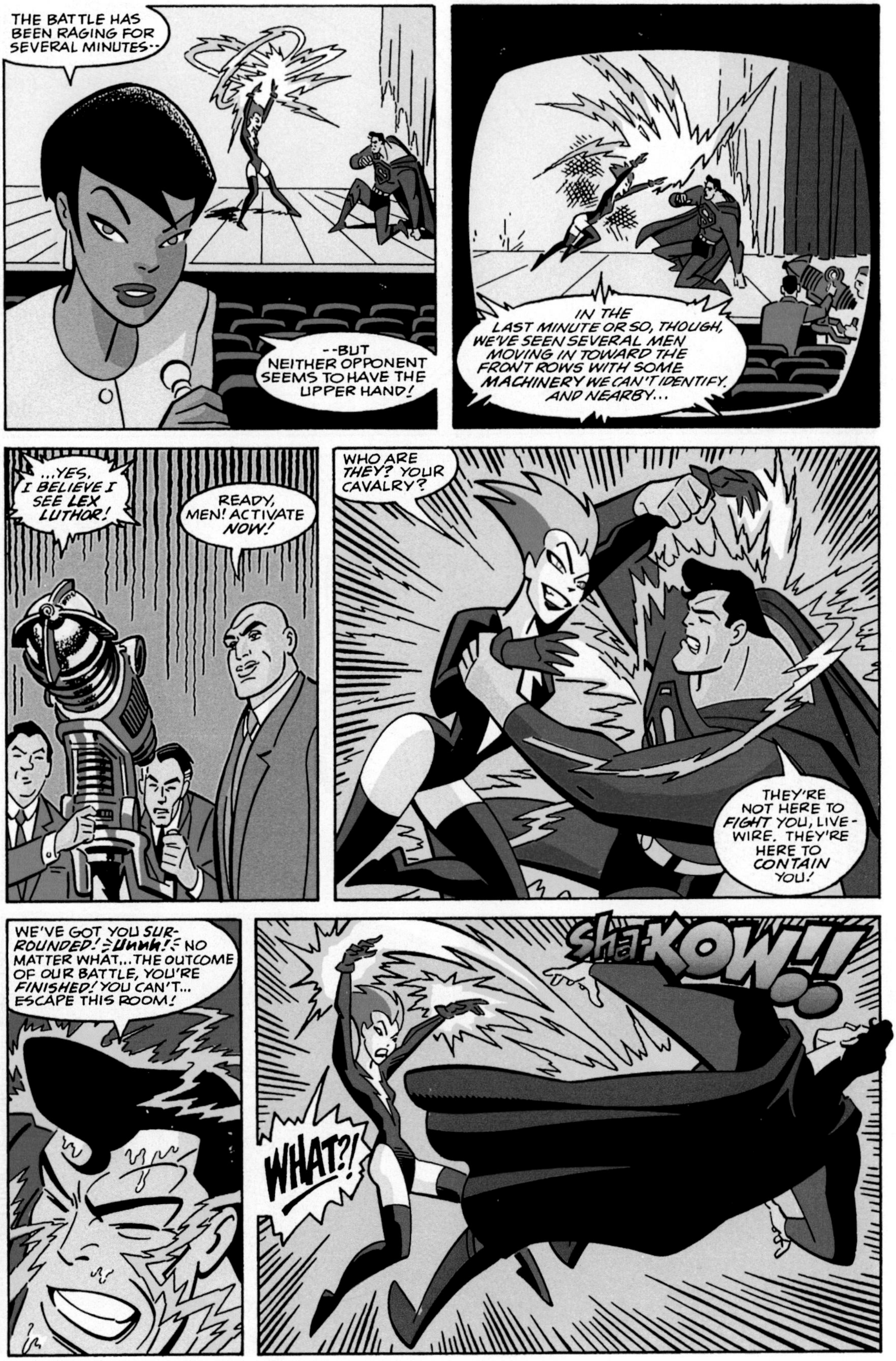
THE BATTLE HAS BEEN RAGING FOR SEVERAL MINUTES--
--BUT NEITHER OPPONENT SEEMS TO HAVE THE UPPER HAND!
IN THE LAST MINUTE OR SO, THOUGH, WE'VE SEEN SEVERAL MEN MOVING IN TOWARD THE FRONT ROWS WITH SOME MACHINERY WE CAN'T IDENTIFY. AND NEARBY...
...YES, I BELIEVE I SEE LEX LUTHOR!
READY, MEN! ACTIVATE NOW!
WHO ARE THEY? YOUR CAVALRY?
THEY'RE NOT HERE TO FIGHT YOU, LIVEWIRE. THEY'RE HERE TO CONTAIN YOU!
WE'VE GOT YOU SURROUNDED! -Unnh!- NO MATTER WHAT...THE OUTCOME OF OUR BATTLE, YOU'RE FINISHED! YOU CAN'T... ESCAPE THIS ROOM!
SHA-KOW!!
WHAT?!

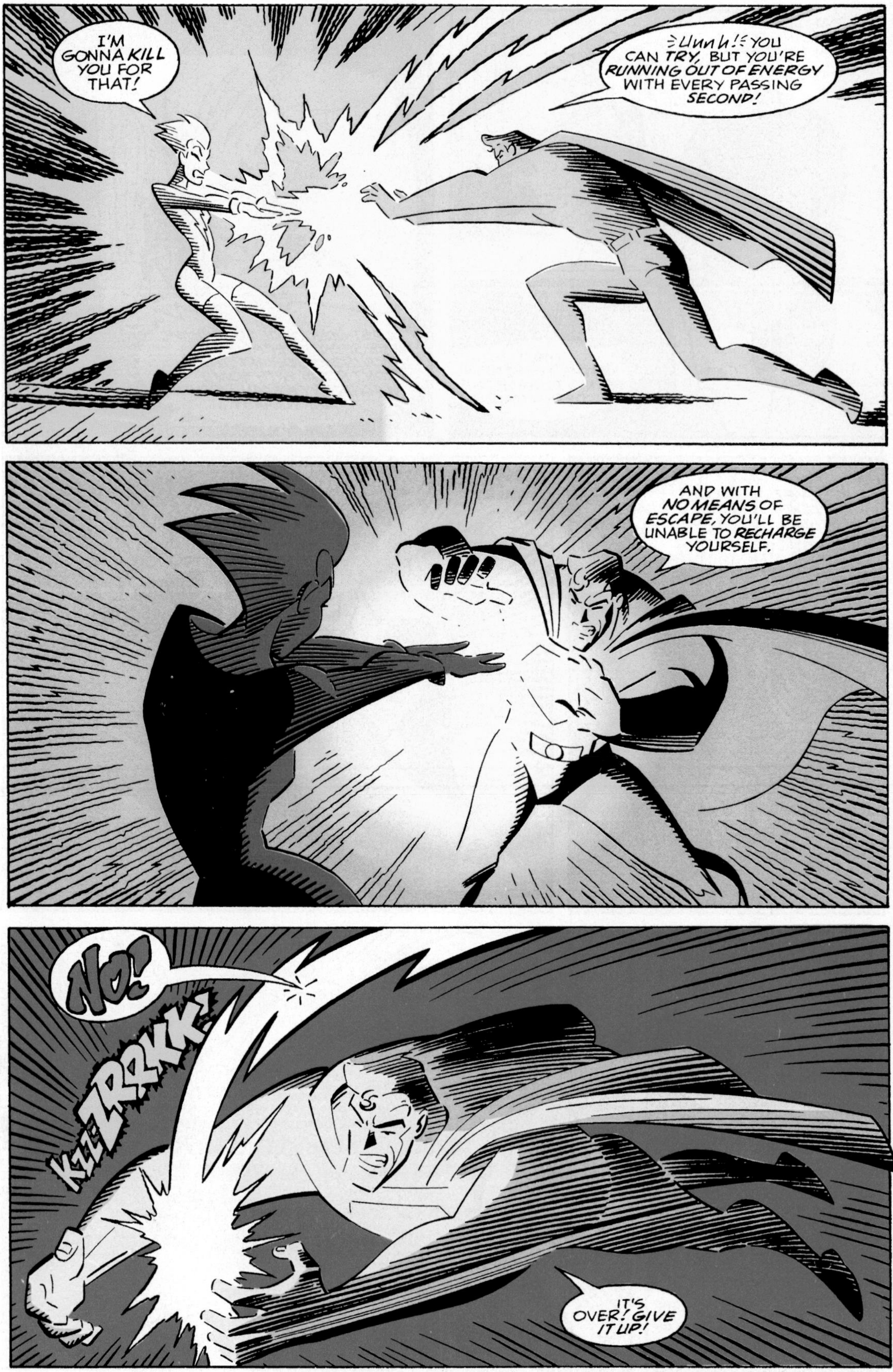
I'M GONNA KILL YOU FOR THAT!
=Unnh!= YOU CAN TRY, BUT YOU'RE RUNNING OUT OF ENERGY WITH EVERY PASSING SECOND!
AND WITH NO MEANS OF ESCAPE, YOU'LL BE UNABLE TO RECHARGE YOURSELF.
NO!
KZZZRRKK!
IT'S OVER! GIVE IT UP!

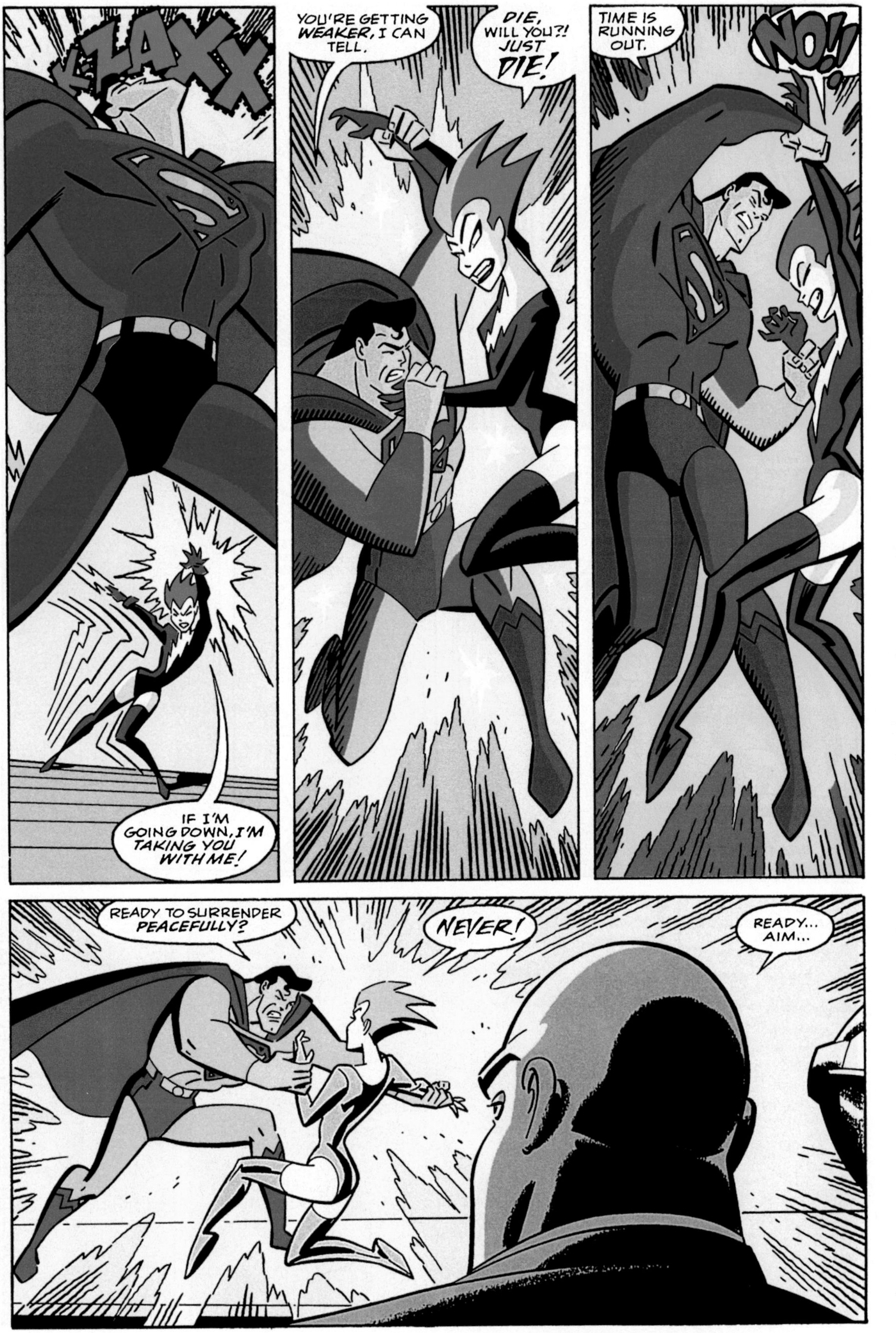

KZAXX
IF I'M GOING DOWN, I'M TAKING YOU WITH ME!
YOU'RE GETTING WEAKER, I CAN TELL.
DIE, WILL YOU?! JUST DIE!
TIME IS RUNNING OUT.
NO!!
READY TO SURRENDER PEACEFULLY?
NEVER!
READY... AIM...

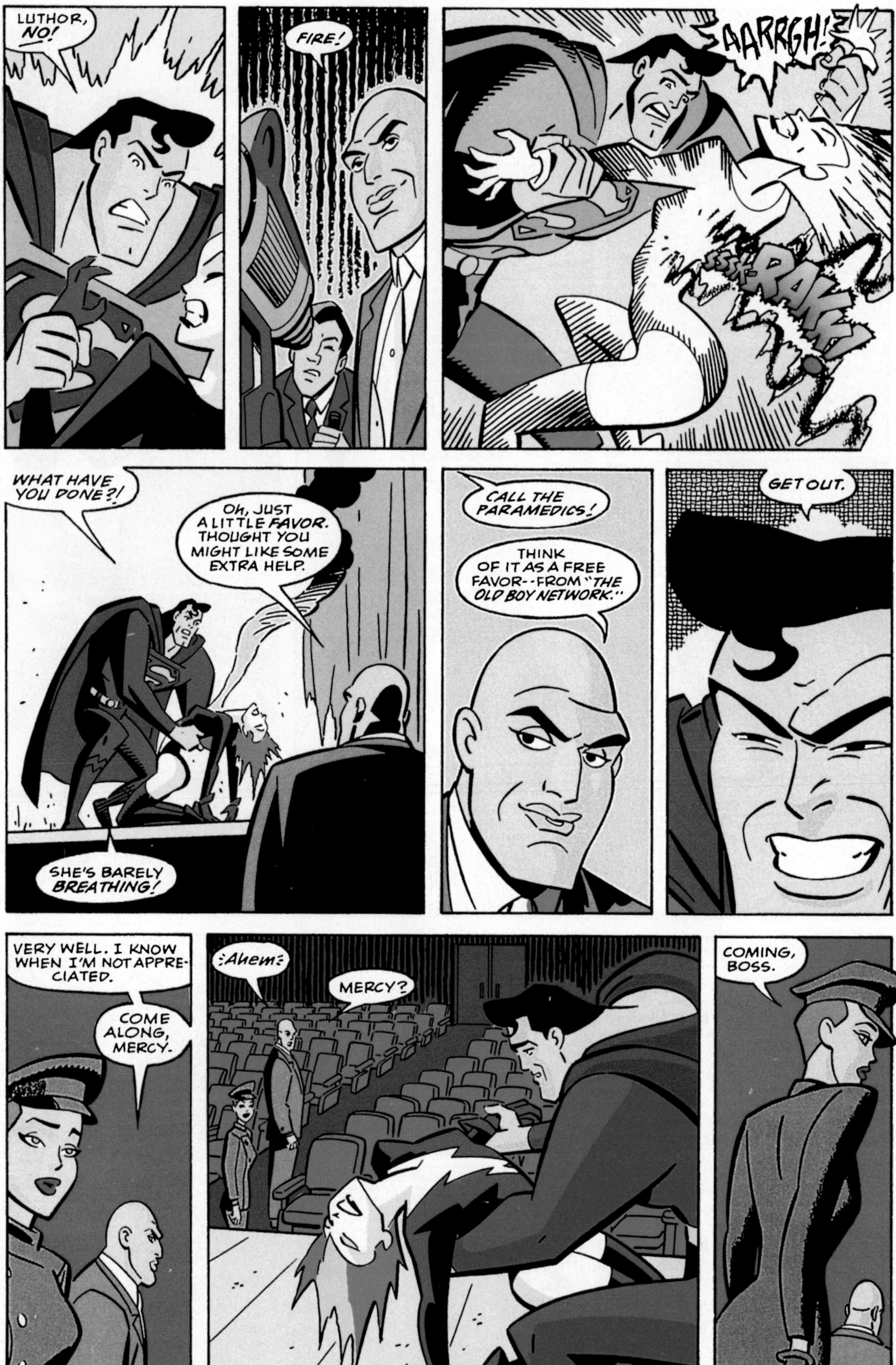
LUTHOR, NO!
FIRE!
AARRGH!
SSSK-RAKK!
WHAT HAVE YOU DONE?!
Oh, JUST A LITTLE FAVOR. THOUGHT YOU MIGHT LIKE SOME EXTRA HELP.
SHE'S BARELY BREATHING!
CALL THE PARAMEDICS!
THINK OF IT AS A FREE FAVOR--FROM "THE OLD BOY NETWORK."
GET OUT.
VERY WELL. I KNOW WHEN I'M NOT APPRECIATED.
COME ALONG, MERCY.
:Ahem:
MERCY?
COMING, BOSS.

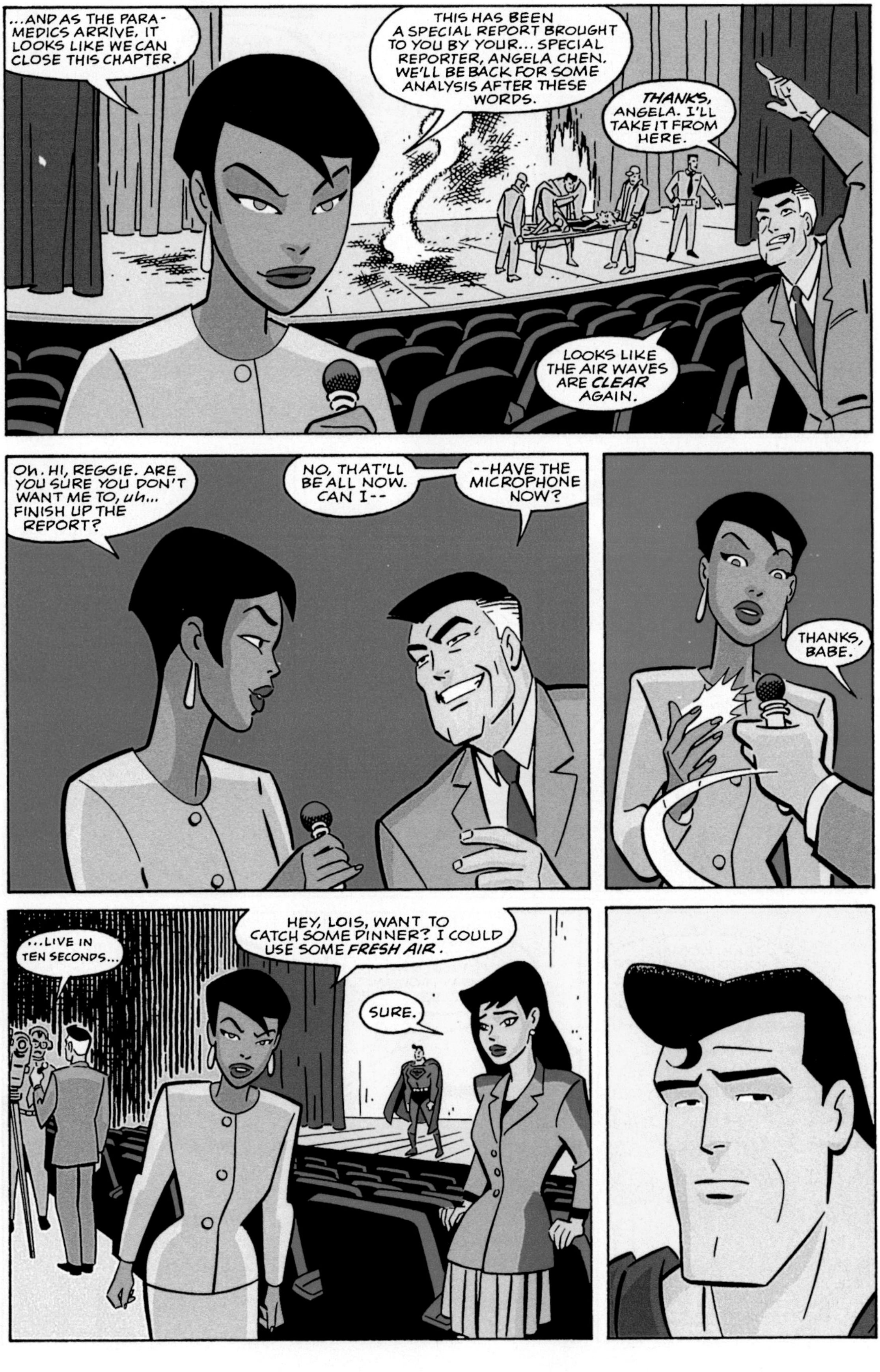

...AND AS THE PARA-MEDICS ARRIVE, IT LOOKS LIKE WE CAN CLOSE THIS CHAPTER.
THIS HAS BEEN A SPECIAL REPORT BROUGHT TO YOU BY YOUR... SPECIAL REPORTER, ANGELA CHEN. WE'LL BE BACK FOR SOME ANALYSIS AFTER THESE WORDS.
THANKS, ANGELA. I'LL TAKE IT FROM HERE.
LOOKS LIKE THE AIR WAVES ARE CLEAR AGAIN.
Oh. HI, REGGIE. ARE YOU SURE YOU DON'T WANT ME TO, uh... FINISH UP THE REPORT?
NO, THAT'LL BE ALL NOW. CAN I--
--HAVE THE MICROPHONE NOW?
THANKS, BABE.
...LIVE IN TEN SECONDS...
HEY, LOIS, WANT TO CATCH SOME DINNER? I COULD USE SOME FRESH AIR.
SURE.

SO WHO'S THE BROAD? IS IT REALLY THAT LIVEWIRE CHICK?
YEAH. NOT A BAD BODY FOR A "SUPER-VILLAIN," huh?
Ahh, I'VE SEEN BETTER.
BOY, THE NERVE OF THIS DAME! THINKING SHE COULD TAKE OVER THE AIR WAVES LIKE THAT!
YEAH, TYPICAL FEMINIST, ALWAYS TELLING US WHAT TO DO.
Y'KNOW, IT REALLY GOES TA SHOW YOU WHAT HAPPENS WHEN WOMEN GET A LITTLE POWER-- IT GOES TO THEIR HEADS!
YEAH, WOMEN SHOULD STAY WHERE THEY BELONG--HOME, TAKING CARE OF THE KIDS.
YEAH, YOU SAID IT. IT'S A MAN'S WORLD. THAT'S THE WAY IT OUGHT TO BE.
YESSIR. IT'S A MAN'S WORLD.
The End

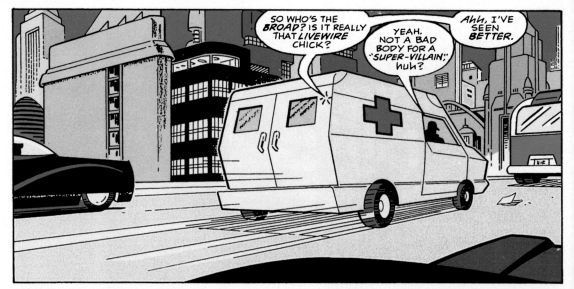

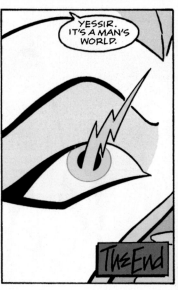

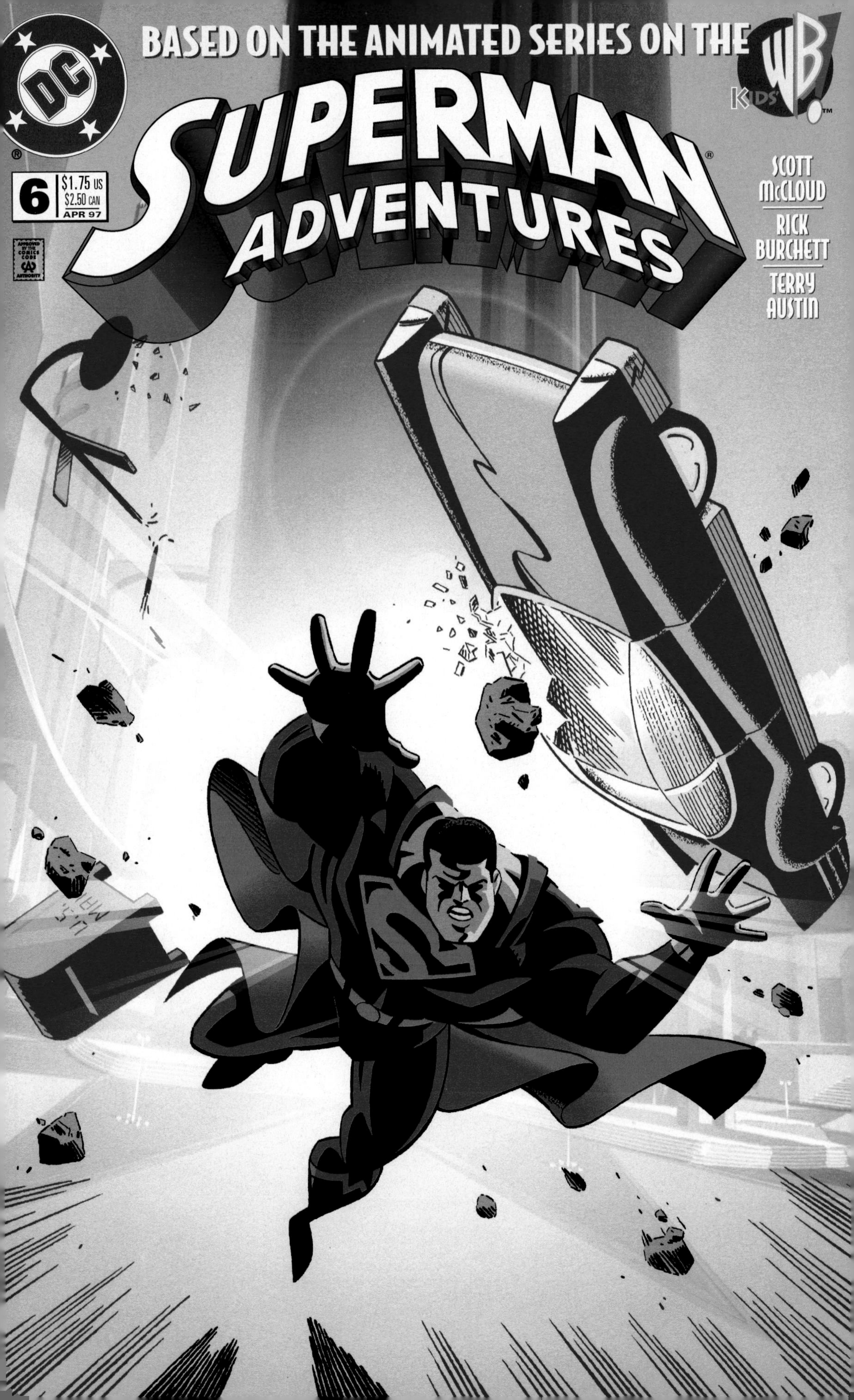
BASED ON THE ANIMATED SERIES ON THE
DC
KIDS' WB!
SUPERMAN ADVENTURES
6
$1.75 US
$2.50 CAN
APR 97
APPROVED BY THE COMICS CODE AUTHORITY
SCOTT McCLOUD
RICK BURCHETT
TERRY AUSTIN

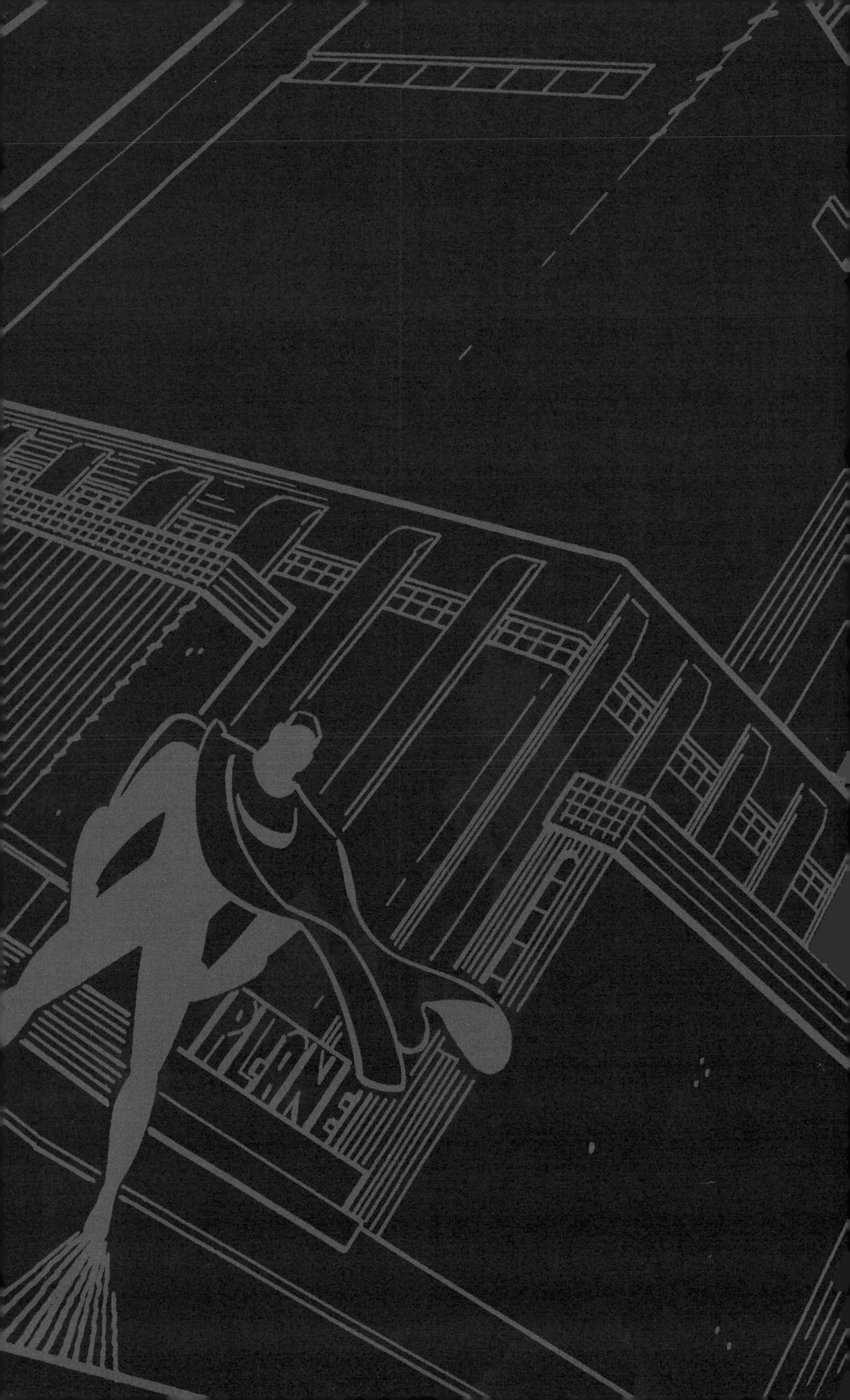

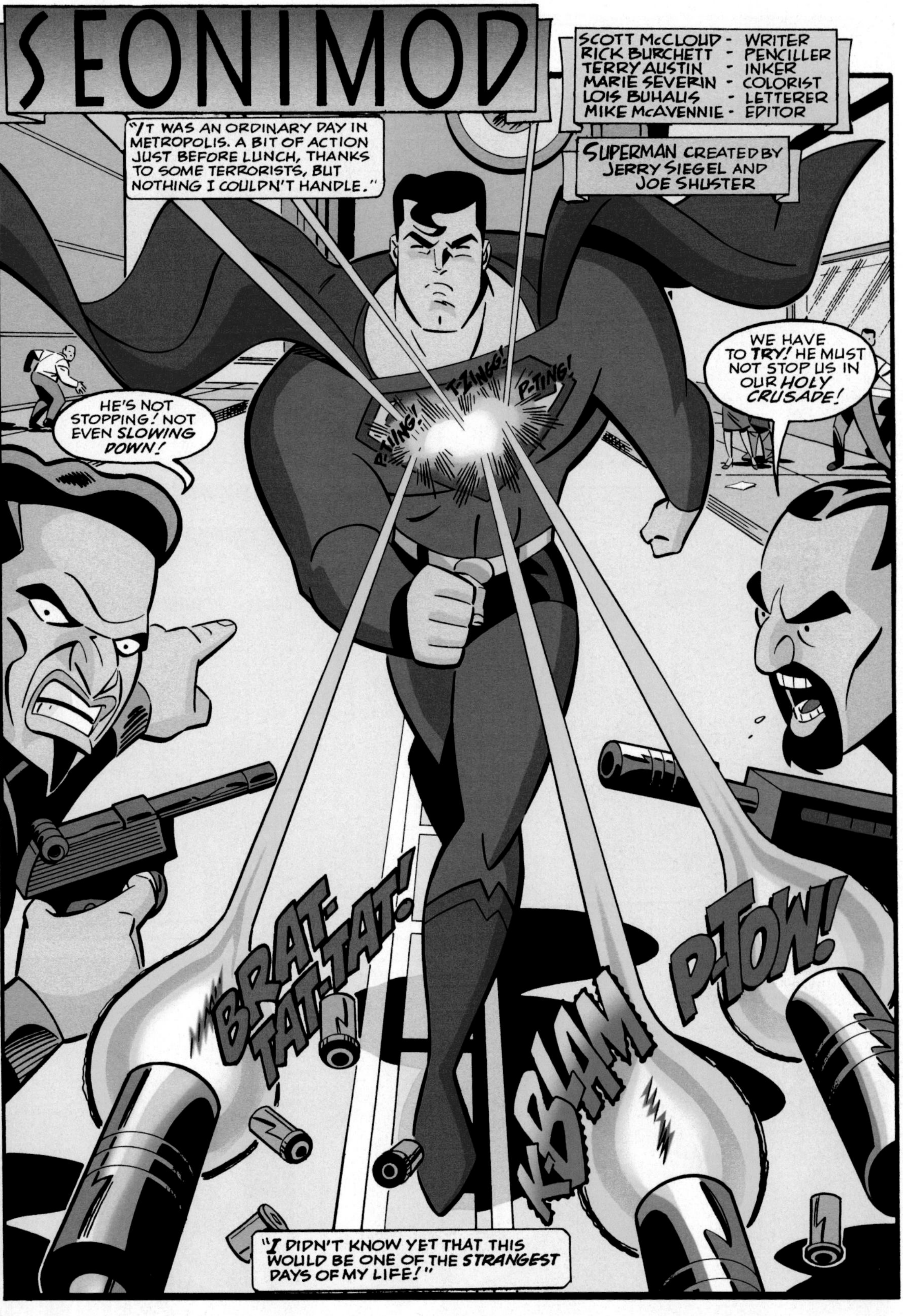
SEONIMOD
SCOTT McCLOUD - WRITER
RICK BURCHETT - PENCILLER
TERRY AUSTIN - INKER
MARIE SEVERIN - COLORIST
LOIS BUHALIS - LETTERER
MIKE McAVENNIE - EDITOR
SUPERMAN CREATED BY JERRY SIEGEL AND JOE SHUSTER
"IT WAS AN ORDINARY DAY IN METROPOLIS. A BIT OF ACTION JUST BEFORE LUNCH, THANKS TO SOME TERRORISTS, BUT NOTHING I COULDN'T HANDLE."
HE'S NOT STOPPING! NOT EVEN SLOWING DOWN!
WE HAVE TO TRY! HE MUST NOT STOP US IN OUR HOLY CRUSADE!
P-TING!
T-ZINGG!
P-TING!
BRAT-TAT-TAT!
K-BLAM
P-TOW!
"I DIDN'T KNOW YET THAT THIS WOULD BE ONE OF THE STRANGEST DAYS OF MY LIFE!"

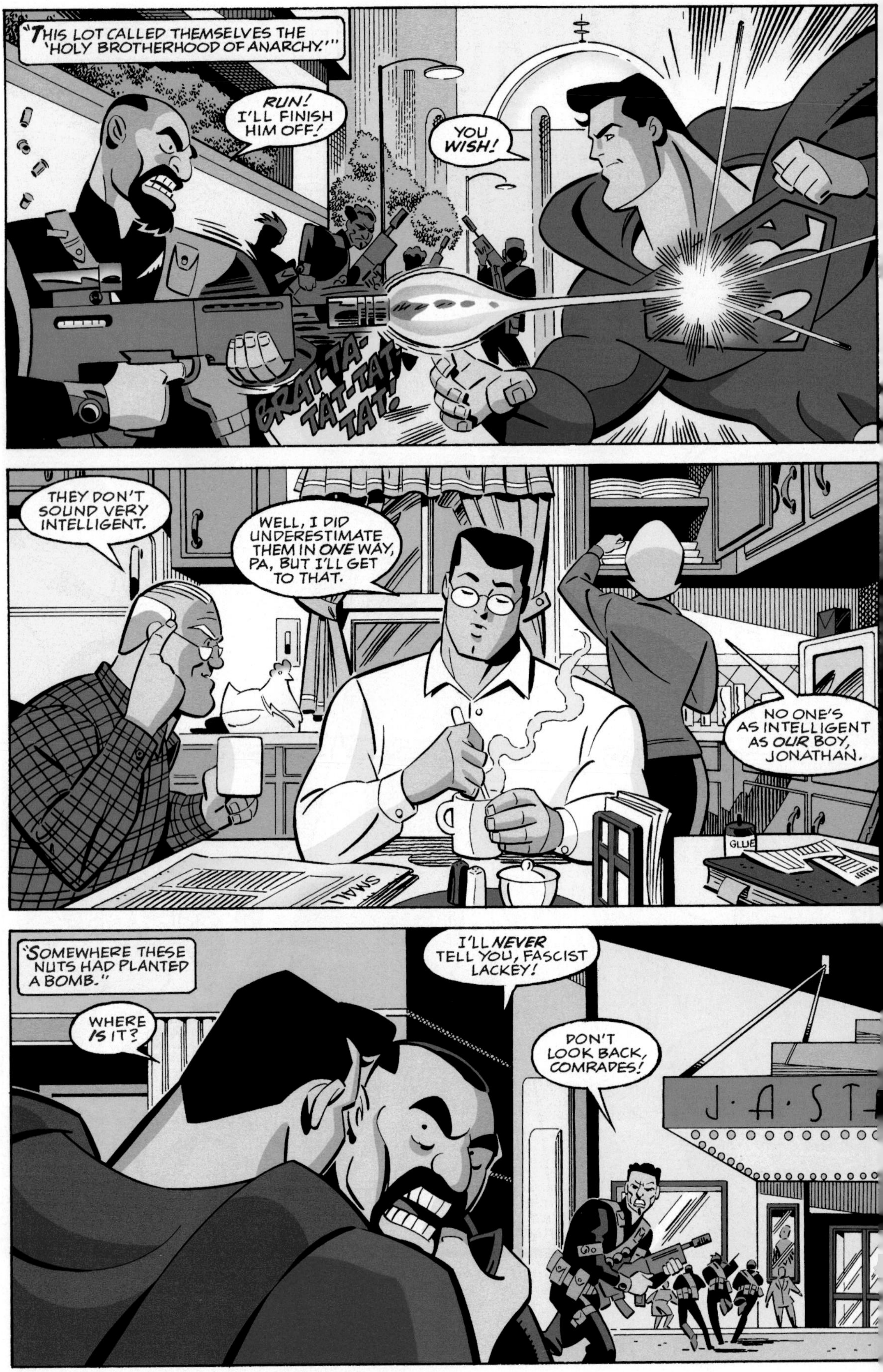

"THIS LOT CALLED THEMSELVES THE 'HOLY BROTHERHOOD OF ANARCHY.'"
RUN! I'LL FINISH HIM OFF!
YOU WISH!
BRAT-TA-TAT-TAT-TAT!
THEY DON'T SOUND VERY INTELLIGENT.
WELL, I DID UNDERESTIMATE THEM IN ONE WAY, PA, BUT I'LL GET TO THAT.
NO ONE'S AS INTELLIGENT AS OUR BOY, JONATHAN.
GLUE
"SOMEWHERE THESE NUTS HAD PLANTED A BOMB."
I'LL NEVER TELL YOU, FASCIST LACKEY!
WHERE IS IT?
DON'T LOOK BACK, COMRADES!

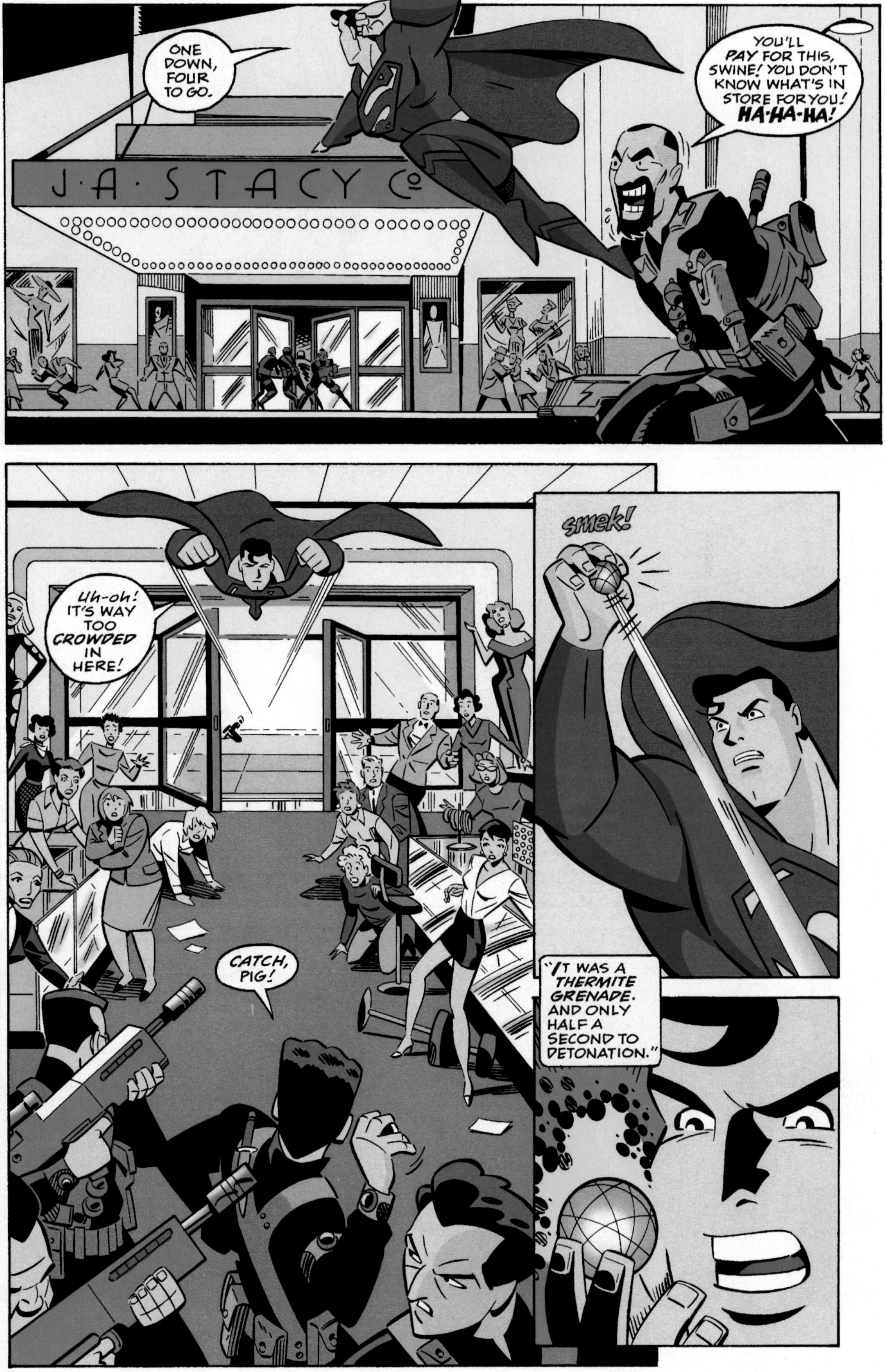
ONE DOWN, FOUR TO GO.
YOU'LL PAY FOR THIS, SWINE! YOU DON'T KNOW WHAT'S IN STORE FOR YOU! HA-HA-HA!
J·A·STACY Co
Uh-oh! IT'S WAY TOO CROWDED IN HERE!
CATCH, PIG!
smek!
"IT WAS A THERMITE GRENADE. AND ONLY HALF A SECOND TO DETONATION."

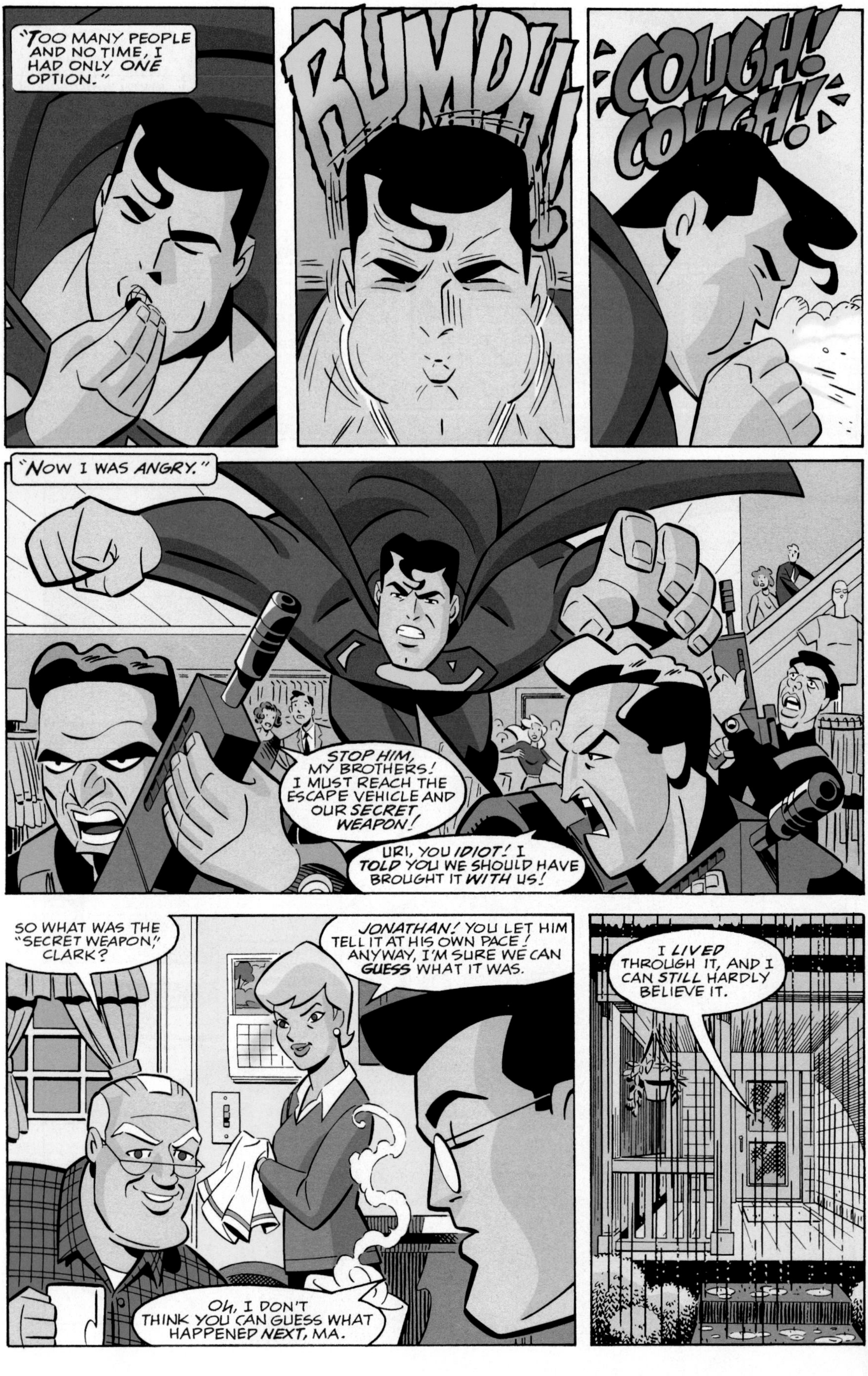
"TOO MANY PEOPLE AND NO TIME, I HAD ONLY ONE OPTION."
BUMPH!
COUGH! COUGH!
"NOW I WAS ANGRY."
STOP HIM, MY BROTHERS! I MUST REACH THE ESCAPE VEHICLE AND OUR SECRET WEAPON!
URI, YOU IDIOT! I TOLD YOU WE SHOULD HAVE BROUGHT IT WITH US!
SO WHAT WAS THE "SECRET WEAPON," CLARK?
JONATHAN! YOU LET HIM TELL IT AT HIS OWN PACE! ANYWAY, I'M SURE WE CAN GUESS WHAT IT WAS.
OH, I DON'T THINK YOU CAN GUESS WHAT HAPPENED NEXT, MA.
I LIVED THROUGH IT, AND I CAN STILL HARDLY BELIEVE IT.

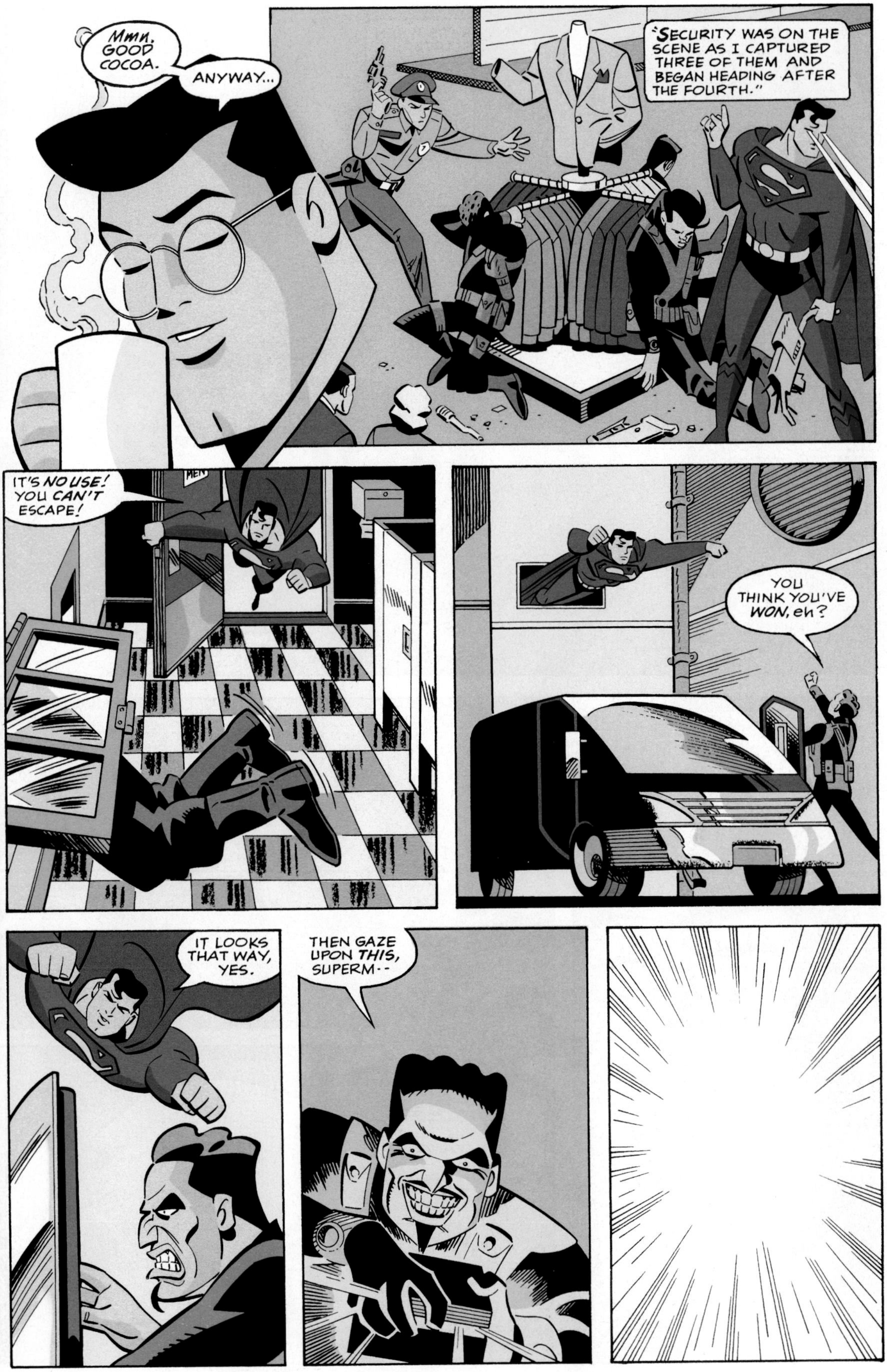
Mmm, GOOD COCOA.
ANYWAY...
"SECURITY WAS ON THE SCENE AS I CAPTURED THREE OF THEM AND BEGAN HEADING AFTER THE FOURTH."
IT'S NO USE! YOU CAN'T ESCAPE!
MEN
YOU THINK YOU'VE WON, eh?
IT LOOKS THAT WAY, YES.
THEN GAZE UPON THIS, SUPERM--

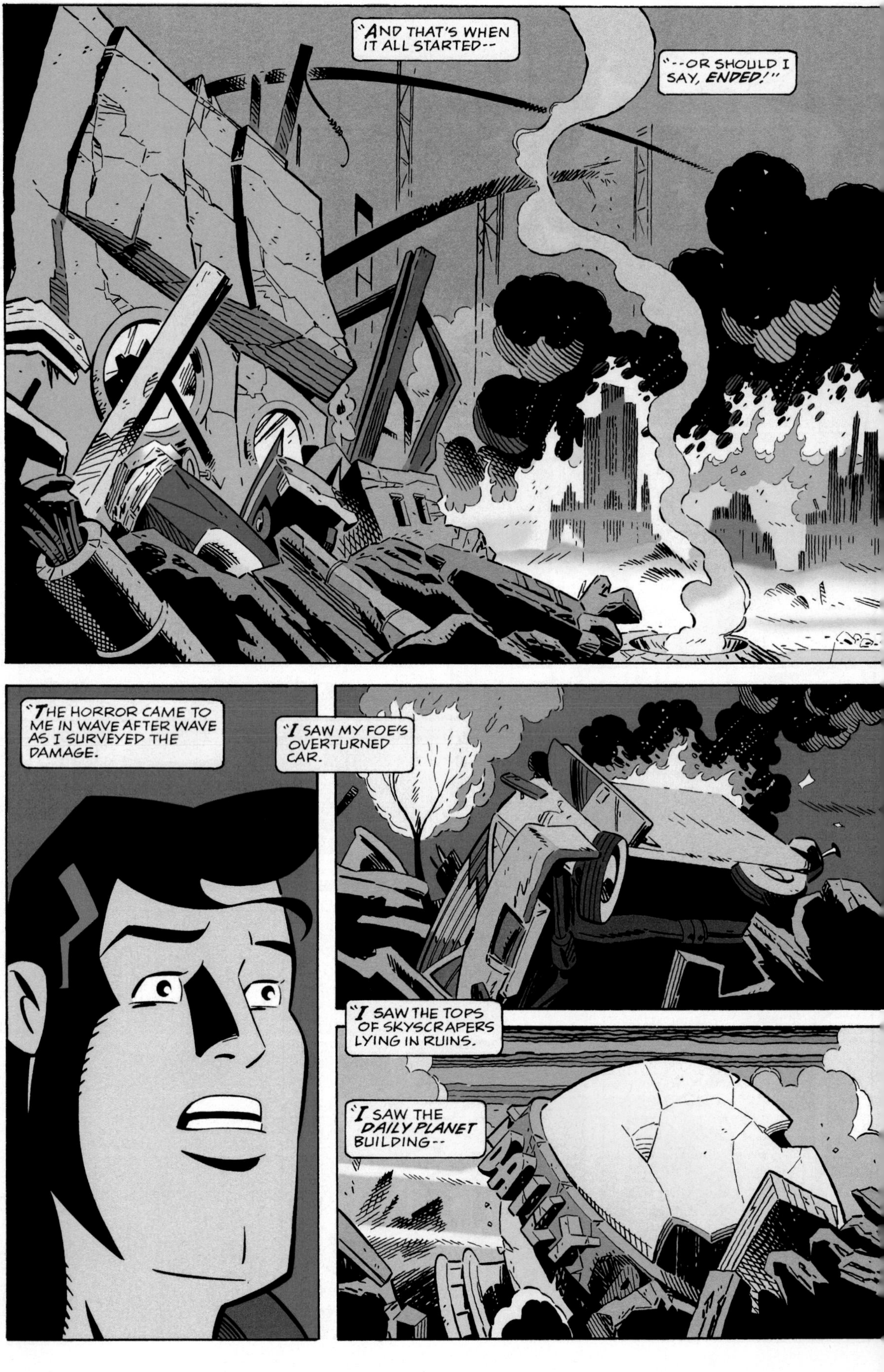
"AND THAT'S WHEN IT ALL STARTED--
"--OR SHOULD I SAY, ENDED!"
"THE HORROR CAME TO ME IN WAVE AFTER WAVE AS I SURVEYED THE DAMAGE.
"I SAW MY FOE'S OVERTURNED CAR.
"I SAW THE TOPS OF SKYSCRAPERS LYING IN RUINS.
"I SAW THE DAILY PLANET BUILDING--

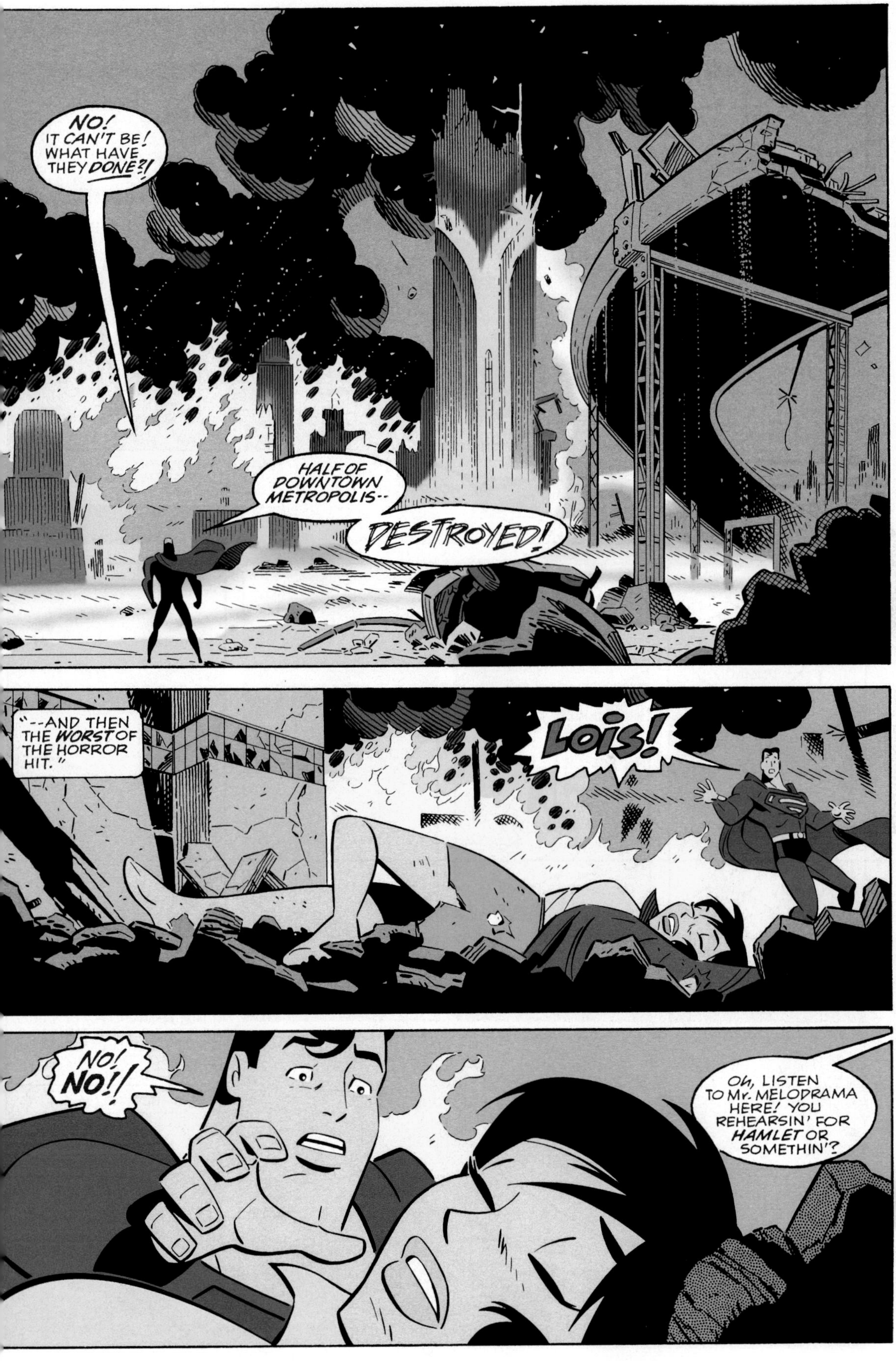
NO! IT CAN'T BE! WHAT HAVE THEY DONE?!
HALF OF DOWNTOWN METROPOLIS--
DESTROYED!
"--AND THEN THE WORST OF THE HORROR HIT."
LOIS!
NO! NO!!
OH, LISTEN TO MR. MELODRAMA HERE! YOU REHEARSIN' FOR HAMLET OR SOMETHIN'?

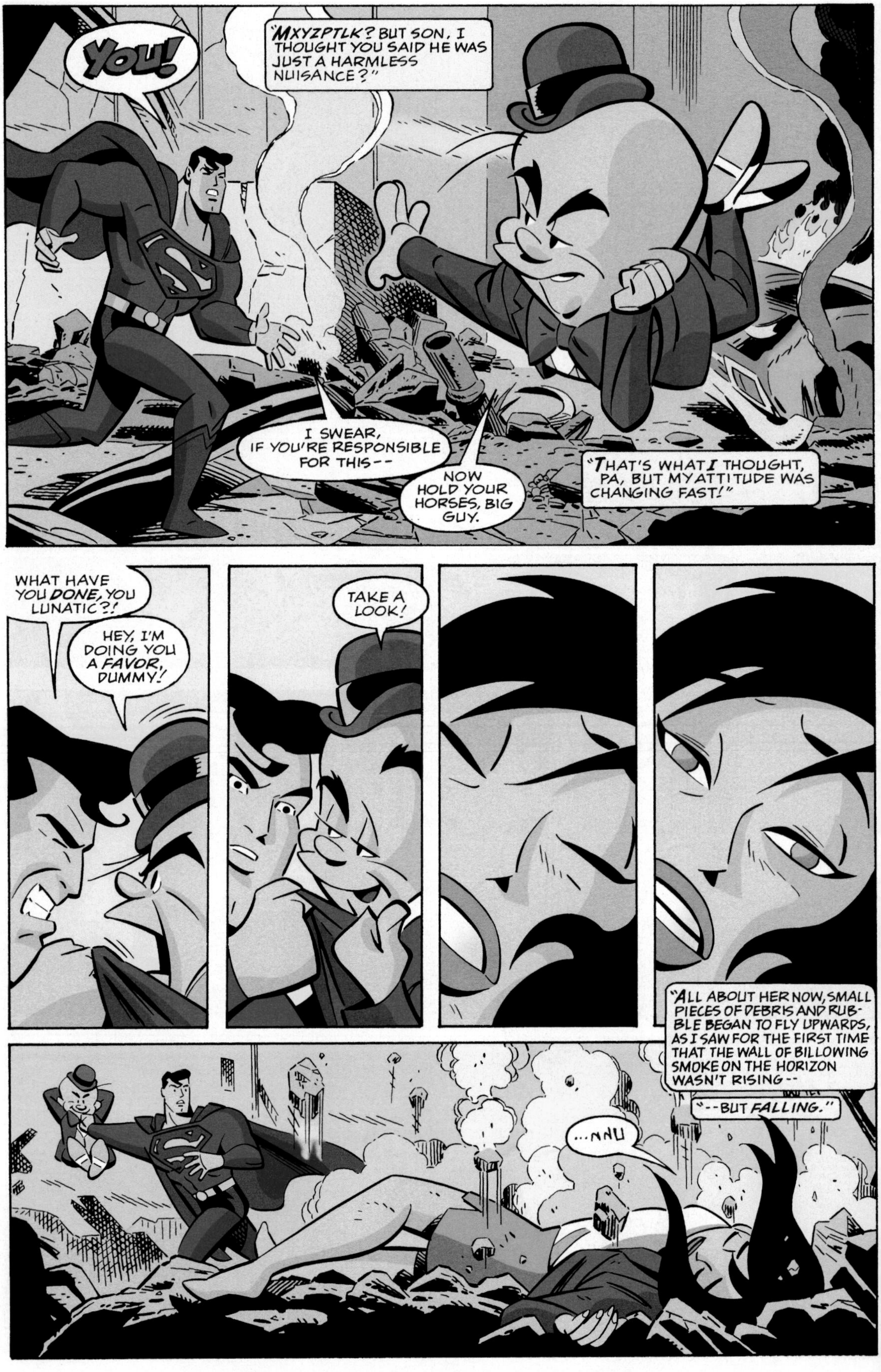
YOU!
"MXYZPTLK? BUT SON, I THOUGHT YOU SAID HE WAS JUST A HARMLESS NUISANCE?"
I SWEAR, IF YOU'RE RESPONSIBLE FOR THIS--
NOW HOLD YOUR HORSES, BIG GUY.
"THAT'S WHAT I THOUGHT, PA, BUT MY ATTITUDE WAS CHANGING FAST!"
WHAT HAVE YOU DONE, YOU LUNATIC?!
HEY, I'M DOING YOU A FAVOR, DUMMY!
TAKE A LOOK!
"ALL ABOUT HER NOW, SMALL PIECES OF DEBRIS AND RUB-BLE BEGAN TO FLY UPWARDS, AS I SAW FOR THE FIRST TIME THAT THE WALL OF BILLOWING SMOKE ON THE HORIZON WASN'T RISING--
"--BUT FALLING."
...NNU

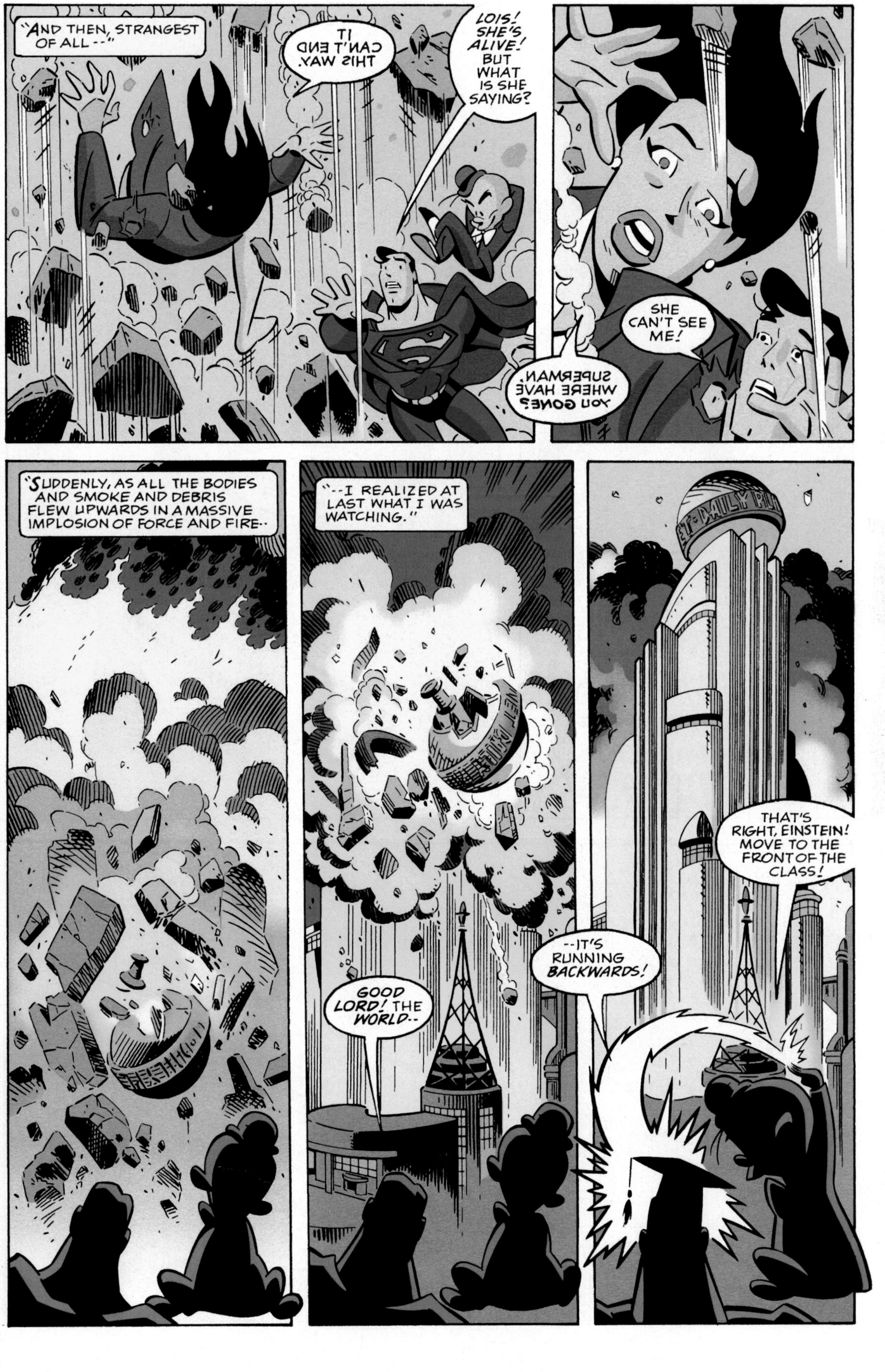
"AND THEN, STRANGEST OF ALL--"
IT CAN'T END THIS WAY.
LOIS! SHE'S ALIVE! BUT WHAT IS SHE SAYING?
SUPERMAN, WHERE HAVE YOU GONE?
SHE CAN'T SEE ME!
"SUDDENLY, AS ALL THE BODIES AND SMOKE AND DEBRIS FLEW UPWARDS IN A MASSIVE IMPLOSION OF FORCE AND FIRE..
"--I REALIZED AT LAST WHAT I WAS WATCHING."
GOOD LORD! THE WORLD..
--IT'S RUNNING BACKWARDS!
THAT'S RIGHT, EINSTEIN! MOVE TO THE FRONT OF THE CLASS!

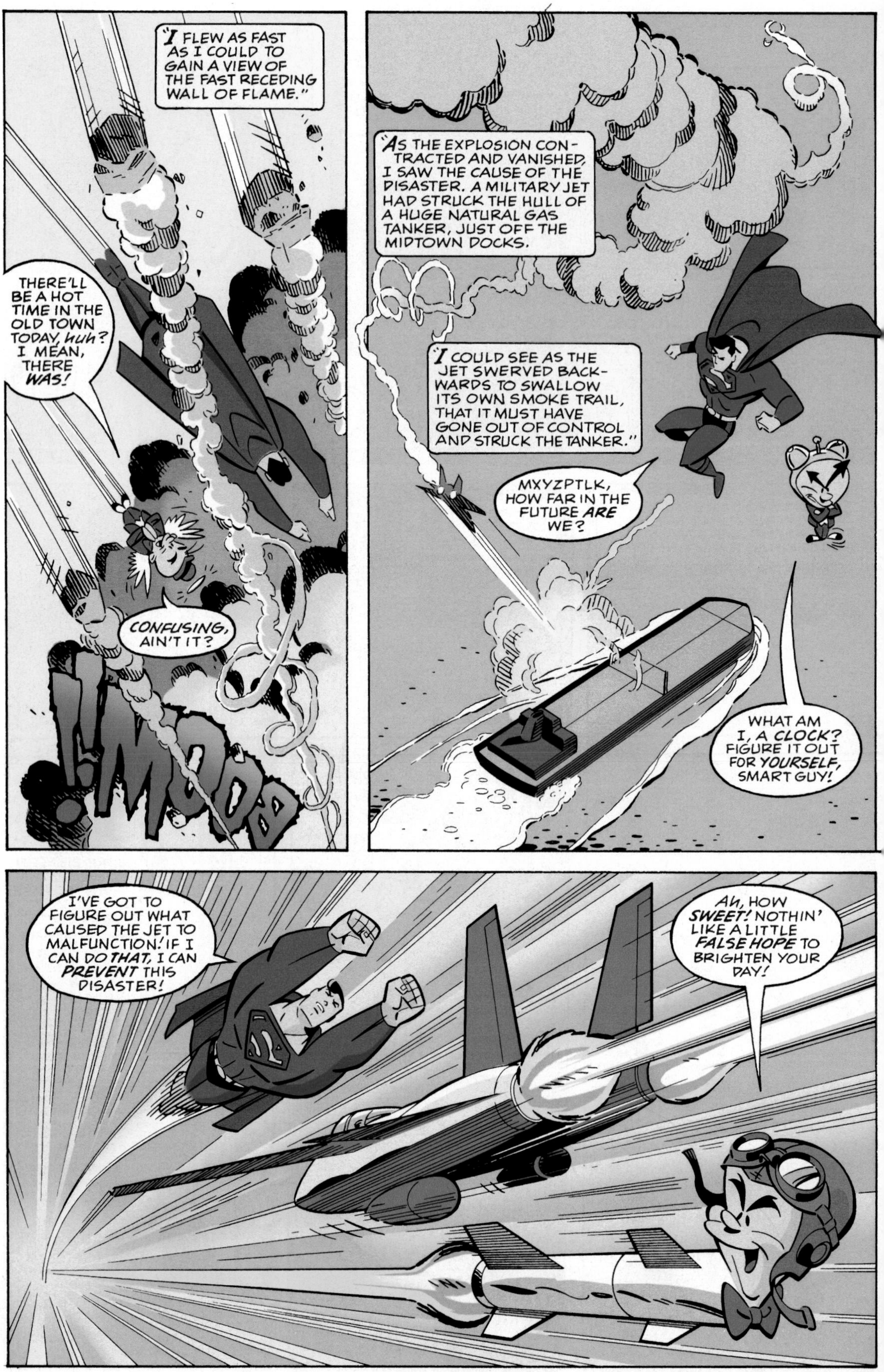
"I FLEW AS FAST AS I COULD TO GAIN A VIEW OF THE FAST RECEDING WALL OF FLAME."
THERE'LL BE A HOT TIME IN THE OLD TOWN TODAY, *huh*? I MEAN, THERE *WAS*!
CONFUSING, AIN'T IT?
!MOOB
"AS THE EXPLOSION CONTRACTED AND VANISHED, I SAW THE CAUSE OF THE DISASTER. A MILITARY JET HAD STRUCK THE HULL OF A HUGE NATURAL GAS TANKER, JUST OFF THE MIDTOWN DOCKS.
"I COULD SEE AS THE JET SWERVED BACKWARDS TO SWALLOW ITS OWN SMOKE TRAIL, THAT IT MUST HAVE GONE OUT OF CONTROL AND STRUCK THE TANKER."
MXYZPTLK, HOW FAR IN THE FUTURE *ARE* WE?
WHAT AM I, A *CLOCK*? FIGURE IT OUT FOR *YOURSELF*, SMART GUY!
I'VE GOT TO FIGURE OUT WHAT CAUSED THE JET TO MALFUNCTION! IF I CAN DO *THAT*, I CAN *PREVENT* THIS DISASTER!
Ah, HOW *SWEET!* NOTHIN' LIKE A LITTLE *FALSE HOPE* TO BRIGHTEN YOUR DAY!

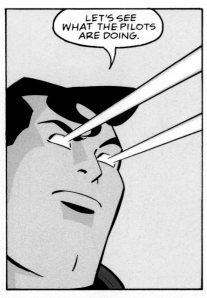

LET'S SEE WHAT THE PILOTS ARE DOING.

"CLEARLY, THE PILOTS DIDN'T HAVE A CLUE WHY THEIR JET WAS OUT OF CONTROL."

"THEN I NOTICED A BREAK IN THE HULL NEAR THE FUEL TANKS."

AN *EXPLOSION* IN THE HULL! *THIS* IS WHERE IT ALL STARTED TO GO WRONG!

"STARTED"?

YOU HAVEN'T EVEN *STARTED* TO FIGURE OUT WHERE IT STARTED, MORON!

LOOKS LIKE IT WAS JUST A ROUTINE TRAINING EXERCISE.

OH, YES. DEFINITELY.

STUPID IS ROUTINE IN THIS DIMENSION, RIGHT? ROUTINE *STUPID* EXERCISE.

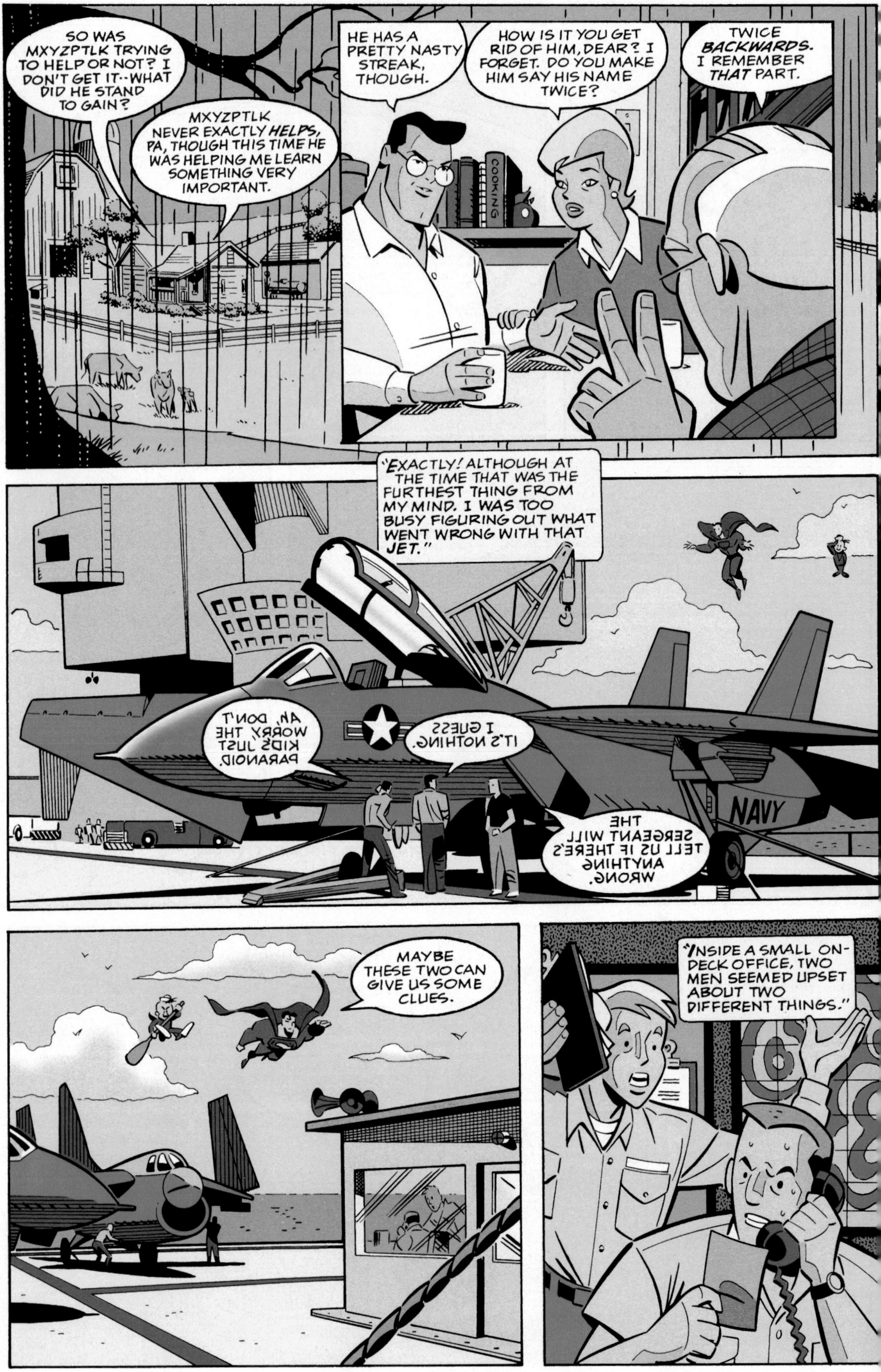
SO WAS MXYZPTLK TRYING TO HELP OR NOT? I DON'T GET IT--WHAT DID HE STAND TO GAIN?
MXYZPTLK NEVER EXACTLY HELPS, PA, THOUGH THIS TIME HE WAS HELPING ME LEARN SOMETHING VERY IMPORTANT.
HE HAS A PRETTY NASTY STREAK, THOUGH.
HOW IS IT YOU GET RID OF HIM, DEAR? I FORGET. DO YOU MAKE HIM SAY HIS NAME TWICE?
TWICE BACKWARDS. I REMEMBER THAT PART.
COOKING
"EXACTLY! ALTHOUGH AT THE TIME THAT WAS THE FURTHEST THING FROM MY MIND. I WAS TOO BUSY FIGURING OUT WHAT WENT WRONG WITH THAT JET."
AH, DON'T WORRY. THE KID'S JUST PARANOID.
I GUESS IT'S NOTHING.
THE SERGEANT WILL TELL US IF THERE'S ANYTHING WRONG.
NAVY
MAYBE THESE TWO CAN GIVE US SOME CLUES.
"INSIDE A SMALL ON-DECK OFFICE, TWO MEN SEEMED UPSET ABOUT TWO DIFFERENT THINGS."

"I PIECED TOGETHER ENOUGH OF THEIR CONVERSATION TO FIGURE OUT THAT THE WRONG FUEL TANK HAD BEEN PLACED IN THE JET, AND THAT THE YOUNG NAVY WORKER HAD BEEN THE ONLY ONE TO NOTICE IT."

"WHY THEN WASN'T HIS SUPERIOR LISTENING, I WONDERED?"

SIR, THERE'S SOMETHING WRONG, I'M SURE OF IT!

"SOMETHING WAS GOING ON, SOMETHING TOO IMPORTANT TO WASTE TIME ON SUBORDINATES."

"LUCKILY, I SPOTTED A CLUE..."

Galaxy Blvd and 49th St

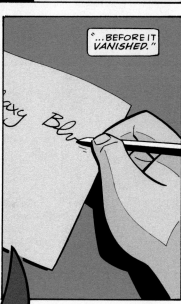

"...BEFORE IT VANISHED."

WHATEVER DISTRACTED THAT MAN MUST HAVE BEEN PRETTY SERIOUS.

MAYBE THE EXPLOSION WASN'T THE ONLY TRAGEDY IN THIS CHAIN OF DOMINOES.

Ooh! BRILLIANT DEDUCTION, WATSON.

NOT!

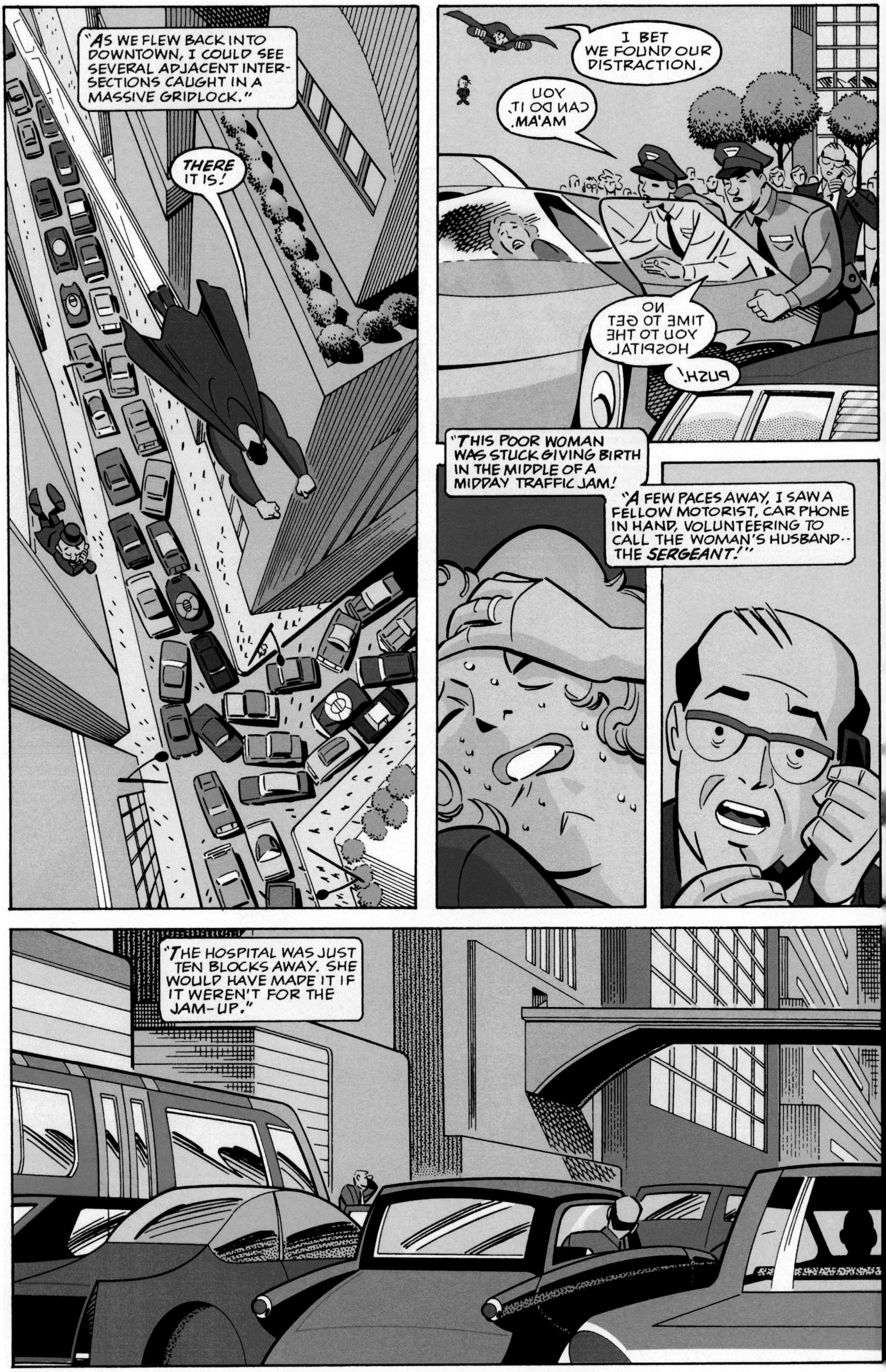
"AS WE FLEW BACK INTO DOWNTOWN, I COULD SEE SEVERAL ADJACENT INTER-SECTIONS CAUGHT IN A MASSIVE GRIDLOCK."
THERE IT IS!
I BET WE FOUND OUR DISTRACTION.
YOU CAN DO IT, MA'AM.
NO TIME TO GET YOU TO THE HOSPITAL.
PUSH!
"THIS POOR WOMAN WAS STUCK GIVING BIRTH IN THE MIDDLE OF A MIDDAY TRAFFIC JAM!
"A FEW PACES AWAY, I SAW A FELLOW MOTORIST, CAR PHONE IN HAND, VOLUNTEERING TO CALL THE WOMAN'S HUSBAND-- THE SERGEANT!"
"THE HOSPITAL WAS JUST TEN BLOCKS AWAY. SHE WOULD HAVE MADE IT IF IT WEREN'T FOR THE JAM-UP."

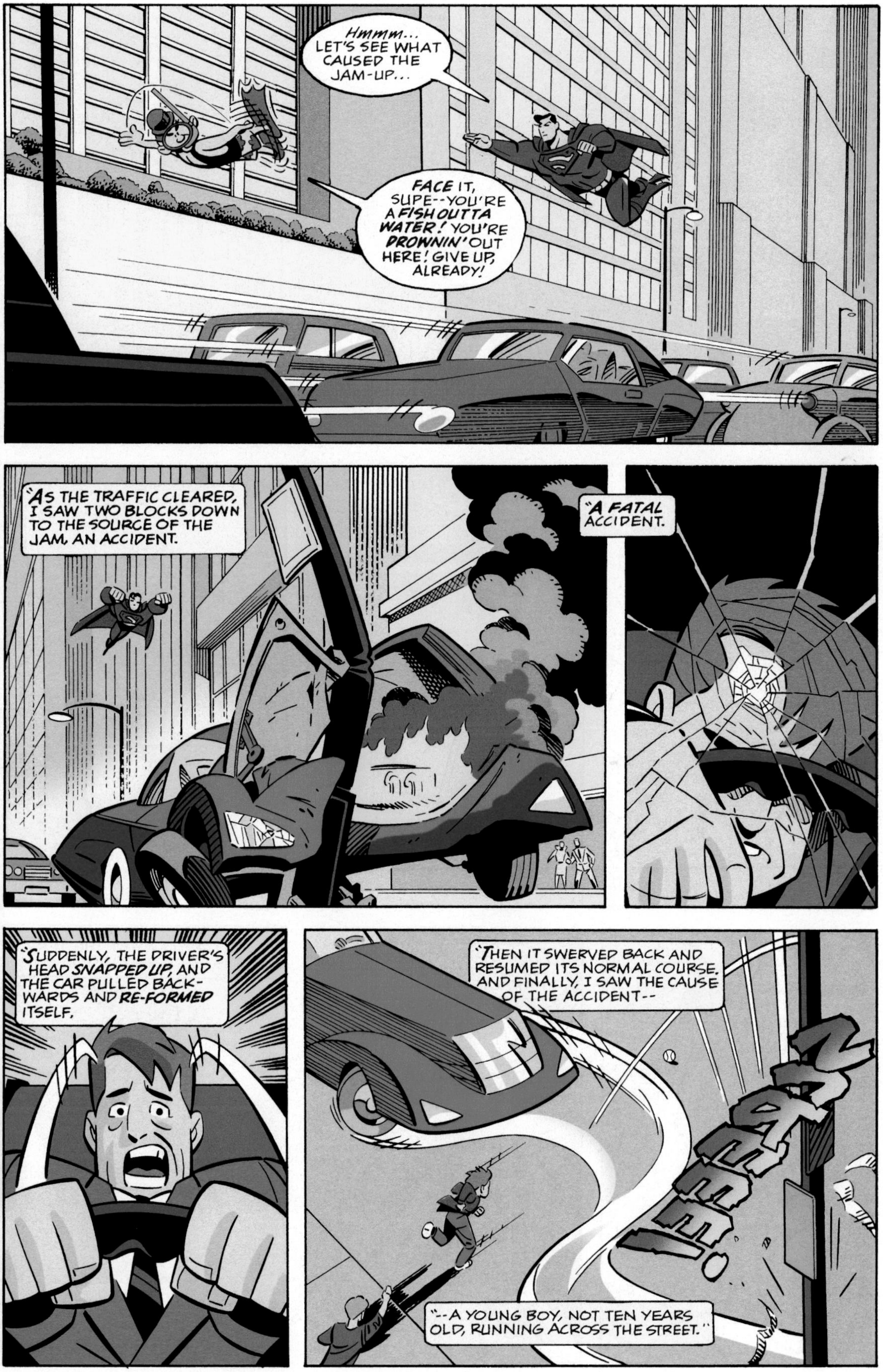
Hmmm... LET'S SEE WHAT CAUSED THE JAM-UP...
FACE IT, SUPE--YOU'RE A FISH OUTTA WATER! YOU'RE DROWNIN' OUT HERE! GIVE UP, ALREADY!
"AS THE TRAFFIC CLEARED, I SAW TWO BLOCKS DOWN TO THE SOURCE OF THE JAM, AN ACCIDENT.
"A FATAL ACCIDENT.
"SUDDENLY, THE DRIVER'S HEAD SNAPPED UP, AND THE CAR PULLED BACK-WARDS AND RE-FORMED ITSELF.
"THEN IT SWERVED BACK AND RESUMED ITS NORMAL COURSE. AND FINALLY, I SAW THE CAUSE OF THE ACCIDENT--
NNEEEEE!
"--A YOUNG BOY, NOT TEN YEARS OLD, RUNNING ACROSS THE STREET."

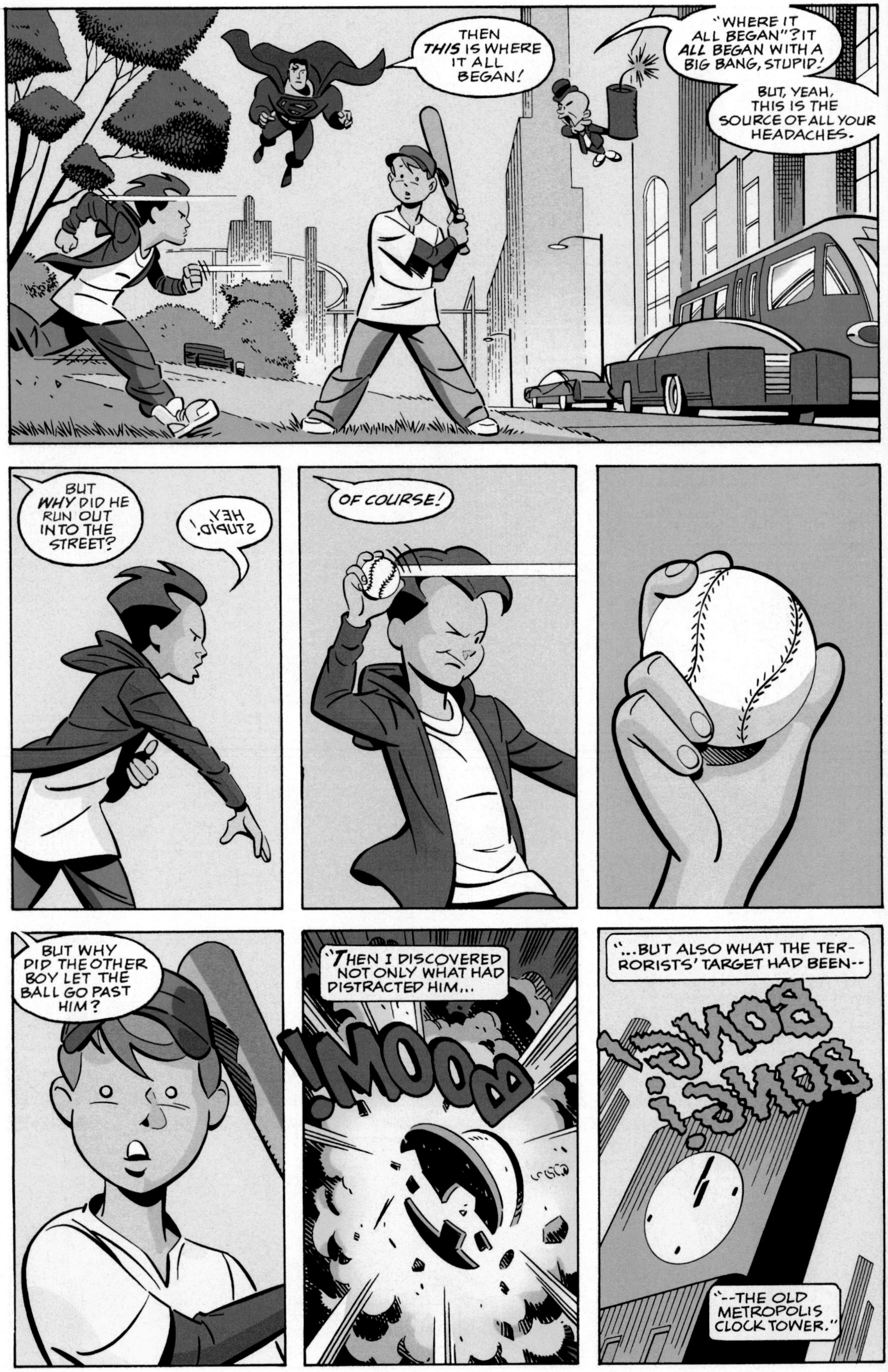

THEN THIS IS WHERE IT ALL BEGAN!
"WHERE IT ALL BEGAN"? IT ALL BEGAN WITH A BIG BANG, STUPID!
BUT, YEAH, THIS IS THE SOURCE OF ALL YOUR HEADACHES.
BUT WHY DID HE RUN OUT INTO THE STREET?
HEY, STUPID!
OF COURSE!
BUT WHY DID THE OTHER BOY LET THE BALL GO PAST HIM?
"THEN I DISCOVERED NOT ONLY WHAT HAD DISTRACTED HIM...
BOOM!
"...BUT ALSO WHAT THE TERRORISTS' TARGET HAD BEEN--
BONG! BONG!
"--THE OLD METROPOLIS CLOCK TOWER."

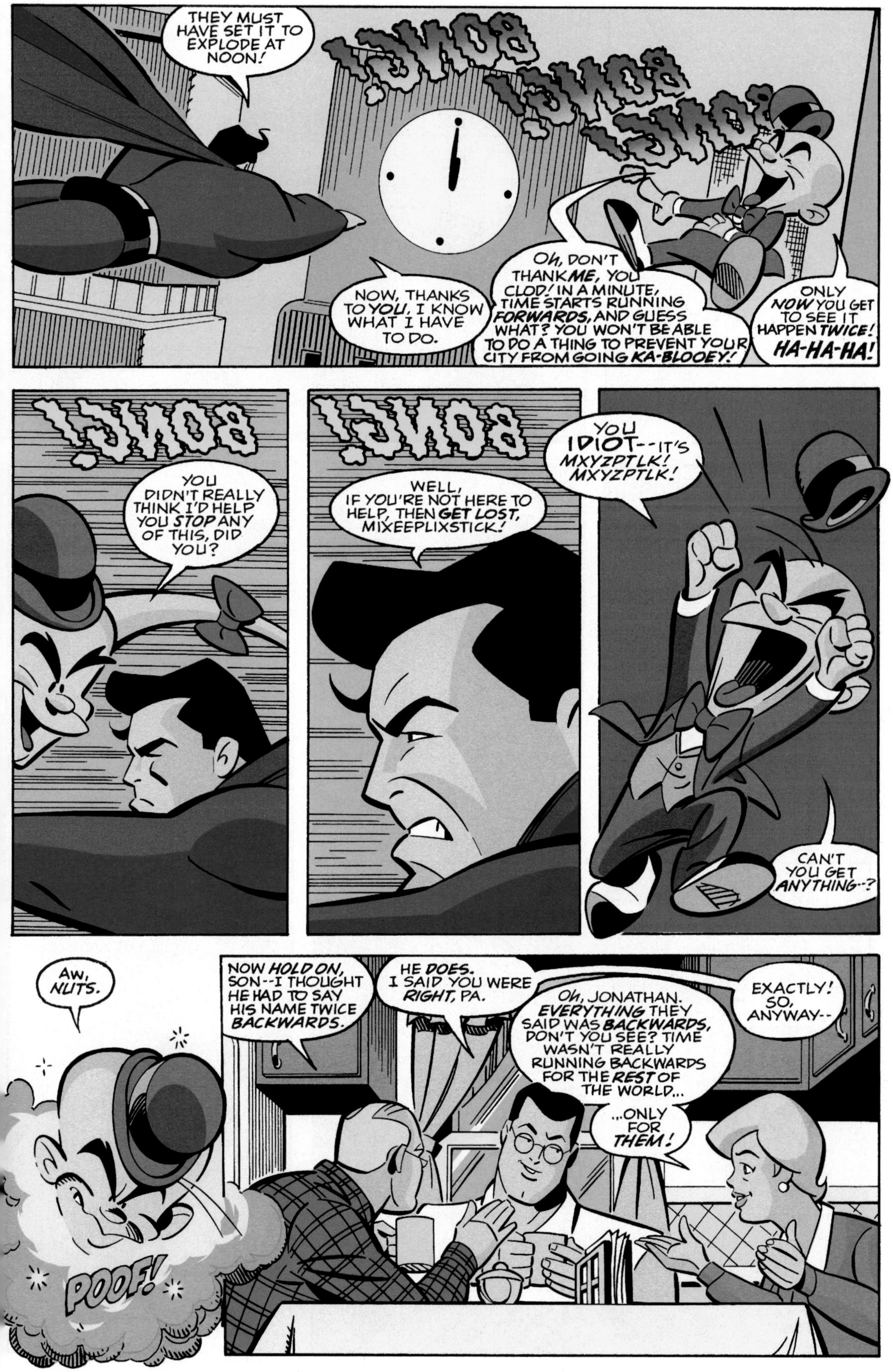

THEY MUST HAVE SET IT TO EXPLODE AT NOON!
BONG! BONG! BONG!
NOW, THANKS TO YOU, I KNOW WHAT I HAVE TO DO.
OH, DON'T THANK ME, YOU CLOD! IN A MINUTE, TIME STARTS RUNNING FORWARDS, AND GUESS WHAT? YOU WON'T BE ABLE TO DO A THING TO PREVENT YOUR CITY FROM GOING KA-BLOOEY!
ONLY NOW YOU GET TO SEE IT HAPPEN TWICE! HA-HA-HA!
BONG!
YOU DIDN'T REALLY THINK I'D HELP YOU STOP ANY OF THIS, DID YOU?
BONG!
WELL, IF YOU'RE NOT HERE TO HELP, THEN GET LOST, MIXEEPLIXSTICK!
YOU IDIOT--IT'S MXYZPTLK! MXYZPTLK!
CAN'T YOU GET ANYTHING--?
AW, NUTS.
POOF!
NOW HOLD ON, SON--I THOUGHT HE HAD TO SAY HIS NAME TWICE BACKWARDS.
HE DOES. I SAID YOU WERE RIGHT, PA.
OH, JONATHAN. EVERYTHING THEY SAID WAS BACKWARDS, DON'T YOU SEE? TIME WASN'T REALLY RUNNING BACKWARDS FOR THE REST OF THE WORLD...
...ONLY FOR THEM!
EXACTLY! SO, ANYWAY--

"--AS I APPROACHED THE SCENE OF MY EARLIER BATTLE, I GLIMPSED MYSELF FOR JUST A MOMENT.

"THEN I WAS BACK, RELIVING THE LAST FEW SECONDS BEFORE I WAS SENT INTO THE FUTURE."

YOU THINK YOU'VE WON, EH?

"AGAIN I SAW THE TERRORIST REACH FOR THE BOX."

IT LOOKS THAT WAY, YES.

THEN GAZE UPON *THIS*, SUPERMAN!

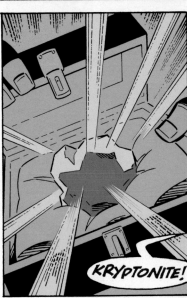

KRYPTONITE!

GUESS I SHOULD HAVE BROUGHT THIS WITH ME, *HUH*? INSTEAD OF LEAVING IT IN OUR GETAWAY CAR.

YOU WERE *FAST*, FASTER THAN WE THOUGHT.

BUT NOT FAST *ENOUGH*!

KER-RUNK!

NO. ≥UHN!≥-- NOT *NOW!* NO TIME!

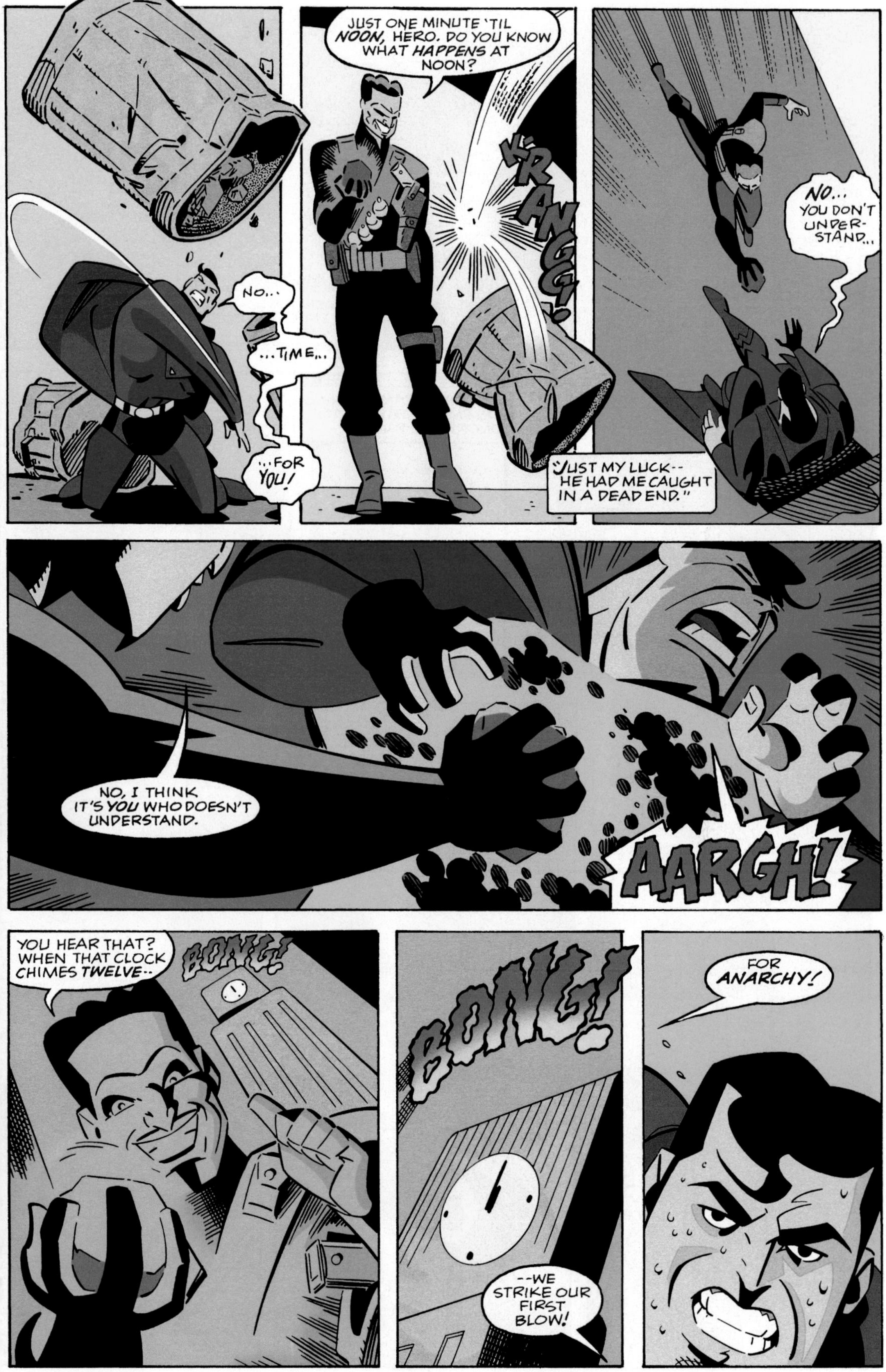

NO...
...TIME...
...FOR YOU!
JUST ONE MINUTE 'TIL NOON, HERO. DO YOU KNOW WHAT HAPPENS AT NOON?
K'RANGG!
NO... YOU DON'T UNDER-STAND...
"JUST MY LUCK-- HE HAD ME CAUGHT IN A DEAD END."
NO, I THINK IT'S YOU WHO DOESN'T UNDERSTAND.
AARGH!
YOU HEAR THAT? WHEN THAT CLOCK CHIMES TWELVE--
BONG!
BONG!
--WE STRIKE OUR FIRST BLOW!
FOR ANARCHY!

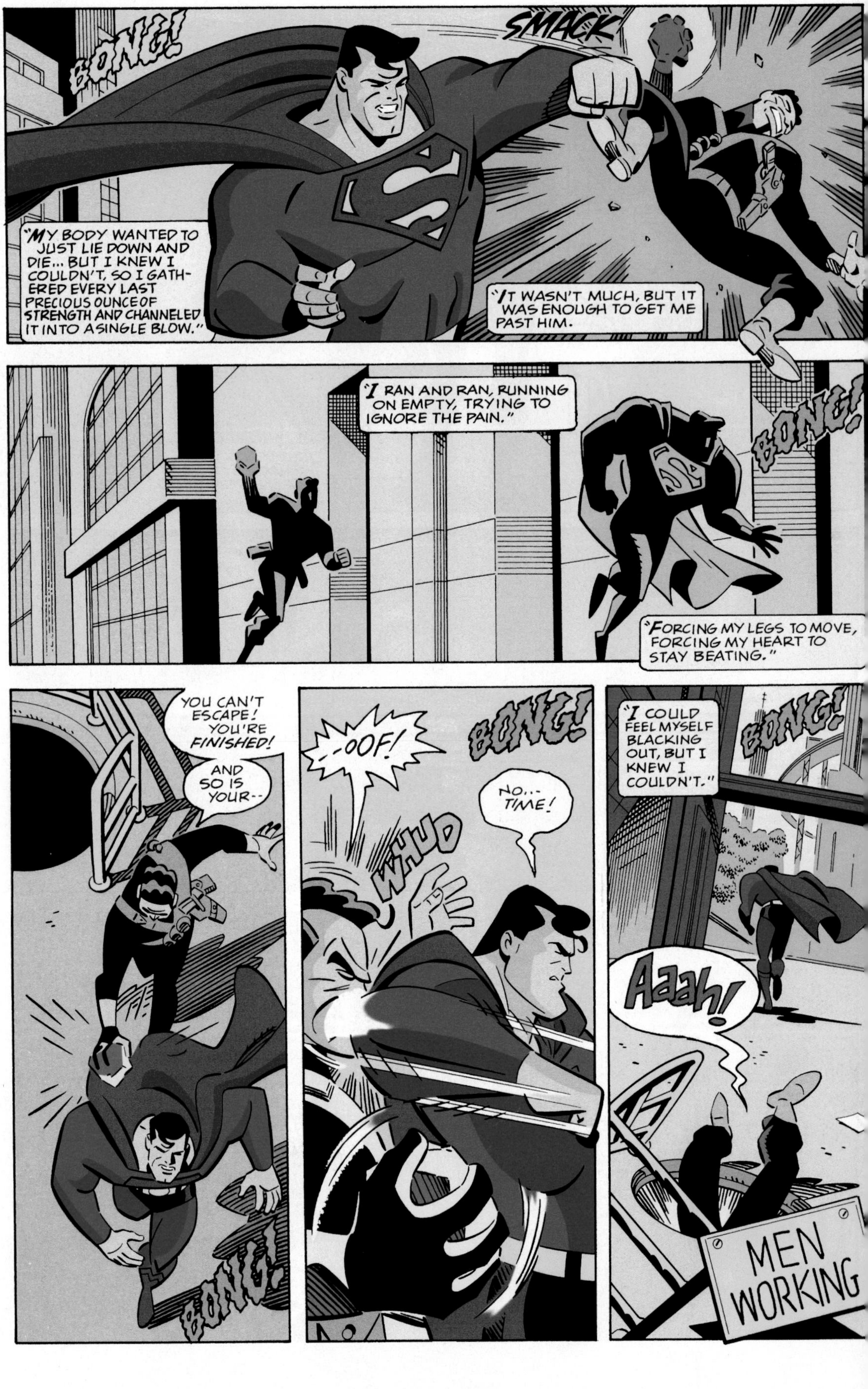
BONG!
SMACK
"MY BODY WANTED TO JUST LIE DOWN AND DIE... BUT I KNEW I COULDN'T, SO I GATHERED EVERY LAST PRECIOUS OUNCE OF STRENGTH AND CHANNELED IT INTO A SINGLE BLOW."
"IT WASN'T MUCH, BUT IT WAS ENOUGH TO GET ME PAST HIM.
"I RAN AND RAN, RUNNING ON EMPTY, TRYING TO IGNORE THE PAIN."
BONG!
"FORCING MY LEGS TO MOVE, FORCING MY HEART TO STAY BEATING."
YOU CAN'T ESCAPE! YOU'RE FINISHED!
AND SO IS YOUR--
BONG!
-OOF!
BONG!
NO... TIME!
WHUD
"I COULD FEEL MYSELF BLACKING OUT, BUT I KNEW I COULDN'T."
BONG!
Aaah!
MEN WORKING

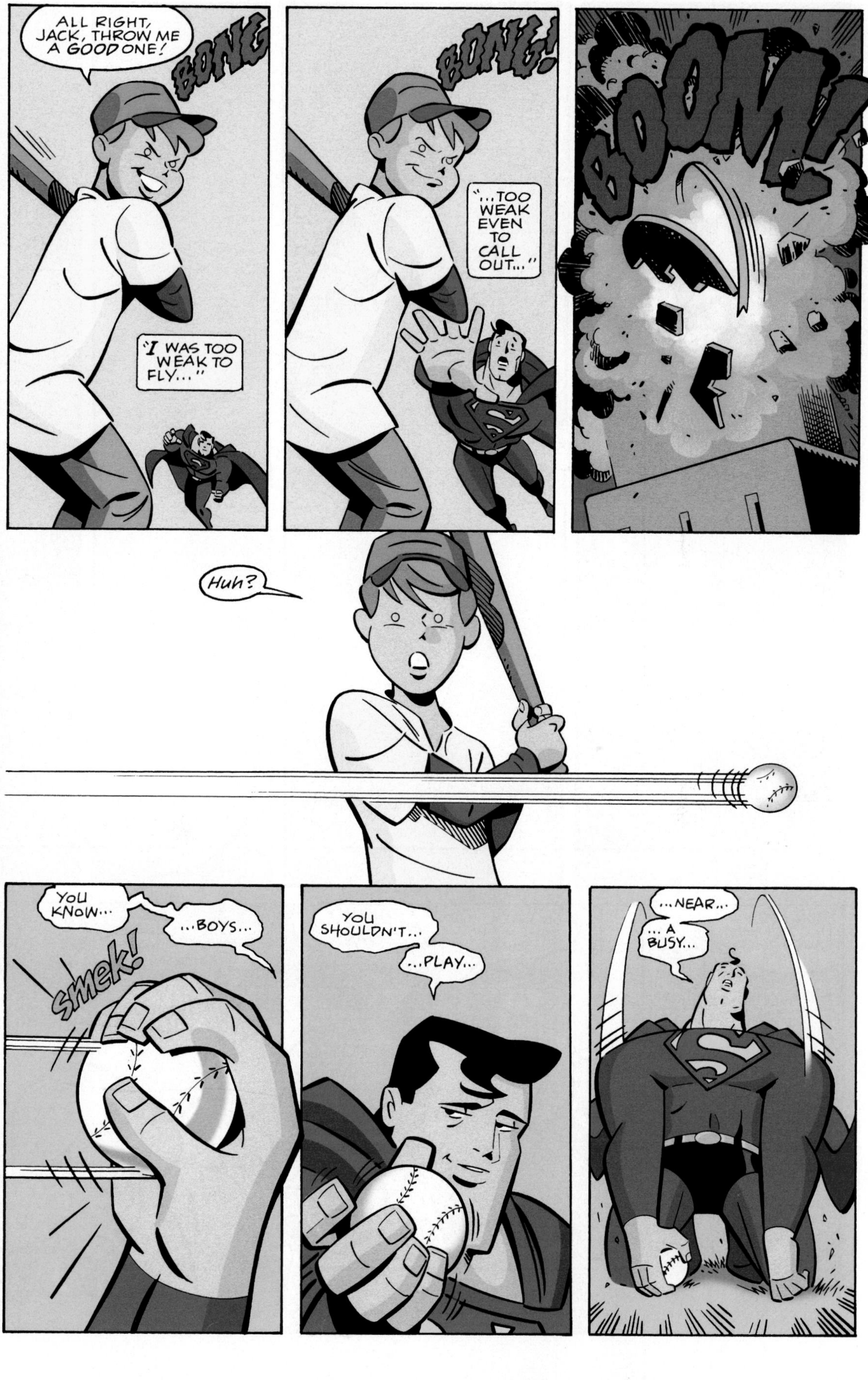
ALL RIGHT, JACK, THROW ME A GOOD ONE!
BONG
"I WAS TOO WEAK TO FLY..."
BONG!
"...TOO WEAK EVEN TO CALL OUT..."
BOOM!
Huh?
YOU KNOW...
...BOYS...
smek!
YOU SHOULDN'T...
...PLAY...
...NEAR...
...A BUSY...

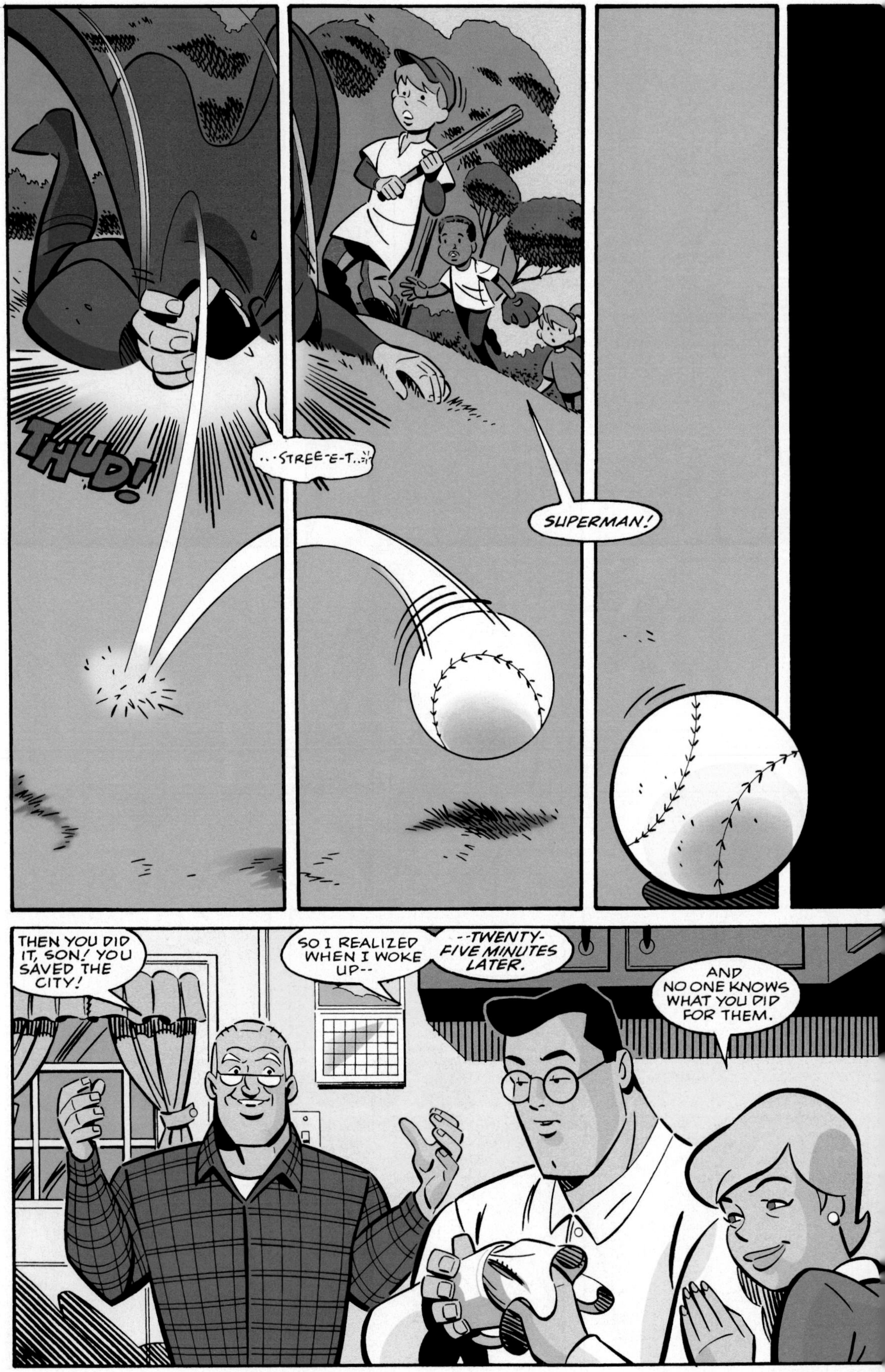
THUD!
...STREE-E-T...
SUPERMAN!
--TWENTY-FIVE MINUTES LATER.
THEN YOU DID IT, SON! YOU SAVED THE CITY!
SO I REALIZED WHEN I WOKE UP--
AND NO ONE KNOWS WHAT YOU DID FOR THEM.

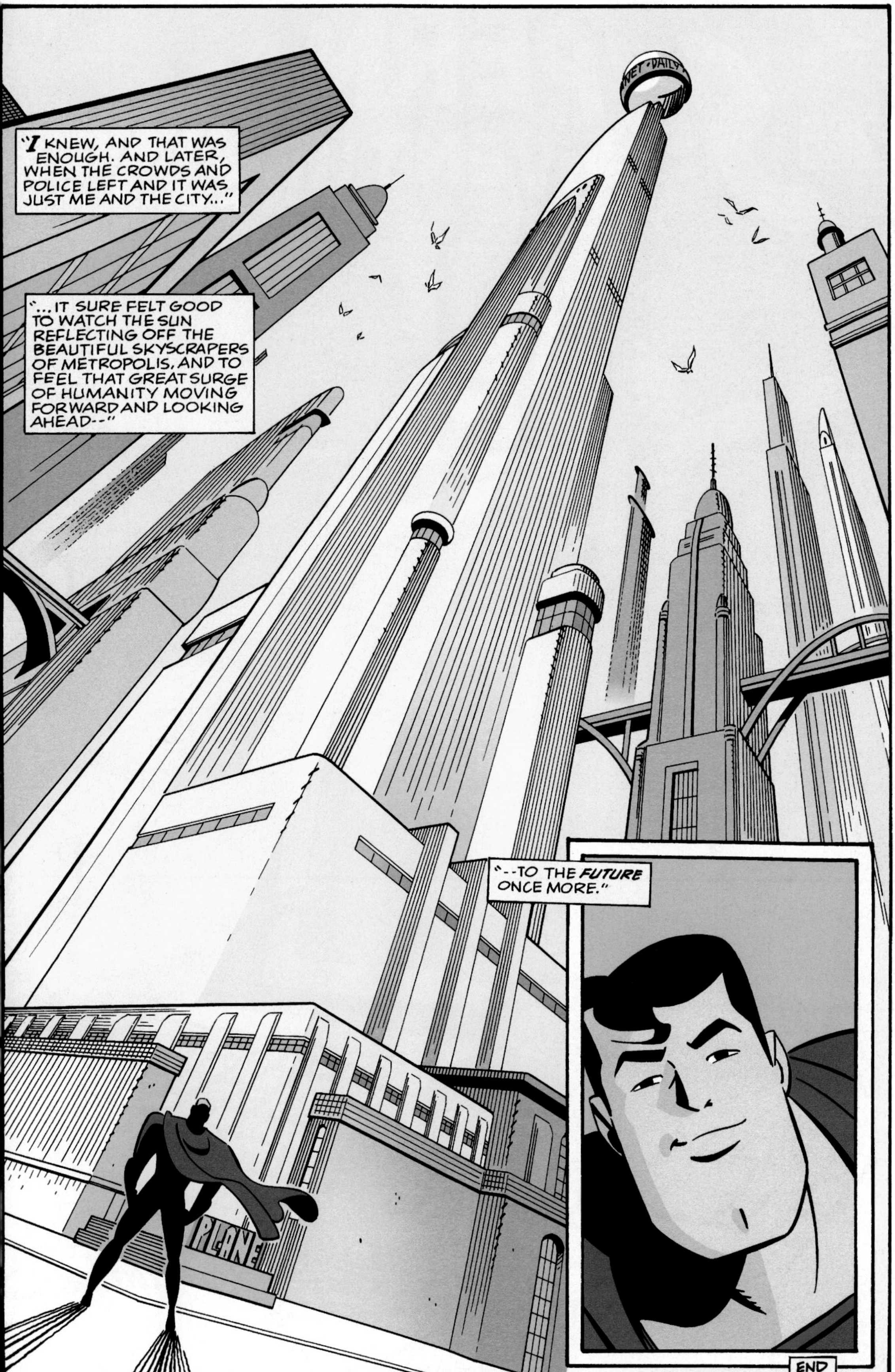
"I KNEW, AND THAT WAS ENOUGH. AND LATER, WHEN THE CROWDS AND POLICE LEFT AND IT WAS JUST ME AND THE CITY..."
"...IT SURE FELT GOOD TO WATCH THE SUN REFLECTING OFF THE BEAUTIFUL SKYSCRAPERS OF METROPOLIS, AND TO FEEL THAT GREAT SURGE OF HUMANITY MOVING FORWARD AND LOOKING AHEAD--"
"--TO THE FUTURE ONCE MORE."
END

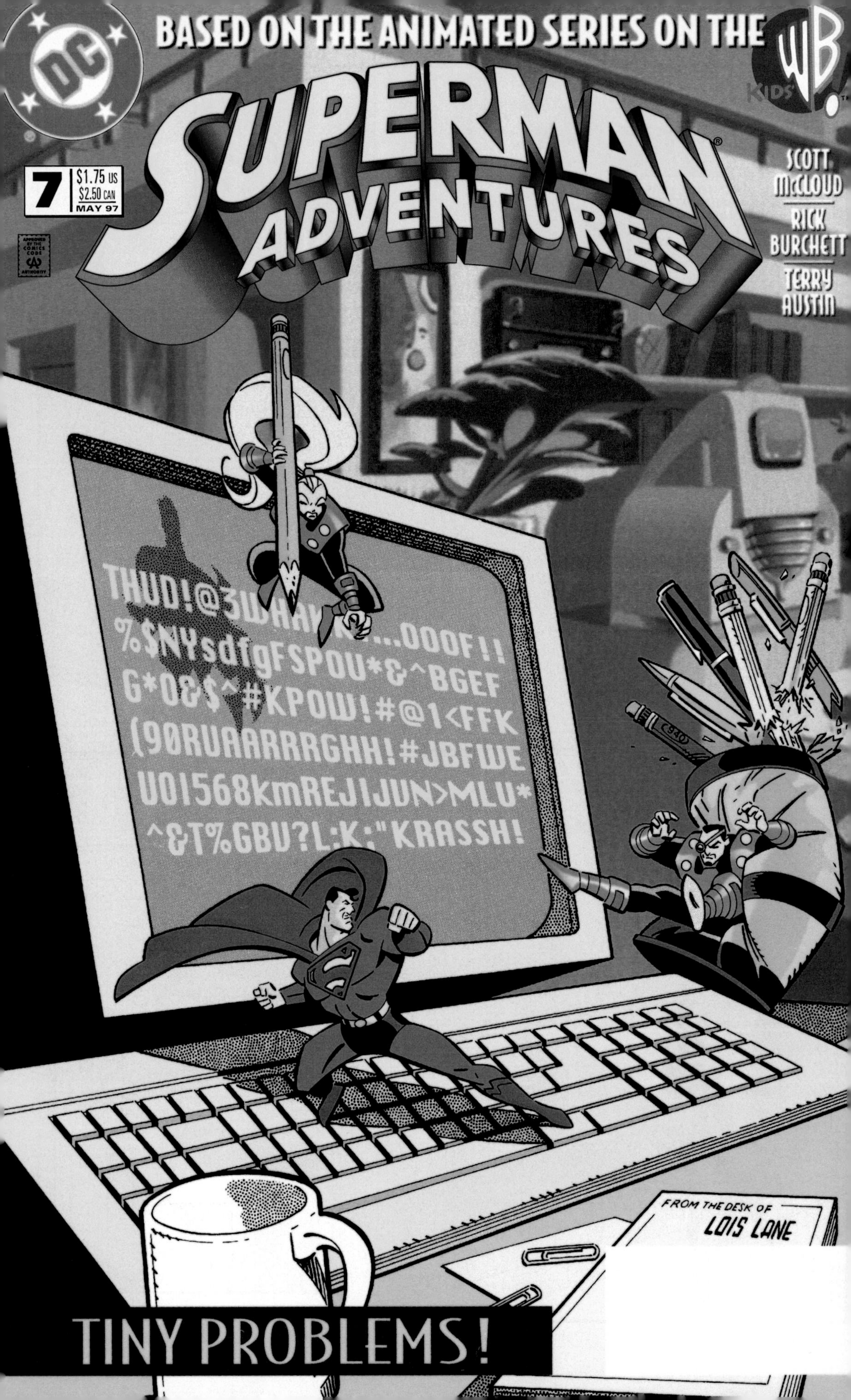
BASED ON THE ANIMATED SERIES ON THE
KIDS WB!
SUPERMAN ADVENTURES
7
$1.75 US
$2.50 CAN
MAY 97
APPROVED BY THE COMICS CODE AUTHORITY
SCOTT McCLOUD
RICK BURCHETT
TERRY AUSTIN
THUD!@3WHA ...OOOF!!
%$NYsdfgFSPOU*&^BGEF
G*0&$^#KPOW!#@1<FFK
(90RUAARRRGHH!#JBFWE
U01568kmREJIJUN>MLU*
^&T%GBU?L:K:"KRASSH!
940
FROM THE DESK OF
LOIS LANE
TINY PROBLEMS!

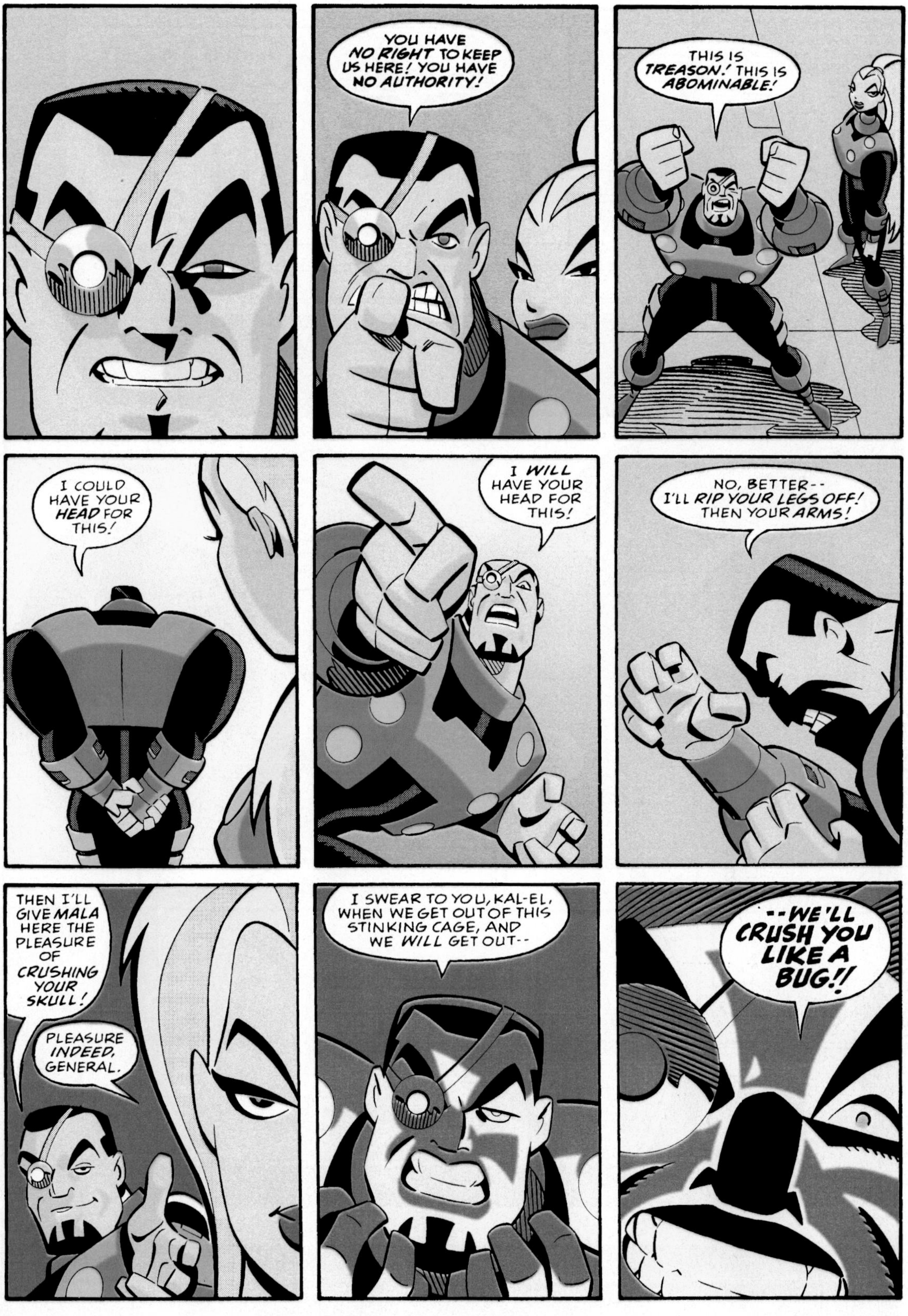
YOU HAVE NO RIGHT TO KEEP US HERE! YOU HAVE NO AUTHORITY!
THIS IS TREASON! THIS IS ABOMINABLE!
I COULD HAVE YOUR HEAD FOR THIS!
I WILL HAVE YOUR HEAD FOR THIS!
NO, BETTER-- I'LL RIP YOUR LEGS OFF! THEN YOUR ARMS!
THEN I'LL GIVE MALA HERE THE PLEASURE OF CRUSHING YOUR SKULL!
PLEASURE INDEED, GENERAL.
I SWEAR TO YOU, KAL-EL, WHEN WE GET OUT OF THIS STINKING CAGE, AND WE WILL GET OUT--
--WE'LL CRUSH YOU LIKE A BUG!!

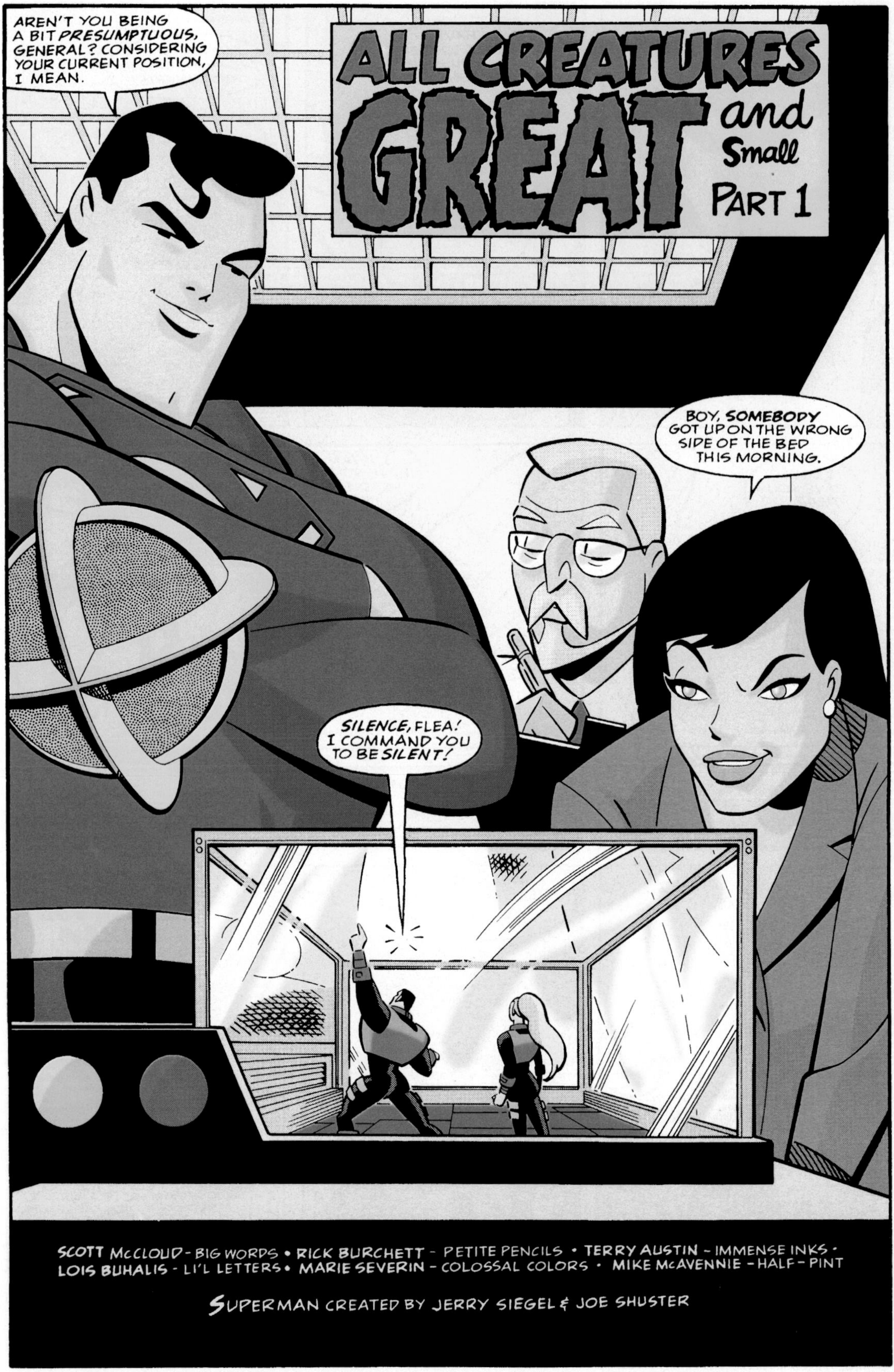
ARE'NT YOU BEING A BIT PRESUMPTUOUS, GENERAL? CONSIDERING YOUR CURRENT POSITION, I MEAN.
ALL CREATURES GREAT and Small PART 1
BOY, SOMEBODY GOT UP ON THE WRONG SIDE OF THE BED THIS MORNING.
SILENCE, FLEA! I COMMAND YOU TO BE SILENT!

SCOTT McCLOUD - BIG WORDS • RICK BURCHETT - PETITE PENCILS • TERRY AUSTIN - IMMENSE INKS • LOIS BUHALIS - LI'L LETTERS • MARIE SEVERIN - COLOSSAL COLORS • MIKE McAVENNIE - HALF-PINT

SUPERMAN CREATED BY JERRY SIEGEL & JOE SHUSTER

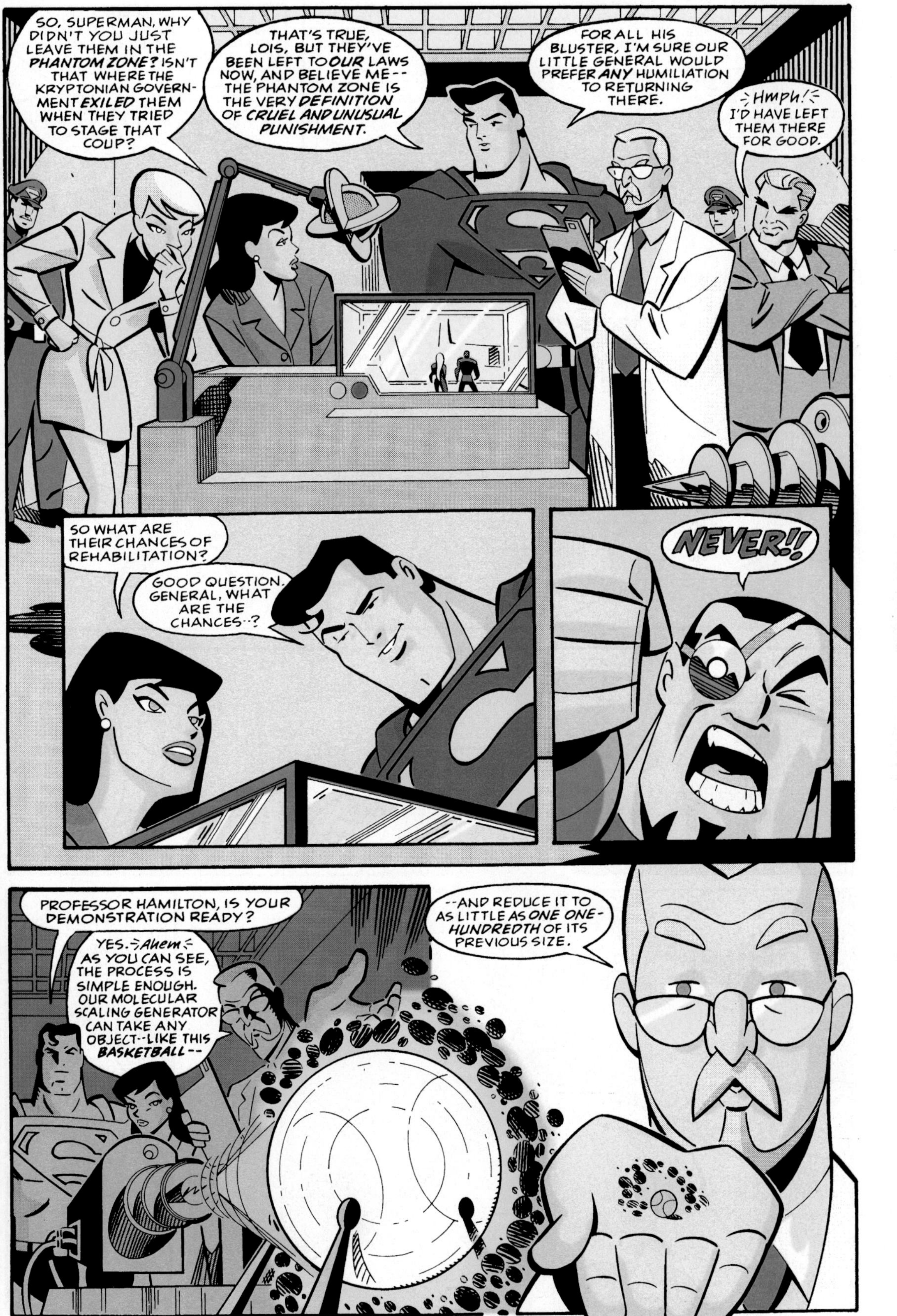
SO, SUPERMAN, WHY DIDN'T YOU JUST LEAVE THEM IN THE PHANTOM ZONE? ISN'T THAT WHERE THE KRYPTONIAN GOVERNMENT EXILED THEM WHEN THEY TRIED TO STAGE THAT COUP?
THAT'S TRUE, LOIS, BUT THEY'VE BEEN LEFT TO OUR LAWS NOW, AND BELIEVE ME-- THE PHANTOM ZONE IS THE VERY DEFINITION OF CRUEL AND UNUSUAL PUNISHMENT.
FOR ALL HIS BLUSTER, I'M SURE OUR LITTLE GENERAL WOULD PREFER ANY HUMILIATION TO RETURNING THERE.
Hmph! I'D HAVE LEFT THEM THERE FOR GOOD.
SO WHAT ARE THEIR CHANCES OF REHABILITATION?
GOOD QUESTION. GENERAL, WHAT ARE THE CHANCES--?
NEVER!!
PROFESSOR HAMILTON, IS YOUR DEMONSTRATION READY?
YES. Ahem AS YOU CAN SEE, THE PROCESS IS SIMPLE ENOUGH. OUR MOLECULAR SCALING GENERATOR CAN TAKE ANY OBJECT--LIKE THIS BASKETBALL--
--AND REDUCE IT TO AS LITTLE AS ONE ONE-HUNDREDTH OF ITS PREVIOUS SIZE.

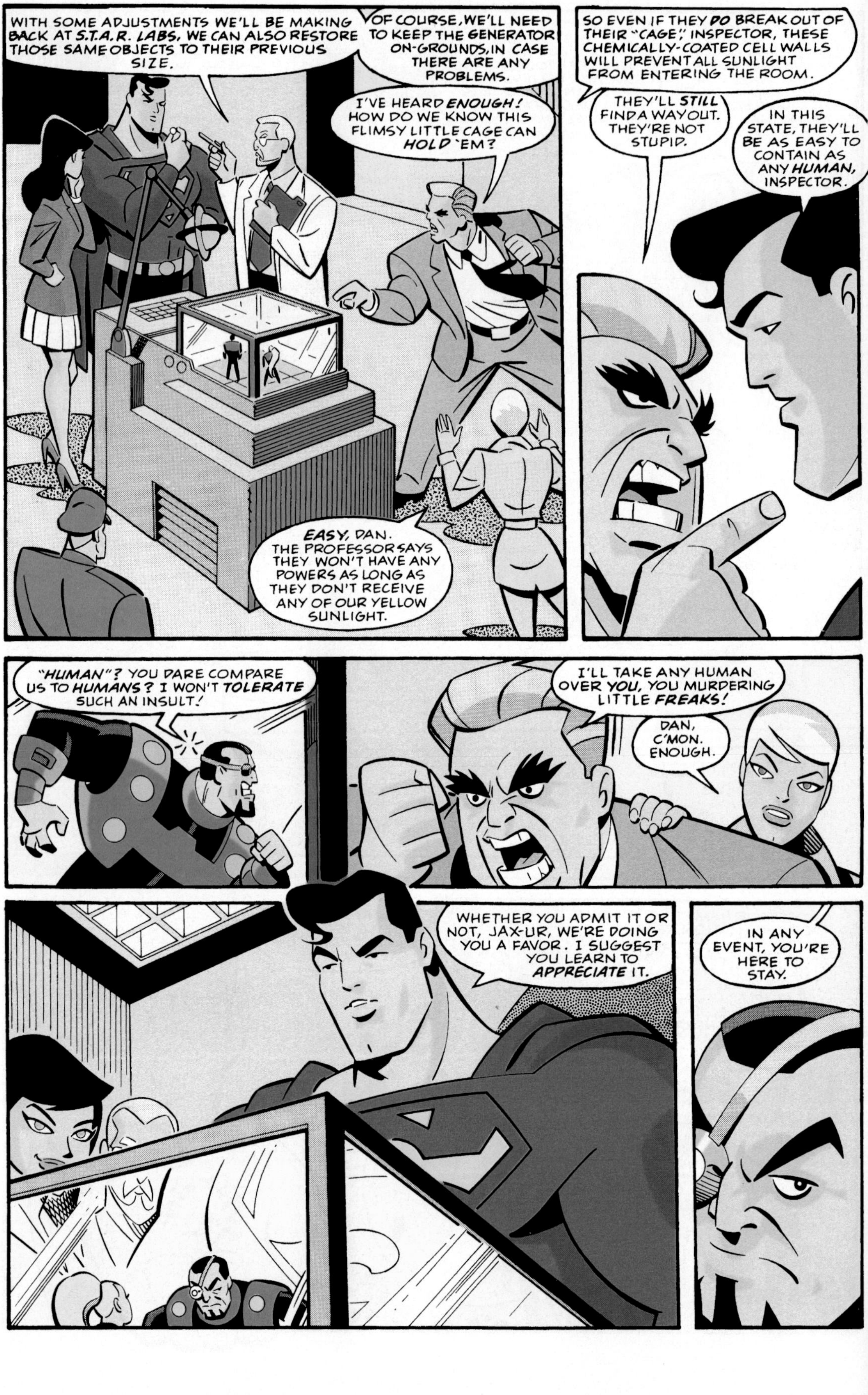
WITH SOME ADJUSTMENTS WE'LL BE MAKING BACK AT S.T.A.R. LABS, WE CAN ALSO RESTORE THOSE SAME OBJECTS TO THEIR PREVIOUS SIZE.
OF COURSE, WE'LL NEED TO KEEP THE GENERATOR ON-GROUNDS, IN CASE THERE ARE ANY PROBLEMS.
I'VE HEARD ENOUGH! HOW DO WE KNOW THIS FLIMSY LITTLE CAGE CAN HOLD 'EM?
EASY, DAN. THE PROFESSOR SAYS THEY WON'T HAVE ANY POWERS AS LONG AS THEY DON'T RECEIVE ANY OF OUR YELLOW SUNLIGHT.
SO EVEN IF THEY DO BREAK OUT OF THEIR "CAGE," INSPECTOR, THESE CHEMICALLY-COATED CELL WALLS WILL PREVENT ALL SUNLIGHT FROM ENTERING THE ROOM.
THEY'LL STILL FIND A WAY OUT. THEY'RE NOT STUPID.
IN THIS STATE, THEY'LL BE AS EASY TO CONTAIN AS ANY HUMAN, INSPECTOR.
"HUMAN"? YOU DARE COMPARE US TO HUMANS? I WON'T TOLERATE SUCH AN INSULT!
I'LL TAKE ANY HUMAN OVER YOU, YOU MURDERING LITTLE FREAKS!
DAN, C'MON. ENOUGH.
WHETHER YOU ADMIT IT OR NOT, JAX-UR, WE'RE DOING YOU A FAVOR. I SUGGEST YOU LEARN TO APPRECIATE IT.
IN ANY EVENT, YOU'RE HERE TO STAY.

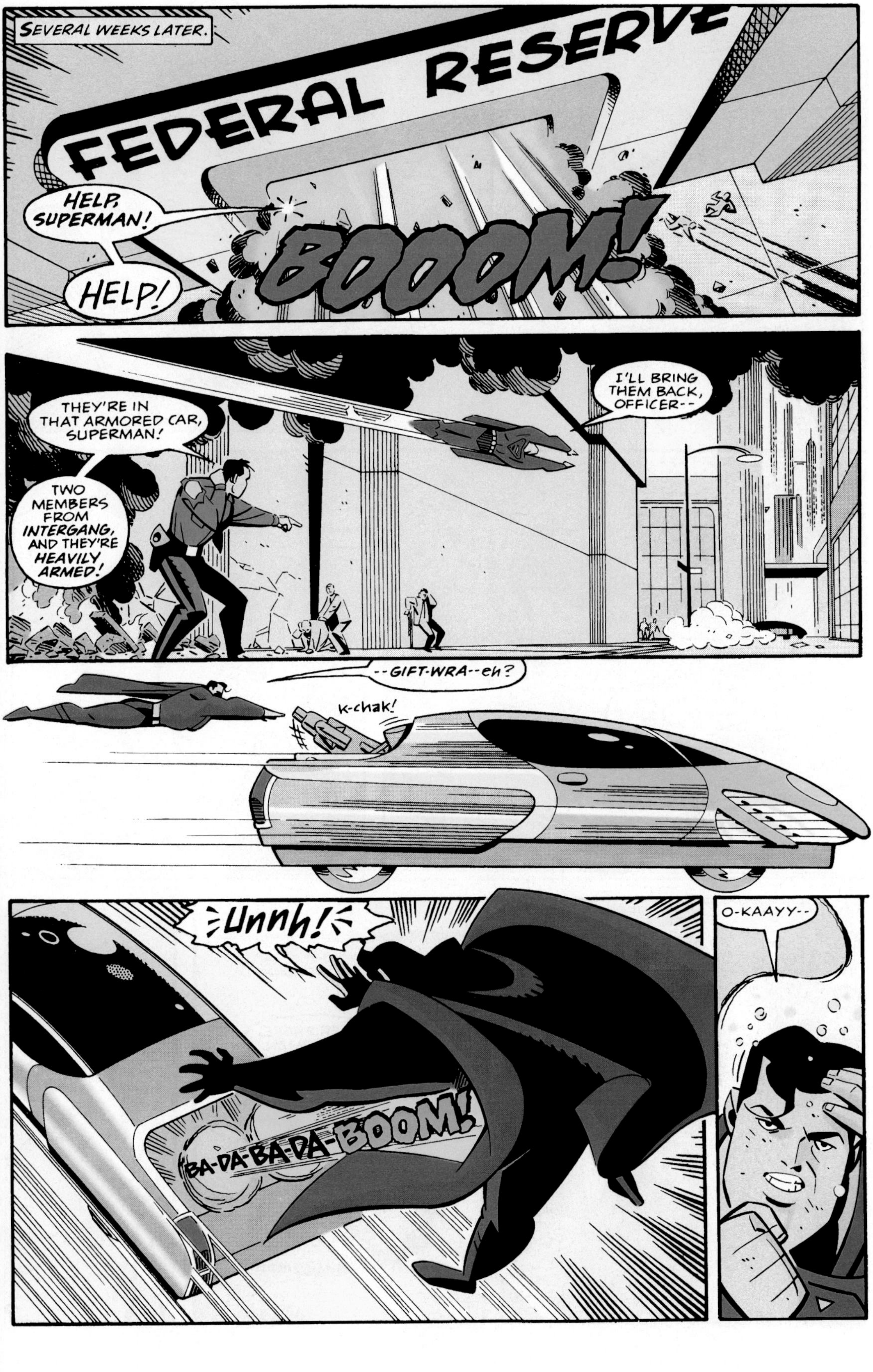
SEVERAL WEEKS LATER.
FEDERAL RESERVE
HELP, SUPERMAN!
HELP!
BOOOM!
THEY'RE IN THAT ARMORED CAR, SUPERMAN!
TWO MEMBERS FROM INTERGANG, AND THEY'RE HEAVILY ARMED!
I'LL BRING THEM BACK, OFFICER--
--GIFT-WRA--eh?
k-chak!
Unnh!
BA-DA-BA-DA-BOOM!
O-KAAYY--

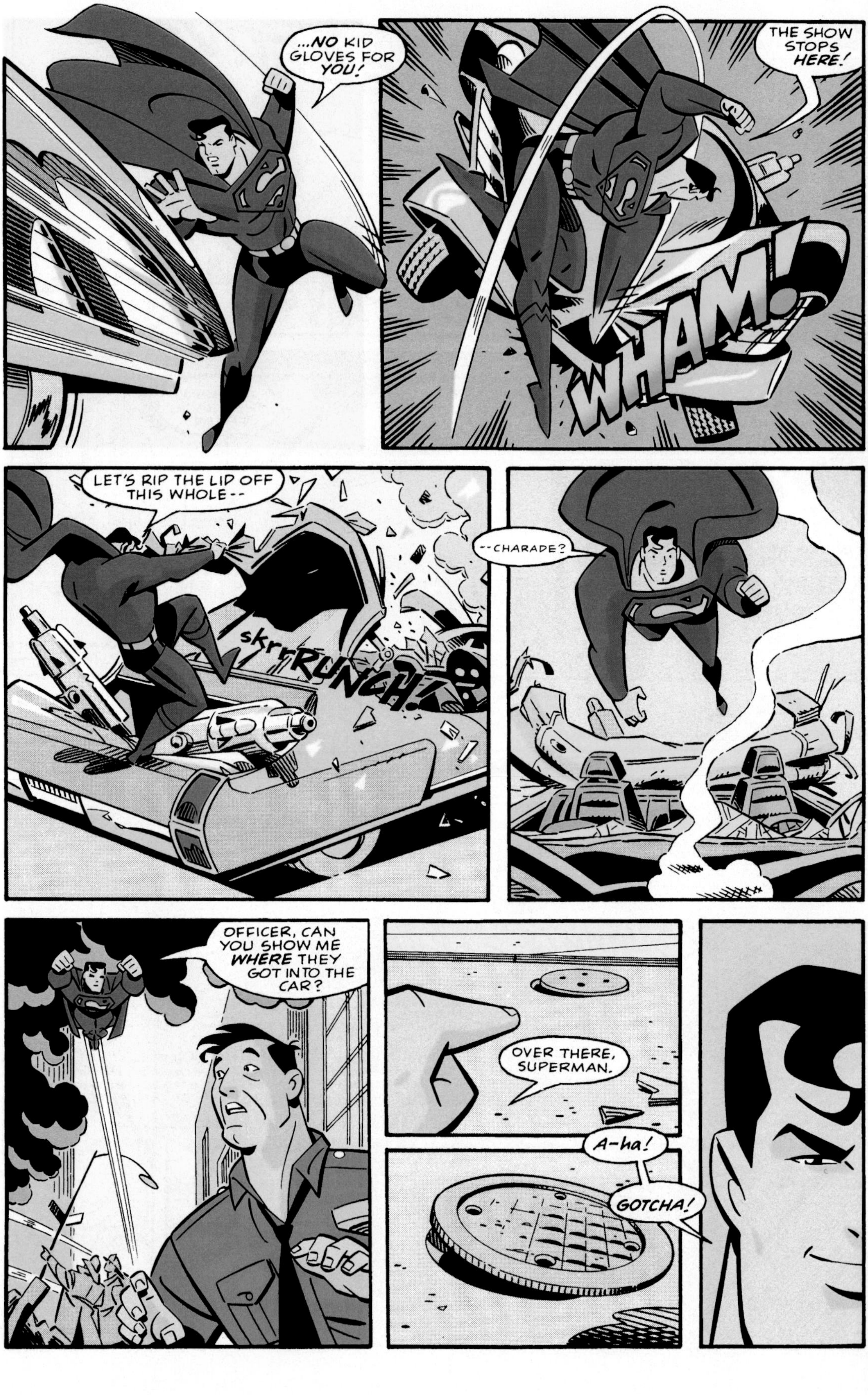
...NO KID GLOVES FOR YOU!
THE SHOW STOPS HERE!
WHAM!
LET'S RIP THE LID OFF THIS WHOLE--
skrrRUNCH!
--CHARADE?
OFFICER, CAN YOU SHOW ME WHERE THEY GOT INTO THE CAR?
OVER THERE, SUPERMAN.
A-ha!
GOTCHA!

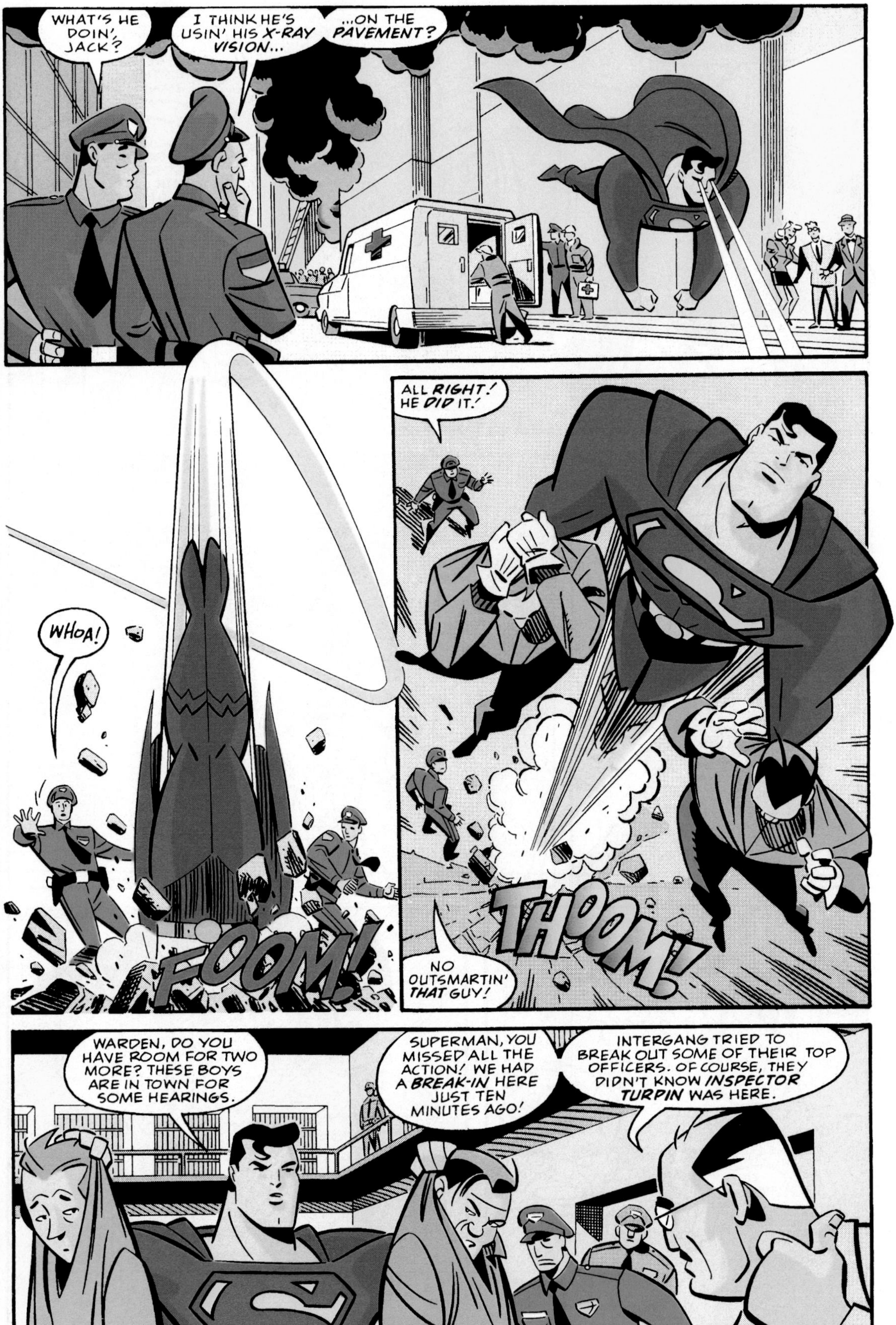
WHAT'S HE DOIN', JACK?
I THINK HE'S USIN' HIS X-RAY VISION...
...ON THE PAVEMENT?
WHOA!
FOOM!
ALL RIGHT! HE DID IT!
THOOM!
NO OUTSMARTIN' THAT GUY!
WARDEN, DO YOU HAVE ROOM FOR TWO MORE? THESE BOYS ARE IN TOWN FOR SOME HEARINGS.
SUPERMAN, YOU MISSED ALL THE ACTION! WE HAD A BREAK-IN HERE JUST TEN MINUTES AGO!
INTERGANG TRIED TO BREAK OUT SOME OF THEIR TOP OFFICERS. OF COURSE, THEY DIDN'T KNOW INSPECTOR TURPIN WAS HERE.

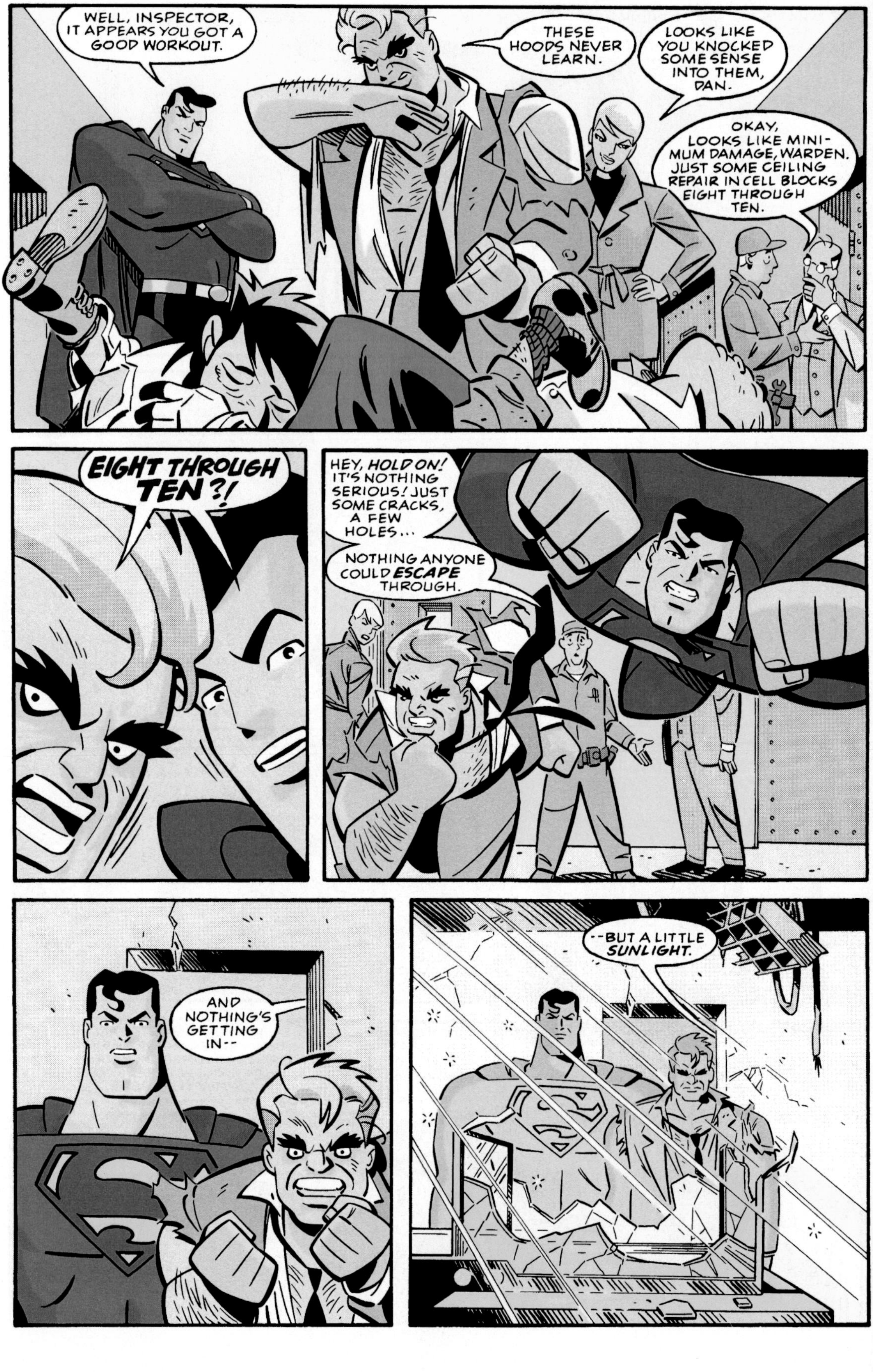
WELL, INSPECTOR, IT APPEARS YOU GOT A GOOD WORKOUT.
THESE HOODS NEVER LEARN.
LOOKS LIKE YOU KNOCKED SOME SENSE INTO THEM, DAN.
OKAY, LOOKS LIKE MINI-MUM DAMAGE, WARDEN. JUST SOME CEILING REPAIR IN CELL BLOCKS EIGHT THROUGH TEN.
EIGHT THROUGH TEN?!
HEY, HOLD ON! IT'S NOTHING SERIOUS! JUST SOME CRACKS, A FEW HOLES...
NOTHING ANYONE COULD ESCAPE THROUGH.
AND NOTHING'S GETTING IN--
--BUT A LITTLE SUNLIGHT.

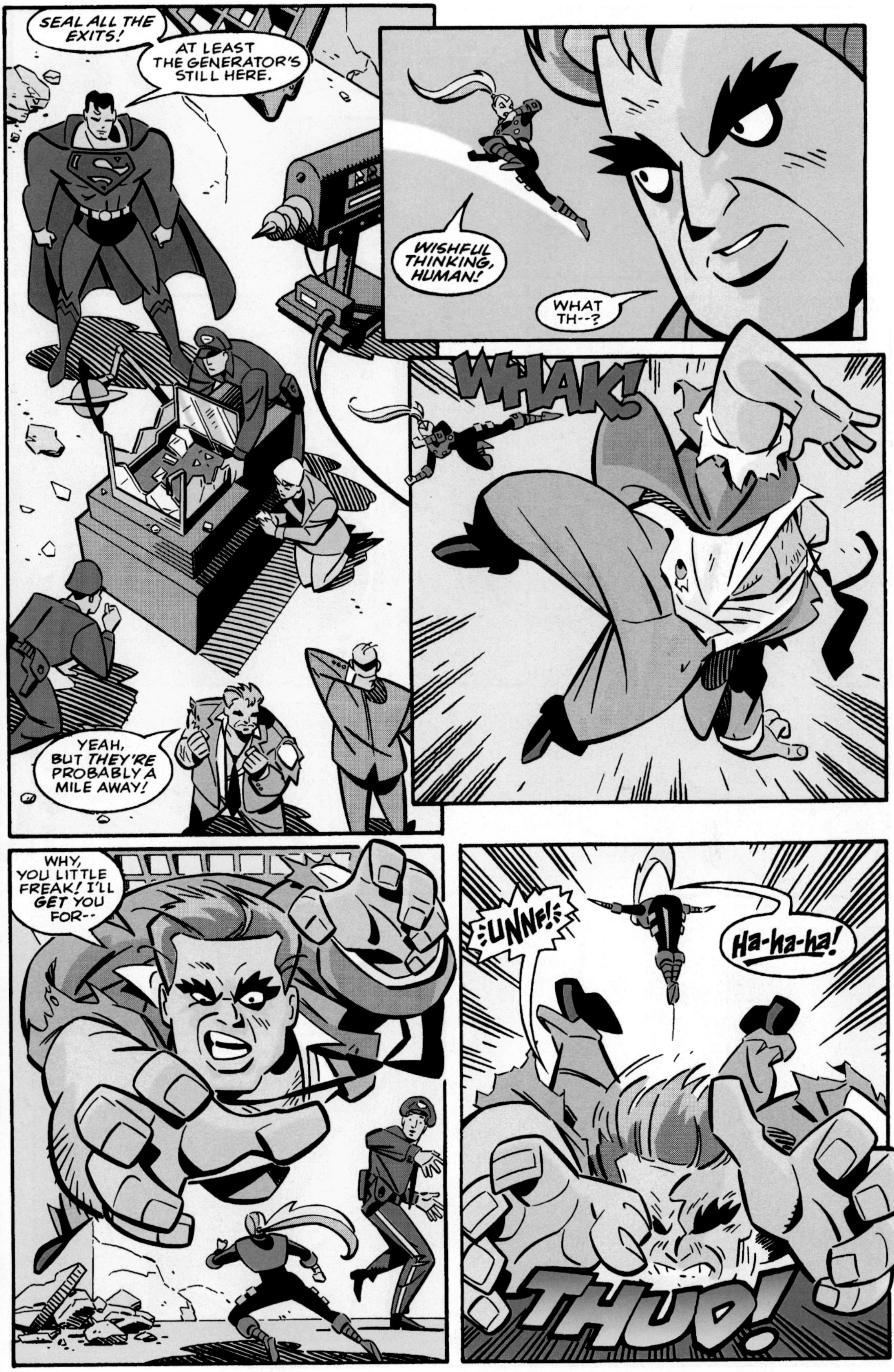
SEAL ALL THE EXITS!
AT LEAST THE GENERATOR'S STILL HERE.
YEAH, BUT THEY'RE PROBABLY A MILE AWAY!
WISHFUL THINKING, HUMAN!
WHAT TH--?
WHAK!
WHY, YOU LITTLE FREAK! I'LL GET YOU FOR--
UNNF!
Ha-ha-ha!
THUD!

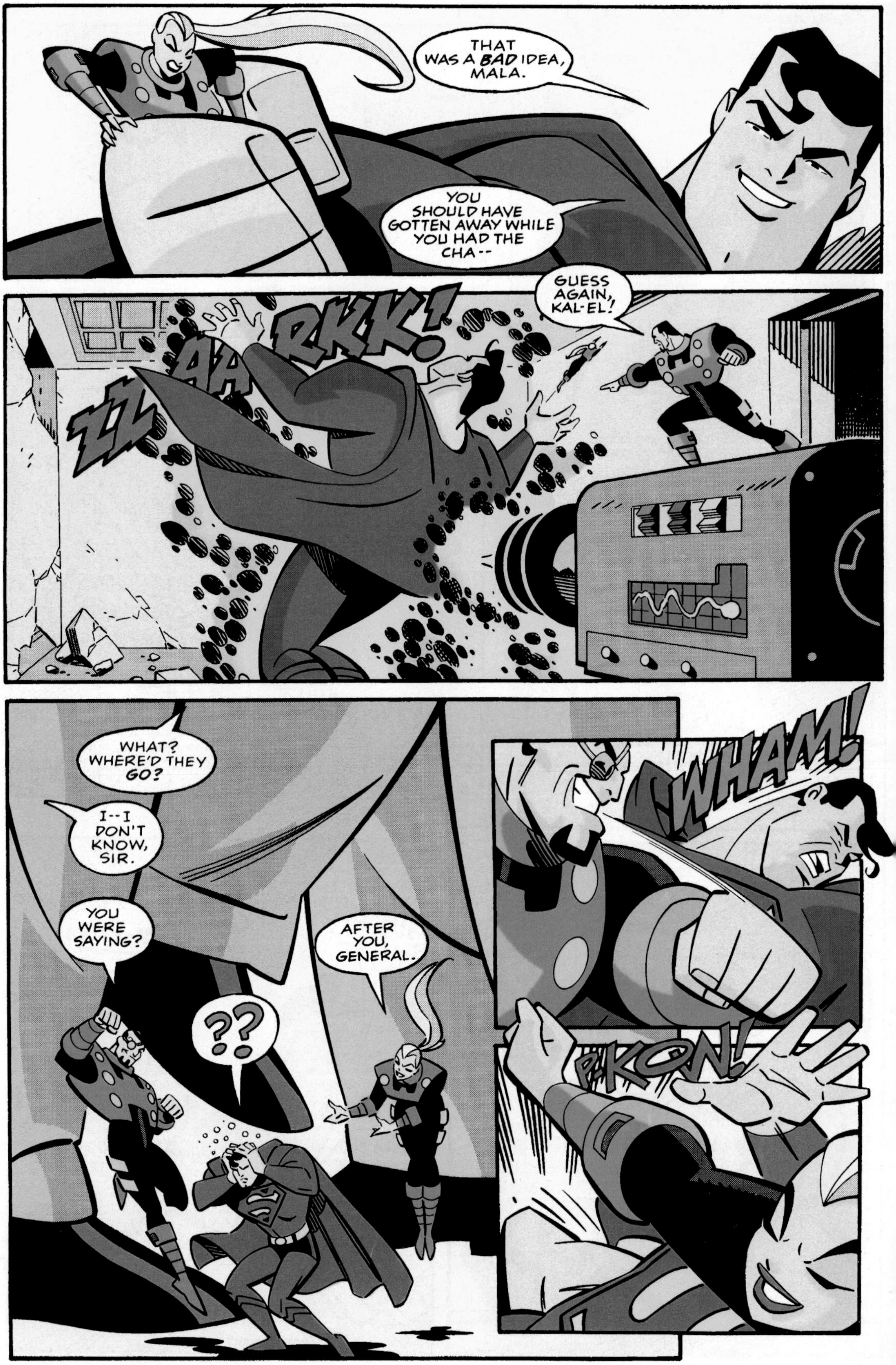
THAT WAS A BAD IDEA, MALA.
YOU SHOULD HAVE GOTTEN AWAY WHILE YOU HAD THE CHA--
GUESS AGAIN, KAL-EL!
ZZAARKK!
WHAT? WHERE'D THEY GO?
I--I DON'T KNOW, SIR.
YOU WERE SAYING?
AFTER YOU, GENERAL.
??
WHAM!
P-KOW!

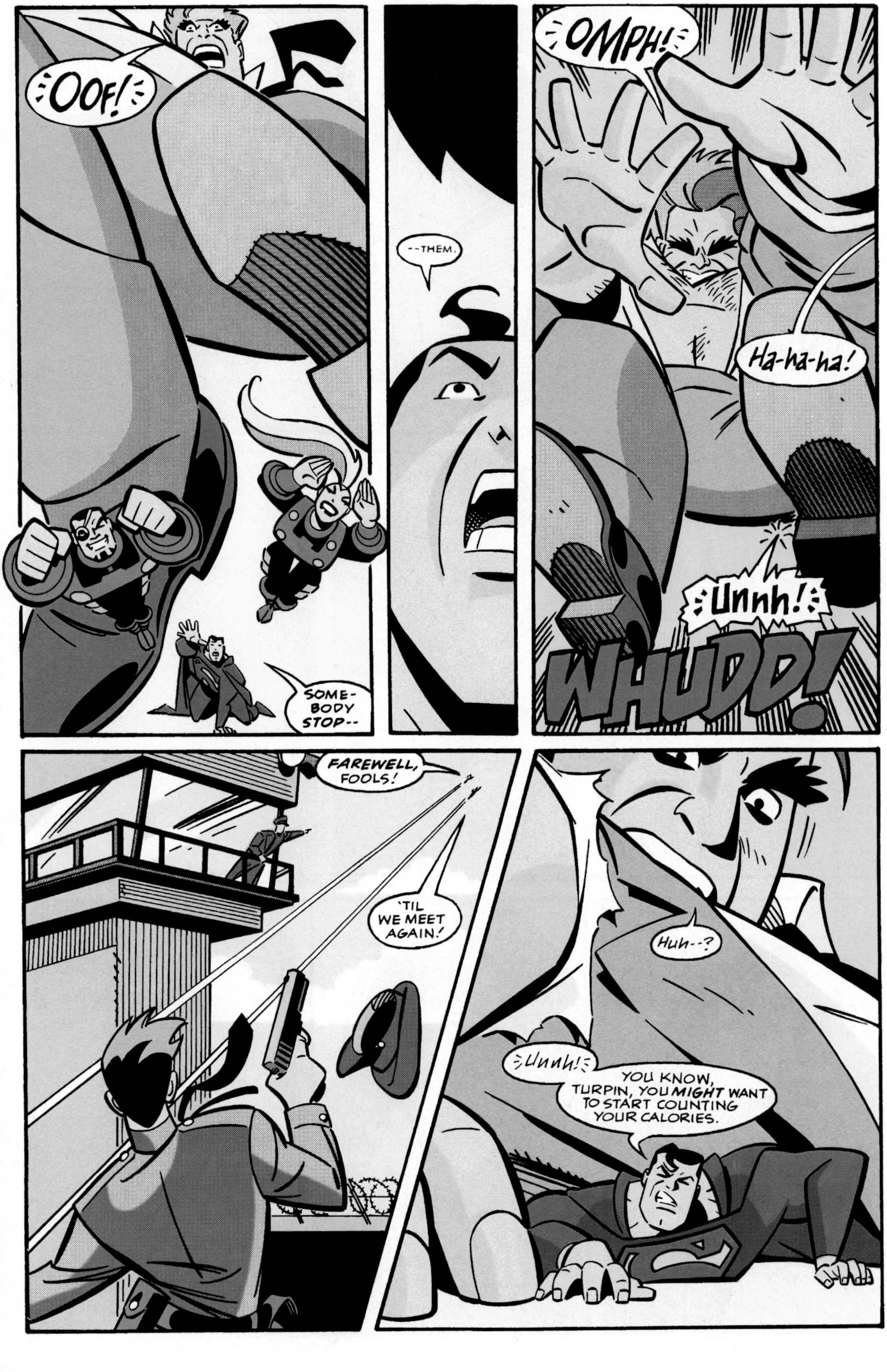
OOF!
SOME-BODY STOP--
--THEM.
OMPH!
Ha-ha-ha!
Unnh!
WHUDD!
FAREWELL, FOOLS!
'TIL WE MEET AGAIN!
Huh--?
Unnh!
YOU KNOW, TURPIN, YOU MIGHT WANT TO START COUNTING YOUR CALORIES.

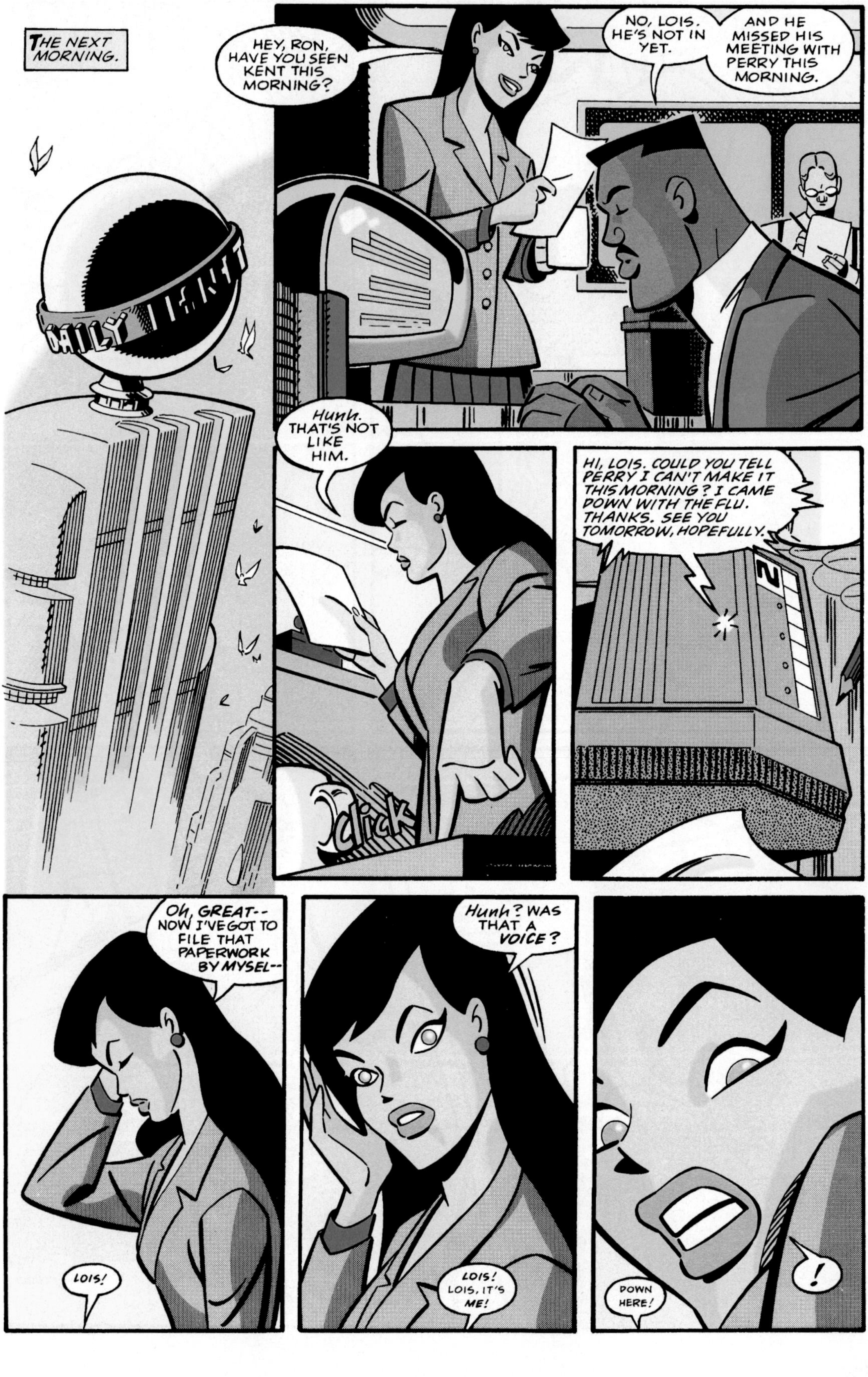
THE NEXT MORNING.
HEY, RON, HAVE YOU SEEN KENT THIS MORNING?
NO, LOIS. HE'S NOT IN YET.
AND HE MISSED HIS MEETING WITH PERRY THIS MORNING.
Hunh. THAT'S NOT LIKE HIM.
click
HI, LOIS. COULD YOU TELL PERRY I CAN'T MAKE IT THIS MORNING? I CAME DOWN WITH THE FLU. THANKS. SEE YOU TOMORROW, HOPEFULLY.
Oh, GREAT-- NOW I'VE GOT TO FILE THAT PAPERWORK BY MYSEL--
LOIS!
Hunh? WAS THAT A VOICE?
LOIS! LOIS, IT'S ME!
DOWN HERE!
!

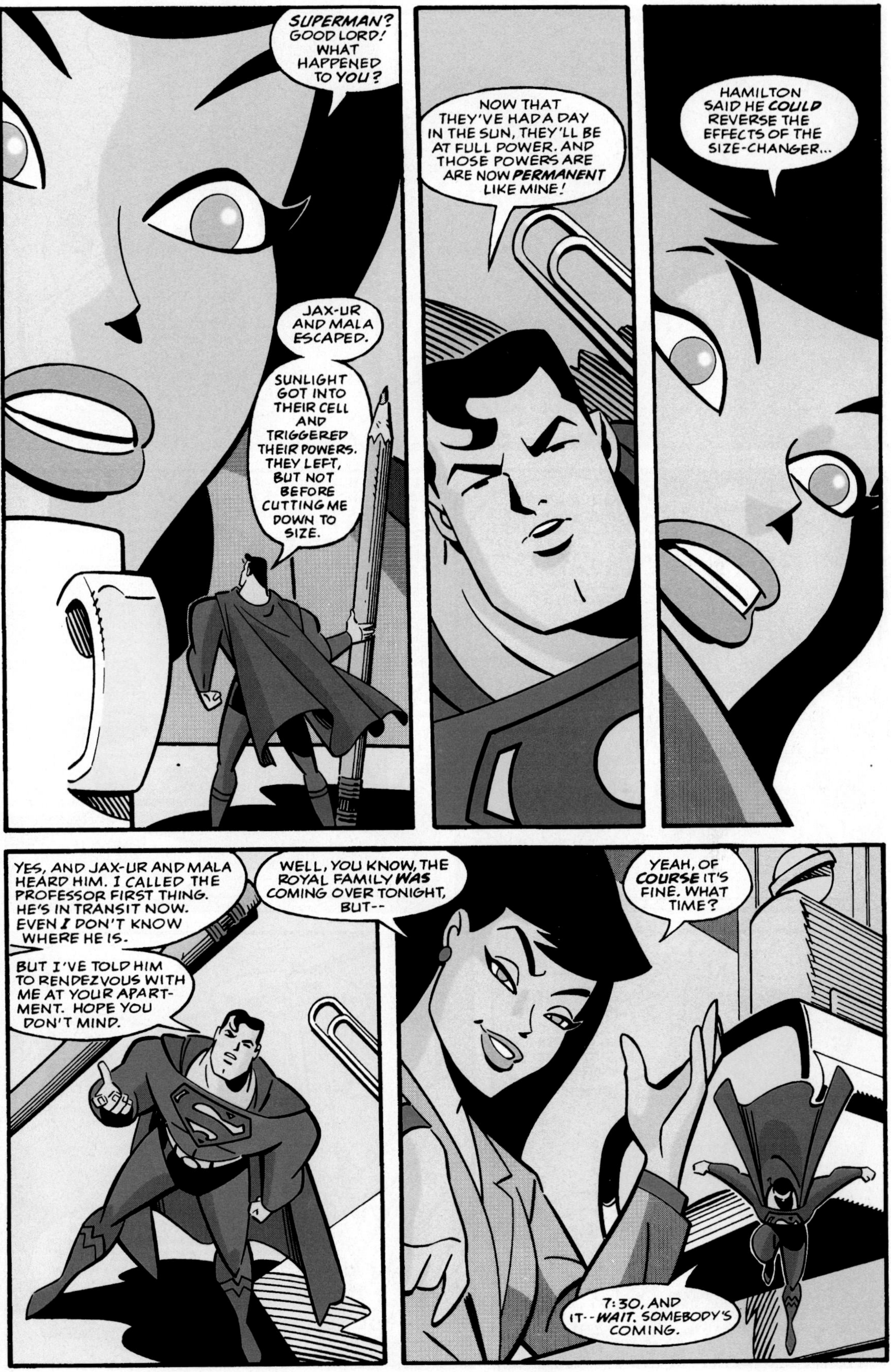
SUPERMAN? GOOD LORD! WHAT HAPPENED TO YOU?
JAX-UR AND MALA ESCAPED.
SUNLIGHT GOT INTO THEIR CELL AND TRIGGERED THEIR POWERS. THEY LEFT, BUT NOT BEFORE CUTTING ME DOWN TO SIZE.
NOW THAT THEY'VE HAD A DAY IN THE SUN, THEY'LL BE AT FULL POWER. AND THOSE POWERS ARE ARE NOW PERMANENT LIKE MINE!
HAMILTON SAID HE COULD REVERSE THE EFFECTS OF THE SIZE-CHANGER...
YES, AND JAX-UR AND MALA HEARD HIM. I CALLED THE PROFESSOR FIRST THING. HE'S IN TRANSIT NOW. EVEN I DON'T KNOW WHERE HE IS.
BUT I'VE TOLD HIM TO RENDEZVOUS WITH ME AT YOUR APART-MENT. HOPE YOU DON'T MIND.
WELL, YOU KNOW, THE ROYAL FAMILY WAS COMING OVER TONIGHT, BUT--
YEAH, OF COURSE IT'S FINE. WHAT TIME?
7:30, AND IT--WAIT. SOMEBODY'S COMING.

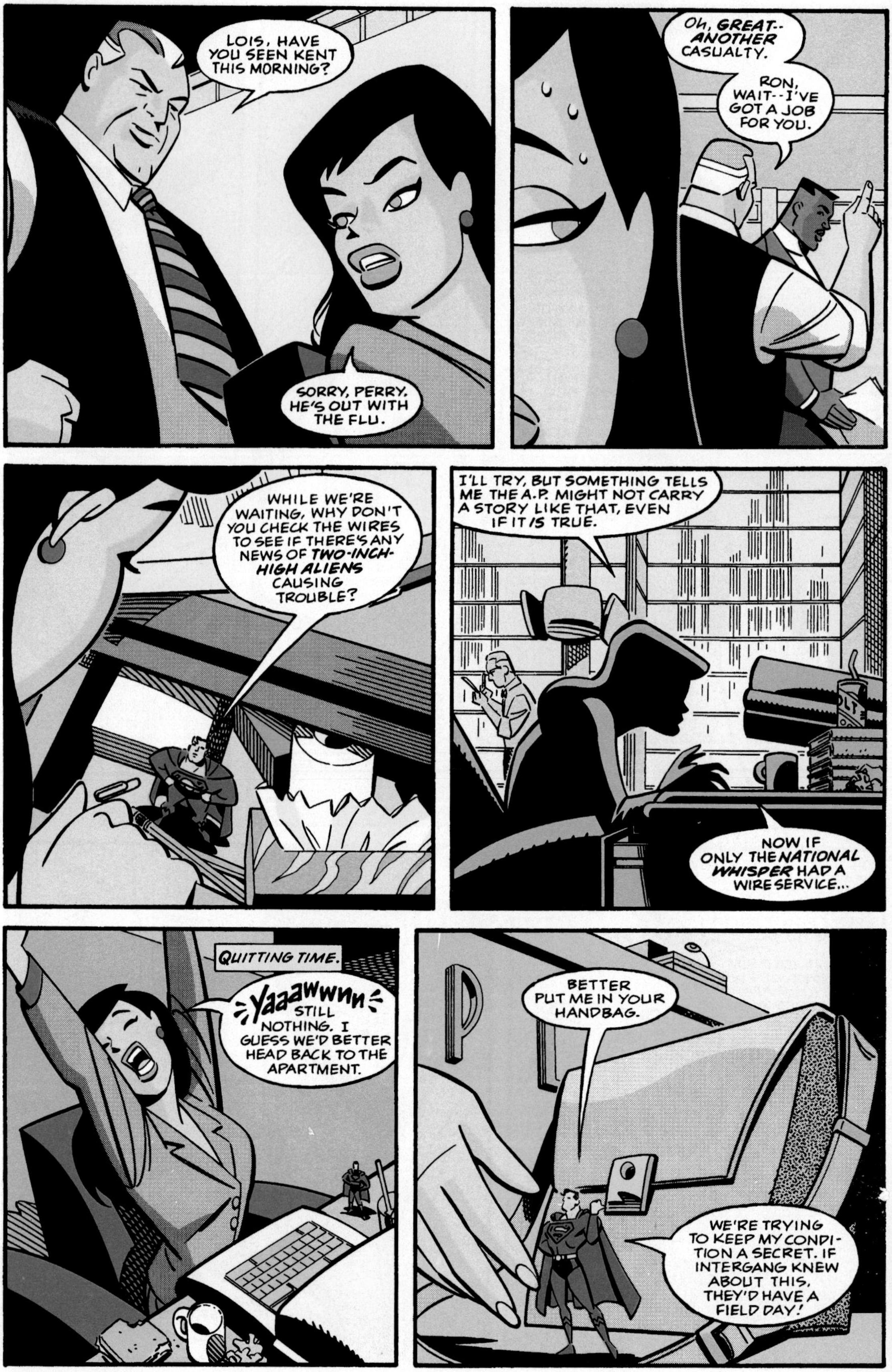
LOIS, HAVE YOU SEEN KENT THIS MORNING?
SORRY, PERRY. HE'S OUT WITH THE FLU.
Oh, GREAT-- ANOTHER CASUALTY.
RON, WAIT--I'VE GOT A JOB FOR YOU.
WHILE WE'RE WAITING, WHY DON'T YOU CHECK THE WIRES TO SEE IF THERE'S ANY NEWS OF TWO-INCH-HIGH ALIENS CAUSING TROUBLE?
I'LL TRY, BUT SOMETHING TELLS ME THE A.P. MIGHT NOT CARRY A STORY LIKE THAT, EVEN IF IT IS TRUE.
NOW IF ONLY THE NATIONAL WHISPER HAD A WIRE SERVICE...
QUITTING TIME.
Yaaawwnn STILL NOTHING. I GUESS WE'D BETTER HEAD BACK TO THE APARTMENT.
BETTER PUT ME IN YOUR HANDBAG.
WE'RE TRYING TO KEEP MY CONDITION A SECRET. IF INTERGANG KNEW ABOUT THIS, THEY'D HAVE A FIELD DAY!

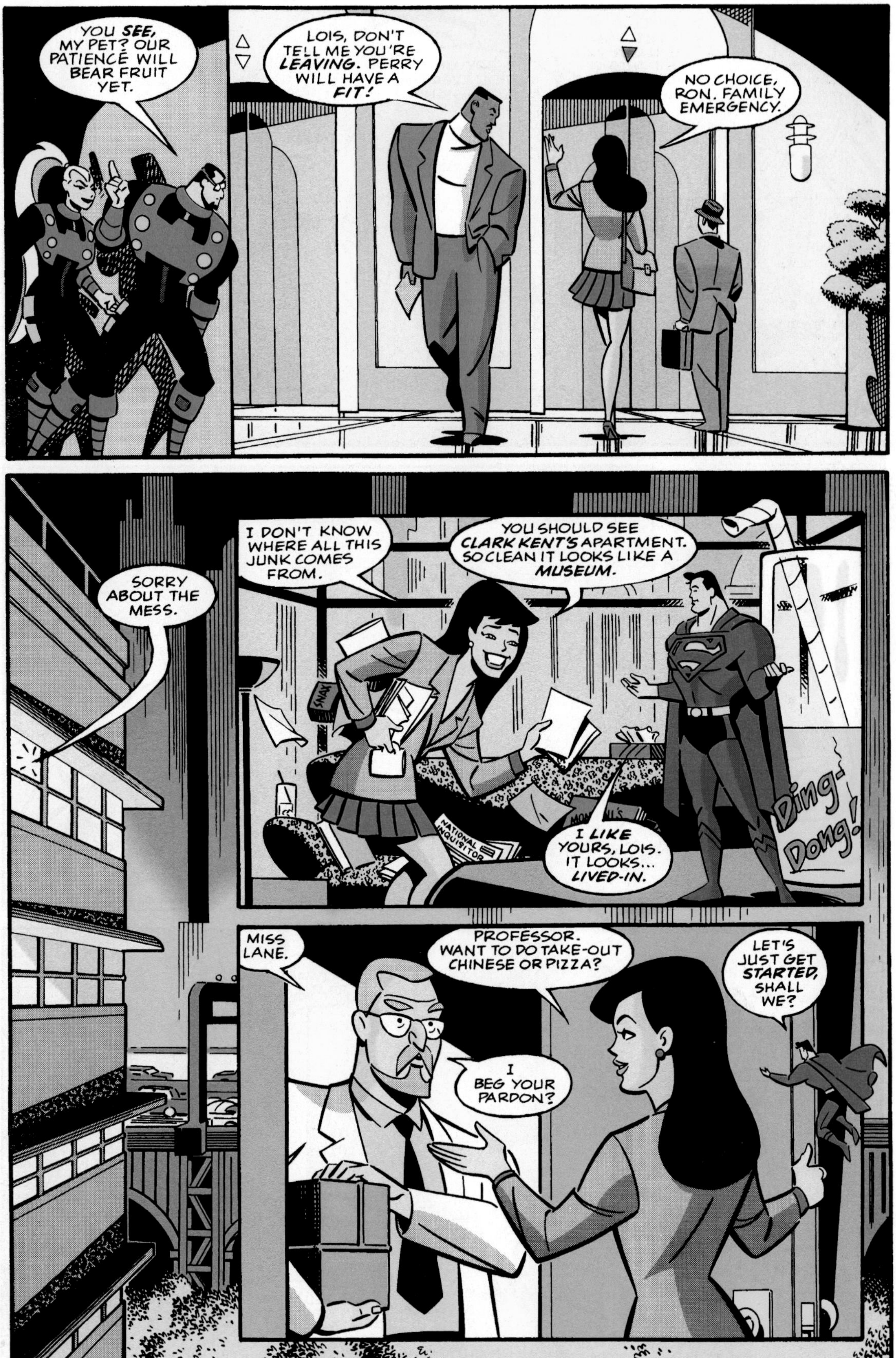
YOU SEE, MY PET? OUR PATIENCE WILL BEAR FRUIT YET.
LOIS, DON'T TELL ME YOU'RE LEAVING. PERRY WILL HAVE A FIT!
NO CHOICE, RON. FAMILY EMERGENCY.
SORRY ABOUT THE MESS.
I DON'T KNOW WHERE ALL THIS JUNK COMES FROM.
YOU SHOULD SEE CLARK KENT'S APARTMENT. SO CLEAN IT LOOKS LIKE A MUSEUM.
SNAX
NATIONAL INQUISITOR
I LIKE YOURS, LOIS. IT LOOKS... LIVED-IN.
Ding-Dong!
MISS LANE.
PROFESSOR. WANT TO DO TAKE-OUT CHINESE OR PIZZA?
I BEG YOUR PARDON?
LET'S JUST GET STARTED, SHALL WE?

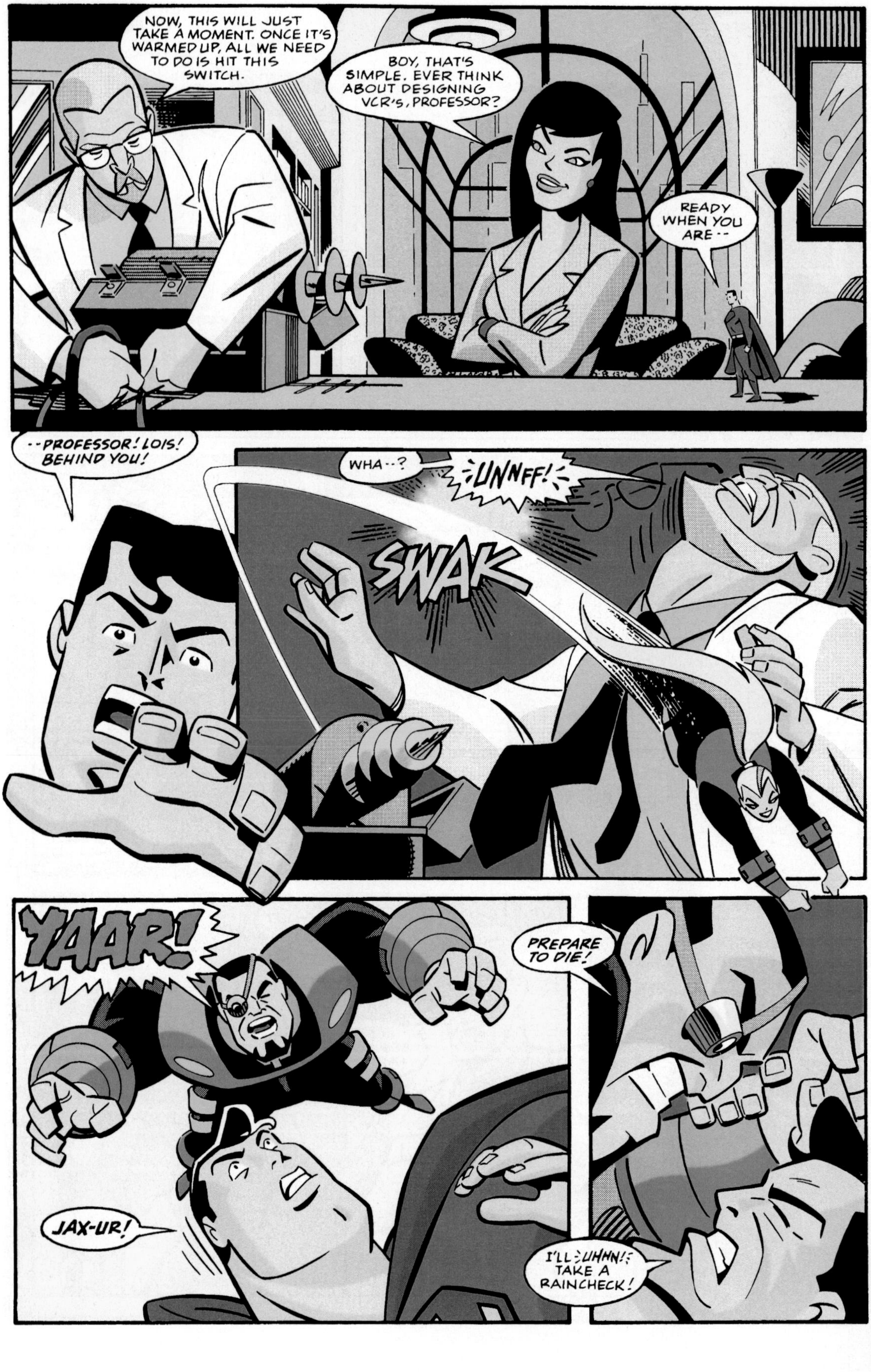
NOW, THIS WILL JUST TAKE A MOMENT. ONCE IT'S WARMED UP, ALL WE NEED TO DO IS HIT THIS SWITCH.
BOY, THAT'S SIMPLE. EVER THINK ABOUT DESIGNING VCR'S, PROFESSOR?
READY WHEN YOU ARE--
--PROFESSOR! LOIS! BEHIND YOU!
WHA--?
UNNFF!
SWAK
YAAR!
JAX-UR!
PREPARE TO DIE!
I'LL UHHN! TAKE A RAINCHECK!

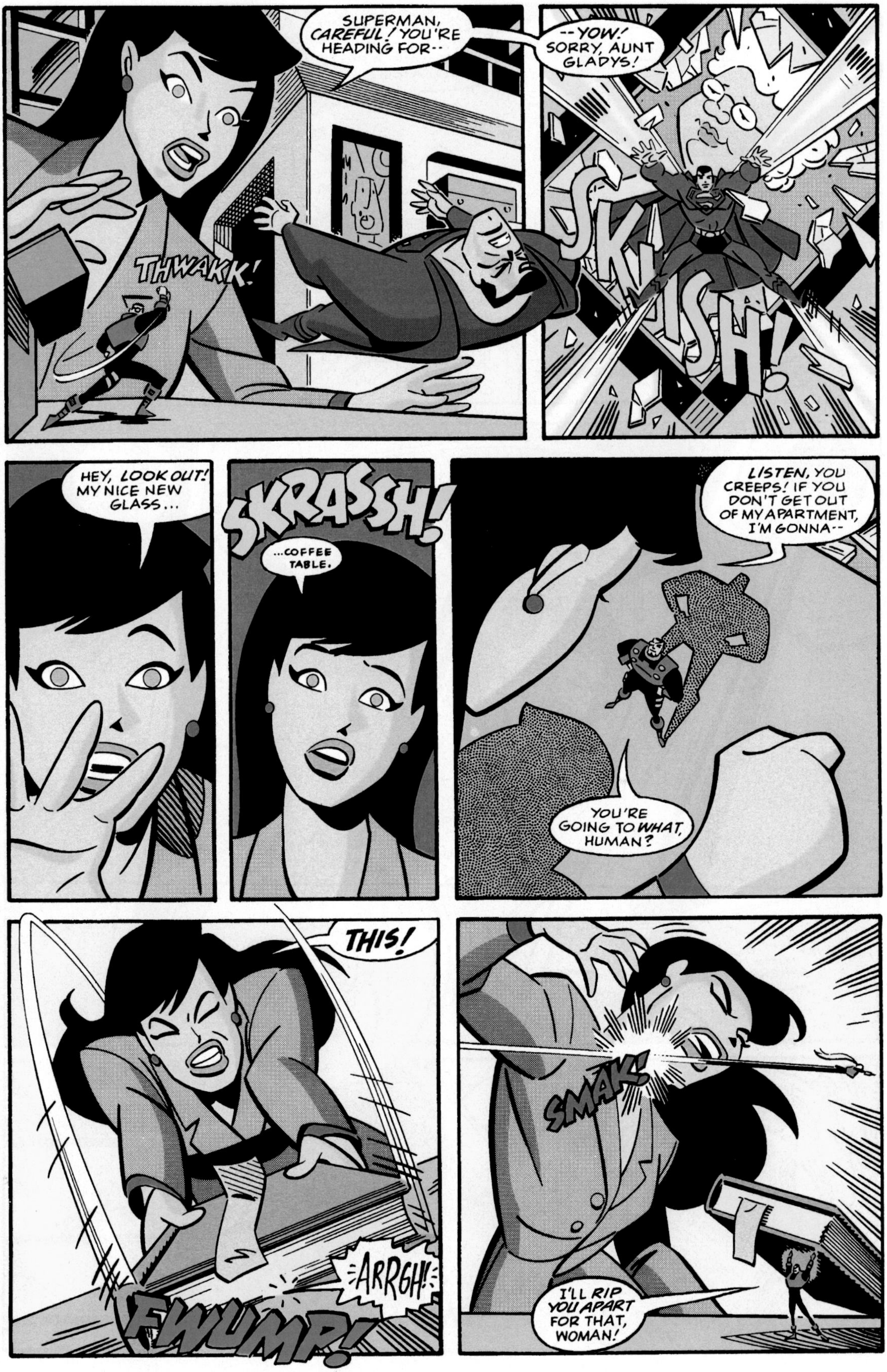
SUPERMAN, CAREFUL! YOU'RE HEADING FOR--
THWAKK!
--YOW! SORRY, AUNT GLADYS!
SKRISH!
HEY, LOOK OUT! MY NICE NEW GLASS...
SKRASSH!
...COFFEE TABLE.
LISTEN, YOU CREEPS! IF YOU DON'T GET OUT OF MY APARTMENT, I'M GONNA--
YOU'RE GOING TO WHAT, HUMAN?
THIS!
ARRGH!
FWUMP!
SMAK!
I'LL RIP YOU APART FOR THAT, WOMAN!

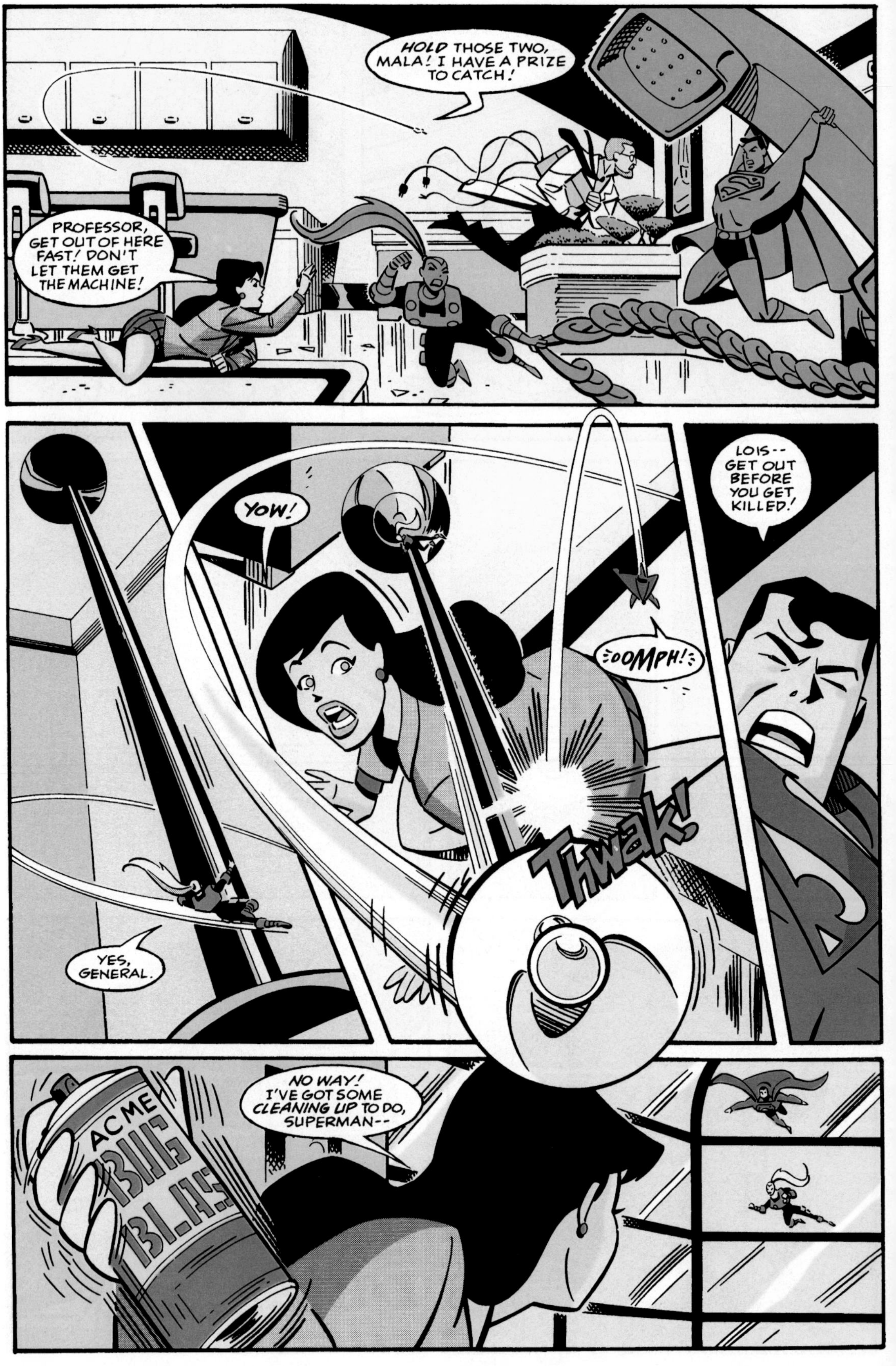
HOLD THOSE TWO, MALA! I HAVE A PRIZE TO CATCH!
PROFESSOR, GET OUT OF HERE FAST! DON'T LET THEM GET THE MACHINE!
YOW!
OOMPH!
LOIS-- GET OUT BEFORE YOU GET KILLED!
THWAK!
YES, GENERAL.
ACME BUG BLAST
NO WAY! I'VE GOT SOME CLEANING UP TO DO, SUPERMAN--

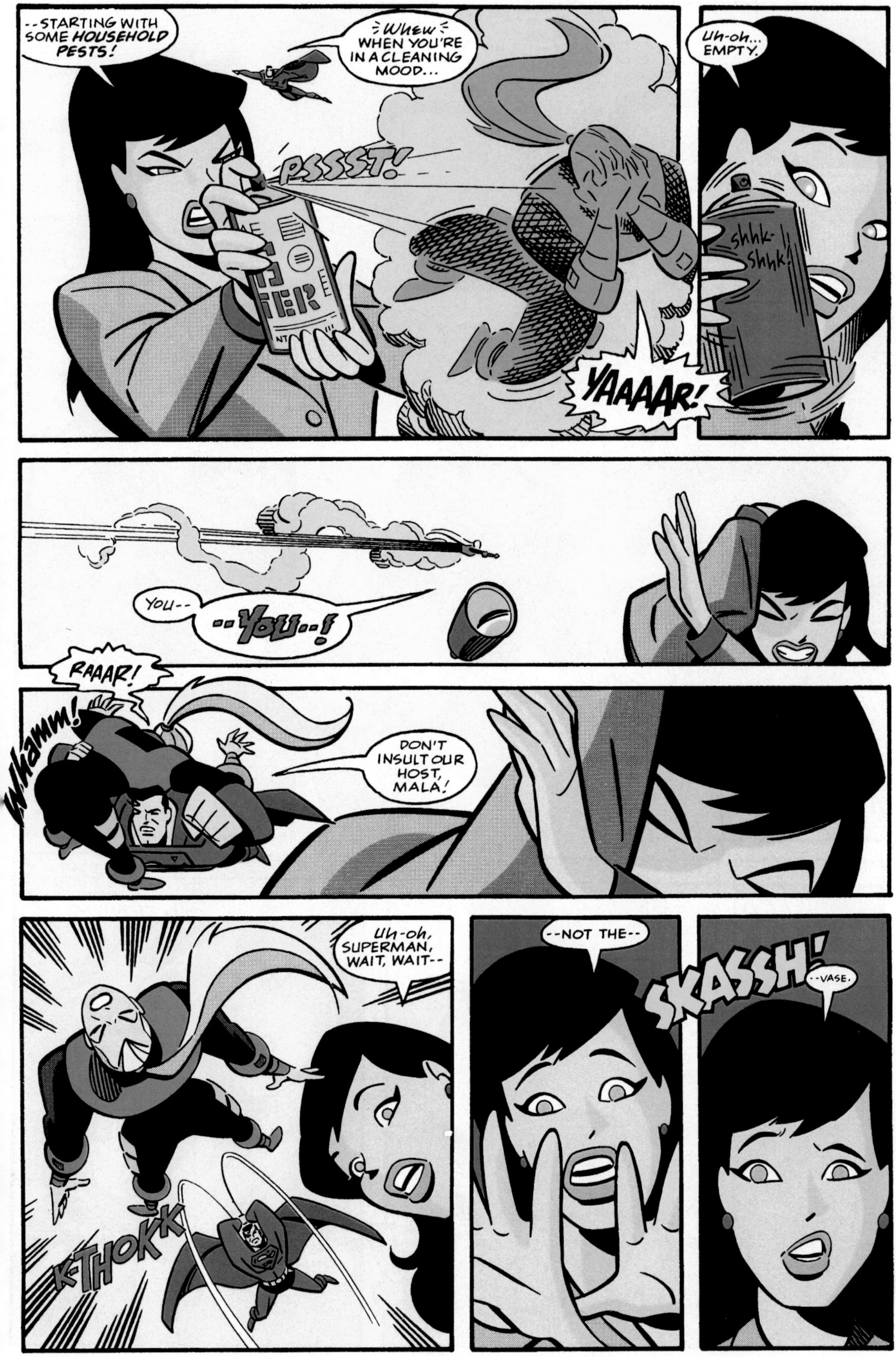
--STARTING WITH SOME HOUSEHOLD PESTS!
PSSSST!
Whew WHEN YOU'RE IN A CLEANING MOOD...
YAAAAR!
Uh-oh... EMPTY.
shhk-shhk!
YOU--
--YOU--!
RAAAR!
WHAMM!
DON'T INSULT OUR HOST, MALA!
Uh-oh, SUPERMAN, WAIT, WAIT--
K-THOKK
--NOT THE--
SKASSH!
--VASE.

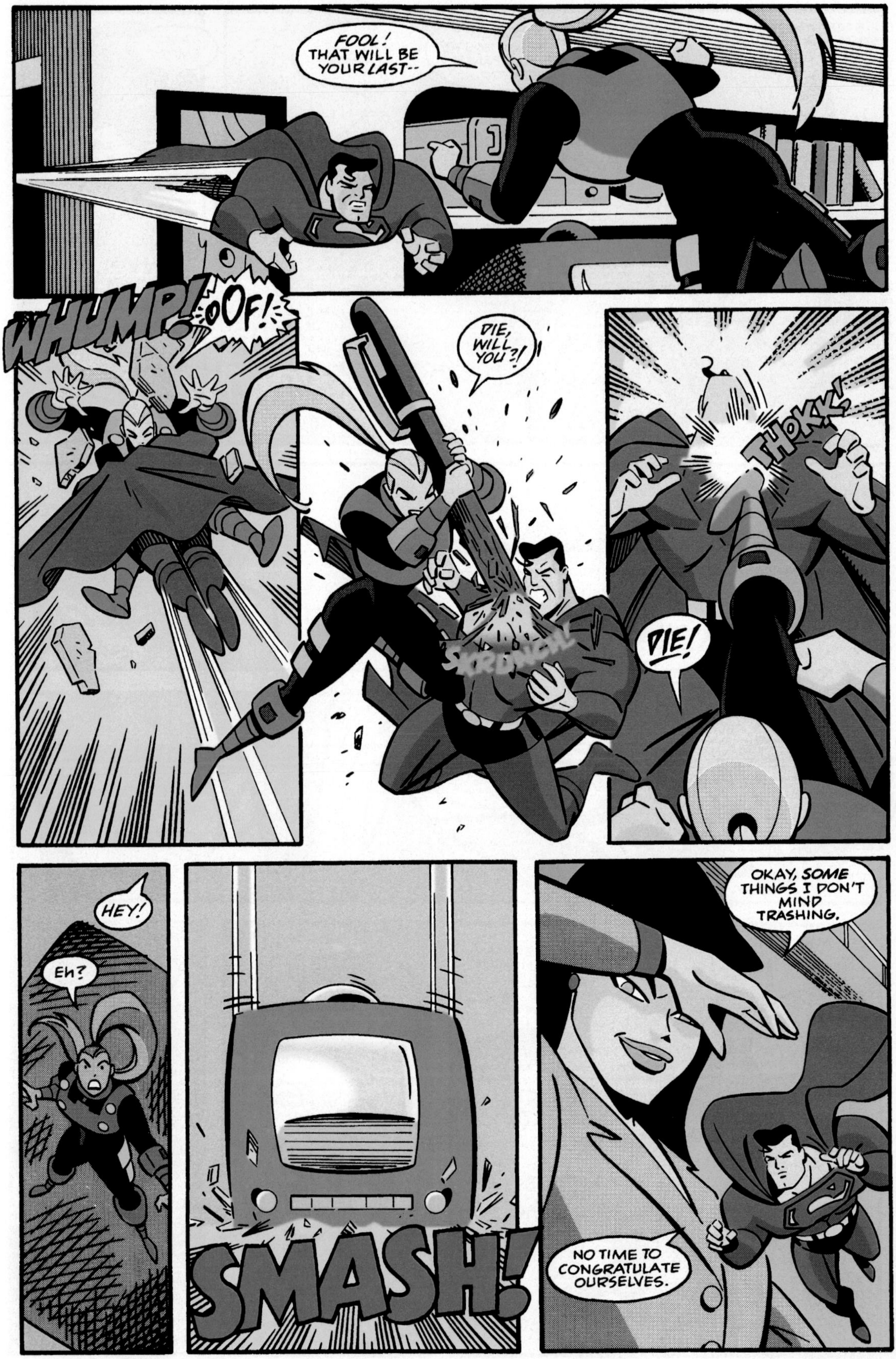
FOOL! THAT WILL BE YOUR LAST--
WHUMP!
OOF!
DIE, WILL YOU?!
SKRUNCH!
THOKK!
DIE!
HEY!
Eh?
SMASH!
OKAY, SOME THINGS I DON'T MIND TRASHING.
NO TIME TO CONGRATULATE OURSELVES.

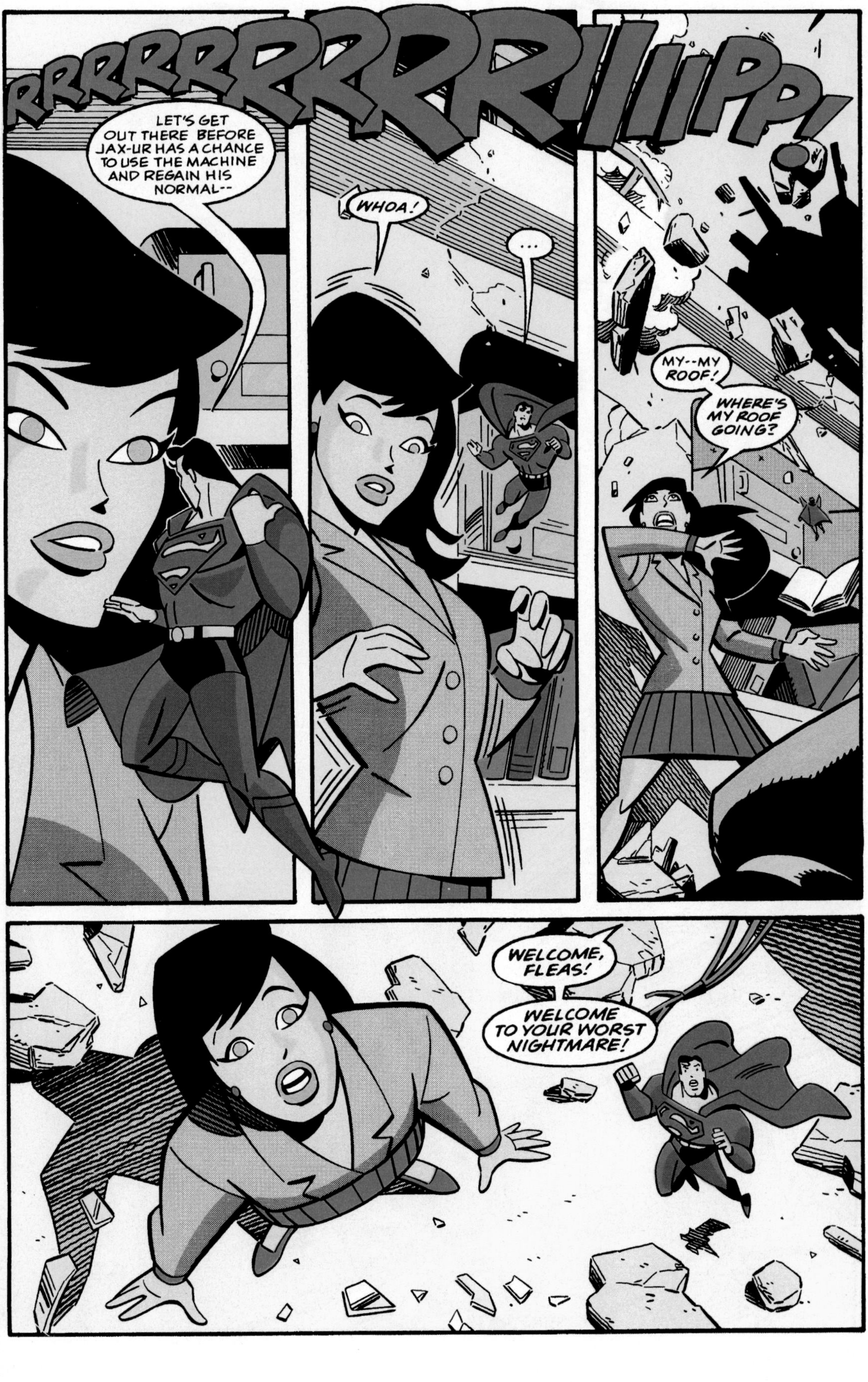
RRRRRRRRRRIIIIPP!
LET'S GET OUT THERE BEFORE JAX-UR HAS A CHANCE TO USE THE MACHINE AND REGAIN HIS NORMAL--
WHOA!
...
MY--MY ROOF!
WHERE'S MY ROOF GOING?
WELCOME, FLEAS!
WELCOME TO YOUR WORST NIGHTMARE!

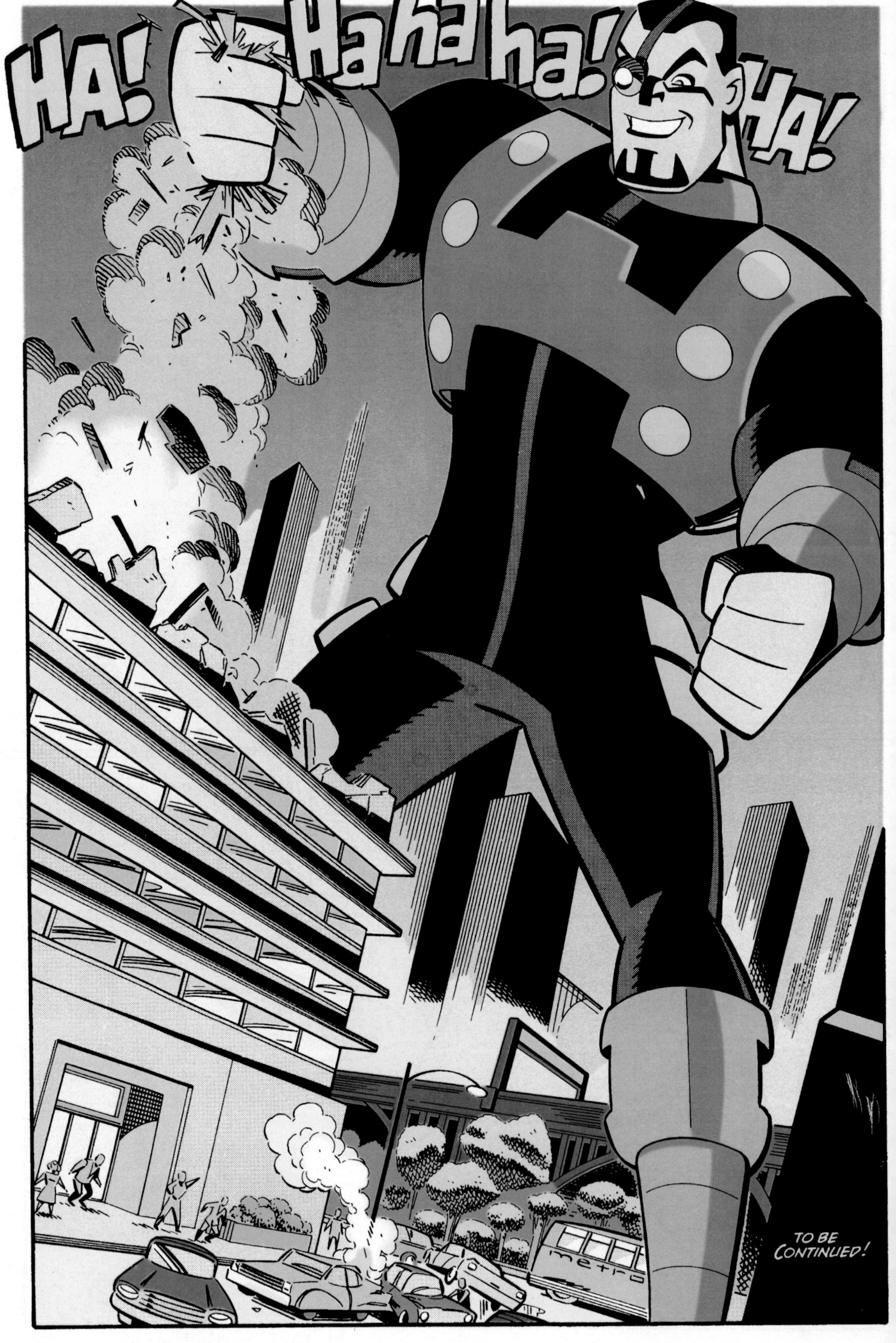
HA! Ha ha ha ha! HA!
metro
TO BE CONTINUED!

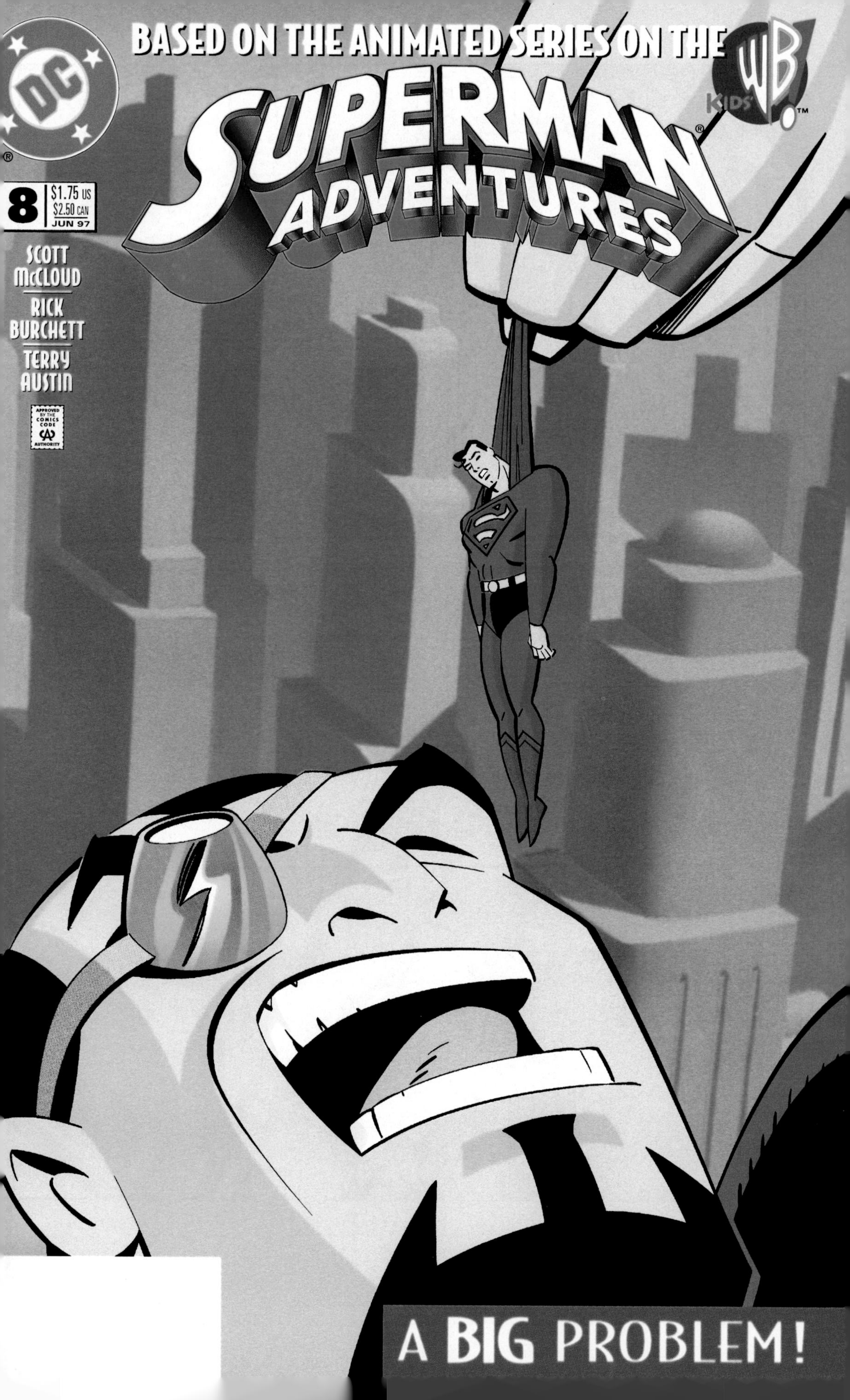
BASED ON THE ANIMATED SERIES ON THE
KIDS' WB!
SUPERMAN ADVENTURES
8 $1.75 US $2.50 CAN JUN 97
SCOTT McCLOUD
RICK BURCHETT
TERRY AUSTIN
APPROVED BY THE COMICS CODE AUTHORITY
A BIG PROBLEM!

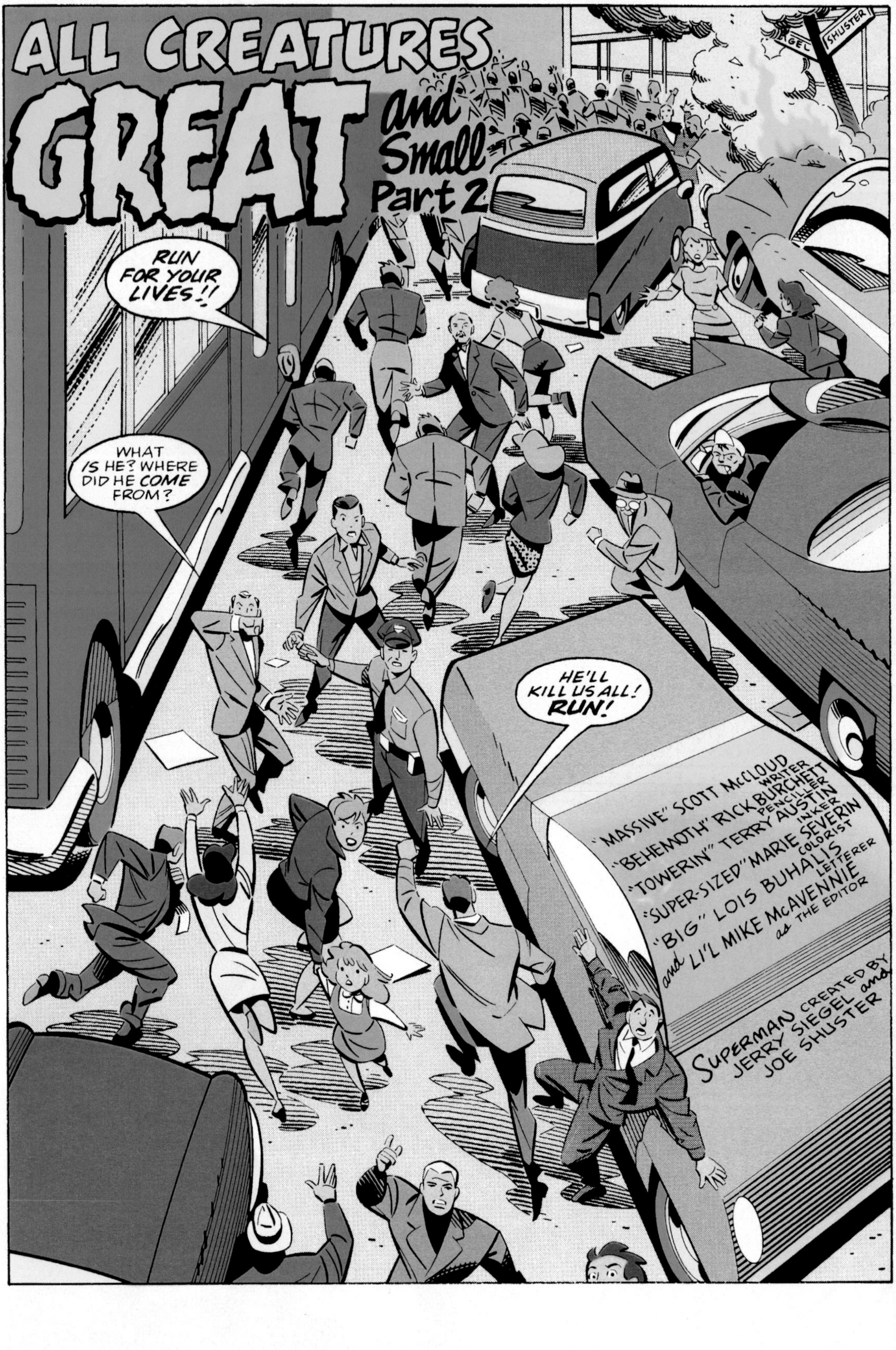
ALL CREATURES GREAT and Small Part 2
SIEGEL
SHUSTER
RUN FOR YOUR LIVES!!
WHAT IS HE? WHERE DID HE COME FROM?
HE'LL KILL US ALL! RUN!
"MASSIVE" SCOTT McCLOUD WRITER
"BEHEMOTH" RICK BURCHETT PENCILLER
"TOWERIN'" TERRY AUSTIN INKER
"SUPER-SIZED" MARIE SEVERIN COLORIST
"BIG" LOIS BUHALIS LETTERER
and LI'L MIKE McAVENNIE as THE EDITOR
SUPERMAN CREATED BY JERRY SIEGEL and JOE SHUSTER

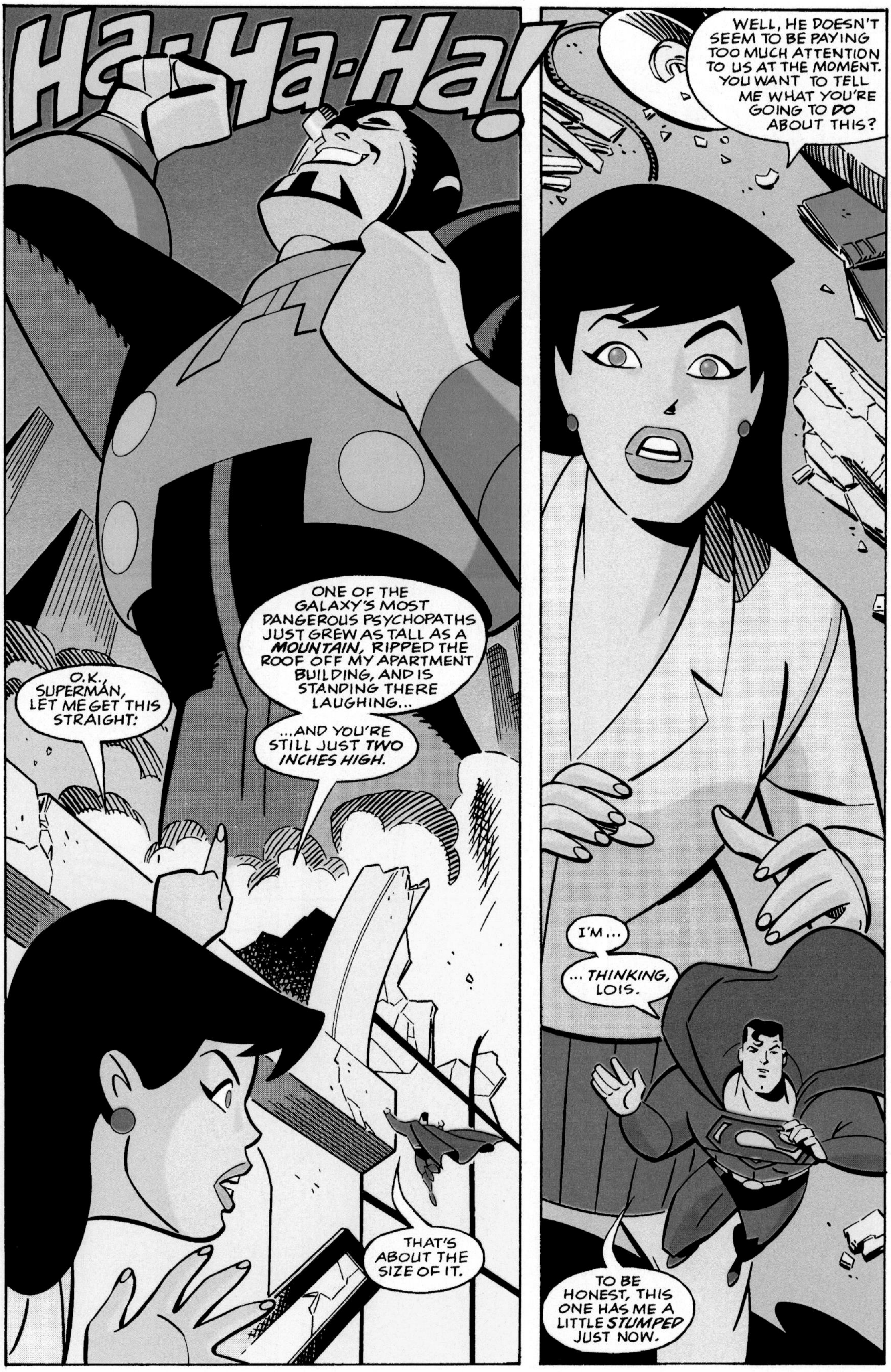

HA-HA-HA-HA!
O.K., SUPERMAN, LET ME GET THIS STRAIGHT:
ONE OF THE GALAXY'S MOST DANGEROUS PSYCHOPATHS JUST GREW AS TALL AS A MOUNTAIN, RIPPED THE ROOF OFF MY APARTMENT BUILDING, AND IS STANDING THERE LAUGHING...
...AND YOU'RE STILL JUST TWO INCHES HIGH.
THAT'S ABOUT THE SIZE OF IT.
WELL, HE DOESN'T SEEM TO BE PAYING TOO MUCH ATTENTION TO US AT THE MOMENT. YOU WANT TO TELL ME WHAT YOU'RE GOING TO DO ABOUT THIS?
I'M...
...THINKING, LOIS.
TO BE HONEST, THIS ONE HAS ME A LITTLE STUMPED JUST NOW.

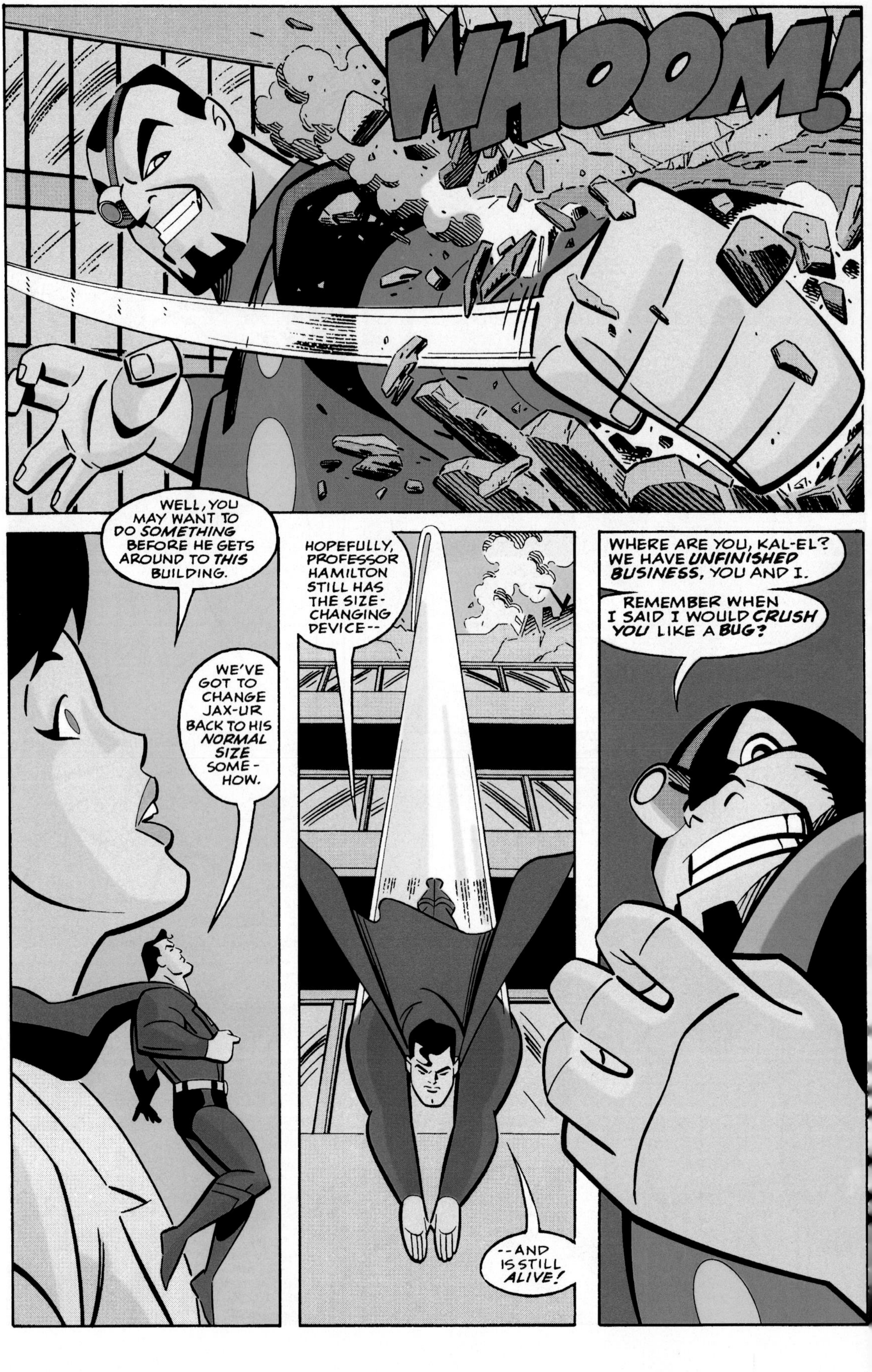
WHOOM!
WELL, YOU MAY WANT TO DO SOMETHING BEFORE HE GETS AROUND TO THIS BUILDING.
WE'VE GOT TO CHANGE JAX-UR BACK TO HIS NORMAL SIZE SOME-HOW.
HOPEFULLY, PROFESSOR HAMILTON STILL HAS THE SIZE-CHANGING DEVICE--
--AND IS STILL ALIVE!
WHERE ARE YOU, KAL-EL? WE HAVE UNFINISHED BUSINESS, YOU AND I.
REMEMBER WHEN I SAID I WOULD CRUSH YOU LIKE A BUG?

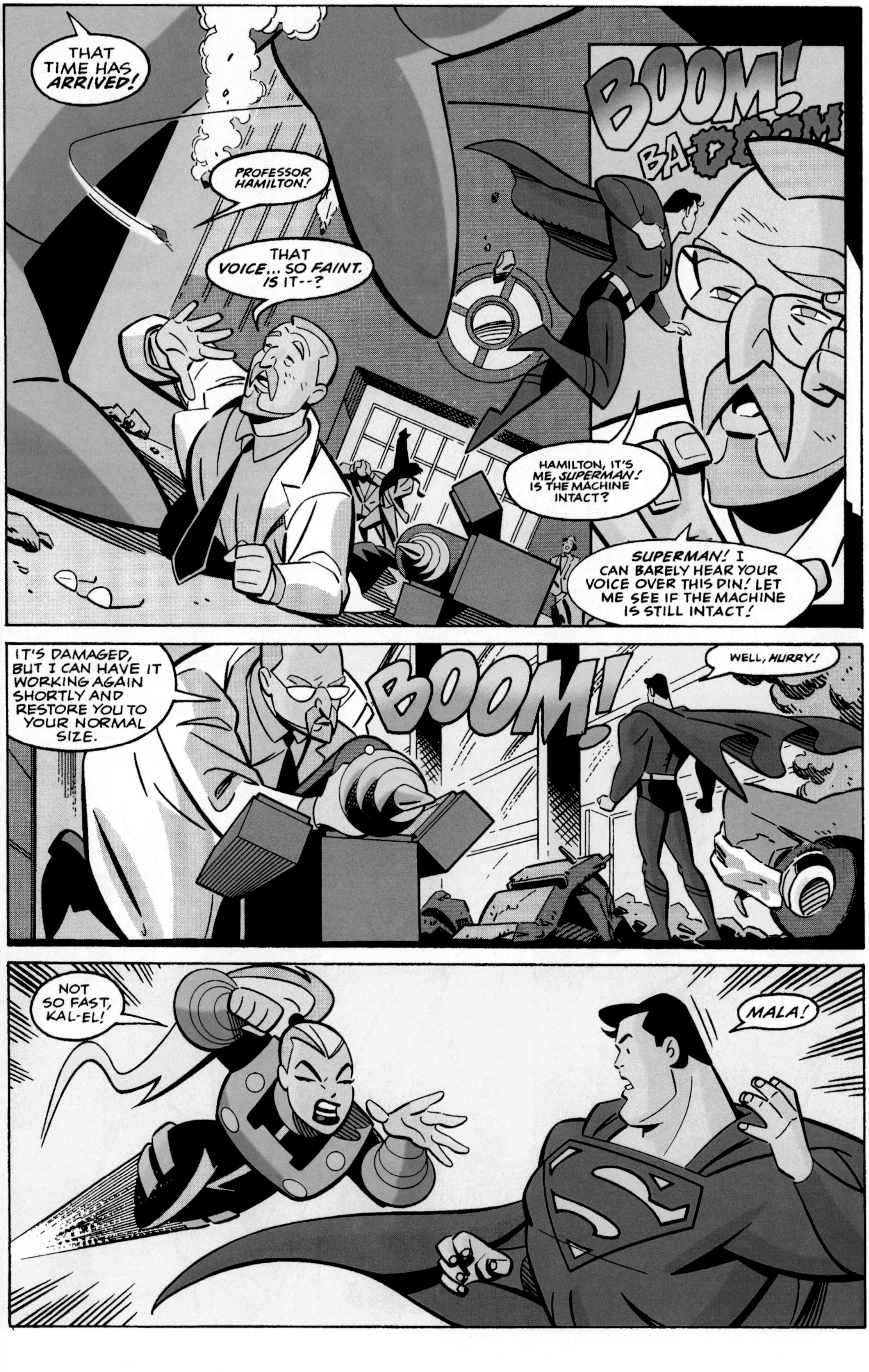
THAT TIME HAS ARRIVED!
PROFESSOR HAMILTON!
THAT VOICE... SO FAINT. IS IT--?
BOOM! BA-DOOM
HAMILTON, IT'S ME, SUPERMAN! IS THE MACHINE INTACT?
SUPERMAN! I CAN BARELY HEAR YOUR VOICE OVER THIS DIN! LET ME SEE IF THE MACHINE IS STILL INTACT!
IT'S DAMAGED, BUT I CAN HAVE IT WORKING AGAIN SHORTLY AND RESTORE YOU TO YOUR NORMAL SIZE.
BOOM!
WELL, HURRY!
NOT SO FAST, KAL-EL!
MALA!

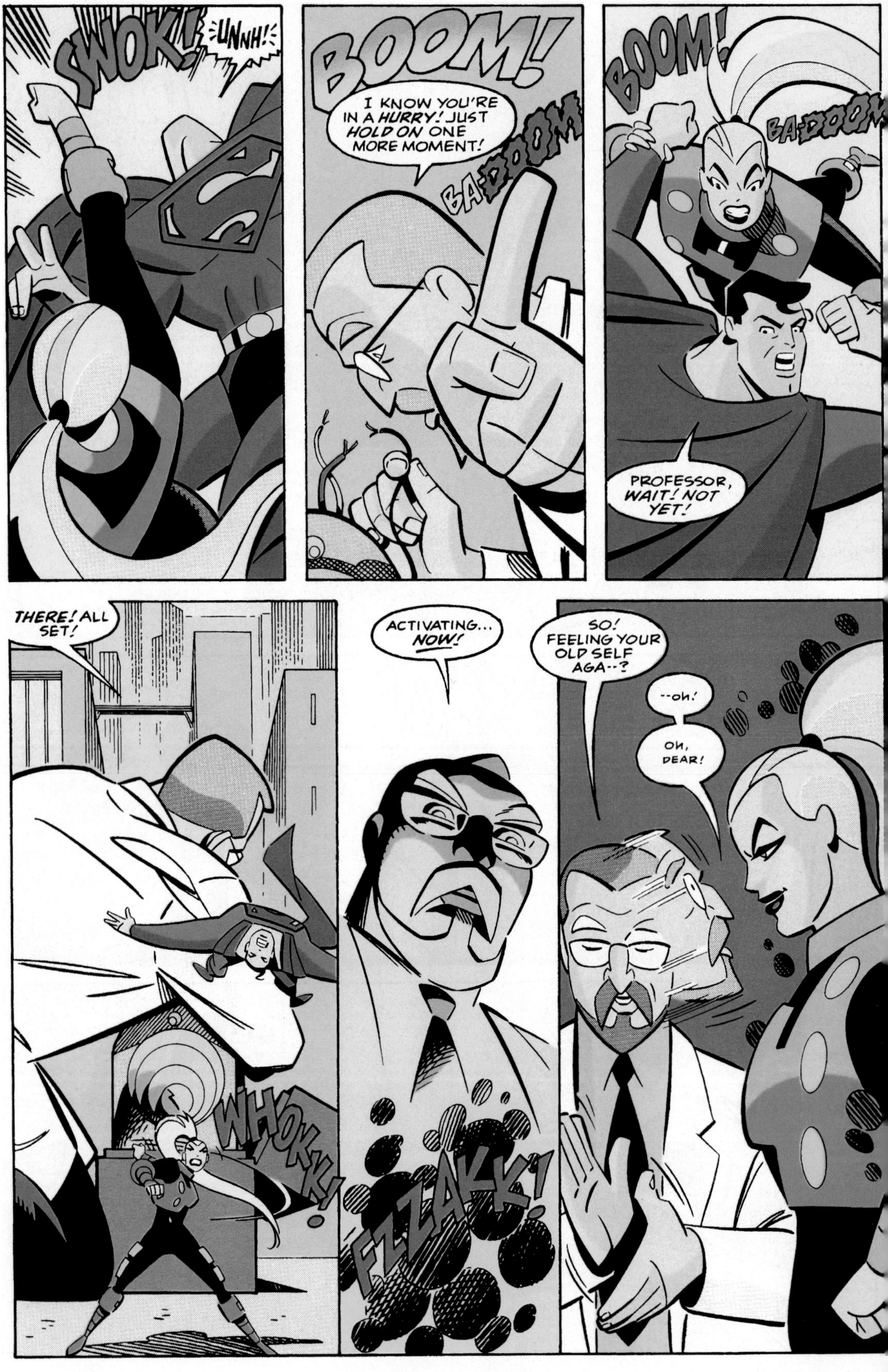
SWOK!
UNNH!
BOOM!
I KNOW YOU'RE IN A HURRY! JUST HOLD ON ONE MORE MOMENT!
BA-DOOM
BOOM!
BA-DOOM
PROFESSOR, WAIT! NOT YET!
THERE! ALL SET!
WHOKK!
ACTIVATING... NOW!
FZZAKK!
SO! FEELING YOUR OLD SELF AGA--?
--oh!
Oh, DEAR!

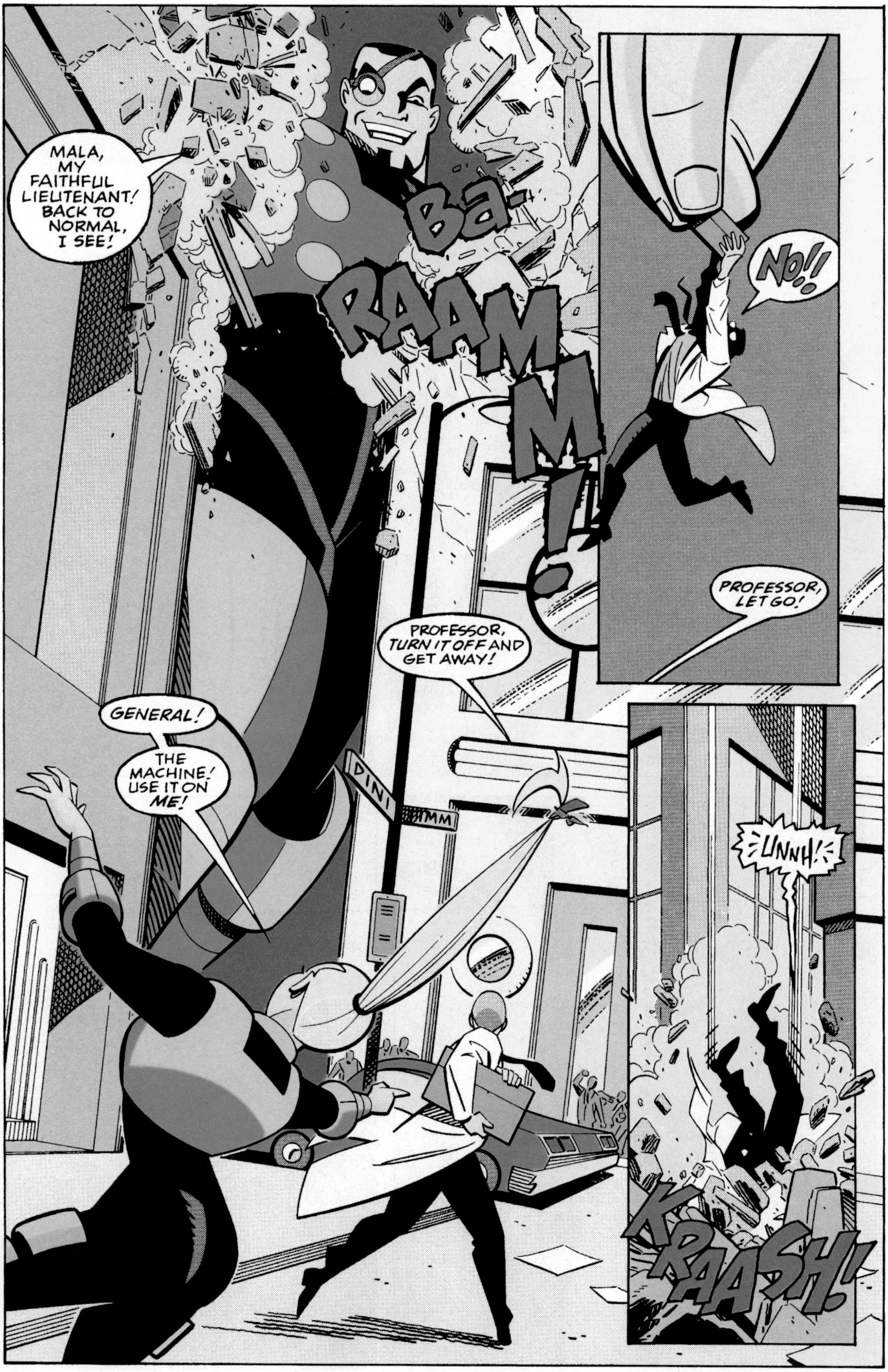
MALA, MY FAITHFUL LIEUTENANT! BACK TO NORMAL, I SEE!
BA-RAAMM!
NO!!
PROFESSOR, LET GO!
PROFESSOR, TURN IT OFF AND GET AWAY!
GENERAL!
THE MACHINE! USE IT ON ME!
DINI
UNNH!
KRAASH!

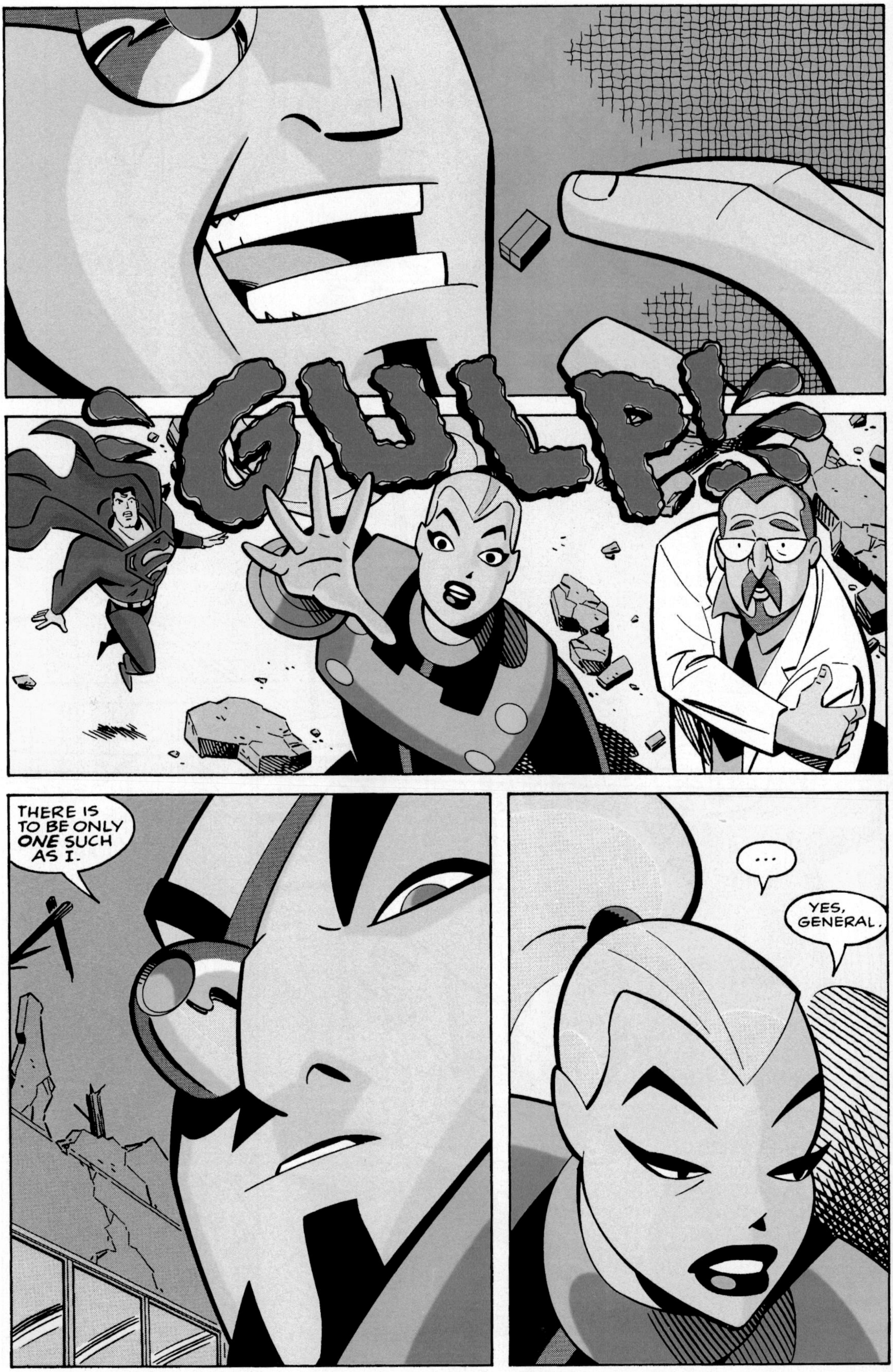
GULP!
THERE IS TO BE ONLY ONE SUCH AS I.
...
YES, GENERAL.

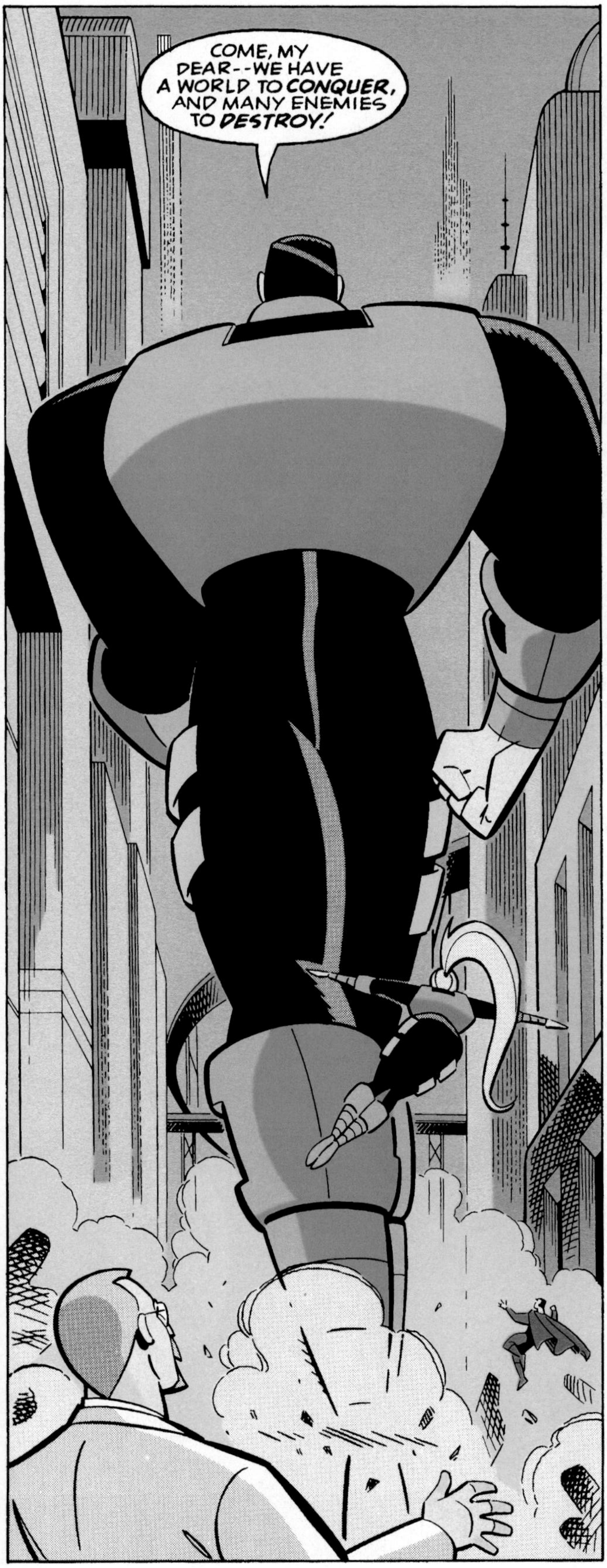
COME, MY DEAR--WE HAVE A WORLD TO CONQUER, AND MANY ENEMIES TO DESTROY!

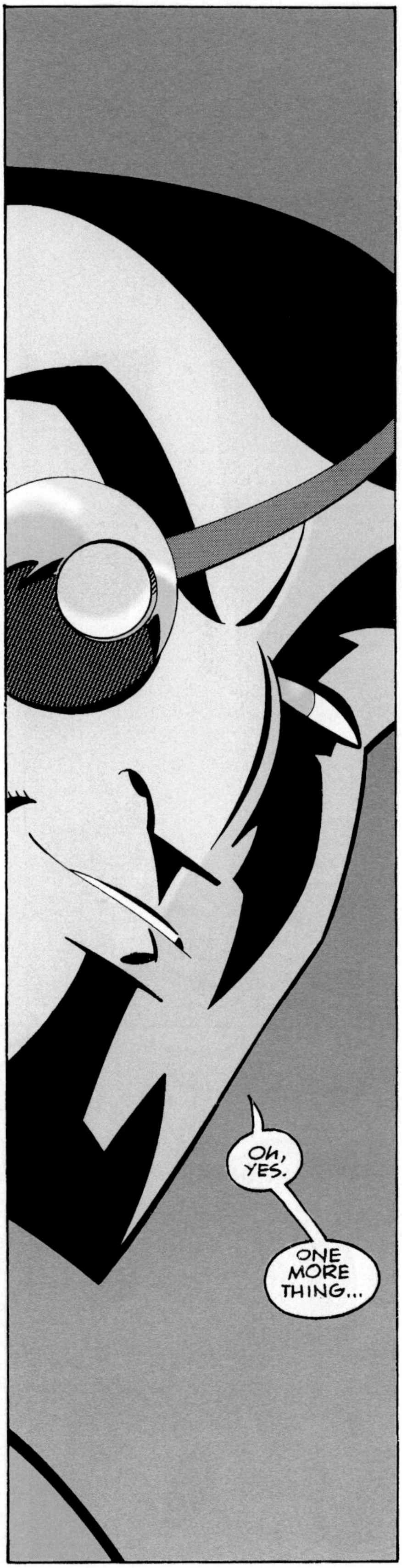
Oh, YES.
ONE MORE THING...

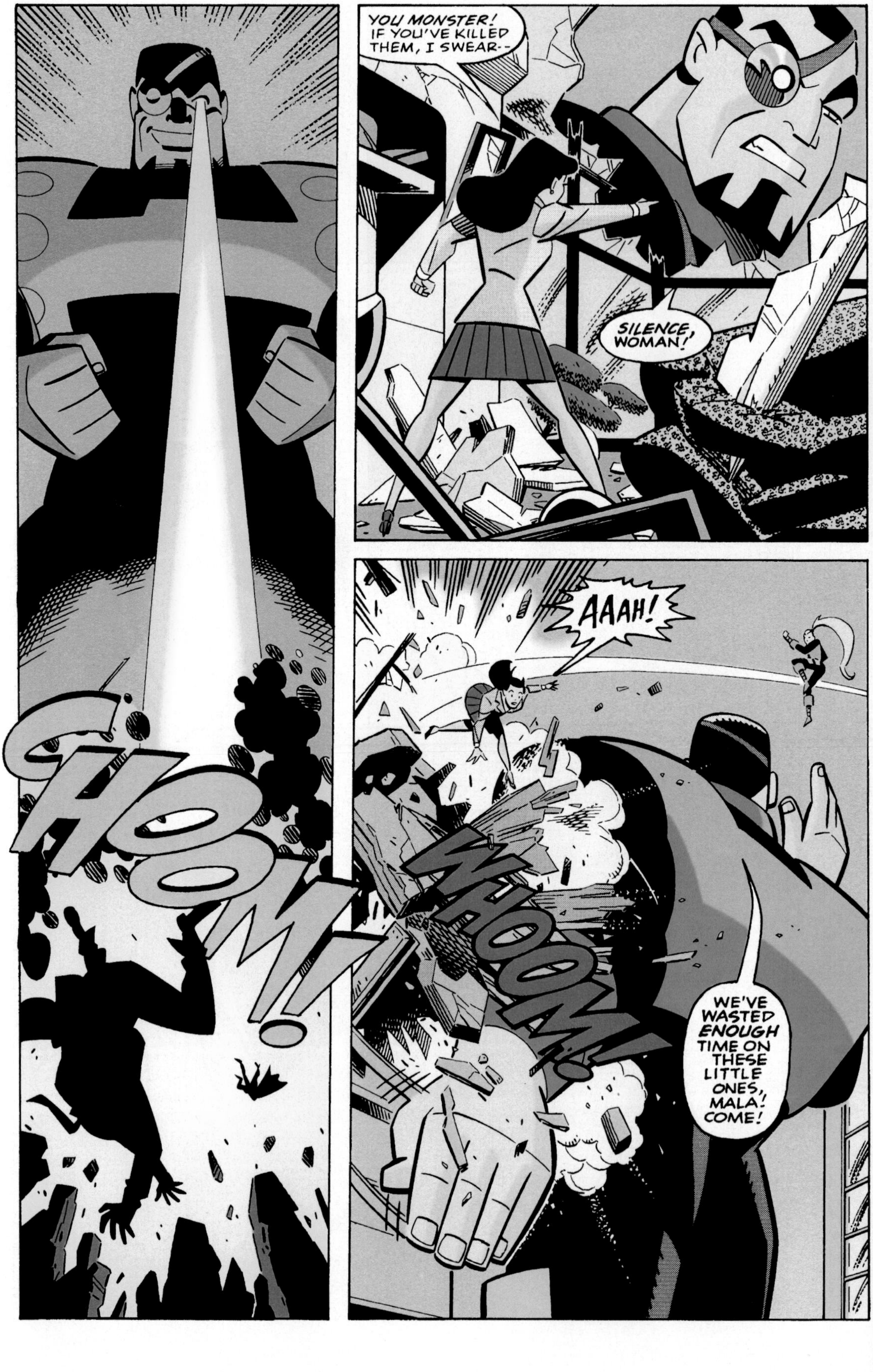
CHOOM!
YOU MONSTER! IF YOU'VE KILLED THEM, I SWEAR--
SILENCE, WOMAN!
AAAH!
WHOOM!
WE'VE WASTED ENOUGH TIME ON THESE LITTLE ONES, MALA! COME!

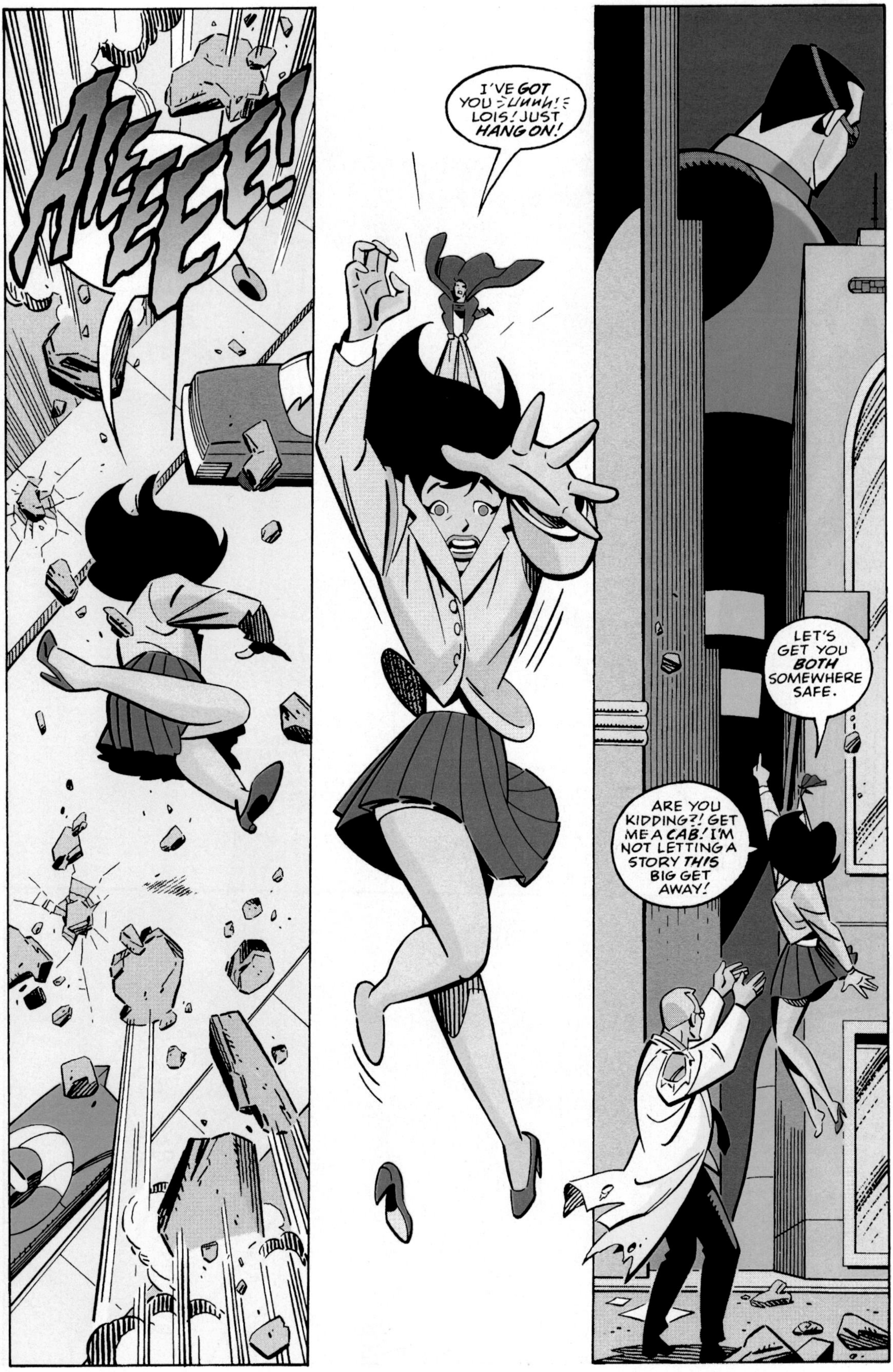
AIEEEE!
I'VE GOT YOU UNNH! LOIS! JUST HANG ON!
LET'S GET YOU BOTH SOMEWHERE SAFE.
ARE YOU KIDDING?! GET ME A CAB! I'M NOT LETTING A STORY THIS BIG GET AWAY!

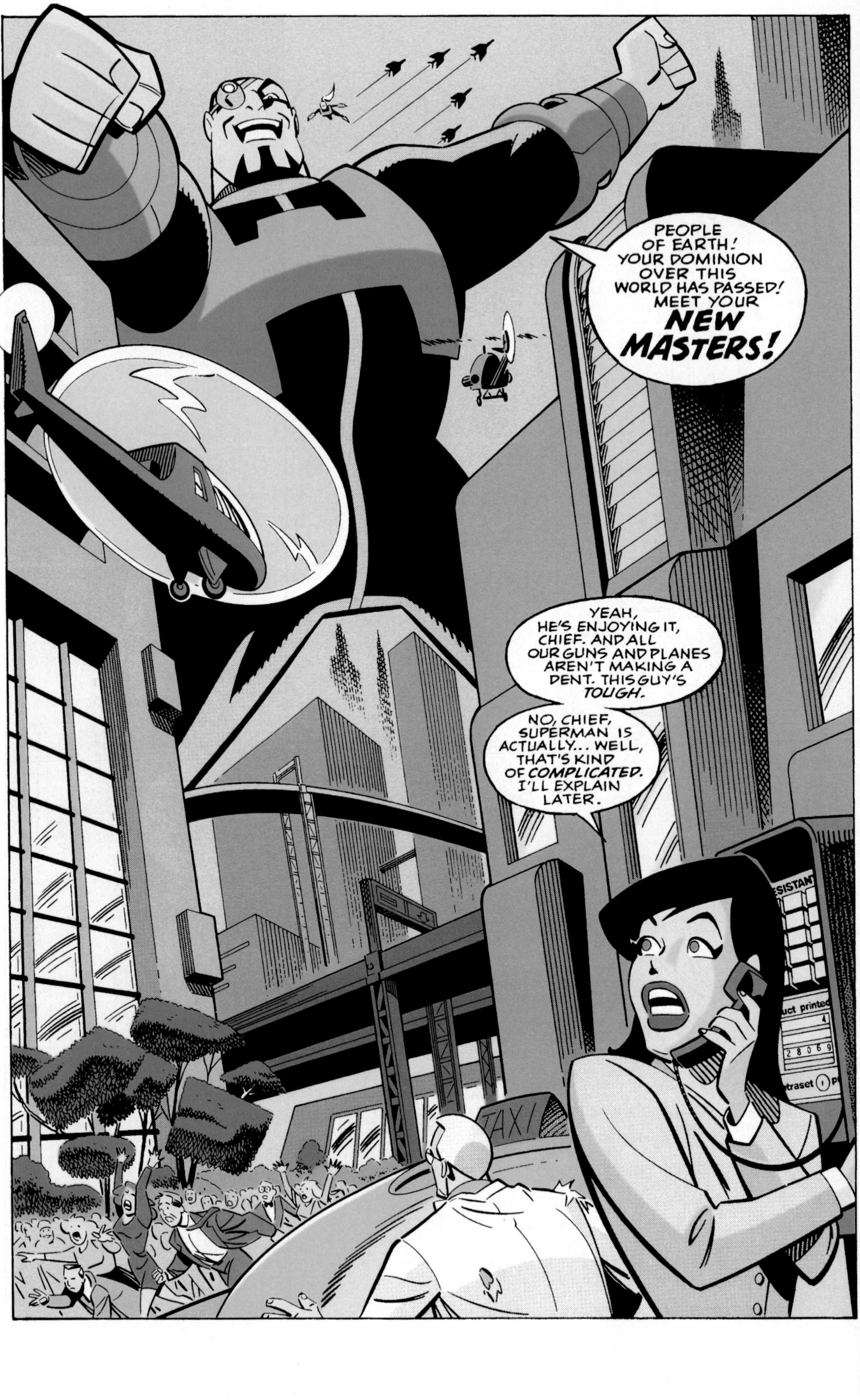
PEOPLE OF EARTH! YOUR DOMINION OVER THIS WORLD HAS PASSED! MEET YOUR *NEW MASTERS!*
YEAH, HE'S ENJOYING IT, CHIEF. AND ALL OUR GUNS AND PLANES AREN'T MAKING A DENT. THIS GUY'S *TOUGH*.
NO, CHIEF, SUPERMAN IS ACTUALLY... WELL, THAT'S KIND OF *COMPLICATED*. I'LL EXPLAIN LATER.
TAXI

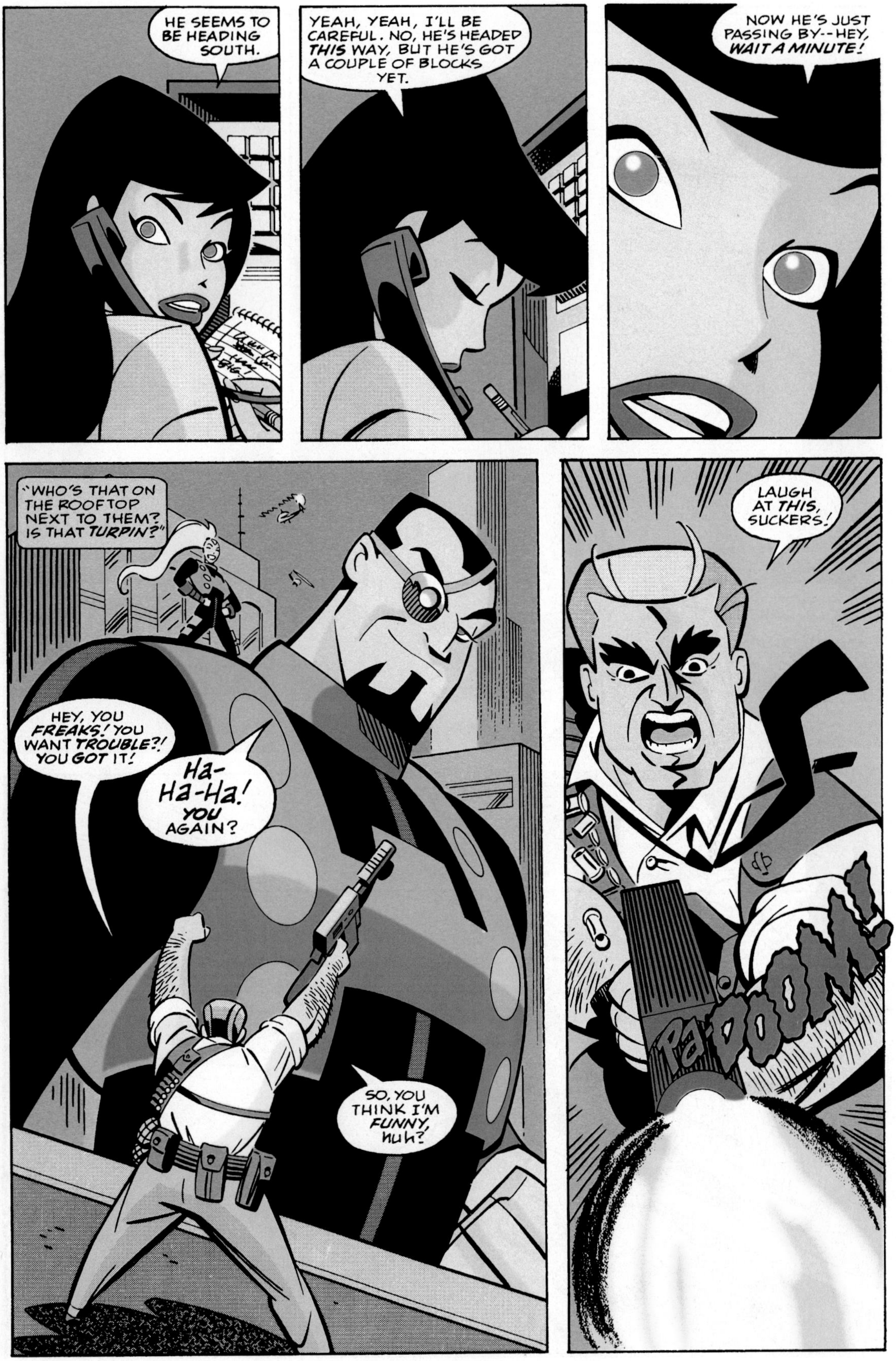
HE SEEMS TO BE HEADING SOUTH.
YEAH, YEAH, I'LL BE CAREFUL. NO, HE'S HEADED THIS WAY, BUT HE'S GOT A COUPLE OF BLOCKS YET.
NOW HE'S JUST PASSING BY--HEY, WAIT A MINUTE!
"WHO'S THAT ON THE ROOFTOP NEXT TO THEM? IS THAT TURPIN?"
HEY, YOU FREAKS! YOU WANT TROUBLE?! YOU GOT IT!
Ha-Ha-Ha! YOU AGAIN?
SO, YOU THINK I'M FUNNY, huh?
LAUGH AT THIS, SUCKERS!
Pa-DOOM!

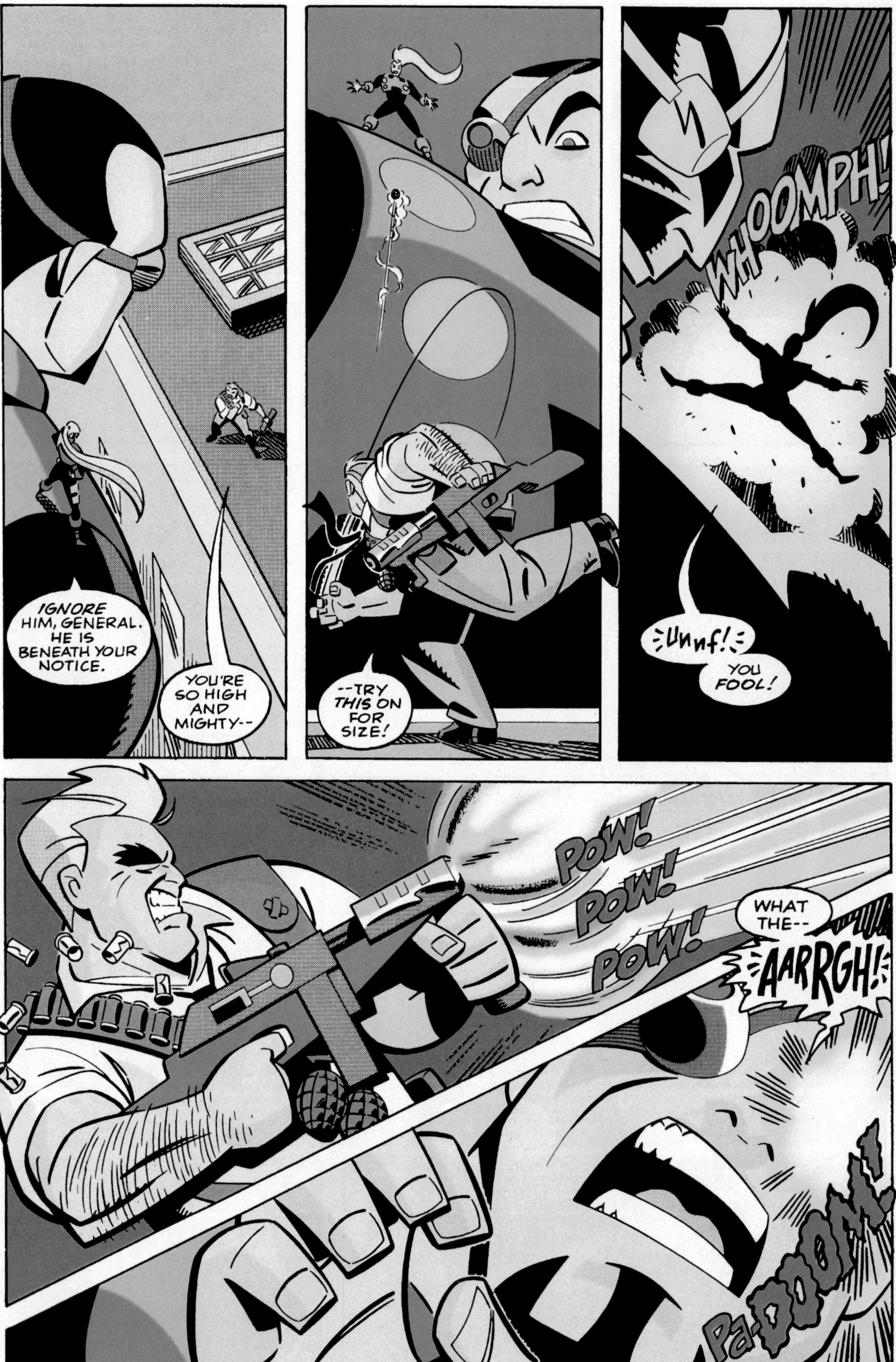
IGNORE HIM, GENERAL. HE IS BENEATH YOUR NOTICE.
YOU'RE SO HIGH AND MIGHTY--
--TRY THIS ON FOR SIZE!
WHOOMPH!
Unnf!
YOU FOOL!
POW!
POW!
POW!
WHAT THE--
AARRGH!
Pa-DOOM!

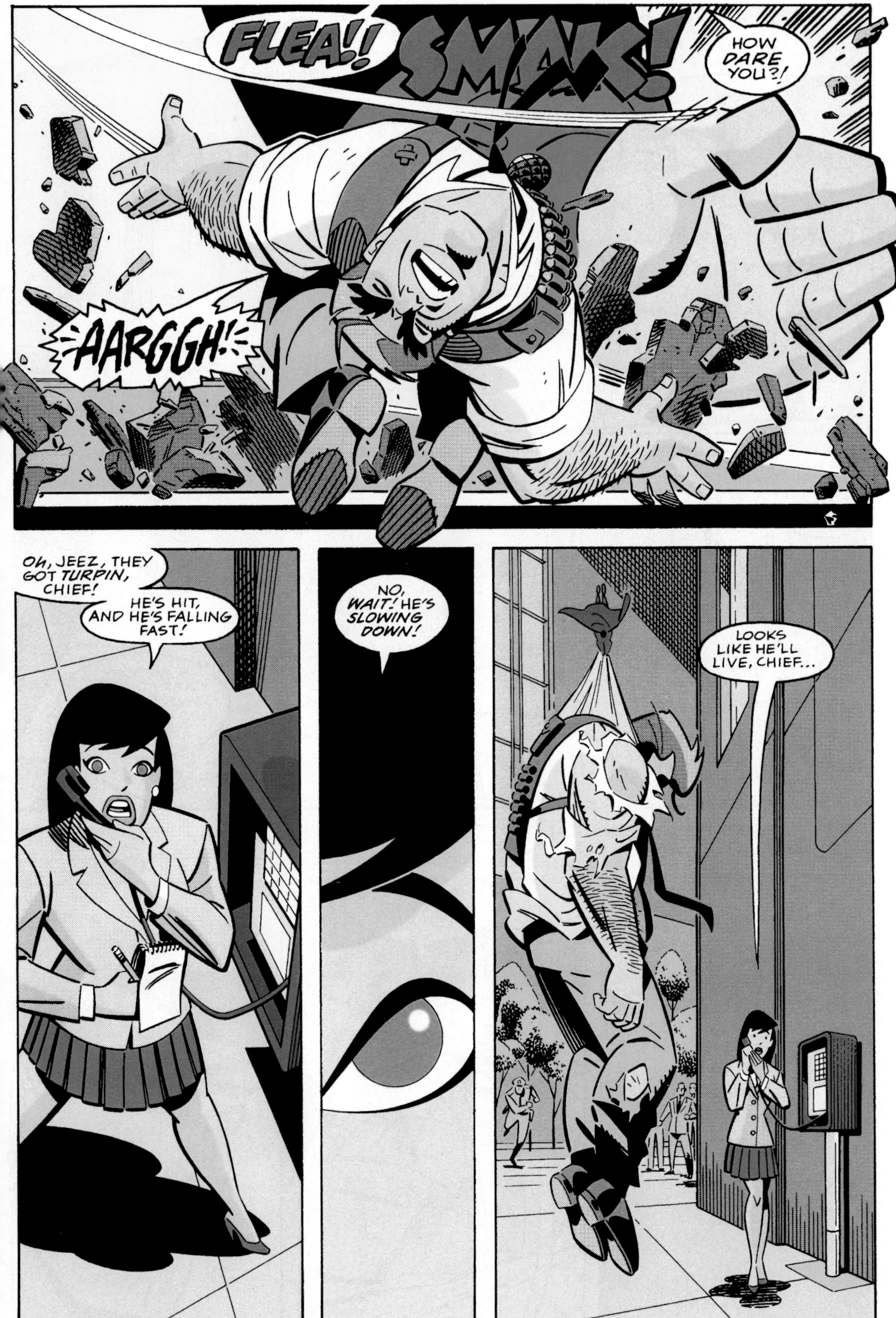
FLEA!!
SMAK!
HOW DARE YOU?!
AARGGH!
Oh, JEEZ, THEY GOT TURPIN, CHIEF!
HE'S HIT, AND HE'S FALLING FAST!
NO, WAIT! HE'S SLOWING DOWN!
LOOKS LIKE HE'LL LIVE, CHIEF...

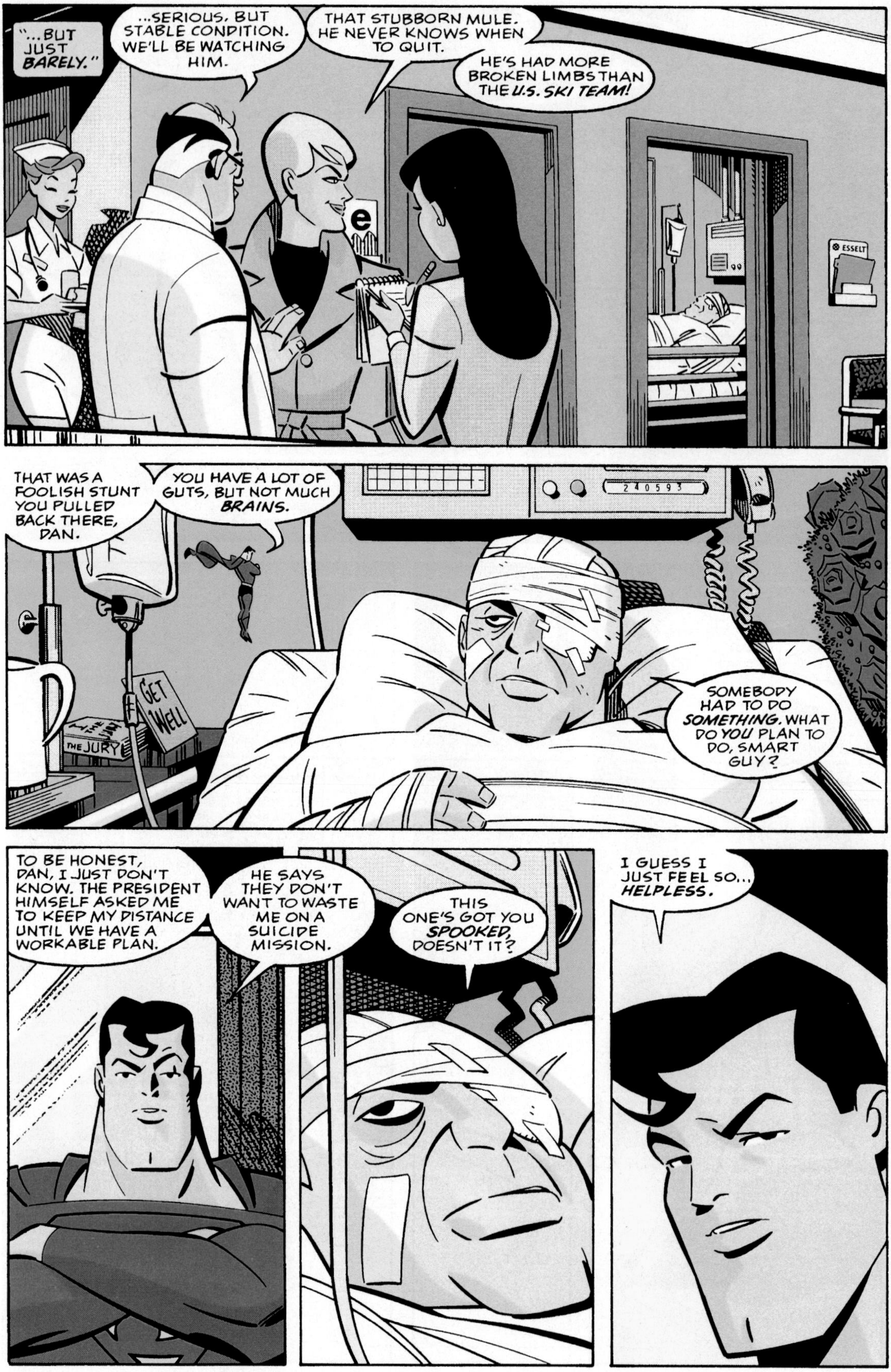

"...BUT JUST BARELY."
...SERIOUS, BUT STABLE CONDITION. WE'LL BE WATCHING HIM.
THAT STUBBORN MULE. HE NEVER KNOWS WHEN TO QUIT.
HE'S HAD MORE BROKEN LIMBS THAN THE U.S. SKI TEAM!
ESSELT
THAT WAS A FOOLISH STUNT YOU PULLED BACK THERE, DAN.
YOU HAVE A LOT OF GUTS, BUT NOT MUCH BRAINS.
240593
GET WELL
THE JURY
SOMEBODY HAD TO DO SOMETHING. WHAT DO YOU PLAN TO DO, SMART GUY?
TO BE HONEST, DAN, I JUST DON'T KNOW. THE PRESIDENT HIMSELF ASKED ME TO KEEP MY DISTANCE UNTIL WE HAVE A WORKABLE PLAN.
HE SAYS THEY DON'T WANT TO WASTE ME ON A SUICIDE MISSION.
THIS ONE'S GOT YOU SPOOKED, DOESN'T IT?
I GUESS I JUST FEEL SO... HELPLESS.

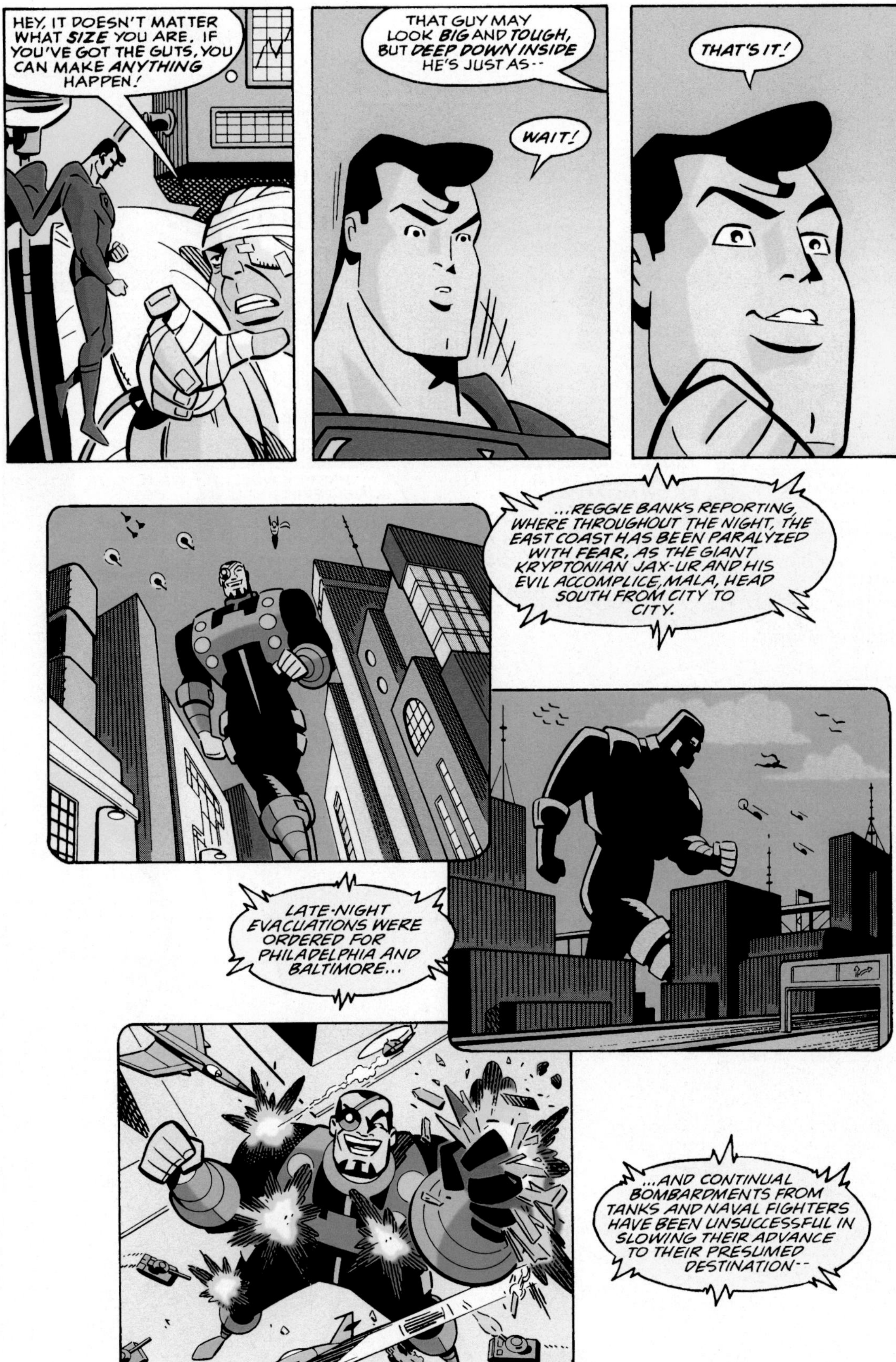
HEY, IT DOESN'T MATTER WHAT SIZE YOU ARE, IF YOU'VE GOT THE GUTS, YOU CAN MAKE ANYTHING HAPPEN!
THAT GUY MAY LOOK BIG AND TOUGH, BUT DEEP DOWN INSIDE HE'S JUST AS--
WAIT!
THAT'S IT!
...REGGIE BANKS REPORTING, WHERE THROUGHOUT THE NIGHT, THE EAST COAST HAS BEEN PARALYZED WITH FEAR, AS THE GIANT KRYPTONIAN JAX-UR AND HIS EVIL ACCOMPLICE, MALA, HEAD SOUTH FROM CITY TO CITY.
LATE-NIGHT EVACUATIONS WERE ORDERED FOR PHILADELPHIA AND BALTIMORE...
...AND CONTINUAL BOMBARDMENTS FROM TANKS AND NAVAL FIGHTERS HAVE BEEN UNSUCCESSFUL IN SLOWING THEIR ADVANCE TO THEIR PRESUMED DESTINATION--

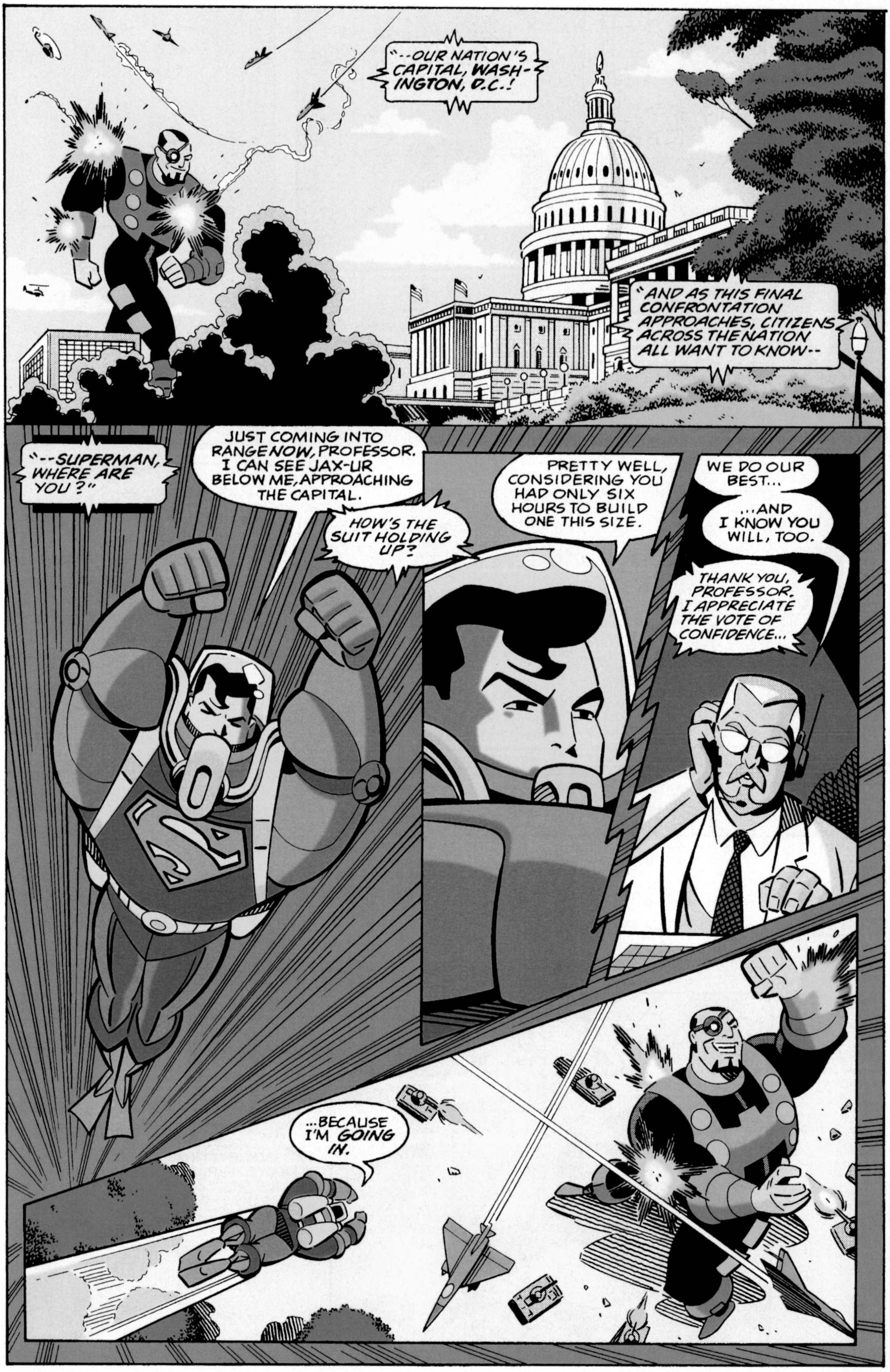
"--OUR NATION'S CAPITAL, WASH-INGTON, D.C.!
"AND AS THIS FINAL CONFRONTATION APPROACHES, CITIZENS ACROSS THE NATION ALL WANT TO KNOW--
"--SUPERMAN, WHERE ARE YOU?"
JUST COMING INTO RANGE NOW, PROFESSOR. I CAN SEE JAX-UR BELOW ME, APPROACHING THE CAPITAL.
HOW'S THE SUIT HOLDING UP?
PRETTY WELL, CONSIDERING YOU HAD ONLY SIX HOURS TO BUILD ONE THIS SIZE.
WE DO OUR BEST...
...AND I KNOW YOU WILL, TOO.
THANK YOU, PROFESSOR. I APPRECIATE THE VOTE OF CONFIDENCE...
...BECAUSE I'M GOING IN.

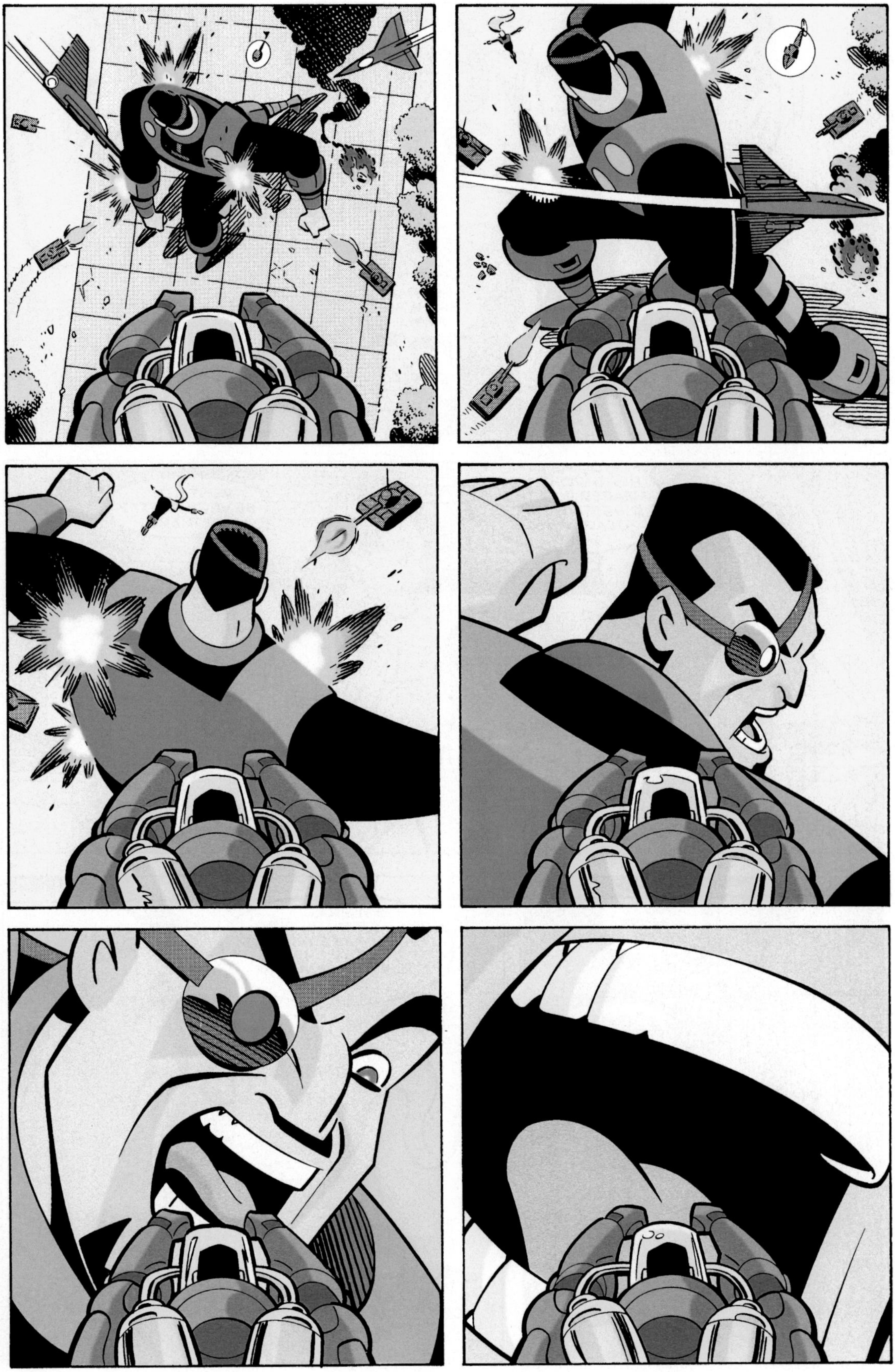

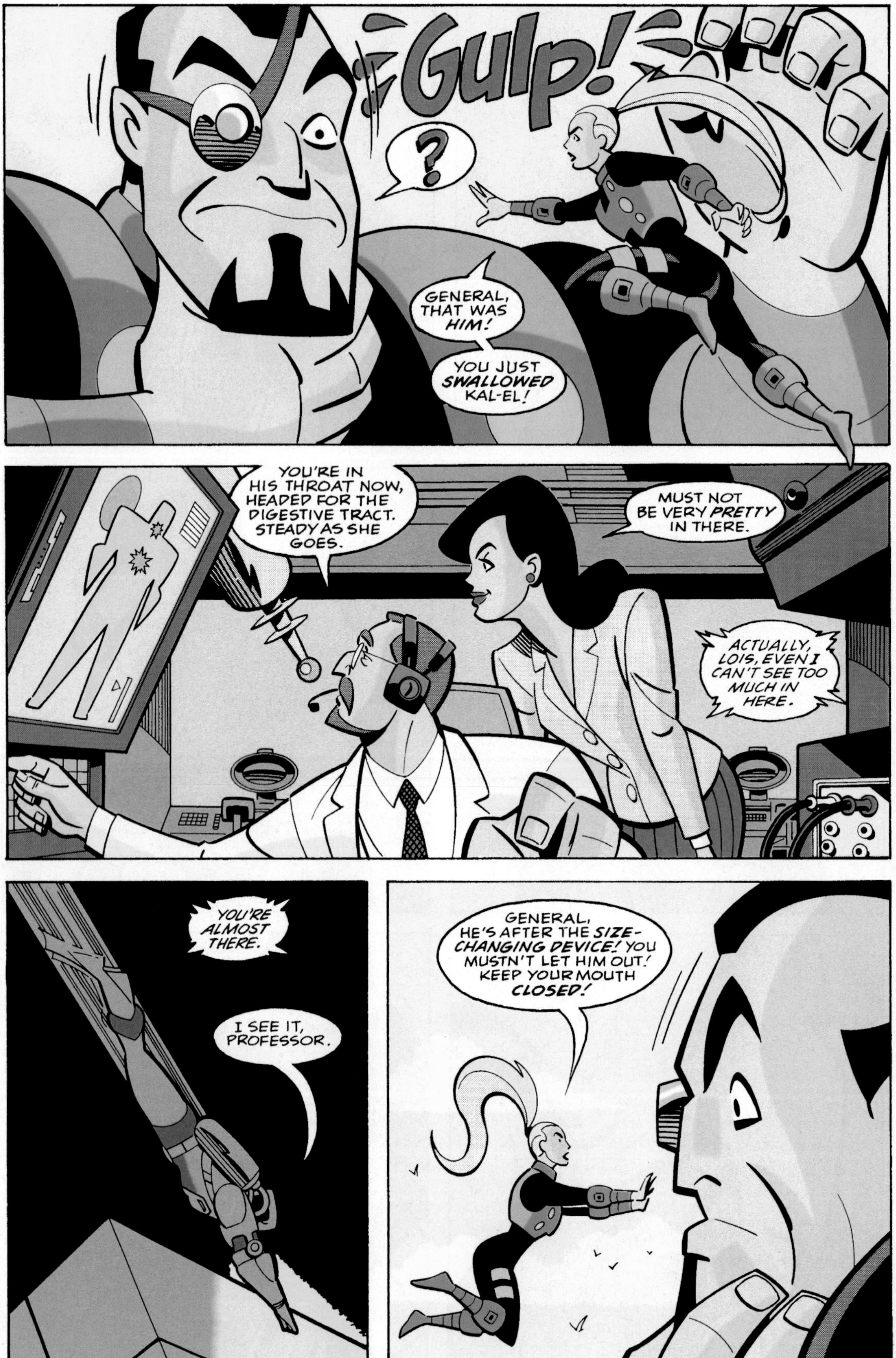
GULP!
?
GENERAL, THAT WAS HIM!
YOU JUST SWALLOWED KAL-EL!
YOU'RE IN HIS THROAT NOW, HEADED FOR THE DIGESTIVE TRACT. STEADY AS SHE GOES.
MUST NOT BE VERY PRETTY IN THERE.
ACTUALLY, LOIS, EVEN I CAN'T SEE TOO MUCH IN HERE.
YOU'RE ALMOST THERE.
I SEE IT, PROFESSOR.
GENERAL, HE'S AFTER THE SIZE-CHANGING DEVICE! YOU MUSTN'T LET HIM OUT! KEEP YOUR MOUTH CLOSED!

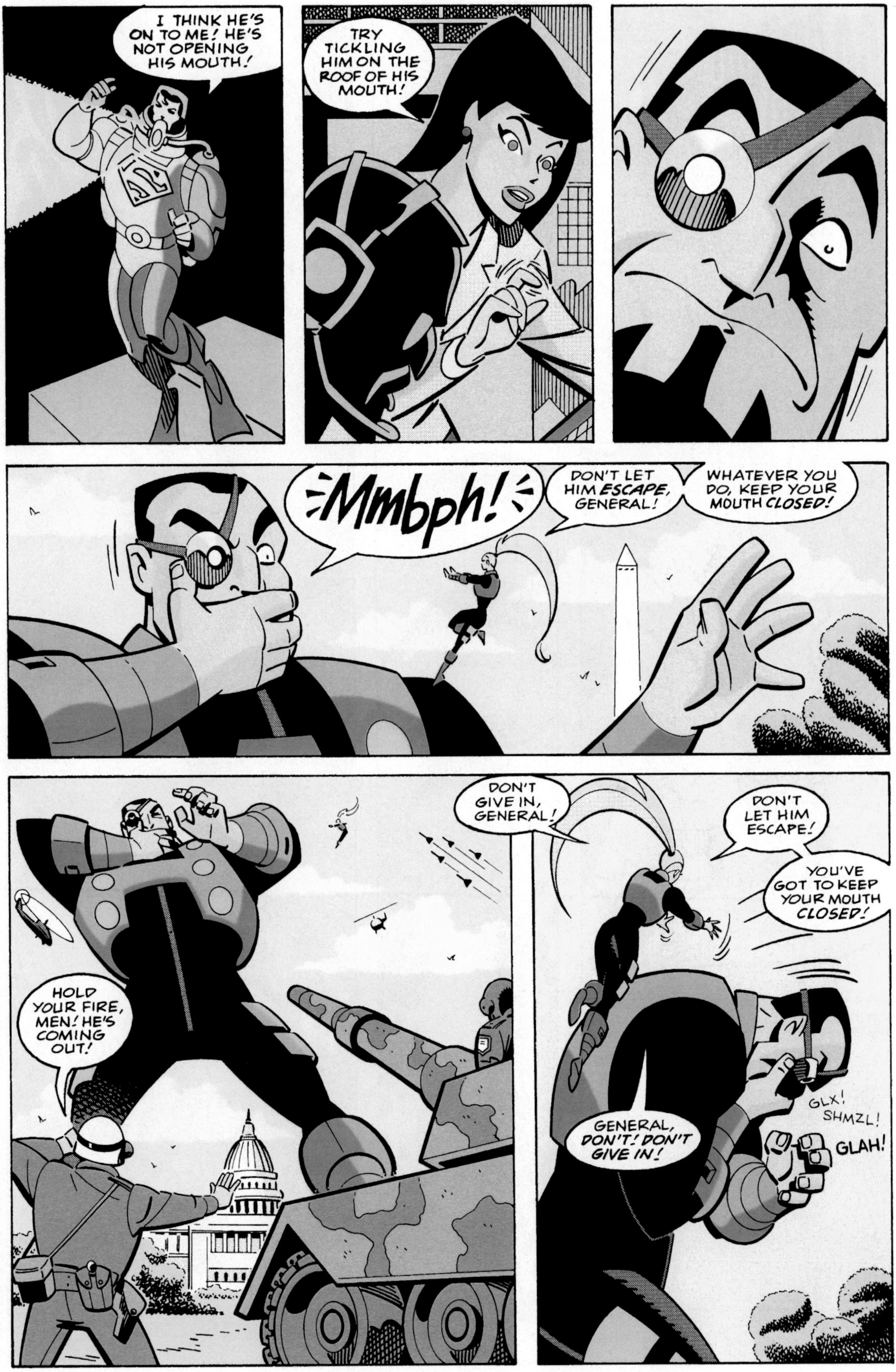
I THINK HE'S ON TO ME! HE'S NOT OPENING HIS MOUTH!
TRY TICKLING HIM ON THE ROOF OF HIS MOUTH!
Mmbph!
DON'T LET HIM ESCAPE, GENERAL!
WHATEVER YOU DO, KEEP YOUR MOUTH CLOSED!
HOLD YOUR FIRE, MEN! HE'S COMING OUT!
DON'T GIVE IN, GENERAL!
DON'T LET HIM ESCAPE!
YOU'VE GOT TO KEEP YOUR MOUTH CLOSED!
GENERAL, DON'T! DON'T GIVE IN!
GLX! SHMZL!
GLAH!

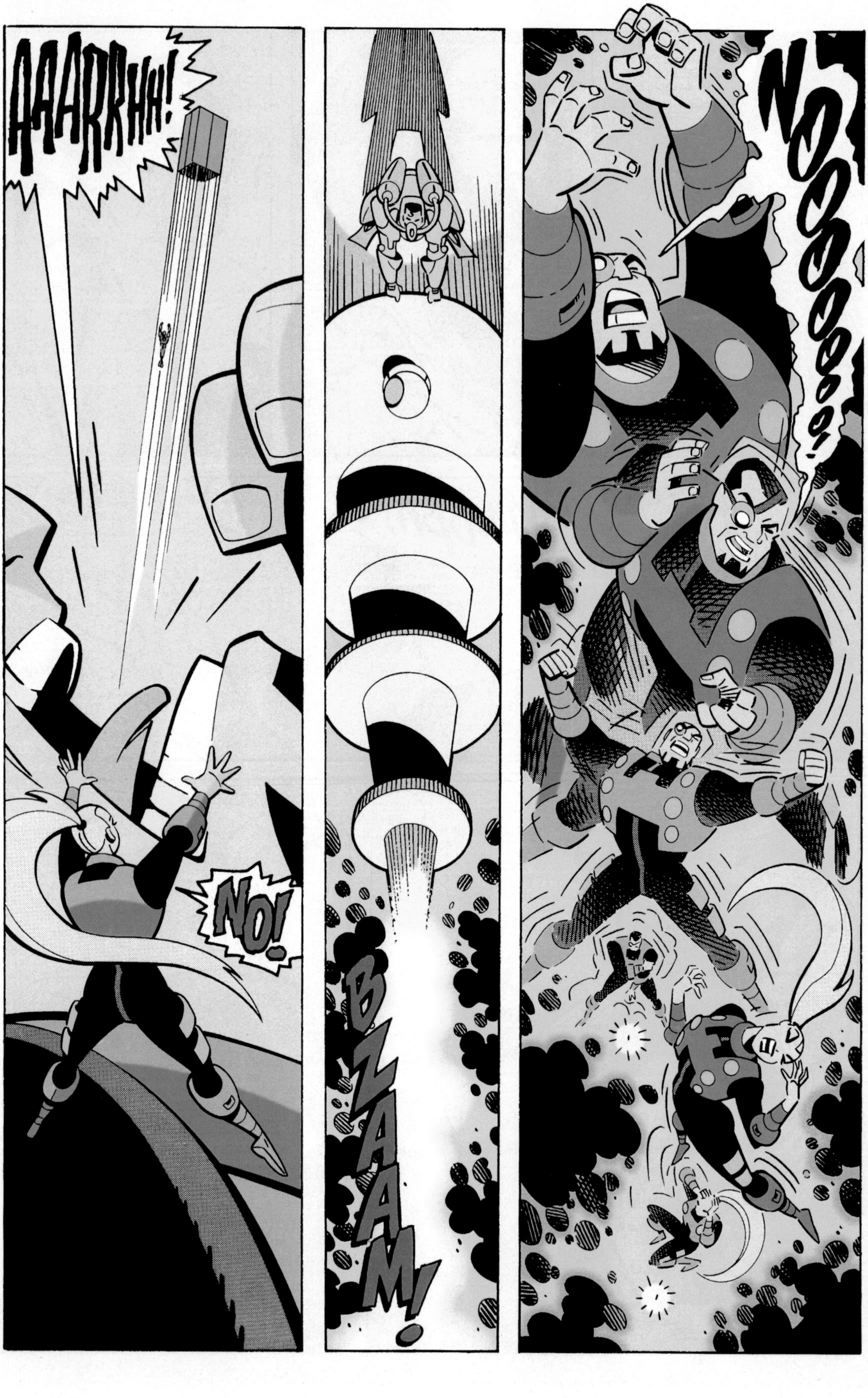
AAARRHH!
NO!
BZZAAM!
NOOOOOOOOOO!

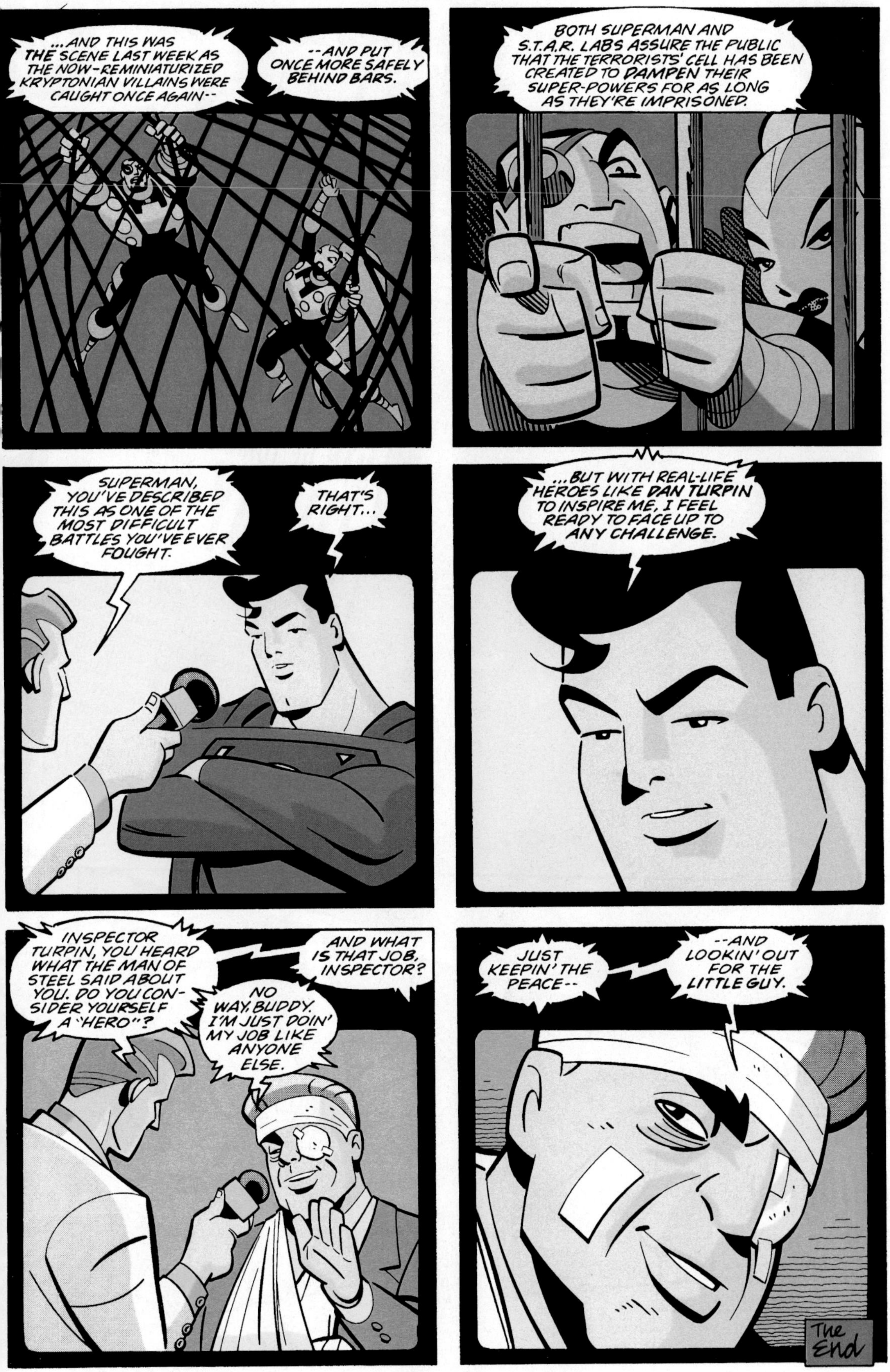
...AND THIS WAS THE SCENE LAST WEEK AS THE NOW-REMINIATURIZED KRYPTONIAN VILLAINS WERE CAUGHT ONCE AGAIN--
--AND PUT ONCE MORE SAFELY BEHIND BARS.
BOTH SUPERMAN AND S.T.A.R. LABS ASSURE THE PUBLIC THAT THE TERRORISTS' CELL HAS BEEN CREATED TO DAMPEN THEIR SUPER-POWERS FOR AS LONG AS THEY'RE IMPRISONED.
SUPERMAN, YOU'VE DESCRIBED THIS AS ONE OF THE MOST DIFFICULT BATTLES YOU'VE EVER FOUGHT.
THAT'S RIGHT...
...BUT WITH REAL-LIFE HEROES LIKE DAN TURPIN TO INSPIRE ME, I FEEL READY TO FACE UP TO ANY CHALLENGE.
INSPECTOR TURPIN, YOU HEARD WHAT THE MAN OF STEEL SAID ABOUT YOU. DO YOU CONSIDER YOURSELF A "HERO"?
NO WAY, BUDDY. I'M JUST DOIN' MY JOB LIKE ANYONE ELSE.
AND WHAT IS THAT JOB, INSPECTOR?
JUST KEEPIN' THE PEACE--
--AND LOOKIN' OUT FOR THE LITTLE GUY.
The End

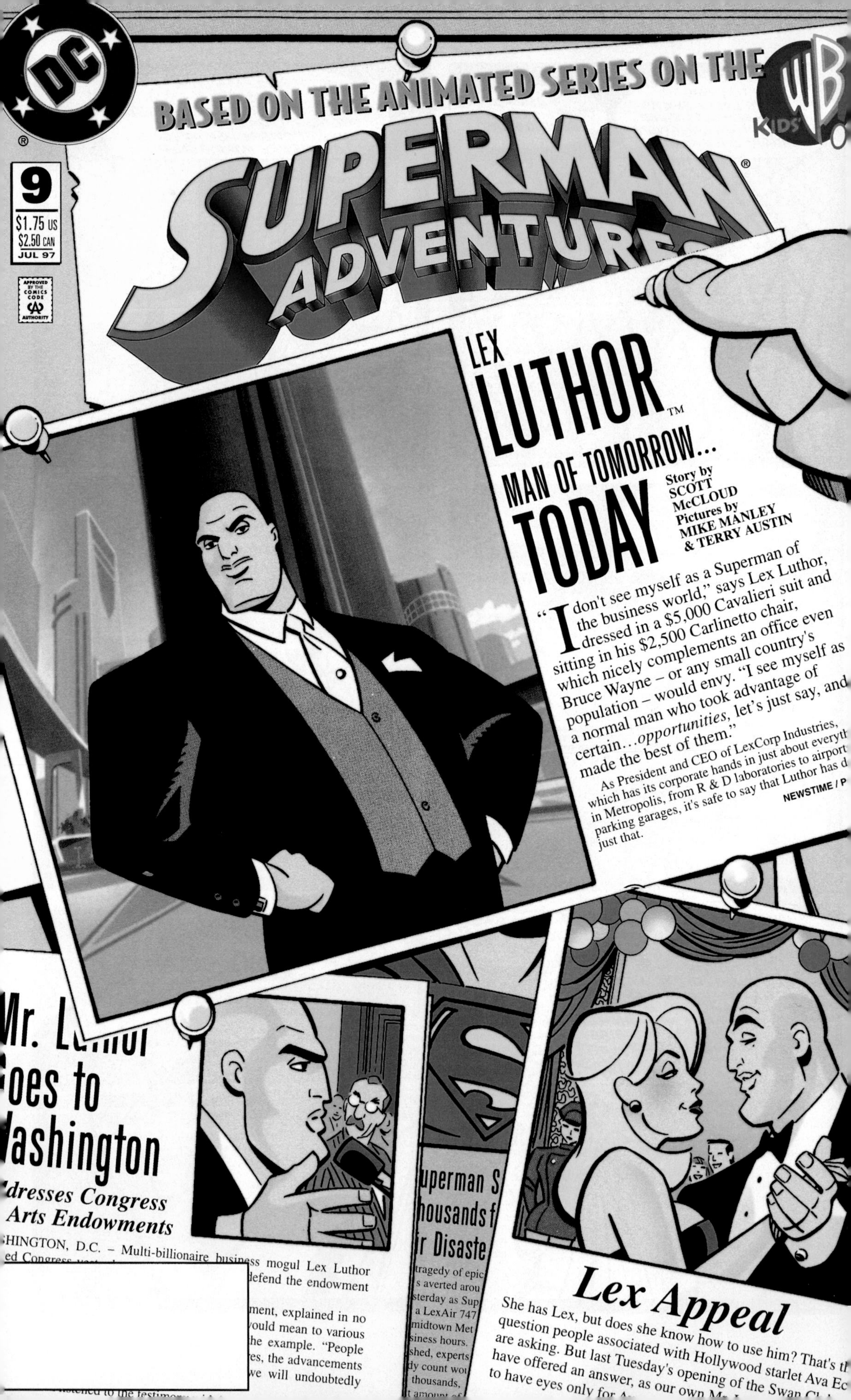

BASED ON THE ANIMATED SERIES ON THE
KIDS' WB!
SUPERMAN ADVENTURES
9
$1.75 US
$2.50 CAN
JUL 97
APPROVED BY THE COMICS CODE AUTHORITY
LEX LUTHOR™
MAN OF TOMORROW... TODAY
Story by SCOTT McCLOUD
Pictures by MIKE MANLEY & TERRY AUSTIN
"I don't see myself as a Superman of the business world," says Lex Luthor, dressed in a $5,000 Cavalieri suit and sitting in his $2,500 Carlinetto chair, which nicely complements an office even Bruce Wayne – or any small country's population – would envy. "I see myself as a normal man who took advantage of certain...*opportunities*, let's just say, and made the best of them."
As President and CEO of LexCorp Industries, which has its corporate hands in just about everyth in Metropolis, from R & D laboratories to airport parking garages, it's safe to say that Luthor has d just that.
NEWSTIME / P
Mr. Luthor Goes to Washington
ddresses Congress Arts Endowments
SHINGTON, D.C. – Multi-billionaire business mogul Lex Luthor
defend the endowment
ment, explained in no
vould mean to various
he example. "People
es, the advancements
we will undoubtedly
uperman S
housands f
ir Disaste
tragedy of epic
s averted arou
sterday as Sup
a LexAir 747
midtown Met
siness hours.
shed, experts
dy count wo
thousands,
Lex Appeal
She has Lex, but does she know how to use him? That's t
question people associated with Hollywood starlet Ava Ec
are asking. But last Tuesday's opening of the Swan Cl
have offered an answer, as our own M
to have eyes only for

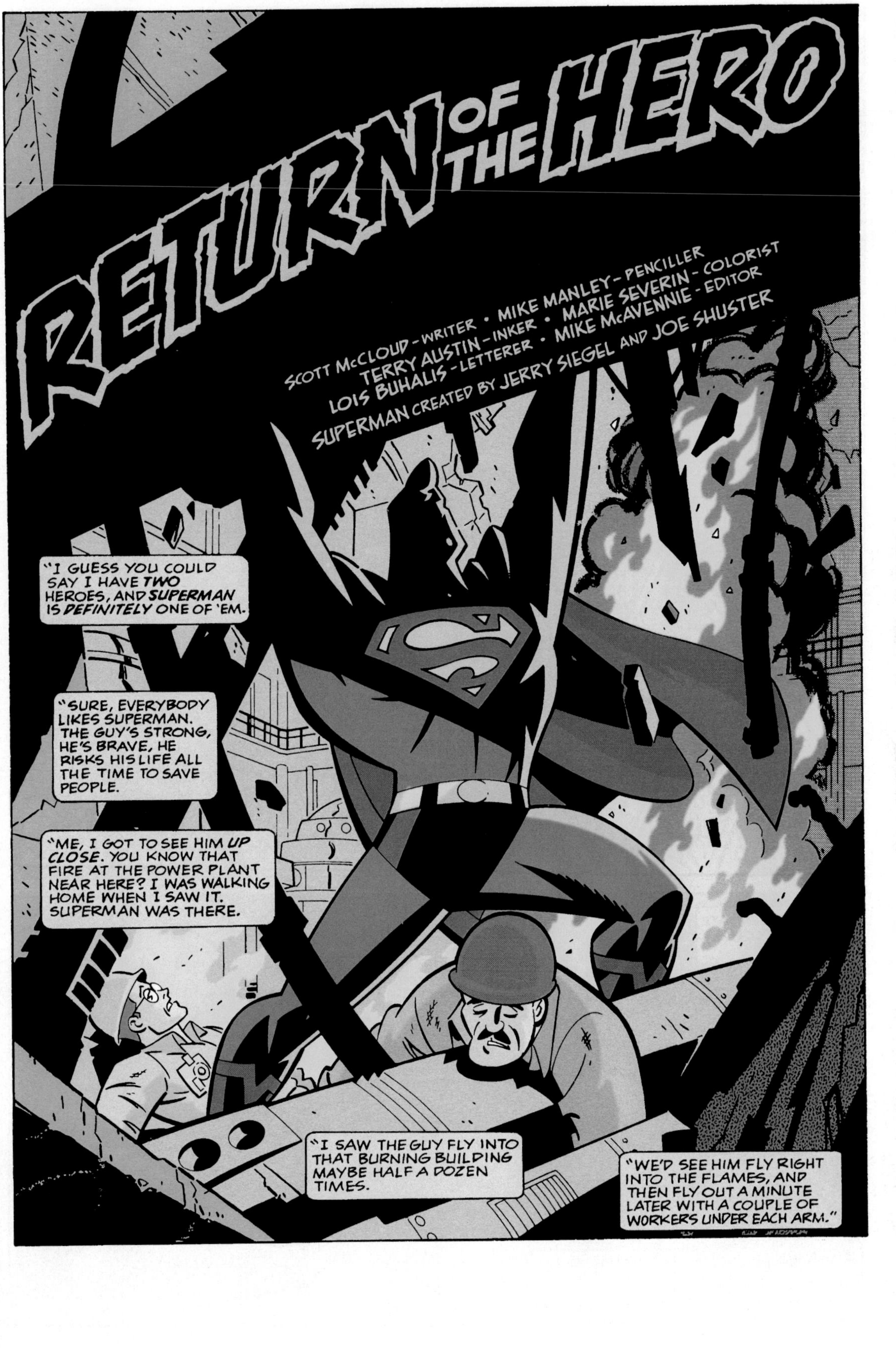
RETURN OF THE HERO
SCOTT McCLOUD - WRITER • MIKE MANLEY - PENCILLER
TERRY AUSTIN - INKER • MARIE SEVERIN - COLORIST
LOIS BUHALIS - LETTERER • MIKE McAVENNIE - EDITOR
SUPERMAN CREATED BY JERRY SIEGEL AND JOE SHUSTER
"I GUESS YOU COULD SAY I HAVE TWO HEROES, AND SUPERMAN IS DEFINITELY ONE OF 'EM.
"SURE, EVERYBODY LIKES SUPERMAN. THE GUY'S STRONG, HE'S BRAVE, HE RISKS HIS LIFE ALL THE TIME TO SAVE PEOPLE.
"ME, I GOT TO SEE HIM UP CLOSE. YOU KNOW THAT FIRE AT THE POWER PLANT NEAR HERE? I WAS WALKING HOME WHEN I SAW IT. SUPERMAN WAS THERE.
"I SAW THE GUY FLY INTO THAT BURNING BUILDING MAYBE HALF A DOZEN TIMES.
"WE'D SEE HIM FLY RIGHT INTO THE FLAMES, AND THEN FLY OUT A MINUTE LATER WITH A COUPLE OF WORKERS UNDER EACH ARM."

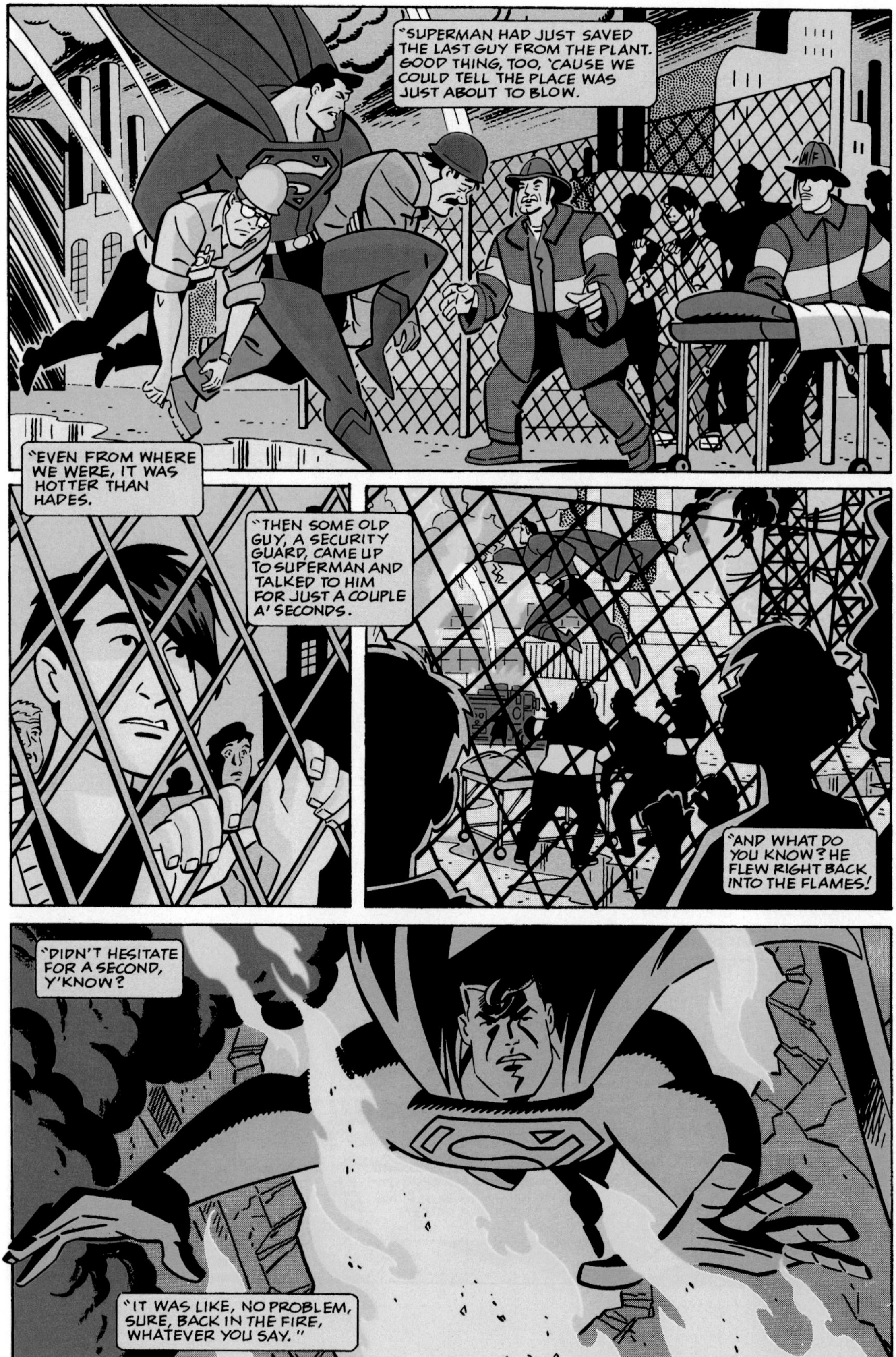

"SUPERMAN HAD JUST SAVED THE LAST GUY FROM THE PLANT. GOOD THING, TOO, 'CAUSE WE COULD TELL THE PLACE WAS JUST ABOUT TO BLOW.
"EVEN FROM WHERE WE WERE, IT WAS HOTTER THAN HADES.
"THEN SOME OLD GUY, A SECURITY GUARD, CAME UP TO SUPERMAN AND TALKED TO HIM FOR JUST A COUPLE A' SECONDS.
"AND WHAT DO YOU KNOW? HE FLEW RIGHT BACK INTO THE FLAMES!
"DIDN'T HESITATE FOR A SECOND, Y'KNOW?
"IT WAS LIKE, NO PROBLEM, SURE, BACK IN THE FIRE, WHATEVER YOU SAY."

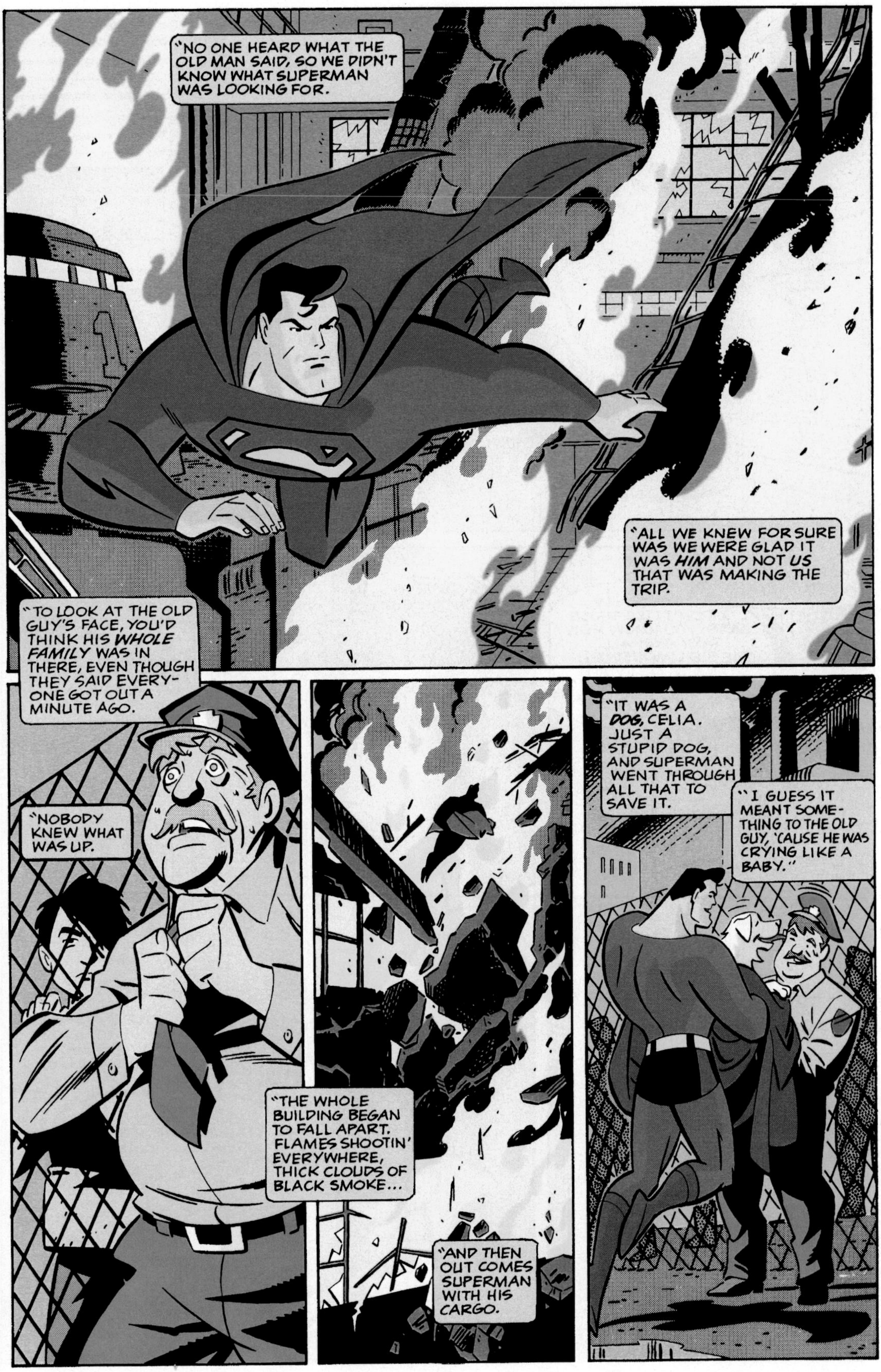
"NO ONE HEARD WHAT THE OLD MAN SAID, SO WE DIDN'T KNOW WHAT SUPERMAN WAS LOOKING FOR.
"ALL WE KNEW FOR SURE WAS WE WERE GLAD IT WAS *HIM* AND NOT *US* THAT WAS MAKING THE TRIP.
"TO LOOK AT THE OLD GUY'S FACE, YOU'D THINK HIS *WHOLE FAMILY* WAS IN THERE, EVEN THOUGH THEY SAID EVERY-ONE GOT OUT A MINUTE AGO.
"NOBODY KNEW WHAT WAS UP.
"THE WHOLE BUILDING BEGAN TO FALL APART. FLAMES SHOOTIN' EVERYWHERE, THICK CLOUDS OF BLACK SMOKE...
"AND THEN OUT COMES SUPERMAN WITH HIS CARGO.
"IT WAS A *DOG*, CELIA. JUST A STUPID DOG, AND SUPERMAN WENT THROUGH ALL THAT TO SAVE IT.
"I GUESS IT MEANT SOME-THING TO THE OLD GUY, 'CAUSE HE WAS CRYING LIKE A BABY."

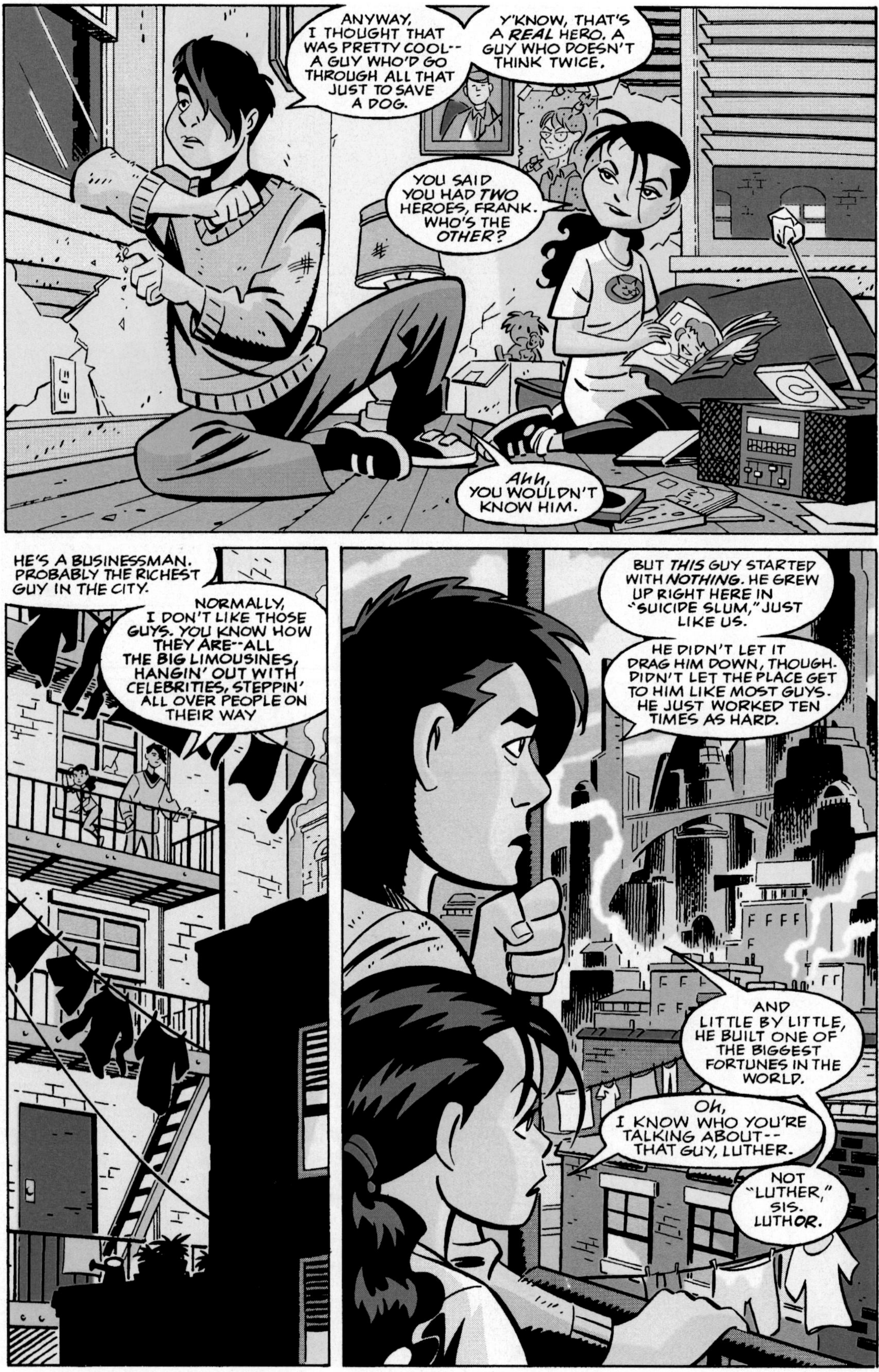

ANYWAY, I THOUGHT THAT WAS PRETTY COOL-- A GUY WHO'D GO THROUGH ALL THAT JUST TO SAVE A DOG.
Y'KNOW, THAT'S A REAL HERO. A GUY WHO DOESN'T THINK TWICE.
YOU SAID YOU HAD TWO HEROES, FRANK. WHO'S THE OTHER?
Ahh, YOU WOULDN'T KNOW HIM.
HE'S A BUSINESSMAN. PROBABLY THE RICHEST GUY IN THE CITY.
NORMALLY, I DON'T LIKE THOSE GUYS. YOU KNOW HOW THEY ARE--ALL THE BIG LIMOUSINES, HANGIN' OUT WITH CELEBRITIES, STEPPIN' ALL OVER PEOPLE ON THEIR WAY
BUT THIS GUY STARTED WITH NOTHING. HE GREW UP RIGHT HERE IN "SUICIDE SLUM," JUST LIKE US.
HE DIDN'T LET IT DRAG HIM DOWN, THOUGH. DIDN'T LET THE PLACE GET TO HIM LIKE MOST GUYS. HE JUST WORKED TEN TIMES AS HARD.
AND LITTLE BY LITTLE, HE BUILT ONE OF THE BIGGEST FORTUNES IN THE WORLD.
Oh, I KNOW WHO YOU'RE TALKING ABOUT-- THAT GUY, LUTHER.
NOT "LUTHER," SIS. LUTHOR.

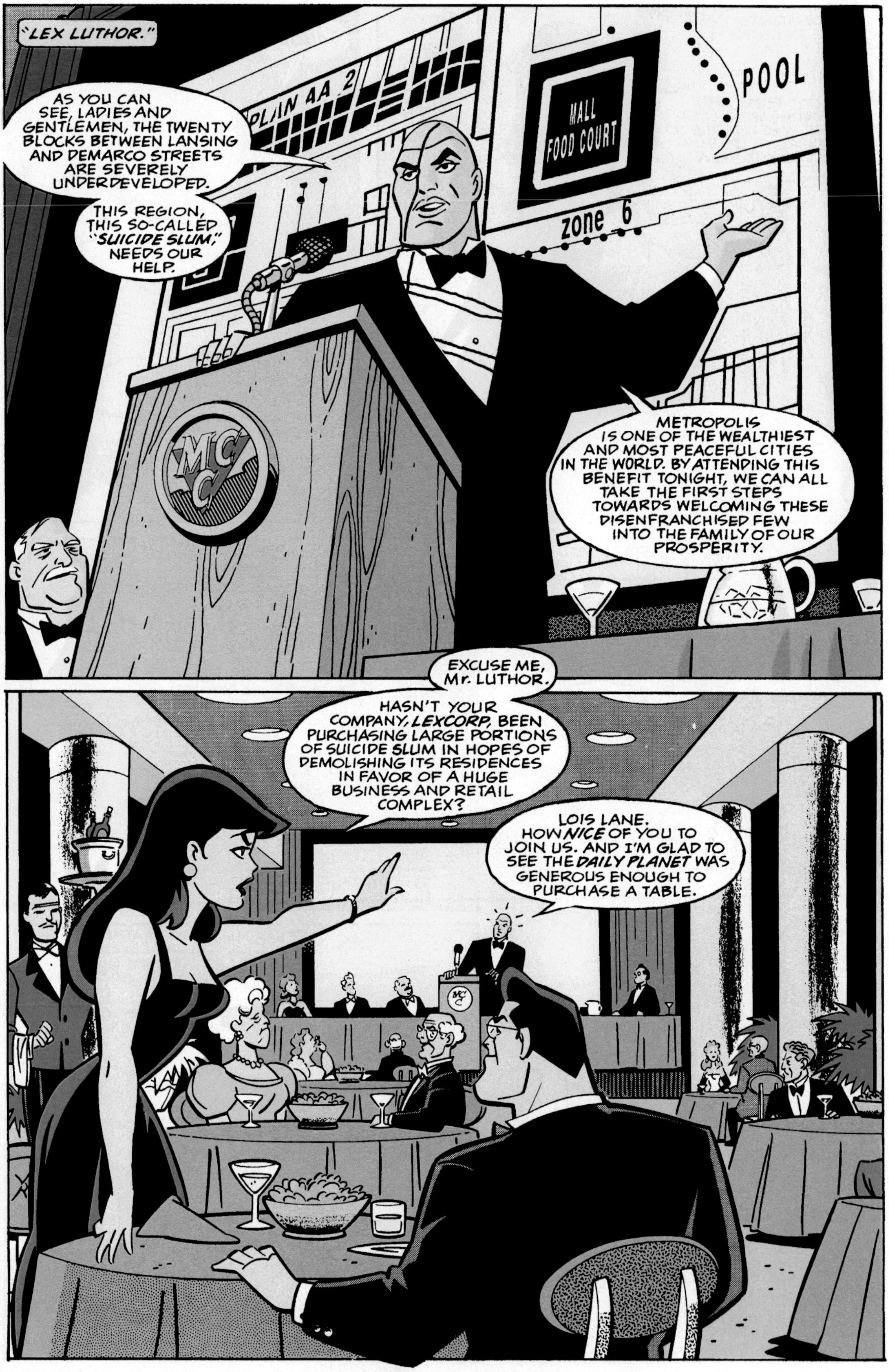
"LEX LUTHOR."
AS YOU CAN SEE, LADIES AND GENTLEMEN, THE TWENTY BLOCKS BETWEEN LANSING AND DEMARCO STREETS ARE SEVERELY UNDERDEVELOPED.
THIS REGION, THIS SO-CALLED "SUICIDE SLUM," NEEDS OUR HELP.
METROPOLIS IS ONE OF THE WEALTHIEST AND MOST PEACEFUL CITIES IN THE WORLD. BY ATTENDING THIS BENEFIT TONIGHT, WE CAN ALL TAKE THE FIRST STEPS TOWARDS WELCOMING THESE DISENFRANCHISED FEW INTO THE FAMILY OF OUR PROSPERITY.
PLAN AA 2
MALL FOOD COURT
POOL
zone 6
EXCUSE ME, Mr. LUTHOR.
HASN'T YOUR COMPANY, LEXCORP, BEEN PURCHASING LARGE PORTIONS OF SUICIDE SLUM IN HOPES OF DEMOLISHING ITS RESIDENCES IN FAVOR OF A HUGE BUSINESS AND RETAIL COMPLEX?
LOIS LANE. HOW NICE OF YOU TO JOIN US. AND I'M GLAD TO SEE THE DAILY PLANET WAS GENEROUS ENOUGH TO PURCHASE A TABLE.

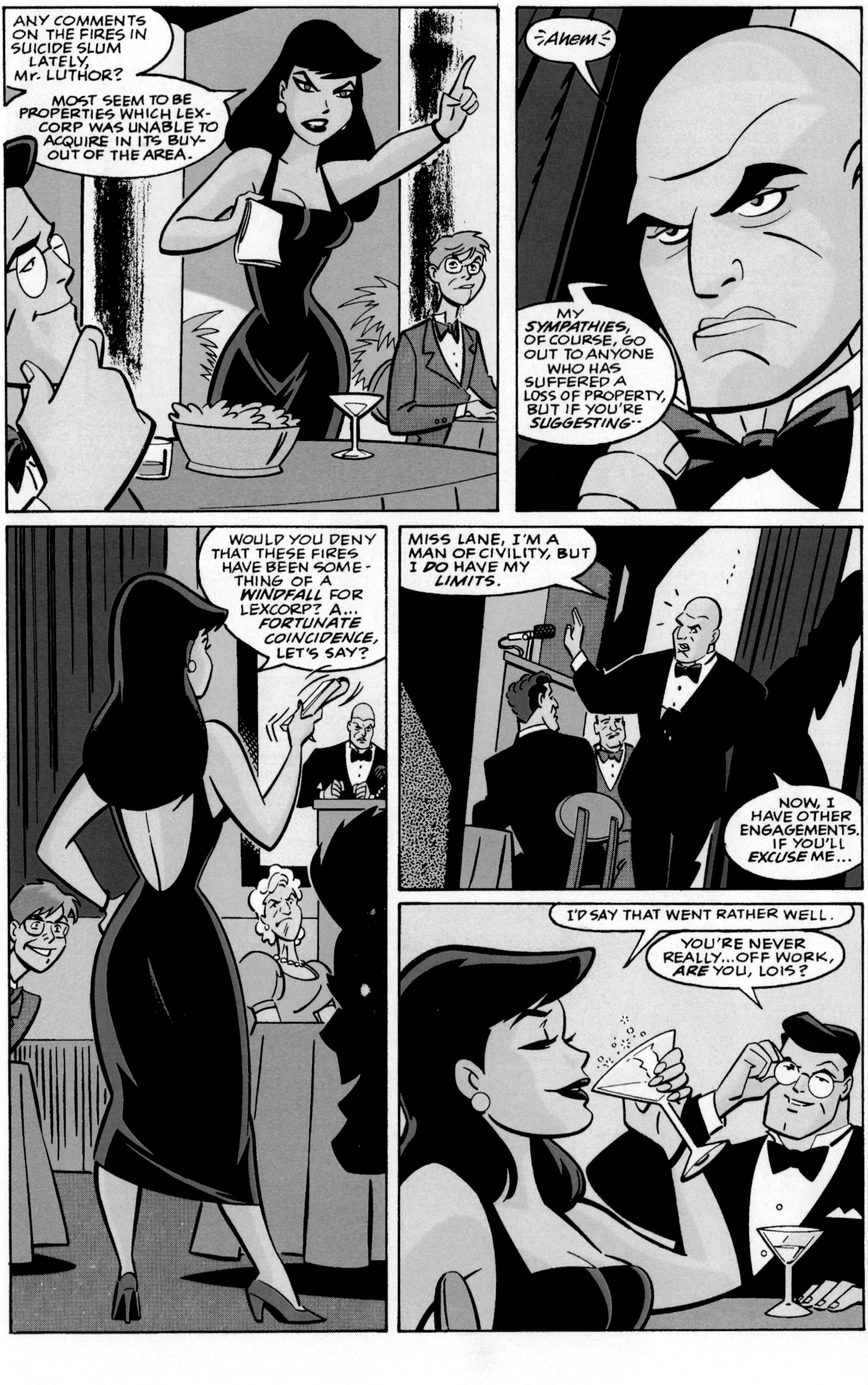
ANY COMMENTS ON THE FIRES IN SUICIDE SLUM LATELY, Mr. LUTHOR?
MOST SEEM TO BE PROPERTIES WHICH LEX-CORP WAS UNABLE TO ACQUIRE IN ITS BUY-OUT OF THE AREA.
Ahem
MY SYMPATHIES, OF COURSE, GO OUT TO ANYONE WHO HAS SUFFERED A LOSS OF PROPERTY, BUT IF YOU'RE SUGGESTING--
WOULD YOU DENY THAT THESE FIRES HAVE BEEN SOME-THING OF A WINDFALL FOR LEXCORP? A... FORTUNATE COINCIDENCE, LET'S SAY?
MISS LANE, I'M A MAN OF CIVILITY, BUT I DO HAVE MY LIMITS.
NOW, I HAVE OTHER ENGAGEMENTS. IF YOU'LL EXCUSE ME...
I'D SAY THAT WENT RATHER WELL.
YOU'RE NEVER REALLY...OFF WORK, ARE YOU, LOIS?

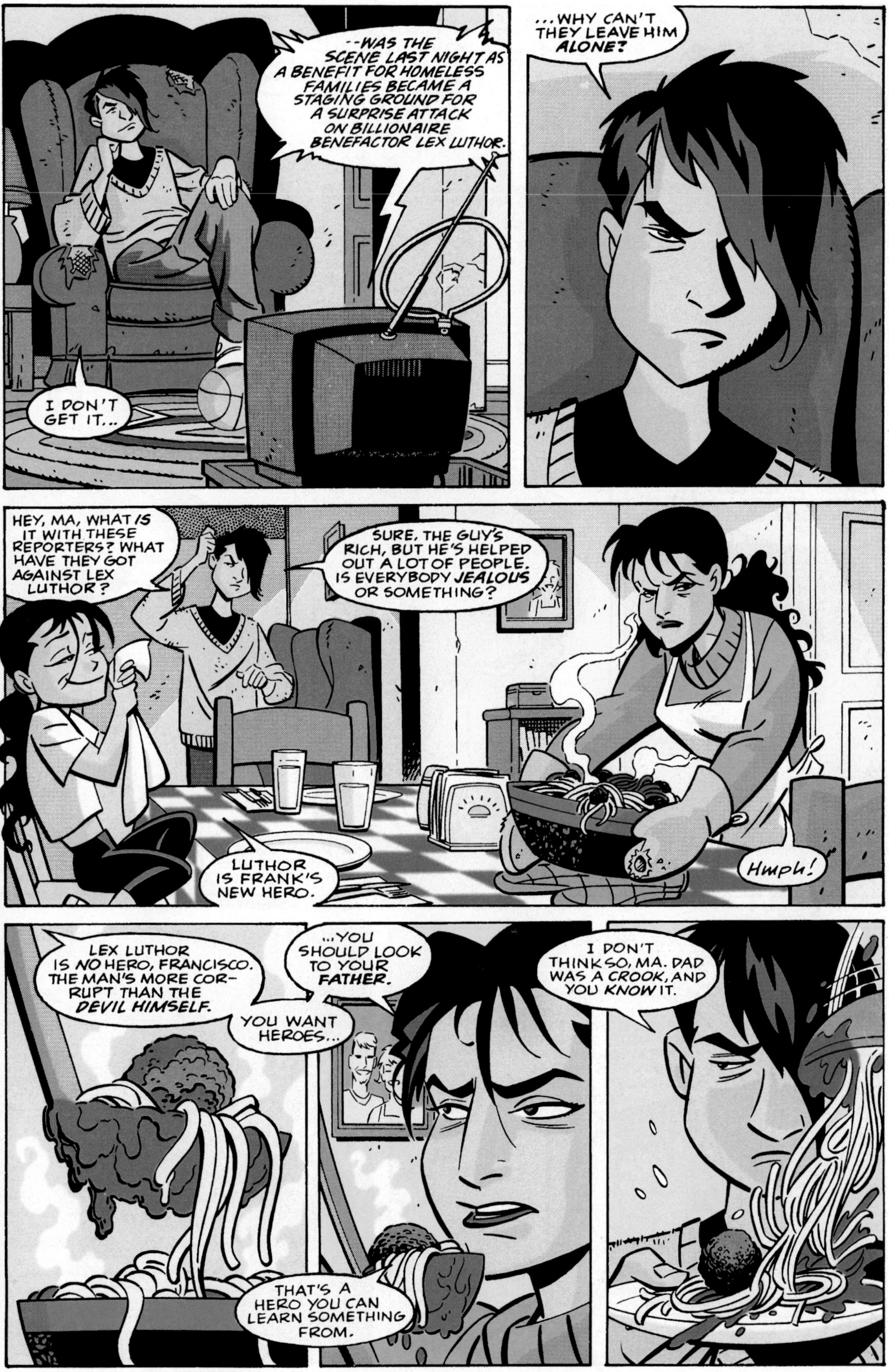
--WAS THE SCENE LAST NIGHT AS A BENEFIT FOR HOMELESS FAMILIES BECAME A STAGING GROUND FOR A SURPRISE ATTACK ON BILLIONAIRE BENEFACTOR LEX LUTHOR.
I DON'T GET IT...
...WHY CAN'T THEY LEAVE HIM ALONE?
HEY, MA, WHAT IS IT WITH THESE REPORTERS? WHAT HAVE THEY GOT AGAINST LEX LUTHOR?
SURE, THE GUY'S RICH, BUT HE'S HELPED OUT A LOT OF PEOPLE. IS EVERYBODY JEALOUS OR SOMETHING?
LUTHOR IS FRANK'S NEW HERO.
Hmph!
LEX LUTHOR IS NO HERO, FRANCISCO. THE MAN'S MORE COR-RUPT THAN THE DEVIL HIMSELF.
YOU WANT HEROES...
...YOU SHOULD LOOK TO YOUR FATHER.
THAT'S A HERO YOU CAN LEARN SOMETHING FROM.
I DON'T THINK SO, MA. DAD WAS A CROOK, AND YOU KNOW IT.

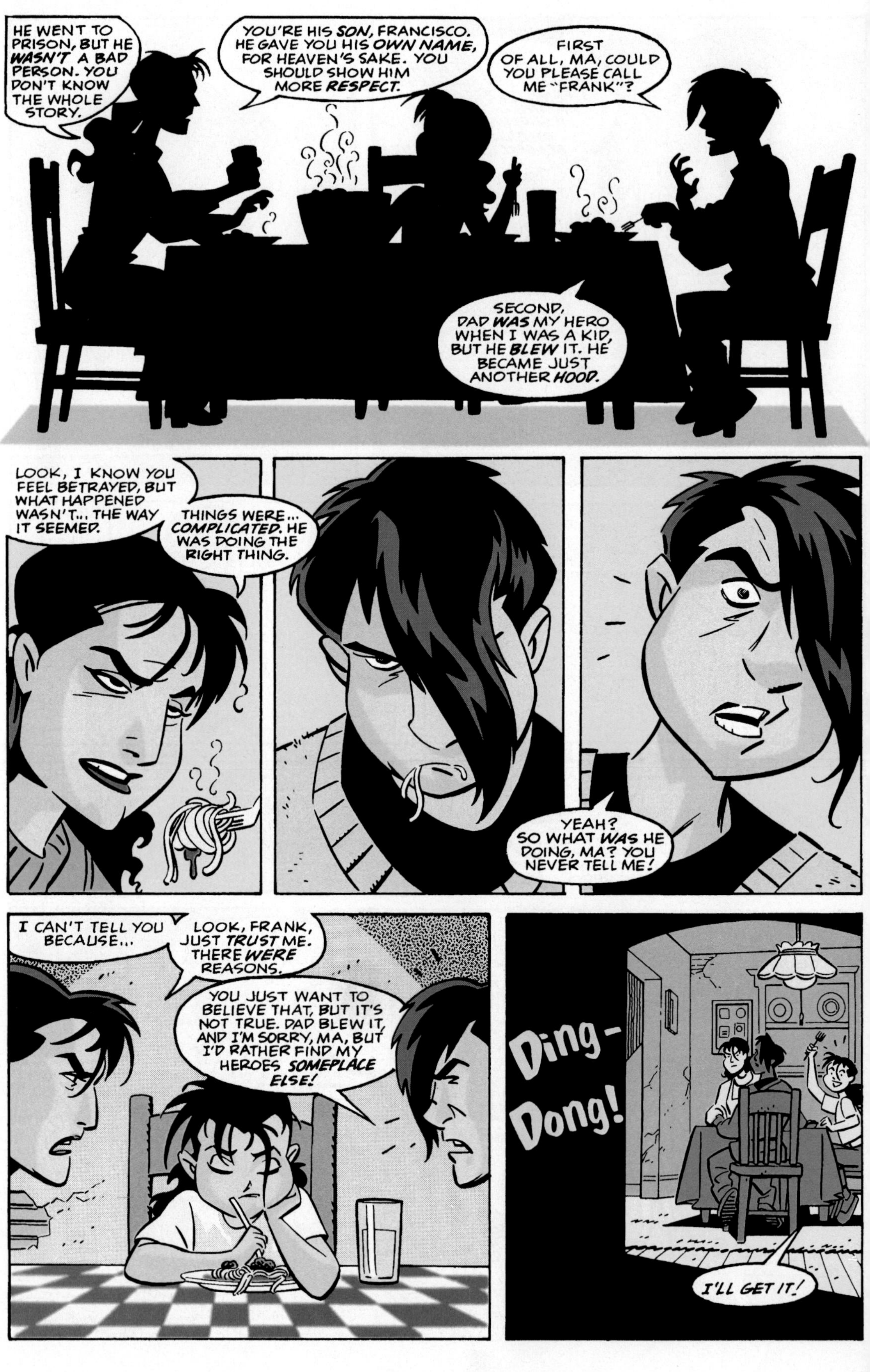
HE WENT TO PRISON, BUT HE WASN'T A BAD PERSON. YOU DON'T KNOW THE WHOLE STORY.
YOU'RE HIS SON, FRANCISCO. HE GAVE YOU HIS OWN NAME, FOR HEAVEN'S SAKE. YOU SHOULD SHOW HIM MORE RESPECT.
FIRST OF ALL, MA, COULD YOU PLEASE CALL ME "FRANK"?
SECOND, DAD WAS MY HERO WHEN I WAS A KID, BUT HE BLEW IT. HE BECAME JUST ANOTHER HOOD.
LOOK, I KNOW YOU FEEL BETRAYED, BUT WHAT HAPPENED WASN'T... THE WAY IT SEEMED.
THINGS WERE... COMPLICATED. HE WAS DOING THE RIGHT THING.
YEAH? SO WHAT WAS HE DOING, MA? YOU NEVER TELL ME!
I CAN'T TELL YOU BECAUSE...
LOOK, FRANK, JUST TRUST ME. THERE WERE REASONS.
YOU JUST WANT TO BELIEVE THAT, BUT IT'S NOT TRUE. DAD BLEW IT, AND I'M SORRY, MA, BUT I'D RATHER FIND MY HEROES SOMEPLACE ELSE!
Ding-Dong!
I'LL GET IT!

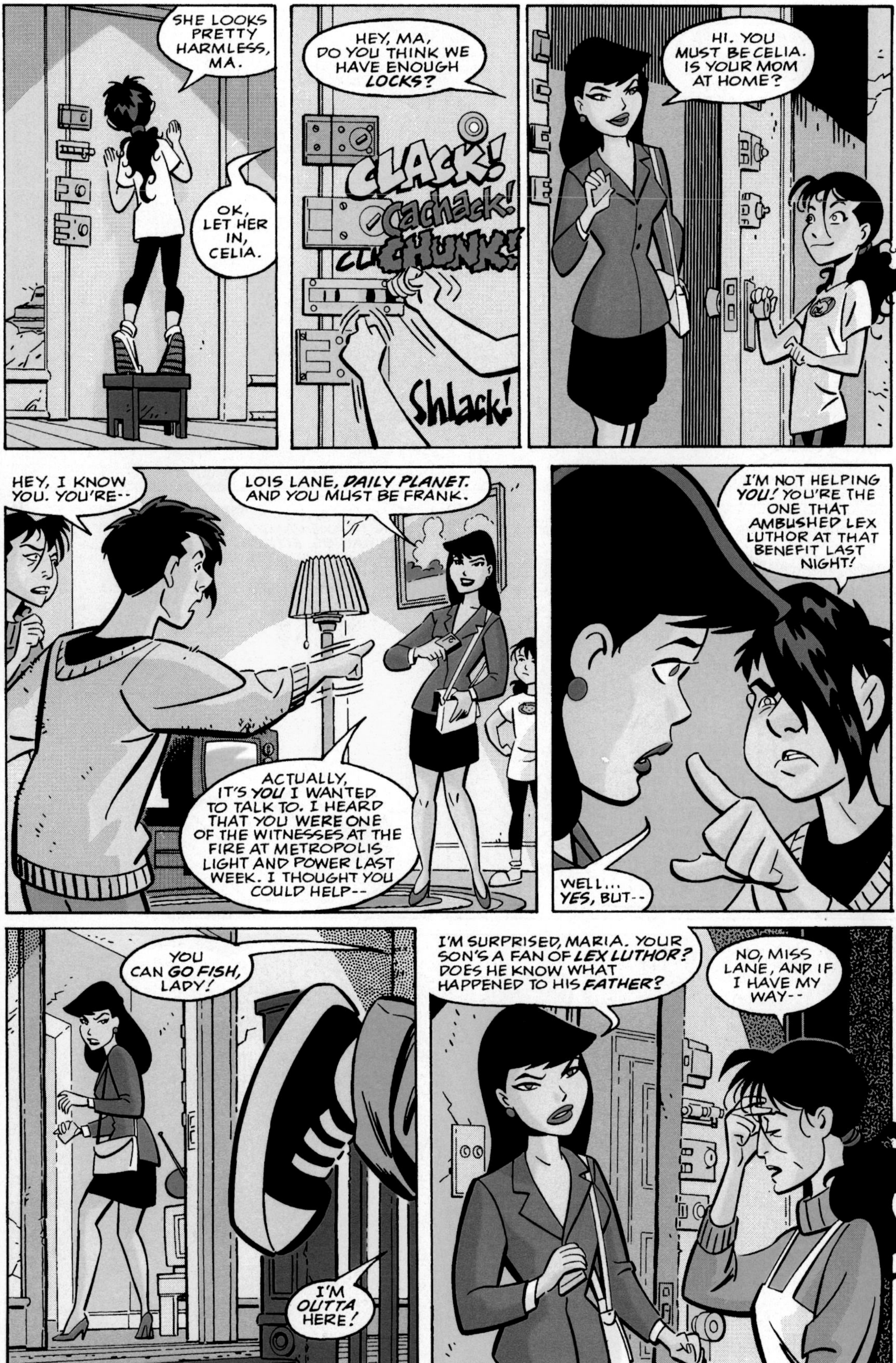
SHE LOOKS PRETTY HARMLESS, MA.
OK, LET HER IN, CELIA.
HEY, MA, DO YOU THINK WE HAVE ENOUGH LOCKS?
CLACK!
CACHACK!
CL
CHUNK!
SHLACK!
HI. YOU MUST BE CELIA. IS YOUR MOM AT HOME?
HEY, I KNOW YOU. YOU'RE--
LOIS LANE, DAILY PLANET. AND YOU MUST BE FRANK.
ACTUALLY, IT'S YOU I WANTED TO TALK TO. I HEARD THAT YOU WERE ONE OF THE WITNESSES AT THE FIRE AT METROPOLIS LIGHT AND POWER LAST WEEK. I THOUGHT YOU COULD HELP--
I'M NOT HELPING YOU! YOU'RE THE ONE THAT AMBUSHED LEX LUTHOR AT THAT BENEFIT LAST NIGHT!
WELL... YES, BUT--
YOU CAN GO FISH, LADY!
I'M OUTTA HERE!
I'M SURPRISED, MARIA. YOUR SON'S A FAN OF LEX LUTHOR? DOES HE KNOW WHAT HAPPENED TO HIS FATHER?
NO, MISS LANE, AND IF I HAVE MY WAY--

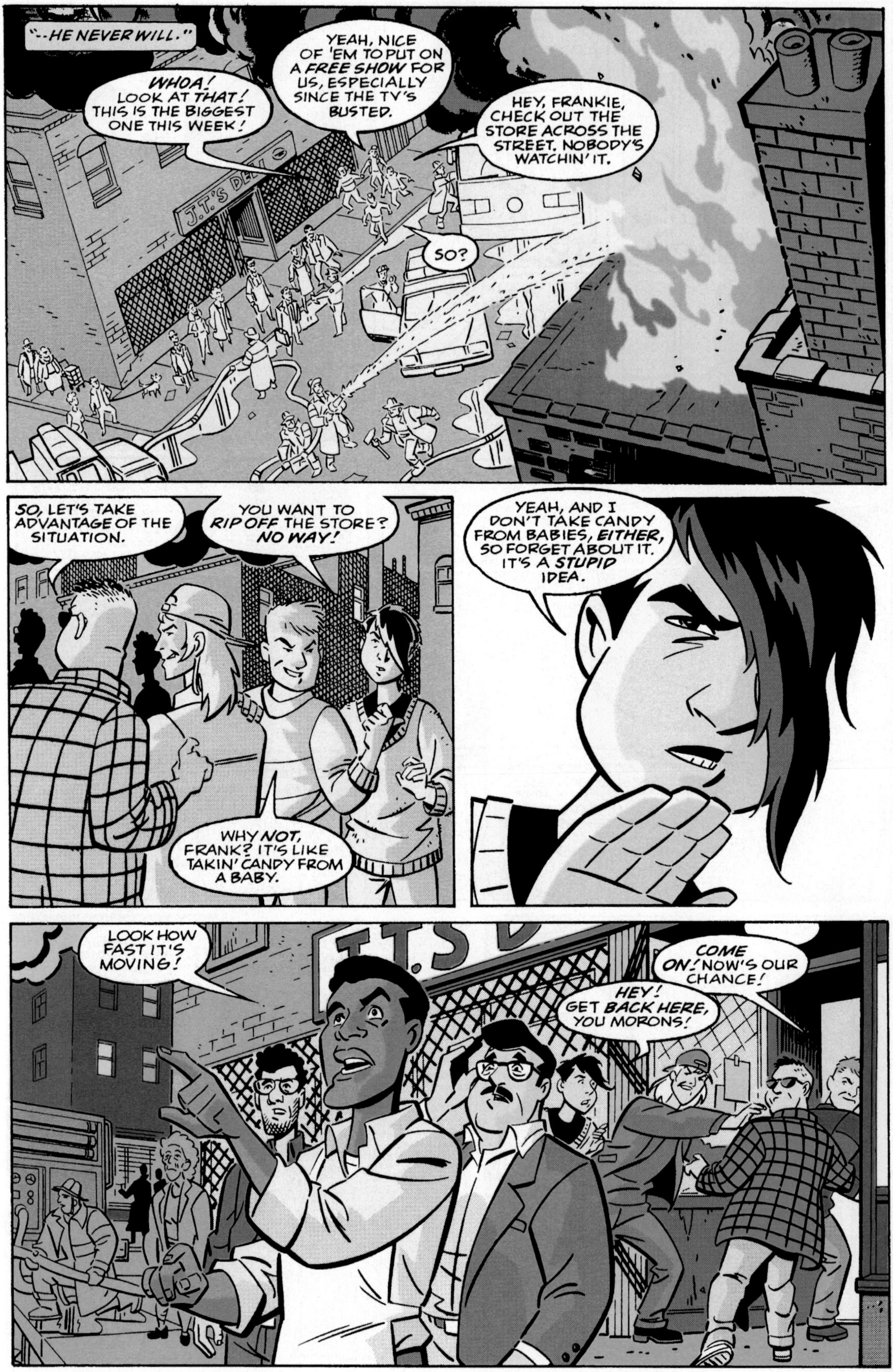
"--HE NEVER WILL."
WHOA! LOOK AT THAT! THIS IS THE BIGGEST ONE THIS WEEK!
YEAH, NICE OF 'EM TO PUT ON A FREE SHOW FOR US, ESPECIALLY SINCE THE TV'S BUSTED.
HEY, FRANKIE, CHECK OUT THE STORE ACROSS THE STREET. NOBODY'S WATCHIN' IT.
SO?
J.T.'S DE
SO, LET'S TAKE ADVANTAGE OF THE SITUATION.
YOU WANT TO RIP OFF THE STORE? NO WAY!
WHY NOT, FRANK? IT'S LIKE TAKIN' CANDY FROM A BABY.
YEAH, AND I DON'T TAKE CANDY FROM BABIES, EITHER, SO FORGET ABOUT IT. IT'S A STUPID IDEA.
LOOK HOW FAST IT'S MOVING!
COME ON! NOW'S OUR CHANCE!
HEY! GET BACK HERE, YOU MORONS!

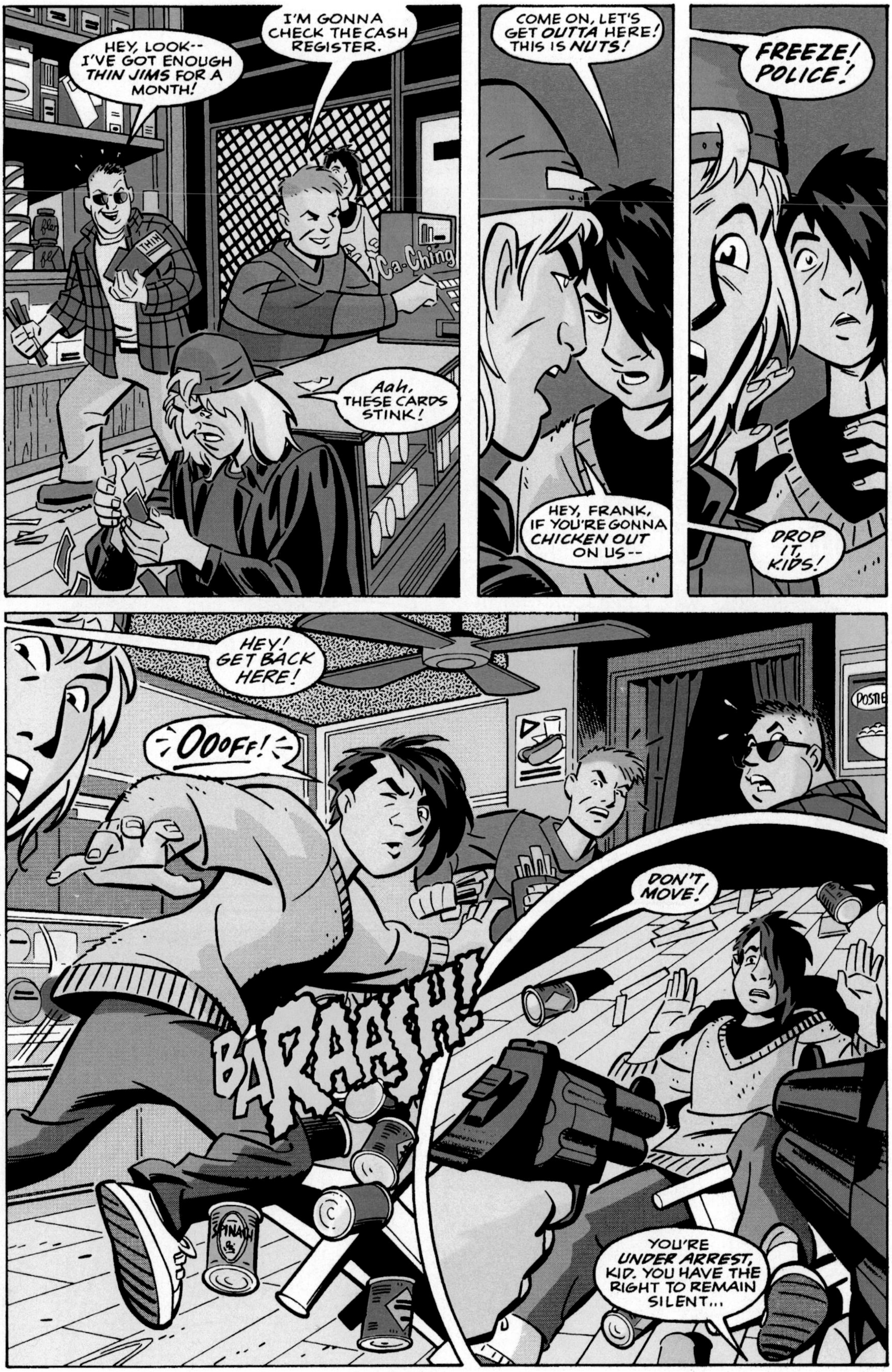
HEY, LOOK-- I'VE GOT ENOUGH THIN JIMS FOR A MONTH!
I'M GONNA CHECK THE CASH REGISTER.
CA-CHING
Aah, THESE CARDS STINK!
COME ON, LET'S GET OUTTA HERE! THIS IS NUTS!
HEY, FRANK, IF YOU'RE GONNA CHICKEN OUT ON US--
FREEZE! POLICE!
DROP IT, KIDS!
HEY! GET BACK HERE!
OOOFF!
DON'T MOVE!
BARAASH!
SPINACH
YOU'RE UNDER ARREST, KID. YOU HAVE THE RIGHT TO REMAIN SILENT...

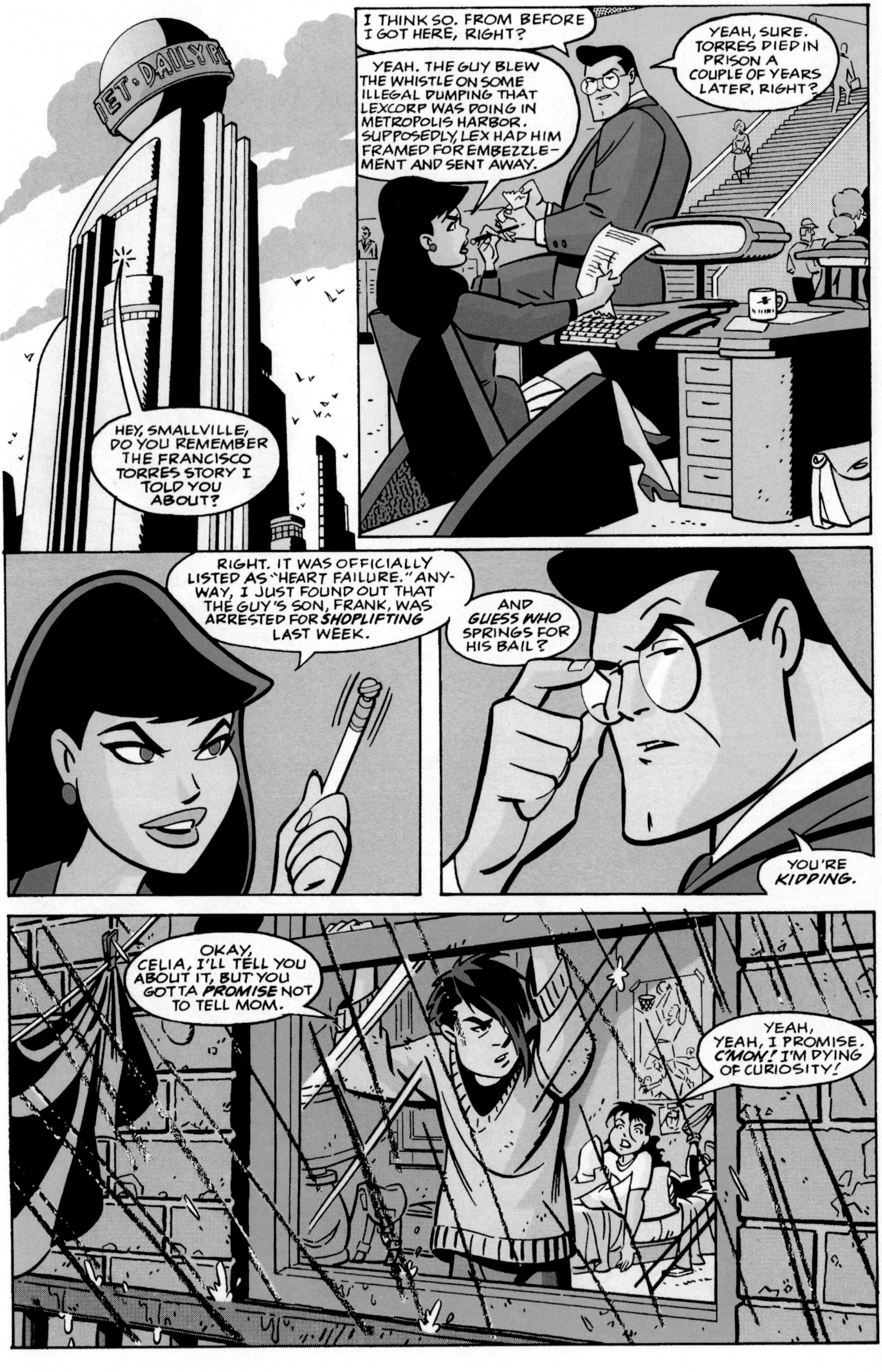
HEY, SMALLVILLE, DO YOU REMEMBER THE FRANCISCO TORRES STORY I TOLD YOU ABOUT?
I THINK SO. FROM BEFORE I GOT HERE, RIGHT?
YEAH. THE GUY BLEW THE WHISTLE ON SOME ILLEGAL DUMPING THAT LEXCORP WAS DOING IN METROPOLIS HARBOR. SUPPOSEDLY, LEX HAD HIM FRAMED FOR EMBEZZLE-MENT AND SENT AWAY.
YEAH, SURE. TORRES DIED IN PRISON A COUPLE OF YEARS LATER, RIGHT?
RIGHT. IT WAS OFFICIALLY LISTED AS "HEART FAILURE." ANY-WAY, I JUST FOUND OUT THAT THE GUY'S SON, FRANK, WAS ARRESTED FOR SHOPLIFTING LAST WEEK.
AND GUESS WHO SPRINGS FOR HIS BAIL?
YOU'RE KIDDING.
OKAY, CELIA, I'LL TELL YOU ABOUT IT, BUT YOU GOTTA PROMISE NOT TO TELL MOM.
YEAH, YEAH, I PROMISE. C'MON! I'M DYING OF CURIOSITY!

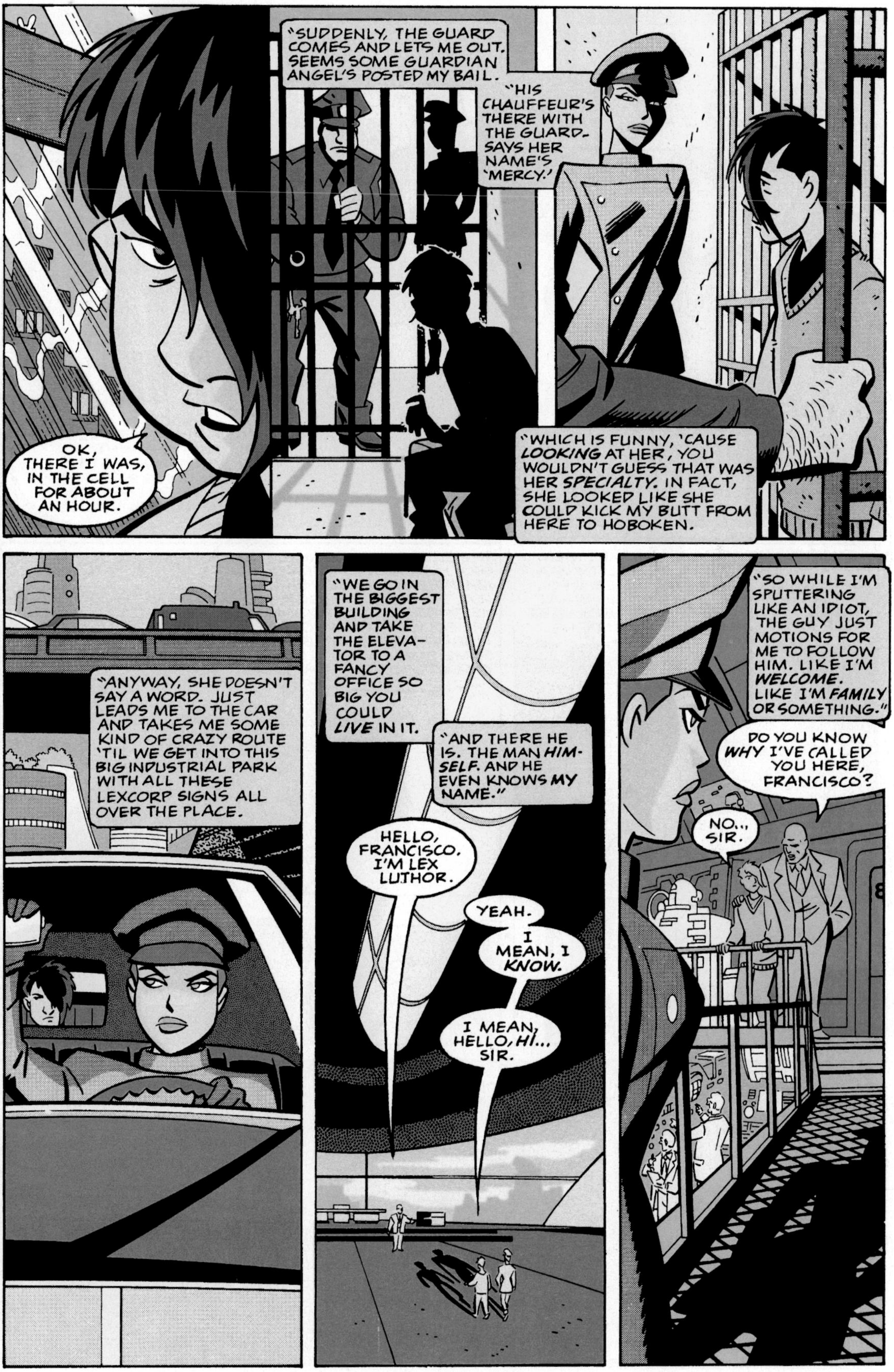
OK, THERE I WAS, IN THE CELL FOR ABOUT AN HOUR.
"SUDDENLY, THE GUARD COMES AND LETS ME OUT. SEEMS SOME GUARDIAN ANGEL'S POSTED MY BAIL.
"HIS CHAUFFEUR'S THERE WITH THE GUARD-- SAYS HER NAME'S 'MERCY.'
"WHICH IS FUNNY, 'CAUSE LOOKING AT HER, YOU WOULDN'T GUESS THAT WAS HER SPECIALTY. IN FACT, SHE LOOKED LIKE SHE COULD KICK MY BUTT FROM HERE TO HOBOKEN.
"ANYWAY, SHE DOESN'T SAY A WORD. JUST LEADS ME TO THE CAR AND TAKES ME SOME KIND OF CRAZY ROUTE 'TIL WE GET INTO THIS BIG INDUSTRIAL PARK WITH ALL THESE LEXCORP SIGNS ALL OVER THE PLACE.
"WE GO IN THE BIGGEST BUILDING AND TAKE THE ELEVATOR TO A FANCY OFFICE SO BIG YOU COULD LIVE IN IT.
"AND THERE HE IS. THE MAN HIMSELF. AND HE EVEN KNOWS MY NAME."
HELLO, FRANCISCO. I'M LEX LUTHOR.
YEAH.
I MEAN, I KNOW.
I MEAN, HELLO, HI... SIR.
"SO WHILE I'M SPUTTERING LIKE AN IDIOT, THE GUY JUST MOTIONS FOR ME TO FOLLOW HIM. LIKE I'M WELCOME. LIKE I'M FAMILY OR SOMETHING."
DO YOU KNOW WHY I'VE CALLED YOU HERE, FRANCISCO?
NO... SIR.

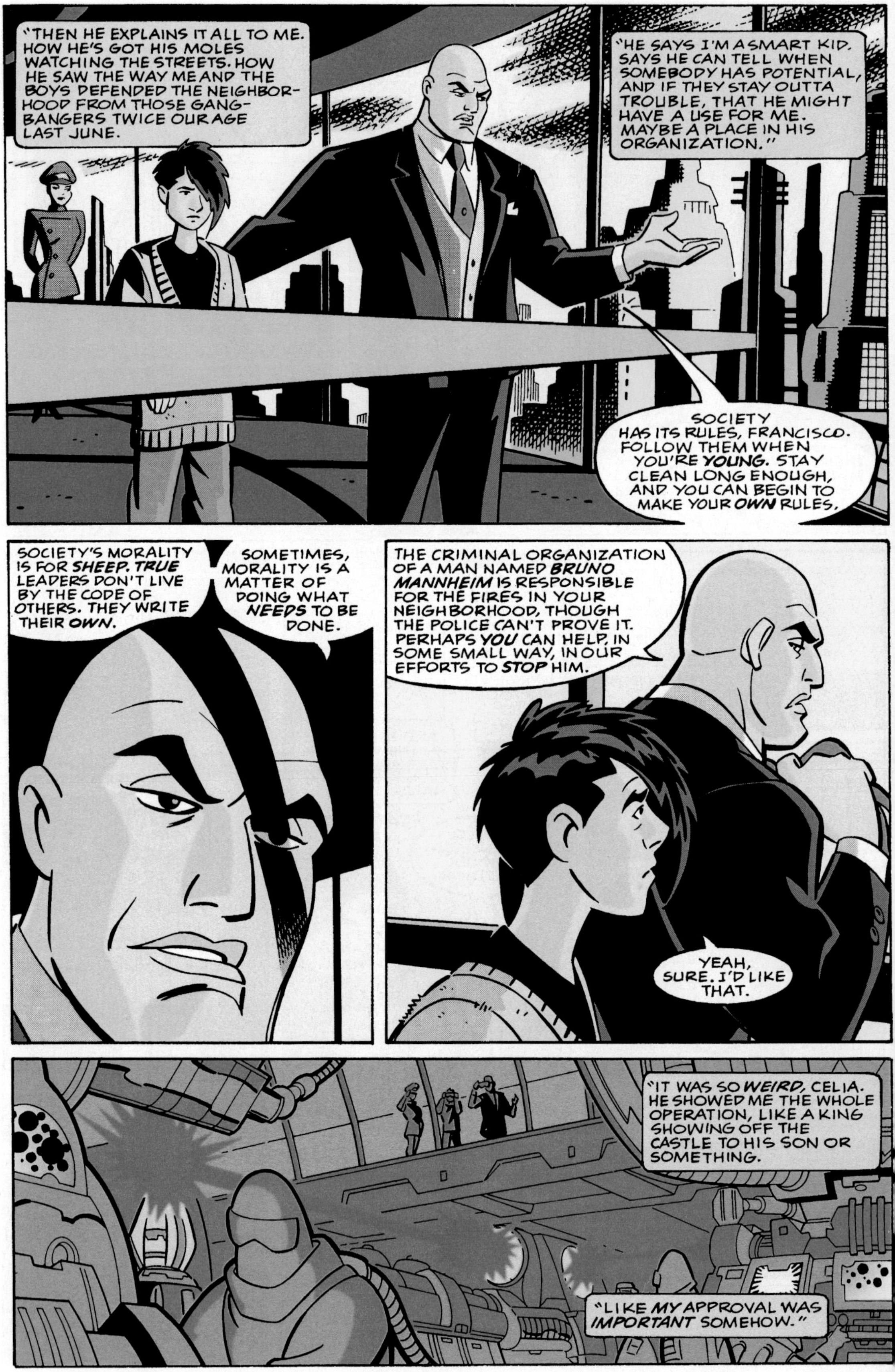
"THEN HE EXPLAINS IT ALL TO ME. HOW HE'S GOT HIS MOLES WATCHING THE STREETS. HOW HE SAW THE WAY ME AND THE BOYS DEFENDED THE NEIGHBORHOOD FROM THOSE GANG-BANGERS TWICE OUR AGE LAST JUNE.
"HE SAYS I'M A SMART KID. SAYS HE CAN TELL WHEN SOMEBODY HAS POTENTIAL, AND IF THEY STAY OUTTA TROUBLE, THAT HE MIGHT HAVE A USE FOR ME. MAYBE A PLACE IN HIS ORGANIZATION."
SOCIETY HAS ITS RULES, FRANCISCO. FOLLOW THEM WHEN YOU'RE YOUNG. STAY CLEAN LONG ENOUGH, AND YOU CAN BEGIN TO MAKE YOUR OWN RULES.
SOCIETY'S MORALITY IS FOR SHEEP. TRUE LEADERS DON'T LIVE BY THE CODE OF OTHERS. THEY WRITE THEIR OWN.
SOMETIMES, MORALITY IS A MATTER OF DOING WHAT NEEDS TO BE DONE.
THE CRIMINAL ORGANIZATION OF A MAN NAMED BRUNO MANNHEIM IS RESPONSIBLE FOR THE FIRES IN YOUR NEIGHBORHOOD, THOUGH THE POLICE CAN'T PROVE IT. PERHAPS YOU CAN HELP, IN SOME SMALL WAY, IN OUR EFFORTS TO STOP HIM.
YEAH, SURE. I'D LIKE THAT.
"IT WAS SO WEIRD, CELIA. HE SHOWED ME THE WHOLE OPERATION, LIKE A KING SHOWING OFF THE CASTLE TO HIS SON OR SOMETHING.
"LIKE MY APPROVAL WAS IMPORTANT SOMEHOW."

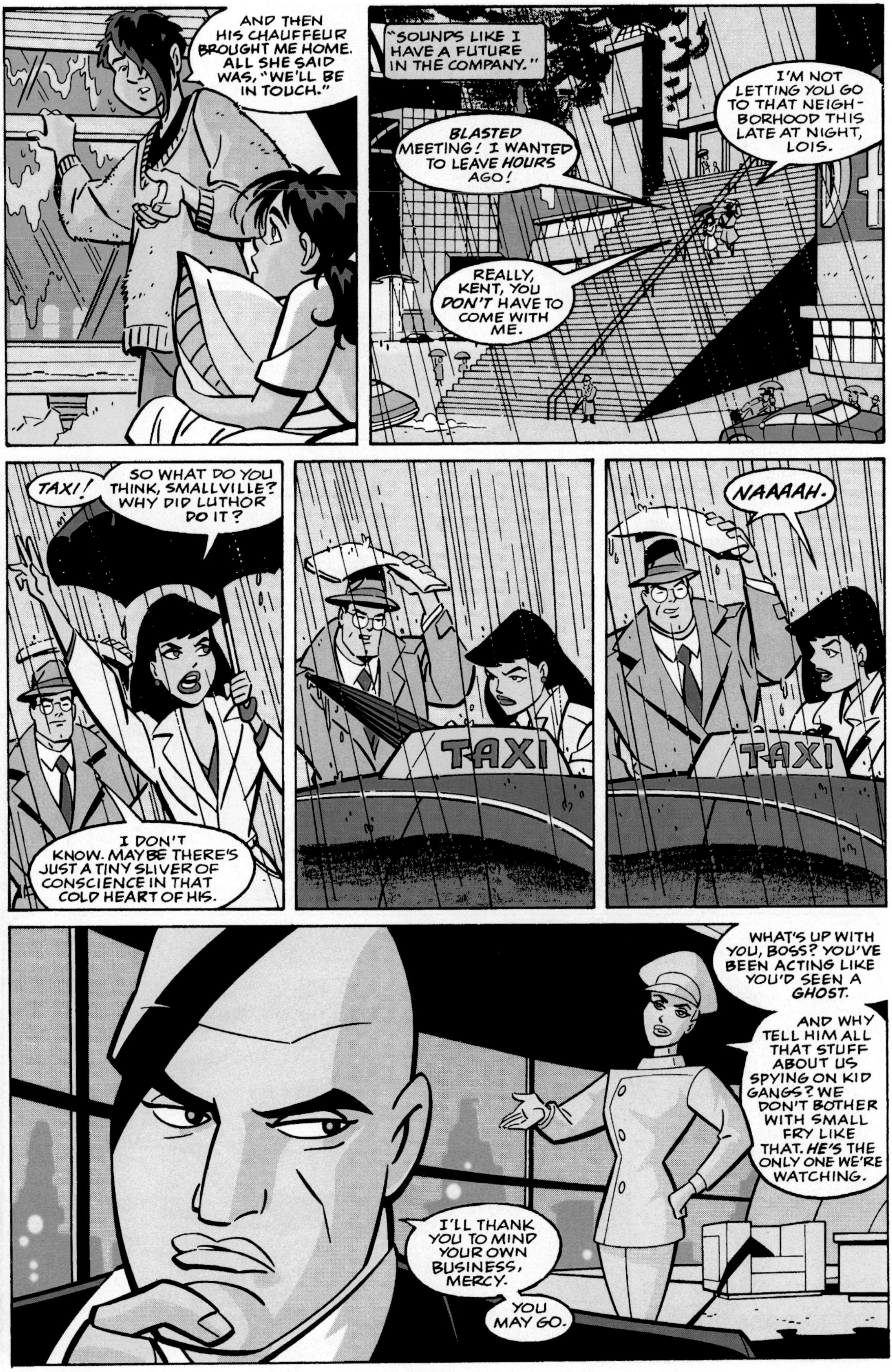
AND THEN HIS CHAUFFEUR BROUGHT ME HOME. ALL SHE SAID WAS, "WE'LL BE IN TOUCH."
"SOUNDS LIKE I HAVE A FUTURE IN THE COMPANY."
BLASTED MEETING! I WANTED TO LEAVE HOURS AGO!
I'M NOT LETTING YOU GO TO THAT NEIGHBORHOOD THIS LATE AT NIGHT, LOIS.
REALLY, KENT, YOU DON'T HAVE TO COME WITH ME.
TAXI!
SO WHAT DO YOU THINK, SMALLVILLE? WHY DID LUTHOR DO IT?
I DON'T KNOW. MAYBE THERE'S JUST A TINY SLIVER OF CONSCIENCE IN THAT COLD HEART OF HIS.
TAXI
NAAAAH.
TAXI
WHAT'S UP WITH YOU, BOSS? YOU'VE BEEN ACTING LIKE YOU'D SEEN A GHOST.
AND WHY TELL HIM ALL THAT STUFF ABOUT US SPYING ON KID GANGS? WE DON'T BOTHER WITH SMALL FRY LIKE THAT. HE'S THE ONLY ONE WE'RE WATCHING.
I'LL THANK YOU TO MIND YOUR OWN BUSINESS, MERCY.
YOU MAY GO.

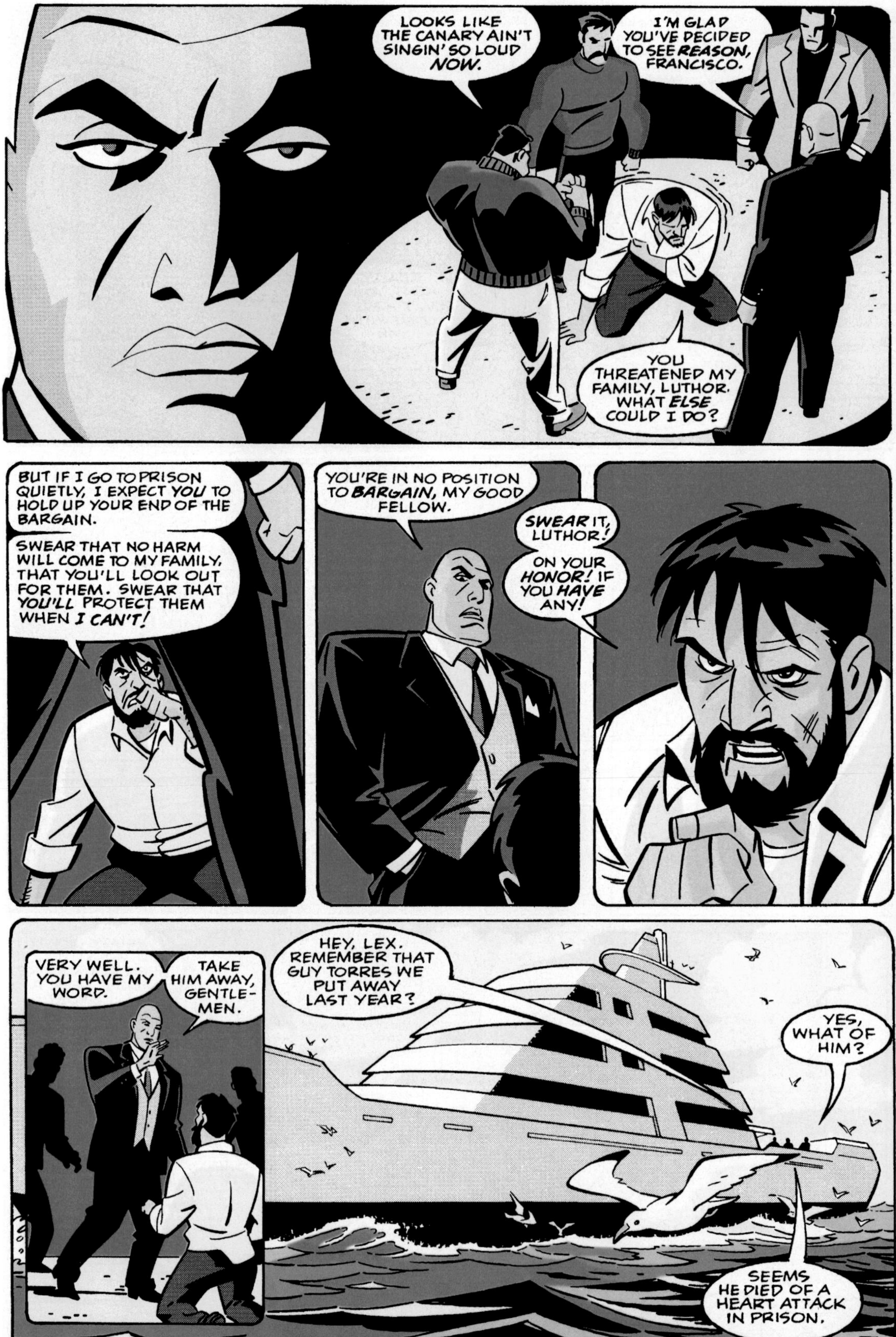
LOOKS LIKE THE CANARY AIN'T SINGIN' SO LOUD NOW.
I'M GLAD YOU'VE DECIDED TO SEE REASON, FRANCISCO.
YOU THREATENED MY FAMILY, LUTHOR. WHAT ELSE COULD I DO?
BUT IF I GO TO PRISON QUIETLY, I EXPECT YOU TO HOLD UP YOUR END OF THE BARGAIN.
SWEAR THAT NO HARM WILL COME TO MY FAMILY, THAT YOU'LL LOOK OUT FOR THEM. SWEAR THAT YOU'LL PROTECT THEM WHEN I CAN'T!
YOU'RE IN NO POSITION TO BARGAIN, MY GOOD FELLOW.
SWEAR IT, LUTHOR!
ON YOUR HONOR! IF YOU HAVE ANY!
VERY WELL. YOU HAVE MY WORD.
TAKE HIM AWAY, GENTLEMEN.
HEY, LEX. REMEMBER THAT GUY TORRES WE PUT AWAY LAST YEAR?
YES, WHAT OF HIM?
SEEMS HE DIED OF A HEART ATTACK IN PRISON.

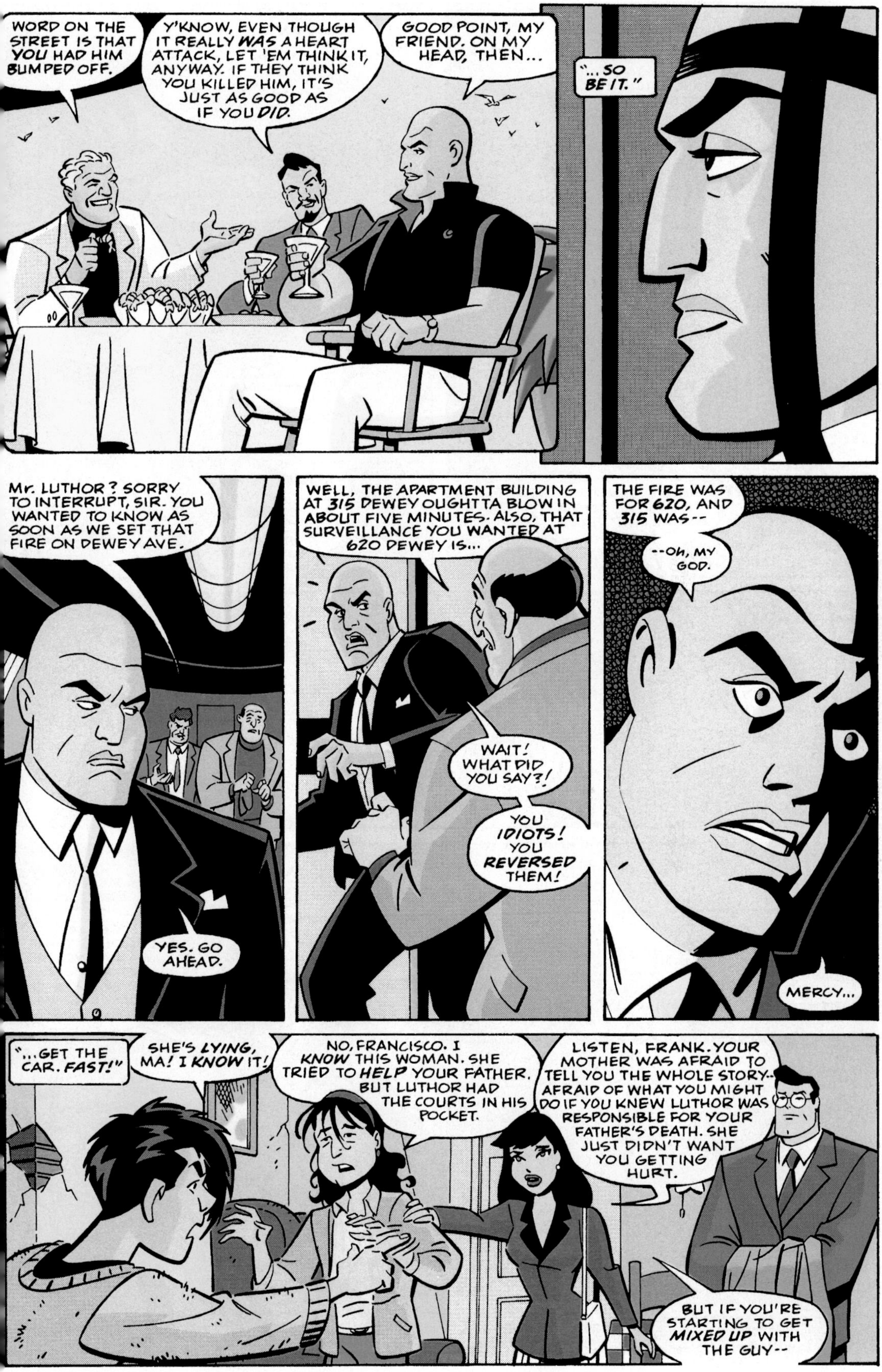
WORD ON THE STREET IS THAT YOU HAD HIM BUMPED OFF.
Y'KNOW, EVEN THOUGH IT REALLY WAS A HEART ATTACK, LET 'EM THINK IT, ANYWAY. IF THEY THINK YOU KILLED HIM, IT'S JUST AS GOOD AS IF YOU DID.
GOOD POINT, MY FRIEND. ON MY HEAD, THEN...
"...SO BE IT."
Mr. LUTHOR? SORRY TO INTERRUPT, SIR. YOU WANTED TO KNOW AS SOON AS WE SET THAT FIRE ON DEWEY AVE.
YES. GO AHEAD.
WELL, THE APARTMENT BUILDING AT 315 DEWEY OUGHTTA BLOW IN ABOUT FIVE MINUTES. ALSO, THAT SURVEILLANCE YOU WANTED AT 620 DEWEY IS...
WAIT! WHAT DID YOU SAY?!
YOU IDIOTS! YOU REVERSED THEM!
THE FIRE WAS FOR 620, AND 315 WAS--
--Oh, MY GOD.
MERCY...
"...GET THE CAR. FAST!"
SHE'S LYING, MA! I KNOW IT!
NO, FRANCISCO. I KNOW THIS WOMAN. SHE TRIED TO HELP YOUR FATHER. BUT LUTHOR HAD THE COURTS IN HIS POCKET.
LISTEN, FRANK. YOUR MOTHER WAS AFRAID TO TELL YOU THE WHOLE STORY-- AFRAID OF WHAT YOU MIGHT DO IF YOU KNEW LUTHOR WAS RESPONSIBLE FOR YOUR FATHER'S DEATH. SHE JUST DIDN'T WANT YOU GETTING HURT.
BUT IF YOU'RE STARTING TO GET MIXED UP WITH THE GUY--

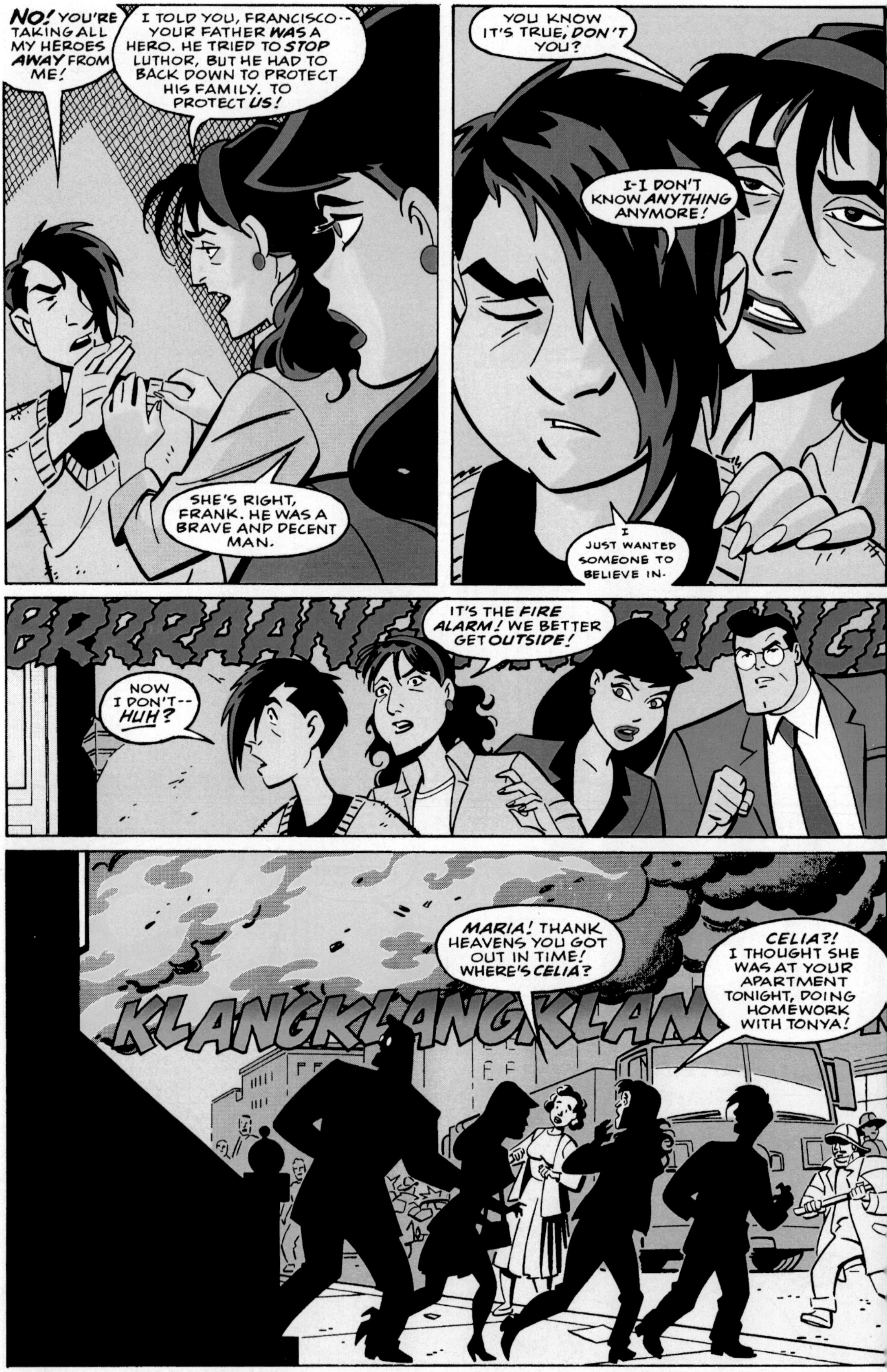
NO! YOU'RE TAKING ALL MY HEROES AWAY FROM ME!
I TOLD YOU, FRANCISCO-- YOUR FATHER WAS A HERO. HE TRIED TO STOP LUTHOR, BUT HE HAD TO BACK DOWN TO PROTECT HIS FAMILY. TO PROTECT US!
SHE'S RIGHT, FRANK. HE WAS A BRAVE AND DECENT MAN.
YOU KNOW IT'S TRUE, DON'T YOU?
I-I DON'T KNOW ANYTHING ANYMORE!
I JUST WANTED SOMEONE TO BELIEVE IN.
BRRRAANG
NOW I DON'T-- HUH?
IT'S THE FIRE ALARM! WE BETTER GET OUTSIDE!
KLANGKLANGKLANG
MARIA! THANK HEAVENS YOU GOT OUT IN TIME! WHERE'S CELIA?
CELIA?! I THOUGHT SHE WAS AT YOUR APARTMENT TONIGHT, DOING HOMEWORK WITH TONYA!

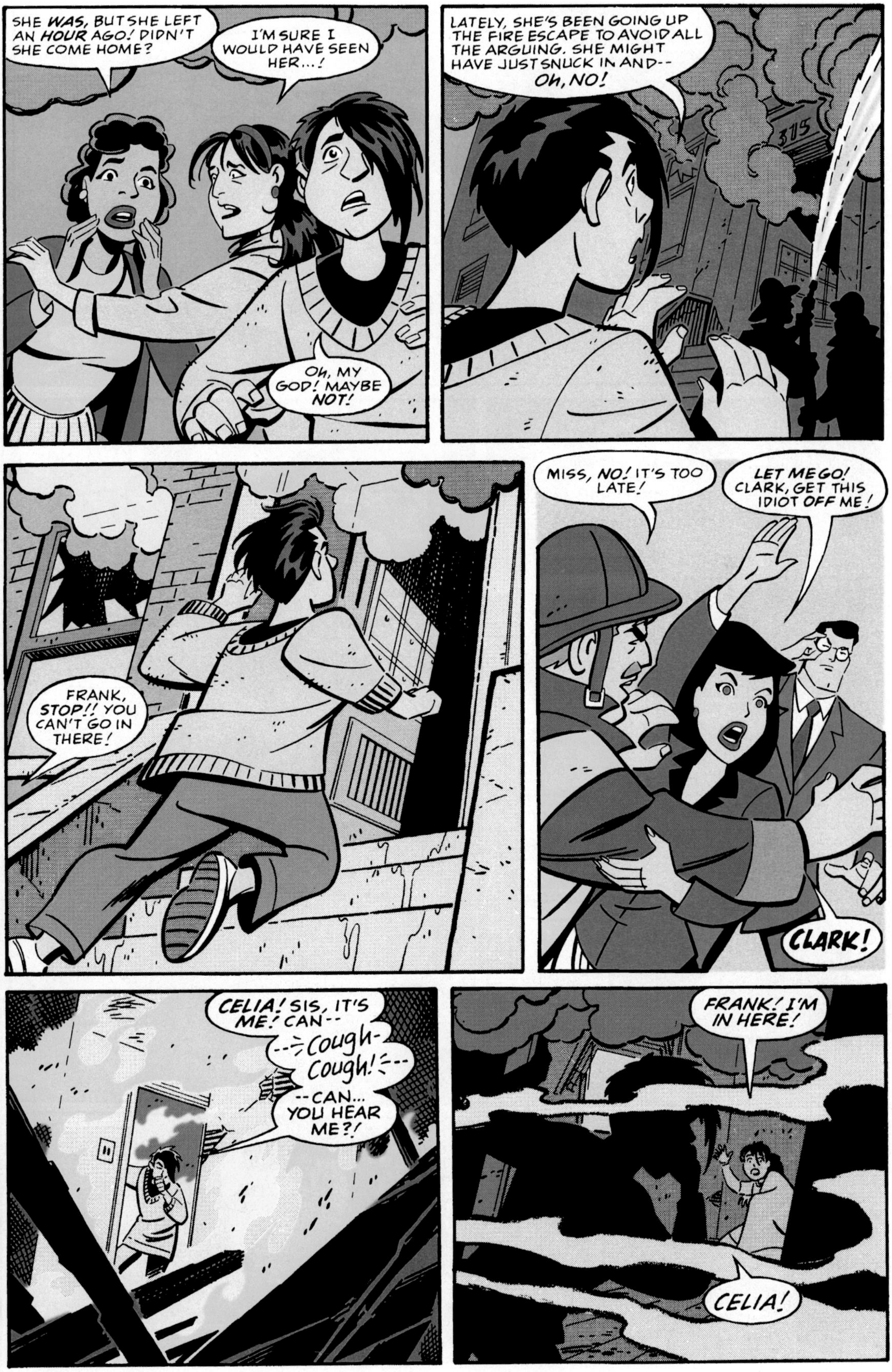
SHE WAS, BUT SHE LEFT AN HOUR AGO! DIDN'T SHE COME HOME?
I'M SURE I WOULD HAVE SEEN HER...!
OH, MY GOD! MAYBE NOT!
LATELY, SHE'S BEEN GOING UP THE FIRE ESCAPE TO AVOID ALL THE ARGUING. SHE MIGHT HAVE JUST SNUCK IN AND-- OH, NO!
315
FRANK, STOP!! YOU CAN'T GO IN THERE!
MISS, NO! IT'S TOO LATE!
LET ME GO! CLARK, GET THIS IDIOT OFF ME!
CLARK!
CELIA! SIS, IT'S ME! CAN-- --COUGH-COUGH!-- --CAN... YOU HEAR ME?!
FRANK! I'M IN HERE!
CELIA!

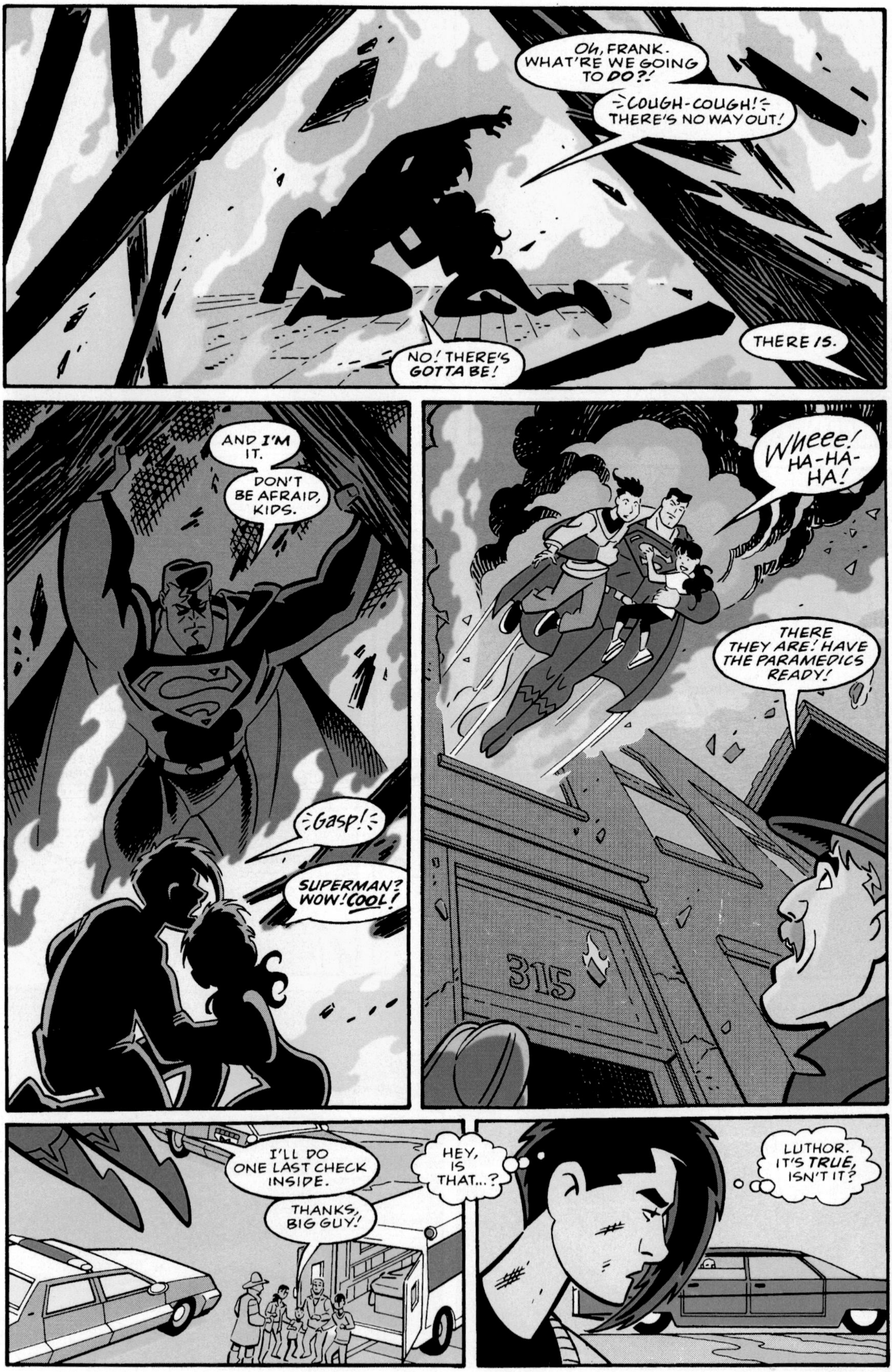
OH, FRANK. WHAT'RE WE GOING TO DO?!
COUGH-COUGH! THERE'S NO WAY OUT!
NO! THERE'S GOTTA BE!
THERE IS.
AND I'M IT.
DON'T BE AFRAID, KIDS.
Gasp!
SUPERMAN? WOW! COOL!
Wheee! HA-HA-HA!
THERE THEY ARE! HAVE THE PARAMEDICS READY!
315
I'LL DO ONE LAST CHECK INSIDE.
THANKS, BIG GUY!
HEY, IS THAT...?
LUTHOR. IT'S TRUE, ISN'T IT?

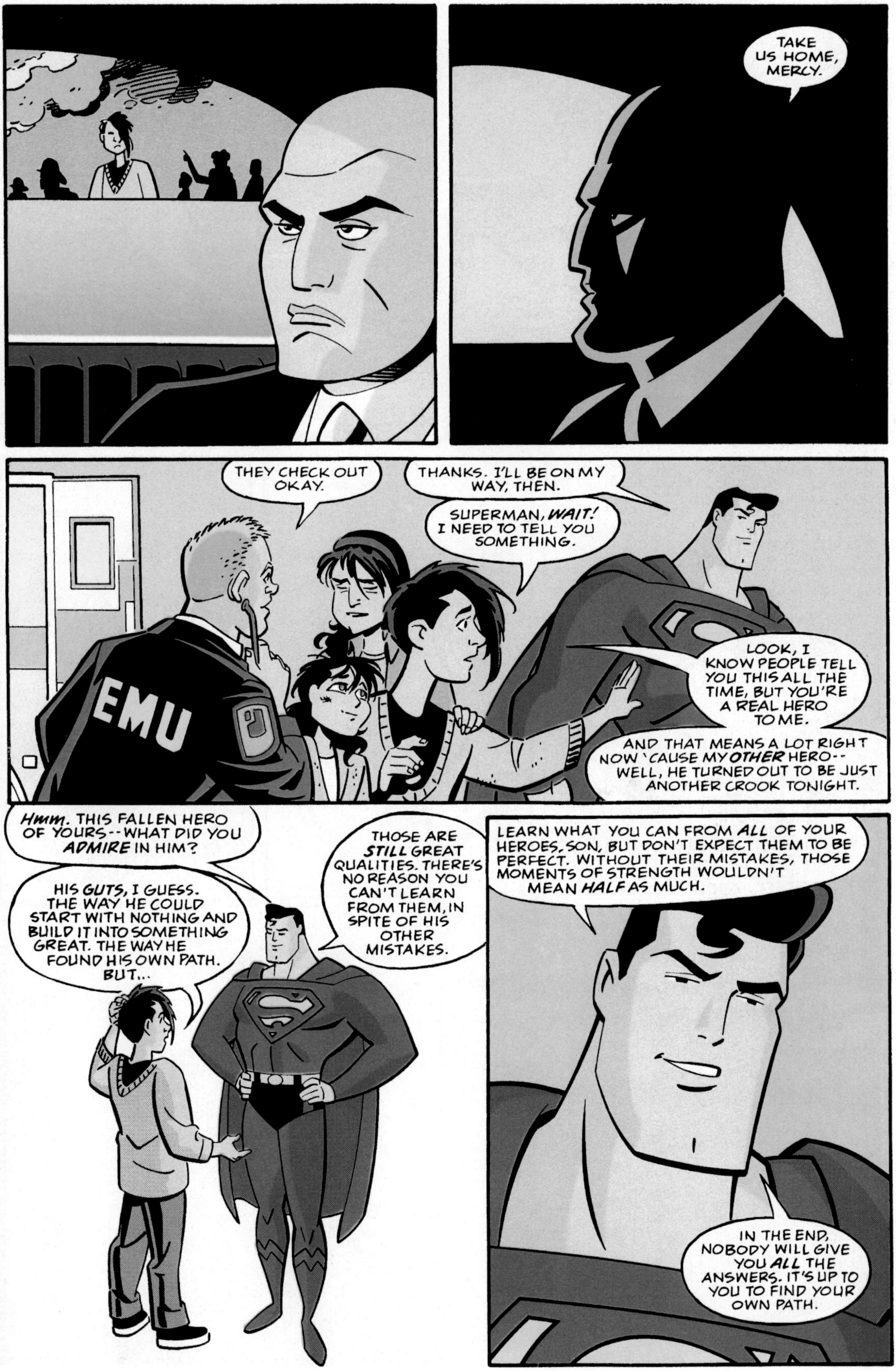
TAKE US HOME, MERCY.
THEY CHECK OUT OKAY.
THANKS. I'LL BE ON MY WAY, THEN.
SUPERMAN, *WAIT!* I NEED TO TELL YOU SOMETHING.
EMU
LOOK, I KNOW PEOPLE TELL YOU THIS ALL THE TIME, BUT YOU'RE A REAL HERO TO ME.
AND THAT MEANS A LOT RIGHT NOW 'CAUSE MY *OTHER* HERO-- WELL, HE TURNED OUT TO BE JUST ANOTHER CROOK TONIGHT.
Hmm. THIS FALLEN HERO OF YOURS--WHAT DID YOU *ADMIRE* IN HIM?
HIS *GUTS,* I GUESS. THE WAY HE COULD START WITH NOTHING AND BUILD IT INTO SOMETHING GREAT. THE WAY HE FOUND HIS OWN PATH. BUT...
THOSE ARE *STILL* GREAT QUALITIES. THERE'S NO REASON YOU CAN'T LEARN FROM THEM, IN SPITE OF HIS OTHER MISTAKES.
LEARN WHAT YOU CAN FROM *ALL* OF YOUR HEROES, SON, BUT DON'T EXPECT THEM TO BE PERFECT. WITHOUT THEIR MISTAKES, THOSE MOMENTS OF STRENGTH WOULDN'T MEAN *HALF* AS MUCH.
IN THE END, NOBODY WILL GIVE YOU *ALL* THE ANSWERS. IT'S UP TO YOU TO FIND YOUR OWN PATH.

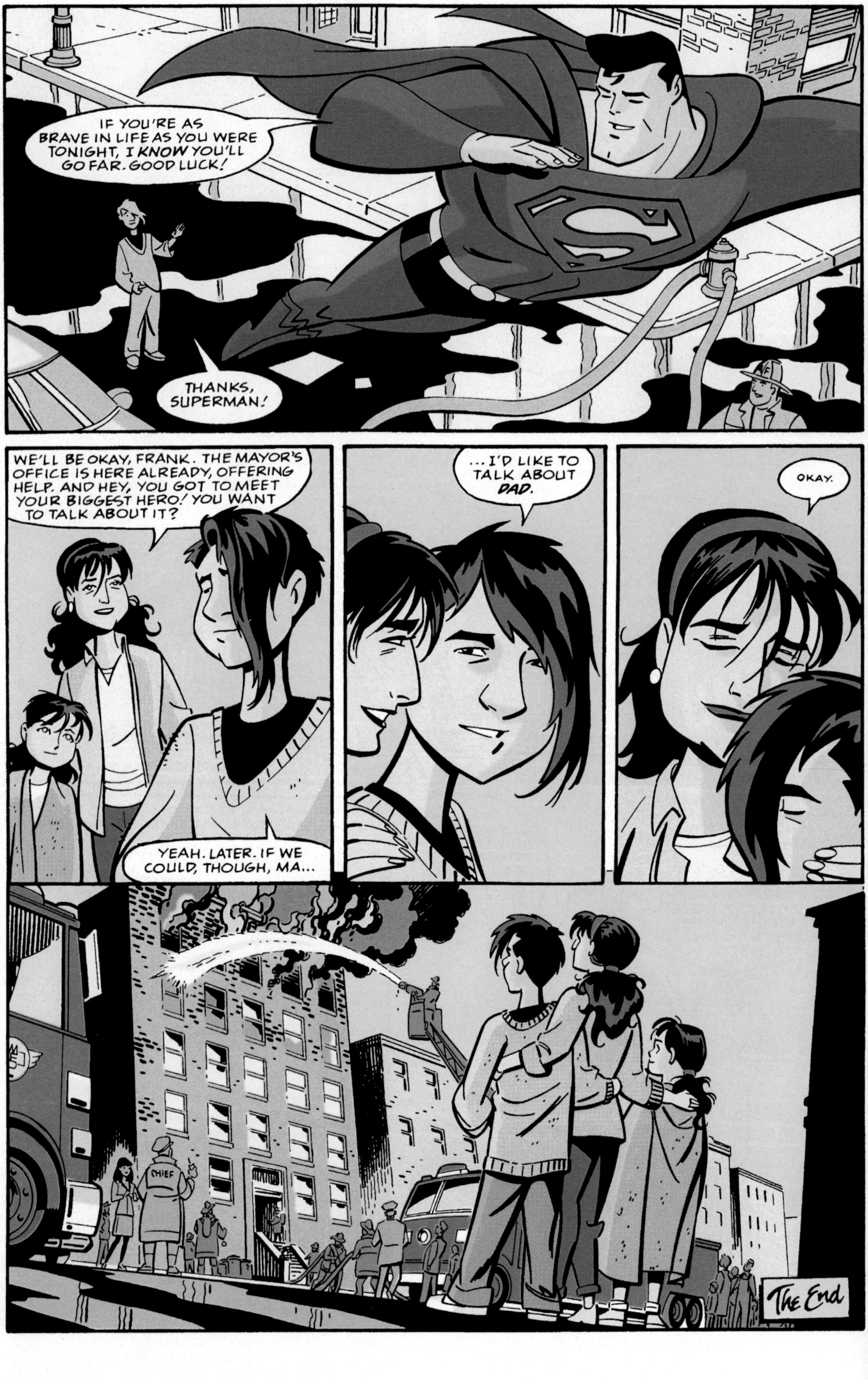
IF YOU'RE AS BRAVE IN LIFE AS YOU WERE TONIGHT, I KNOW YOU'LL GO FAR. GOOD LUCK!
THANKS, SUPERMAN!
WE'LL BE OKAY, FRANK. THE MAYOR'S OFFICE IS HERE ALREADY, OFFERING HELP. AND HEY, YOU GOT TO MEET YOUR BIGGEST HERO! YOU WANT TO TALK ABOUT IT?
YEAH. LATER. IF WE COULD, THOUGH, MA...
...I'D LIKE TO TALK ABOUT DAD.
OKAY.
CHIEF
The End

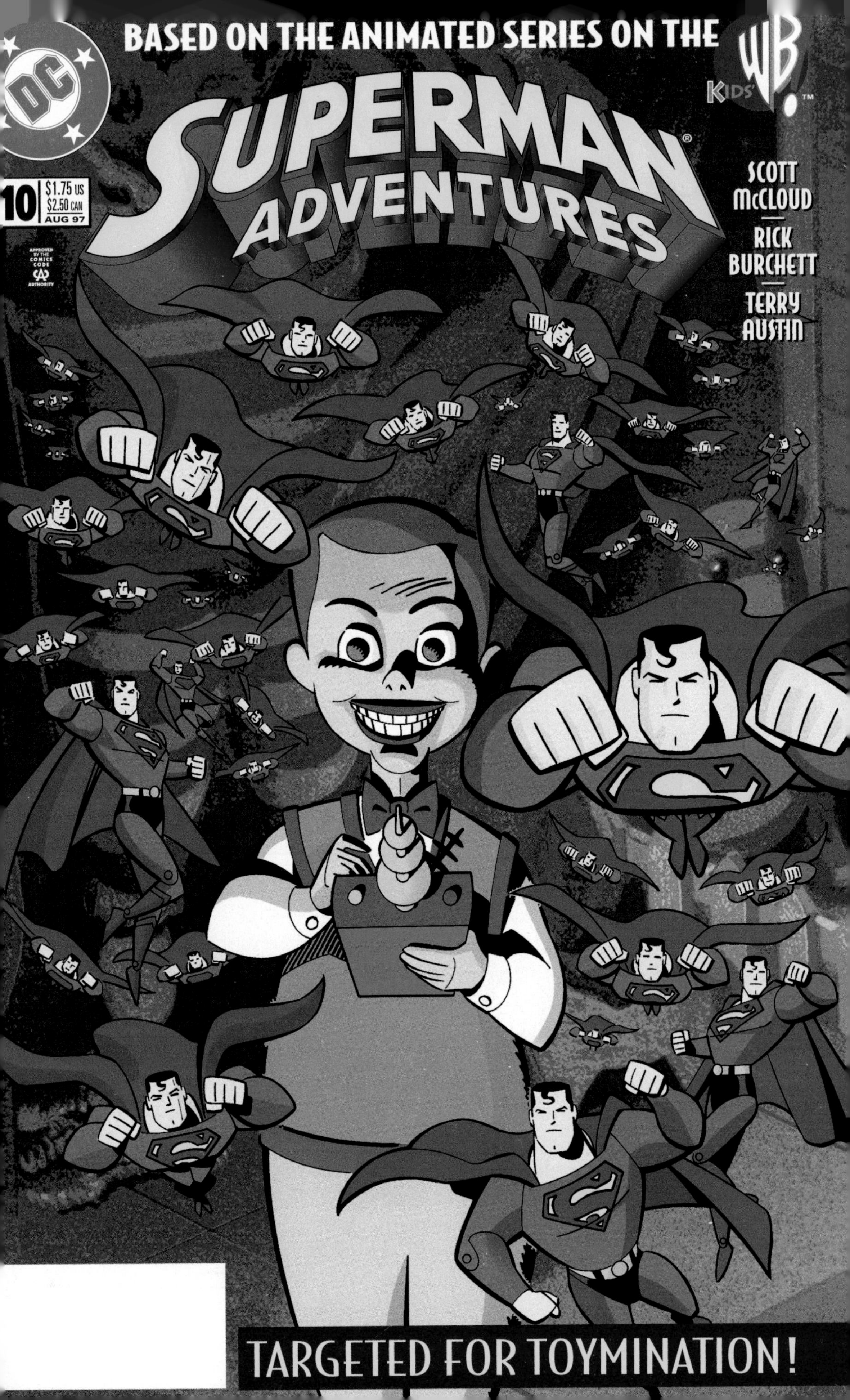

BASED ON THE ANIMATED SERIES ON THE
KIDS' WB!
DC
SUPERMAN ADVENTURES
10
$1.75 US
$2.50 CAN
AUG 97
APPROVED BY THE COMICS CODE AUTHORITY
SCOTT McCLOUD
RICK BURCHETT
TERRY AUSTIN
TARGETED FOR TOYMINATION!

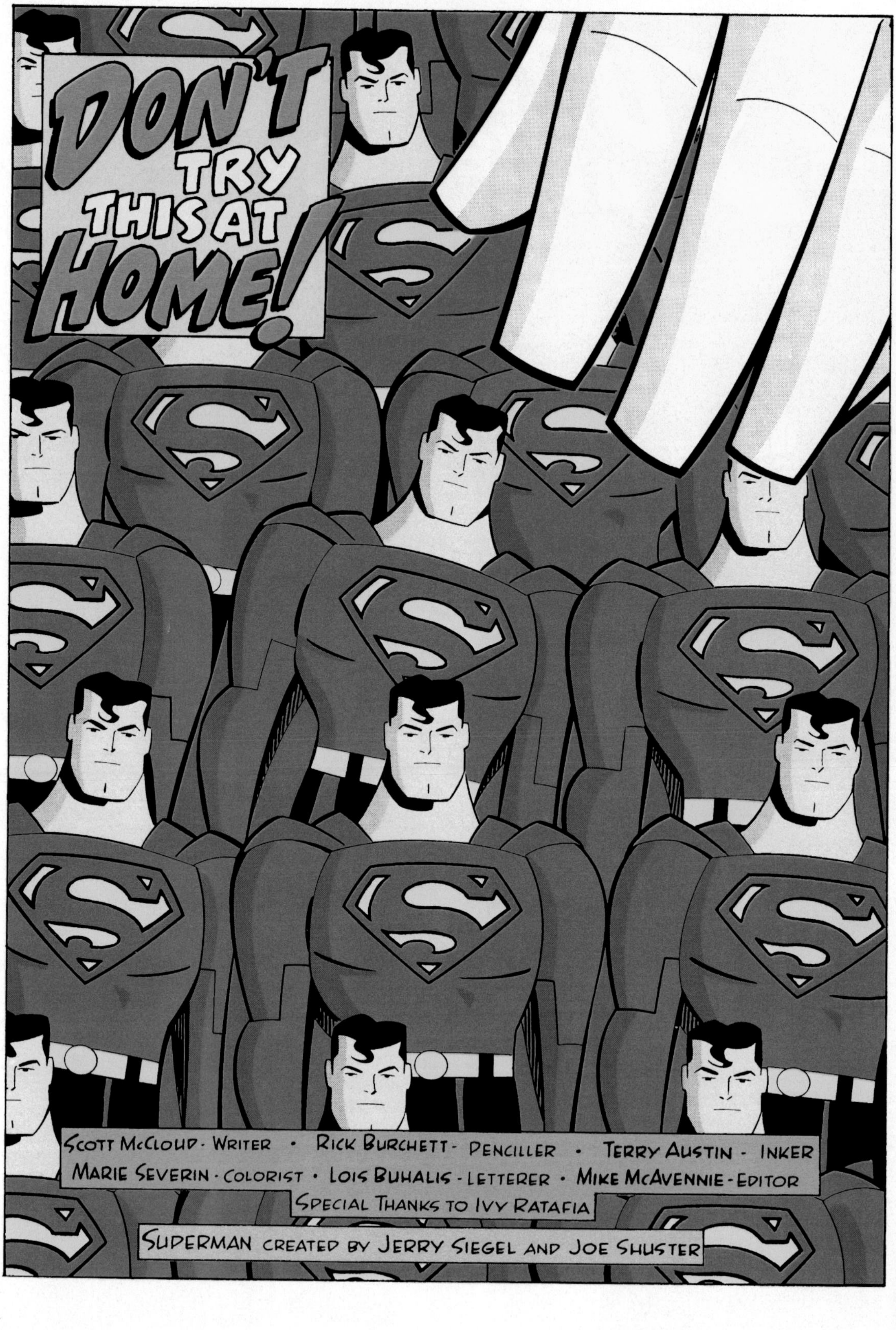

DON'T TRY THIS AT HOME!
SCOTT McCLOUD - WRITER • RICK BURCHETT - PENCILLER • TERRY AUSTIN - INKER
MARIE SEVERIN - COLORIST • LOIS BUHALIS - LETTERER • MIKE McAVENNIE - EDITOR
SPECIAL THANKS TO IVY RATAFIA
SUPERMAN CREATED BY JERRY SIEGEL AND JOE SHUSTER

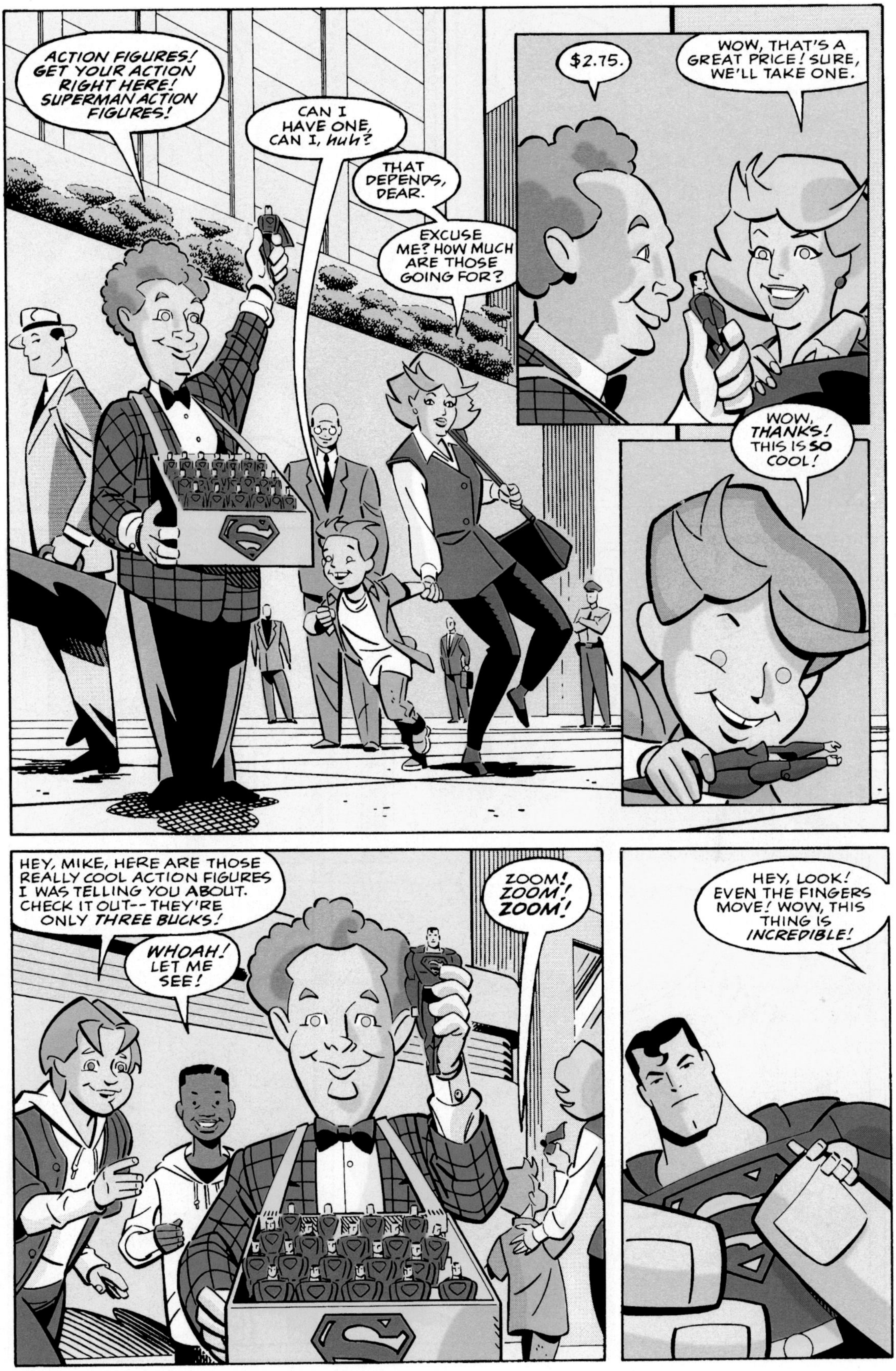
ACTION FIGURES! GET YOUR ACTION RIGHT HERE! SUPERMAN ACTION FIGURES!
CAN I HAVE ONE, CAN I, *huh*?
THAT DEPENDS, DEAR.
EXCUSE ME? HOW MUCH ARE THOSE GOING FOR?
$2.75.
WOW, THAT'S A GREAT PRICE! SURE, WE'LL TAKE ONE.
WOW, *THANKS!* THIS IS *SO* COOL!
HEY, MIKE, HERE ARE THOSE REALLY COOL ACTION FIGURES I WAS TELLING YOU ABOUT. CHECK IT OUT-- THEY'RE ONLY *THREE BUCKS!*
WHOAH! LET ME SEE!
ZOOM! *ZOOM!* *ZOOM!*
HEY, LOOK! EVEN THE FINGERS MOVE! WOW, THIS THING IS *INCREDIBLE!*

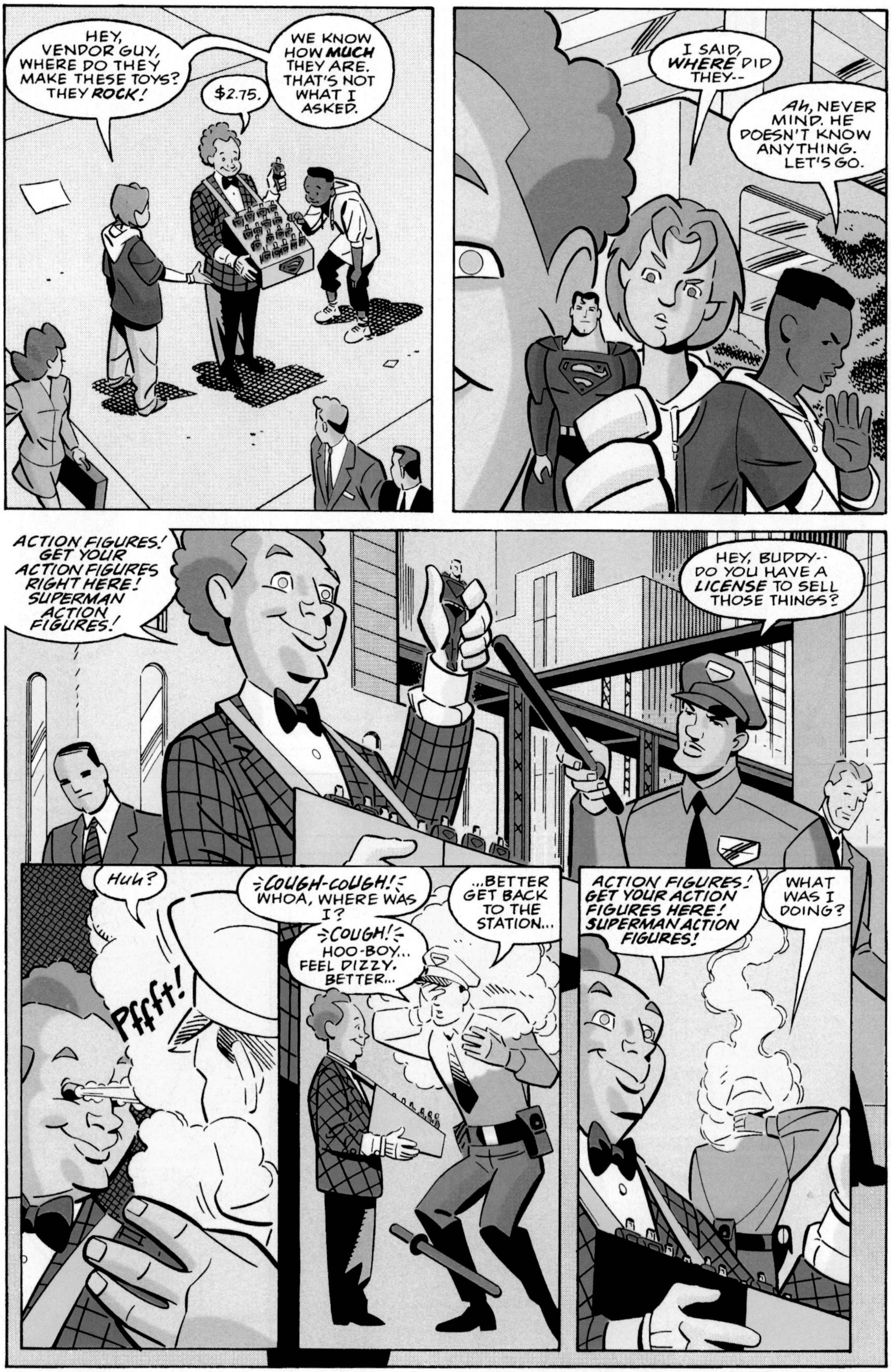
HEY, VENDOR GUY, WHERE DO THEY MAKE THESE TOYS? THEY ROCK!
$2.75.
WE KNOW HOW MUCH THEY ARE. THAT'S NOT WHAT I ASKED.
I SAID, WHERE DID THEY--
AH, NEVER MIND. HE DOESN'T KNOW ANYTHING. LET'S GO.
ACTION FIGURES! GET YOUR ACTION FIGURES RIGHT HERE! SUPERMAN ACTION FIGURES!
HEY, BUDDY-- DO YOU HAVE A LICENSE TO SELL THOSE THINGS?
HUH?
PFFFT!
COUGH-COUGH! WHOA, WHERE WAS I?
COUGH! HOO-BOY... FEEL DIZZY. BETTER...
...BETTER GET BACK TO THE STATION...
ACTION FIGURES! GET YOUR ACTION FIGURES HERE! SUPERMAN ACTION FIGURES!
WHAT WAS I DOING?

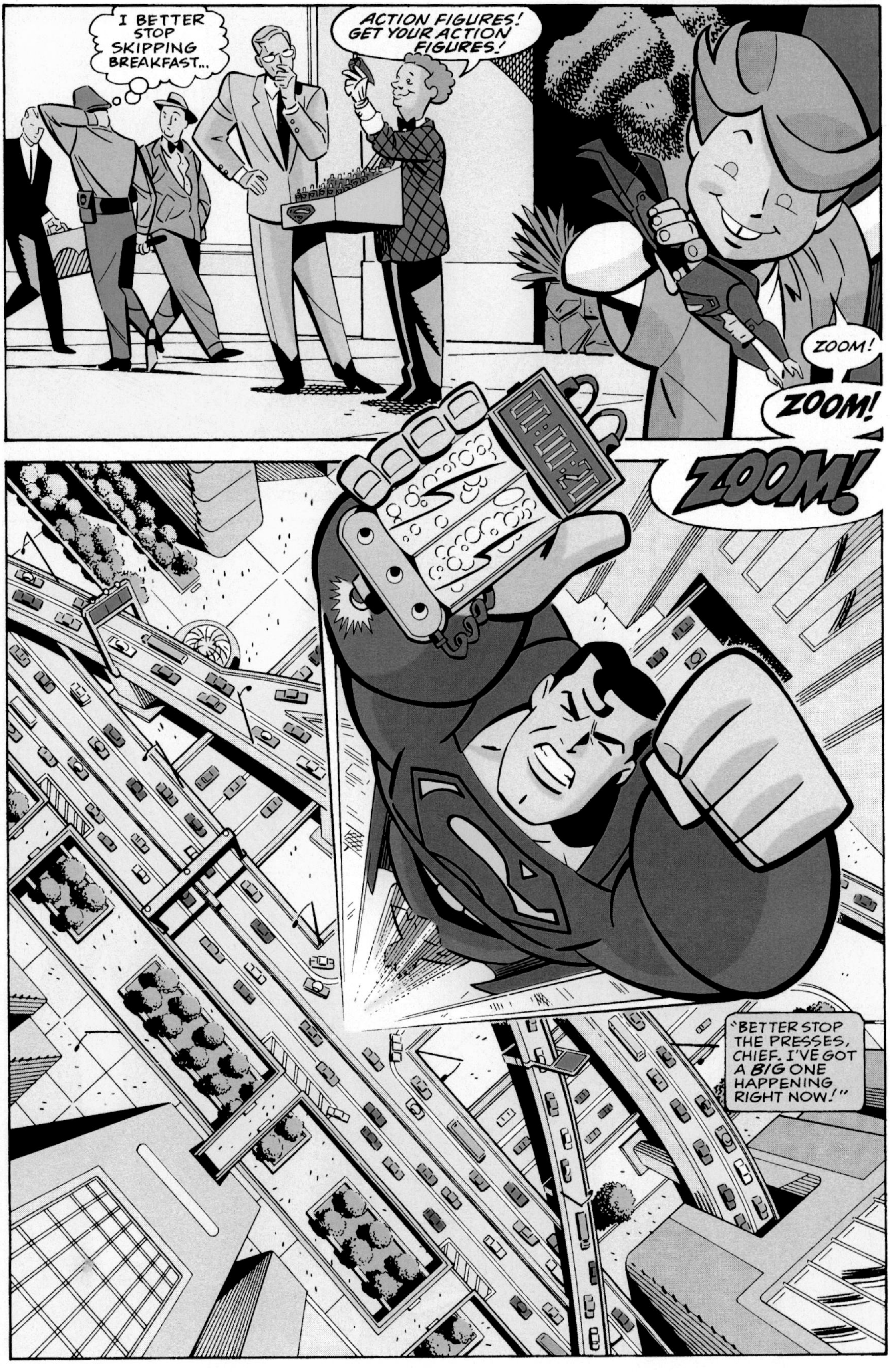
I BETTER STOP SKIPPING BREAKFAST...
ACTION FIGURES! GET YOUR ACTION FIGURES!
ZOOM!
ZOOM!
ZOOM!
"BETTER STOP THE PRESSES, CHIEF. I'VE GOT A BIG ONE HAPPENING RIGHT NOW!"

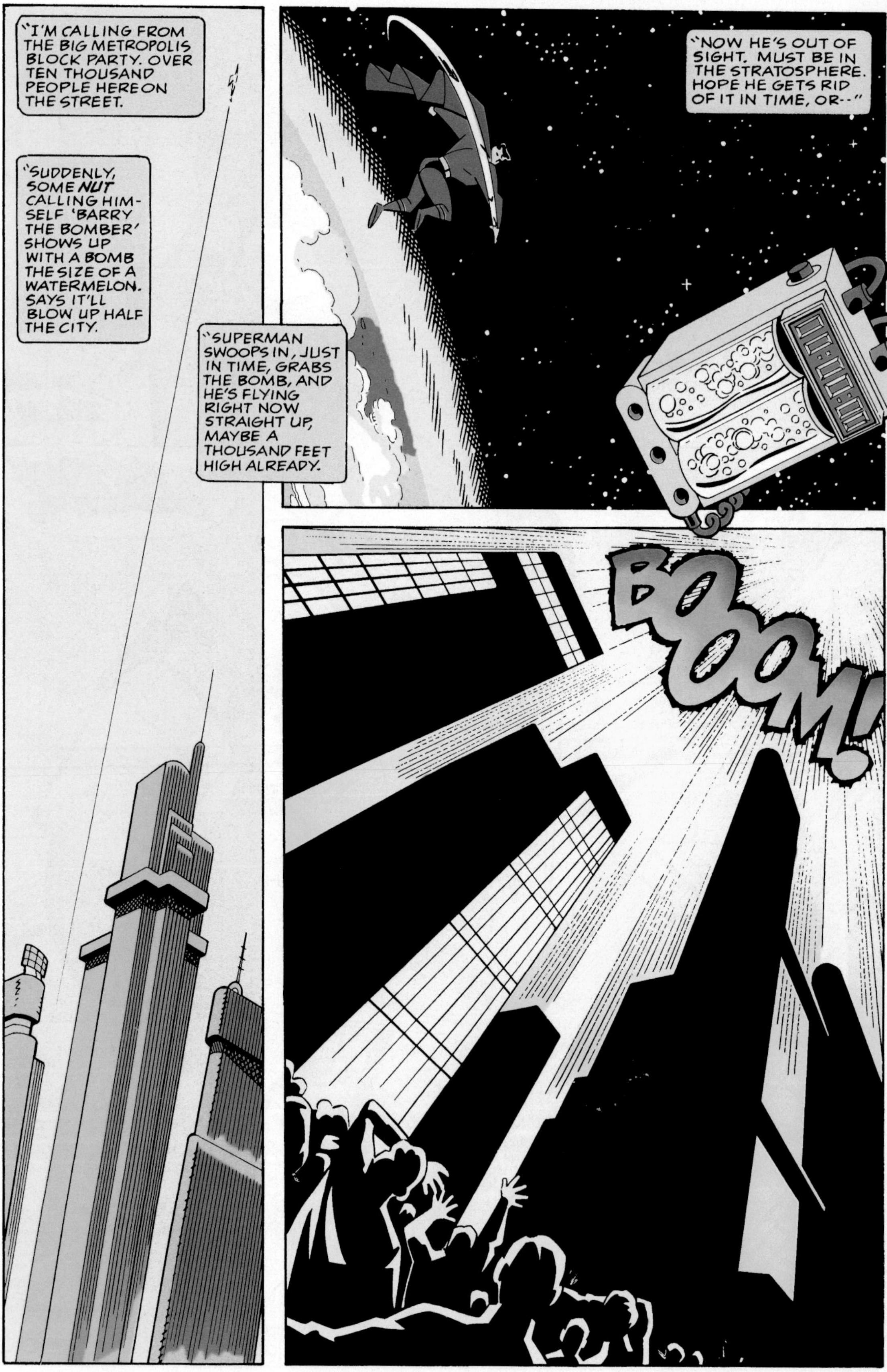
"I'M CALLING FROM THE BIG METROPOLIS BLOCK PARTY. OVER TEN THOUSAND PEOPLE HERE ON THE STREET.
"SUDDENLY, SOME NUT CALLING HIMSELF 'BARRY THE BOMBER' SHOWS UP WITH A BOMB THE SIZE OF A WATERMELON. SAYS IT'LL BLOW UP HALF THE CITY.
"SUPERMAN SWOOPS IN, JUST IN TIME, GRABS THE BOMB, AND HE'S FLYING RIGHT NOW STRAIGHT UP, MAYBE A THOUSAND FEET HIGH ALREADY.
"NOW HE'S OUT OF SIGHT. MUST BE IN THE STRATOSPHERE. HOPE HE GETS RID OF IT IN TIME, OR--"
BOOOOM!

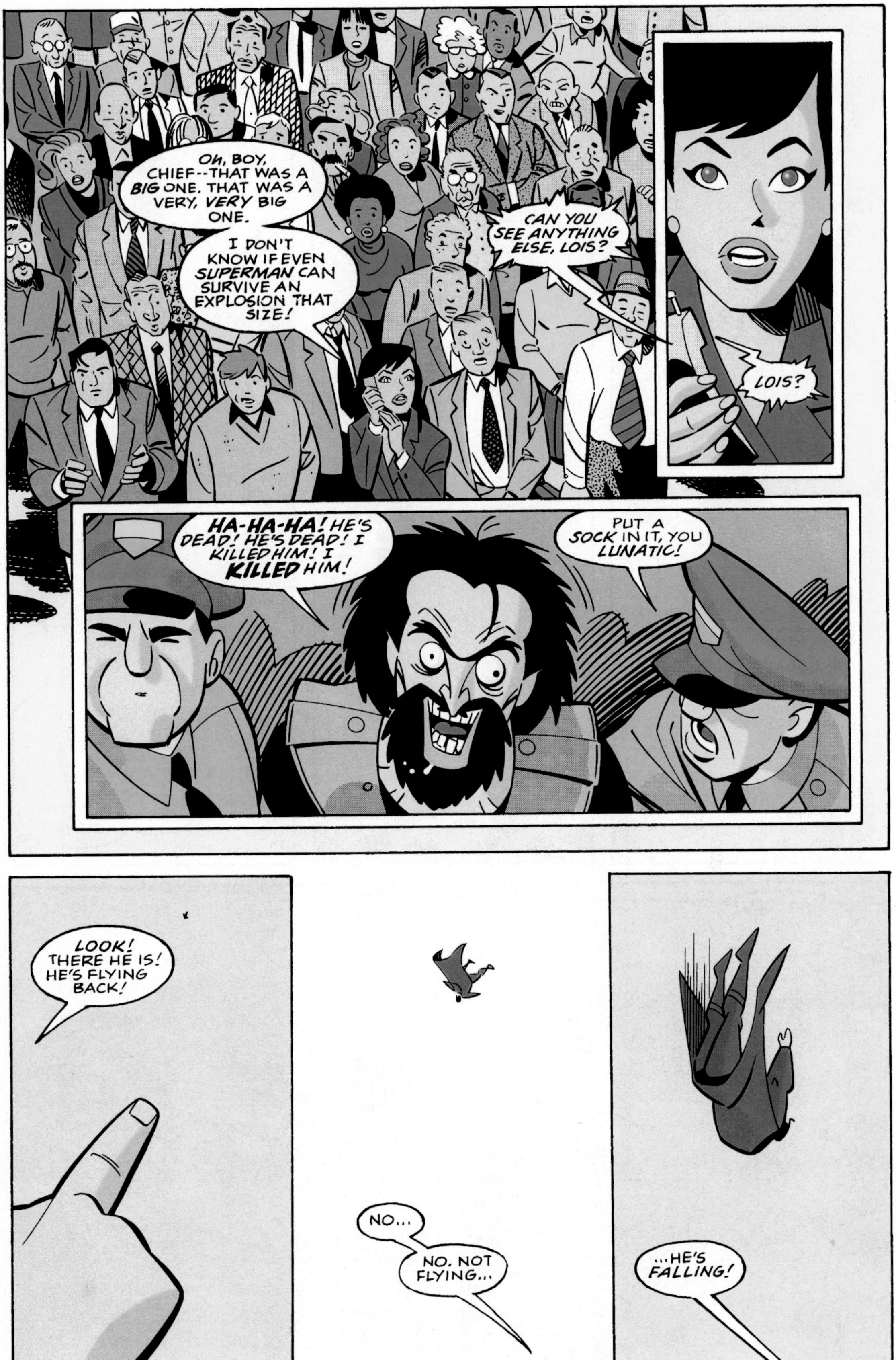
OH, BOY, CHIEF--THAT WAS A BIG ONE. THAT WAS A VERY, VERY BIG ONE.
I DON'T KNOW IF EVEN SUPERMAN CAN SURVIVE AN EXPLOSION THAT SIZE!
CAN YOU SEE ANYTHING ELSE, LOIS?
LOIS?
HA-HA-HA! HE'S DEAD! HE'S DEAD! I KILLED HIM! I KILLED HIM!
PUT A SOCK IN IT, YOU LUNATIC!
LOOK! THERE HE IS! HE'S FLYING BACK!
NO...
NO. NOT FLYING...
...HE'S FALLING!

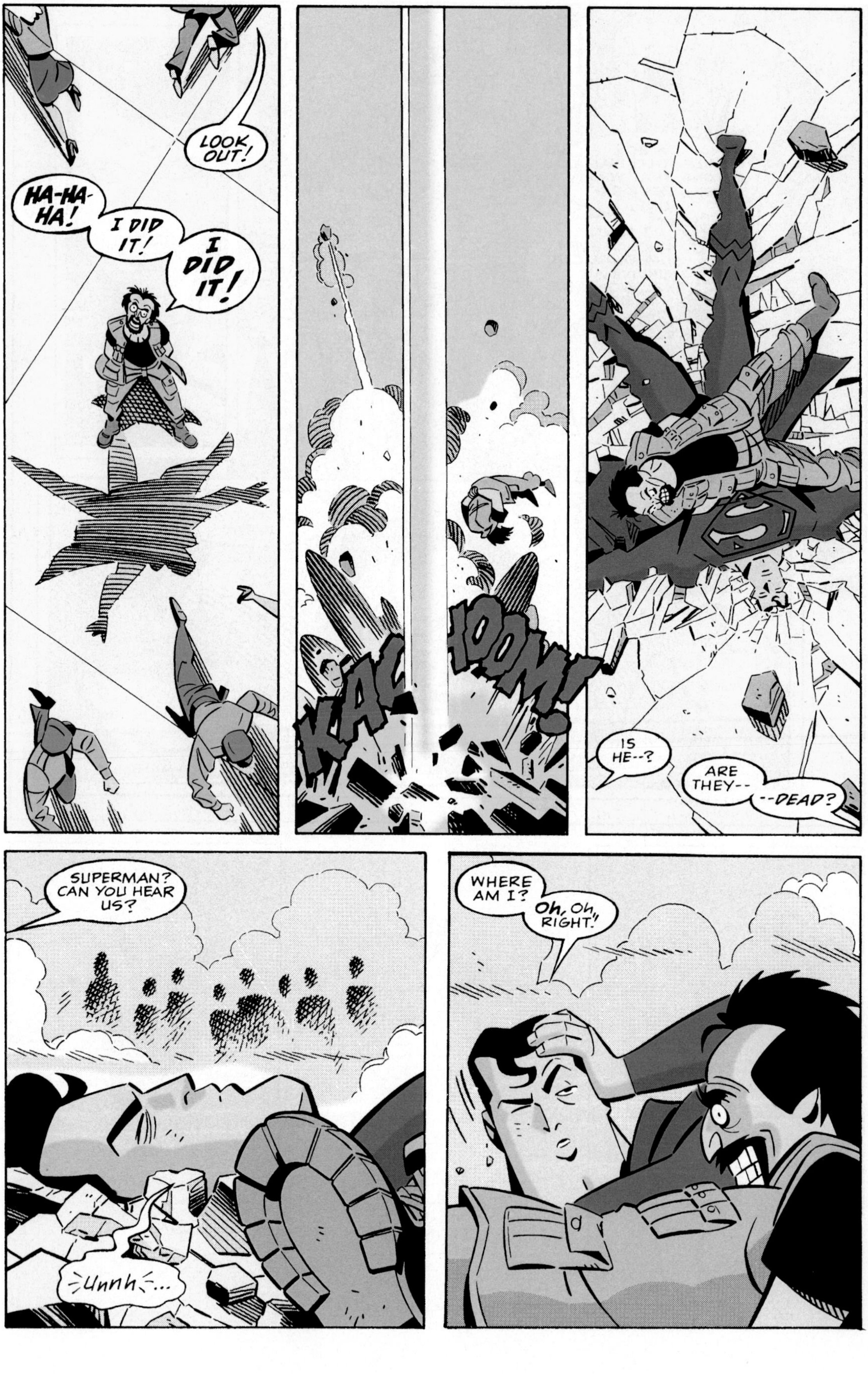
LOOK, OUT!
HA-HA-HA!
I DID IT!
I DID IT!
KAC-HOOM!
IS HE--?
ARE THEY--
--DEAD?
SUPERMAN? CAN YOU HEAR US?
Unnh...
WHERE AM I?
Oh, Oh, RIGHT.

NICE TRY BARRY.

NO! *NO!* YOU'RE *DEAD!*

DEAD, I SAY, *DEAD!*

WE'LL TAKE CARE OF HIM FROM HERE, SUPERMAN. SOUNDS LIKE A *LIVELY* ONE, huh?

YOU *COULD* SAY THAT.

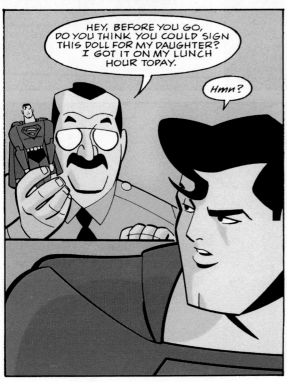

HEY, BEFORE YOU GO, DO YOU THINK YOU COULD SIGN THIS DOLL FOR MY DAUGHTER? I GOT IT ON MY LUNCH HOUR TODAY.

Hmn?

THEY'RE SELLING 'EM ALL OVER THE CITY. DIDN'T YOU KNOW ABOUT IT?

NO...THIS IS THE FIRST I'VE HEARD.

Oh, well...

"...I GUESS THERE'S NO HARM IN IT."

HEY, HANNAH! LOOK WHAT DADDY GOT FOR YOU TODAY!

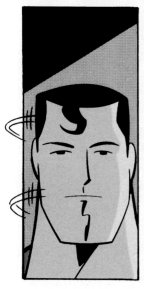

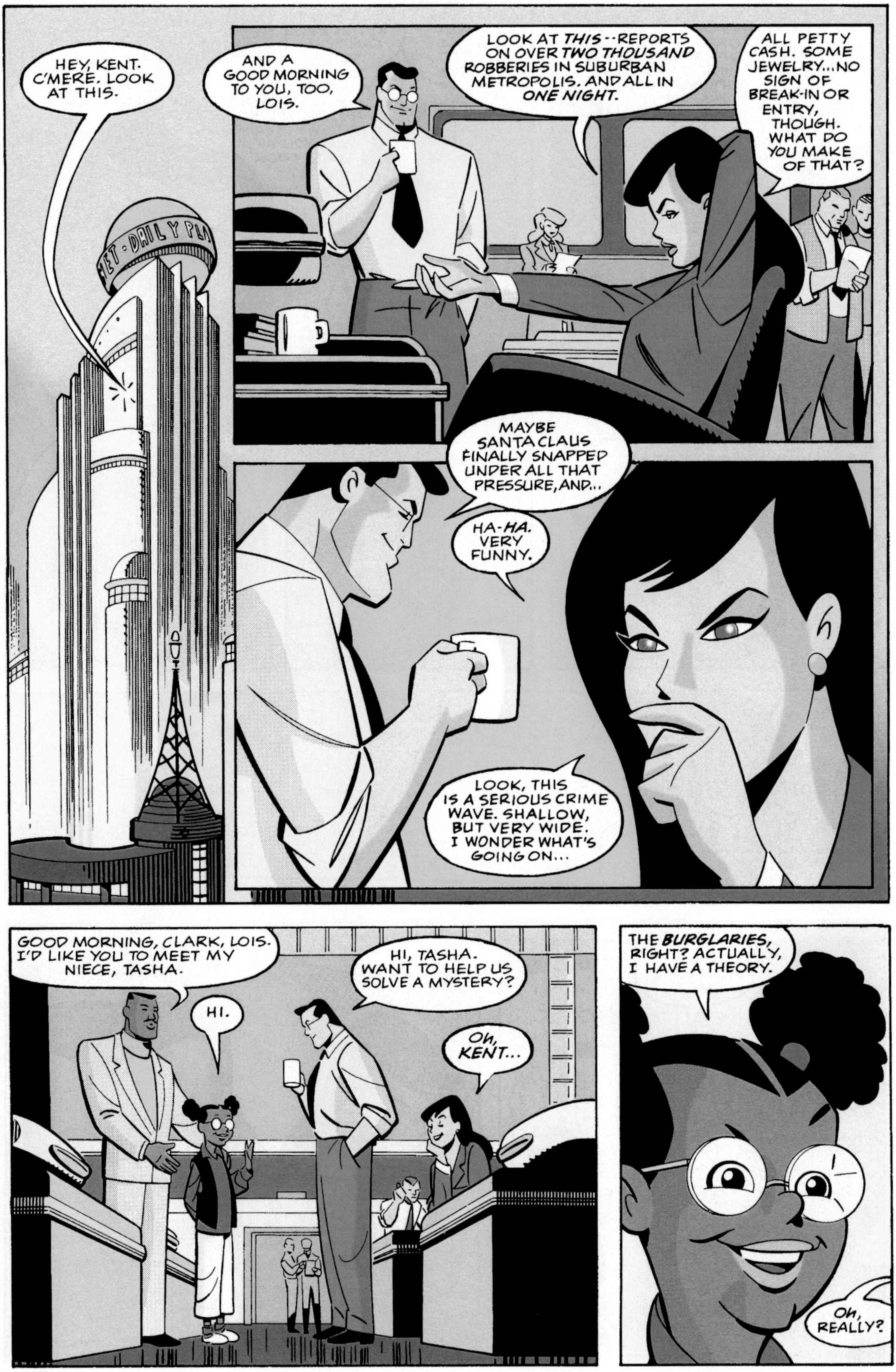
HEY, KENT. C'MERE. LOOK AT THIS.
AND A GOOD MORNING TO YOU, TOO, LOIS.
LOOK AT THIS--REPORTS ON OVER TWO THOUSAND ROBBERIES IN SUBURBAN METROPOLIS. AND ALL IN ONE NIGHT.
ALL PETTY CASH. SOME JEWELRY...NO SIGN OF BREAK-IN OR ENTRY, THOUGH. WHAT DO YOU MAKE OF THAT?
MAYBE SANTA CLAUS FINALLY SNAPPED UNDER ALL THAT PRESSURE, AND...
HA-HA. VERY FUNNY.
LOOK, THIS IS A SERIOUS CRIME WAVE. SHALLOW, BUT VERY WIDE. I WONDER WHAT'S GOING ON...
GOOD MORNING, CLARK, LOIS. I'D LIKE YOU TO MEET MY NIECE, TASHA.
HI.
HI, TASHA. WANT TO HELP US SOLVE A MYSTERY?
Oh, KENT...
THE BURGLARIES, RIGHT? ACTUALLY, I HAVE A THEORY.
Oh, REALLY?

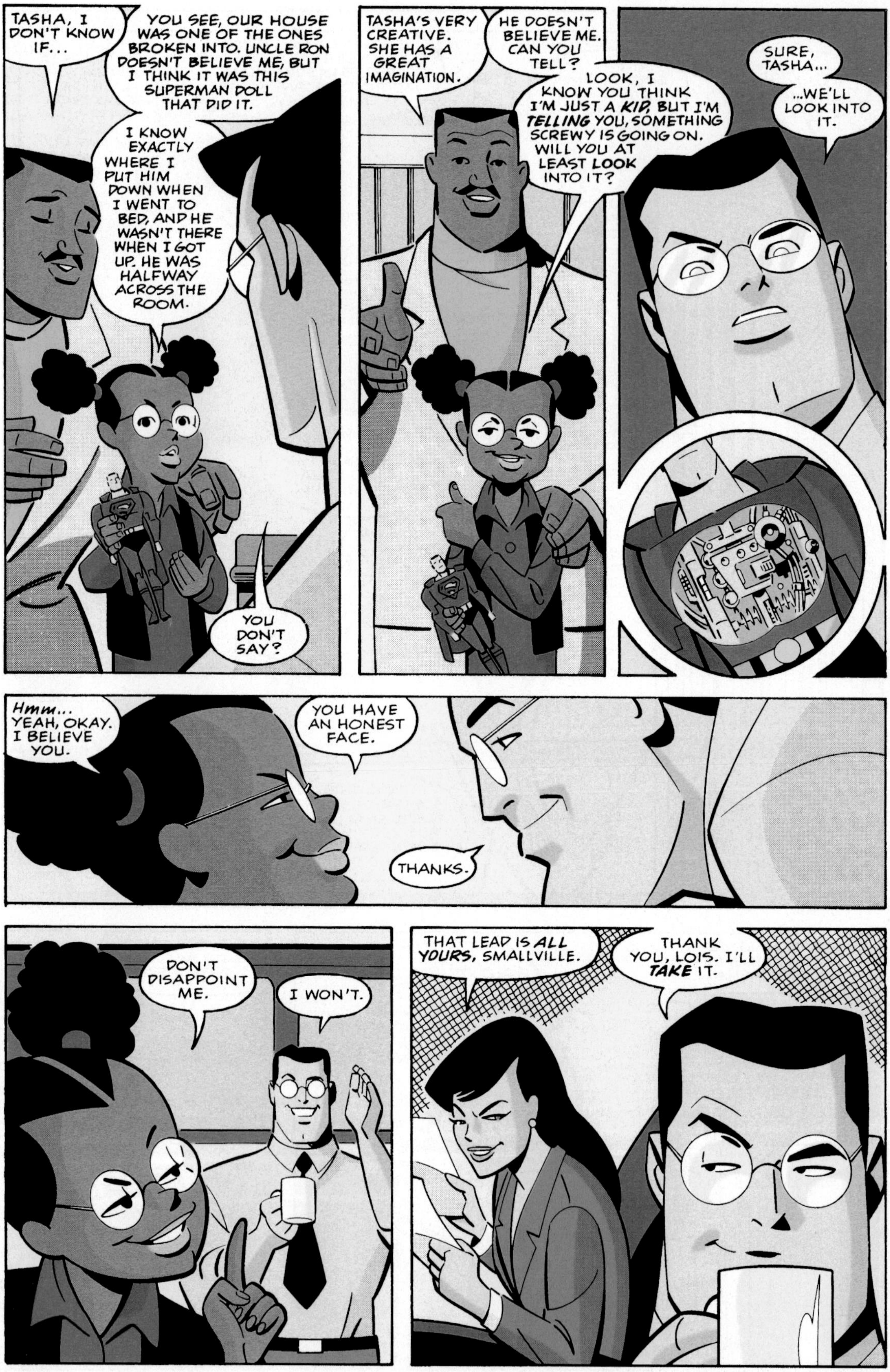
TASHA, I DON'T KNOW IF...
YOU SEE, OUR HOUSE WAS ONE OF THE ONES BROKEN INTO. UNCLE RON DOESN'T BELIEVE ME, BUT I THINK IT WAS THIS SUPERMAN DOLL THAT DID IT.
I KNOW EXACTLY WHERE I PUT HIM DOWN WHEN I WENT TO BED, AND HE WASN'T THERE WHEN I GOT UP. HE WAS HALFWAY ACROSS THE ROOM.
YOU DON'T SAY?
TASHA'S VERY CREATIVE. SHE HAS A GREAT IMAGINATION.
HE DOESN'T BELIEVE ME. CAN YOU TELL?
LOOK, I KNOW YOU THINK I'M JUST A KID, BUT I'M TELLING YOU, SOMETHING SCREWY IS GOING ON. WILL YOU AT LEAST LOOK INTO IT?
SURE, TASHA...
...WE'LL LOOK INTO IT.
Hmm... YEAH, OKAY. I BELIEVE YOU.
YOU HAVE AN HONEST FACE.
THANKS.
DON'T DISAPPOINT ME.
I WON'T.
THAT LEAD IS ALL YOURS, SMALLVILLE.
THANK YOU, LOIS. I'LL TAKE IT.

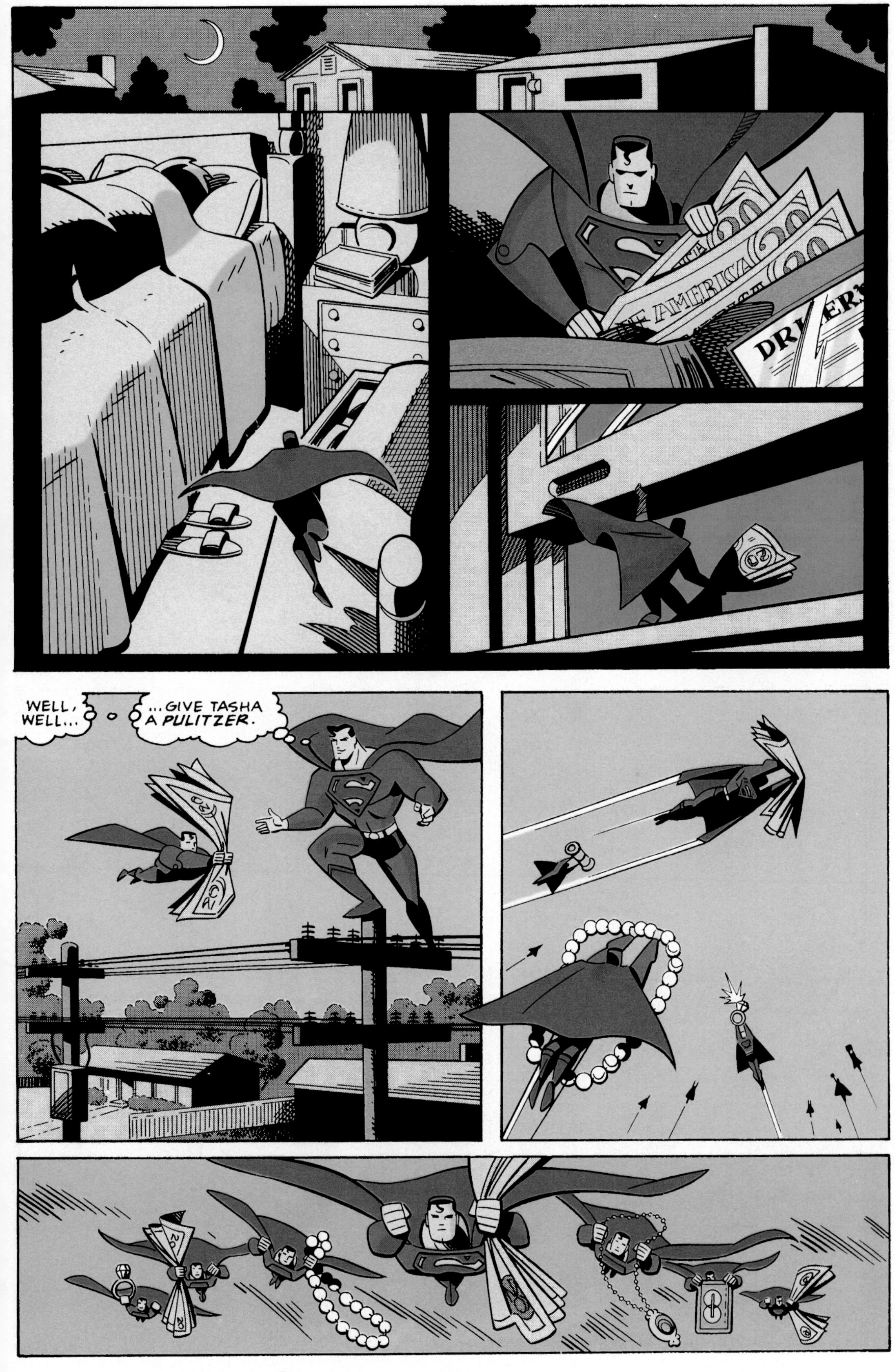

WELL, WELL...
...GIVE TASHA A *PULITZER*.

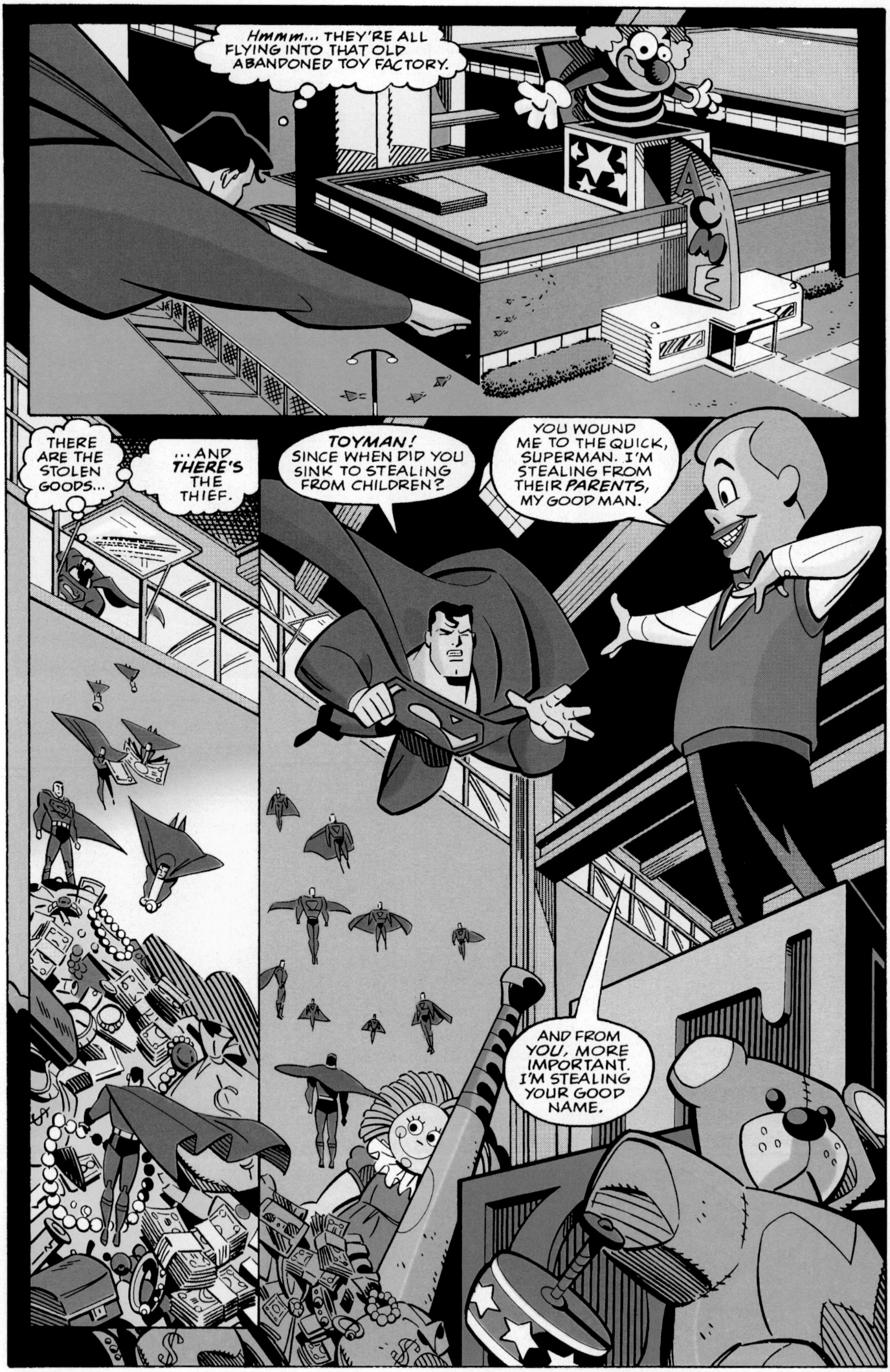
Hmmm... THEY'RE ALL FLYING INTO THAT OLD ABANDONED TOY FACTORY.
ACME
THERE ARE THE STOLEN GOODS...
...AND THERE'S THE THIEF.
TOYMAN! SINCE WHEN DID YOU SINK TO STEALING FROM CHILDREN?
YOU WOUND ME TO THE QUICK, SUPERMAN. I'M STEALING FROM THEIR PARENTS, MY GOOD MAN.
AND FROM YOU, MORE IMPORTANT. I'M STEALING YOUR GOOD NAME.

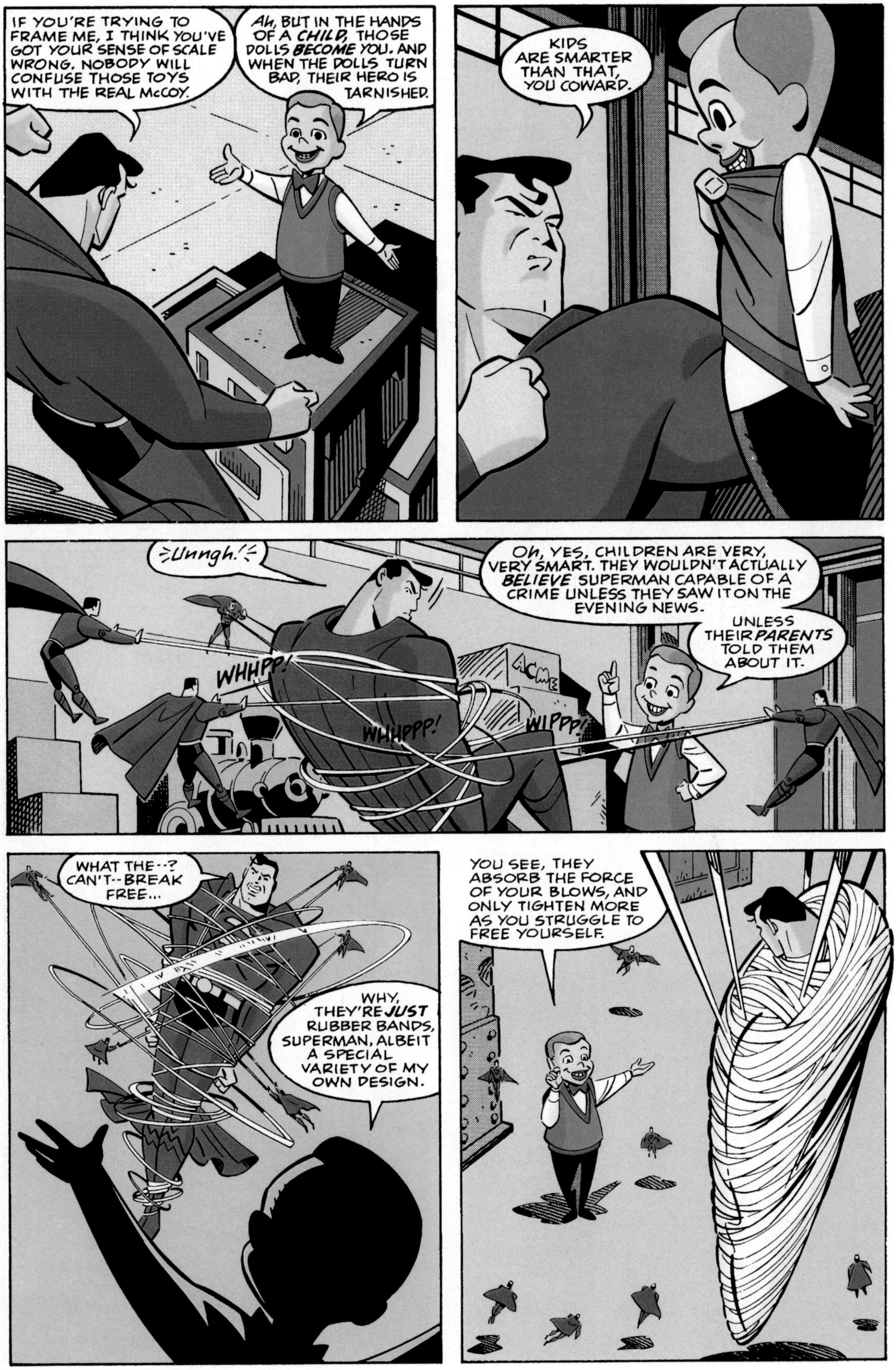
IF YOU'RE TRYING TO FRAME ME, I THINK YOU'VE GOT YOUR SENSE OF SCALE WRONG. NOBODY WILL CONFUSE THOSE TOYS WITH THE REAL McCOY.
Ah, BUT IN THE HANDS OF A CHILD, THOSE DOLLS BECOME YOU. AND WHEN THE DOLLS TURN BAD, THEIR HERO IS TARNISHED.
KIDS ARE SMARTER THAN THAT, YOU COWARD.
Unngh!
Oh, YES, CHILDREN ARE VERY, VERY SMART. THEY WOULDN'T ACTUALLY BELIEVE SUPERMAN CAPABLE OF A CRIME UNLESS THEY SAW IT ON THE EVENING NEWS.
UNLESS THEIR PARENTS TOLD THEM ABOUT IT.
WHHPP!
ACME
WHHPPP!
WIPPP!
WHAT THE--? CAN'T--BREAK FREE...
WHY, THEY'RE JUST RUBBER BANDS, SUPERMAN, ALBEIT A SPECIAL VARIETY OF MY OWN DESIGN.
YOU SEE, THEY ABSORB THE FORCE OF YOUR BLOWS, AND ONLY TIGHTEN MORE AS YOU STRUGGLE TO FREE YOURSELF.

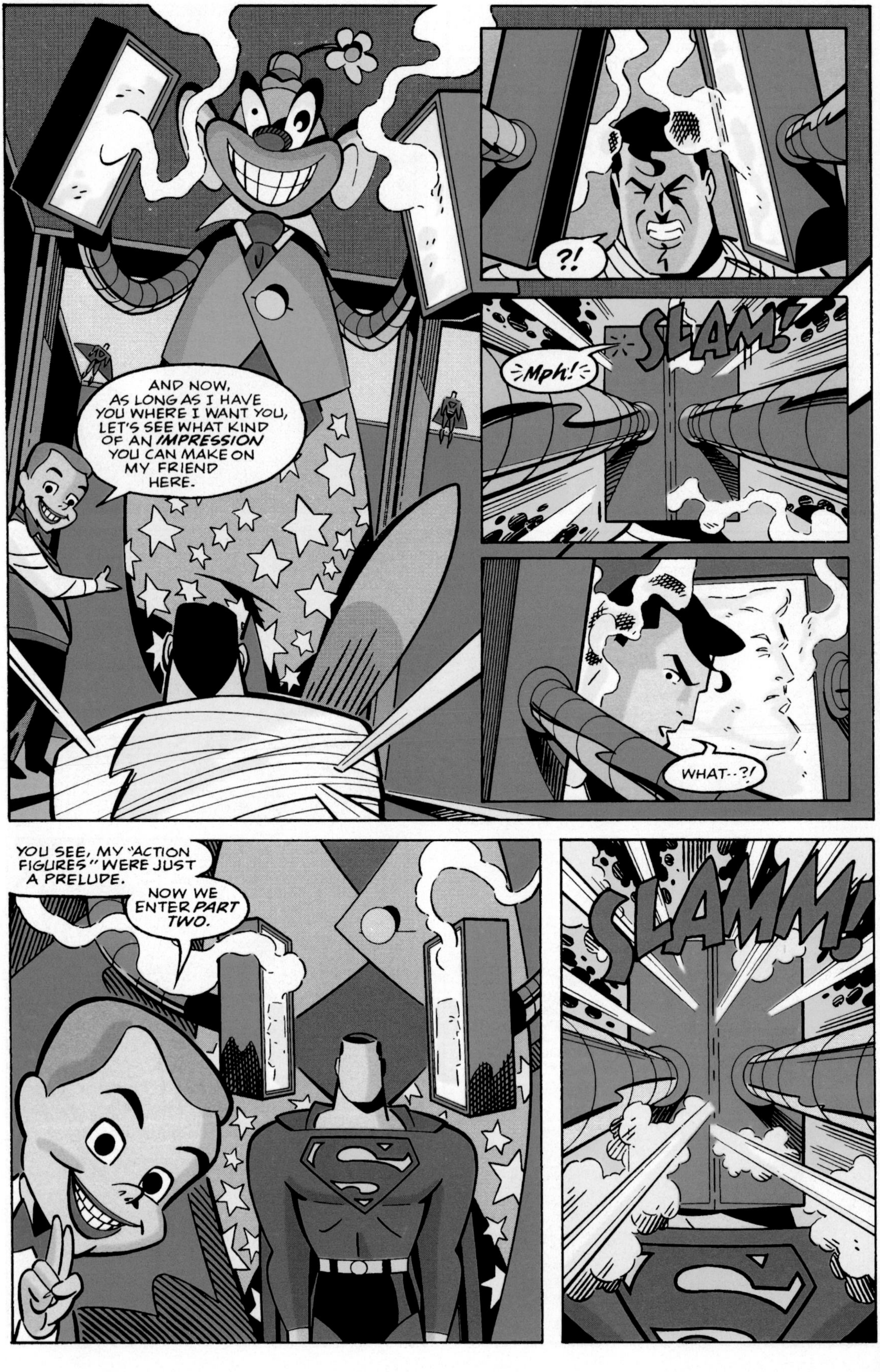
?!
SLAM!
Mph!
AND NOW, AS LONG AS I HAVE YOU WHERE I WANT YOU, LET'S SEE WHAT KIND OF AN *IMPRESSION* YOU CAN MAKE ON MY FRIEND HERE.
WHAT--?!
YOU SEE, MY "ACTION FIGURES" WERE JUST A PRELUDE.
NOW WE ENTER *PART TWO.*
SLAMM!

NOW FOR SOME *LIFE-SIZED* FUN.

"YOU SEE, SUPERMAN, YOU WOULDN'T LET ME DESTROY THE MEN WHO DESTROYED MY FATHER'S GOOD NAME.

"NOW *YOU* GET TO SEE HOW IT FEELS.

"MY FATHER WAS A GOOD MAN, AND *HE* WENT TO JAIL. MAYBE THERE ARE OTHERS LIKE HIM THERE. SO, AS HIS FIRST ASSIGNMENT...

"...MY TOY WILL BE DELIVERING SOME *EARLY* PAROLES."

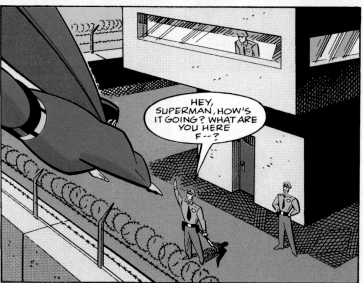

HEY, SUPERMAN, HOW'S IT GOING? WHAT ARE YOU HERE F--?

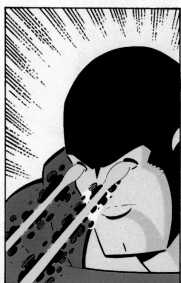

BOOM!

WHOA! WHAT THE--!

GO. YOU-ARE-ALL-FREE.

WOW!

THANKS, BUDDY!

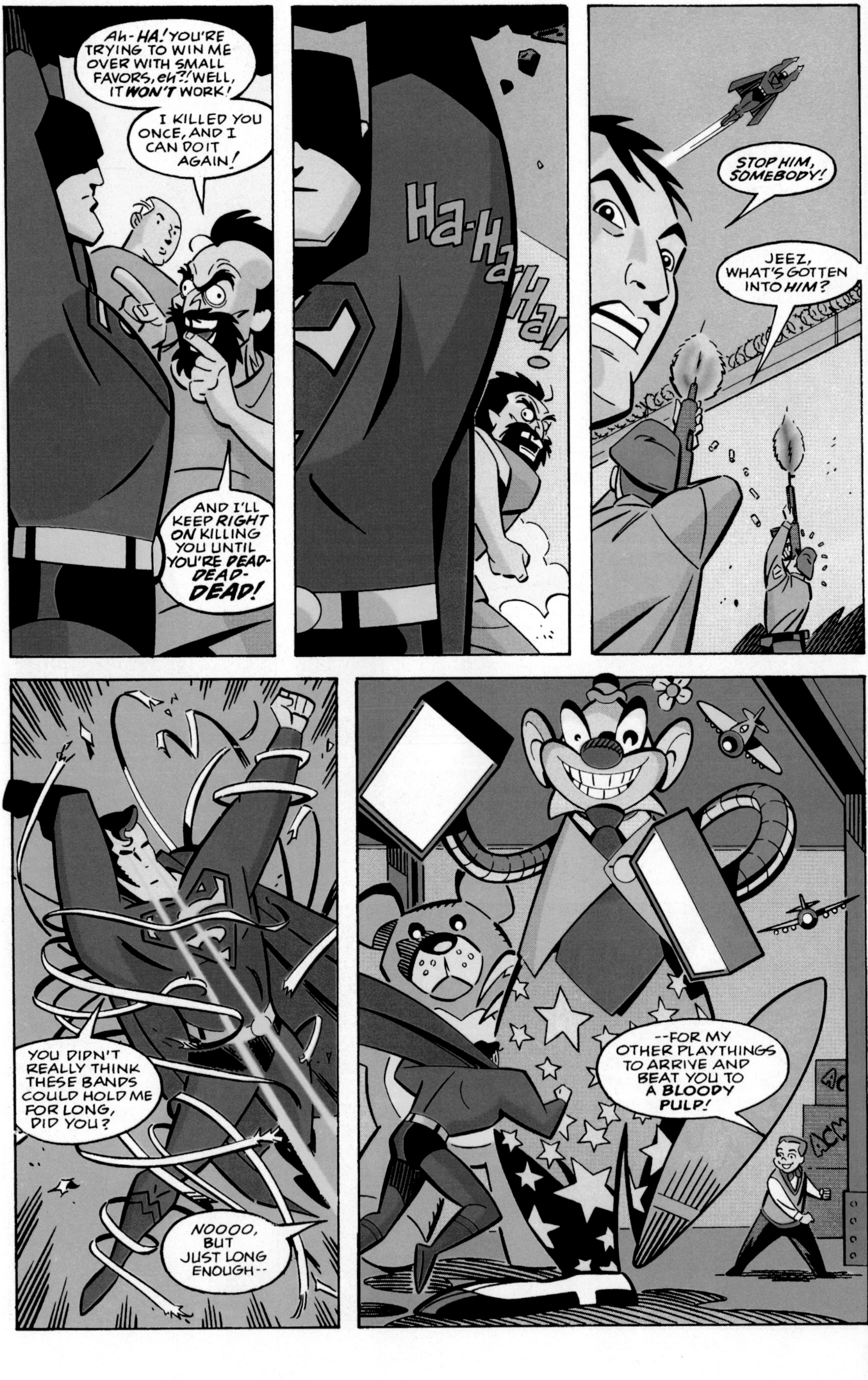
Ah-HA! YOU'RE TRYING TO WIN ME OVER WITH SMALL FAVORS, eh?! WELL, IT WON'T WORK!
I KILLED YOU ONCE, AND I CAN DO IT AGAIN!
AND I'LL KEEP RIGHT ON KILLING YOU UNTIL YOU'RE DEAD-DEAD-DEAD!
Ha-Ha-Ha-Ha!
STOP HIM, SOMEBODY!
JEEZ, WHAT'S GOTTEN INTO HIM?
YOU DIDN'T REALLY THINK THESE BANDS COULD HOLD ME FOR LONG, DID YOU?
NOOOO, BUT JUST LONG ENOUGH--
--FOR MY OTHER PLAYTHINGS TO ARRIVE AND BEAT YOU TO A BLOODY PULP!

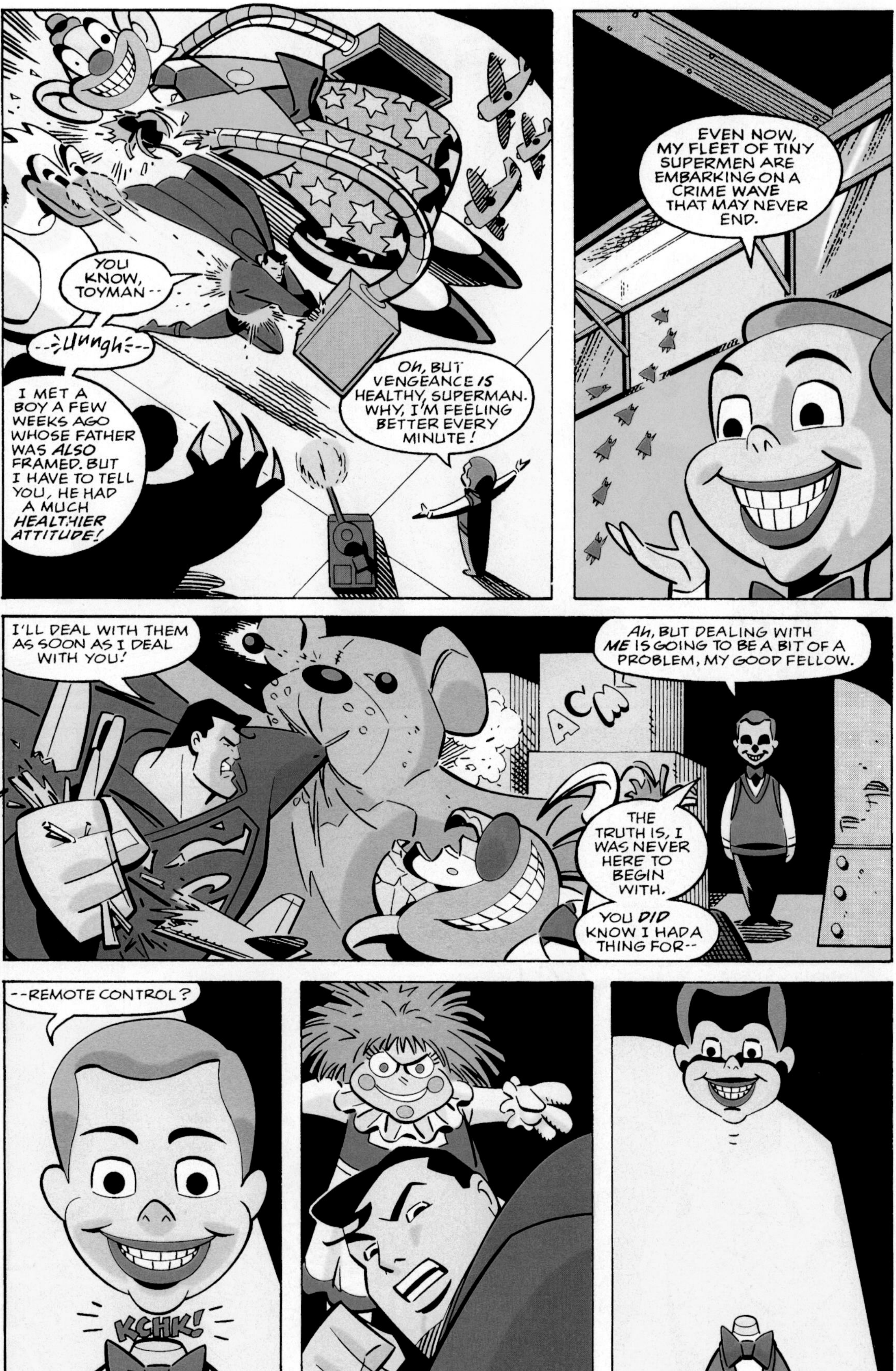
YOU KNOW, TOYMAN--
--Uungh--
I MET A BOY A FEW WEEKS AGO WHOSE FATHER WAS ALSO FRAMED. BUT I HAVE TO TELL YOU, HE HAD A MUCH HEALTHIER ATTITUDE!
Oh, BUT VENGEANCE IS HEALTHY, SUPERMAN. WHY, I'M FEELING BETTER EVERY MINUTE!
EVEN NOW, MY FLEET OF TINY SUPERMEN ARE EMBARKING ON A CRIME WAVE THAT MAY NEVER END.
I'LL DEAL WITH THEM AS SOON AS I DEAL WITH YOU!
Ah, BUT DEALING WITH ME IS GOING TO BE A BIT OF A PROBLEM, MY GOOD FELLOW.
THE TRUTH IS, I WAS NEVER HERE TO BEGIN WITH.
YOU DID KNOW I HAD A THING FOR--
--REMOTE CONTROL?
KCHK!

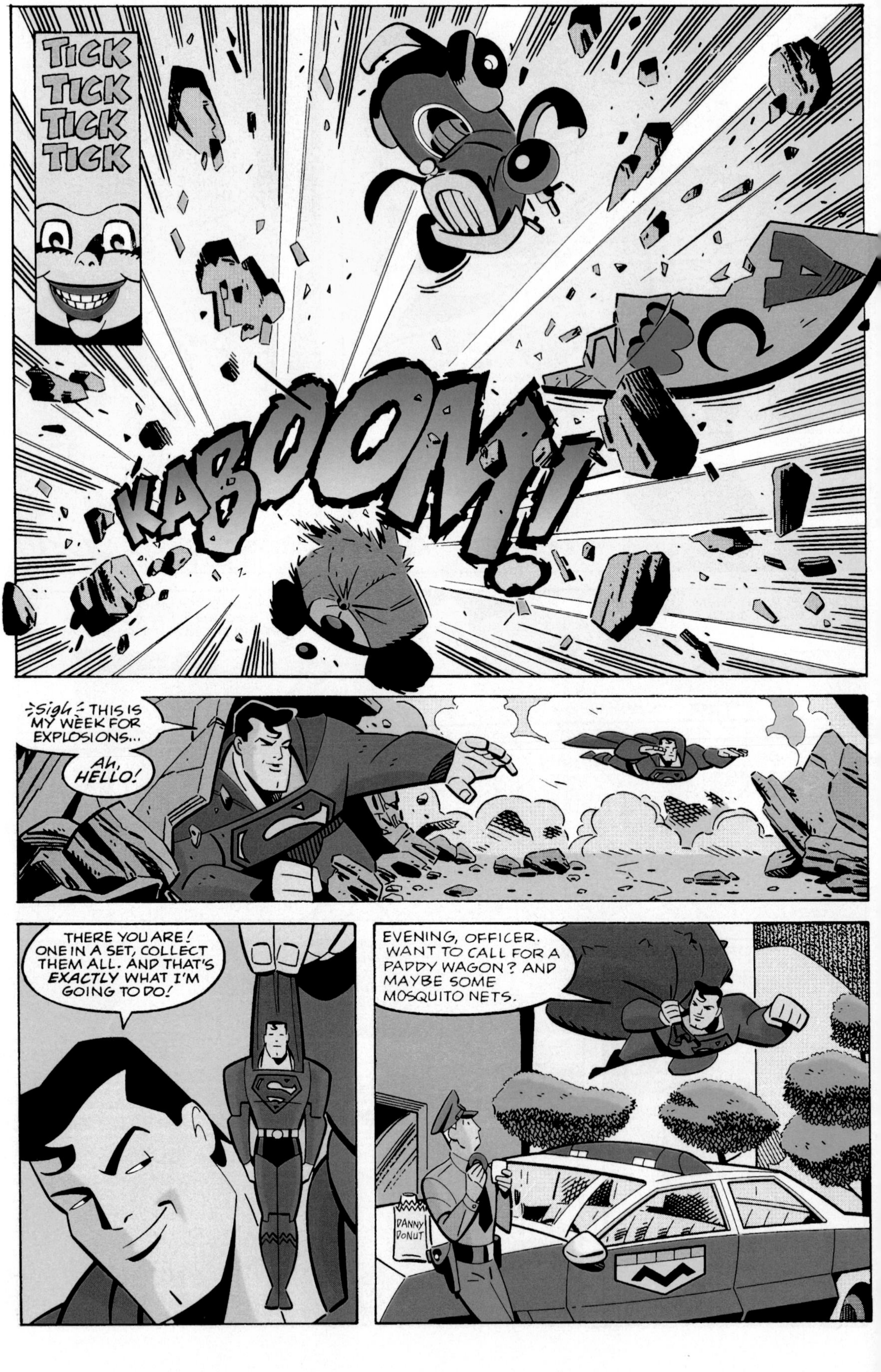
TICK
TICK
TICK
TICK
KABOOM!
-Sigh- THIS IS MY WEEK FOR EXPLOSIONS...
Ah, HELLO!
THERE YOU ARE! ONE IN A SET, COLLECT THEM ALL. AND THAT'S EXACTLY WHAT I'M GOING TO DO!
EVENING, OFFICER. WANT TO CALL FOR A PADDY WAGON? AND MAYBE SOME MOSQUITO NETS.
DANNY DONUT

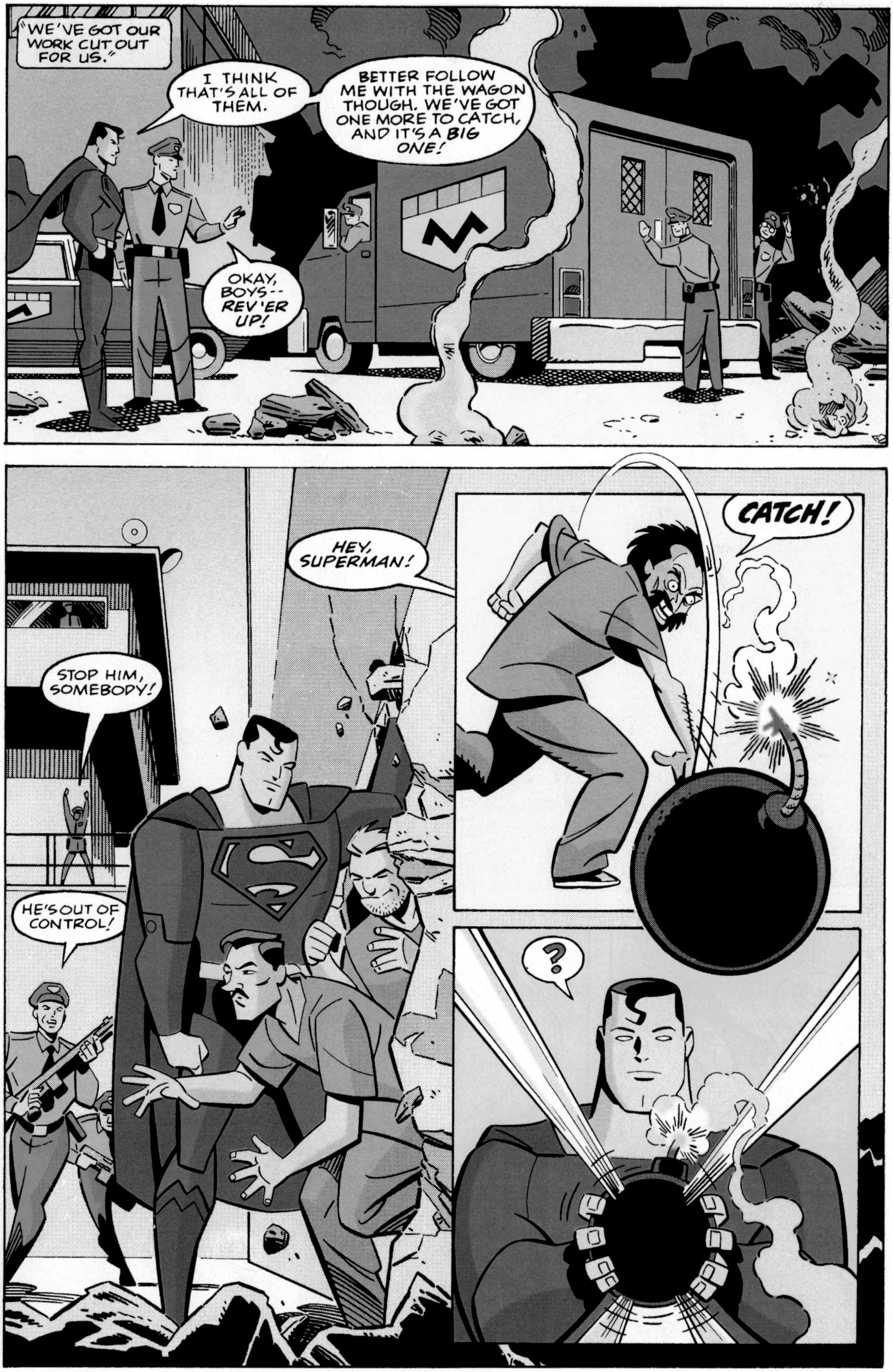
"WE'VE GOT OUR WORK CUT OUT FOR US."
I THINK THAT'S ALL OF THEM.
BETTER FOLLOW ME WITH THE WAGON THOUGH. WE'VE GOT ONE MORE TO CATCH, AND IT'S A BIG ONE!
OKAY, BOYS-- REV 'ER UP!
HEY, SUPERMAN!
CATCH!
STOP HIM, SOMEBODY!
HE'S OUT OF CONTROL!
?

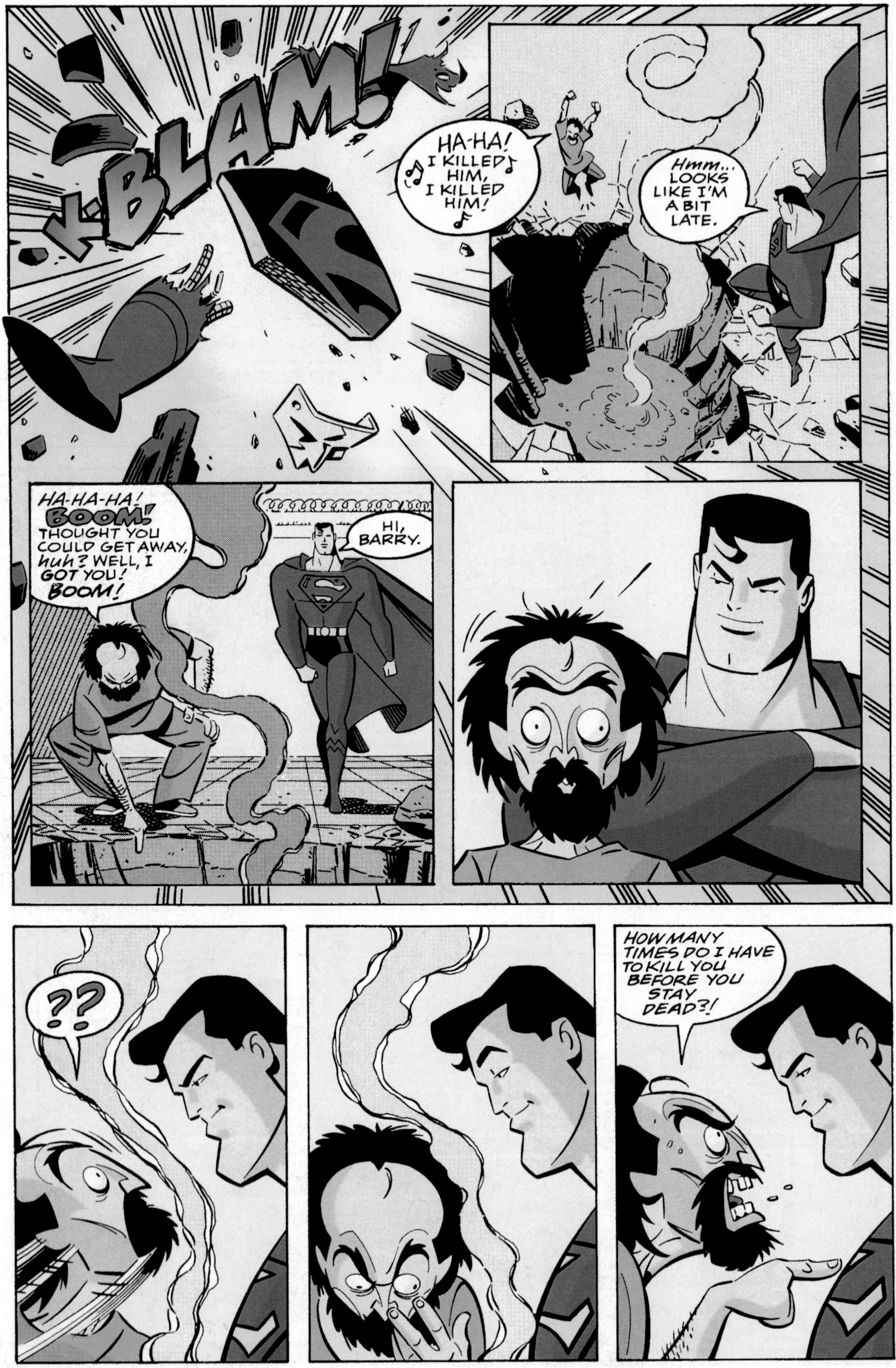
K-BLAM!
HA-HA! I KILLED HIM, I KILLED HIM!
Hmm... LOOKS LIKE I'M A BIT LATE.
HA-HA-HA! BOOM! THOUGHT YOU COULD GET AWAY, huh? WELL, I GOT YOU! BOOM!
HI, BARRY.
??
HOW MANY TIMES DO I HAVE TO KILL YOU BEFORE YOU STAY DEAD?!

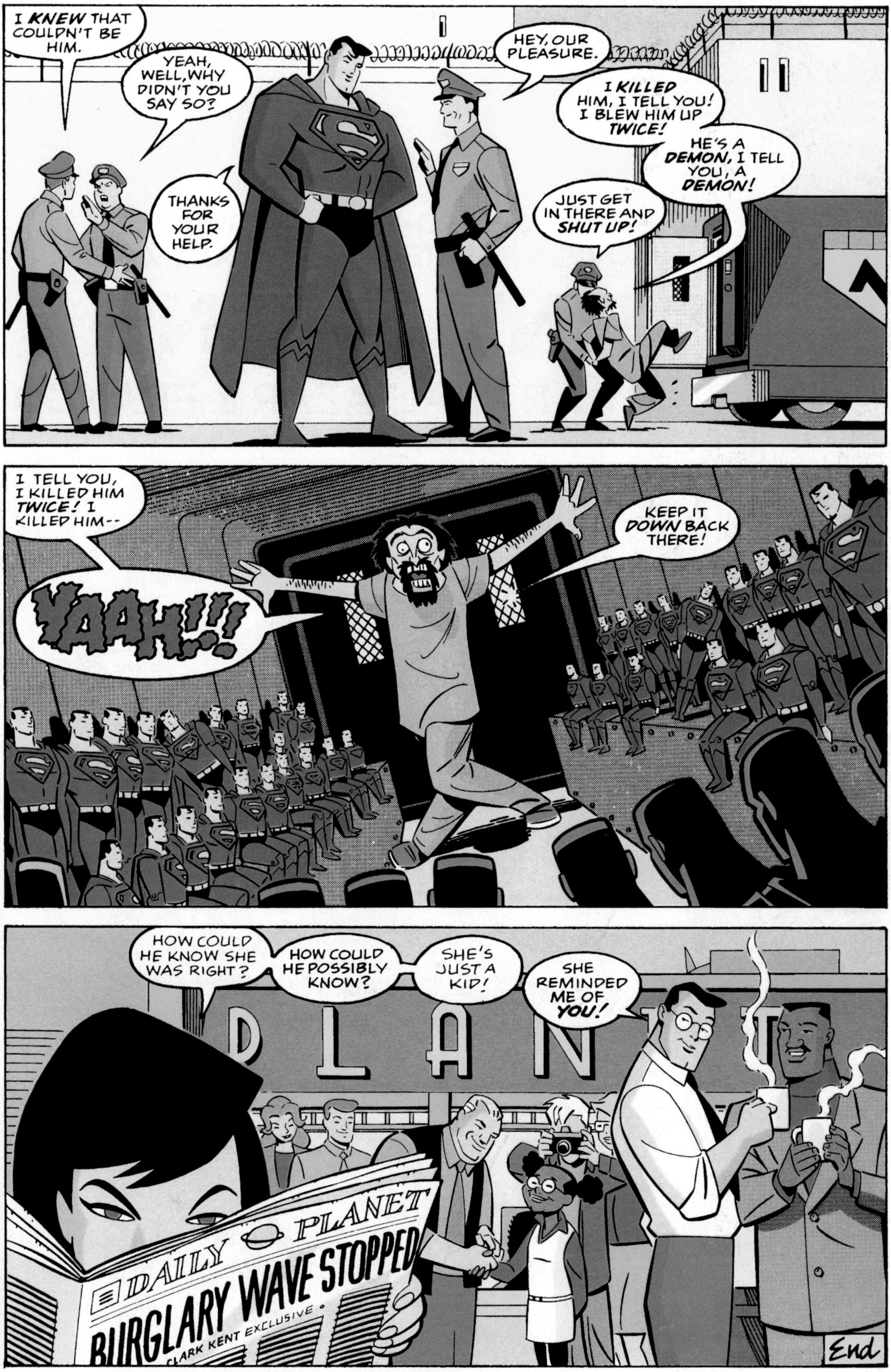
I KNEW THAT COULDN'T BE HIM.
YEAH, WELL, WHY DIDN'T YOU SAY SO?
THANKS FOR YOUR HELP.
HEY, OUR PLEASURE.
I KILLED HIM, I TELL YOU! I BLEW HIM UP TWICE!
HE'S A DEMON, I TELL YOU, A DEMON!
JUST GET IN THERE AND SHUT UP!
I TELL YOU, I KILLED HIM TWICE! I KILLED HIM--
YAAH!!!
KEEP IT DOWN BACK THERE!
HOW COULD HE KNOW SHE WAS RIGHT?
HOW COULD HE POSSIBLY KNOW?
SHE'S JUST A KID!
SHE REMINDED ME OF YOU!
PLANET
DAILY PLANET
BURGLARY WAVE STOPPED
CLARK KENT EXCLUSIVE
BURGLARY
End

EISNER AWARD-WINNING GRAPHIC
NOVELS FOR READERS OF ANY AGE

TINY TITANS

BY ART BALTAZAR & FRANCO

TINY TITANS:
THE FIRST RULE OF
PET CLUB...

TINY TITANS:
ADVENTURES IN
AWESOMENESS

READ THE ENTIRE
SERIES!

TINY TITANS:
ADVENTURES IN
AWESOMENESS

TINY TITANS:
SIDEKICKIN' IT

TINY TITANS: THE FIRST
RULE OF PET CLUB...

TINY TITANS: FIELD
TRIPPIN'

TINY TITANS: THE TREE-
HOUSE AND BEYOND

TINY TITANS:
GROWING UP TINY

TINY TITANS:
AW YEAH TITANS!